ESSENTIAL DIALOGUES
OF PLATO

TRANSLATED BY BENJAMIN JOWETT
TRANSLATION REVISED BY PEDRO DE BLAS

EDITED WITH AN INTRODUCTION AND NOTES
BY PEDRO DE BLAS

GEORGE STADE
CONSULTING EDITORIAL DIRECTOR

BARNES & NOBLE CLASSICS
NEW YORK

$\mathcal{AB}$

BARNES & NOBLE CLASSICS

NEW YORK

Published by Barnes & Noble Books
122 Fifth Avenue
New York, NY 10011

www.barnesandnoble.com/classics

Benjamin Jowett's English translation of Plato's dialogues first appeared in 1871.

Published in 2005 by Barnes & Noble Classics with new Introductions,
Notes, Biography, Chronology, Inspired By, Comments & Questions,
and For Further Reading.

Essential Dialogues of Plato
ISBN-13: 978-1-59308-269-7
ISBN-10: 1-59308-269-X
LC Control Number 2005923979

Produced and published in conjunction with:
Fine Creative Media, Inc.
322 Eighth Avenue
New York, NY 10001

Michael J. Fine, President and Publisher

Printed in the United States of America

QM

5   7   9   10   8   6   4

PLATO

Plato was born into a wealthy, aristocratic Athenian family in 428 or 427 B.C.E., and he lived until 348 or 347. He had kinship ties on both sides of his family with many prominent men in Athens. His father, Ariston, died when he was a child, and his mother, Perictione, was subsequently married to Pyrilampes. Plato was raised in Pyrilampes' household along with his older brothers (Glaucon and Adeimantus), a stepbrother (Demos), and a half-brother (Antiphon). As young men, Plato and his brothers were close to Socrates.

Plato's familial connections and wealth would have made it easy for him to embark on a political career in Athens. But he did not become politically active, perhaps because he became disillusioned with politics after witnessing, first, the brutal oligarchic regime of the Thirty Tyrants, who seized control of Athens at the end of the Peloponnesian War in 404 B.C.E., and then the execution of Socrates, who was condemned to die in 399 under the restored democratic government for "not recognizing the gods recognized by the city and corrupting the youth."

Plato traveled in the years after Socrates' death, and he almost certainly spent time in Megara (near Corinth) and Syracuse (on Sicily). He became close friends with Dion, a kinsman of the tyrant of Syracuse, Dionysius I. Plato probably traveled to Syracuse three times during the period from the early 380s to the late 360s. He and Dion evidently planned to educate the tyrant's son, Dionysius II, in the hopes that, upon succeeding his father, he would put into practice the political ideals they cherished. But these hopes were never fulfilled. Upon taking power in the early 360s, Dionysius II broke with both his kinsman and his tutor.

In the early 380s, Plato began teaching what he called "philosophy" at a place near the grove of the hero Academus on the outskirts of Athens. The school came to be called the "Academy" because of its location, and Plato remained at its head until his death, when his nephew Speusippus took over its administration. After Plato's death, the Academy continued to be an important center of research and study for many centuries, attracting students from all over the Mediterranean world.

Plato probably started to compose dialogues before he established the Academy. All but a few of his dialogues feature Socrates as the main interlocutor, and most are peopled with figures who would have been well known, especially in Athens' elite circles, during the fifth century. A large body of writing attributed to Plato survives from antiquity, including *Apology* (a recreation of Socrates' defense speech), numerous dialogues, and a series of letters. Most of these works are considered to be truly by Plato, although the authenticity of some texts (including some of the letters and a handful of dialogues) has been doubted at various points in the last 2,400 years.

TABLE OF CONTENTS

THE WORLD OF PLATO

508
B.C.E.
Cleisthenes, son of Megacles, introduces sweeping political reforms to the Athenian constitution, marking the beginning of democratic government in Athens.

490 At the battle of Marathon (26.3 miles from Athens in Attica), Greek land forces, under the command of the Athenian Miltiades, son of Cimon, defeat an invading army of Persians. Most of the Greek troops who fight at Marathon come from Athens.

480 At the battle of Thermopylae (a mountain pass in northeastern Greece), Persian land forces fight against elite Spartan soldiers under the command of Leonidas, one of the Spartan kings. The entire Spartan force is killed in the battle.

480 At the battle of Salamis (an island near the port city Piraeus in Attica), Greek naval forces, under the leadership of the Athenian Themistocles, son of Neocles, defeat the Persian navy.

479 In the battle of Plataea (in Boeotia), Greek land forces decisively defeat the Persian army, which subsequently withdraws from Greece. Under the leadership of the Spartans and then the Athenians, city-states in Greece band together in the fight to free Hellenic city-states on the coast of Asia Minor from Persian dominion. This alliance is soon called the Delian League, because its treasury is kept on the sacred island of Delos; it eventually will come under the total control of the Athenians.

c.469 Socrates, son of Sophroniscus, is born.

462 Ephialtes, son of Sophronides, and Pericles, son of Xanthippus, introduce reforms to the democratic constitution, which expands the franchise of Athenian citizens and provides more opportunities for political involvement to greater numbers of men, regardless of economic class.

458 Aeschylus of Eleusis (in Attica) produces his *Oresteia* tetralogy (the tragedies *Agamemnon*, *Libation Bearers*, and *Eumenides*, and the satyr-drama *Proteus*) in the annual theatrical competition held at the Greater Dionysia festival in the Theater of Dionysus on the southern slope of the Athenian Acropolis.

454 The treasury of the Delian League is transferred from the island of Delos to Athens. Under the leadership of Pericles, funds from the treasury are used to finance the construction of buildings on the Acropolis, including the Parthenon, which was destroyed by the Persian invasion of 480.

450s– 440s The relationships between Athens and other prominent city-states (notably Sparta, Corinth, and Thebes) deteriorate, as Athens expands its influence throughout the Aegean area.

c.450 The astronomer and natural scientist Anaxagoras (from Clazomenae), who is closely associated with Pericles, is said to be prosecuted on the charge of impiety. Sources reporting this event claim that Anaxagoras flees Athens with Pericles' assistance and goes to Lampsacus (on the eastern entrance to the Hellespont).

c.432 Protagoras of Abdera (in Thrace), a "Sophist" and professional teacher of rhetoric, visits Athens.

431 Full-scale hostilities break out between the Peloponnesian alliance, led by Sparta, and Athens and its allies, marking the beginning of the Peloponnesian War. Euripides, son of Mnesarchides (or Mnesarchos), produces *Medea* in a tetralogy with two other tragedies (*Philoctetes* and *Dictys*) and a satyr-drama (*Theristai*) at the Greater Dionysia festival in Athens.

c.429? Sophocles, son of Sophilus, produces *Oedipus Tyrannus* (*Oedipus the King*) in a tragic tetralogy at the Greater Dionysia festival in Athens.

429 Pericles dies during the plague that falls upon Athens in the first years of the Peloponnesian War. Cleon, son of Cleaenetus, becomes the leading politician in Athens until his death in battle at Amphipolis in 422.

428 or 427 Plato is born into a wealthy and influential family. His father, Ariston, dies when Plato is a boy; his mother, Perictione, is subsequently married to her uncle Pyrilampes, who is politically prominent and closely associated with Pericles.

427 Gorgias (from Leontini on Sicily), a professional teacher of rhetoric, visits Athens.

423 At the Greater Dionysia festival, Aristophanes, son of Philippus, produces his comedy *Clouds*, in which Socrates is portrayed as a professional teacher of rhetoric and natural science who runs a "Think Factory." The comedy is awarded third prize (out of three).

415– 413 Under the leadership of Alcibiades, son of Clinias and former ward of Pericles, Athens sends an armada to attack the city of Syracuse on Sicily. After Alcibiades' defection to Sparta and other major setbacks, the Athenian forces are defeated, and the Sicilian expedition ends with many lives lost and almost all ships in the armada destroyed.

411– During an oligarchic coup in Athens, democratic political
410   institutions are temporarily dissolved. Resistance by loyalists leads
to the restoration of the democratic constitution in 410.

405   The Spartans defeat the Athenian navy at Aegospotami off the
coast of Asia Minor.

404   The Peloponnesian War ends as Athens surrenders to the Spartans. The Spartans impose strict terms of surrender upon the
Athenians, including the destruction of the Long Walls connecting Athens to the port city Piraeus. They also foment another oligarchic coup and install in power a group of men, led by Plato's
kinsman Critias, who come to be known as the Thirty Tyrants.

403   Democratic loyalists, who take refuge in Piraeus, defeat the
Thirty Tyrants and their supporters, and the democratic constitution is once again restored. To reduce lingering factional strife
between loyal "democrats" and those who supported the second coup, a general amnesty is declared in 403. Only those
deemed directly involved with the Thirty Tyrants are liable for
prosecution for crimes against the *demos* (people).

399   Socrates, who has been closely associated with Alcibiades and
other men known for their hostility to the democratic constitution, is charged with impiety and corrupting youth. He is convicted of both charges and ordered to commit suicide by
drinking hemlock.

390s Plato, along with other members of the Socratic circle (Antisthenes, Phaedo, Eucleides, Aristippus, Aeschines, and Xenophon), begins to write "Socratic dialogues." Athens reemerges
as an important naval power in the Aegean area.

early Plato travels to Syracuse in or around 387, when he befriends
380s Dion, a kinsman of Dionysius I, the tyrant of Syracuse. It is
probably upon his return to Athens from this trip that he begins teaching "philosophy" near the grove of the hero Academus on the outskirts of Athens, in a school that comes to be
known as the Academy.

384   Aristotle, son of Nicomachus, is born at Stageira (in Chal-
cidice). He will study at the Academy from 367 until Plato's
death.

378   In Thebes, the general Gorgidas forms an elite force of 300 men
that legendarily comprises pairs of lovers. The corps, known as
the Sacred Band, reportedly remains undefeated until the battle
at Chaeronea in 338.

360s After the death of Dionysius I of Syracuse (in 367), Plato is said
to make two trips to Sicily in order to facilitate the restoration

of Dion, who has been exiled by Dionysius I. He and Dion apparently hope to exert political influence on Dionysius II, the tyrant's son and successor. Plato probably visits Syracuse for the last time in 361 or 360.

354   Dion is assassinated.

348   Plato dies. Speusippus (the son of Plato's sister Potone) becomes
or   head of the Academy, and Aristotle leaves Athens, eventually
347   arriving at the court of King Philip II of Macedon, where he will serve for a few years as the tutor to Philip's son, Alexander.

344   Dionysius II is exiled to Corinth.

339   Speusippus dies.

338   In the battle of Chaeronea (in Boeotia), the Macedonians under the leadership of Philip II defeat the combined forces of the Athenians and Thebans. The defeat brings Athens, Thebes, and other Greek city-states under the sway of Macedon.

335   Aristotle returns to Athens and founds a school near a grove outside the city that was sacred to Apollo Lyceius. The school will come to be known as the Lyceum.

323   Alexander the Great dies in Babylon. Anti-Macedonian feeling runs high in Athens after Alexander's death, causing Aristotle to leave the city and take up residence in Chalcis (on Euboea). Upon his departure, his pupil Theophrastus takes over leadership of the Lyceum.

322   Aristotle dies in Chalcis.

GENERAL INTRODUCTION

The extraordinary range of Plato's interests and his formidable command of the Greek language and cultural tradition make him appear as the inventor of philosophy, and make classical Athens appear as its birthplace. Yet some of the questions that Plato addressed had been opened in different ways by other thinkers elsewhere in the Greek world, many still remain open, and no systematic elaboration of his thought has proved possible—partly because Plato is almost never present, and he certainly never speaks in the first person in any of the dialogues that he wrote. Consequently, reading Plato's dialogues is a rather unusual experience, perhaps more akin to reading drama than to reading philosophy, at least as the latter is conventionally understood today: On the one hand, we are drawn into the dialogues in order to witness discussions about the nature of love, the power of language, the best way to live one's life, and the best way to face death, among many others; on the other hand, it takes a considerable interpretive effort to be reasonably certain about what Plato himself thought about these questions.

The open-ended nature of Plato's dialogues has prompted other thinkers to continue the tradition of philosophical discussion for twenty-four centuries: Plato died a long time ago, but we still rely on ordinary language in order to deal with the most profound questions of human existence. Hence A. N. Whitehead's famous characterization of the history of Western philosophy as "a series of footnotes to Plato," which is commonly taken as a praise of Plato but can also be taken as a description of a state of affairs that later thinkers have regarded as a problem (the list includes Nietzsche, Heidegger, and Derrida). In this respect, I have assumed that the readers of this volume are less interested in taking sides in this controversy than in getting to know what the fuss is all about in the first place.

There can be little doubt that Plato's claim to fame today is the utopian vision of the ideal city that Socrates (on whom more shortly) puts forward in the dialogue *Republic*. Many universities include this dialogue in their undergraduate reading lists, and it is the one most frequently translated and printed in popular editions. Unfortunately, readers who do not go further in their exploration of philosophy or the ancient world may not read more by Plato than *Republic*, which is, in my opinion, misleading about what Plato was really up to, although that dialogue is admittedly an important and memorable work.

In the history of philosophy, other dialogues have been considered to provide readers with a better approach to Platonic philosophy. Sometimes this role has fallen to *Timaeus*, the dialogue about the origin and structure of the universe, or to *Alcibiades* (of disputed authenticity), which deals with the moral education of the eponymous Athenian military and political superstar. Recently, the scholarly attention paid to sexuality in the ancient world has caused the fascinating discussion of the nature of love in *Symposium* to be regarded as a suitable introduction to Plato's thought.

The truth of the matter is that no single dialogue is the best way into Plato. Readers familiar only with *Republic* will soon discover that Plato dealt with important issues addressed in that dialogue more extensively elsewhere. For instance, the limits of verbal persuasion are more amply discussed in *Gorgias*, and both the discussion of the Ideas and the theory of knowledge become a lot more elaborate in the conversations that take place in *Parmenides*, *Theaetetus*, and *Sophist*. Moreover, those willing to venture into the dialogues that Plato wrote later in life (for example, *Statesman* and *Laws*) may come to pose themselves the question of whether Plato agreed with everything Socrates says in *Republic* about the ideal city and the ideal ruler.

Philosophical thought in general hardly ever follows a straight line or can be condensed at the rate of one work per author, but there is a peculiar "networking" quality to Plato's writings: Only after reading (and rereading) enough of his dialogues can the reader form in his mind a tentative outline of Plato's enterprise. Whitehead was right: To a large extent, the practice of philosophy (at least in the Western tradition) consists of striving toward an ever better definition of that enterprise, even if that means jettisoning part of the baggage during the journey. Any traveler knows, however, that the items you leave behind on your trip may be the ones you later find yourself most in need of.

In view of all the above, it would be irresponsible to pretend that a sufficient discussion of even a selection of Plato's dialogues can be contained in the span of this volume; therefore, I have limited the scope of this general introduction to what I consider an essential historical and cultural background for a first reading. In the individual introductions that immediately precede each of the dialogues, I have identified the speakers and suggested condensed outlines of the arguments, since a continuous reading of any but the shortest of the dialogues is too difficult for most of us in the beginning. Although a few critical insights are given, my aim has been to facilitate an intelligent and enjoyable first contact with the dialogues themselves, rather than to put forward interpretive views. Footnotes and endnotes follow the same principle. Readers who want to engage more deeply with the background and intricacies of Plato's thought will find guidance in the recommendations for further reading.

Every author should be studied in the context of his time, and Plato wrote a very long time ago. Consequently, the dialogues lose a lot of their immediacy with readers who are not familiar with the cultural context of classical Athens. In this respect, it is not enough to say that the reading lens of history is always imperfect; especially when we read Plato for the first time, we should learn as much as we can about him and his world, or else we are certain to miss too much.

Who Was Plato?

A brief answer to this question is that Plato was a Greek philosopher whose lifetime bridged the fifth and fourth centuries B.C.E.*—a period often referred to by historians as "classical Greece"—but there are several reasons why the brevity of that answer is achieved only if we accept a good deal of inaccuracy.

First, the word "Greek" is generally used today of people or things belonging to Greece as a nation, and Greece as a nation did not exist in Plato's time. The Greek world was then composed of a number of independent city-states (including Athens and Sparta) with different traditions, customs, laws, and political regimes whose main unifying trait was a common language, in spite of dialectal differences—much as English is today the common language of a Texas rancher, an engineer from Bangalore, and the British prime minister. Greeks referred collectively to speakers of other languages as "barbarians" (*barbaroi*) perhaps because any foreign language sounded to them like an unintelligible "bar-bar." Whether or not this is a true etymology, to a large extent being Greek meant speaking Greek and understanding Greek cultural references in speech. Regarding their political allegiance, however, people in classical Greece thought of themselves as belonging to their respective cities: Greeks were first Spartans, Thebans, Corinthians, and so on. Plato himself was first and foremost an Athenian; as such, he was concerned with philosophical problems as they arose from human experience as seen from the perspective of a male Athenian aristocrat, although, to his credit, he shows a keen awareness of past and current cultural developments throughout the Greek world.

Second, the word "philosopher" is generally used today of a person who explicates his or her own thoughts about a specialized set of ques-

---

*All dates given in this introduction are B.C.E. unless otherwise indicated or self-evident.

tions in sophisticated technical language. But Plato does neither of these two things: As noted earlier, Plato never speaks in the first person in his dialogues, and his characters conduct conversations about topics and in a language that would be understood by every educated Athenian. As C. Kahn explains in his *Plato and the Socratic Dialogue* (references to this and other modern works mentioned in this introduction are given in the section "For Further Reading," at the end of this volume), Plato began his writing career within the conventions of the "Socratic stories" *(sokratikoi logoi)*, a literary genre mentioned by Aristotle in his *Poetics* (1447b) that seems to have been individualized by the presence of Socrates as the main character. Nothing suggests that the dialogues were written for an intellectual audience only; on the contrary, some of their features, especially at the beginning of Plato's career, suggest that Plato wrote for intellectuals and other readers at the same time.

Socrates (c.469–399) was an Athenian thinker who never wrote anything himself and was sentenced to death by his fellow citizens on the charge of corrupting their youth and standing outside the religious mainstream. It is difficult to form a clear idea of Socrates the man; our picture of him comes mainly from Plato's dialogues,* Xenophon's narrative accounts, and Aristophanes' comedy *Clouds*, in which Socrates is presented as the leader of a "Thinkery." For our purposes here, it will suffice to say that what makes Plato's Socrates different from that of other writers is Plato's own philosophical interests, which he sought to explore in the dialogical form that he himself helped to develop.

Third, Plato's lifetime bridged the fifth and fourth centuries (c.427–c.347), and that places him at a crucial point in the history of Athens and of the Western world, as well as of the development of philosophical thinking and literary culture, two areas in which he was extremely influential. However, an awareness of Plato's influence on other writers does not in and of itself help us better understand his writings. On the contrary, reading Plato through other philosophers can make initial comprehension more difficult, since later authors necessarily had to interpret Plato and often did so in questionable ways.

The business of literary criticism consists mainly of disentangling interpretive webs and offering new and better interpretations, hopefully without creating too many new entanglements in the process. But our business here is different: Readers meeting Plato for the first time will do well to bear in mind the truism that neither Plato nor his con-

---

*Plato was not the only one to write "Socratic stories." Other writers (for example, Antisthenes, Phaedo, Aeschines) also practiced this genre, but their works have survived only in fragments.

temporaries were aware that they lived in classical Greece, since the division of historical time into periods, centuries, and millennia is arbitrary and came only later. Our strategy, then, should be to gain information about Plato's own historical perspective.

Athens in Plato's Time

Plato was born into an aristocratic Athenian family during the Peloponnesian War (431–404). Given that a state of war in ancient Greece was the norm rather than the exception, this fact may not seem particularly relevant. But the war that Plato was born in the middle of was indeed of special significance, as was recognized by the historian Thucydides, whose work is our main source for the events. According to Thucydides, the union of all the Greeks against the Persian invasion led by Xerxes* (490–479) was shattered fifty years later by a struggle for hegemony in the Greek world. The ensuing armed confrontation would split that world in two: on the one hand, Sparta and its Peloponnesian allies, among whom oligarchic forms of government were common; on the other, Athens and the cities that remained in the alliance formed at the end of the Persian Wars and known as the Delian League, a group that can be characterized by more participatory or "soft" political systems, under the strong leadership of Athens.

The financial resources of the Delian League were severely diminished by a war of unprecedented duration, but private business seems to have benefited from a war economy. Although Athens basically remained an agricultural society, the Athenian port of the Piraeus saw an expansion of commercial enterprises, including some owned by metics, or "displaced people" (metoikoi), who settled in Athens during the fifth century as resident aliens excluded from political participation. Consequently, a notion of classical Athens as a placid community of poets and philosophers would be seriously misleading: Plato's fellow Athenians undoubtedly lived in troubled times that involved significant demographic, economic, and political changes.

In the fifth century, political decisions in Athens had come to be taken with the participation of all male citizens in two main bodies: the Assembly and the Council. All male citizens, without distinction by wealth or birth, had the right to participate and vote in the decisions to be taken by the Assembly and in scrutinizing the chosen magistrates at the end of their term of office. A Council of 500 citizens (fifty from

---

*Our source for the Persian Wars is the historian Herodotus.

each of the ten Athenian administrative divisions known as *demes*) ran the day-to-day public affairs and prepared the meetings of the Assembly. The presidency (Prytaneis) of the Council rotated among the *demes*. The judicial system was also highly participatory: There were no judges in the modern sense, but cases were decided instead by the vote of a popular jury that may have had as many as 500 members in the most prominent cases. Such was, in a nutshell, the political regime that the emblematic Athenian leader Pericles praises in the famous passage of Thucydides' history that is known as the Funeral Oration (*Thucydides* 2.35–46).

Because of the Peloponnesian War, the democratic system was briefly suspended in 411 and, after the defeat of Athens by Sparta, briefly replaced in 404 by an oligarchy known as the Thirty Tyrants, in which Plato's relative Critias was very actively involved. Plato himself, however, kept out of this regime and out of active Athenian politics in general. Nevertheless, he was obviously very sensitive to the political and social transformations that were underway in Athens. Plato's ideology was clearly conservative: In times of change, he tried to preserve and improve what he considered the intellectual and moral core of Athenian life. Whether or not we can fully work out Plato's program and whether we can agree with it is hardly the point. In my opinion, his merit is to have identified the fracture lines of a great city and empire, and to have discussed the competing strategies that are available in order to deal, individually and collectively, with major upheavals in our surrounding reality and our own view of the world.

Democracy was restored in 403, but Athens faced a fundamental ideological division among its citizens, partly because the democratic system was an expensive one, and the financial burden that had been borne by the tribute-paying allies of the Delian League had now come to rest on the shoulders of a minority of wealthy Athenians. In addition, the supremacy of Athens in the Greek world was over; from now on, Athens would have to interact with other cities on a more level field. Eventually, Athens came under the Macedonian empire of Philip II and Alexander the Great, but these were developments that Plato did not live to see. During Plato's lifetime, Athens remained an independent city-state with a culture that was very much its own.

Athenian culture was very deeply imbued with religion, but Athenian religion must be understood as a social phenomenon consisting mainly of collective practices in honor of the gods, rather than personal belief. As R. Parker says in his *Athenian Religion*, religious practices in Athens were "a medium of association not between man and god, but between man and man." Religious practices assumed a good knowledge of mythology, since it was through myth that the Athenians got to know about their gods and heroes, of which they had many in common with the rest of the Greek world. Mythology, in this sense, included Hesiod's *Theogony* (a poem about the origin of the world and the ascent of Zeus as the supreme god) and *Works and Days*, as well as Homer's *Iliad* and *Odyssey*. Homer was also used for educational and entertainment purposes, and he became the single most important literary reference of all the Greeks.

The *Iliad*, probably composed in the second half of the eighth century, is a lengthy epic poem describing the battle between Greeks and Trojans fought at the city of Troy in Asia Minor (modern Turkey). The leader of the Greek army is Agamemnon, king of Mycenae, who rallied kings from all over Greece to attack Troy in order to vindicate his brother Menelaus, king of Sparta, whose bride Helen, reputed to be the most beautiful woman in the world as well as the daughter of Zeus, had been seduced and abducted by the Trojan prince Paris. While both Agamemnon and Menelaus were effective warriors, they were neither the strongest nor the cleverest men on the battlefield, and the Greek army suffered many setbacks because of their ineffective leadership. As the *Iliad* opens, Agamemnon's pride leads him to offend and alienate Achilles, the Greeks' finest warrior, by stealing his concubine. Achilles, filled with divine wrath, complains to his mother, the goddess Thetis, and withdraws from fighting. While out of combat, he wrestles with the knowledge of his fate: He will either live a long life if he stays away from war and glorious deeds, or die at Troy but win fame and glory. Without Achilles, the Greeks have little hope for victory and must rely heavily on their other key players, such as the aged but wise Nestor, who came to Troy with his son in order to serve as an adviser to the leaders, and wily Odysseus, the hero of the eponymous *Odyssey*, who was famous for his shrewd mind and stunning powers of persuasion.

On the Trojan side, Paris fought as one of fifty brothers, all sons of King Priam. While Paris was seen as a foppish dandy, an oriental prince spoiled by luxuries, his brother Hector was seen as the savior of the Trojans and the one hero who could save the city. All heroes in Homer are larger than life, but they are also flawed: Agamemnon is too proud; Odysseus' cleverness and persuasion often border on deceit; Nestor persists in retelling the exploits of his youth at every given opportunity; and Achilles is too ready to sulk in his tent and whine to his mother when he is treated unfairly. Hector is the exception: Through his character, Homer constantly reinforces the horrors of war—Hector fights not in order to win glory but to save his city and family from destruction.

Achilles is finally persuaded to rejoin the Greeks in battle after his best friend, Patroclus, is killed by Hector. Patroclus and Achilles' deep affection for each other, whether sexual or not, has been studied carefully as the archetypal friendship of Western literature. The poem's action ends with the death of Hector at Achilles' hands and his funeral among the Trojans. In the *Odyssey* and other sources, including fifth-century tragedy, we learn of the death of Achilles at Troy, the victory of the Greeks through the trick of the Trojan Horse, and the difficult return journeys (*nostoi*) of the victorious Greeks to their respective cities.

The most difficult and celebrated story of such returns is the *Odyssey*, which chronicles the ten-year journey that Odysseus makes in order to return to his home in Ithaca and to his faithful wife, Penelope. (Penelope keeps hoping for his return and staves off her many suitors by the stratagem of postponing her new marriage until she finishes a piece of weaving, which she works on during the day and undoes at night.) Odysseus' journey takes him in a wide circuit around the Mediterranean; it includes sea wrecks and difficult encounters with witches and monsters, as well as a visit to the underworld, all of which he alone survives out of his entire crew, thanks to his gift of persuasiveness and his determination.

One cannot emphasize enough the essential role of Homer for an understanding of the ancient Greek world. I cannot think of a single American equivalent: Homer was to the Greeks what the Bible, Hollywood's movies, and Dr. Seuss' books are to American culture, all in one. The sociological effect of the 1980s television broadcast in India of the epic poem *Ramayana* may provide a closer comparison: According to some reports, political meetings were scheduled outside the show's viewing time, during which life in the whole country came to a halt; celebratory music was heard, incense burnt atop TV sets, and phones were not answered.* The factual details may be discussed endlessly, but there is enough evidence for the strong grip of the story on the imagination of a country that regards it as an integral part of its religious, moral, political, and literary backbone, as well as for the critical voices that advocated a modern-day perspective on it.

Myth also provided the basis for the plots of many of the tragedies that were produced during religious festivals, the most important of which was the yearly Athenian one known as the City Dionysia (the main festival in honor of the god Dionysus). During their heyday in the fifth century, these festivals would last several days, from dawn till dusk, and would feature poetic competitions: Of the three tragic trilogies

---

*See report by the Buddhist activist Fuengsin Trafford at www.chezpaul.org.uk/fuengsin/index.htm; accessed April 27, 2005.

produced at each of these festivals, one would be chosen as the winner, as would one of the five comedies that were also produced on this
occasion.* The dramatic competitions engaged the collective memory
of the city, and their staging and attendance were both a religious and
a civic duty; the City Dionysia was the largest annual gathering in
Athens. It is not altogether surprising that, as A. W. Nightingale has
shown in her *Genres in Dialogue*, Plato's dialogues are much closer relatives of Athenian stage writing than earlier scholars had recognized.

During the fifth century, Athens also witnessed a considerable rise
of the individuals known collectively as "Sophists," although we must
note that the Greek word *sophistēs* simply means "expert," and we do
not know that it was used in Athens with any other meaning. We do
know that the most celebrated Sophists were not Athenians, but visited
Athens from other cities, and made money there by charging fees to
those who retained their services in order to be trained to excel in public life by means of persuasive speech, which Plato considered a threat
to the pursuit of truth by means of rational argumentation.

Very little has survived from the work of the Sophists, but many
of them appear in Plato's dialogues, and some of them were thinkers in
their own right. It is clear that Plato recognized that fact, judging from
the prominent role that he gave in his dialogues to Protagoras of Abdera or Gorgias of Leontini, who confront Socrates in discussions about
the possibility of teaching political virtue and the morality of rhetorical training, respectively. The well-respected and bigmouthed speaker
Thrasymachus of Chalcedon, the polymath Hippias of Elis, and Prodicus of Ceos, who seems to have been very interested in linguistic theory and in the ascription of fixed meanings to words (much in the way
of our modern dictionaries), are also featured as speakers in several dialogues.

In addition to writing dialogues, Plato founded the Academy,
which came to be known by that name because it was located near a
grove that had been consecrated to the hero Academus, and which
would keep its doors open until the first century B.C.E. The Academy
was an institution of higher learning, but it is surely wrong to assume
that its early members spent most of their time reading and discussing
Plato's dialogues. The Academy was the place of work of individuals
like the mathematician Eudoxus of Cnidus (c.408–c.354), and there
are reasons to believe that the study of mathematics played an impor-

---

*The tragedies from Aeschylus, Sophocles, and Euripides, and the comedies of Aristo-
phanes were produced at such festivals. The only extant trilogy is Aeschylus' *Oresteia*
(*Agamemnon*, *Libation-Bearers*, and *Eumenides*).

tant role. Nevertheless, as A. W. Nightingale also discusses in her *Genres in Dialogue*, an allegiance to the Academy probably set any intellectual at odds with another very important school of thought in fourth-century Athens. The school in question is that of Isocrates (436–338), another Athenian writer who stayed out of active politics and tried instead to influence their course by means of rhetorical instruction and speech-writing. Isocrates' views on rhetoric, however, are different from those of the Sophists: He disapproved of rhetorical skills geared solely toward winning an argument, but, in contrast with Socrates, he demanded that clear benefits, including that of rational persuasion, be derived from the practice of philosophy. He also had Panhellenic political views that were at odds with Plato's uncompromising belief in Athenian supremacy. Isocrates' gift as a writer cannot be compared with Plato's, but the current reevaluation of his thought is a welcome contribution to a better understanding of the development of philosophy in classical Athens and of Plato's role therein. Initially, *philosophia* is defined both by Plato and by Isocrates as something other than what the Sophists did: It is more than the techniques required to win an argument, the ascription of fixed meanings to words, or the drafting of good constitutions for the colonies. And it is Athenian, not foreign.

Aristotle (384–322) studied at the Academy for about twenty years, and he stands witness to Plato's philosophical stature in his deliberate efforts to present his own thinking as an improvement on Plato's. Plato himself, however, was more concerned with the teachings of the Sophists and with the work of the thinkers that were active before him, who are commonly referred to as the pre-Socratics.

The Pre-Socratics

The title "pre-Socratics" is a conventional way to lump together many Greek thinkers who lived before or at the same time as Socrates and whose work we know from relatively scarce fragments, derived mostly from quotations by other writers, especially by Aristotle and his pupil Theophrastus (c.371–c.287). That title, however, must not be taken to imply that they all formed a school or lived in the same place, or even that they were contemporaries.

The lifetimes of the pre-Socratics span the sixth and fifth centuries B.C.E., and their locations spread over a wide geographical area of the ancient Greek world: several cities in Asia Minor (modern Turkey), the Greek islands, southern Italy, and Sicily. Partly because we have only fragments of their works, their thought is difficult to understand, let alone to summarize. In very general terms, they were concerned with mathematics and the physical world; even those of the pre-Socratics who were interested in ethical questions refused to seek explanations based on the doings of the gods but relied instead on rational argumentation. In this sense, and together with the medical writings of Hippocrates of Cos (of imprecise date), the pre-Socratics can be considered the precursors of what we call Greek philosophy.

Some of Plato's writings show an obvious interest in Pythagorean doctrines, and it is clear that he gave a great deal of thought to the work of Parmenides of Elea, whom he made converse with Socrates during a visit of the Elean thinker to Athens around 450, for which the dialogue named after him is the only evidence. Parmenides is of particular significance for an understanding of Plato's philosophical project, since he was the author of a poem about the "Way of Truth" and the "Way of Appearance" that is essential for an understanding of the development of the notion of rational thought and, consequently, distinguishes him as the most important of the pre-Socratics, in spite of his undeniable obscurity, which may have dumbfounded even Plato at times.

More generally, we can think of Plato's writings as a point of inflection between the rise of the scientific thinking of the pre-Socratics and the development of philosophy as a specialized activity that would begin to split into different branches thanks to Aristotle's talent for systematization. Readers interested in the work of the pre-Socratics will find a selection of their fragments (and of those of the Sophists) in the recent translation by R. Waterfield published under the title *The First Philosophers*.

General Features and Chronology of Plato's Dialogues

In contrast with the pre-Socratics, who wrote very often in verse, Plato responded to the rise of political debate, court cases, and historical writing in Athens with the use of philosophical prose in the genre of the Socratic dialogue. The dialogues are part and parcel of the development of prose as a literary genre aimed at readers, rather than hearers, although they obviously rest on a resemblance to the oral nature of poetry, which was either recited or performed in the theater. Consequently, Plato's prose is very far from the prose of philosophers like Kant or Russell: Plato's dialogues are full of colloquialisms, proverbs, puns, fanciful etymologies, unusual exclamations (for example, "by the dog," often out of Socrates' mouth), mythological allusions, and myths invented by Plato himself in order to explain a point to readers without philosophical training or to address questions that cannot be reduced to rational terms. In addition, the dialogues are peppered with frequent quotations from epic, lyric, and tragic poetry, as well as with names of well-known people and places, and references to historical events. Since all these elements must be regarded as an integral part of the arguments, I have tried to help the reader through the maze by means of this introduction, the individual introductions to each of the dialogues, and the footnotes and endnotes in this volume, for which Debra Nails' *The People of Plato* has been a tremendous help. I have tried to provide as much information as was possible within the limits of this series and without becoming obtrusive; accordingly, topography and the Greek gods and heroes are dealt with only minimally here; readers with a geographical interest may refer to Robert Morkot's *The Penguin Historical Atlas of Ancient Greece* and, as far as myth is concerned, to the many good retellings that are available of the origins, attributes, and actions of the Greek gods, including my favorite, J.-P. Vernant's *The Universe, the Gods, and Men*.

Every reader of Plato would like to know the order in which the dialogues were written. Unfortunately, even computerized analyses of the Greek text of the dialogues have failed to yield a generally agreed sequence of composition. The dialogues themselves do not give us enough indications of their relative chronology, and we cannot trust the occasional internal references to contemporary events for dating purposes other than the "dramatic" dates of the dialogues, since Plato sets many of them in the past—Socrates and many of the Sophists featured in the dialogues were dead for most of Plato's lifetime. We must also note that the arrangement in tetralogies by Thrasyllus,* to which some editors have kept, is not to be taken as a guide for chronological purposes either.

Nevertheless, some stylistic differences, together with changes in topics and mode of argumentation, have yielded a conventional grouping of the dialogues into early, middle, and late, although there is some disagreement about a few dialogues. The twenty-six dialogues that are generally recognized as authentic can be grouped as follows:†

---

*A Greek philosopher from Alexandria who was also the astrologer of the Roman emperor Tiberius in the first century C.E.

†See Charles Kahn's *Plato and the Socratic Dialogue*, pp. 47–48. The ascription of the dialogues to different periods is generally agreed; the sequence of composition within each period follows Kahn's conjecture, which I find plausible.

Early

1. *Apology, Crito*
2. *Ion, Shorter Hippias* (also known as *Lesser Hippias* or *Hippias Minor*)
3. *Gorgias, Menexenus*
4. *Laches, Charmides, Euthyphro, Protagoras*
5. *Meno, Lysis, Euthydemus*
6. *Symposium, Phaedo, Cratylus*

Middle

Republic, Phaedrus, Parmenides, Theaetetus

Late

Sophist, Statesman, Philebus, Timaeus, Critias, Laws

Some of the early dialogues are often called "aporetic" because they leave the interlocutors (and the readers) at a loss (*aporia*) regarding the conclusion about the issue under examination (for example, lying in *Shorter Hippias*; best training of the youth in *Laches*). Nevertheless, one comes away from reading these early dialogues with a clear idea of the difference between the search for definitions by means of philosophical discussion, on the one hand, and idle talk, on the other.

Also in the early dialogues, Socrates often confronts Sophists about topics on which they were famous experts. The mode of Socratic argumentation is known as "elenchus" (examination by means of refutation); it consists mainly of Socrates' preliminary admission of a statement from his interlocutor and his subsequent deduction of several other statements that eventually lead to a contradiction with the first, from which it follows that the first must be wrong. The reader will no doubt soon recognize that this is an annoying way of practicing philosophy, and perhaps Plato expects to create such annoyance as an indirect explanation of the reaction that Socrates provoked in his fellow citizens. In any event, the elenctic mode of argumentation is consistent with Socrates' claim that he neither knew nor taught anything (a recurring Socratic statement) but simply aimed to discover the truth with the help of his interlocutors, who were never charged tuition fees.

The middle dialogues are clearly a transitional phase: *Republic* still displays Socrates and his elenctic method very prominently, and takes his particular version of dialectical discussion to its ultimate consequences, which are expounded one night at a businessman's house in the Piraeus, away from the Agora, while a festival in honor of the

Thracian goddess Bendis that has never been seen before in Athens takes place outdoors, featuring a spectacular torch-race on horseback attended by a gathering of young men (*Republic* 328a).* *Phaedrus* is a discussion of the value of rhetoric and writing, and *Parmenides* is a consideration of the problem of Being that exceeds by far in complexity the metaphysics of previous dialogues. *Theaetetus* adumbrates the philosophical methodology of the late period with a re-elaboration of the theory of knowledge that will be continued in *Sophist*.

In the late dialogues, Plato departs from the Socratic elenchus and develops a new system of "division," in which he seems to have been especially interested later in life. The question-and-answer way of conducting the conversation is never completely abandoned, but in dialogues like *Statesman* (perhaps the best example of this method), it seems to give way to an effort in precise philosophical definition that is closer to a modern notion of the task of a philosopher. *Philebus* contains a very interesting assessment of the role of pleasure in life that is very often overlooked. *Timaeus* is Plato's contribution to cosmology, and was historically very influential. *Laws*, the last of Plato's dialogues, is the closest that Plato came to a continuous exposition of philosophical views as applied to "real-world" problems.

The lack of a precise chronology should not be taken as a stumbling block in the reading of Plato, for the dialogues, from *Apology* to *Laws*, are clearly interconnected. In fact, one should read the early dialogues again after becoming acquainted with the middle and late ones, since this is sometimes the only way to understand why some of the Socratic questions that appear early on are dealt with in one particular way versus another. When proceeding in this manner, it is also interesting to see what is left out from the discussion in the early dialogues and taken up in later ones. In this respect, scholars have asked themselves the question of whether Plato had all the dialogues planned out from the beginning or had little idea of where his thinking and his writing would take him. In my opinion, that question is ultimately irrelevant; what matters are the connections between the dialogues, whether planned or unplanned.

One more thing needs to be said before moving on to the dialogues themselves: Plato could not anticipate that some of the contents of his writings, such as Socrates' mention of the final judgment in the afterlife (*Gorgias* 523a–524a), would later coalesce with philosophical

---

*After reading the dialogues in this selection, some may want to consider the question whether *Republic* is truly one of Plato's most representative works and/or whether it is Plato's philosophical "fireworks."

and religious doctrines that have held immense sway. Christian thought in particular drew heavily on Plato, with the result that, in the work of authors like Gregory of Nyssa (c.330–c.395 C.E.), it is hard to tell whether Platonism has adopted a Christian face or Christian thought has become Platonic. However, one must keep in mind that Christianity and Platonic philosophy should not be conflated; this is true at the general level, as well as at the specific one that has to do with the use and translation of certain Greek words. For example, the Greek word that is often translated as "virtue" (aretē) does not mean Christian virtues such as faith, hope, and charity, but refers to personal characteristics, like cunning or physical strength, that are needed in order to excel in one's undertakings.

Nevertheless, it is true that Plato is responsible for bringing the moral aspects of virtue (in the Greek sense) into philosophical debate; therefore, from the historical point of view, the conceptual demarcation of cardinal Christian virtues like temperance and fortitude is philosophically indebted to Plato. Similar considerations apply to his doctrine of the immortality of the soul and the judgment in the afterlife.

On This Selection

The publication of Republic in a separate volume of the Barnes & Noble Classics is a fortunate event, since it has allowed this selection to be wider than usual in a book of this kind. Still, given space limitations, I have opted to select dialogues that are crucial for an understanding of Plato's political thought, rather than his metaphysics or his theory of knowledge. I have also tried to enable the reader to compare Plato's different philosophical stances throughout his life.

A few words are in order about the sequence to be followed in the reading. It makes sense to begin with the early dialogues, in order to gain some familiarity with the character of Socrates and his style of argumentation. Accordingly, I have first presented Ion, Shorter Hippias, and Laches, as representatives of the kinds of Socratic questions that may have sparked Plato's interest in his master.

For the rest, however, I have not kept to the chronological groupings, and I have next presented three dialogues on love, rhetoric, and writing (Symposium, Gorgias, and Phaedrus). My arrangement of these three is meant to help in the reader's appreciation of the thematic unity of Phaedrus, which has often proved difficult to elucidate.

The third group of dialogues in this volume concerns the prosecution and death of Socrates (Euthyphro, Apology, Crito, and Phaedo). Given their dramatic continuity, it seems natural to read them in a row, although *Phaedo* stands out among these four early dialogues because of its complexity: It presents Socrates' theory of knowledge, an intimation of the Ideas, the "proof" of the immortality of the soul, and a myth of judgment in the afterlife, all of them topics to which Plato returns in other dialogues.

The fourth and last group of dialogues in this selection features three different works on virtue and politics, two topics that can be traced here from the early dialogue *Protagoras* to the late dialogue *Statesman*, which I personally regard as the crucial dialogue for a correct understanding of Platonic political thought, and the first three books of *Laws*. Some readers may find it interesting (and eye-opening) to read *Republic* between *Protagoras* and *Statesman*, in a sequence that not only is coherent with the generally agreed chronology but also shows Plato taking great pains to deal with the possibility that the best way of life may, in fact, be learned during our lifetime by applying rational thought to the evolving needs of a society, as opposed to relying on the immutable truth that is known only to philosophers. The end product of this particular one of Plato's many philosophical efforts is *Laws*, his last and longest dialogue, from which Socrates is completely absent, and in which an ideal legal code is laid out in painstaking detail.

Stephanus Numbering

The numbers and letters in the margin of this edition correspond to those of the edition of the Platonic dialogues prepared by Henri Estienne (Stephanus is his Latin name) in 1578. Since most scholars use Stephanus numbering when they refer to passages in Plato, the reader should become comfortable with it as soon as possible. However, since the arrangement of the dialogues in this edition does not follow Stephanus' own order, the numbering is not necessarily consecutive from one dialogue to the next. Note also that the Stephanus numbering corresponds to a text in Greek, so there may be minor occasional discrepancies in the lettering between this and other modern language editions, due to the different turns of phrase of the respective translators.

Note on the Translation

Plato had an extraordinary gift to marshal the linguistic resources of the Greek language with remarkable ease and to inimitable effect. As a result, even the best translation necessarily remains painfully distant from the original. For an advanced reader of Plato, and indeed of any Greek author, learning Greek is a much better investment of time and energy than the search for a perfect translation that will never exist.

The landmark rendition into English by Benjamin Jowett (1817–1893) is still serviceable for introductory purposes and has been used in this edition, with corrections proposed by Paul Shorey in the *American Journal of Philology* 13 (1892) and others that I have deemed necessary in order to take into account Greek texts to which Jowett did not have access. Finally, and in line with Jowett's ruling concern about readability, I have also edited the English when it seemed too different from current American idiom.

In the preparation of this edition, I have often turned to the Greek texts of J. Burnet (Oxford: Oxford University Press, 1900–1907), except for *Gorgias*, where I have used the one of E. R. Dodds (Oxford: Oxford University Press, 1959), and for *Euthyphro*, *Apology*, *Crito*, *Phaedo*, and *Statesman*, where I have benefited from the recent edition by E. A. Duke, W. F. Hicken, W. S. M. Nicoll, D. B. Robinson, and J. C. G. Strachan (Oxford: Oxford University Press, 1995).

Acknowledgments

Several faculty members and fellow doctoral students at Columbia University have helped me greatly to complete this project. I owe a special debt to James Coulter, Suzanne Saïd, Elizabeth Scharffenberger, Jackie Elliott, and Michael Mordine. I am also grateful to Jeffrey Broesche and his staff for carrying the burden of book production. Henry Nardi, my longtime friend and independent Americanist, deserves personal thanks for his encouragement, as does my brother Miguel, for keeping me grounded, and Silvia, who knows a lot more than I do about Greek poetry and mythology, and could get tired of Plato without getting tired of me.

Pedro de Blas holds degrees in Law and Classics. He has worked as counsel for several international organizations, including the United Nations and the World Bank, and he is currently a Ph.D. candidate in Classics at Columbia University. He has taught classical languages and literature at Columbia, the CUNY Latin and Greek Institute, and New York University's Gallatin School.

ESSENTIAL DIALOGUES OF PLATO

I. SOCRATIC QUESTIONS

Ion
Shorter Hippias
Laches

ION

Introduction

THIS SHORT DIALOGUE PORTRAYS a conversation between Socrates and the rhapsode Ion, who is otherwise unknown to us. We know that rhapsodes were singers of Homeric epics and that they probably also lectured to their audiences about the interpretation of Homer's poetry. The dialogue tells us that Ion is from the city of Ephesus (530a) in Asia Minor (modern Turkey), and we know that this city was under Athenian control at that time. We also know that the Athenian fleet had been lost at that time in the Sicilian expedition,[1] and that Athens was in the process of appointing foreign generals as a result of an acute shortage of military personnel; therefore, the discussion of whether excellence as a rhapsode is an indication of ability as a general (540d–542a) is not as surprising as it may seem, and Socrates' admission in the last lines of the dialogue of the divine nature of the rhapsode's inspiration should not be mistaken for a stock praise of Ion's gift.

The dialogue can be structured as follows:

- (530a–533c) Is the performance of poetry a skill that requires knowledge?
- (533d–536d) What is poetic inspiration?
- (536e–542b) Rhapsodes do not possess true skill but are divinely inspired.

ION

SOCRATES. Welcome, Ion. Have you come to us now from your native city of Ephesus?*

ION. No, Socrates; but from Epidaurus, where I attended the festival of Asclepius.†

SOC. And do the Epidaurians have contests of rhapsodes‡ at the festival?

ION. O yes; and of all sorts of musical performers.

SOC. And were you one of the competitors—and did you succeed?

ION. I won first prize, Socrates.

SOC. Well done; I hope that you will do the same for us at the Panathenaea.§

ION. I will, god willing.

SOC. I often envy the profession of a rhapsode, Ion; you always wear fine clothes, and looking as beautiful as you can is part of your art. In addition, you are obliged to be continually in the company of many good poets; and especially of Homer, who is the best and most divine of them; understanding him, and not merely learning his words by rote, is a thing to be envied greatly. And no man can be a rhapsode who does not understand the meaning of the poet, for the rhapsode ought to interpret the mind of the poet to his hearers. But how can he interpret him well unless he knows what he means? All this is to be envied greatly.

ION. Very true, Socrates; interpretation has certainly been the most laborious part of my art; and I believe I am able to speak about Homer better than any man: Neither Metrodorus of Lampsacus, nor Stesimbrotus of Thasos, nor Glaucon, nor any one else ever, had as good ideas about Homer as I have, or as many!²

SOC. I am glad to hear you say so, Ion; I see that you will not refuse to acquaint me with them.

ION. Certainly, Socrates; and you really ought to hear how exquisitely I render Homer. I think that the Homeridae‖ should give me a golden crown.

---

*Ancient Greek city in Asia Minor (modern Turkey).

†God of healing, honored by a festival every four years at Epidaurus, an ancient city in the Peloponnese (the southern peninsula of mainland Greece).

‡The rhapsodes were singers who often included the recitation of the Homeric poems in their repertoire.

§Yearly Athenian festival in honor of the goddess Athena.

‖Homeric rhapsodes; at one point they claimed descent from Homer himself.

Soc. I will take the opportunity of hearing your embellishments of
531   him at some other time. But now I would like to ask you a question:
does your art extend to Hesiod and Archilochus,* or to Homer only?

Ion. To Homer only; he is enough, I think.

Soc. Are there any things about which Homer and Hesiod agree?

Ion. Yes; in my opinion there are many.

Soc. And can you interpret better what Homer says, or what Hesiod says, about the matters in which they agree?

Ion. I can interpret them equally well, Socrates, when they agree.

b   Soc. But what about matters in which they do not agree?—for example, about divination, of which both Homer and Hesiod have something to say.

Ion. Very true.

Soc. Would you or a good prophet be a better interpreter of what
these two poets say about divination, not only when they agree, but
when they disagree?

Ion. A prophet.

Soc. And if you were a prophet, would you be able to interpret
them when they disagree as well as when they agree?

Ion. Clearly.

c   Soc. But how did you come to have this skill about Homer only,
and not about Hesiod or the other poets? Does not Homer speak of the
same themes which all other poets handle? Is not war his great argument? and does he not speak of human society and of intercourse of
men, good and bad, skilled and unskilled, and of the gods conversing
with one another and with mankind, and about what happens in heaven
d   and in the world below, and the generations of gods and heroes? Are
not these the themes of which Homer sings?

Ion. Very true, Socrates.

Soc. And do not the other poets sing of the same?

Ion. Yes, Socrates; but not in the same way as Homer.

Soc. What, in a worse way?

Ion. Yes, in a far worse.

Soc. And Homer in a better way?

Ion. He is incomparably better.

Soc. And yet surely, my dear friend Ion, in a discussion about
arithmetic, where many people are speaking, and one speaks better
than the rest, there is somebody who can judge which of them is the
good speaker?

Ion. Yes.

---

*Greek poets of the eighth and seventh centuries B.C.E., respectively.

Soc. And he who judges of the good will be the same as he who   *e*
judges of the bad speakers?

Ion. The same.

Soc. And he will be the arithmetician?

Ion. Yes.

Soc. Well, and in discussions about the wholesomeness of food,
when many persons are speaking, and one speaks better than the rest,
will he who recognizes the better speaker be a different person from
him who recognizes the worse, or the same?

Ion. Clearly the same.

Soc. And who is he, and what is his name?

Ion. The physician.

Soc. And speaking generally, in all discussions in which the subject is
the same and many men are speaking, will not he who knows the good
know the bad speaker also? For if he does not know the bad, neither   532
will he know the good when the same topic is being discussed.

Ion. True.

Soc. Is not the same person skilful in both?

Ion. Yes.

Soc. And you say that Homer and the other poets, such as Hesiod
and Archilochus, speak of the same things, although not in the same
way; but the one speaks well and the other not so well?

Ion. Yes; and I am right in saying so.

Soc. And if you knew the good speaker, you would also know the   *b*
inferior speakers to be inferior?

Ion. That is true.

Soc. Then, my dear friend, can I be mistaken in saying that Ion is
equally skilled in Homer and in other poets, since he himself acknowledges that the same person will be a good judge of all those who speak
of the same things; and that almost all poets do speak of the same things?

Ion. Why then, Socrates, do I lose attention and go to sleep and
have absolutely no ideas of the least value, when any one speaks of any   *c*
other poet; but when Homer is mentioned, I wake up at once and am
all attention and have plenty to say?

Soc. The reason, my friend, is obvious. No one can fail to see that
you speak of Homer without any art or knowledge. If you were able to
speak of him by rules of art, you would have been able to speak of all
other poets; for poetry is a whole.

Ion. Yes.

Soc. And when any one acquires any other art as a whole, the same   *d*
may be said of them. Would you like me to explain my meaning, Ion?

Ion. Yes, indeed, Socrates; I very much wish that you would: for I
love to hear you wise men talk.

Soc. I wish we were wise, Ion, and that you could truly call us so; but you rhapsodes and actors, and the poets whose verses you sing, are wise; whereas I am a common man, who only speaks the truth. For

e   consider what a very commonplace and trivial thing is this which I have said—a thing which any man might say: that when a man has acquired a knowledge of a whole art, the enquiry into good and bad is one and the same. Let us consider this matter; is not the art of painting a whole?

Ion. Yes.

Soc. And there are and have been many painters good and bad?

Ion. Yes.

Soc. And did you ever know any one who was skilful in pointing out the excellences and defects of Polygnotus* the son of Aglaophon,

533   but incapable of criticizing other painters; and when the work of any other painter was produced, went to sleep and was at a loss, and had no ideas; but when he had to give his opinion about Polygnotus, or whoever the painter might be, and about him only, woke up and was attentive and had plenty to say?

Ion. No indeed, I have never known such a person.

Soc. Or did you ever know of any one in sculpture, who was skilful in expounding the merits of Daedalus the son of Metion, or of

b   Epeius the son of Panopeus, or of Theodorus† the Samian, or of any individual sculptor; but when the works of sculptors in general were produced, was at a loss and went to sleep and had nothing to say?

Ion. No indeed; no more than the other.

Soc. And if I am not mistaken, you never met with any one among flute-players or harp-players or singers to the harp or rhapsodes who was able to discourse of Olympus or Thamyras or Orpheus,‡ or Phemius

c   the rhapsode of Ithaca, but was at a loss when he came to speak of Ion of Ephesus, and had no notion of his merits or defects?

Ion. I cannot deny what you say, Socrates. Nevertheless I am conscious in my own self, and the world agrees with me in thinking that I do speak better and have more to say about Homer than any other man. But I do not speak equally well about others—tell me the reason of this.

d   Soc. All right, Ion; I will proceed to explain to you what I imagine

---

*Famous Athenian painter (c.500–c.440 B.C.E.) who decorated the painted colonnade (stoa poikilē), located near the Agora (marketplace and civic center of Athens).

†Daedalus: mythical craftsman of exceptional talent; Epeius: builder of the Trojan horse (Iliad 8.493); Theodorus: famous artist of the sixth century B.C.E.

‡Olympus: mythical inventor of pipe-playing; Thamyras: Thracian lyre player; Orpheus: mythical Thracian musician who sang so sweetly that he charmed trees and animals.

to be the reason of this. The gift which you possess of speaking excellently about Homer is not an art, but, as I was just saying, an inspiration; there is a divinity moving you, like that contained in the stone which Euripides calls a magnet, but which is commonly known as the stone of Heraclea. This stone not only attracts iron rings, but also imparts to them a similar power of attracting other rings; and sometimes e you may see a number of pieces of iron and rings suspended from one another so as to form quite a long chain: and all of them derive their power of suspension from the original stone. In like manner the Muse first of all inspires men herself; and from these inspired persons a chain of other persons is suspended, who take the inspiration. For all good poets, epic as well as lyric, compose their beautiful poems not by art, but because they are inspired and possessed. And as the Corybantian revelers when they dance are not in their right mind,[3] so the lyric poets are 534 not in their right mind when they are composing their beautiful strains: but when falling under the power of music and metre they are inspired and possessed; like Bacchic maidens who draw milk and honey from the rivers when they are under the influence of Dionysus but not when they are in their right mind. And the soul of the lyric poet does the same, as they themselves say; for they tell us that they bring songs from honeyed fountains, culling them out of the gardens and dells of the Muses; they, b like the bees, winging their way from flower to flower. And this is true. For the poet is a light and winged and holy thing, and there is no invention in him until he has been inspired and is out of his senses, and the mind is no longer in him: when he has not attained to this state, he is powerless and is unable to utter his oracles. Many are the noble words in which poets speak concerning the actions of men; but like yourself when speaking about Homer, they do not speak of them by any rules of art: they are simply inspired to utter that to which the Muse impels them, and that only; and when inspired, one of them will make c dithyrambs, another hymns of praise, another choral strains, another epic or iambic verses—and he who is good at one is not good at any other kind of verse: for not by art does the poet sing, but by power divine. Had he learned by rules of art, he would have known how to speak not of one theme only, but of all; and therefore god takes away the minds of poets, and uses them as his ministers, as he also uses di- d viners and holy prophets, in order that we who hear them may know them to be speaking not of themselves who utter these priceless words in a state of unconsciousness, but that god himself is the speaker, and that through them he is conversing with us. Tynnichus* the Chalcidian

---

*Little-known poet, perhaps of the early fifth century B.C.E.

affords a striking instance of what I am saying: he wrote nothing that any one would care to remember but the famous paean which is in every one's mouth, one of the finest poems ever written, simply an invention of the Muses, as he himself says. For in this way the god would seem to indicate to us and not allow us to doubt that these beautiful poems are not human, or the work of man, but divine and the work of god; and that the poets are only the interpreters of the gods by whom they are severally possessed. Was not this the lesson which the god intended to teach when by the mouth of the worst of poets he sang the best of songs? Am I not right, Ion?

ION. Yes, indeed, Socrates, I feel that you are; for your words touch my soul, and I am persuaded that good poets by a divine inspiration interpret the things of the gods to us.

SOC. And you rhapsodes are the interpreters of the poets?

ION. There again you are right.

SOC. Then you are the interpreters of interpreters?

ION. Precisely.

SOC. I wish you would frankly tell me, Ion, what I am going to ask you: when you produce the greatest effect upon the audience in the recitation of some striking passage, such as the apparition of Odysseus leaping forth on the floor, recognized by the suitors and casting his arrows at his feet, or the description of Achilles rushing at Hector, or the sorrows of Andromache, Hecuba, or Priam,—are you in your right mind? Are you not carried out of yourself, and does not your soul in an ecstasy seem to be among the persons or places of which you are speaking, whether they are in Ithaca or in Troy or whatever may be the scene of the poem?

ION. That proof strikes home to me, Socrates. For I must frankly confess that at the tale of pity my eyes are filled with tears, and when I speak of horrors, my hair stands on end and my heart throbs.

SOC. Well, Ion, and what are we to say of a man who at a sacrifice or festival, when he is dressed in holiday attire, and has golden crowns upon his head, of which nobody has robbed him, appears weeping or panic-stricken in the presence of more than twenty thousand friendly faces, when there is no one despoiling or wronging him; is he in his right mind or is he not?

ION. No, indeed, Socrates, I must say that, strictly speaking, he is not in his right mind.

SOC. And are you aware that you produce similar effects on most spectators?

ION. Only too well; for I look down upon them from the stage, and behold the various emotions of pity, wonder, sternness, stamped upon their countenances when I am speaking: and I am obliged to give my very best attention to them; for if I make them cry I myself shall laugh, and if I make them laugh I myself shall cry when the time of payment arrives.

Soc. Do you know that the spectator is the last of the rings which, as I was saying, receive the power of the original magnet from one another? The rhapsode like yourself and the actor are intermediate links, and the poet himself is the first of them. Through all these the god sways 536 the souls of men in any direction which he pleases, and makes one man hang down from another. Thus there is a vast chain of dancers and masters and under-masters of choruses, who are suspended, as if from the stone, at the side of the rings which hang down from the Muse. And every poet has some Muse from whom he is suspended, and by whom he is said to be possessed, which is nearly the same thing; for he is taken hold of. And from these first rings, which are the poets, b depend others, some deriving their inspiration from Orpheus, others from Musaeus;* but the greater number are possessed and held by Homer. Of whom, Ion, you are one, and are possessed by Homer; and when anyone repeats the words of another poet you go to sleep, and don't know what to say; but when anyone recites a strain of Homer you wake up in a moment, and your soul leaps within you, and you have plenty to say; for not by art or knowledge about Homer do you say c what you say, but by divine inspiration and by possession; just as the Corybantian revellers too have a quick perception of that strain only which is appropriated to the god by whom they are possessed, and have plenty of dances and words for that, but take no heed of any other. And you, Ion, when the name of Homer is mentioned have plenty to say, and have nothing to say of others. You ask, 'Why is this?' The answer is that you praise Homer not by art but by divine inspira- d tion.

Ion. That is good, Socrates; and yet I doubt whether you will ever have eloquence enough to persuade me that I praise Homer only when I am mad and possessed; and if you could hear me speak of him I am sure you would never think this to be the case.

Soc. I would like very much to hear you, but not until you have answered a question which I have to ask. On what part of Homer do you e speak well?—not surely about every part.

Ion. There is no part, Socrates, about which I do not speak well: of that I can assure you.

---

*Singer and priest often connected with Orpheus.

Soc. Surely not about things in Homer of which you have no knowledge?

Ion. And what is there in Homer of which I have no knowledge?

Soc. Why, does not Homer speak in many passages about arts? For 537 example, about driving chariots; if I can only remember the lines I will repeat them.

Ion. I remember, and will repeat them.

Soc. Tell me then, what Nestor says to Antilochus, his son, where he bids him be careful of the turn at the horse-race in honour of Patroclus.

Ion. 'Bend gently,' he says, 'in the polished chariot to the left of them, b   and urge the horse on the right hand with whip and voice; and slacken the rein. And when you are at the goal, let the left horse draw near, yet so that the nave of the well-wrought wheel may not even seem to touch the extremity; and avoid catching the stone.'*

c   Soc. Enough. Now, Ion, will the charioteer or the physician be the better judge of the propriety of these lines?

Ion. The charioteer, clearly.

Soc. And will the reason be that this is his art, or will there be any other reason?

Ion. No, that will be the reason.

Soc. And every art is appointed by god to have knowledge of a certain work; for what we know by the art of the pilot we do not know by the art of medicine?

d   Ion. Certainly not.

Soc. Nor do we know by the art of the carpenter that which we know by the art of medicine?

Ion. Certainly not.

Soc. And this is true of all the arts: that which we know by one art we do not know by the other? But let me ask a prior question: You admit that there are different arts?

Ion. Yes.

Soc. You would argue, as I should, that when one art is of one kind of knowledge and another of another, they are different?

Ion. Yes.

e   Soc. Yes, surely; for if the subject of knowledge were the same, there would be no meaning in saying that the arts were different—if they both gave the same knowledge. For example, I know that here are

---

*Iliad 23.335.

five fingers, and you know the same. And if I were to ask whether I and you became acquainted with this fact with the help of the same art of arithmetic, you would acknowledge that we did?

ION. Yes.

SOC. Tell me, then, what I was intending to ask you—whether this holds universally? Must the same art have the same subject of knowledge, and different arts other subjects of knowledge?   538

ION. That is my opinion, Socrates.

SOC. Then one who has no knowledge of a particular art will have no right judgment of the sayings and doings of that art?

ION. Very true.   b

SOC. Then which one will be a better judge of the lines which you were reciting from Homer, you or the charioteer?

ION. The charioteer.

SOC. Why, yes, because you are a rhapsode and not a charioteer.

ION. Yes.

SOC. And the art of the rhapsode is different from that of the charioteer?

ION. Yes.

SOC. And if a different knowledge, then a knowledge of different matters?

ION. True.

SOC. You know the passage in which Hecamede, the concubine of Nestor, is described as giving to the wounded Machaon a potion, as he says,   c

'Made with Pramnian wine; and she grated cheese of goat's milk with a grater of bronze, and at his side placed an onion which gives a relish to drink.'*

Now would you say that the art of the rhapsode or the art of medicine was better able to judge of the propriety of these lines?

ION. The art of medicine.

SOC. And when Homer says,

'And she descended into the deep like a leaden plummet, which, set in   d
the horn of ox that ranges in the fields, rushes along carrying death among the ravenous fishes,'†

---

*Iliad 11.638.
†Iliad 24.80.

will the art of the fisherman or of the rhapsode be better able to judge whether these lines are rightly expressed or not?

ION. Clearly, Socrates, the art of the fisherman.

SOC. Come now, suppose that you were to say to me: 'Since you, Socrates, are able to assign different passages in Homer to their corresponding arts, I wish that you would tell me what are the passages of which the excellence ought to be judged by the prophet and prophetic art'; and you will see how readily and truly I shall answer you. For there are many such passages, particularly in the Odyssey; as, for example, the passage in which Theoclymenus the prophet of the house of Melampus says to the suitors:

539   'Wretched men! what is happening to you? Your heads and your faces and your limbs underneath are shrouded in night; and the voice of lamentation bursts forth, and your cheeks are wet with tears. And the vestibule is full, and the court is full, of ghosts descending into the darkness of Erebus, and the sun has perished out of heaven, and an evil mist is spread abroad.'*

And there are many such passages in the Iliad also; as for example in the description of the battle near the rampart, where he says:

'As they were eager to pass the ditch, there came to them an omen: a soaring eagle, holding back the people on the left, bore a huge bloody dragon in his talons, still living and panting; nor had he yet resigned the strife, for he bent back and smote the bird which carried him on the breast by the neck, and he in pain let him fall from him to the ground into the midst of the multitude. And the eagle, with a cry, was borne afar on the wings of the wind.'†

These are the sort of things which I should say that the prophet ought to consider and determine.

ION. And you are quite right, Socrates, in saying so.

SOC. Yes, Ion, and you are right also. And as I have selected from the Iliad and Odyssey for you passages which describe the office of the prophet and the physician and the fisherman, do you, who know Homer so much better than I do, Ion, select for me passages which relate to the rhapsode and the rhapsode's art, and which the rhapsode ought to examine and judge of better than other men.

---

*Odyssey 20.351.
†Iliad 12.200.

Ion. All passages, I should say, Socrates.

Soc. Not all, Ion, surely. Have you already forgotten what you were saying? A rhapsode ought to have a better memory.

Ion. Why, what am I forgetting? 540

Soc. Do you not remember that you declared the art of the rhapsode to be different from the art of the charioteer?

Ion. Yes, I remember.

Soc. And you admitted that being different they would have different subjects of knowledge?

Ion. Yes.

Soc. Then upon your own showing the rhapsode, and the art of the rhapsode, will not know everything?

Ion. I should exclude certain things, Socrates.

Soc. You mean to say that you would exclude pretty much the subjects of the other arts. As he does not know all of them, which of them will he know? b

Ion. He will know what a man and what a woman ought to say, and what a freeman and what a slave ought to say, and what a ruler and what a subject.

Soc. Do you mean that a rhapsode will know better than the pilot what the ruler of a sea-tossed vessel ought to say?

Ion. No; the pilot will know best.

Soc. Or will the rhapsode know better than the physician what the ruler of a sick man ought to say? c

Ion. He will not.

Soc. But he will know what a slave ought to say?

Ion. Yes.

Soc. Suppose the slave to be a cowherd; the rhapsode will know better than the cowherd what he ought to say in order to soothe the infuriated cows?

Ion. No, he will not.

Soc. But he will know what a spinning-woman ought to say about the working of wool?

Ion. No.

Soc. At any rate he will know what a general ought to say when exhorting his soldiers? d

Ion. Yes, that is the sort of thing which the rhapsode will be sure to know.

Soc. Well, but is the art of the rhapsode the art of the general?

Ion. I am sure that I should know what a general ought to say.

Soc. Why, yes, Ion, because you may possibly have a knowledge of the art of the general as well as of the rhapsode; and you may also have a knowledge of horsemanship as well as of the lyre: and then you would

know when horses were well or ill managed. But suppose I were to ask
you: With the help of which art, Ion, do you know whether horses are
e   well managed, by your skill as a horseman or as a performer on the
lyre—what would you answer?

Ion. I should reply, by my skill as a horseman.

Soc. And if you judged of performers on the lyre, you would
admit that you judged of them as a performer on the lyre, and not as
a horseman?

Ion. Yes.

Soc. And in judging of the general's art, do you judge of it as a general or a rhapsode?

Ion. To me there appears to be no difference between them.

541   Soc. What do you mean? Do you mean to say that the art of the
rhapsode and of the general is the same?

Ion. Yes, one and the same.

Soc. Then he who is a good rhapsode is also a good general?

Ion. Certainly, Socrates.

Soc. And he who is a good general is also a good rhapsode?

Ion. No; I do not say that.

b   Soc. But you do say that he who is a good rhapsode is also a good
general.

Ion. Certainly.

Soc. And you are the best of Greek rhapsodes?

Ion. By far, Socrates.

Soc. And are you the best general, Ion?

Ion. To be sure, Socrates; and Homer was my master.

Soc. But then, Ion, what in the name of goodness can be the reason why you, who are the best of generals as well as the best of rhapsodes in the entire Greek world, go about as a rhapsode when you might
c   be a general? Do you think that the Hellenes want a rhapsode with his
golden crown, and do not want a general?

Ion. Why, Socrates, the reason is that my countrymen, the Ephesians, are the servants and soldiers of Athens, and do not need a general; and you and Sparta are not likely to have me, for you think that
you have enough generals of your own.

Soc. My good Ion, did you never hear of Apollodorus* of Cyzicus?

Ion. Who may he be?

Soc. One who, though a foreigner, has often been chosen their
d   general by the Athenians: and there is Phanosthenes† of Andros, and

---

*He became an Athenian citizen around 410 B.C.E.

†Not a general, but he also became an Athenian citizen around 410 B.C.E.

Heraclides* of Clazomenae, whom they have also appointed to the command of their armies and to other offices, although aliens, after they had shown their merit. And will they not choose Ion the Ephesian to be their general, and honour him, if he proved himself worthy? Were not the Ephesians originally Athenians, and Ephesus is no mean city? But, indeed, Ion, if you are correct in saying that by art and knowledge you are able to praise Homer, you do not deal fairly with me, and after all your professions of knowing many glorious things about Homer, and promises that you would exhibit them, you are only a deceiver, and so far from exhibiting the art of which you are a master, will not, even after my repeated entreaties, explain to me the nature of it. You have literally as many forms as Proteus;† and now you go all manner of ways, twisting and turning, and, like Proteus, become all manner of people at once, and at last slip away from me in the disguise of a general, in order that you may escape exhibiting your Homeric lore. And if you have art, then, as I was saying, in falsifying your promise that you would exhibit Homer, you are not dealing fairly with me. But if, as I believe, you have no art, but speak all these beautiful words about Homer unconsciously under his inspiring influence, then I acquit you of dishonesty, and shall only say that you are inspired. Which do you prefer to be thought, dishonest or inspired?

e

542

ION. There is a great difference, Socrates, between the two alternatives; and inspiration is by far the nobler.

b

SOC. Then, Ion, I shall assume the nobler alternative; and attribute to you in your praises of Homer divine inspiration, not skill.

---

*Benefactor of Athens; he became an Athenian in the early fourth century B.C.E.
†Shape-shifting god of the sea who has knowledge of the future (*Odyssey* 4.382ff.).

SHORTER HIPPIAS

Introduction

SHORTER HIPPIAS (WHOSE TITLE distinguishes it from another dialogue with Hippias, of disputed authenticity) portrays a conversation of Socrates with the Sophist and polymath Hippias of Elis (470–395 B.C.E.). It is a short dialogue that has received little scholarly attention, and yet it points at one of the issues that would become central to Plato—namely, the examination from the moral point of view of the willingness or unwillingness to act justly.

The discussion is introduced by Eudicus, of whom we know nothing. He is probably in the dialogue only to ask Socrates to comment on Hippias' lecture, because Plato did not want to show Socrates engaging in a discussion with a Sophist on his own accord.

The ensuing conversation between Socrates and Hippias proceeds along the following lines:

- (363a–364c) At a lecture on Homer by Hippias: Is Achilles better than Odysseus?

- (364c–369b) Is there a difference between a person who tells the truth and a liar?

- (369b–373c) Socrates shows that Homer can be used to support either answer.

- (373c–376c) Lying on purpose is better than lying unintentionally.

The above conclusion is one that neither Hippias nor Socrates himself is ready to accept, and the dialogue comes to an inconclusive end, although not without Socrates pointing at Hippias' failure to resolve the question. The issue will reappear in later dialogues (*Gorgias* and *Republic*), in which Socrates will argue that it is impossible for a moral subject with a truly intelligent design to act wrongly, and therefore that anyone (for we are all moral subjects) who acts wrongly does so unknowingly.

SHORTER HIPPIAS

EUDICUS. Why are you silent, Socrates, after the magnificent display which Hippias has made? Why do you not either refute his words, if it seems to you that he was wrong in any point, or join us in commending him? Especially since we are now alone, and all of us may claim to take part in philosophical discussions.

SOCRATES. I would really like, Eudicus, to ask Hippias the meaning of what he was saying just now about Homer. I have heard your father, Apemantus, declare that the Iliad of Homer is a finer poem than the Odyssey in the same degree that Achilles was a better man than Odysseus; Odysseus, he would say, is the central figure of the latter poem and Achilles of the former. Now, I would like to know, if Hippias has no objection to tell me, what he thinks about these two heroes, and which of them he maintains to be the better one; he has already told us in the course of his exhibition many things of various kinds about Homer and various other poets.

EUD. I am sure that Hippias will be delighted to answer anything which you would like to ask; tell me, Hippias, if Socrates asks you a question, will you answer him?

HIPPIAS. Indeed, Eudicus, I would be strangely inconsistent if I refused to answer Socrates, when at each Olympic festival, as I went up from my house at Elis to the temple of Olympia, where all the Greeks were assembled, I continually professed my willingness to perform any of the exhibitions which I had prepared, and to answer any questions which anyone had.

SOC. Lucky you, Hippias, if at every Olympic festival you have such an encouraging opinion of your own wisdom when you go up to the temple. I doubt whether any muscular hero would be so fearless and confident in offering his body to the combat at Olympia as you are in offering your mind.

HIP. And with good reason, Socrates; since the day I first entered the lists at Olympia, I have never found any man who was my superior in anything.

SOC. What an ornament, Hippias, will the reputation of your wis- dom be to the city of Elis and to your parents! But to return to my question: what do you say of Odysseus and Achilles? Which is the better one of the two? and in what particular does either surpass the other? For when you were exhibiting and there was company in the room, though I could not follow you, I hesitated to ask what you meant, because a crowd of people were present, and I was afraid that the question might interrupt your exhibition. But now that there are not so many of us, and my friend Eudicus bids me ask, I wish you would tell me what you were saying about these two heroes, so that I may clearly understand; how did you distinguish them?

Hip. It will be my pleasure, Socrates, to explain to you more clearly than I could in public my views about these and also about other heroes. I say that Homer intended Achilles to be the bravest of the men who went to Troy, Nestor the wisest, and Odysseus the wiliest.

Soc. Hippias! Will you be so good as not to laugh, if I find it difficult to follow you, and repeat my questions several times over? Please answer me kindly and gently.

Hip. I would be greatly ashamed of myself, Socrates, if I, who teach others and take money from them, could not, when I was asked by you, answer in a civil and agreeable manner.

Soc. Thank you: You know, I seemed to understand what you meant when you said that the poet intended Achilles to be the bravest of men, and also that he intended Nestor to be the wisest; but when you said that he meant Odysseus to be the wiliest, I must confess that I could not understand what you were saying. Will you tell me, and then I shall perhaps understand you better; has not Homer made Achilles wily?

Hip. Certainly not, Socrates; he is the most straightforward of mankind, and when Homer has them talk to each other in the passage called the Prayers,[1] Achilles is supposed by the poet to say to Odysseus:—

'Son of Laertes, sprung from heaven, crafty Odysseus, I will speak out plainly the word which I intend to carry out in act, and which will, I believe, be accomplished. For I hate him like the gates of death who thinks one thing and says another. But I will speak that which shall be accomplished.'

Now, in these verses he clearly indicates the character of the two men; he shows Achilles to be true and simple, and Odysseus to be wily and false; for he supposes Achilles to be addressing Odysseus in these lines.

Soc. Now, Hippias, I think that I understand your meaning; when you say that Odysseus is wily, you clearly mean that he is false?

Hip. Exactly so, Socrates; it is the character of Odysseus, as he is represented by Homer in many passages both of the Iliad and the Odyssey.

Soc. And Homer must be presumed to have meant that the true man is not the same as the false?

Hip. Of course, Socrates.

Soc. And is that your own opinion, Hippias?

Hip. Certainly; how can I have any other?

Soc. Well, then, as there is no possibility of asking Homer what he *d* meant in these verses of his, let us leave him; but as you show a willingness to take up his cause, and your opinion agrees with what you declare to be his, will you answer on behalf of yourself and him?

Hip. I will; ask anything you like, without delay.

Soc. Do you say that the false, like the sick, have no power to do things, or that they have the power to do things?

Hip. I should say that they have power to do many things, and in particular to deceive mankind.

Soc. Then, according to you, they are both powerful and wily, are *e* they not?

Hip. Yes.

Soc. And are they wily, and do they deceive by reason of their simplicity and folly, or by reason of their cunning and a certain sort of good sense?

Hip. By reason of their cunning and good sense, most certainly.

Soc. Then they are sensible, I suppose?

Hip. So they are—very.

Soc. And if they are sensible, do they know or do they not know what they do?

Hip. Of course they know very well; and that is why they do mischief to others.

Soc. And having this knowledge, are they ignorant, or are they wise?

Hip. Wise, certainly; at least, in so far as they can deceive.

Soc. Stop, and let us recall to mind what you are saying; are you not *366* saying that the false are powerful and sensible and knowing and wise in those things about which they are false?

Hip. To be sure.

Soc. And the true differ from the false—the true and the false are the very opposite of each other?

Hip. That is my view.

Soc. Then, according to your view, it would seem that the false are to be ranked in the class of the powerful and wise?

Hip. Assuredly.

Soc. And when you say that the false are powerful and wise in so far as they are false, do you mean that they have or have not the power *b* of uttering their falsehoods if they like?

Hip. I mean to say that they have the power.

Soc. In a word, then, the false are the ones who are wise and have the power to speak falsely?

Hip. Yes.

Soc. Then a man who has not the power to speak falsely and is ignorant cannot be false?

Hip. You are right.

Soc. And every man who has power does what he wishes and when he wishes. I am not speaking of any special case in which he is prevented by disease or something of that sort, but I am speaking generally, as I might say of you, that you are able to write my name when you like. Would you not call a man able who could do that?

Hip. Yes.

Soc. And tell me, Hippias, are you not a skilful calculator and arithmetician?

Hip. Yes, Socrates, assuredly I am.

Soc. And if some one were to ask you what is 3 times 700, you would tell him the right answer in a moment, if you wished?

Hip. Certainly I would.

Soc. Is not that because you are the wisest and ablest of men in these matters?

Hip. Yes.

Soc. And being as you are the wisest and ablest of men in these matters of calculation, are you not also the best?

Hip. To be sure, Socrates, I am the best.

Soc. And therefore you would be the most able to tell the truth about these matters, would you not?

Hip. Yes, I should.

Soc. And could you speak falsehoods about them equally well? I must beg, Hippias, that you answer me with the same frankness and magnanimity which has hitherto characterized you. If a person were to ask you what is 3 times 700, would not you be the best and most consistent teller of a falsehood, having always the power of speaking falsely as you have of speaking truly, about these same matters, if you wanted to tell a falsehood, and not to answer truly? Would the ignorant man be better able to tell a falsehood in matters of calculation than you would be, if you chose? Might he not sometimes stumble upon the truth, when he wanted to tell a lie, because he did not know, whereas you who are the wise man, if you wanted to tell a lie would always lie consistently?

Hip. Yes; there you are quite right.

Soc. Does the false man tell lies about other things, but not about numbers, or when he is making a calculation?

Hip. To be sure; he would tell as many lies about numbers as about other things.

Soc. Then may we further assume, Hippias, that there are men who are false about calculation and numbers?

Hip. Yes.

Soc. Who can they be? For you have already admitted that he who b
is false must have the ability to be false: you said, as you will remember, that he who is unable to be false will not be false?

Hip. Yes, I remember; it was so said.

Soc. And were you not yourself just now shown to be best able to
speak falsely about calculation?

Hip. Yes; that was another thing which was said.

Soc. And are you not likewise said to speak truly about calculation? c

Hip. Certainly.

Soc. Then the same person is able to speak both falsely and truly
about calculation? And is that person the one who is good at calculation—
the arithmetician?

Hip. Yes.

Soc. Who, then, Hippias, is discovered to be false at calculation? Is
he not the good man? For the good man is the able man, and he is the
true man.

Hip. That is evident.

Soc. Do you not see, then, that the same man is false and also true
about the same matters? And the true man is not at all better than the
false; for indeed he is the same with him and not the very opposite, as d
you were just now imagining.

Hip. Not in that instance, clearly.

Soc. Shall we examine other instances?

Hip. Certainly, if you are disposed.

Soc. Are you not also skilled in geometry?

Hip. I am.

Soc. Well, and does not the same hold in that science also? Is not the
same person best able to speak falsely or to speak truly about diagrams—
the geometrician?

Hip. Yes.

Soc. He and no one else is good at it?

Hip. Yes, he and no one else.

Soc. Then the good and wise geometer has this double power in e
the highest degree; and if there is a man who is false about diagrams,
it will be the good man, for he is able to be false; whereas the bad is
unable, and for this reason is not false, as has been admitted.

Hip. True.

Soc. Once more—let us examine a third case; that of the astronomer,
in whose art, again, you, Hippias, profess to be a still greater proficient
than in the preceding—do you not?

Hip. Yes, I am.

Soc. And does not the same hold of astronomy?

Hip. True, Socrates.

Soc. And in astronomy, too, if any man be able to speak falsely he will be the good astronomer, but he who is not able will not speak falsely, for he has no knowledge.

Hip. Clearly not.

Soc. Then in astronomy also, the same man will be true and false?

Hip. It would seem so.

Soc. And now, Hippias, consider the question at large about all the
b   sciences, and see whether the same principle does not always hold. I know that in most disciplines you are the wisest of men, as I have heard you boasting in the agora at the tables of the money-changers, when you were setting forth the great and enviable stores of your wisdom; and you said that upon one occasion, when you went to the Olympic games, all that you had on your person was made by yourself. You began
c   with your ring, which was of your own workmanship, and you said that you could engrave rings; and you had another seal which was also of your own workmanship, and a strigil* and an oil flask, which you had made yourself; you said also that you had made the shoes which you had on your feet, and the cloak and the short tunic; but what appeared to us all most extraordinary and a proof of singular skill, was the girdle of your tunic, which, you said, was as fine as the most costly Persian fabric, and of your own weaving; moreover, you told us that you had
d   brought with you poems, epic, tragic, and dithyrambic as well as prose writings of the most various kinds; and you said that your skill was also pre-eminent in the arts which I was just now mentioning, and in the true principles of rhythm and harmony and of orthography; and if I remember rightly, there were a great many other accomplishments in which you excelled. I have forgotten to mention your art of memory, which you regard as your special glory, and I dare say that I have forgotten many other
e   things; but, as I was saying, only look to your own skills—and there are plenty of them—and to those of others; tell me, having regard to the admissions which you and I have made, whether you discover any department of art or any description of wisdom or cunning, whichever name you use, in which the true and false are different and not the same:
369 tell me, if you can, of any. But you cannot.

Hip. Not without consideration, Socrates.

Soc. Nor will consideration help you, Hippias, I believe; but then if I am right, remember what the consequence will be.

Hip. I do not know what you mean, Socrates.

Soc. I suppose that you are not using your art of memory, doubtless because you think that such an accomplishment is not needed on

---

*A small, curved tool used to scrape dirt and sweat from the body.

the present occasion. I will therefore remind you of what you were saying: were you not saying that Achilles was a true man, and Odysseus   b
false and wily?

HIP. I was.

SOC. And now do you perceive that the same person has turned out
to be false as well as true? If Odysseus is false he is also true, and if
Achilles is true he is also false, and so the two men are not opposed to
one another, but they are alike.

HIP. Socrates, you are always weaving the meshes of an argument,
selecting the most difficult point, and fastening upon details instead of   c
grappling with the matter in hand as a whole. Come now, I will demonstrate to you, if you will allow me, by many satisfactory proofs, that
Homer has made Achilles a better man than Odysseus, and a truthful
man too; and that he has made the other crafty, and a teller of many
untruths, and inferior to Achilles. Then, if you please, you will make a
speech on the other side, in order to prove that Odysseus is the better
man; and this may be compared to mine, and then the company will
know which of us is the better speaker.

SOC. Hippias, I do not doubt that you are wiser than I am. But I have   d
a way, when anybody else says anything, of giving close attention to
him, especially if the speaker appears to me to be a wise man. Having
a desire to understand, I question him, and I examine and analyse and
put together what he says, in order that I may understand; but if the
speaker appears to me to be a poor hand, I do not interrogate him, or
trouble myself about him, and you may know by this who they are
whom I deem to be wise men, for you will see that when I am talking
with a wise man, I am very attentive to what he says; and I ask ques-   e
tions of him, in order that I may learn, and be improved by him. And
I could not help remarking while you were speaking, that when you
recited the verses in which Achilles, as you argued, attacks Odysseus as
a deceiver, you must be strangely mistaken, because Odysseus, the man   370
of wiles, is never found to tell a lie; but Achilles is found to be wily on
your own showing. At any rate he speaks falsely; for first he utters these
words, which you just now repeated—

'He is hateful to me even as the gates of death who thinks one thing and
says another:'—

And then he says, a little while afterwards, he will not be persuaded by   b
Odysseus and Agamemnon, neither will he remain at Troy; but, says he,

'Tomorrow, when I have offered sacrifices to Zeus and all the Gods,
having loaded my ships well, I will drag them down into the deep; and

then you shall see, if you have a mind, and if such things are a care to
you, early in the morning my ships sailing over the fishy Hellespont,
and my men eagerly plying the oar; and, if the illustrious shaker of the
c   earth gives me a good voyage, on the third day I shall reach the fertile
Phthia.'*

And before that, when he was reviling Agamemnon, he said,

'And now to Phthia I will go, since to return home in the beaked ships
is far better, nor am I inclined to stay here in dishonour and amass
d   wealth and riches for you.'†

But although on that occasion, in the presence of the whole army, he
spoke after this fashion, and on the other occasion to his companions,
he appears never to have made any preparation or attempt to draw
down the ships, as if he had the least intention of sailing home; so
nobly regardless was he of the truth. Now I, Hippias, originally asked
e   you the question, because I was in doubt as to which of the two heroes was intended by the poet to be the best, and because I thought that
both of them were the best, and that it would be difficult to decide
which was the better of them, not only in respect of truth and falsehood, but of virtue generally, for even in this matter of speaking the
truth they are much upon a par.

HIP. There you are wrong, Socrates; for in so far as Achilles speaks
falsely, the falsehood is obviously unintentional. He is compelled against
his will to remain and rescue the army in their misfortune. But when
Odysseus speaks falsely he is voluntarily and intentionally false.

SOC. You, dear Hippias, like Odysseus, are a deceiver yourself.

HIP. Certainly not, Socrates; what makes you say so?

371   SOC. Because you say that Achilles does not speak falsely from
design, when he is not only a deceiver, but besides being a braggart,
in Homer's description of him is so cunning, and so far superior to
Odysseus in lying and pretending, that he dares to contradict himself,
and Odysseus does not find him out; at any rate he does not appear to
b   say anything to him which would imply that he perceived his falsehood.

HIP. What do you mean, Socrates?

SOC. Did you not observe that afterwards, when he is speaking to
Odysseus, he says that he will sail away with the early dawn, but to Ajax
he tells quite a different story?

---

*Iliad 9.357–363.
†Iliad 1.169–171.

HIP. Where is that?

SOC. Where he says:

'I will not think about bloody war until the son of warlike Priam, illus-   c
trious Hector, comes to the tents and ships of the Myrmidons, slaugh-
tering the Argives, and burning the ships with fire; and about my tent
and dark ship, I suspect that Hector, although eager for the battle, will
nevertheless stay his hand.'*

Now, do you really think, Hippias, that the son of Thetis, who had been   d
the pupil of the sage Cheiron,† had such a bad memory, or would have
carried the art of lying to such an extent (when he had been assailing
liars in the most violent terms only the instant before) as to say to
Odysseus that he would sail away, and to Ajax that he would remain,
and that he was not rather practising upon the simplicity of Odysseus,
whom he regarded as an ancient, and thinking that he would get the
better of him by his own cunning and falsehood?

HIP. No, I do not agree with you, Socrates; but I believe that Achilles
is induced to say one thing to Ajax, and another to Odysseus because   e
he was well-disposed toward the former, whereas Odysseus, whether
he speaks falsely or truly, speaks always with a purpose.

SOC. Then Odysseus would appear after all to be better than Achilles?

HIP. Certainly not, Socrates.

SOC. Why, were not the voluntary liars only just now shown to be
better than the involuntary?

HIP. And how, Socrates, can those who intentionally err, and voluntarily and designedly commit iniquities, be better than those who err
and do wrong involuntarily? Surely there is a great excuse to be made for   372
a man telling a falsehood, or doing an injury or any sort of harm to another in ignorance. And the laws are obviously far more severe on those
who lie or do evil voluntarily, than on those who do evil involuntarily.

SOC. You see, Hippias, as I have already told you, how pertinacious
I am in asking questions of wise men. And I think that this is the only   b
good point about me, for I am full of defects, and always going wrong
in some way or other. My deficiency is proved to me by the fact that
when I meet one of you who are famous for wisdom, and to whose
wisdom all the Hellenes are witnesses, I am found out to know nothing. For speaking generally, I hardly ever have the same opinion about

---

*Iliad 9.650–655.

†Also spelled Chiron; wise and most famous centaur of Greek mythology; teacher of
Achilles and many other heroes.

c anything which you have, and what proof of ignorance can be greater than to differ from wise men? But I have one singular good quality, which is my salvation: I am not ashamed to learn, and I ask and enquire, and am very grateful to those who answer me, and never fail to give them my grateful thanks; and when I learn a thing I never deny my teacher, or pretend that the lesson is a discovery of my own, but I praise his wisdom, and proclaim what I have learned from him. And now I can-

d not agree with what you are saying, but I strongly disagree. Well, I know that this is my own fault, and is a defect in my character, but I will not pretend to be more than I am; and my opinion, Hippias, is the very contrary of what you are saying. For I maintain that those who hurt or injure mankind, and speak falsely and deceive, and err voluntarily, are better far than those who do wrong involuntarily. Sometimes, however, I am of the opposite opinion; for my ideas about this matter are

e all over the place, a condition obviously occasioned by ignorance. And just now I happen to be in a crisis of my disorder at which those who err voluntarily appear to me better than those who err involuntarily. My present state of mind is due to our previous argument, which inclines me to believe that in general those who do wrong involuntarily are worse than those who do wrong voluntarily, and therefore I hope that you will be good to me, and not refuse to heal me; for you will do me a much greater benefit if you cure my soul of ignorance, than you would if you

373 were to cure my body of disease. I must, however, tell you beforehand, that if you talk to me at length you will not cure me, for I shall not be able to follow you; but if you will answer me, as you did just now, you will do me a great deal of good, and I do not think that you will be any the worse yourself. And I have some claim upon you also, son of Ape-mantus, for you incited me to converse with Hippias; and now, if Hippias will not answer me, you must entreat him on my behalf.

EUD. But I do not think, Socrates, that Hippias will require any en-

b treaty of mine; for he has already said that he will refuse to answer no man. Did you not say so, Hippias?

HIP. Yes, I did; but then, Eudicus, Socrates is always troublesome in an argument, and appears to be dishonest.

SOC. Excellent Hippias, I do not do so intentionally (if I did, I would be a wise man and a master of wiles, according to you), but un-intentionally, and therefore you must pardon me; for, as you say, who-ever is unintentionally dishonest should be pardoned.

c EUD. Yes, Hippias, do as he says; and for our sake, and also that you may not belie yourself, answer whatever Socrates asks you.

HIP. I will answer, as you request me; ask whatever you like.

SOC. I am very desirous, Hippias, of examining this question, as to which are the better—those who err voluntarily or involuntarily? And if you will answer me, I think that I can put you in the best way of approaching the subject: You would admit, would you not, that there are good runners?

HIP. Yes.　　　　　　　　　　　　　　　　　　　　　　　　　　　　*d*

SOC. And there are bad runners?

HIP. Yes.

SOC. And he who runs well is a good runner, and he who runs badly is a bad runner?

HIP. Very true.

SOC. And he who runs slowly runs badly, and he who runs quickly runs well?

HIP. Yes.

SOC. Then in a race, and in running, swiftness is a good quality, and slowness is an evil one?

HIP. To be sure.

SOC. Which of the two then is a better runner? He who runs slowly　　*e* voluntarily, or he who runs slowly involuntarily?

HIP. He who runs slowly voluntarily.

SOC. And is not running a species of doing?

HIP. Certainly.

SOC. And if a species of doing, a species of action?

HIP. Yes.

SOC. Then he who runs badly does a bad and dishonourable action in a race?

HIP. Yes; a bad action, certainly.

SOC. And he who runs slowly runs badly?

HIP. Yes.

SOC. Then the good runner does this bad and disgraceful action voluntarily, and the bad involuntarily?

HIP. That is to be inferred.

SOC. Then he who involuntarily does evil actions, is worse in a race than he who does them voluntarily?

HIP. Yes, in a race.

SOC. Well, but at a wrestling match—which is the better wrestler,　374 he who falls voluntarily or involuntarily?

HIP. He who falls voluntarily, doubtless.

SOC. And is it worse or more dishonourable at a wrestling match, to fall, or to throw another?

HIP. To fall.

SOC. Then, at a wrestling match, he who voluntarily does base and dishonourable actions is a better wrestler than he who does them involuntarily?

HIP. That appears to be the truth.

Soc. And what would you say of any other bodily exercise—is not he who is better made able to do both that which is strong and that

b   which is weak—that which is fair and that which is foul?—so that when he does bad actions with the body, he who is better made does them voluntarily, and he who is worse made does them involuntarily.

Hip. Yes, that appears to be true about strength.

Soc. And what do you say about grace, Hippias? Is not he who is better made able to assume evil and disgraceful figures and postures voluntarily, as he who is worse made assumes them involuntarily?

Hip. True.

Soc. Then voluntary ungracefulness comes from excellence of the

c   bodily frame, and involuntary from the defect of the bodily frame?

Hip. True.

Soc. And what would you say of an unmusical voice; would you prefer the voice which is voluntarily or involuntarily out of tune?

Hip. That which is voluntarily out of tune.

Soc. The involuntary is the worse of the two?

Hip. Yes.

Soc. And would you choose to possess goods or evils?

Hip. Goods.

Soc. And would you rather have feet which are voluntarily or involuntarily lame?

Hip. Feet which are voluntarily lame.

d   *Soc.* But is not lameness a defect or deformity?

Hip. Yes.

Soc. And is not blinking a defect in the eyes?

Hip. Yes.

Soc. And would you rather always have eyes with which you might voluntarily blink and not see, or with which you might involuntarily blink?

Hip. I would rather have eyes which voluntarily blink.

Soc. Then in your own case you deem that which voluntarily acts ill better than that which involuntarily acts badly?

Hip. Yes, certainly, in cases such as you mention.

Soc. And does not the same hold of ears, nostrils, mouth, and of all

e   the senses—those which involuntarily act badly are not to be desired, as being defective; and those which voluntarily act badly are to be desired as being good?

Hip. I agree.

Soc. And what would you say of instruments;—which are the better sort of instruments to have to do with?—those with which a man acts badly voluntarily or involuntarily? For example, had a man better have a rudder with which he will steer badly, voluntarily or involuntarily?

Hip. He had better have a rudder with which he will steer badly voluntarily.

Soc. And does not the same hold of the bow and the lyre, the flute and all other things?

Hip. Very true.

Soc. And would you rather have a horse of such a temper that you 375 may ride him badly voluntarily or involuntarily?

Hip. I would rather have a horse which I could ride badly voluntarily.

Soc. That would be the better horse?

Hip. Yes.

Soc. Then with a horse of better temper, vicious actions would be produced voluntarily; and with a horse of bad temper involuntarily?

Hip. Certainly.

Soc. And that would be true of a dog, or of any other animal?

Hip. Yes.

Soc. And is it better to possess the mind of an archer who volun- b tarily or involuntarily misses the mark?

Hip. Of him who voluntarily misses.

Soc. This would be the better mind for the purposes of archery?

Hip. Yes.

Soc. Then the mind which involuntarily errs is worse than the mind which errs voluntarily?

Hip. Yes, certainly, in the use of the bow.

Soc. And what would you say of the art of medicine—does not the mind which voluntarily harms the body have more of the healing art?

Hip. Yes.

Soc. Then in the art of medicine the voluntary is better than the involuntary?

Hip. Yes.

Soc. Well, and in lute-playing and in flute-playing, and in all arts and sciences, is not that mind the better which voluntarily does what c is evil and dishonourable, and goes wrong, and is not the worse that which does so involuntarily?

Hip. That is evident.

Soc. And what would you say of the characters of slaves? Should we not prefer to have those who voluntarily do wrong and make mistakes, and are they not better in their mistakes than those who commit them involuntarily?

Hip. Yes.

Soc. And should we not desire to have our own minds in the best state possible?

Hip. Yes.

d   *Soc.* And will our minds be better if they do wrong and make mistakes voluntarily or involuntarily?

Hip. Socrates, it would be a monstrous thing to say that those who do wrong voluntarily are better than those who do wrong involuntarily!

Soc. And yet that appears to be the only inference.

Hip. I do not think so.

Soc. But I imagined, Hippias, that you did. Please, answer once more: Is not justice a power, or knowledge, or both? Must not justice, at all events, be one of these?

Hip. Yes.

e   *Soc.* But if justice is a power of the soul, then the soul which has the greater power is also the more just; for that which has the greater power, my good friend, has been proved by us to be the better.

Hip. Yes, that has been proved.

Soc. And if justice is knowledge, then the wiser will be the juster soul, and the more ignorant the more unjust?

Hip. Yes.

Soc. But if justice be power as well as knowledge—then will not the soul which has both knowledge and power be the more just, and that which is the more ignorant be the more unjust? Must it not be so?

Hip. Clearly.

Soc. And is not the soul which has the greater power and wisdom also better, and better able to do both good and evil in every action?

Hip. Certainly.

376   *Soc.* The soul, then, which acts badly, acts voluntarily by power and art—and either one or both of these are elements of justice?

Hip. That seems to be true.

Soc. And to do injustice is to act badly, and not to do injustice is to act well?

Hip. Yes.

Soc. And will not the better and abler soul when it does wrong, do wrong voluntarily, and the bad soul involuntarily?

Hip. Clearly.

b   *Soc.* And the good man is the one who has the good soul, and the bad man is the one who has the bad?

Hip. Yes.

Soc. Then the good man will voluntarily do wrong, and the bad man involuntarily, if the good man is the one who has the good soul?

Hip. Which he certainly has.

Soc. Then, Hippias, he who voluntarily does wrong and disgraceful things, if there be such a man, will be the good man?

Hip. There I cannot agree with you, Socrates.

Soc. Nor can I agree with myself, Hippias; and yet that seems to be the conclusion which, as far as we can see at present, must follow from our argument. As I was saying before, I am all over the place, and, being in perplexity, I am always changing my opinion. Now, that I or any ordinary man should wander in perplexity is not surprising; but if you wise men also wander, and we cannot come to you and put an end to our wandering, the matter begins to be serious both for us and for you.

LACHES

Introduction

THE TOPIC OF THIS dialogue is the best possible training for a young man; one may perhaps think of it as the Platonic version of career counseling. The conversation takes place at a site in which two young men have just finished a training session for combat in armor. Their fathers are present: Lysimachus is reputedly a very well-educated man (*Meno* 94a; not included in this volume), and his friend Melesias is a trained wrestler (*Meno* 94c) and a member of the Thirty Tyrants (*Thucydides* 8.86.9; see also "General Introduction," p. xviii). Also present are Nicias, a prominent Athenian politician and general who died during the Sicilian expedition (see endnote 1 to *Ion*), and Laches, another Athenian general in the Peloponnesian War who died at the battle of Mantinea in 418 B.C.E. Given the cast of characters, it is not surprising that the dialogue begins with the question of the value of military training.

Starting from this question, the dialogue proceeds as follows:

- (178a–184c) Nicias praises military training; Laches disagrees: Courage cannot be learned, but depends on one's character.

- (184d–190d) Socrates is brought into the discussion and establishes the need to define courage.

- (190d–194c) Laches' two definitions of courage are: (a) standing and fighting; and (b) endurance. Socrates criticizes both definitions and demands a more general one; he also brings up the question of the role of wisdom in this matter. Nicias is asked to help.

- (194c–197e) Nicias defines courage as knowledge of the probable outcome of fighting.

- (198a–201c) Socrates objects that Nicias' definition depends entirely on what the agent considers good (desirable outcome) and bad (undesirable outcome), and not on present, past, or future. Hence: (a) knowledge and courage are the same, and (b) Nicias has not provided a complete definition. Since the attempt to define courage has failed, the generals suggest that Socrates become the teacher of their sons. Socrates declines and advises all present to find a proper teacher to take classes from together with their sons.

LACHES

LYSIMACHUS. You have seen the exhibition of the man fighting in armour, Nicias and Laches, but we did not tell you at the time the reason why my friend Melesias and I asked you to come with us and see him. I think that we may as well confess what this was, for we certainly ought not to have any reserve with you. The reason was that we were intending to ask your advice. Some laugh at the very notion of advising others, and when they are asked will not say what they think. They guess at the wishes of the person who asks them, and answer according- b ing to his, and not according to their own, opinion. But as we know that you are good judges, and will say exactly what you think, we have taken you into our counsels. The matter about which I am making all this preface is as follows: Melesias and I have two sons; that is his son, and he is named Thucydides,* after his grandfather; and this is mine, 179 who is also called after his grandfather, Aristides.† We are resolved to take the greatest care of the youths, and not to let them run about as they like, which is too often the way with the young, when they are no longer children, but to begin at once and do the utmost that we can for them. And knowing that you have sons of your own, we thought that b you were most likely to have attended to their training and improvement, and, if perchance you have not attended to them, we may remind you that you ought to have done so, and would invite you to assist us in the fulfilment of a common duty. I will tell you, Nicias and Laches, even at the risk of being tedious, how we came to think of this. Melesias and I live together, and our sons live with us; and now, as I was say- c ing at first, we are going to speak openly to you. Both of us often talk to the lads about the many noble deeds which our own fathers did in war and peace—in the management of the allies, and in the administration of the city; but neither of us has any deeds of his own to speak of. The truth is that we are ashamed of this contrast being seen by them, and we blame our fathers for letting us be spoiled in the days of our d youth, while they were occupied with the concerns of others; and we urge all this upon the lads, pointing out to them that they will not grow

---

*Not the historian but a political opponent of Pericles, an extremely influential Athenian statesman of the fifth century B.C.E. who was the leader of the city at the start of the Peloponnesian War.
†Prominent general in the Persian Wars and framer of the Delian League (see "General Introduction," p. xvii).

up to be honored if they are rebellious and take no pains about themselves; but that if they take pains they may, perhaps, become worthy of the names which they bear. They, on their part, promise to comply with our wishes; and our care is to discover what studies or pursuits
e   are likely to be most improving to them. Someone commended to us the art of fighting in armour, which he thought an excellent accomplishment for a young man to learn; and he praised the man whose exhibition you have seen, and told us to come and see him. And we determined that we would do so, and get you to accompany us; and we were intending at the same time, if you did not object, to take counsel
180 with you about the education of our sons. That is the matter which we wanted to talk over with you; and we hope that you will give us your opinion about this art of fighting in armour, and about any other studies or pursuits which may or may not be desirable for a young man to learn. Please tell us whether you agree to our proposal.

NICIAS. As far as I am concerned, Lysimachus and Melesias, I applaud your purpose, and will gladly assist you; and I believe that Laches here will be equally glad.

b   LACHES. Certainly, Nicias; and I quite approve of the remark which Lysimachus made about his own father and the father of Melesias, which is applicable not only to them, but also to us and to every one who is occupied with public affairs. As he says, such persons are too apt to be negligent and careless of their own children and private concerns. There is much truth in that remark of yours, Lysimachus. But why, instead of consulting us, do you not consult our friend Socrates about the
c   education of the youths? He is of your deme, and is always passing his time in places where the youth have noble studies or pursuits, such as you are enquiring after.

LYS. Why, Laches, has Socrates ever attended to matters of this sort?

LA. Certainly, Lysimachus.

NIC. That I can attest to no less than Laches; for recently he supplied
d   me with a teacher of music for my son—Damon,* the disciple of Agathocles,† who is a most accomplished man in every way, as well as a musician, and a companion of inestimable value for young men at their age.

LYS. I and those who have reached my time of life, Socrates and Nicias and Laches, fall out of acquaintance with the young, because we are generally detained at home by old age; but you, son of Sophroniscus,

---

*Greek musicologist (fifth century B.C.E.) interested in the moral effects of musical modes.

†A Sophist; otherwise unknown to us.

should let your fellow demesman have the benefits of any advice which you are able to give. Moreover I have a claim upon you as an old friend *e* of your father; for I and he were always companions and friends, and to the hour of his death there never was a difference between us; and now it comes back to me, at the mention of your name, that I have heard these lads talking to one another at home, and often speaking of Socrates in terms of the highest praise; but I have never thought to ask them whether 181 the son of Sophroniscus was the person whom they meant. Tell me, boys, whether this is the Socrates of whom you have often spoken?

SON. Certainly, father, this is he.

LYS. I am delighted to hear, Socrates, that you maintain the good name of your father, who was a excellent man; and I further rejoice at the prospect of our connection being renewed.

LA. Indeed, Lysimachus, you ought not to give him up; for I can assure you that I have seen him upholding not only his father's, but also *b* his country's name. He was my companion in the retreat from Delium,* and I can tell you that if others had only been like him, the honour of our country would have been maintained, and the great defeat would never have occurred.

LYS. That is very high praise which is accorded to you, Socrates, by faithful witnesses and for actions like those which they praise. Let me tell you the pleasure which I feel in hearing of your fame; and I hope that you will regard me as one of your warmest friends. You ought to have visited us long ago, and made yourself at home with us; but now, *c* from this day forward, as we have at last found one another out, do as I say—come and make acquaintance with me, and with these young men, so that I may continue your friend, as I was your father's. I shall expect you to do so, and shall venture at some future time to remind you of your duty. But what do you say about the matter of which we were beginning to speak—the art of fighting in armour? Is that a practice in which the lads may be advantageously instructed?

SOCRATES. I will endeavour to advise you, Lysimachus, as far as I can *d* in this matter, and also in every way will comply with your wishes; but as I am younger and not so experienced, I think that I ought certainly to hear first what my elders have to say, and to learn from them, and if I have anything to add, then I may venture to give my opinion to them as well as to you. Suppose, Nicias, that one or other of you begin.

NIC. I have no objection, Socrates; and my opinion is that the acquisition of this art is in many ways useful to young men. It is an advantage *e*

---

*Ancient Greek seaport; site of an Athenian defeat at the hands of the Boeotians, during the Peloponnesian War (*Thucydides* 4.91–96).

to them that instead of the favourite amusements of their leisure hours
they should have one which improves their bodily health. No gymnastics
182 could be better or harder exercise; at the same time this, and the art of
riding, are of all arts the most befitting to a freeman; for only those
who are thus trained in the use of arms are the athletes of our military
profession, trained in that on which the conflict turns. Moreover in actual battle, when you have to fight in a line with many others, such an
acquisition will be of some use, and will be of the greatest whenever
the ranks are broken and you have to fight singly, either in pursuit,
b   when you are attacking someone who is defending himself, or in
flight, when you have to defend yourself against an assailant. Certainly
he who possessed the art could not meet with any harm at the hands
of a single person, or perhaps of several; and in any case he would have
a great advantage. Further, this sort of skill inclines a man to the love of
other noble subjects; for every man who has learned how to fight in
armour will desire to learn the proper arrangement of an army, which
is the sequel: and when he has learned this, and his ambition is fired,
he will go on to learn the complete art of generalship. There is no dif-
c   ficulty in seeing that the knowledge and practice of other military arts
will be honourable and valuable to a man; and this lesson may be the
beginning of them. Let me add a further advantage, which is by no means
a slight one—that this science will make any man a great deal more
valiant and self-possessed in the field. And I will not disdain to mention, what by some may be thought to be a small matter—he will make
d   a better appearance at the right time; that is to say, at the time when his
appearance will strike terror into his enemies. My opinion then, Lysimachus, is, as I say, that the youths should be instructed in this art for
the reasons I have given. But Laches may take a different view; and I
will be very glad to hear what he has to say.

LA. It is difficult to say, Nicias, that any kind of knowledge is not to
be learned; for all knowledge appears to be a good thing: and if, as
e   Nicias and as the teachers of the art affirm, this use of arms is really a
species of knowledge, then it ought to be learned; but if not, and if
those who profess to teach it are deceivers only; or if it be knowledge,
but not of a valuable sort, then what is the use of learning it? I say this,
183 because I think that if it had been really valuable, the Spartans, whose
whole life is passed in finding out and practising the arts which give
them an advantage over other nations in war, would have discovered
this one. And even if they had not, still these professors of the art would
certainly not have failed to discover that of all the Greeks the Spartans
have the greatest interest in such matters, and that a master of the art
who was honoured among them would be sure to make his fortune
among other nations, just as a tragic poet would who is honoured

among ourselves; which is the reason why he who fancies that he can write a tragedy does not go about itinerating in the neighbouring states, but rushes hither straight, and exhibits at Athens; and this is nat-   b
ural. Whereas I perceive that these fighters in armour regard Lacedae-mon as a sacred inviolable territory, which they do not touch with the point of their foot; but they make a circuit of the neighbouring states, and would rather exhibit to any others than to the Spartans; and par-ticularly to those who would themselves acknowledge that they are by no means first-rate in the arts of war. Further, Lysimachus, I have en-countered a good many of these gentlemen in actual service, and have   c
taken their measure, which I can give you at once; for none of these masters of fence have ever been distinguished in war,—there has been a sort of fatality about them; while in all other arts the men of note have been always those who have practised the art, they appear to be a most unfortunate exception. For example, this very Stesilaus, whom you and I have just witnessed exhibiting in all that crowd and making   d
such great professions of his powers, I have seen at another time mak-ing, in sober truth, an involuntary exhibition of himself, which was a far better spectacle. He was a marine on board a ship which struck a transport vessel, and was armed with a weapon, half spear, half scythe; the singularity of this weapon was worthy of the singularity of the man. To make a long story short, I will only tell you what happened to this notable invention of the scythe-spear. He was fighting, and the   e
scythe was caught in the rigging of the other ship, and stuck fast; and he tugged, but was unable to get his weapon free. The two ships were passing one another. He first ran along his own ship holding on to the spear; but as the other ship passed by and drew him after as he was holding on, he let the spear slip through his hand until he retained   184
only the end of the handle. The people in the transport clapped their hands, and laughed at his ridiculous figure; and when some one threw a stone, which fell on the deck at his feet, and he let go of the scythe-spear, the crew of his own trireme also burst out laughing; they could not refrain when they saw the weapon waving in the air, suspended from the transport. Now I do not deny that there may be something in such an art, as Nicias asserts, but I tell you my experience; and, as I said at   b
first, whether this be an art of which the advantage is so slight, or not an art at all, but only an imposition, in either case such an acquisition is not worth having. For my opinion is that if the professor of this art is a coward, he will be likely to become rash, and his character will be only more notorious; or if he is brave, and fail ever so little, other men will be on the watch, and he will be greatly scorned; for there is a jeal-   c
ousy of such pretenders; and unless a man is pre-eminent in valor, he cannot help being ridiculous, if he says that he has this sort of skill.

Such is my judgment, Lysimachus, of the desirableness of this art; but, as I said at first, ask Socrates, and do not let him go until he has given you his opinion about the matter.

d   LYS. I am going to ask this favour of you, Socrates; it is all the more necessary because the two councillors disagree. Had they agreed, no arbiter would have been required. But as Laches has voted one way and Nicias another, I would like to hear with which of our two friends you agree.

SOC. What, Lysimachus, are you going to accept the opinion of the majority?

LYS. Why, yes, Socrates; what else am I to do?

SOC. And would you do so too, Melesias? If you were deliberating
e   about the gymnastic training of your son, would you follow the advice of the majority of us, or the opinion of the one who had been trained and exercised under a skilful master?

MELESIAS. The latter, Socrates; as would surely be reasonable.

SOC. His one vote would be worth more than the vote of all us four?

MEL. Certainly.

SOC. And for this reason, as I imagine,—because a good decision is based on knowledge and not on numbers?

MEL. To be sure.

185   SOC. Must we not then first of all ask whether there is any one of us who has knowledge of that about which we are deliberating? If there is, let us take his advice, though he be one only, and not mind the rest; if there is not, let us seek further counsel. Is this a slight matter about which you and Lysimachus are deliberating? Are you not risking the greatest of your possessions? For children are your riches; and upon their turning out well or badly depends the whole order of their father's house.

MEL. That is true.

SOC. Great care, then, is required in this matter.

MEL. Certainly.

b   SOC. Suppose, as I was just now saying, that we were considering, or wanting to consider, who was the best trainer. Should we not select the one who knew and had practised the art, and had the best teachers?

MEL. I think that we should.

SOC. But would there not arise a prior question about the nature of the art of which we want to find the masters?

MEL. I do not understand.

SOC. Let me try to make my meaning plainer, then. I do not think that we have as yet decided what that is about which we are consulting, when we ask which of us is or is not skilled in the art, and has or
c   has not had a teacher of the art.

Nɪᴄ. Why, Socrates, is not the question whether young men ought or ought not to learn the art of fighting in armour?

Soᴄ. Yes, Nicias; but there is also a prior question, which I may illustrate in this way: When a person considers applying a medicine to the eyes, would you say that he is consulting about the medicine or about the eyes?

Nɪᴄ. About the eyes.

Soᴄ. And when he considers whether he shall set a bridle on a horse and at what time, he is thinking of the horse and not of the bridle?

Nɪᴄ. True.

Soᴄ. And in a word, when he considers anything for the sake of another thing, he thinks of the end and not of the means?

Nɪᴄ. Certainly.

Soᴄ. And when you call in an adviser, you should see whether he too is skilful in the accomplishment of the end which you have in view?

Nɪᴄ. Most true.

Soᴄ. And at present we have in view some knowledge, of which the end is the soul of youth?

Nɪᴄ. Yes.

Soᴄ. And we are enquiring as to which of us is skilful or successful in the treatment of the soul, and which of us has had good teachers?

Lᴀ. Well but, Socrates; did you never observe that some persons, who have had no teachers, are more skilful than those who have, in some things?

Soᴄ. Yes, Laches, I have observed that; but you would not be very willing to trust them if they only professed to be masters of their art, unless they could show some proof of their skill or excellence in one or more works.

Lᴀ. That is true.

Soᴄ. And therefore, Laches and Nicias, as Lysimachus and Melesias, in their anxiety to improve the minds of their sons, have asked our advice about them, we too should tell them who our teachers were, if we say that we have had any, and prove them to be in the first place men of merit and experienced trainers of the minds of youth and also to have been really our teachers. Or if any of us says that he has no teacher, but that he has works of his own to show, then he should point out to them what Athenians or strangers, slave or free men, he is generally acknowledged to have improved. But if he can show neither teachers nor works, then he should tell them to look out for others; and not run the risk of spoiling the children of friends, thereby incurring the most formidable accusation which can be brought against any one by those nearest to him. As for myself, Lysimachus and Melesias, I am the first to

c   confess that I have never had a teacher of this kind, although I have al-
    ways from my earliest youth desired to have one. But I am too poor to
    give money to the sophists, who are the only professors of moral im-
    provement; and to this day I have never been able to discover the art
    myself, though I should not be surprised if Nicias or Laches may have
    discovered or learned it; for they are far wealthier than I am, and may
    therefore have learnt from others. And they are older too; so that they
d   have had more time to make the discovery. And I really believe that
    they are able to educate a man; for unless they had been confident
    in their own knowledge, they would never have spoken so decidedly of
    the pursuits which are advantageous or hurtful to a young man. I put
    my confidence in both of them, but I am surprised to find that they dif-
    fer from one another. Therefore, Lysimachus, as Laches suggested that
    you should detain me, and not let me go until I answered, I in turn
    earnestly beseech and advise you to detain Laches and Nicias, and
e   question them. I would have you say to them: Socrates avers that he has
    no knowledge of the matter—he is unable to decide which of you speaks
    truly; neither discoverer nor student is he of anything of the kind. But
    both of you, Laches and Nicias, should tell us who is the most skilful
    educator whom you have ever known, and whether you invented the
187 art yourselves, or learned from another; and if you learned, who were
    your respective teachers, and who were their brothers in the art; and
    then, if you are too much occupied in politics to teach us yourselves,
    let us go to them, and present them with gifts, or favors, or both, in
    the hope that they may be induced to take charge of our children and
    of yours; and then they will not grow up inferior, and disgrace their
    ancestors. But if you are yourselves original discoverers in that field,
    give us some proof of your skill. Who are they who, having been infe-
    rior persons, have become good and noble under your care? For if this
    is your first attempt at education, there is a danger that you may be try-
b   ing the experiment, not on the 'vile corpus' of a Carian slave, but on
    your own sons, or the sons of your friend, and, as the proverb says,
    'break the large vessel in learning to make pots.' Tell us then, what qual-
    ities you claim or do not claim. Make them tell you that, Lysimachus,
    and do not let them off.

        LYS. I very much approve of the words of Socrates, my friends; but
    you, Nicias and Laches, must determine whether you will be ques-
c   tioned, and give an explanation about matters of this sort. Assuredly, I
    and Melesias would be greatly pleased to hear you answer the ques-
    tions which Socrates asks, if you will: for I began by saying that we
    took you into our counsels because we thought that you would have
    attended to the subject, especially as you have children who, like our
d   own, are of an age to be educated. Well, then, if you have no objection,

suppose that you take Socrates into partnership; and you and he ask and answer one another's questions: for, as he has well said, we are deliberating about the most important of our concerns. I hope that you will see fit to comply with our request.

NIC. I see very clearly, Lysimachus, that you have only known Socrates' father, and have no acquaintance with Socrates himself: at least, you can only have known him when he was a child, and may have met him among his fellow-wardsmen, in company with his father, at a sacrifice, or at some other gathering. You clearly show that you have never known him since he arrived at manhood.

LYS. Why do you say that, Nicias?

NIC. Because you seem not to be aware that any one who has an intellectual affinity to Socrates and enters into conversation with him is liable to be drawn into an argument; and whatever subject he may start, he will be continually carried round and round by him, until at last he finds that he has to give an account both of his present and past life; and when he is once entangled, Socrates will not let him go until he has completely and thoroughly sifted him. Now I am used to his ways; and I know that he will certainly do that, and also that I myself shall be the sufferer; for I am fond of his conversation, Lysimachus. And I think that there is no harm in being reminded of any wrong thing which we are, or have been, doing: he who does not fly from reproof will be sure to take more heed of his life from that point onward; as Solon says, he will wish and desire to be learning so long as he lives, and will not think that old age of itself brings wisdom. To me, to be cross-examined by Socrates is neither unusual nor unpleasant; indeed, I knew all along that where Socrates was, the argument would soon pass from our sons to ourselves; and therefore, I say that for my part, I am quite willing to discuss with Socrates in his own manner; but you had better ask our friend Laches how he feels about this.

LA. I have but one feeling, Nicias, or (shall I say?) two feelings, about discussions. Some would think that I am a lover, and to others I may seem to be a hater of discourse; for when I hear a man discoursing of virtue, or of any sort of wisdom, who is a true man and worthy of his theme, I am delighted beyond measure: and I compare the man and his words, and note the harmony and correspondence of them. And such a one I deem to be the true musician, attuned to a fairer harmony than that of the lyre, or any pleasant instrument of music; for truly he has in his own life a harmony of words and deeds arranged, not in the Ionian, or in the Phrygian mode, nor yet in the Lydian, but in the true Greek mode, which is the Dorian, and no other.[1] Such a one makes me merry with the sound of his voice; and when I hear him I am thought to be a lover of discourse; so eager am I to hear his words. But a man whose actions do not agree with his words is an annoyance to me; and the better he speaks the more I hate him, and then I seem to be a hater of discourse. As to Socrates, I have no knowledge of his words, but of old, as would seem, I have had experience of his deeds; and his deeds show that free and noble sentiments are natural to him. And if his words accord, then I am of one mind with him, and will be delighted to be interrogated by a man such as he is, and shall not be annoyed at having to learn from him: for I too agree with Solon, 'that I wish to grow old learning many things.' But I must be allowed to add 'of the good only.' Let him (Solon) concede me this, that the teacher himself be a good man, or I shall appear dull, because I shall take no pleasure in his teaching. But that the teacher is younger, or not as yet in repute—anything of that sort is of no account with me. Therefore, Socrates, I give you notice that you may teach and refute me as much as you like, and also learn from anything I know. So high is the opinion which I have entertained of you ever since the day on which you were my companion in danger, and gave a proof of your valor such as only a man of merit can give. Therefore, say whatever you like, and do not mind the difference of our ages.

Soc. I cannot say that either of you show any reluctance to take counsel and advise with me.

Lys. But this is our proper business; and yours as well as ours, for I reckon you as one of us. Please, take my place, and find out from Nicias and Laches what we want to know, for the sake of the youths, and talk and consult with them: for I am old, and my memory is bad; and I do not remember the questions which I am going to ask, or the answers to them; and if there is any interruption I am quite lost. I will therefore beg you to carry on the proposed discussion by yourselves; I will listen, and Melesias and I will act upon your conclusions.

Soc. Let us, Nicias and Laches, comply with the request of Lysimachus and Melesias. There will be no harm in asking ourselves the question which was first proposed to us: 'Who have been our own instructors in this sort of training, and whom have we made better?' But the other mode of carrying on the enquiry will bring us equally to the same point, and will be more like proceeding from first principles. For if we knew that the addition of something would improve some other thing, and were able to make the addition, then, clearly, we must know how that about which we are advising may be best and most easily attained. Perhaps you do not understand what I mean. Let me make my meaning plainer in this way. Suppose we knew that the addition of sight makes better the eyes which possess this gift, and also were able to impart sight to the eyes. Then, clearly, we should know the nature of sight, and should be able to advise how this gift of sight may be best and most easily attained; but if we knew neither what sight is, nor what hearing is, we would not be very good medical advisers about the eyes or the ears, or about the best mode of giving sight and hearing to them. b

LA. That is true, Socrates.

Soc. And are not our two friends, Laches, at this very moment, inviting us to consider in what way the gift of virtue may be imparted to their sons for the improvement of their minds?

LA. Very true.

Soc. Then must we not first know the nature of virtue? For how can we advise any one about the best mode of attaining something of c which we are wholly ignorant?

LA. I do not think that we can, Socrates.

Soc. Then, Laches, we may presume that we know the nature of virtue?

LA. Yes.

Soc. And that which we know we must surely be able to tell?

LA. Certainly.

Soc. I would not have us begin, my friend, with enquiring about the whole of virtue; for that may be more than we can accomplish: let us first consider whether we have a sufficient knowledge of a part; the enquiry will thus probably be made easier to us. d

LA. Let us do as you say, Socrates.

Soc. Then which of the parts of virtue shall we select? Must we not select that to which the art of fighting in armour is supposed to conduce? And is not that generally thought to be courage?

LA. Yes, certainly.

Soc. Then, Laches, suppose that we first set about determining the nature of courage, and in the second place proceed to enquire how the young men may attain this quality by the help of studies and pursuits. e Tell me, if you can, what is courage.

LA. Indeed, Socrates, I see no difficulty in answering; a man of courage does not run away, but remains at his post and fights against the enemy; there can be no mistake about that.

Soc. Very good, Laches; and yet I fear that I did not express myself clearly; and therefore you have answered not the question which I intended to ask, but another.

LA. What do you mean, Socrates?   191

Soc. I will endeavour to explain; you would call a man courageous who remains at his post, and fights with the enemy?

LA. Certainly.

Soc. And so would I; but what would you say of another man, who fights flying, instead of remaining?

LA. How flying?

Soc. Why, as the Scythians are said to fight, flying as well as pursuing; and as Homer says in praise of the horses of Aeneas, that they knew
b   'how to pursue, and fly quickly hither and thither;' and he passes an encomium on Aeneas himself, as having a knowledge of fear or flight, and calls him 'an author of fear or flight.'

LA. Yes, Socrates, and there Homer is right: for he was speaking of chariots, as you were speaking of the Scythian cavalry, who have that way of fighting; but the heavy-armed Greek fights, as I say, remaining in his rank.

Soc. And yet, Laches, you must except the Spartans at Plataea,*
c   who, when they came upon the light shields of the Persians, are said not to have been willing to stand and fight, and to have fled; but when the ranks of the Persians were broken, they turned upon them like cavalry, and won the battle of Plataea.

LA. That is true.

Soc. That was my meaning when I said that I was to blame for having put my question badly, and that this was the reason of your answering badly. For I meant to ask you not only about the courage of
d   heavy-armed soldiers, but about the courage of cavalry and every other style of soldier; and not only those courageous in war, but also those courageous in perils by sea, and in disease, or in poverty, or again in politics; and not only courageous against pain or fear, but mighty to contend against desires and pleasures, either fixed in their rank or turn-
e   ing upon their enemy. There is this sort of courage—is there not, Laches?

LA. Certainly, Socrates.

Soc. And all these are courageous, but some have courage in pleasures, and some in pains: some in desires, and some in fears, and some are cowards under the same conditions, I would imagine.

LA. Very true.

Soc. Now I was asking about courage and cowardice in general. And I will begin with courage, and once more ask: what is that common quality, which is the same in all these cases, and which is called courage? Do you now understand what I mean?

LA. Not completely.

192   Soc. I mean this: as I might ask what is that quality which is called quickness, and which is found in running, in playing the lyre, in speaking, in learning, and in many other similar actions, or rather which we

---

*Ancient Greek city; site of a Persian defeat at the hands of the Greek army led by the Spartan king Pausanias (*Herodotus* 9.53—but the account given there is different from Socrates').

possess in nearly every action that is worth mentioning of arms, legs, mouth, voice, mind; would you not apply the term quickness to all of them?

LA. Yes.

SOC. And suppose I were to be asked by someone: what is that common quality, Socrates, which, in all these uses of the word, you call quickness? I would say the quality which accomplishes much in a little time—whether in running, speaking, or in any other sort of action.   b

LA. You would be quite correct.

SOC. And now, Laches, try and tell me in like manner, what is that common quality called courage, which includes all the various uses of the term when applied both to pleasure and pain, and in all cases to which I was just now referring?

LA. I would say that courage is a sort of endurance of the soul, if I am to speak of the universal nature which pervades them all.   c

SOC. But that is what we must do if we are to answer the question. And yet I cannot say that every kind of endurance is, in my opinion, to be deemed courage. Here is my reason: I am sure, Laches, that you would consider courage to be a very noble quality.

LA. Most noble, certainly.

SOC. And you would say that a wise endurance is also good and noble?

LA. Very noble.

SOC. But what would you say of a foolish endurance? Is not that, on   d the other hand, to be regarded as evil and hurtful?

LA. True.

SOC. And is anything noble which is evil and hurtful?

LA. I ought not to say that, Socrates.

SOC. Then you would not admit that sort of endurance to be courage—for it is not noble, but courage is noble?

LA. You are right.

SOC. Then, according to you, only the wise endurance is courage?

LA. True.

SOC. But as to the epithet 'wise,'—wise in what? In all things small as well as great? For example, if a man shows the quality of endurance in spending his money wisely, knowing that by spending he will acquire more in the end, do you call him courageous?

LA. Certainly not.

SOC. Or, for example, if a man is a physician, and his son, or some patient of his, has inflammation of the lungs, and begs that he may be allowed to eat or drink something, and the other is firm and refuses; is that courage?

LA. No; that is not courage at all, any more than the last.

Soc. Again, take the case of one who endures in war, and is willing to fight, and wisely calculates and knows that others will help him, and that there will be fewer and inferior men against him than there are with him; and suppose that he has also advantages of position; would you say of such a one who endures with all this wisdom and preparation, that he, or some man in the opposing army who is in the opposite circumstances to these and yet endures and remains at his post, is the braver?

b   La. I should say that the latter, Socrates, was the braver.

Soc. But, surely, this is a foolish endurance in comparison with the other?

La. That is true.

Soc. Then you would say that he who in an engagement of cavalry endures, having the knowledge of horsemanship, is not so courageous as he who endures, having no such knowledge?

La. So I should say.

Soc. And he who endures, having a knowledge of the use of the sling, or the bow, or of any other art, is not so courageous as he who endures, without having such a knowledge?

La. True.

c   Soc. And the one that descends into a well, and dives, and holds out in this or any similar action, having no knowledge of diving, or the like, is, as you would say, more courageous than those who have this knowledge?

La. Why, Socrates, what else can a man say?

Soc. Nothing, if that is what he thinks.

La. But that is what I do think.

Soc. And yet men who thus run risks and endure are foolish, Laches, in comparison of those who do the same things, having the skill to do them.

La. Obviously.

d   Soc. But foolish boldness and endurance appeared before to be base and hurtful to us.

La. Quite true.

Soc. Whereas courage was acknowledged to be a noble quality.

La. True.

Soc. And now on the contrary we are saying that the foolish endurance, which was before held in dishonour, is courage.

La. Very true.

Soc. And are we right in saying so?

La. Indeed, Socrates, I am sure that we are not right.

Soc. Then according to your statement, you and I, Laches, are not
e   attuned to the Dorian mode, which is a harmony of words and deeds;

for our deeds are not in accordance with our words. Anyone who saw us in action would say that we had courage, but not, I imagine, the one that heard us talking about courage just now.

LA. That is most true.

SOC. And is this condition of ours satisfactory?

LA. Not at all.

SOC. Suppose, however, that we admit the principle of which we are speaking to a certain extent.

LA. To what extent and what principle do you mean?

194

SOC. The principle of endurance. We too must endure and persevere in the enquiry, and then courage will not laugh at our faint-heartedness in searching for courage; which after all may, very likely, be endurance.

LA. I am ready to go on, Socrates; and yet I am unused to investigations of this sort. But the spirit of controversy has been aroused in me by what has been said; and I am really grieved at being thus unable to express my meaning. For I fancy that I do know the nature of courage; but, somehow or other, it has slipped away from me, and I cannot get hold of it and tell its nature.

b

SOC. But, my dear friend, should not the good hunter follow the track, and not be lazy?

LA. Certainly, he should.

SOC. And shall we invite Nicias to join us? He may be better at this than we are. What do you say?

LA. I would like that.

c

SOC. Come then, Nicias, and do what you can to help your friends, who are tossing on the waves of argument, and at the last gasp: you see our extremity, and may save us and also settle your own opinion, if you will tell us what you think about courage.

NIC. I have been thinking, Socrates, that you and Laches are not defining courage in the right way; for you have forgotten an excellent saying which I have heard from your own lips.

SOC. What is it, Nicias?

NIC. I have often heard you say that 'Every man is good in that in which he is wise, and bad in that in which he is unwise.'

d

SOC. That is certainly true, Nicias.

NIC. And therefore if the brave man is good, he is also wise.

SOC. Do you hear him, Laches?

LA. Yes, I hear him, but I do not understand him completely.

SOC. I think that I understand him; he seems to me to mean that courage is a sort of wisdom.

LA. What can he possibly mean, Socrates?

SOC. That is a question which you must ask him.

e

LA. Yes.

Soc. Tell him then, Nicias, what you mean by this wisdom, for you surely do not mean the wisdom which plays the flute?

Nic. Certainly not.

Soc. Nor the wisdom which plays the lyre?

Nic. No.

Soc. But what is this knowledge then, and of what?

La. I think that you put the question to him very well, Socrates; I would like him to say what it is.

195　　　　Nic. I mean to say, Laches, that courage is the knowledge of that which inspires fear or confidence in war, or in anything.

La. How strangely he is talking, Socrates.

Soc. Why do you say so, Laches?

La. Why, surely courage is one thing, and wisdom another.

Soc. That is just what Nicias denies.

La. Yes, that is what he denies; but he is talking nonsense.

Soc. Suppose that we instruct instead of abusing him?

Nic. Laches does not want to instruct me, Socrates; but having been proved to be talking nonsense himself, he wants to prove that I have

b　　been doing the same.

La. Very true, Nicias; and you are talking nonsense, as I shall endeavour to show. Let me ask you a question: do not physicians know the dangers of disease? or do the courageous know them? or are the physicians the same as the courageous?

Nic. Not at all.

La. No more than the farmers who know the dangers of farming, or than other craftsmen, who have a knowledge of that which inspires them with fear or confidence in their own arts, and yet they are not

c　　more courageous at all for that.

Soc. What is Laches saying, Nicias? He appears to be saying something of importance.

Nic. Yes, he is saying something, but it is not true.

Soc. How so?

Nic. Because he does not see that the physician's knowledge only extends to the nature of health and disease: he can tell who is sick, but that is all. Do you imagine, Laches, that the physician knows whether health or disease is the more terrible to a man? Had not many a man better never get up from a sick bed? I would like to know whether you

d　　think that life is always better than death. May not death often be the better of the two?

La. Yes, certainly so in my opinion.

Nic. And do you think that the same things are terrible to those who had better die, and to those who had better live?

La. Certainly not.

NIC. And do you suppose that the physician or any other artist knows this, or any one indeed, except he who is skilled in the grounds of fear and hope? Him I call the courageous.

SOC. Do you understand his meaning, Laches?

LA. Yes; I suppose that, in his way of speaking, the soothsayers are *e* courageous. For who but one of them can know to whom to die or to live is better? And yet, Nicias, would you allow that you are yourself a soothsayer, or are you neither a soothsayer nor courageous?

NIC. What! do you mean to say that the soothsayer ought to know the grounds of hope or fear?

LA. Indeed I do: who but he?

NIC. Much rather I would say he of whom I speak; for the sooth-sayer ought to know only the signs of things that are about to come to pass, whether death or disease, or loss of property, or victory, or defeat in war, or in any sort of contest; but to whom the suffering or not suf- 196 fering of these things will be for the best, can no more be decided by the soothsayer than by one who is no soothsayer.

LA. I cannot understand what Nicias means, Socrates; for he repre-sents the courageous man as neither a soothsayer, nor a physician, nor in any other character, unless he means to say that he is a god. My opin-ion is that he does not like honestly to confess that he is talking non-sense, but that he shuffles up and down in order to conceal the difficulty *b* into which he has got himself. You and I, Socrates, might have practised a similar shuffle just now, if we had only wanted to avoid the appear-ance of inconsistency. And if we had been arguing in a court of law there might have been reason in so doing; but why should a man deck himself out with vain words at a meeting of friends such as this?

SOC. I quite agree with you, Laches, that he should not. But perhaps *c* Nicias is serious, and not merely talking for the sake of talking. Let us ask him just to explain what he means, and if he has reason on his side we will agree with him; if not, we will instruct him.

LA. You, Socrates, if you like, ask him: I think that I have asked enough.

SOC. I do not see why I should not; and my question will do for both of us.

LA. Very good.

SOC. Then tell me, Nicias, or rather tell us, for Laches and I are part-ners in the argument: Do you mean to affirm that courage is the knowl- *d* edge of the grounds of hope and fear?

NIC. I do.

SOC. And not every man has this knowledge; the physician and the soothsayer have it not; and they will not be courageous unless they ac-quire it—that is what you were saying?

NIC. I was.

SOC. Then this is certainly not a thing which every pig would know, as the proverb says, and therefore he could not be courageous.

NIC. I think not.

e SOC. Clearly not, Nicias; not even such a big pig as the Crommyonian sow would be called by you courageous. And this I say not as a joke, but because I think that anyone who assents to your doctrine, that courage is the knowledge of the grounds of fear and hope, cannot allow that any wild beast is courageous, unless he admits that a lion, or a leopard, or perhaps a boar, or any other animal, has such a degree of wisdom that he knows things which but a few human beings ever know, on account of their difficulty. He who takes your view of courage must affirm that a lion, and a stag, and a bull, and a monkey, have equally little pretensions to courage.

197 LA. Great, Socrates; by the gods, that is truly good. I hope, Nicias, that you will tell us whether these animals, which we all admit to be courageous, are really wiser than mankind; or whether you will have the boldness, in the face of universal opinion, to deny their courage.

NIC. Laches, I do not call animals or any other things which have no fear of dangers, because they are ignorant of them, courageous, but only fearless and senseless. Do you imagine that I should call little chil-
b dren courageous, which fear no dangers because they know none? There is a difference, to my way of thinking, between fearlessness and courage. I am of the opinion that thoughtful courage is a quality possessed by very few, but that rashness and boldness, and fearlessness, which has no forethought, are very common qualities possessed by many men, many women, many children, and many animals. And you, and men in general, call by the term 'courageous' actions which I call rash—my courageous
c actions are wise actions.

LA. Look, Socrates, how admirably—he thinks—he dresses himself out in words, while seeking to deprive of the honour of courage those whom all the world acknowledges to be courageous.

NIC. Not so, Laches, but do not be alarmed; for I am quite willing to say of you and also of Lamachus,* and of many other Athenians, that you are courageous and therefore wise.

LA. I could answer that; but I will not give you the chance to say that I am a haughty Aexonian.†

---

*Athenian general who accompanied the general Nicias—and died—on the Sicilian expedition (see note 1 to Ion).
†Like Laches, natives of the ancient Greek city of Aexone had a reputation for sharp and abusive speech.

Soc. Do not answer him, Laches; I see that you are not aware of the d
source from which his wisdom is derived. He has got all this from my
friend Damon, and Damon is always with Prodicus, who, of all the
Sophists, is considered to be the best hair-splitter of this sort.

La. Yes, Socrates; and the examination of such niceties is a much
more suitable employment for a sophist than for a great statesman
whom the city chooses to preside over it.

Soc. Yes, my good friend, but a great statesman is likely to have a e
great intelligence. And I think that the view which is implied in Nicias'
definition of courage is worthy of examination.

La. Then examine for yourself, Socrates.

Soc. That is what I am going to do, my dear friend. Do not, however, suppose I shall let you out of the partnership; for I shall expect
you to apply your mind, and join me in the consideration of the question.

La. I will, if you think that I ought.

Soc. Yes, I do; but I must beg you, Nicias, to begin again. You re- 198
member that we originally considered courage to be a part of virtue.

Nic. Very true.

Soc. And you yourself said that it was a part; and there were many
other parts, all of which taken together are called virtue.

Nic. Certainly.

Soc. Do you agree with me about the parts? For I say that justice,
temperance, and the like, are all of them parts of virtue, as is courage.
Would you not say the same? b

Nic. Certainly.

Soc. Well then, so far we are agreed. And now let us proceed a step,
and try to arrive at a similar agreement about the fearful and the hopeful: I do not want you to be thinking one thing and I another. Let me
then tell you my own opinion, and if I am wrong you shall set me right:
in my opinion the terrible and the hopeful are the things which do or
do not create fear, and fear is not of the present, nor of the past, but is
of future and expected evil. Do you not agree to that, Laches?

La. Yes, Socrates, entirely. c

Soc. That is my view, Nicias; the terrible things, as I should say, are
the evils which are future; and the hopeful are the good or not evil
things which are future. Do you or do you not agree with me?

Nic. I agree.

Soc. And the knowledge of these things you call courage?

Nic. Precisely.

Soc. And now let me see whether you agree with Laches and myself as to a third point.

Nic. What is that?

d   SOC. I will tell you. He and I have a notion that there is not one knowledge or science of the past, another of the present, a third of what is likely to be best and what will be best in the future; but that of all three there is one science only: for example, there is one science of medicine which is concerned with the inspection of health equally in all times, present, past, and future; and one science of farming in like manner, which is concerned with the productions of the earth in all times. As to the art of the general, you yourselves will be my witnesses that he has an excellent foreknowledge of the future, and that he claims to be the master and not the servant of the soothsayer, because he knows better what is happening or is likely to happen in war: and
199 accordingly the law places the soothsayer under the general, and not the general under the soothsayer. Am I not correct in saying so, Laches?

LA. Quite correct.

SOC. And do you, Nicias, also acknowledge that the same science has understanding of the same things, whether future, present, or past?

NIC. Yes, indeed Socrates; that is my opinion.

SOC. And courage, my friend, is, as you say, a knowledge of the fear-
b   ful and of the hopeful?

NIC. Yes.

SOC. And the fearful, and the hopeful, are admitted to be future goods and future evils?

NIC. True.

SOC. And the same science has to do with the same things in the future or at any time?

NIC. Also true.

SOC. Then courage is not the science which is concerned with the fearful and hopeful, for they are future only; courage, like the other sci-
c   ences, is concerned not only with good and evil of the future, but of the present and past, and of any time?

NIC. So it seems.

SOC. Then the answer which you have given, Nicias, includes only a third part of courage; but our question extended to the whole nature of courage: and according to your view, that is, according to your present view, courage is not only the knowledge of the hopeful and the fearful, but seems to include nearly every good and evil without refer-
d   ence to time. What do you say to that alteration in your statement?

NIC. I agree, Socrates.

SOC. But then, my dear friend, if a man knew all good and evil, and how they are, and have been, and will be produced, would he not be perfect, and wanting in no virtue, whether justice, or temperance, or holiness? He would possess them all, and he would know which were dangers and which were not, and guard against them whether they were supernatural or natural; and he would provide the good, as he would know how to deal both with gods or men.   e

NIC. I think, Socrates, that there is truth in what you say.

SOC. But then, Nicias, courage, according to this new definition of yours, instead of being a part of virtue only, will be all virtue?

NIC. It would seem so.

SOC. But we were saying that courage is one of the parts of virtue?

NIC. Yes, that was what we were saying.

SOC. And that is in contradiction with our present view?

NIC. That appears to be the case.

SOC. Then, Nicias, we have not discovered what courage is.

NIC. We have not.

LA. And yet, friend Nicias, I imagined that you would have made   200 the discovery, when you were so contemptuous of the answers which I gave Socrates. I had very great hopes that you would have been enlightened by the wisdom of Damon.

NIC. I perceive, Laches, that you think nothing of having displayed your ignorance of the nature of courage, but you look only to see whether I have not made a similar display; if we are both equally ignorant of the things which a man who is good for anything should know, that, I suppose, will be of no consequence. You certainly appear to me very like the rest of the world, looking at your neighbour and   b not at yourself. I am of the opinion that enough has been said on the subject which we have been discussing; and if anything has been imperfectly said, that may be hereafter corrected with the help of Damon, whom you think to laugh down, although you have never seen him, and with the help of others. And when I am satisfied myself, I will freely impart my satisfaction to you, for I think that you are very much   c in want of knowledge.

LA. You are wise, Nicias; of that I am aware: nevertheless I would recommend Lysimachus and Melesias not to take you and me as advisers about the education of their children; but, as I said at first, they should ask Socrates and not let him off; if my own sons were old enough, I would have asked him myself.

NIC. To that I quite agree, if Socrates is willing to take them under his charge. I should not wish for any one else to be the tutor of Niceratus. But I observe that when I mention the matter to him he recom-   d mends to me some other tutor and refuses himself. Perhaps he may be more ready to listen to you, Lysimachus.

LYS. He ought, Nicias: for certainly I would do things for him which I would not do for many others. What do you say, Socrates—will you comply? And are you ready to give assistance in the improvement of the youths?

e   Soc. Indeed, Lysimachus, I should be very wrong in refusing to aid in the improvement of anybody. And if I had shown in this conversation that I had a knowledge which Nicias and Laches have not, then I admit that you would be right in inviting me to perform this duty; but as we are all in the same perplexity, why should one of us be preferred

201 to another? I certainly think that no one should; and under these circumstances, let me offer you a piece of advice (and this need not go further than ourselves). I maintain, my friends, that every one of us should seek out the best teacher whom he can find, first for ourselves, who are greatly in need of one, and then for the youth, regardless of expense or anything. But I cannot advise that we remain as we are. And

b if any one laughs at us for going to school at our age, I would quote to them the authority of Homer, who says that

'Modesty is not good for a needy man.'*

Let us, then, regardless of what may be said of us, make the education of the youths our own education.

      Lys. I like your proposal, Socrates; and as I am the oldest, I am also the most eager to go to school with the boys. Let me beg a favour of you: Come to my house tomorrow at dawn, and we will deliberate

c about these matters. For the present, let us make an end of the conversation.

      Soc. I will come to you tomorrow, Lysimachus, as you propose, god willing.

---

*Odyssey 17.347.

II. LOVE, RHETORIC, AND WRITING

———◆———

Symposium
Gorgias
Phaedrus

SYMPOSIUM

Introduction

DRINKING PARTIES (*SYMPOSIA*) WERE a common practice in classical Athens. They did not involve the consumption of food, which took place in advance, but were instead entirely given over to drinking, talking, and enjoying the company of courtesans that raised the sexual temperature of the room, with a flute player providing background music. Wine cups, sometimes decorated with erotic images, would go around from one symposiast's lips to another's. How much sexual intercourse actually took place at the symposia is anybody's guess, but it is clear that the atmosphere was one of relaxed conversation and erotic tension in equal parts.

The setting of Plato's *Symposium* is at a remove from that of a real symposium: The symposiasts are so hung over from a celebration held on the previous day that they decide not to drink too much; the flute player is sent away; there are no courtesans; and the conversation is not spontaneous, as each participant must take his turn and deliver a speech in praise of Love (*Erōs*). The end of the dialogue reveals Socrates' own views on love, and through the expedient of the sudden arrival of the drunk Alcibiades, we learn a little about Socrates' own sex life, or the absence thereof.

Symposium takes place at the house of Agathon, an Athenian tragic poet and a near-contemporary of Plato. Present are Phaedrus (a member of the Socratic circle), Pausanias (Agathon's lover and a disciple of the Sophist Prodicus), Eryximachus (a doctor), the comic poet Aristophanes, and Socrates himself. Alcibiades, who joins the company at the end of the dialogue, was a young, beautiful, rich, and very famous politician and general who was accused of religious crimes and changed sides more than once during the Peloponnesian War.

The dialogue unfolds in the following stages:

- (172a–178a) Apollodorus (a very emotional follower of Socrates) narrates to a friend the speeches on Love that were delivered at Agathon's house, which he himself heard from Aristodemus (a fellow demesman of Aristophanes) and had already narrated to Glaucon (Plato's brother). In Apollodorus' version, Socrates invites Aristodemus to join him on his way to Agathon's house, on the day following a celebration of Agathon's victory at a tragedy competition. Since much drinking had already taken

65

place on the previous evening, this one will have not drink, but speeches in praise of Love—at Phaedrus' initiative—as its main purpose.

- (178b–180c) Quoting Hesiod, Phaedrus characterizes Love as one of the most ancient gods. He next praises male homosexual love for the special bond of honor it generates among men, and refers to Achilles and Patroclus as an ideal pair of lovers.

- (180d–185e) Pausanias makes a distinction between two kinds of Love, which is inseparably linked to Aphrodite (sexual desire). There are two Aphrodites, Pausanias says, the heavenly one and the common one, and they must be kept apart. The common one is responsible for raw sexual drive, while the heavenly one is associated exclusively with male homosexual attachments and masters the sexual drive. He then specifically praises the Athenian custom of male homosexuality as involving an attachment of a younger lover to an older one for the sake of teaching the former how to become excellent in life.

- (185e–189d) The doctor Eryximachus points out that the two kinds of Love are inseparable in the human body. He then summarizes the role of Love in several domains of human existence, and emphasizes the need to achieve harmony by recognizing and promoting the higher form of Love and curing the vices to which the lower kind leads us.

- (189d–194e) Aristophanes tells a memorable myth: Humans were initially round beings with two faces, and there were three kinds of these beings: all male, all female, and male-female. Zeus split them in half because of their attempt to attack the gods. As a result, each half looks now for the other half: Some males desire union with males, some females with females, and some desire union with the opposite sex. Moreover, the myth accounts for the fact that the desired attachment to another goes beyond sex: We are unable to define what it is that we want, yet unwilling to let go of it when we have found it.

- (194e–199c) Agathon speaks next. He begins by stating that the previous speakers have not delivered a praise of Love so much as they have discussed the effects of Love on human beings. He then delivers a highly poetic praise of Love as a god who is young, delicate, beautiful, moderate, just, and wise. It is because of Love that there can be order and beauty in human affairs.

- (199c–203b) Socrates is impressed with Agathon's poetic prowess but raises a question: If Love desires beauty, surely this is because it does not have it. And so, if good things are beautiful, no good is to be found in Love. After deflating Agathon's poetic praise of Love, Socrates tells the story that was told to him by the priestess Diotima about how Love is neither beautiful nor ugly, and neither a god nor a mortal, but a spirit between these extremes.

- (203b–212c) According to Diotima, Socrates says, Love is the child of Poros (Plenty) and Penia (Poverty), and has the attributes of both. Love, therefore, is a constant pursuit of Beauty and Wisdom, which humans seek—in many areas, and not only in sexual love—in order to be happy. Moreover, according to Diotima, the true object of love is reproduction and giving birth "in beauty." Examples of such births are the poems of Homer and Hesiod and the laws of Lycurgus and Solon. Given all this, it makes no sense to love the beauty of looks or clothing, but one should strive to behold the true Beauty instead.

- (212c–222c) At this point, Alcibiades enters, drunk, and it is only after a while that he recognizes Socrates. Alcibiades tells the story of his sexual pursuit of Socrates, which was prompted by the latter's fascinating allure but turned out to be in vain. He also praises Socrates for his steadfastness in battle.

- (222c–223d) The end of the dialogue portrays Socrates carrying on his conversation all through the night. All his interlocutors fall asleep, lastly Agathon and Aristophanes (the two poets). Apollodorus wakes up in time to see Socrates depart to his daily routine.

Symposium has justly been acclaimed as a literary masterpiece, and it is undoubtedly a central dialogue for the understanding of Plato's philosophical endeavors. In fact, it addresses the very root of such endeavors, for, through the speech of Diotima, Socrates defines the search for Beauty and Wisdom as a kind of Love that shares in the power and resourcefulness of the most burning erotic pursuits.

SYMPOSIUM

CONCERNING THE THINGS ABOUT which you ask I believe that I am not ill-prepared to answer. For the day before yesterday I was coming from my own home at Phalerum to the city, and one of my acquaintances, who had caught a sight of me from behind, calling out playfully in the distance, said: Apollodorus, Phalerian, halt![1] So I did as I was asked; and then he said: I was looking for you, Apollodorus, just now, in order to ask you about the speeches in praise of love which were delivered by Socrates, Alcibiades, and others at Agathon's supper. Phoenix,* the son of Philip, told another person who told me of them; his narrative was very indistinct, but he said that you knew, and I wish that you would give me an account of them. Who, if not you, should be the reporter of the words of your friend? Tell me, he said, were you present at this meeting?

Your informant, Glaucon,† I said, must have been very indistinct indeed, if you imagine that the occasion was recent; or that I could have been at the party.

Why, yes, he replied, I thought so.

Impossible, I said. Do you not know that for many years Agathon has not resided at Athens; and not three have elapsed since I became acquainted with Socrates, and have made it my daily business to know all that he says and does? There was a time when I was running about the world, fancying myself to be well employed, but I was really a most wretched being, no better than you are now. I thought that I ought to do anything rather than be a philosopher.

Well, he said, jesting apart, tell me when the meeting occurred.

In our boyhood, I replied, when Agathon won the prize with his first tragedy, on the day after that on which he and his chorus offered the sacrifice of victory.

Then it must have been a long while ago, he said; and who told you—Socrates?

No, indeed, I replied, but the same person who told Phoenix;—he was a little fellow, who never wore any shoes, Aristodemus,‡ of the deme of Cydathenaeum. He had been at Agathon's feast; and I think

172

b

c

173

b

---

*Unknown character; the name is unusual.
†One of Plato's brothers, and the main interlocutor of Socrates in Plato's *Republic*.
‡Apparently of low birth, and a fellow demesman of Aristophanes (that is, a member of the same administrative division).

that in those days there was no one who was a more devoted admirer of Socrates. Moreover, I have asked Socrates about the truth of some parts of his narrative, and he confirmed them. Then, said Glaucon, let us have the tale over again; is not the road to Athens just made for con-
c versation? And so we walked, and talked of the discourses on love; and therefore, as I said at first, I am not ill-prepared to comply with your request, and will repeat them if you like. For to speak or to hear others speak of philosophy always gives me the greatest pleasure, to say nothing of the benefit. But when I hear another strain, especially that of you rich men and traders, such conversation displeases me; and I pity you
d who are my companions, because you think that you are doing something when in reality you are doing nothing. And I dare say that you pity me in return, whom you regard as an unhappy creature, and very probably you are right. But I certainly know of you, while you only think of me—there is the difference.

COMPANION. I see, Apollodorus, that you are just the same—always speaking evil of yourself, and of others; and I do believe that you pity all mankind, with the exception of Socrates, yourself first of all, true in this to your old name, which, however deserved, I know not how you acquired, of Apollodorus the madman; for you are always raging against yourself and everybody but Socrates.
e   APOLLODORUS. Yes, friend, and the reason why I am said to be mad, and out of my wits, is just because I have these notions of myself and you; no other evidence is required.

COM. No more of that, Apollodorus; but let me renew my request that you would repeat the conversation.
174   APOLL. Well, the tale of love was on this wise—but perhaps I had better begin at the beginning, and endeavour to give you the exact words of Aristodemus:

He said that he met Socrates fresh from the bath and sandalled; and as the sight of the sandals was unusual, he asked him whither he was going so beautified.

To a banquet at Agathon's, he replied, whose invitation to his sacrifice of victory I refused yesterday, fearing a crowd, but promising that I would come today instead; and so I have put on my finery, because he
b is such a fine man. What say you to going with me uninvited?

I will do as you bid me, I replied.

Follow then, he said, and let us change the proverb to say:

'To the feasts of the good the good unbidden go'[2]

and this alteration may be supported by the authority of Homer himself, who not only demolishes but literally outrages the proverb. For, after picturing Agamemnon as the most valiant of men, he makes Menelaus, who is but a faint-hearted warrior, come unbidden to the banquet of Agamemnon, who is feasting and offering sacrifices, not the better to the worse, but the worse to the better.

I rather fear, Socrates, said Aristodemus, lest this may still be my case; and that, like Menelaus in Homer, I shall be the inferior person, who

'To the feasts of the wise unbidden goes.'

Mind you, I shall say that I was bidden of you, and then you will have to make an excuse.

'Two going together,'

he replied, in Homeric fashion, one or the other will come up with an excuse along the way.

This was the style of their conversation as they went along. Socrates dropped behind in a fit of abstraction, and ordered Aristodemus, who was waiting, to go on before him. When he reached the house of Agathon he found the doors wide open, and a comical thing happened. A servant coming out met him, and led him at once into the banqueting-hall in which the guests were reclining, for the banquet was about to begin. 'Welcome, Aristodemus,' said Agathon, as soon as he appeared— 'you are just in time to sup with us; if you come on any other matter put it off, and make one of us, as I was looking for you yesterday and meant to have asked you, if I could have found you. But what have you done with Socrates?'

I turned round, but Socrates was nowhere to be seen; and I had to explain that he had been with me a moment before, and that I came by his invitation to the supper.

You were quite right in coming, said Agathon; but where is he himself?

He was behind me just now, as I entered, he said, and I cannot think what has become of him.

Go and look for him, boy, said Agathon, and bring him in; and you, Aristodemus, meanwhile sit by Eryximachus.

The servant then assisted him to wash, and he lay down, and presently another servant came in and reported that our friend Socrates had retired into the portico of the neighbouring house. 'There he is fixed,' said he, 'and when I call to him he will not stir.'

How strange, said Agathon; then you must call him again, and keep calling him.

Let him alone, said my informant; he has a way of stopping

anywhere and losing himself without any reason. I believe that he will soon appear; do not disturb him.

Well, if you think so, I will leave him, said Agathon. And then, turning to the servants, he added, 'Let us have supper without waiting for him. Serve up whatever you please, for there is no one to give you orders; hitherto I have never left you to yourselves. But on this occasion imagine that you are our hosts, and that I and the company are your guests; treat us well, and then we shall commend you.' After this, supper was served, but still no Socrates; and during the meal Agathon several times expressed a wish to send for him, but Aristodemus objected; and at last when the feast was about half over—for the fit, as usual, was not of long duration—Socrates entered. Agathon, who was reclining alone at the end of the table, begged that he would take the place next to him; so that 'I may touch you,' he said, 'and have the benefit of that wise thought which came into your mind in the portico, and is now in your possession; for I am certain that you would not have come away until you had found what you sought.'

How I wish, said Socrates taking his place, that wisdom could be infused by touch, out of the fuller into the emptier man, as water runs through wool out of a fuller cup into an emptier one; if that were so, how greatly should I value the privilege of reclining at your side! For you would have filled me full with a stream of wisdom plentiful and fair; whereas my own is of a very mean and questionable sort, no better than a dream. But yours is bright and full of promise, and was manifested in all the splendour of youth the day before yesterday, in the presence of more than thirty thousand Greeks.

You are mocking, Socrates, said Agathon, and before long you and I will have to determine who bears off the palm of wisdom—of this Dionysus shall be the judge; but at present you are better occupied with supper.

Socrates took his place on the couch, and supped with the rest; then libations were offered, and after a hymn had been sung to the god, and there had been the usual ceremonies, they were about to commence drinking, when Pausanias said: now, my friends, how can we drink with least injury to ourselves? I can assure you that I feel severely the effect of yesterday's drinking, and must have time to recover; I suspect that most of you are in the same predicament, for you were at the party yesterday. Consider then: How can the drinking be made easiest on us?

I entirely agree, said Aristophanes, that we should, by all means, avoid hard drinking, for I was myself one of those who were yesterday drowned in drink.

I think that you are right, said Eryximachus, the son of Acumenus;

but I should still like to hear one other person speak: Is Agathon able to drink hard?

No way, said Agathon.

Then, said Eryximachus, the weak heads like myself, Aristodemus,   c
Phaedrus, and others who can never drink, are fortunate in finding that the stronger ones are not in a drinking mood. (I do not include Socrates, who is able either to drink or to abstain, and will not mind, whichever we do.) Well, as none of the company seem disposed to drink much, I may be forgiven for saying, as a physician, that drinking a lot is a bad practice, which I never follow, if I can help it, and certainly do not rec-   d
ommend to another, least of all to any one who still feels the effects of yesterday's binge.

'I always do what you advise, and especially what you prescribe as a physician,' rejoined Phaedrus the Myrrhinusian, 'and the rest of the company, if they are wise, will do the same.'

It was agreed that drinking was not to be the order of the day, but   e
that they were all to drink only so much as they pleased.

Then, said Eryximachus, as you are all agreed that drinking is to be voluntary, and that there is to be no compulsion, I move, in the next place, that the flute-girl, who has just made her appearance, be told to go away and play to herself, or, if she likes, to the women who are within. Today let us have conversation instead; and, if you will allow   177
me, I will tell you what sort of conversation. This proposal having been accepted, Eryximachus proceeded as follows:—

I will begin, he said, after the manner of Melanippe in Euripides,*

'Not mine the word'

which I am about to speak, but that of Phaedrus. For often he says to me in an indignant tone:—'What a strange thing it is, Eryximachus, that, whereas other gods have poems and hymns made in their honor, the great and glorious god, Love, has no encomiast among all the   b
poets, who are so many. There are the worthy sophists too—the excellent Prodicus† for example, who have written in prose about the virtues of Heracles and other heroes; and, what is still more extraordinary, I have met with a philosophical work in which the utility of salt has been made the theme of an eloquent discourse; and many other like things have had a like honor bestowed upon them. And only to think that   c

---

*Greek playwright (fifth century B.C.E.); the play alluded to is not extant.
†A well-known Sophist and diplomat, Prodicus of Ceos was a contemporary of Socrates.

there should have been an eager interest created about them, and yet that to this day no one has ever dared worthily to hymn Love's praises! So entirely has this great deity been neglected.' Now in this Phaedrus seems to me to be quite right, and therefore I want to offer him a contribution; also I think that at the present moment we who are here assembled cannot do better than honour the god Love. If you agree with me, there will be no lack of conversation; for I mean to propose that each of us in turn, going from left to right, shall make a speech in honor of Love. Let him give us the best which he can; Phaedrus, because he is sitting first on the left hand, and because he is the father of the thought, shall begin.

No one will vote against you, Eryximachus, said Socrates. How can I oppose your motion, who profess to understand nothing but matters of love; nor, I presume, will Agathon and Pausanias; and there can be no doubt of Aristophanes, whose whole concern is with Dionysus and Aphrodite; nor will any one disagree with those whom I see around me. The proposal, though, is rather hard upon us whose place is last; but we shall be contented if we hear some good speeches first. Let Phaedrus begin the praise of Love, and good luck to him. All the company expressed their assent, and desired him to do as Socrates bade him.

Aristodemus did not recollect all that was said, nor do I recollect all that he related to me; but I will tell you what I thought most worthy of remembrance, and what the chief speakers said.

Phaedrus began by affirming that Love is a mighty god, and wonderful among gods and men, but especially wonderful in his birth. For he is the eldest of the gods, which is an honor to him; and a proof of his claim to this honor is that there is no memorial of his parents; neither poet nor prose writer has ever affirmed that he had any. As Hesiod says:

> 'First Chaos came, and then broad-bosomed Earth,
> The everlasting seat of all that is,
> And Love.'*

In other words, after Chaos, the Earth and Love, these two, came into being. Also Parmenides† sings of Generation:

> 'First in the train of gods, she‡ fashioned Love.'

---

*Theogony 116–120, with 118 omitted.
†The most important of the pre-Socratics (see "General Introduction," p. xxii).
‡I've changed the wording of Jowett's translation from "he" to "she," since in the extant text the subject is the goddess of the previous line.

And Acusilaus* agrees with Hesiod. Thus numerous are the witnesses c
who acknowledge Love to be the eldest of the gods. And not only is he
the eldest, he is also the source of the greatest benefits to us. For I know
not any greater blessing to a young man who is beginning life than a
virtuous lover, or to the lover than a beloved youth. For the principle
which ought to be the guide of men who would nobly live—that principle, I say, neither kindred, nor honour, nor wealth, nor any other motive is able to implant so well as love. Of what am I speaking? Of the
sense of honour and dishonour, without which neither states nor indi- d
viduals ever do any good or great work. And I say that a lover who is
caught doing any dishonourable act, or submitting through cowardice
when any dishonour is done to him by another, will be more pained
at being caught by his beloved than at being seen by his father, or by
his companions, or by any one else. The beloved too, when he is found e
in any disgraceful situation, has the same feeling about his lover. And if
there were only some way of contriving that a state or an army should
be made up of lovers and their beloved, they would be the very best
governors of their own city, abstaining from all dishonour, and emulating one another in honour; and when fighting at each other's side, 179
although a mere handful, they would overcome the world. For what
lover would not choose rather to be seen by all mankind than by his
beloved, either when abandoning his post or throwing away his arms?
He would be ready to die a thousand deaths rather than endure this. Or
who would desert his beloved or fail him in the hour of danger? The
worst coward would become an inspired hero, equal to the bravest, at
such a time; Love would inspire him. That courage which, as Homer b
says, the god breathes into the souls of some heroes, Love of his own
nature infuses into the lover.

Love will make men dare to die for their beloved—love alone; and
women as well as men. Of this, Alcestis,† the daughter of Pelias, is a
monument to all the Greek world; for she was willing to lay down her
life on behalf of her husband, when no one else would, although he c
had a father and mother; but the tenderness of her love so far exceeded
theirs, that she made them seem to be strangers in blood to their own
son, and related to him in name only; and so noble did this action of
hers appear to the gods, as well as to men, that among the many who
have done virtuously she is one of the very few to whom, in admiration
of her noble action, they have granted the privilege of returning alive to
earth; such exceeding honor is paid by the gods to the devotion and d

---

*Genealogist from Argos who wrote in the beginning of the fifth century B.C.E.
†The myth of Alcestis is best known from the eponymous play by Euripides.

virtue of love. But Orpheus,* the son of Oeagrus, the harper, they sent empty away, and presented to him an apparition only of her whom he sought, but herself they would not give up, because he showed no spirit; he was only a harp-player, and did not dare like Alcestis to die for love, but was contriving how he might enter Hades alive; moreover, they afterwards caused him to suffer death at the hands of women, as the pun-
e ishment of his cowardliness. Very different was the reward of the true love of Achilles towards his lover Patroclus—his lover and not his love (the notion that Patroclus was the beloved one is a foolish error into which Aeschylus has fallen, for Achilles was surely the fairer of the two, fairer also than all the other heroes; and, as Homer informs us, he was
180 still beardless, and far younger). And greatly as the gods honor the virtue of love, still the return of love on the part of the beloved to the lover is more admired and valued and rewarded by them, for the lover is more divine; because he is inspired by god. Now Achilles was quite aware, for he had been told by his mother, that he might avoid death and return home, and live to a good old age, if he abstained from slaying Hector. Nevertheless he gave his life to revenge his friend, and
b dared to die, not only in his defence, but after he was dead. Wherefore the gods honored him even above Alcestis, and sent him to the Islands of the Blessed. These are my reasons for affirming that Love is the eldest and noblest and mightiest of the gods, and the chiefest author and giver of virtue in life, and of happiness after death.

c This, or something like this, was the speech of Phaedrus; and some other speeches followed which Aristodemus did not remember; the next which he repeated was that of Pausanias. Phaedrus, he said, the argument has not been set before us, I think, quite in the right form; we should not be called upon to praise Love in such an indiscriminate manner. If there were only one Love, then what you said would be well enough; but since there are more Loves than one, you should have begun by determining which of them was to be the theme of our
d praises. I will correct this mistake; and first of all I will tell you which Love is deserving of praise, and then try to hymn the praiseworthy one in a manner worthy of him. For we all know that Love is inseparable from Aphrodite, and if there were only one Aphrodite there would be only one Love; but as there are two goddesses there must be two Loves. And am I not right in asserting that there are two goddesses? The elder one, having no mother, who is called the heavenly Aphrodite—she

---

*The mythical Thracian singer (see footnote on p. 10) went to the underworld to rescue his wife, Eurydice.

is the daughter of Uranus; the younger, who is the daughter of Zeus and
Dione—her we call common; and the Love who is her fellow-worker   *e*
is rightly named common, as the other love is called heavenly. All the
gods ought to have praise given to them, but not without distinction
of their natures; and therefore I must try to distinguish the characters
of the two Loves. Now actions vary according to the manner of their   181
performance. Take, for example, that which we are now doing, drinking, singing and talking—these actions are not in themselves either
good or evil, but they turn out in this or that way according to the
mode of their performance; and when well done they are good, and
when wrongly done they are evil; and in like manner not every love,
but only that which has a noble purpose, is noble and worthy of praise.
The Love who is the offspring of the common Aphrodite is essentially
common, and has no discrimination, being such as the meaner sort of   *b*
men feel, and is apt to be of women as well as of youths, and is of the
body rather than of the soul—the most foolish beings are the objects
of this love which desires only to gain an end, but never thinks of accomplishing the end nobly, and therefore does good and evil quite indiscriminately. The goddess who is his mother is far younger than the
other, and she was born of the union of the male and female, and partakes of both. But the offspring of the heavenly Aphrodite is derived
from a mother in whose birth the female has no part,—she is from the   *c*
male only; this is that love which is of youths, and the goddess being
older, there is nothing of wantonness in her. Those who are inspired
by this love turn to the male, and delight in him who is the more
valiant and intelligent nature; any one may recognise the pure enthusi-
asts in the very character of their attachments. For they love not boys, *d*
but intelligent beings whose reason is beginning to be developed, much
about the time at which their beards begin to grow. And in choosing
young men to be their companions, they mean to be faithful to them,
and pass their whole life in company with them, not to take them in
their inexperience, and deceive them, and play the fool with them, or
run away from one to another of them. But the love of young boys
should be forbidden by law, because their future is uncertain; they may
turn out good or bad, either in body or soul, and much noble enthusiasm may be spent on them; in this matter the good are a law to them-   *e*
selves, and the coarser sort of lovers ought to be restrained by force, as
we restrain or attempt to restrain them from fixing their affections on
women of free birth. These are the persons who bring a reproach on   182
love; and some have been led to deny the lawfulness of such attachments because they see the impropriety and evil of them; for surely
nothing that is decorously and lawfully done can justly be censured.

b   Now here and in Sparta the rules about love are perplexing, but in most cities they are simple and easily intelligible; in Elis and Boeotia, and in countries having no gifts of eloquence, they are very straightforward; the law is simply in favour of these attachments and no one, whether young or old, has anything to say to their discredit; the reason being, as I suppose, that they are men of few words in those parts, and therefore the lovers do not like the trouble of pleading their suit. In Ionia and other places, and generally in countries which are subject to the barbarians, the custom is held to be dishonourable; loves of youths share the evil repute in which philosophy and gymnastics are held, be-

c   cause they are inimical to tyranny; for the interests of rulers require that their subjects should be poor in spirit and that there should be no strong bond of friendship or society among them, which love, above all other motives, is likely to inspire, as our Athenian tyrants learned by experience: the love of Aristogeiton and the constancy of Harmodius

d   had a strength which undid their power.[3] And, therefore, the ill-repute into which these attachments have fallen is to be ascribed to the evil condition of those who make them to be ill-reputed; that is to say, to the self-seeking of the governors and the cowardice of the governed; on the other hand, the indiscriminate honor which is given to them in some countries is attributable to the laziness of those who hold this opinion of them. In our own country a far better principle prevails, but, as I was saying, the explanation of it is rather perplexing. For, observe that open loves are held to be more honorable than secret ones, and that the love of the noblest and highest, even if their persons are less beautiful than others, is especially honorable. Consider, too, how great is the encouragement which all the world gives to the lover; neither is he supposed to be doing anything dishonourable; but if he succeeds he is praised, and if he fail he is blamed. And in the pursuit of his

e   love the custom allows him to do many strange things, which philos-
183   ophy would bitterly censure if they were done from any motive of interest, or wish for office or power. He may pray, and entreat, and supplicate, and swear, and lie on a mat at the door, and endure a slavery worse than that of any slave—in any other case friends and enemies would be equally ready to prevent him, but now there is no friend who

b   will be ashamed of him and admonish him, and no enemy will charge him with meanness or flattery; the actions of a lover have a grace which ennobles them; and custom has decided that they are highly commendable and that there is no loss of character in them; and, what is strangest of all, he alone may swear falsely (so people say), and the gods will forgive his transgression, for there is no such thing as a lover's

c   oath. Such is the entire liberty which gods and men have allowed the lover, according to the custom which prevails in our part of the world. From this point of view a man fairly argues that in Athens to love and to be loved is held to be a very honorable thing. But when parents forbid their sons to talk with their lovers, and place them under a tutor's care, who is appointed to see to these things, and their companions and equals reprove them if they catch them in the act, and their elders refuse to silence the reprovers and do not rebuke them—any one who reflects on all this will, on the contrary, think that we hold these practices to be most disgraceful. But, as I was saying at first, the truth, as I imagine, is that whether such practices are honorable or whether they are dishonorable is not a simple question; they are honorable to him who follows them honorably, dishonorable to him who follows them dishonorably. There is dishonor in yielding to the evil, or in an evil manner; but there is honor in yielding to the good, or in an honorable manner. Evil is the vulgar lover who loves the body rather than the soul, inasmuch as he is not even stable, because he loves a thing which is in itself unstable, and therefore when the bloom of youth which he was desiring is over, he takes wing and flies away, in spite of all his words and promises; whereas the love of the noble disposition is lifelong, for it is bound to the permanent. The custom of our country would have both of them proven well and truly, and would have us yield to the one sort of lover and avoid the other, and therefore encourages some to pursue, and others to fly; testing both the lover and beloved in contests and trials, until they show to which of the two classes they respectively belong. And this is the reason why, in the first place, a hasty attachment is held to be dishonorable, because time is the true test of this as of most other things; and secondly there is dishonor in being overcome by the love of money, wealth, or political power, whether a man is frightened into surrender by the loss of them, or, having experienced the benefits of money and political corruption, is unable to rise above their seductions. For none of these things are of a permanent or lasting nature; not to mention that no generous friendship ever sprang from them. There remains, then, only one way of honorable attachment which custom allows in the beloved, and this is the way of virtue; for as we admitted that any service which the lover does to him is not to be accounted flattery or a dishonor to himself, so the beloved has one way only of voluntary service which is not dishonorable, and this is virtuous service.

For we have a custom, and according to our custom any one who does service to another under the idea that he will be improved by him either in wisdom, or in some other particular of virtue—such a voluntary service, I say, is not to be regarded as a dishonor, and is not open

d

e

184

b

c

d   to the charge of flattery. And these two customs, one the love of youth, and the other the practice of philosophy and virtue in general, ought to meet in one, and then the beloved may honorably indulge the lover. For when the lover and beloved come together, having each of them a law, and the lover thinks that he is right in doing any service which he can to his gracious loving one; and the other that he is right in showing any kindness he can to him who is making him wise and good; the

e   one capable of communicating wisdom and virtue, the other seeking to acquire them with a view to education and wisdom; when the two laws of love are fulfilled and meet in one—then, and then only, may the beloved yield with honor to the lover. Nor when love is of this disinterested sort is there any disgrace in being deceived, but in every other case there is equal disgrace in being or not being deceived. For he who

185 is gracious to his lover under the impression that he is rich, and is disappointed of his gains because he turns out to be poor, is disgraced all the same: for he has done his best to show that he would do anything for anybody for the sake of money; and this is not honorable. And, on the same principle, he who gives himself to a lover because he is a good man, and in the hope that he will be improved by his company, shows himself to be virtuous, even though the object of his affection

b   turn out to be a villain, and to have no virtue; and if he is deceived he has committed a noble error. For he has proved that for his part he will do anything for anybody with a view to virtue and improvement, and there can be nothing nobler. Thus noble in every case is the acceptance of another for the sake of virtue. This is that love which is the love of the heavenly goddess, and is heavenly, and of great value to individuals and cities, making the lover and the beloved alike eager in the work of their

c   own improvement. But all other loves are the offspring of the other, who is the common goddess. To you, Phaedrus, I offer this my contribution in praise of love, which is as good as I could make offhand.

     Pausanias came to a pause—this is the balanced way in which I have been taught by the wise to speak; and Aristodemus said that the turn of Aristophanes was next, but either he had eaten too much, or for some other reason he had the hiccups, and was obliged to change turns with Eryximachus the physician, who was reclining on the couch after

d   him. Eryximachus, he said, you ought either to stop my hiccups, or to speak in my turn until they stop.

     I will do both, said Eryximachus: I will speak in your turn, and you in mine; and while I am speaking, let me recommend you to hold your breath, and if after you have done so for some time the hiccups are not gone, then gargle with a little water; and if it still continues, tickle your

e   nose with something and sneeze; and if you sneeze once or twice, even the most violent hiccups is sure to go. I will do as you prescribe, said Aristophanes. Now get on.

Eryximachus spoke as follows: Seeing that Pausanias made a fair beginning, but a lame ending, I must endeavor to provide a better one. **186** I think that he has rightly distinguished two kinds of love. But my training further informs me that the double love is not merely an affection of the soul of man towards the fair, or towards anything, but is to be found in the bodies of all animals and in productions of the earth, and I may say in all that exists; such is the conclusion which I have gathered from my own practice of medicine, whence I learn how great and wonderful and universal is the deity of Love, whose empire **b** extends over all things, divine and human. And from medicine I will begin and do honor to my practice. There are in the human body these two kinds of love, which are confessedly different and unlike, and being unlike, they have loves and desires which are unlike; and the desire of the healthy is one, and the desire of the diseased is another; and as Pausanias was just now saying that to indulge good men is honorable, and bad men dishonorable, so too in the body the good and healthy **c** elements are to be indulged, and the bad elements and the elements of disease are not to be indulged, but discouraged. And this is what the physician has to do, and of this medicine consists: for medicine may be regarded generally as the knowledge of the loves and desires of the body, and how to satisfy them or not; and the best physician is the one who is able to separate fair love from foul, or to convert one into **d** the other; and the one who knows how to eradicate and how to implant love, whichever is required, and can reconcile the most hostile elements in the constitution and make them loving friends, is a skilful practitioner. Now the most hostile are the most opposite, such as hot and cold, bitter and sweet, moist and dry, and the like. And my ancestor, Asclepius, knowing how to implant friendship and accord in these **e** elements, was the creator of our art, as our friends the poets here tell us, and I believe them; and not only medicine in every branch, but the arts of gymnastics and farming are under his dominion. Any one who pays the least attention to the subject will also perceive that in music **187** there is the same reconciliation of opposites; and I suppose that this must have been the meaning of Heraclitus, although his words are not accurate; for he says that The One is united by disunion, like the harmony of the bow and the lyre. Now there is an absurdity in saying that harmony is discord or is composed of elements which are still in a state of discord. But what he probably meant was, that harmony is composed of differing notes of higher or lower pitch which disagreed **b** once, but are now reconciled by the art of music; for if the higher and

lower notes still disagreed, there could be no harmony—clearly not.
For harmony is a symphony, and symphony is an agreement; but an
agreement of disagreements while they disagree there cannot be; you
c   cannot harmonize that which disagrees. In like manner rhythm is compounded of elements short and long, once differing and now in accord; which accordance, as in the former instance, medicine, so in all
these other cases, music implants, making love and unison to grow up
among them; and thus music, too, is concerned with the principles of
love in their application to harmony and rhythm. Again, in the essential nature of harmony and rhythm there is no difficulty in discerning
love which has not yet become double. But when you want to use
d   them in actual life, either in the composition of songs or in the correct
performance of airs or metres composed already, which latter is called
education, then the difficulty begins, and the good artist is needed.
Then the old tale has to be repeated of fair and heavenly love—the love
of Urania the fair and heavenly muse,* and of the duty of accepting the
temperate, and those who are as yet intemperate in order that they may
become temperate, and of preserving their love; and again, of the vul-
e   gar Polyhymnia,† who must be used with circumspection for the pleasure to be enjoyed, but may not generate licentiousness; just as in my
own art it is a great matter so to regulate the desires of the hedonist in
order that he may gratify his tastes without the attendant evil of disease. Whence I infer that in music, in medicine, and in all other things
human and divine, both loves ought to be noted as far as may be, for
188 they are both present.

The course of the seasons is also full of both these principles; and
when, as I was saying, the elements of hot and cold, moist and dry, attain the harmonious love of one another and blend in temperance
and harmony, they bring to men, animals, and plants health and plenty,
and do them no harm; whereas the wanton love, getting the upper
hand and affecting the seasons of the year, is very destructive and injurious, being the source of pestilence, and bringing many other kinds
b   of diseases on animals and plants; for hoar-frost and hail and blight
spring from the excesses and disorders of these elements of love, which
to know in relation to the revolutions of the heavenly bodies and the
seasons of the year is termed astronomy. Furthermore all sacrifices and
the whole province of divination, which is the art of communion be-
c   tween gods and men—these, I say, are concerned only with the preservation of the good and the cure of the evil love. For all manner of impiety

---

*Theogony 75–79 contains a list of the Muses but does not specify different functions.
†Another Muse.

is likely to ensue if, instead of accepting and honoring and revering the harmonious love in all his actions, a man honors the other love, whether in his feelings towards gods or parents, towards the living or the dead. Wherefore the business of divination is to see to these loves and to heal them, and divination is the peacemaker of gods and men, working by a knowledge of the religious or irreligious tendencies which exist in human loves. Such is the great and mighty, or rather omnipotent force of love in general. And the love, more especially, which is concerned with the good, and which is perfected in company with temperance and justice, whether among gods or men, has the greatest power, and is the source of all our happiness and harmony, and makes us friends with the gods who are above us, and with one another. I dare say that I too have omitted several things which might be said in praise of Love, but this was not intentional, and you, Aristophanes, may now supply the omission or take some other line of commendation; since you are now rid of the hiccups.

Yes, said Aristophanes, who followed, the hiccups are gone; not, however, until I applied the sneezing; and I wonder whether the harmony of the body has a love of such noises and ticklings, for I no sooner applied the sneezing than I was cured.

Eryximachus said: Beware, friend Aristophanes, although you are going to speak, you are making fun of me; and I shall have to watch and see whether I cannot have a laugh at your expense, when you might speak in peace.

You are quite right, said Aristophanes, laughing. I will unsay my words; but you please do not watch me, as I fear that in the speech which I am about to make, instead of others laughing with me, which is in the manner born of our muse and would be all the better, I shall only be laughed at by them.

Do you expect to shoot your bolt and escape, Aristophanes? Well, perhaps if you are very careful and bear in mind that you will be called to account, I may be induced to let you off.

Aristophanes professed to open another vein of discourse; he had a mind to praise Love in another way, unlike that either of Pausanias or Eryximachus. Mankind, he said, judging by their neglect of him, have never, as I think, at all understood the power of Love. For if they had understood him they would surely have built noble temples and altars, and offered solemn sacrifices in his honor; but this is not done, and most certainly ought to be done: since of all the gods he is the best friend of men, the helper and the healer of the ills which are the great impediment to the happiness of the race. I will try to describe his power to you, and you shall teach the rest of the world what I am teaching you. In the first place, let me treat of the nature of man and what has happened to it; for the original human nature was not like the present one. The sexes were not two as they are now, but originally three in number; there was man, woman, and the union of the two, having a name corresponding to this double nature, which had once a real existence, but is now lost, and the word 'Androgynous' is only preserved as a term of reproach. In the second place, the primeval man was round, his back and sides forming a circle; and he had four hands and four feet, one head with two faces, looking opposite ways, set on a round neck and precisely alike; also four ears, two privy members, and the remainder to correspond. He could walk upright as men do now, backwards or forwards as he pleased, and he could also roll over and over at a great pace, turning on his four hands and four feet, eight in all, like tumblers going over and over with their legs in the air; he did that when he wanted to run fast. Now the sexes were three, such as I have described them; because the sun, moon, and earth are three; and the man was originally the child of the sun, the woman of the earth, and the man-woman of the moon, which is made up of sun and earth, and they were all round and moved round and round like their parents. Terrible was their might and strength, and the thoughts of their hearts were great, and they made an attack upon the gods; of them is told the tale of Otys and Ephialtes who, as Homer says, dared to scale heaven, and would have laid hands upon the gods. Doubt reigned in the celestial councils. Should they kill them and annihilate the race with thunderbolts, as they had done with the giants,[4] then there would be an end of the sacrifices and worship which men offered to them; but, on the other hand, the gods could not suffer their insolence to be unrestrained. At last, after a good deal of reflection, Zeus found a way. He said: 'I think I have a plan which will humble their pride and improve their manners; men shall continue to exist, but I will cut them in two and then they will be diminished in strength and increased in numbers; this will have the advantage of making them more profitable to us. They shall walk upright on two legs, and if they continue insolent and will not be quiet, I will split them again and they shall hop about on a single leg.' He spoke and cut men in two, like a sorb-apple which is halved for pickling, or as you might divide an egg with a hair; and as he cut them one after another, he bade Apollo give the face and the half of the neck a turn in order that the man might contemplate the section of himself: he would thus learn a lesson of humility. Apollo was also bidden to heal their wounds and compose their forms. So he gave a turn to the face and pulled the skin from the sides all over that which in our language is called the belly, like the purses which draw in, and he made one mouth at the centre, which he fastened in a knot (the same which is called the navel); he also moulded the breast and took out most of the wrinkles, much as a shoemaker might smooth leather upon a last; he left a few, however, in the region of the belly and navel, as a memorial of the primeval state. After the division, the two parts of man, each desiring his other half, came together, and throwing their arms about one another, entwined in mutual embraces, longing to grow into one, they were on the point of dying from hunger and self-neglect, because they did not like to do anything apart; and when one of the halves died and the other survived, the survivor sought another mate, man or woman as we call them,—being the sections of entire men or women,—and clung to that. They were being destroyed, when Zeus in pity of them invented a new plan: he turned the parts of generation round to the front, for this had not been always their position, and they sowed the seed no longer as hitherto like grasshoppers in the ground,⁵ but in one another; and after the transposition the male sowed his seed in the female in order that by the mutual embraces of man and woman they might breed, and the race might continue; or if man came to man they might be satisfied, and rest, and go their ways to the business of life: so ancient is the desire of one another which is implanted in us, reuniting our original nature, making one of two, and healing the state of man. Each of us when separated, having one side only, like a flat fish, is but the indenture of a man, and he is always looking for his other half. Men who are a section of that double nature which was once called Androgynous are lovers of women; adulterers are generally of this breed, and also adulterous women who lust after men: the women who are a section of the woman do not care for men, but have female attachments; the female companions are of this sort. But they who are a section of the male follow the male, and while they are young, being slices of the original man, they hang about men and embrace them, and they are themselves the best of boys and youths, because they have the most manly nature. Some indeed assert that they are shameless, but this is not true; for they do not act thus from any want of shame, but because they are valiant and manly, and have a manly countenance, and they embrace that which is like them. And these when they grow up become our statesmen, and these only, which is a great proof of the truth of what I am saying. When they reach manhood they are lovers of youth, and are not naturally inclined to marry or beget children. If at all, they do so only in response to the demands of society; but they are satisfied if they may be allowed to live with one another unwedded; and such a nature is prone to love and ready to return love, always embracing that which is akin to him. And when one of them meets with his other half, the actual half of himself, whether c   he be a lover of youth or a lover of another sort, the pair are lost in an amazement of love and friendship and intimacy, and will not be out of the other's sight, as I may say, even for a moment: these are the people who pass their whole lives together; yet they could not explain what they desire of one another. For the intense yearning which each of them has towards the other does not appear to be the desire of lover's intercourse, but of something else which the soul of either evidently desires and cannot tell, and of which she has only a dark and doubtful presentiment. Suppose Hephaestus, with his instruments, should come to

d   the pair who are lying side by side and say to them: 'What do you people want of one another?' they would be unable to explain. And suppose further, that when he saw their perplexity he said: 'Do you desire to be wholly one; always day and night to be in one another's company? for if this is what you desire, I am ready to melt you into one and let you grow together, so that being two you shall become one, and

e   while you live live a common life as if you were a single man, and after your death in the world below still be one departed soul instead of two? I ask whether this is what you lovingly desire and whether you are satisfied to attain this.' There is not one of them who when he heard the proposal would deny or would not acknowledge that this meeting and melting into one another, this becoming one instead of two, was the very expression of his ancient need. And the reason is that human nature was originally one and we were a whole, and the desire and

193   pursuit of the whole is called love. There was a time, I say, when we were one. But now because of the wickedness of mankind, god has dispersed us, as the Arcadians were dispersed into villages by the Spartans. And if we are not obedient to the gods, there is a danger that we shall be split up again and go about in bas relief, like the profile figures having only half a nose which are sculptured on monuments. Wherefore let us exhort all men to piety, that we may avoid evil, and

b   obtain the good, of which Love is to us the lord and minister; and let no one oppose him—whoever would oppose him is the enemy of the gods. For if we are friends of the god and at peace with him we shall find our own true loves, which rarely happens in this world at present. I am serious, and therefore I must beg Eryximachus not to make fun or to find any allusion in what I am saying to Pausanias and Agathon, who,

c   as I suspect, are both of the manly nature, and belong to the class which I have been describing. My words have a wider application: they include men and women everywhere; and I believe that if our loves were perfectly accomplished, and each one returning to his primeval nature had his original true love, then our race would be happy. And if this would be best of all, the next best thing under present circumstances must be the nearest approach to such an union; and that will be the attainment of a congenial love. Wherefore, if we would praise him who has given to us the benefit, we must praise the god Love, who is our greatest benefactor, both leading us in this life back to our own nature, and giving us high hopes for the future, for he promises that if we are pious, he will restore us to our original state, and heal us and make us happy and blessed. This, Eryximachus, is my discourse of Love, which, although different to yours, I must beg you to leave unassailed by the arrows of your ridicule, in order that each may have his turn; each, or rather either, for Agathon and Socrates are the only ones left.

Indeed, I am not going to attack you, said Eryximachus, for I thought your speech charming, and if I did not know that Agathon and Socrates are masters in the art of love, I would be really afraid that they would have nothing to say, after the world of things which have been said already. But, for all that, I am not without hopes.

Socrates said: You played your part well, Eryximachus; but if you were as I am now, or rather as I shall be when Agathon has spoken, you would, indeed, be in a great strait.

You want to cast a spell over me, Socrates, said Agathon, in the hope that I may be disconcerted at the expectation raised among the audience that I shall speak well.

I would be strangely forgetful, Agathon, replied Socrates, of the courage and magnanimity which you showed when your own compositions were about to be exhibited, and you came upon the stage with the actors and faced the vast theatre altogether undismayed, if I thought that your nerves could be fluttered at a small party of friends.

Do you think, Socrates, said Agathon, that my head is so full of the theatre as not to know how much more formidable to a man of sense a few good judges are than many fools?

Nay, replied Socrates, I should be very wrong in attributing to you, Agathon, that or any other lack of refinement. And I am quite aware that if you happened to meet with anyone whom you thought wise, you would care for their opinion much more than for that of most people. But then we, having been a part of the foolish many in the theatre, cannot be regarded as the select wise; though I know that if you chanced to be in the presence, not of one of us, but of some really wise man, you would be ashamed of disgracing yourself before him— would you not?

Yes, said Agathon.

But before the crowd you would not be ashamed, if you thought that you were doing something disgraceful in their presence?

d   Here Phaedrus interrupted them, saying: Do not answer him, my
dear Agathon; for if he can only get a partner with whom he can talk,
especially a good-looking one, he will no longer care about the completion of our plan. I love to hear him talk; but at present I must not
forget the encomium on Love which I ought to receive from him and
from every one. When you and he have paid your tribute to the god,
then you may talk.

e   Very good, Phaedrus, said Agathon; I see no reason why I should
not proceed with my speech, as I shall have many other opportunities
of conversing with Socrates. Let me say first how I ought to speak, and
then speak.

          The previous speakers, Agathon began, instead of praising the god
Love, or unfolding his nature, appear to have congratulated mankind
195 on the benefits which he confers upon them. But I would rather praise
the god first, and then speak of his gifts; this is always the right way of
praising everything. May I say without impiety or offence, that of all the
blessed gods he is the most blessed because he is the fairest and best?

b   And he is the fairest: for, in the first place, he is the youngest, and of
his youth he is himself the witness, fleeing out of the way of old age,
who is swift enough, swifter truly than most of us would like: Love
hates old age and will not come near it; but youth and love live and
move together—like to like, as the proverb says. Many things were said
by Phaedrus about Love in which I agree with him; but I cannot agree that
he is older than Iapetus and Kronos: I maintain him to be the youngest
of the gods, and ever youthful. The ancient doings among the gods of

c   which Hesiod and Parmenides spoke, if their tradition is true, were
done of Necessity and not of Love; had Love been in those days, there
would have been no chaining or mutilation of the gods, or other violence, but peace and sweetness, as there is now in heaven, since the rule
of Love began. Love is young and also tender; he ought to have a poet
like Homer to describe his tenderness, as Homer says of Ate, that she is

d   a goddess and tender:

          'Her feet are tender, for she sets her steps,
          Not on the ground but on the heads of men:'*

herein is an excellent proof of her tenderness,—that she walks not
e   upon the hard but upon the soft. Let us adduce a similar proof of the
tenderness of Love; for he walks not upon the earth, nor yet upon the
skulls of men, which are not so very soft, but in the hearts and souls

---

*Iliad 19.92–93.

of both gods and men, which are of all things the softest: in them he
walks and dwells and makes his home. Not in every soul without exception, for where there is hardness he departs, where there is softness,
there he dwells; and nestling always with his feet and in all manner of
ways in the softest of soft places, how can he be other than the softest
of all things? Truly he is the tenderest as well as the youngest, and also   196
he is of flexible form; for if he were hard and inflexible he could not
enfold all things, or wind his way into and out of every soul of man
undiscovered. And a proof of his flexibility and symmetry of form is
his grace, which is universally admitted to be in an especial manner the
attribute of Love; ungrace and love are always at war with one another.
The fairness of his complexion is revealed by his habitation among the
flowers; for he dwells not amid bloomless or fading beauties, whether   b
of body or soul or anything else, but in the place of flowers and scents,
there he sits and abides. Concerning the beauty of the god I have said
enough; and yet there remains much more which I might say. Of his
virtue I have now to speak: his greatest glory is that he can neither do
nor suffer wrong to or from any god or any man; for he suffers not by
force if he suffers; force comes not near him, neither when he acts does   c
he act by force. For all men in all things serve him of their own free
will, and where there is voluntary agreement, there, as the laws which
are the lords of the city say, is justice. And not only is he just but exceedingly temperate, for Temperance is the acknowledged ruler of the
pleasures and desires, and no pleasure ever masters Love; he is their
master and they are his servants; and if he conquers them he must be
temperate indeed. As to courage, even the god of war is no match for   d
him; he is the captive and Love is the Lord, for love, the love of
Aphrodite, masters him, as the tale runs;[6] and the master is stronger
than the servant. And if he conquers the bravest of all others, he must
be himself the bravest. Of his courage and justice and temperance I have
spoken, but I have yet to speak of his wisdom; and according to the
measure of my ability I must try to do my best. In the first place he is   e
a poet (and here, like Eryximachus, I magnify my art), clever enough
to make others poets too, which he could not do if he were not one
himself. And at his touch everyone becomes a poet, even if he had no
inspiration in him before; this also is a proof that Love is a good poet
and accomplished in all the fine arts; for no one can give to another
that which he has not himself, or teach that of which he has no knowledge. Who will deny that the creation of the animals is his doing? Are   197
they not all the work of his wisdom, born and begotten of him? And
as to the artists, do we not know that only those of them whom Love
inspires have the light of fame?—he whom Love touches does not walk
in darkness. The arts of medicine and archery and divination were

discovered by Apollo, under the guidance of love and desire; so that he
b too is a disciple of Love. Also the melody of the Muses, the metallurgy
of Hephaestus, the weaving of Athene, the empire of Zeus over gods
and men, are all due to Love, who was the inventor of them. And so
Love set in order the empire of the gods—the love of beauty, as is evident, for with deformity Love has no concern. In the days of old, as I
began by saying, dreadful deeds were done among the gods, for they
were ruled by Necessity; but now since the birth of Love, and from the
Love of the beautiful, has sprung every good in heaven and earth.
c Therefore, Phaedrus, I say of Love that he is the fairest and best in himself, and the cause of what is fairest and best in all other things. And
there comes into my mind a line of poetry in which he is said to be
the god who

> 'Gives peace on earth and calms the stormy deep,
> Who stills the winds and bids the sufferer sleep.'*

d This is he who empties men of disaffection and fills them with affection, who makes them meet together at banquets such as these: In sacrifices, feasts, dances, he is our lord—who sends courtesy and sends
away discourtesy, who gives kindness ever and never gives unkindness;
the friend of the good, the wonder of the wise, the amazement of the
gods; desired by those who have no part in him, and precious to those
who have the better part in him; parent of delicacy, luxury, desire,
fondness, softness, grace; regardful of the good, regardless of the evil:
in every word, work, wish, fear—saviour, pilot, comrade, helper; glory
e of gods and men, leader best and brightest: in whose footsteps let every
man follow, sweetly singing in his honor and joining in that sweet
strain with which love charms the souls of gods and men. Such is the
speech, Phaedrus, half-playful, yet having a certain measure of seriousness, which, according to my ability, I dedicate to the god.

198   When Agathon had done speaking, Aristodemus said that there
was a general cheer; the young man was thought to have spoken in
a manner worthy of himself, and of the god. And Socrates, looking
at Eryximachus, said: Tell me, son of Acumenus, was there not reason in my fears? and was I not a true prophet when I said that
Agathon would make a wonderful oration, and that I should be in a
strait?

---

*The lines are Agathon's. His entire speech displays metrical effects in Greek, in line
with Gorgias' teachings; comparing with what we have of Gorgias, Plato seems better
at them.

The part of the prophecy which concerns Agathon, replied Eryximachus, appears to me to be true; but not the other part—that you will be in a strait.

Why, my dear friend, said Socrates, must not I or any one be in a   b
strait who has to speak after he has heard such a rich and varied discourse? I am especially struck with the beauty of the concluding words—who could listen to them without amazement? When I reflected on the immeasurable inferiority of my own powers, I was ready to run away for shame, if there had been a possibility of escape. For I was reminded of Gorgias, and at the end of his speech I fancied that   c
Agathon was shaking at me the Gorginian or Gorgonian head of that gifted speaker, which was simply to turn me and my speech into stone, as Homer says,* and strike me dumb. And then I perceived how foolish I had been in consenting to take my turn with you in praising love,   d
and saying that I too was a master of the art, when I really had no conception how anything ought to be praised. For in my simplicity I imagined that the topics of praise should be true, and that this being presupposed, out of the true the speaker was to choose the best and set them forth in the best manner. And I felt quite proud, thinking that I knew the nature of true praise, and should speak well. Whereas I now see that the intention was to attribute to Love every species of greatness   e
and glory, whether really belonging to him or not, without regard to truth or falsehood—that was no matter; for the original proposal seems to have been not that each of you should really praise Love, but only that you should appear to praise him. And so you attribute to Love every imaginable form of praise which can be gathered anywhere; and you say that 'he is all this,' and 'the cause of all that,' making him appear the   199
fairest and best of all to those who do not know him, for you cannot impose upon those who know him. A noble and solemn hymn of praise have you rehearsed. But as I misunderstood the nature of the praise when I said that I would take my turn, I must beg to be absolved from the promise which I made in ignorance, and which (as Euripides would say)† was a promise of the lips and not of the mind. Farewell then to such a strain: for I do not praise in that way; no, indeed, I cannot. But if   b
you like to hear the truth about love, I am ready to speak in my own manner, though I will not make myself ridiculous by entering into any rivalry with you. Say then, Phaedrus, whether you would like to have the truth about love, spoken in any words and in any order which may happen to come into my mind at the time. Will that be agreeable to you?

---

*Odyssey 11.633–635.
†Hyppolytus 612.

Aristodemus said that Phaedrus and the company bid him speak in any manner which he thought best. Then, he added, let me have your permission first to ask Agathon a few more questions, in order that I may take his admissions as the premises of my discourse.

c   I grant the permission, said Phaedrus: put your questions. Socrates then proceeded as follows:

In the magnificent oration which you have just uttered, I think that you were right, my dear Agathon, in proposing to speak of the nature of Love first and afterwards of his works—that is a way of beginning which I very much approve. And as you have spoken so eloquently of

d his nature, may I ask you further, is love the love of something or of nothing? And here I must explain myself: I do not want you to say that love is the love of a father or the love of a mother—that would be ridiculous; but to answer as you would, if I asked is a father a father of something? to which you would find no difficulty in replying, of a son or daughter: and the answer would be right.

Very true, said Agathon.

And you would say the same of a mother?

He assented.

e   Yet let me ask you one more question in order to illustrate my meaning: Is not a brother to be regarded essentially as a brother of something?

Certainly, he replied.

That is, of a brother or sister?

Yes, he said.

And now, said Socrates, I will ask about Love:—Is Love of something or of nothing?

Of something, surely, he replied.

200   Keep in mind what this is, and tell me what I want to know— whether Love desires what there is love of.

Yes, surely.

And does he possess, or does he not possess, that which he loves and desires?

Probably not, I should say.

Nay, replied Socrates, I would have you consider whether 'necessarily' is not rather the word. The inference that he who desires something is in want of something, and that he who desires nothing is in

b want of nothing, is in my judgment, Agathon, absolutely and necessarily true. What do you think?

I agree with you, said Agathon.

Very good. Would the one who is great, desire to be great, or the one who is strong, desire to be strong?

That would be inconsistent with our previous admissions.

True. For the one who is anything cannot want to be what he is?
Very true.

And yet, added Socrates, if a man being strong desired to be strong, or being swift desired to be swift, or being healthy desired to be healthy, in that case he might be thought to desire something which he already has or is. I give the example in order that we may avoid misconception. For the possessors of these qualities, Agathon, must be supposed to have their respective advantages at the time, whether they choose or not; and who can desire that which he has? Therefore, when a person says, I am well and wish to be well, or I am rich and wish to be rich, and I desire simply to have what I have—to him we shall reply: 'You, my friend, having wealth and health and strength, want to have the continuance of them; for at this moment, whether you choose or not, you have them. And when you say, I desire that which I have and nothing else, is not your meaning that you want to have what you now have in the future?' He must agree with us—must he not?

He must, replied Agathon.

Then, said Socrates, he desires that what he has at present may be preserved to him in the future, which is equivalent to saying that he desires something which is non-existent to him, and which as yet he has not got.

Very true, he said.

Then he and every one who desires, desires that which he has not already, and which is future and not present, and which he has not, and is not, and of which he is in want; are these the sort of things which love and desire seek?

Very true, he said.

Then now, said Socrates, let us recapitulate the argument. First, is not love of something, and of something too which is wanting to a man?

Yes, he replied.

Remember further what you said in your speech, or if you do not remember I will remind you: you said that the love of the beautiful set in order the empire of the gods, for that of deformed things there is no love—did you not say something of that kind?

Yes, said Agathon.

Yes, my friend, and the remark was a just one. And if this is true, Love is the love of beauty and not of deformity?

He assented.

And the admission has been already made that Love is of something which a man wants and has not?

True, he said.

Then Love wants and has not beauty?

Certainly, he replied.

And would you call that beautiful which wants and does not possess beauty?

Certainly not.

Then would you still say that Love is beautiful?

Agathon replied: I fear that I did not understand what I was saying.

c   You made a very good speech, Agathon, replied Socrates; but there is yet one small question which I would like to ask: Is not the good also the beautiful?

Yes.

Then in wanting the beautiful, Love wants also the good?

I cannot refute you, Socrates, said Agathon. Let us assume that what you say is true.

Say rather, beloved Agathon, that you cannot refute the truth; for Socrates is easily refuted.

d   And now, taking my leave of you, I will repeat a tale of love which I heard from Diotima of Mantineia, a woman wise in this and in many other kinds of knowledge, who in the days of old, when the Athenians offered sacrifice before the coming of the plague, delayed the disease ten years. She was my instructress in the art of love, and I shall repeat to you what she said to me, beginning with the admissions made by Agathon, which are nearly if not quite the same which I made to the wise woman when she questioned me: I think that this will be the easiest way, and I shall take both parts myself as well as I can. As you, Agathon, suggested, I must speak first of the being and nature of Love,

e   and then of his works. First I said to her in nearly the same words which he used, that Love was a mighty god, and likewise fair; and she proved to me as I proved to him that, by my own showing, Love was neither fair nor good. 'What do you mean, Diotima,' I said, 'is love then evil and foul?' 'Hush,' she shouted; 'must that be foul which is

202   not fair?' 'Certainly,' I said. 'And is that which is not wise, ignorant? do you not see that there is a mean between wisdom and ignorance?' 'And what may that be?' I said. 'Right opinion,' she replied; 'which, as you know, being incapable of giving a reason, is not knowledge (for how can knowledge be devoid of reason?) nor, again, ignorance, (for neither can ignorance attain the truth), but is clearly something which is a mean between ignorance and wisdom.' 'Quite true,' I replied. 'Do not

b   then insist,' she said, 'that what is not fair is of necessity foul, or what is not good evil; or infer that because Love is not fair and good he is therefore foul and evil; for he is in a mean between them.' 'Well,' I said, 'Love is surely admitted by all to be a great god.' 'By those who know or by those who do not know?' 'By all.' 'And how, Socrates,' she said with a smile, 'can Love be acknowledged to be a great god by those who say that he is not a god at all?' 'And who are they?' I said. 'You and I are two of them,' she replied. 'How can that be?' I said. 'It is quite intelligible,' she replied; 'for you yourself would acknowledge that the gods are happy and fair—of course you would—would you dare to say that any god was not?' 'Certainly not,' I replied. 'And you mean by happy, those who are the possessors of things good or fair?' 'Yes.' 'And you admitted that Love, because he was in want, desires those good and fair things of which he is in want?' 'Yes, I did.' 'But how can he be a god who has no portion in what is either good or fair?' 'Impossible.' 'Then you see that you also deny the divinity of Love.'

'What then is Love?' I asked; 'Is he mortal?' 'No.' 'What then?' 'As in the former instance, he is neither mortal nor immortal, but in a mean between the two.' 'What is he, Diotima?' 'He is a great spirit, and like all spirits he is intermediate between the divine and the mortal.' 'And what,' I said, 'is his power?' 'He interprets,' she replied, 'between gods and men, conveying and taking across to the gods the prayers and sacrifices of men, and to men the commands and replies of the gods; he is the mediator who spans the chasm which divides them, and therefore in him all is bound together, and through him the arts of the prophet and the priest, their sacrifices and mysteries and charms, and all prophecy and incantation, find their way. For god mingles not with man; but through Love all the intercourse and converse of god with man, whether awake or asleep, is carried on. The knowledge which understands this is spiritual; all other knowledge, such as that of arts and handicrafts, is mean and vulgar. Now these spirits or intermediate powers are many and diverse, and one of them is Love.' 'And who,' I said, 'was his father, and who his mother?' 'The tale,' she said, 'will take time; nevertheless I will tell you. On the birthday of Aphrodite there was a feast of the gods, at which the god Poros or Plenty, who is the son of Metis or Discretion, was one of the guests. When the feast was over, Penia or Poverty, as the manner is on such occasions, came about the doors to beg. Now Plenty, who was drunk with nectar (there was no wine in those days), went into the garden of Zeus and fell into a heavy sleep; and Poverty considering her own straitened circumstances, plotted to have a child by him, and accordingly she lay down at his side and conceived Love, who partly because he is naturally a lover of the beautiful, because Aphrodite is herself beautiful, and also because he was born on her birthday, is her follower and attendant. And as his parentage is, so also are his fortunes. In the first place he is always poor, and anything but tender and fair, as the many imagine him; he is *d*   rough and squalid, and has no shoes, nor a house to dwell in; on the bare earth exposed he lies under the open heaven, in the streets, or at the doors of houses, taking his rest; and like his mother he is always in distress. Like his father too, whom he also partly resembles, he is always plotting against the fair and good; he is bold, enterprising, strong, a mighty hunter, always weaving some intrigue or other, keen in the pursuit of wisdom, fertile in resources: a philosopher at all times, terrible

e   as an enchanter, sorcerer, sophist. He is by nature neither mortal nor immortal, but alive and flourishing at one moment when he is in plenty, and dead at another moment, and again alive by reason of his father's nature. But that which is always flowing in is always flowing out, and so he is never in want and never in wealth; and, further, he is in a mean between ignorance and knowledge. The truth of the matter is this: no god is a philosopher or seeker after wisdom, for he is wise already; nor does any man who is wise seek after wisdom. Neither do the ignorant seek after wisdom. For herein is the evil of ignorance, that he who is

204   neither good nor wise is nevertheless satisfied with himself: he has no desire for that of which he feels no want.' 'But who then, Diotima,' I said, 'are the lovers of wisdom, if they are neither the wise nor the

b   foolish?' 'A child may answer that question,' she replied; 'they are those who are in a mean between the two; Love is one of them. For wisdom is a most beautiful thing, and Love is of the beautiful; and therefore Love is also a philosopher or lover of wisdom, and being a lover of wisdom is in a mean between the wise and the ignorant. And of this too his birth is the cause; for his father is wealthy and wise, and his mother poor and foolish. Such, my dear Socrates, is the nature of

c   the spirit Love. The error in your conception of him was very natural, and as I imagine from what you say, has arisen out of a confusion of Love and the beloved, which made you think that Love was all beautiful. For the beloved is the truly beautiful, and delicate, and perfect, and blessed; but the principle of Love is of another nature, and is such as I have described.'

       I said: 'Woman stranger, you speak well; but, assuming Love to be

d   such as you say, what is the use of him to men?' 'That, Socrates,' she replied, 'I will attempt to unfold: of his nature and birth I have already spoken; and you acknowledge that Love is of the beautiful. But some one will say: of the beautiful in what, Socrates and Diotima?—Or rather let me put the question more clearly, and ask: when a man loves the beautiful, what does he desire?' I answered her, 'That the beautiful may be his.' 'Still,' she said, 'the answer suggests a further question: What is given by the possession of beauty?' 'To what you have asked,' I replied, 'I have no answer ready.' 'Then,' she said, 'let me put the

word "good" in the place of the beautiful, and repeat the question once   e
more: If he who loves loves the good, what is it then that he loves?'
'The possession of the good,' I said. 'And what does he gain who possesses the good?' 'Happiness,' I replied; 'there is less difficulty in answering that question.' 'Yes,' she said, 'the happy are made happy by the
acquisition of good things. Nor is there any need to ask why a man de-   205
sires happiness; the answer is already final.' 'You are right,' I said. 'And
is this wish and this desire common to all? and do all men always desire their own good, or only some men?—what do you say?' 'All men,'
I replied; 'the desire is common to all.' 'Why, then,' she rejoined, 'are
not all men, Socrates, said to love, but only some of them? whereas you   b
say that all men are always loving the same things.' 'I myself wonder,' I
said, 'why this is.' 'There is nothing to wonder at,' she replied; 'the reason is that one part of love is separated off and receives the name of the
whole, but the other parts have other names.' 'Give an illustration,' I
said. She answered me as follows: 'There is poetry, which, as you know,
is complex and manifold. All creation or passage of non-being into   c
being is poetry or making, and the processes of all art are creative; and
the masters of arts are all poets or makers.' 'Very true.' 'Still,' she said,
'you know that they are not called poets, but have other names; only
that portion of the art which is separated off from the rest, and is concerned with music and metre, is termed poetry, and they who possess
poetry in this sense of the word are called poets.' 'Very true,' I said.
'And the same holds of Love. For you may say generally that all desire   d
of good and happiness is only the great and subtle power of Love; but
they who are drawn towards him by any other path, whether the path
of money-making or gymnastics or philosophy, are not called lovers—
the name of the whole is appropriated to those whose affection takes
one form only—they alone are said to love, or to be lovers.' 'I dare say,'
I replied, 'that you are right.' 'Yes,' she added, 'and you hear people say
that lovers are seeking for their other half; but I say that they are seeking neither for the half of themselves, nor for the whole, unless the half   e
or the whole be also a good. And they will cut off their own hands and
feet and cast them away, if they are evil; for they love not what is their
own, unless perchance there is someone who calls what belongs to
him the good, and what belongs to another the evil. For there is noth-   206
ing which men love but the good. Is there anything?' 'Certainly, I
should say, that there is nothing.' 'Then,' she said, 'the simple truth is,
that men love the good.' 'Yes,' I said. 'To which must be added that
they love the possession of the good?' 'Yes, that must be added.' 'And
not only the possession, but the everlasting possession of the good?'
'That must be added too.' 'Then Love,' she said, 'may be described

generally as the love of the everlasting possession of the good?' 'That
is most true.'

b   'Then, if this is the nature of Love, can you tell me further,' she said,
'what is the manner of the pursuit? what are they doing, those who
show all this eagerness and heat which is called Love? and what is the
object which they have in view? Answer me.' 'Diotima,' I replied, 'if I had
known, I should not have wondered at your wisdom, nor should I have
come to learn from you about this very matter.' 'Well,' she said, 'I will
teach you:—The object which they have in view is birth in beauty,
whether of body or soul.' 'I do not understand you,' I said; 'the oracle
c   requires an explanation.' 'I will make my meaning clearer,' she replied.
'I mean to say that all men are giving birth in their bodies and in their
souls. There is a certain age at which human nature is desirous of procreation—procreation which must be in beauty and not in deformity;
and this procreation is the union of man and woman, and is a divine
thing; for conception and generation are an immortal principle in the
mortal creature, and in the inharmonious they can never be. But the de-
d   formed is always inharmonious with the divine, and the beautiful harmonious. Beauty, then, is the destiny or goddess of parturition who
presides at birth, and therefore, when approaching beauty, the con-
ceiving power is propitious, and diffusive, and benign, and begets and
bears fruit: At the sight of ugliness, she frowns and contracts and has a
sense of pain, and turns away, and shrivels up, and not without a pang
refrains from conception. And this is the reason why, when the hour of
conception arrives, and the teeming nature is full, there is such a flutter and ecstasy about beauty whose approach is the alleviation of the
e   pain of travail. For Love, Socrates, is not, as you imagine, the love of the
beautiful only.' 'What then?' 'The love of generation and of birth in
beauty.' 'Yes,' I said. 'Yes, indeed,' she replied. 'But why of generation?'
'Because to the mortal creature, generation is a sort of eternity and immortality,' she replied; 'and if, as has been already admitted, love is of
the everlasting possession of the good, all men will necessarily desire
207 immortality together with good: Wherefore love is of immortality.'
         All this she taught me at various times when she spoke of love. And
I remember her once saying to me, 'What is the cause, Socrates, of love,
and the attendant desire? Do you not see how all animals, birds, as well
as beasts, in their desire of procreation, are in agony when they take the
infection of love, which begins with the desire of union; whereto is
b   added the care of offspring, on whose behalf the weakest are ready to
battle against the strongest even to the uttermost, and to die for them,
and will let themselves be tormented with hunger or suffer anything
in order to maintain their young? People may be supposed to act thus
from reason; but why should animals have these passionate feelings?

Can you tell me why?' Again I replied that I did not know. She said to $\quad$ c
me: 'And do you expect ever to become a master in the art of love, if
you do not know this?' 'But I have told you already, Diotima, that my
ignorance is the reason why I come to you; for I am conscious that I
want a teacher; tell me then the cause of this and of the other mysteries of love.' 'Marvel not,' she said, 'if you believe that love is of the immortal, as we have several times acknowledged; for here again, and on
the same principle too, the mortal nature is seeking as far as possible $\quad$ d
to be everlasting and immortal: and this is only to be attained by generation, because generation always leaves behind a new existence in the
place of the old. Nay, even in the life of the same individual there is succession and not absolute unity: a man is called the same, and yet in the
short interval which elapses between youth and age, and in which
every animal is said to have life and identity, he is undergoing a per-
petual process of loss and reparation—hair, flesh, bones, blood, and the $\quad$ e
whole body are always changing. Which is true not only of the body,
but also of the soul, whose habits, tempers, opinions, desires, pleasures, pains, fears, never remain the same in any one of us, but are always coming and going; and equally true of knowledge, and what is
still more surprising to us mortals, not only do the sciences in general $\quad$ 208
spring up and decay, so that in respect of them we are never the same;
but each of them individually experiences a like change. For what is
implied in the word "recollection," but the departure of knowledge,
which is ever being forgotten, and is renewed and preserved by recollection, and appears to be the same although in reality new, according
to that law of succession by which all mortal things are preserved, not
absolutely the same, but by substitution, the old worn-out mortality
leaving another new and similar existence behind—unlike the divine,
which is always the same and not another? And in this way, Socrates, $\quad$ b
the mortal body, or mortal anything, partakes of immortality; but the
immortal in another way. Marvel not then at the love which all men
have of their offspring; for that universal love and interest is for the
sake of immortality.'

    I was astonished at her words, and said: 'Is this really true, wise
Diotima?' And she answered with all the authority of an accomplished
sophist: 'Of that, Socrates, you may be assured;—think only of the am- $\quad$ c
bition of men, and you will wonder at the senselessness of their
ways, unless you consider how they are stirred by the love of an immortality of fame. They are ready to run all risks far greater than they
would have run for their children, and to spend money and undergo
any sort of toil, and even to die, for the sake of leaving behind them
a name which shall be eternal. Do you imagine that Alcestis would $\quad$ d
have died to save Admetus, or Achilles to avenge Patroclus, or your

own Codrus* in order to preserve the kingdom for his sons, if they had not imagined that the memory of their virtues, which still survives among us, would be immortal? No,' she said, 'I am persuaded that all men do all things and the better they are the more they do them in hope of the glorious fame of immortal virtue; for they de-
e sire the immortal.

'Those who are pregnant in the body only, betake themselves to women and beget children—this is the character of their love; their offspring, as they hope, will preserve their memory and give them the blessedness and immortality which they desire in the future. But souls
209 which are pregnant—for there certainly are men who are more creative in their souls than in their bodies—conceive that which is proper for the soul to conceive or contain. And what are these conceptions?—wisdom and virtue in general. And such creators are poets and all artists who are deserving of the name inventor. But the greatest and fairest sort of wisdom by far is that which is concerned with the ordering of states and families, and which is called temperance and justice. And he who in youth has the seed of these implanted in him and is himself in-
b spired, when he comes to maturity desires to beget and generate. He wanders about seeking beauty that he may beget offspring—for in deformity he will beget nothing—and naturally embraces the beautiful rather than the deformed body; above all when he finds a fair and noble and well-nurtured soul, he embraces the two in one person, and to such a one he is full of speech about virtue and the nature and pur-
c suits of a good man; and he tries to educate him; and at the touch of the beautiful which is ever present to his memory, even when absent, he brings forth that which he had conceived long before, and in company with him tends that which he brings forth; and they are married by a far nearer tie and have a closer friendship than those who beget mortal children, for the children who are their common offspring are fairer and more immortal. Who, when he thinks of Homer and Hesiod
d and other great poets, would not rather have their children than ordinary human ones? Who would not emulate them in the creation of children such as theirs, which have preserved their memory and given them everlasting glory? Or who would not have such children as Lycurgus left behind him to be the saviors, not only of Sparta, but of all the Greeks, as one may say? There is Solon, too, who is the revered father of Athenian laws; and many others there are in many other places, both among Greeks and barbarians, who have given to the world many

---

*Legendary last king of Athens; he gave his life to save Athens from the Dorian invasion of the Peloponnese in the eleventh century B.C.E.

noble works, and have been the parents of virtue of every kind; and   e
many temples have been raised in their honor for the sake of children
like theirs, which were never raised in honor of anyone for the sake of
his mortal children.

'These are the lesser mysteries of love, into which even you,
Socrates, may enter; the greater and more hidden ones which are the   210
crown of these, and to which, if you pursue them in a right spirit, they
will lead, I do not know whether you will be able to attain. But I will
do my utmost to inform you. Follow if you can. For he who would
proceed aright in this matter should begin in youth to visit beautiful
forms; and first, if he is guided by his instructor aright, to love one
such form only—out of that he should create fair thoughts; and soon
he will of himself perceive that the beauty of one form is akin to the   b
beauty of another; and then if beauty of form in general is his pursuit,
how foolish would he be not to recognize that the beauty in every form
is one and the same! And when he perceives this he will abate his violent love of the one, which he will despise and deem a small thing, and
will become a lover of all beautiful forms; in the next stage he will consider that the beauty of the mind is more honourable than the beauty
of the outward form. So that if a virtuous soul have but a little comeli-
ness, he will be content to love and tend him, and will search out and   c
give birth to thoughts which may improve the young, until he is compelled to contemplate and see the beauty of institutions and laws, and
to understand that the beauty of them all is of one family, and that personal beauty is a trifle; and after laws and institutions he will go on to
the sciences, that he may see their beauty, being not like a servant in   d
love with the beauty of one youth or man or institution, himself a slave
mean and narrow-minded, but drawing towards and contemplating
the vast sea of beauty, he will create many fair and noble thoughts and
notions in boundless love of wisdom; until on that shore he grows and
waxes strong, and at last the vision is revealed to him of a single sci-   e
ence, which is the science of beauty everywhere. To this I will proceed;
please give me your very best attention.

'He who has been instructed thus far in the things of love, and
who has learned to see the beautiful in due order and succession, when
he comes toward the end will suddenly perceive a nature of wondrous
beauty (and this, Socrates, is the final cause of all our former toils)—a   211
nature which in the first place is everlasting, not growing and decay-
ing, or waxing and waning; secondly, not fair in one point of view and
foul in another, or at one time or in one relation or at one place fair, at
another time or in another relation or at another place foul, as if fair to
some and foul to others, or in the likeness of a face or hands or any
other part of the bodily frame, or in any form of speech or knowledge,

or existing in any other being, as for example, in an animal, or in
b heaven, or in earth, or in any other place; but beauty absolute, separate,
simple, and everlasting, which without diminution and without increase, or any change, is imparted to the ever-growing and perishing
beauties of all other things. He who from these ascending under the
influence of true love, begins to perceive that beauty, is not far from the
end. And the true order of going, or being led by another, to the things
c of love, is to begin from the beauties of earth and mount upwards for
the sake of that other beauty, using these as steps only, and from one
going on to two, and from two to all fair forms, and from fair forms
to fair practices, and from fair practices to fair notions, until from fair
notions he arrives at the notion of absolute beauty, and at last knows
what the essence of beauty is. This, my dear Socrates,' said the stranger
d of Mantineia, 'is that life above all others which man should live, in the
contemplation of beauty absolute; a beauty which if you once beheld,
you would see not to be after the measure of gold, and garments, and
fair boys and youths, whose presence now entrances you; and you and
many would be content to live seeing them only and conversing with
them without meat or drink, if that were possible—you only want to
look at them and to be with them. But what if man had eyes to see the
e true beauty—the divine beauty, I mean, pure and clear and unalloyed,
not clogged with the pollutions of mortality and all the colours and
vanities of human life—thither looking, and holding converse with the
212 true beauty simple and divine? Remember how in that communion
only, beholding beauty with the eye of the mind, he will be enabled to
bring forth, not images of beauty, but realities (for he has hold not of
an image but of a reality), and bringing forth and nourishing true
virtue to become the friend of God and be immortal, if a mortal may.
Would that be an ignoble life?'

b   Such, Phaedrus—and I speak not only to you, but to all of you—
were the words of Diotima; and I am persuaded of their truth. And
being persuaded of them, I try to persuade others, that in the attainment of this end human nature will not easily find a helper better than
Love. And therefore, also, I say that every man ought to honor him as I
myself honor him, and walk in his ways, and exhort others to do the
same, and praise the power and spirit of Love according to the measure
of my ability now and ever.

c   The words which I have spoken, you, Phaedrus, may call an encomium of Love, or anything else which you please.

When Socrates had finished speaking, the company applauded, and
Aristophanes was beginning to say something in answer to the allusion
which Socrates had made to his own speech, when suddenly there was

a great knocking at the door of the house, as of revellers, and the sound of a flute-girl was heard. Agathon told the attendants to go and see who were the intruders. 'If they are friends of ours,' he said, 'invite them in, but if not, say that the drinking is over.' A little while afterwards they heard the voice of Alcibiades resounding in the court; he was in a great state of intoxication, and kept roaring and shouting, 'Where is Agathon? Lead me to Agathon,' and at length, supported by the flute-girl and some of his attendants, he found his way to them. 'Hail, friends,' he said, appearing at the door crowned with a massive garland of ivy and violets, his head flowing with ribands. 'Will you have a very drunken man as a companion of your revels? Or shall I crown Agathon, which was my intention in coming, and go away? For I was unable to come yesterday, and therefore I am here today, carrying on my head these ribands, in order to take them from my own head and crown the head of this fairest and wisest of men, as I may be allowed to call him. Will you laugh at me because I am drunk? Yet I know very well that I am speaking the truth, although you may laugh. But first tell me; if I come in shall we have the understanding of which I spoke? Will you drink with me or not?'

The company were vociferous in begging that he would take his place among them, and Agathon specially invited him. Thereupon he was led in by the people who were with him; and as he was being led, intending to crown Agathon, he took the ribands from his own head and held them in front of his eyes; he was thus prevented from seeing Socrates, who made way for him, and Alcibiades took the vacant place between Agathon and Socrates, and in taking the place he embraced Agathon and crowned him. Take off his sandals, said Agathon, and let him be the third on the same couch.

By all means; but who makes the third partner in our revels? said Alcibiades, turning round and starting up as he caught sight of Socrates. By Heracles, he said, what is this? here is Socrates always lying in wait for me, and always, as is his way, coming out at all sorts of unsuspected places: and now, what have you to say for yourself, and why are you lying here, where I perceive that you have contrived to find a place, not by a joker or lover of jokes, like Aristophanes, but by the fairest of the company?

Socrates turned to Agathon and said: I must ask you to protect me, Agathon; for the passion of this man has grown quite a serious matter to me. Since I became his admirer I have never been allowed to speak to any other fair one, or so much as to look at them. If I do, he goes wild with envy and jealousy, and not only abuses me but can hardly keep his hands off me, and at this moment he may do me some harm.

Please see to this, and either reconcile me to him, or, if he attempts violence, protect me, as I am in bodily fear of his mad and passionate attempts.

There can never be reconciliation between you and me, said Alcibiades; but for the present I will defer your chastisement. And I must beg e you, Agathon, to give me back some of the ribands so that I may crown the marvellous head of this universal despot—I would not have him complain of me for crowning you, and neglecting him, who in conversation is the conqueror of all mankind; and this not only once, as you were the day before yesterday, but always. Whereupon, taking some of the ribands, he crowned Socrates, and again reclined.

Then he said: You seem, my friends, to be sober, which is a thing not to be endured; you must drink—for that was the agreement under which I was admitted—and I elect myself master of the feast until you are well drunk. Let us have a large goblet, Agathon, or rather, he said, addressing the attendant, bring me that wine-cooler. The wine-cooler 214 which had caught his eye was a vessel holding more than two quarts— this he filled and emptied, and bade the attendant fill it again for Socrates. Observe, my friends, said Alcibiades, that this ingenious trick of mine will have no effect on Socrates, for he can drink any quantity of wine and not be at all nearer being drunk. Socrates drank the cup which the attendant filled for him.

Eryximachus said: What is this, Alcibiades? Are we to have neither b conversation nor singing over our cups; but simply to drink as if we were thirsty?

Alcibiades replied: Hail, worthy son of a most wise and worthy sire!

The same to you, said Eryximachus; but what shall we do?

That I leave to you, said Alcibiades.

'The wise physician skilled our wounds to heal'*

shall prescribe and we will obey. What do you want?

Well, said Eryximachus, before you appeared we had passed a resolution that each one of us in turn should make a speech in praise of Love, c and as good a one as he could: the turn was passed round from left to right; and as all of us have spoken, and you have not spoken but have well drunken, you ought to speak, and then impose upon Socrates any task which you please, and he on his right hand neighbour, and so on.

That is good, Eryximachus, said Alcibiades; and yet the comparison

---

*Iliad 11.514.

of a drunken man's speech with those of sober men is hardly fair; and I should like to know, sweet friend, whether you really believe what Socrates was just now saying; for I can assure you that the very reverse is the fact, and that if I praise any one but himself in his presence, *d* whether God or man, he will hardly keep his hands off me.

Shut up, said Socrates.

Hold your tongue, said Alcibiades, for by Poseidon, there is no one else whom I will praise when you are of the company.

Well then, said Eryximachus, if you like praise Socrates.

What do you think, Eryximachus? said Alcibiades: shall I attack *e* him and inflict the punishment before you all?

What are you going to do? said Socrates; are you going to raise a laugh at my expense? Is that the meaning of your praise?

I am going to speak the truth, if you will permit me.

I not only permit, but exhort you to speak the truth.

Then I will begin at once, said Alcibiades, and if I say anything which is not true, you may interrupt me if you will, and say, 'That is a lie,' though my intention is to speak the truth. But do not wonder if I speak as things come into my mind; for the fluent and orderly enumeration of all your singularities is not a task which is easy to a man in my condition.

And now, my boys, I shall praise Socrates in a figure which will 215 appear to him to be a caricature, and yet I speak, not to make fun of him, but only for the truth's sake. I say, that he is exactly like the busts of Silenus,* which are set up in the statuaries' shops, holding pipes *b* and flutes in their mouths; and they are made to open in the middle, and have images of gods inside them. I say also that he is like Marsyas the satyr.† You yourself will not deny, Socrates, that your face is like that of a satyr. And there is a resemblance in other points too: for example, you are a bully, as I can prove by witnesses, if you will not confess. And are you not a flute-player? That you are, and a performer far more wonderful than Marsyas. He indeed with instruments used to charm the souls of men by the powers of his breath, and the players of his music do so still: for the melodies of Olympus are derived from *c* Marsyas who taught them, and these, whether they are played by a great master or by a miserable flute-girl, have a power which no others have; they alone possess the soul and reveal the wants of those

---

*Mythical male inhabitant of the wild, known for his great appetite for sex and wine; father of the satyrs (goat-men), which had similar characteristics.

†He was skinned alive for daring to compete in music with Apollo, the god of music and poetry.

who have need of gods and mysteries, because they are divine. But you produce the same effect with your words only, and do not require the flute; that is the difference between you and him. When we hear any other speaker, even a very good one, he produces absolutely no

d   effect upon us, or not much, whereas the mere fragments of you and your words, even at second-hand, and however imperfectly repeated, amaze and possess the souls of every man, woman, and child who comes within hearing of them. And if I were not afraid that you would think me hopelessly drunk, I would have sworn as well as spoken to the influence which they have always had and still have over me. For my heart leaps within me more than that of any Corybantian

e   reveler,* and my eyes rain tears when I hear them. And I observe that many others are affected in the same manner. I have heard Pericles and other great orators, and I thought that they spoke well, but I never had any similar feeling; my soul was not stirred by them, nor was I angry at the thought of my own slavish state. But this Marsyas has often brought me to such a pass, that I have felt as if I could hardly endure

216 the life which I am leading (this, Socrates, you will admit); and I am conscious that if I did not shut my ears against him, and fly as from the voice of the sirens, my fate would be like that of others,—he would transfix me, and I should grow old sitting at his feet. For he makes me confess that I ought not to live as I do, neglecting the wants of my own soul, and busying myself with the concerns of the Athe-

b   nians; therefore I hold my ears and tear myself away from him. And he is the only person who ever made me ashamed, which you might think not to be in my nature, and there is no one else who does the same. For I know that I cannot answer him or say that I ought not to do as he bids, but when I leave his presence the love of popularity gets the better of me. And therefore I run away and fly from him, and when I see him I am ashamed of what I have confessed to him. Many a time have I wished that he were dead, and yet I know that I should

c   be much more sorry than glad, if he were to die: so that I am at my wits' end.

　　And this is what I and many others have suffered from the flute-playing of this satyr. Yet hear me once more while I show you how exact the image is, and how marvellous his power. For let me tell you; none of you know him; but I will reveal him to you; having begun, I

d   must go on. See you how fond he is of the fair? He is always with them

---

*Corybantians worshiped Cybele (a nature goddess) and Dionysus (god of wine) with plenty of wine, dance, and sex.

and is always being smitten by them, and then again he knows nothing and is ignorant of all things—such is the appearance which he puts
on. Is he not like a Silenus in this? To be sure he is: his outer mask is
the carved head of the Silenus; but, my companions in drink, when he
is opened, what temperance there is residing within! Know that beauty   e
and wealth and honour, at which the many wonder, are of no account
with him, and are utterly despised by him: he regards not at all the persons who are gifted with them; mankind are nothing to him; all his life
is spent in mocking and flouting at them. But when I opened him, and
looked within at his serious purpose, I saw in him divine and golden
images of such fascinating beauty that I was ready to do in a moment   217
whatever Socrates commanded: they may have escaped the observation
of others, but I saw them. Now I fancied that he was seriously enam-
ored of my beauty, and I thought that I should therefore have a grand
opportunity of hearing him tell what he knew, for I had a wonderful
opinion of the attractions of my youth. In the prosecution of this design, when I next went to him, I sent away the attendant who usually
accompanied me (I will confess the whole truth, and beg you to listen;   b
and I speak falsely, you, Socrates, expose the falsehood). Well, he and I
were alone together, and I thought that when there was nobody with
us, I should hear him speak the language which lovers use to their loves
when they are by themselves, and I was delighted. Nothing of the sort;
he conversed as usual, and spent the day with me and then went away.
Afterwards I challenged him to the palaestra; and he wrestled and
closed with me several times when there was no one present; I fancied   c
that I might succeed in this manner. Not a bit; I made no way with him.
Lastly, as I had failed hitherto, I thought that I must take stronger measures and attack him boldly, and, as I had begun, not give him up, but
see how matters stood between him and me. So I invited him to sup
with me, just as if he were a fair youth, and I a designing lover. He was
not easily persuaded to come; he did, however, after a while accept the
invitation, and when he came the first time, he wanted to go away at
once as soon as supper was over; I had not the face to detain him. The   d
second time, still in pursuance of my design, after we had supped, I
went on conversing far into the night, and when he wanted to go away,
I pretended that the hour was late and that he had much better remain.
So he lay down on the couch next to me, the same on which he had
supped, and there was no one but ourselves sleeping in the apartment.
All this may be told without shame to any one. But what follows I   e
could hardly tell you if I were sober. Yet as the proverb says, 'there is
truth in wine,' whether with boys, or without them;[7] and therefore I
must speak. Nor, again, should I be justified in concealing the lofty

actions of Socrates when I come to praise him. Moreover I have felt the serpent's sting; and the one who had suffered, as they say, is willing to
218 tell his fellow-sufferers only, as they alone will be likely to understand him, and will not be extreme in judging of the sayings or doings which have been wrung from his agony. For I have been bitten by a more than viper's tooth; I have known in my soul, or in my heart, or in some other part, that worst of pangs, more violent in ingenuous youth than any serpent's tooth, the pang of philosophy, which will make a man say or do anything. And you whom I see around me, Phaedrus and Agathon and Eryximachus and Pausanias and Aristodemus and
b Aristophanes, all of you, and I need not say Socrates himself, have had experience of the same madness and passion in your longing after wisdom. Therefore listen and excuse my doings then and my sayings now. But let the attendants and other profane and unmannered persons close up the doors of their ears.

c   When the lamp was put out and the servants had gone away, I thought that I must be plain with him and have no more ambiguity. So I gave him a shake, and I said: 'Socrates, are you asleep?' 'No,' he said. 'Do you know what I am meditating?' 'What are you meditating?' he said. 'I think,' I replied, 'that of all the lovers whom I have ever had you are the only one who is worthy of me, and you appear to be too modest to speak. Now I feel that I should be a fool to refuse you this or any
d other favour, and therefore I come to lay at your feet all that I have and all that my friends have, in the hope that you will assist me in the way of virtue, which I desire above all things, and in which I believe that you can help me better than any one else. And I should certainly have more reason to be ashamed of what wise men would say if I were to refuse a favour to someone like you, than of what the world, who are mostly fools, would say of me if I granted it.' To these words he replied in the ironical manner which is so characteristic of him: 'Alcibiades, my friend, you have indeed an elevated aim if what you say is true, and if there really is in me any power by which you may become better;
e truly you must see in me some rare beauty of a kind infinitely higher than any which I see in you. And therefore, if you mean to share with me and to exchange beauty for beauty, you will have greatly the advantage of me; you will gain true beauty in return for appearance—like
219 Diomedes,* gold in exchange for brass. But look again, sweet friend, and see whether you are not deceived in me. The mind begins to grow critical when the bodily eye fails, and it will be a long time before you

---

*Iliad 6.232–236.

get old.' Hearing this, I said: I have told you my purpose, which is quite serious; consider what you think best for you and me.' 'That is good,'   b
he said; 'at some other time then we will consider and act as seems best about this and about other matters.' Whereupon, I fancied that he was smitten, and that the words which I had uttered like arrows had wounded him, and so without waiting to hear more I got up, and throwing my coat about him crept under his threadbare cloak, as the time of year was winter, and there I lay during the whole night having this wonderful monster in my arms. This again, Socrates, will not be   c
denied by you. And yet, notwithstanding all, he was so superior to my solicitations, so contemptuous and derisive and disdainful of my beauty—which really, as I fancied, had some attractions. Hear, judges; for judges you shall be of the haughty virtue of Socrates: nothing more happened, but in the morning when I awoke (let all the gods and goddesses be my witnesses) I arose as from the couch of a father or an   d
elder brother.

What do you suppose must have been my feelings, after this rejection, at the thought of my own dishonor? And yet I could not help wondering at his natural temperance and self-restraint and manliness. I never imagined that I could have met with a man such as he is in wisdom and endurance. And therefore I could not be angry with him or renounce his company, any more than I could hope to win him. For I well knew that if Ajax could not be wounded by steel, much less he by   e
money; and my only chance of captivating him by my personal attractions had failed. So I was at my wits' end; no one was ever more hopelessly enslaved by another. All this happened before he and I went on the expedition to Potidaea; there we dined together, and I had the opportunity of observing his extraordinary power of sustaining fatigue. His endurance was simply marvellous when, being cut off from our supplies, we were compelled to go without food—on such occasions,   220
which often happen in time of war, he was superior not only to me but to everybody; there was no one to be compared to him. Yet at a festival he was the only person who had any real powers of enjoyment; though not willing to drink, he could if compelled beat us all at that— wonderful to relate! No human being had ever seen Socrates drunk; and his powers, if I am not mistaken, will be tested before long. His   b
fortitude in enduring cold was also surprising. There was a severe frost, for the winter in that region is really tremendous, and everybody else either remained indoors, or if they went out had on an amazing quantity of clothes, and were well shod, and had their feet swathed in felt and fleeces: in the midst of this, Socrates with his bare feet on the ice and in his ordinary dress marched better than the other soldiers who

had shoes, and they looked daggers at him because he seemed to despise them.

    I have told you one tale, and now I must tell you another, which is

c   worth hearing,

'Of the doings and suffering of the enduring man'*

while he was on the expedition. One morning he was thinking about something which he could not resolve; he would not give it up, but continued thinking from early dawn until noon—there he stood fixed in thought; and at noon attention was drawn to him, and the rumour ran through the wondering crowd that Socrates had been standing and thinking about something ever since the break of day. At last, in the evening after supper, some Ionians out of curiosity (I should explain

d   that this was not in winter but in summer), brought out their mats and slept in the open air in order to watch him and see whether he would stand all night. There he stood until the following morning; and with the return of light he offered up a prayer to the sun, and went his way. I will also tell, if you please—and indeed I am bound to tell—of his courage in battle; for who but he saved my life? Now this was the engagement in which I received the prize of valour: for I was

e   wounded and he would not leave me, but he rescued me and my arms; and he ought to have received the prize of valour which the generals wanted to confer on me partly on account of my rank, and I told them so (this, again, Socrates will not impeach or deny), but he was more eager than the generals that I and not he should have the

221   prize. There was another occasion on which his behaviour was very remarkable—in the light of the army after the battle of Delium,† where he served among the heavy-armed. I had a better opportunity to see him than at Potidaea,‡ for I was myself on horseback, and therefore comparatively out of danger. He and Laches§ were retreating, for the troops were in flight, and I met them and told them not to be discouraged, and promised to remain with them; and there you might see him, Aristophanes, as you describe,‖ just as he is in the streets of

b   Athens, stalking like a pelican, and rolling his eyes, calmly contem-

---

*Odyssey 4.242, 271.
†Athenian defeat at the hands of the Boeotians during the Peloponnesian War (Thucydides 4.91–96); Delium was a seaport of ancient Greece.
‡An intense battle between the Corinthians and the Athenians took place in Potidaea, an ancient city of Macedonia, in 432 B.C.E., just before the Peloponnesian War.
§See "Introduction" to Laches.
‖Clouds 362.

plating enemies as well as friends, and making very intelligible to anybody, even from a distance, that whoever attacked him would be likely to meet with a stout resistance; and in this way he and his companion escaped—for this is the sort of man who is never touched in war; those only are pursued who are running away headlong. I particularly observed how superior he was to Laches in presence of mind. Many *c* are the marvels which I might narrate in praise of Socrates; most of his ways might perhaps be paralleled in another man, but his absolute *d* unlikeness to any human being that is or ever has been is perfectly astonishing. You may imagine Brasidas* and others to have been like Achilles; or you may imagine Nestor and Antenor to have been like Pericles; and the same may be said of other famous men, but of this strange being you will never be able to find any likeness, however remote, either among men who now are or who ever have been—other than that which I have already suggested of Silenus and the satyrs; and they represent in a figure not only himself, but his words. For, although I forgot to mention this to you before, his words are like the *e* images of Silenus which open; they are ridiculous when you first hear them; he clothes himself in language that is like the skin of the wanton satyr—for his talk is of pack-asses and smiths and cobblers and curriers, and he is always repeating the same things in the same words, so that any ignorant or inexperienced person might feel disposed to laugh at him; but he who opens the bust and sees what is 222 within will find that they are the only words which have a meaning in them, and also the most divine, abounding in fair images of virtue, and of the widest comprehension, or rather extending to the whole duty of a good and honourable man.

This, friends, is my praise of Socrates. I have added my blame of him for his ill-treatment of me; and he has ill-treated not only me, but *b* Charmides† the son of Glaucon, and Euthydemus‡ the son of Diocles, and many others in the same way—beginning as their lover he has ended by making them pay their addresses to him. Wherefore I say to you, Agathon, 'Be not deceived by him; learn from me and take warning, and do not be a fool and learn by experience, as the proverb says.'

When Alcibiades had finished, there was a laugh at his outspokenness; for he seemed to be still in love with Socrates. You are sober, Alcibiades, said Socrates, or you would never have gone so far to hide the

---

*Outstanding Spartan general in the Peloponnesian War; he died in combat at the Athenian colony of Amphipolis.
†An Athenian orphan, reared by a wealthy family.
‡Neither the orator Lysias' brother nor the character of Plato's homonymous dialogue, but a handsome follower of Socrates.

purpose of your satyr's praises, for all this long story is only an ingenious circumlocution, of which the point comes in by the way at the end; you want to get up a quarrel between me and Agathon, and your notion is that I ought to love you and nobody else, and that you and

d you only ought to love Agathon. But the plot of this Satyric or Silenic drama has been detected, and you must not allow him, Agathon, to set us at variance.

I believe you are right, said Agathon, and I am disposed to think

e that his intention in placing himself between you and me was only to divide us; but he shall gain nothing by that move; for I will go and lie on the couch next to you.

Yes, yes, replied Socrates, by all means come here and lie on the couch below me.

Alas, said Alcibiades, how I am fooled by this man; he is determined to get the better of me at every turn. I do beseech you, allow Agathon to lie between us.

Certainly not, said Socrates, as you praised me, and I in turn ought to praise my neighbour on the right, he will be out of order in praising me again when he ought rather to be praised by me, and I must entreat you to consent to this, and not be jealous, for I have a great de-

223 sire to praise the youth.

Hurrah! cried Agathon, I will rise instantly, that I may be praised by Socrates.

The usual way, said Alcibiades; where Socrates is, no one else has any chance with the fair; and now how readily has he invented a specious reason for attracting Agathon to himself.

b Agathon arose in order that he might take his place on the couch by Socrates, when suddenly a band of revellers entered, and spoiled the order of the banquet. Someone who was going out left the door open, they had found their way in, and made themselves at home; great confusion ensued, and everyone was compelled to drink large quantities of wine. Aristodemus said that Eryximachus, Phaedrus, and others went away—he himself fell asleep, and as the nights were long took a good

c rest: he was awakened towards daybreak by a crowing of cocks, and when he awoke, the others were either asleep, or had gone away; there remained only Socrates, Aristophanes, and Agathon, who were drinking out of a large goblet which they passed round, and Socrates was discoursing to them. Aristodemus was only half awake, and he did not hear the beginning of the discourse; the chief thing which he remem-

d bered was Socrates compelling the other two to acknowledge that the genius of comedy was the same with that of tragedy, and that the true artist in tragedy was an artist in comedy also. To this they were constrained to assent, being drowsy, and not quite following the argument. And first of all Aristophanes dropped off, then, when the day was already dawning, Agathon. Socrates, having laid them to sleep, rose to depart; Aristodemus, as his manner was, following him. At the Lyceum* he took a bath, and passed the day as usual. In the evening he retired to rest at his own home.

e

---

*Gymnasium that Socrates visited frequently.

GORGIAS

Introduction

AFTER LAWS AND REPUBLIC, *Gorgias* is the third-longest of Plato's dialogues. This attests to the importance Plato attached in his early period to effects of the rhetorical instruction imparted by the Sophists in Athens, in particular by the master rhetoricians Gorgias of Leontini and Polus of Acragas, who are both speakers in this dialogue. Gorgias is staying at the house of the young politician Callicles, who shows signs of nervousness at the end of the dialogue when the conversation turns to the actual purpose of the leaders of the masses. Chaerephon, another speaker in the dialogue, is a close friend of Socrates and also knows Gorgias; he seems to have been well respected in Athens, although he was "a little mad" (*Charmides* 153b; not included in this volume). He is mentioned by Socrates in *Apology* (21a, p. 280) as the man who consulted the oracle of Delphi and was told that Socrates was the wisest man alive.

The case against rhetoric as the skill exclusively oriented to win an argument is made forcibly and at length in this dialogue, since Socrates has to face two rhetorical heavyweights and a politician. Nevertheless, the result is far from conclusive, and Plato will need to return to the topic of rhetoric in *Phaedrus*.

We can outline the conversation as follows:

- (447a–449c) Socrates and Chaerephon meet Callicles, who offers to arrange for a meeting with Gorgias, who has just finished an exhibition of his rhetorical skills. Socrates wants to know what kind of expertise is rhetoric.

(449c–461b) Socrates and Gorgias

- (449c–455a) Gorgias provides answers to which Socrates objects: Rhetoric is about words (Socrates' objection: too general); it has discourse as an instrument (also true of mathematics and games of dice); it is about the most important of human interests (too vague); it is the art of persuading in civic assemblies. After this last answer, Socrates asks a new question: What kind of conviction does it produce, and about what? Gorgias' fifth answer is that it produces conviction in juries and crowds, and about matters of right and wrong. Socrates objects that such conviction is not true knowledge, but opinion.

- (455a–461b) Socrates claims that the orator is useless in technical matters. Gorgias retorts that it is the orator, and not the expert, who achieves results, and that rhetoric is a "neutral" power. Socrates objects that the conviction produced in juries and crowds is produced among nonexperts. Gorgias claims that the orator is more powerful than the expert. Socrates then asks about the difference between right and wrong: Does Gorgias teach that too? Gorgias says that he teaches it if his students do not already know it. Socrates then concludes that the good speaker cannot do wrong, and therefore rhetoric is not a "neutral" power after all. The teacher of rhetoric is responsible for what his students do with the rhetorical skills they learn from him.

(461b–481b) Socrates and Polus

- (461b–463e) Polus interrupts and asks Socrates for his opinion about rhetoric. Socrates says rhetoric is a skill that produces pleasure, which is a statement that applies equally to cooking skills. Rhetoric is, in fact, a false version of a branch of politics. Gorgias asks for clarification.

- (463e–466a) Socrates classifies skills as: (a) pertaining to the body or the soul; (b) regulative or corrective; and (c) genuine or spurious. Rhetoric is a spurious, corrective skill aimed at minds (the mental counterpart of cooking skills).

- (466a–469c) Polus is tired of classifications and states that politicians are powerful because they do what they want. To this Socrates retorts that they do what they decide, and what they decide is a means to an end. As a means, it cannot be what anyone wants.

- (469c–472d) Polus is forced to agree that we can only do what we want when what we want is beneficial to us. And what is beneficial is just. What about, Polus says, the unjust but prosperous king? Socrates states that he would not accept that kind of prosperity, even if most people would.

- (472d–481b) In a lengthy dialectical argument, Socrates demonstrates that the wicked man is unhappy, and even more so if he goes unpunished. Therefore, the best use of rhetoric would be to get oneself punished for evil deeds or to help enemies escape punishment for theirs. This is, of course, a way to return to the initial question about the value of rhetoric.

(481b–522e) Socrates and Callicles

- (481b–486d) Callicles interrupts: Is Socrates serious? Only the law, not nature, says that doing wrong is more dishonorable than suffering it. Examples of this, Callicles says, are animal behavior and foreign relations, Socrates is wasting too much time with philosophy; instead, he should be getting ready to defend himself in case he has to go to trial.

- (486d–495e) Socrates objects that the laws are the laws for all, and "all" are by nature stronger than one, so violating the laws is violating nature. Callicles replies that the better people must not be identified with the stronger, but with the more intelligent. Socrates asks whether the expert in dietetics has a right to a double ration. Callicles says that this is a ridiculous example and asserts that the strongest in politics and the happiest are those who get their way without bothering with justice or self-control. Socrates denies that happiness consists of satisfying every desire.

- (495e–506c) Socrates offers dialectical proof that pleasure is not the good. A distinction needs to be made between good and bad pleasures. Good pleasure is not the one aimed at pleasing an audience. Callicles offers Pericles as an example of a good politician who pleased the masses, and Socrates replies that the good is gratifying one's own and other people's desires, but that the good politician tries to impose the good, and this will involve repressing people's desires.

- (506c–518c) Socrates continues: The good depends on self-control. The man without moral sense has no place in the community and cannot be happy. It's more important to not do wrong than to not have wrong done upon oneself. How can we ensure that we do not do wrong, given that identifying with the current regime is no guarantee? Callicles senses that these are dangerous waters. Socrates says that Athens has never produced a true statesman who would give the people what is good for them, instead of what they want.

- (518c–522e) Socrates continues in this vein: Some politicians, he says, are acclaimed as benefactors because the effects of their actions are not immediately obvious; if they are later abandoned by the people, they have no right to complain, since they did not educate them. They are, in fact, worse than Sophists, since Sophists are caricatures of legislators, while politicians ape judges, whose skills fall in the domain of the corrective ones. Callicles senses that they are treading on dangerous ground again, but Socrates would rather be convicted by a jury of unfair people than to be wicked by his own standards.

- (523a–527e) In closing, Socrates tells the myth of the judgment in the afterlife, where all men will be judged, stripped of all their possessions and friends, by the judges appointed by Zeus. He then tells Gorgias and his friends to prepare for that judgment, next to which all mortal issues are trivial.

GORGIAS

CALLICLES. The wise man, as the proverb says, is late for a fray, but not for a feast.

SOCRATES. And are we late for a feast?

CAL. Yes, and a delightful one; for Gorgias has just been exhibiting to us many fine things.

SOC. It is not my fault, Callicles; our friend Chaerephon is to blame; for he would keep us loitering in the Agora.*

CHAEREPHON. Never mind, Socrates; the misfortune of which I have been the cause I will also repair; for Gorgias is a friend of mine, and I will make him give the exhibition again either now, or, if you prefer, at some other time. **b**

CAL. What is the matter, Chaerephon—does Socrates want to hear Gorgias?

CHAER. Yes, that was our intention in coming.

CAL. Come into my house, then; for Gorgias is staying with me, and he shall exhibit to you.

SOC. Very good, Callicles; but will he answer our questions? for I want to hear from him what is the nature of his art, and what it is which he professes and teaches; he may, as you, Chaerephon, suggest, defer the exhibition to some other time. **c**

CAL. There is nothing like asking him, Socrates; and indeed to answer questions is a part of his exhibition, for he was saying only just now, that any one in my house might put any question to him, and that he would answer.

SOC. How fortunate! will you ask him, Chaerephon?

CHAER. What shall I ask him? **d**

SOC. Ask him who he is.

CHAER. What do you mean?

SOC. I mean such a question as would elicit from him, if he had been a maker of shoes, the answer that he is a cobbler. Do you understand?

CHAER. I understand, and will ask him: Tell, me, Gorgias, is our friend Callicles right in saying that you undertake to answer any questions which you are asked?

GORGIAS. Quite right, Chaerephon: I was saying as much only just now; and I may add that many years have elapsed since any one has asked me a new one. **448**

---

*Athens' marketplace and civic center.

CHAER. Then you must be very ready, Gorgias.

GOR. Of that, Chaerephon, you can make trial.

POLUS. Yes, indeed, and if you like, Chaerephon, you may make trial of me too, for I think that Gorgias, who has been talking a long time, is tired.

CHAER. And do you, Polus, think that you can answer better than Gorgias?

b POL. What does that matter if I answer well enough for you?

CHAER. Not at all; answer if you like.

POL. Ask.

CHAER. My question is this: If Gorgias had the skill of his brother Herodicus, what ought we to call him? Ought he not to have the name which is given to his brother?

POL. Certainly.

CHAER. Then we should be right in calling him a physician?

POL. Yes.

CHAER. And if he had the skill of Aristophon the son of Aglaophon, or of his brother Polygnotus, what ought we to call him?

c POL. Clearly, a painter.

CHAER. But now what shall we call him—what is the art in which he is skilled?

POL. Chaerephon, there are many arts among mankind which are experimental, and have their origin in experience, for experience makes the days of men to proceed according to art, and inexperience according to chance, and different persons in different ways are proficient in different arts, and the best persons in the best arts. And our friend Gorgias is one of the best, and the art in which he is a proficient is the noblest.

SOC. Polus has been taught how to make a fine speech, Gorgias, but
d he is not fulfilling the promise which he made to Chaerephon.

GOR. What do you mean, Socrates?

SOC. I mean that he has not exactly answered the question which he was asked.

GOR. Then why not ask him yourself?

SOC. But I would much rather ask you, if you are disposed to answer: for I see, from the few words which Polus has uttered, that he has
e attended more to the art which is called rhetoric than to dialectic.

POL. What makes you say so, Socrates?

SOC. Because, Polus, when Chaerephon asked you what was the art which Gorgias knows, you praised it as if you were answering someone who found fault with it, but you never said what the art was.

POL. Why, did I not say that it was the noblest of arts?

SOC. Yes, indeed, but that was no answer to the question: nobody asked what was the quality, but what was the nature of the art, and by what name we were to describe Gorgias. And I would still beg you briefly and clearly, as you answered Chaerephon when he asked you at first, to say what this art is, and what we ought to call Gorgias: Or rather, Gorgias, let me turn to you, and ask the same question: what are we to call you, and what is the art which you profess? 449

GOR. Rhetoric, Socrates, is my art.

SOC. Then I am to call you a rhetorician?

GOR. Yes, Socrates, and a good one too, if you would call me that which, in Homeric language, 'I boast myself to be.'

SOC. I would wish to do so.

GOR. Then pray do.

SOC. And are we to say that you are able to make other men rhetoricians? b

GOR. Yes, that is exactly what I profess to make them, not only at Athens, but in all places.

SOC. And will you continue to ask and answer questions, Gorgias, as we are at present doing, and reserve for another occasion the longer mode of speech which Polus was attempting? Will you keep your promise, and answer shortly the questions which are asked of you?

GOR. Some answers, Socrates, are of necessity longer; but I will do c my best to make them as short as possible; for a part of my profession is that I can be as short as any one.

SOC. That is what is wanted, Gorgias; exhibit the shorter method now, and the longer one at some other time.

GOR. Well, I will; and you will certainly say that you never heard a man use fewer words.

SOC. Very good then; as you profess to be a rhetorician, and a maker of rhetoricians, let me ask you, with what is rhetoric concerned: d I might ask with what is weaving concerned, and you would reply (would you not?), with the making of garments?

GOR. Yes.

SOC. And music is concerned with the composition of melodies?

GOR. It is.

SOC. By Hera, Gorgias, I admire the surpassing brevity of your answers.

GOR. Yes, Socrates, I do think myself good at that.

SOC. I am glad to hear it; answer me in like manner about rhetoric: with what is rhetoric concerned?

GOR. With discourse. e

SOC. What sort of discourse, Gorgias?—such discourse as would teach the sick under what treatment they might get well?

GOR. No.

Soc. Then rhetoric does not treat of all kinds of discourse?

Gor. Certainly not.

Soc. And yet rhetoric makes men able to speak?

Gor. Yes.

Soc. And to understand that about which they speak?

Gor. Of course.

450 Soc. But does not the art of medicine, which we were just now mentioning, also make men able to understand and speak about the sick?

Gor. Certainly.

Soc. Then medicine also treats of discourse?

Gor. Yes.

Soc. Of discourse concerning diseases?

Gor. Just so.

Soc. And does not gymnastic also treat of discourse concerning the good or evil condition of the body?

Gor. Very true.

b Soc. And the same, Gorgias, is true of the other arts: all of them treat of discourse concerning the subjects with which they severally have to do.

Gor. Clearly.

Soc. Then why, if you call rhetoric the art which treats of discourse, and all the other arts treat of discourse, do you not call them arts of rhetoric?

Gor. Because, Socrates, the knowledge of the other arts has only to do with some sort of external action, as of the hand; but there is no such action of the hand in rhetoric which works and takes effect only c through the medium of discourse. And therefore I am justified in saying that rhetoric treats of discourse.

Soc. I am not sure whether I entirely understand you, but I dare say I shall soon know better; please answer me a question: you would allow that there are arts?

Gor. Yes.

Soc. As to the arts generally, they are for the most part concerned with doing, and require little or no speaking; in painting, and statuary, and many other arts, the work may proceed in silence; and of such arts d I suppose you would say that they do not come within the province of rhetoric.

Gor. You perfectly conceive my meaning, Socrates.

Soc. But there are other arts which work wholly through the medium of language, and require either no action or very little, as, for example, the arts of arithmetic, of calculation, of geometry, and of playing draughts; in some of these speech is pretty nearly coextensive with action, but in most of them the verbal element is greater—they depend wholly on words for their efficacy and power: and I take your meaning to be that rhetoric is an art of this latter sort?   *e*

GOR. Exactly.

SOC. And yet I do not believe that you really mean to call any of these arts rhetoric; although the precise expression which you used was, that rhetoric is an art which works and takes effect only through the medium of discourse; and an adversary who wished to be captious might say, 'And so, Gorgias, you call arithmetic rhetoric.' But I do not think that you really call arithmetic rhetoric any more than geometry would be so called by you.   451

GOR. You are quite right, Socrates, in your apprehension of my meaning.

SOC. Well, then, let me now have the rest of my answer: Seeing that rhetoric is one of those arts which works mainly by the use of words, and there are other arts which also use words, tell me what is that quality in words with which rhetoric is concerned. Suppose that a person asks me about some of the arts which I was mentioning just now; he might say, 'Socrates, what is arithmetic?' and I should reply to him, as   *b* you replied to me, that arithmetic is one of those arts which take effect through words. And then he would proceed to ask: 'Words about what?' and I should reply, Words about odd and even numbers, and how many there are of each. And if he asked again: 'What is the art of calculation?' I should say, That also is one of the arts which is concerned wholly with words. And if he further said, 'Concerned with what?' I should say, like the clerks in the assembly, 'as aforesaid' of arithmetic, but with   *c* a difference, the difference being that the art of calculation considers not only the quantities of odd and even numbers, but also their numerical relations to themselves and to one another. And suppose, again, I were to say that astronomy is only words—he would ask, 'Words about what, Socrates?' and I should answer, that astronomy tells us about the motions of the stars and sun and moon, and their relative swiftness.

GOR. You would be quite right, Socrates.

SOC. And now let us have from you, Gorgias, the truth about rhet-   *d* oric, which you would admit (would you not?) to be one of those arts which act always and fulfil all their ends through the medium of words?

GOR. True.

SOC. Words which do what? I should ask. To what class of things do the words which rhetoric uses relate?

GOR. To the greatest, Socrates, and the best of human things.

SOC. That again, Gorgias, is ambiguous; I am still in the dark: for *e*   which are the greatest and best of human things? I dare say that you have heard men singing at feasts the old drinking song, in which the singers enumerate the goods of life, first health, beauty next, thirdly, as the writer of the song says, wealth honestly obtained.

452   GOR. Yes, I know the song; but what is your drift?

SOC. I mean to say, that the producers of those things which the author of the song praises, that is to say, the physician, the trainer, the money-maker, will at once come to you, and first the physician will say: Socrates, Gorgias is deceiving you, for my art is concerned with the greatest good of men and not his.' And when I ask, Who are you? he will reply, 'I am a physician.' What do you mean? I shall say. Do you mean that your art produces the greatest good? 'Certainly,' he will answer, 'for is not health the greatest good? What greater good can men

b   have, Socrates?' And after him the trainer will come and say, 'I too, Socrates, shall be greatly surprised if Gorgias can show more good of his art than I can show of mine.' To him again I shall say, Who are you, honest friend, and what is your business? 'I am a trainer,' he will reply, 'and my business is to make men beautiful and strong in body.' When

c   I have done with the trainer, there arrives the money-maker, and he, as I expect, will utterly despise them all. 'Consider, Socrates,' he will say, 'whether Gorgias or any one else can produce any greater good than wealth.' Well, you and I say to him, and are you a creator of wealth? 'Yes,' he replies. And who are you? 'A money-maker.' And do you consider wealth to be the greatest good of man? 'Of course,' will be his reply. And we shall rejoin: Yes; but our friend Gorgias contends that his art produces a greater good than yours. And then he will be sure to go

d   on and ask, 'What good? Let Gorgias answer.' Now I want you, Gorgias, to imagine that this question is asked of you by them and by me: What is that which, as you say, is the greatest good of man, and of which you are the creator? Answer us.

GOR. That good, Socrates, which is truly the greatest, being that which gives to men freedom in their own persons, and to individuals the power of ruling over others in their several states.

SOC. And what would you consider this to be?

e   GOR. What is there greater than the word which persuades the judges in the courts, or the members of the Council, or the citizens in the assembly, or at any other political meeting? If you have the power of uttering this word, you will have the physician your slave, and the trainer your slave, and the money-maker of whom you talk will be found to gather treasures, not for himself, but for you who are able to speak and to persuade the multitude.

SOC. Now I think, Gorgias, that you have very accurately explained what you conceive to be the art of rhetoric; and you mean to say, if I

am not mistaken, that rhetoric is the artificer of persuasion, having this 453
and no other business, and that this is her crown and end. Do you
know any other effect of rhetoric over and above that of producing persuasion?

GOR. No: the definition seems to me very fair, Socrates; for persuasion is the chief end of rhetoric.

SOC. Then hear me, Gorgias, for I am quite sure that if there ever b
was a man who entered on the discussion of a matter from a pure love
of knowing the truth, I am such a one, and I should say the same of
you.

GOR. What is coming, Socrates?

SOC. I will tell you: I am very well aware that I do not know what,
according to you, is the exact nature, or what are the topics of that persuasion of which you speak, and which is given by rhetoric; although
I have a suspicion about both the one and the other. And I am going to
ask: what is this power of persuasion which is given by rhetoric, and c
about what? But why, if I have a suspicion, do I ask instead of telling
you? Not for your sake, but in order that the argument may proceed in
such a manner as is most likely to set forth the truth. And I would have
you observe, that I am right in asking this further question: If I asked,
'What sort of a painter is Zeuxis?'* and you said, 'The painter of figures,' should I not be right in asking, 'What kind of figures, and where
do you find them?'

GOR. Certainly.

SOC. And the reason for asking this second question would be, that d
there are other painters besides, who paint many other figures?

GOR. True.

SOC. But if there had been no one but Zeuxis who painted them,
then you would have answered very well?

GOR. Quite so.

SOC. Now I want to know about rhetoric in the same way: is rhetoric the only art which brings persuasion, or do other arts have the
same effect? I mean to say: Does he who teaches anything persuade
men of that which he teaches or not?

GOR. He persuades, Socrates; there can be no mistake about that.

SOC. Again, if we take the arts of which we were just now speaking: e
do not arithmetic and the arithmeticians teach us the properties of
number?

GOR. Certainly.

---

*Famous Greek painter (fifth century B.C.E.); he may be the same as the Zeuxippus of
Protagoras 318b.

Soc. And therefore persuade us of them?

Gor. Yes.

Soc. Then arithmetic as well as rhetoric is an artificer of persuasion?

Gor. Clearly.

Soc. And if any one asks us what sort of persuasion, and about what, we shall answer: persuasion which teaches the quantity of odd and even; and we shall be able to show that all the other arts of which we were just now speaking are artificers of persuasion, and of what sort, and about what.

Gor. Very true.

Soc. Then rhetoric is not the only artificer of persuasion?

Gor. True.

Soc. Seeing, then, that not only rhetoric works by persuasion, but that other arts do the same, as in the case of the painter, a question has arisen which is a very fair one: Of what persuasion is rhetoric the artificer, and about what? Is not that a fair way of putting the question?

Gor. I think so.

Soc. Then, if you approve of the question, Gorgias, what is the answer?

Gor. I answer, Socrates, that rhetoric is the art of persuasion in courts of law and other assemblies, as I was just now saying, and about the just and unjust.

Soc. And that, Gorgias, was what I was suspecting to be your notion; yet I would not have you wonder if by-and-by I am found repeating a seemingly plain question; for I ask not in order to confute you, but, as I was saying, in order that the argument may proceed consecutively, and that we may not get into the habit of anticipating and suspecting the meaning of one another's words; I would have you develop your own views in your own way, whatever may be your hypothesis.

Gor. I think that you are quite right, Socrates.

Soc. Then let me raise another question; there is such a thing as 'having learned'?

Gor. Yes.

Soc. And there is also 'having believed'?

Gor. Yes.

Soc. And is the 'having learned' the same as 'having believed,' and are learning and belief the same things?

Gor. In my judgment, Socrates, they are not the same.

Soc. And your judgment is right, as you may ascertain in this way: If a person were to say to you, 'Is there, Gorgias, a false belief as well as a true one?' you would reply, if I am not mistaken, that there is.

GOR. Yes.

SOC. Well, but is there a false knowledge as well as a true one?

GOR. No.

SOC. No, indeed; and this again proves that knowledge and belief differ.

GOR. Very true.

SOC. And yet those who have learned as well as those who have be-   e
lieved are persuaded?

GOR. Just so.

SOC. Shall we then assume two sorts of persuasion, one which is the source of belief without knowledge, as the other is of knowledge?

GOR. By all means.

SOC. And which sort of persuasion does rhetoric create in courts of law and other assemblies about the just and unjust, the sort of persuasion which gives belief without knowledge, or that which gives knowledge?

GOR. Clearly, Socrates, that which only gives belief.   455

SOC. Then rhetoric, as would appear, is the artificer of a persuasion which creates belief about the just and unjust, but gives no instruction about them?

GOR. True.

SOC. And the rhetorician does not instruct the courts of law or other assemblies about things just and unjust, but he creates belief about them; for no one can be supposed to instruct such a vast multitude about such high matters in a short time?

GOR. Certainly not.

SOC. Come, then, and let us see what we really mean about rheto-   b
ric; for I do not know what my own meaning is as yet. When the assembly meets to elect a physician or a shipwright or any other craftsman, will the rhetorician be taken into counsel? Surely not. For at every election he ought to be chosen who is most skilled; and, again, when walls have to be built or harbours or docks to be constructed, not the rhetorician but the master workman will advise; or when generals have   c
to be chosen and an order of battle arranged, or a proposition taken, then the military will advise and not the rhetoricians: what do you say, Gorgias? Since you profess to be a rhetorician and a maker of rhetoricians, I cannot do better than learn the nature of your art from you. And here let me assure you that I have your interest in view as well as my own. For likely enough someone or other of the young men present might desire to become your pupil, and in fact I see some, and a good many too, who have this wish, but they would be too modest to   d
question you. And therefore when you are interrogated by me, I would have you imagine that you are interrogated by them. 'What is the use

of coming to you, Gorgias?' they will say—'about what will you teach us to advise the state?—about the just and unjust only, or about those other things also which Socrates has just mentioned?' How will you answer them?

GOR. I like your way of leading us on, Socrates, and I will endeavour to reveal to you the whole nature of rhetoric. You must have heard, I think, that the docks and the walls of the Athenians and the plan of the harbour were devised in accordance with the counsels, partly of Themistocles,* and partly of Pericles, and not at the suggestion of the builders.

SOC. Such is the tradition, Gorgias, about Themistocles; and I myself heard the speech of Pericles when he advised us about the middle wall.

GOR. And you will observe, Socrates, that when a decision has to be given in such matters the rhetoricians are the advisers; they are the men who win their point.

SOC. I had that in my admiring mind, Gorgias, when I asked what is the nature of rhetoric, which always appears to me, when I look at the matter in this way, to be a marvel of greatness.

GOR. A marvel, indeed, Socrates, if you only knew how rhetoric comprehends and holds under her sway all the inferior arts. Let me offer you a striking example of this. On several occasions I have been with my brother Herodicus or some other physician to see one of his patients, who would not allow the physician to give him medicine, or apply a knife or hot iron to him; and I have persuaded him to do for me what he would not do for the physician just by the use of rhetoric. And I say that if a rhetorician and a physician were to go to any city, and had there to argue in the Ecclesia or any other assembly as to which of them should be elected state-physician, the physician would have no chance; but he who could speak would be chosen if he wished; and in a contest with a man of any other profession the rhetorician more than anyone would have the power of getting himself chosen, for he can speak more persuasively to the multitude than any of them, and on any subject. Such is the nature and power of the art of rhetoric! And yet, Socrates, rhetoric should be used like any other competitive art, not against everybody. The rhetorician ought not to abuse his strength any more than a pugilist or pancratiast† or other master of fence; because he has powers which are more than a match either for friend or enemy, he ought not therefore to strike, stab, or slay his friends. Suppose a man trained in the palestra and a skilful boxer, in the

---

*Athenian statesman (fifth-century B.C.E.) who strengthened the Athenian navy.
†A participant in a pancratium, an athletic contest involving both wrestling and boxing.

fulness of his strength, goes and strikes his father or mother or one of   e
his familiars or friends; that is no reason why the trainers or fencing-
masters should be held in detestation or banished from the city—
surely not. For they taught their art for a good purpose, to be used
against enemies and evil-doers, in self-defence not in aggression, and
others have perverted their instructions, and turned to a bad use their
own strength and skill. But not on this account are the teachers bad,   457
neither is the art in fault, or bad in itself; I should rather say that those
who make a bad use of the art are to blame. And the same argument
holds good of rhetoric; for the rhetorician can speak against all men
and upon any subject; in short, he can persuade the multitude better
than any other man of anything which he pleases, but he should not
therefore seek to defraud the physician or any other artist of his repu-   b
tation merely because he has the power; he ought to use rhetoric fairly,
as he would also use his athletic powers. And if after having become a
rhetorician he makes a bad use of his strength and skill, his instructor
surely ought not on that account to be held in detestation or banished.
For he was intended by his teacher to make a good use of his instruc-   c
tions, but he abuses them. And therefore he is the person who ought
to be held in detestation, banished, and put to death, and not his instructor.

Soc. You, Gorgias, like myself, have had great experience of disputations, and you must have observed, I think, that they do not always
terminate in mutual edification, or in the definition by either party of
the subjects which they are discussing; but disagreements are apt to   d
arise—somebody says that another has not spoken truly or clearly; and
then they get into a passion and begin to quarrel, both parties con-
ceiving that their opponents are arguing from personal feeling only
and jealousy of themselves, not from any interest in the question at
issue. And sometimes they will go on abusing one another until the
company at last are quite vexed at themselves for ever listening to such   e
fellows. Why do I say this? Why, because I cannot help feeling that you
are now saying what is not quite consistent or accordant with what you
were saying at first about rhetoric. And I am afraid to point this out to
you, lest you should think that I have some animosity against you, and
that I speak, not for the sake of discovering the truth, but from jealousy
of you. Now if you are one of my sort, I should like to cross-examine
you, but if not I will let you alone. And what is my sort? you will ask.   458
I am one of those who are very willing to be refuted if I say anything
which is not true, and very willing to refute anyone else who says what
is not true, and quite as ready to be refuted as to refute; for I hold that
this is the greater gain of the two, just as the gain is greater of being
cured of a very great evil than of curing another. For I imagine that

there is no evil which a man can endure so great as an erroneous opinion about the matters of which we are speaking; and if you claim to be
b   one of my sort, let us have the discussion out, but if you would rather
have done, no matter—let us make an end of it.

GOR. I should say, Socrates, that I am quite the man whom you indicate; but, perhaps, we ought to consider the audience, for, before you
c   came, I had already given a long exhibition, and if we proceed the argument may run on to a great length. And therefore I think that we
should consider whether we may not be detaining some part of the
company when they are wanting to do something else.

CHAER. You hear the audience cheering, Gorgias and Socrates, which
shows their desire to listen to you; and for myself, heaven forbid that I
should have any business on hand which would take me away from a
discussion so interesting and so ably maintained.

d   CAL. By the gods, Chaerephon, although I have been present at
many discussions, I doubt whether I was ever so much delighted before, and therefore if you go on discoursing all day I shall be the better pleased.

SOC. I may truly say, Callicles, that I am willing, if Gorgias is.

GOR. After all this, Socrates, I should be disgraced if I refused, especially as I have promised to answer all comers; in accordance with
e   the wishes of the company, then, do begin, and ask of me any question
which you like.

SOC. Let me tell you then, Gorgias, what surprises me in your
words; though I dare say that you may be right, and I may have misunderstood your meaning. You say that you can make any man, who
will learn from you, a rhetorician?

GOR. Yes.

SOC. Do you mean that you will teach him to gain the ears of the
459   multitude on any subject, and this not by instruction but by persuasion?

GOR. Quite so.

SOC. You were saying, in fact, that the rhetorician will have greater
powers of persuasion than the physician even in a matter of health?

GOR. Yes, with the multitude, that is.

SOC. You mean to say, with the ignorant; for with those who know
he cannot be supposed to have greater powers of persuasion.

GOR. Very true.

SOC. But if he is to have more power of persuasion than the physician, he will have greater power than he who knows?

GOR. Certainly.

b   SOC. Although he is not a physician; is he?

GRO. No.

Soc. And he who is not a physician must, obviously, be ignorant of what the physician knows.

Gor. Clearly.

Soc. Then, when the rhetorician is more persuasive than the physician, the ignorant is more persuasive with the ignorant than he who has knowledge? is not that the inference?

Gor. In the case supposed, yes.

Soc. And the same holds of the relation of rhetoric to all the other arts; the rhetorician need not know the truth about things; he has only c to discover some way of persuading the ignorant that he has more knowledge than those who know?

Gor. Yes, Socrates, and is not this a great comfort, not to have learned the other arts, but the art of rhetoric only, and yet to be in no way inferior to the professors of them?

Soc. Whether the rhetorician is or is not inferior on this account is a question which we will hereafter examine if the enquiry is likely to be of any service to us; but I would rather begin by asking, whether he is or is not as ignorant of the just and unjust, base and honorable, good d and evil, as he is of medicine and the other arts; I mean to say, does he really know anything of what is good and evil, base or honorable, just or unjust in them, or has he only a way with the ignorant of persuading them that he, not knowing, is to be esteemed to know more about these things than some one else who knows? Or must the pupil know e these things and come to you knowing them before he can acquire the art of rhetoric? If he is ignorant, you who are the teacher of rhetoric will not teach him—it is not your business; but you will make him seem to the multitude to know them, when he does not know them; and seem to be a good man, when he is not. Or will you be unable to 460 teach him rhetoric at all, unless he knows the truth of these things first? What is to be said about all this? By heavens, Gorgias, I wish that you would reveal to me the power of rhetoric, as you were saying that you would.

Gor. Well, Socrates, I suppose that if the pupil does chance not to know them, he will have to learn from me these things as well.

Soc. Say no more, for there you are right; and so he whom you make a rhetorician must either know the nature of the just and unjust already, or he must be taught by you.

Gor. Certainly. b

Soc. Well, and is not he who has learned carpentering a carpenter?

Gor. Yes.

Soc. And he who has learned music a musician?

Gor. Yes.

Soc. And he who has learned medicine is a physician, in like manner?

He who has learned anything whatever is that which his knowledge makes him.

GOR. Certainly.

SOC. And in the same way, he who has learned what is just is just?

GOR. To be sure.

SOC. And he who is just may be supposed to do what is just?

GOR. Yes.

SOC. And must not the rhetorician be just, and the just man always

c desire to do what is just?

GOR. That is clearly the inference.

SOC. Surely, then, the just man will never consent to do injustice?

GOR. Certainly not.

SOC. And according to the argument the rhetorician must be a just man?

GOR. Yes.

SOC. And will therefore never be willing to do injustice?

GOR. Clearly not.

d   SOC. But do you remember saying just now that the trainer is not to be accused or banished if the pugilist makes a wrong use of his pugilistic art; in like manner, if the rhetorician makes a bad and unjust use of rhetoric, that is not to be laid to the charge of his teacher, who is not to be banished, but the wrong-doer himself who made a bad use of his rhetoric—he is to be banished—was not that said?

GOR. Yes, it was.

e   SOC. But now we are affirming that the aforesaid rhetorician will never have done injustice at all?

GOR. True.

SOC. And at the very outset, Gorgias, it was said that rhetoric treated of discourse, not about odd and even,* but about just and unjust? Was not this said?

GOR. Yes.

SOC. I was thinking at the time, when I heard you saying so, that rhetoric, which is always discoursing about justice, could not possibly be an unjust thing. But when you added, shortly afterwards, that the rhetorician might make a bad use of rhetoric, I noted with surprise the

461 inconsistency into which you had fallen; and I said, that if you thought, as I did, that there was a gain in being refuted, there would be an advantage in going on with the question, but if not, I would leave off. And in the course of our investigations, as you will see yourself, the rhetorician has been acknowledged to be incapable of making an

---

*That is to say, about arithmetic.

unjust use of rhetoric, or of willingness to do injustice. By the dog, Gorgias, there will be a great deal of discussion, before we get at the truth of all this.

POL. And do even you, Socrates, seriously believe what you are now saying about rhetoric? What! because Gorgias was ashamed to deny that the rhetorician knew the just and the honorable and the good, and admitted that to any one who came to him ignorant of them he could teach them, and then out of this admission there arose a contradiction—the thing which you so dearly love, and to which not he, but you, brought the argument by your captious questions. Will any one ever acknowledge that he does not know, or cannot teach, the nature of justice? The truth is, that there is great lack of manners in bringing the argument to such a pass.

SOC. Illustrious Polus, the reason why we provide ourselves with friends and children is so that, when we get old and stumble, a younger generation may be at hand to set us on our legs again in our words and in our actions: and now, if I and Gorgias are stumbling, here are you who should raise us up; and I for my part engage to retract any error into which you may think that I have fallen—upon one condition.

POL. What condition?

SOC. That you contract, Polus, the length of speech in which you indulged at first.

POL. What! do you mean that I may not use as many words as I please?

SOC. Only to think, my friend, that having come on a visit to Athens, which is the most free-spoken state in the Greek World,[1] you when you got there, and you alone, should be deprived of the power of speech—that would be hard indeed. But then consider my case: shall not I be very hardly used, if, when you are making a long oration, and refusing to answer what you are asked, I am compelled to stay and listen to you, and may not go away? I say rather, if you have a real interest in the argument, or, to repeat my former expression, have any desire to set it on its legs, take back any statement which you please; and in your turn ask and answer, like myself and Gorgias—refute and be refuted. For I suppose that you would claim to know what Gorgias knows—would you not?

POL. Yes.

SOC. And you, like him, invite anyone to ask you about anything which he pleases, and you will know how to answer him?

POL. To be sure.

SOC. And now, which will you do, ask or answer?

POL. I will ask; answer me, Socrates, the same question which Gorgias, as you suppose, is unable to answer: What is rhetoric?

Soc. Do you mean what sort of an art?

Pol. Yes.

Soc. To say the truth, Polus, it is not an art at all, in my opinion.

Pol. Then what, in your opinion, is rhetoric?

c   Soc. A thing which, as I was lately reading in a book of yours, you say that you have made an art.

Pol. What thing?

Soc. I should say a sort of experience.

Pol. Does rhetoric seem to you to be an experience?

Soc. That is my view, but you may be of another mind.

Pol. An experience in what?

Soc. An experience in producing a sort of delight and gratification.

Pol. And if able to gratify others, must not rhetoric be a fine thing?

Soc. What are you saying, Polus? Why do you ask me whether rhet-

d   oric is a fine thing or not, when I have not as yet told you what rhetoric is?

Pol. Did I not hear you say that rhetoric was a sort of experience?

Soc. Will you, who are so desirous to gratify others, afford a slight gratification to me?

Pol. I will.

Soc. Will you ask me what sort of an art is cookery?

Pol. What sort of an art is cookery?

Soc. Not an art at all, Polus.

Pol. What then?

Soc. I should say an experience.

Pol. In what? I wish that you would explain to me.

e   Soc. An experience in producing a sort of delight and gratification, Polus.

Pol. Then are cookery and rhetoric the same?

Soc. No, they are only different parts of the same profession.

Pol. Of what profession?

Soc. I am afraid that the truth may seem discourteous; and I hesitate to answer, lest Gorgias should imagine that I am making fun of his

463 own profession. For whether or not this is that art of rhetoric which Gorgias practises I really cannot tell. From what he was just now saying, nothing appeared of what he thought of his art, but the rhetoric which I mean is a part of a not very creditable whole.

Gor. A part of what, Socrates? Say what you mean, and never mind me.

Soc. In my opinion then, Gorgias, the whole of which rhetoric is a part is not an art at all, but the habit of a bold and ready wit, which knows how to manage mankind: this habit I sum up under the word

b   'flattery'; and it appears to me to have many other parts, one of which is cookery, which may seem to be an art, but, as I maintain, is only an experience or routine and not an art; another part is rhetoric, and the art of attiring and sophistry are two others. Thus there are four branches, and four different things answering to them. And Polus may ask, if he likes, for he has not as yet been informed, what part of flattery is rhetoric: he did not see that I had not yet answered him when he proceeded to ask the further question of whether I think rhetoric a fine thing. But I shall not tell him whether rhetoric is a fine thing or not, until I have first answered, 'What is rhetoric?' For that would not be right, Polus; but I shall be happy to answer, if you will ask me: What part of flattery is rhetoric?

POL. I will ask, and you will answer. What part of flattery is rhetoric?

SOC. Will you understand my answer? Rhetoric, according to my view, is the ghost or counterfeit of a part of politics.

POL. And noble or ignoble?

SOC. Ignoble, I should say, if I am compelled to answer, for I call what is bad ignoble; though I doubt whether you understand what I was saying before.

GOR. Indeed, Socrates, I cannot say that I understand myself.

SOC. I am not surprised, Gorgias; for I have not as yet explained myself, and our friend Polus, colt by name and colt by nature, is apt to run away.

GOR. Never mind him, but explain to me what you mean by saying that rhetoric is the counterfeit of a part of politics.

SOC. I will try, then, to explain my notion of rhetoric, and if I am mistaken, my friend Polus shall refute me. We may assume the existence of bodies and of souls?

GOR. Of course.

SOC. You would further admit that there is a good condition of either of them?

GOR. Yes.

SOC. A condition that may not be really good, but good only in appearance? I mean to say, that there are many persons who appear to be in good health, and whom only a physician or trainer will discern at first sight not to be in good health.

GOR. True.

SOC. And this applies not only to the body, but also to the soul: in either there may be that which gives the appearance of health and not the reality?

GOR. Yes, certainly.

SOC. Now I will endeavour to explain to you more clearly what I mean: The soul and body being two, have two arts corresponding to them: there is the art of politics attending on the soul, and another art

attending on the body, of which I know no single name, but which
may be described as having two divisions, one of them gymnastic, and
the other medicine. And in politics there is a legislative part, which an-

c   swers to gymnastic, as justice does to medicine; and the two parts run
into one another, justice having to do with the same subject as legislation, and medicine with the same subject as gymnastic, but with a difference. There are these four arts, two attending on the body and two
on the soul for their highest good; flattery knowing, or rather guessing
their natures, has distributed herself into four shams or simulations
of them; she puts on the likeness of one or other of them, and pretends

d   to be that which she simulates, and having no regard for men's highest interests, is always making pleasure the bait of the unwary, and deceiving them into the belief that she is of the highest value to them.
Cookery simulates the disguise of medicine, and pretends to know
what food is the best for the body; and if the physician and the cook
had to enter into a competition in which children were the judges, or
men who had no more sense than children, as to which of them best

e   understands the goodness or badness of food, the physician would be
465 starved to death. A flattery I deem this to be and of an ignoble sort,
Polus, for to you I am now addressing myself, because it aims at pleasure without any thought of the best. An art I do not call it, but only
an experience, because it is unable to explain or to give a reason of the
nature of its own applications. And I do not call any irrational thing an
art; but if you dispute my words, I am prepared to argue for them.

b   Cookery, then, I maintain to be a flattery which takes the form of
medicine; and cosmetics, in like manner, is a flattery which takes the
form of gymnastic, and is knavish, false, ignoble, illiberal, working de-
ceitfully by the help of lines, and colors, and enamels, and garments,
and making men affect a spurious beauty to the neglect of the true
beauty which is given by gymnastic.
        I would rather not be tedious, and therefore I will only say, after

c   the manner of the geometricians (for I think that by this time you will
be able to follow)

            as cosmetics : gymnastic : : cookery : medicine;

or rather,

            as cosmetics : gymnastic : : sophistry : legislation;

and

            as cookery : medicine : : rhetoric : justice.

And this, I say, is the natural difference between the rhetorician and the sophist, but by reason of their near connection, they are apt to be jumbled up together; neither do they know what to make of themselves, nor do other men know what to make of them. For if the body   *d* presided over itself, and were not under the guidance of the soul, and the soul did not discern and discriminate between cookery and medicine, but the body was made the judge of them, and the rule of judgment was the bodily delight which was given by them, then the word of Anaxagoras, that word with which you, friend Polus, are so well acquainted, would prevail far and wide: 'Chaos' would come again, and cookery, health, and medicine would mingle in an indiscriminate mass. And now I have told you my notion of rhetoric, which is, in relation to the soul, what cookery is to the body. I may have been inconsistent   *e* in making a long speech, when I would not allow you to discourse at length. But I think that I may be excused, because you did not understand me, and could make no use of my answer when I spoke shortly, and therefore I had to enter into an explanation. And if I show an equal   466 inability to make use of yours, I hope that you will speak at equal length; but if I am able to understand you, let me have the benefit of your brevity, as is only fair: And now you may do what you please with my answer.

POL. What do you mean? do you think that rhetoric is flattery?

SOC. Nay, I said a part of flattery; if at your age, Polus, you cannot remember, what will you do by-and-by, when you get older?

POL. And are the good rhetoricians meanly regarded in states, under the idea that they are flatterers?

SOC. Is that a question or the beginning of a speech?   *b*

POL. I am asking a question.

SOC. Then my answer is that they are not regarded at all.

POL. How not regarded? Have they not very great power in states?

SOC. Not if you mean to say that power is a good to the possessor.

POL. And that is what I do mean to say.

SOC. Then, if so, I think that they have the least power of all the citizens.

POL. What! are they not like tyrants? They kill and despoil and exile   *c* anyone whom they please.

SOC. By the dog, Polus, I cannot make out at each deliverance of yours, whether you are giving an opinion of your own, or asking a question of me.

POL. I am asking a question of you.

SOC. Yes, my friend, but you ask two questions at once.

POL. How two questions?

SOC. Why, did you not say just now that the rhetoricians are like   *d* tyrants, and that they kill and despoil or exile any one whom they please?

Pol. I did.

Soc. Well then, I say to you that here are two questions in one, and I will answer both of them. And I tell you, Polus, that rhetoricians and tyrants have the least possible power in states, as I was just now saying; for they do literally nothing which they will, but only what they think best.

Pol. And is not that a great power?

Soc. Polus has already said the reverse.

Pol. What! Me? But I agree, of course.

Soc. No, by the great—what do you call him?—not you, for you say that power is a good to him who has the power.

Pol. I do.

Soc. And would you maintain that if a fool does what he thinks best, this is a good, and would you call this great power?

Pol. I would not.

Soc. Then you must prove that the rhetorician is not a fool, and that rhetoric is an art and not a flattery—and so you will have refuted me; but if you leave me unrefuted, why, the rhetoricians who do what they think best in states, and the tyrants, will have nothing upon which to congratulate themselves, if as you say, power be indeed a good, admitting at the same time that what is done without sense is an evil.

Pol. Yes; I admit that.

Soc. How then can the rhetoricians or the tyrants have great power in states, unless Polus can refute Socrates, and prove to him that they do as they will?

Pol. This fellow . . .

Soc. I say that they do not do as they will; now refute me.

Pol. Why, have you not already said that they do as they think best?

Soc. And I say so still.

Pol. Then surely they do as they will?

Soc. I deny it.

Pol. But they do what they think best?

Soc. Aye.

Pol. That, Socrates, is monstrous and absurd.

Soc. Good words, good Polus, as I may say in your own peculiar style; but if you have any questions to ask of me, either prove that I am in error or give the answer yourself.

Pol. Very well, I am willing to answer so that I may know what you mean.

Soc. Do men appear to you to will that which they do, or to will that further end for the sake of which they do a thing? when they take medicine, for example, at the bidding of a physician, do they will the drinking of the medicine which is painful, or the health for the sake of which they drink?

POL. Clearly, the health.   d

SOC. And when men go on a voyage or engage in business, they do not will that which they are doing at the time; for who would desire to take the risk of a voyage or the trouble of business?—But they will, to have the wealth for the sake of which they go on a voyage.

POL. Certainly.

SOC. And is not this universally true? If a man does something for the sake of something else, he wills not that which he does, but that for the sake of which he does it.   e

POL. Yes.

SOC. And are not all things either good or evil, or intermediate and indifferent?

POL. To be sure, Socrates.

SOC. Wisdom and health and wealth and the like you would call goods, and their opposites evils?

POL. I would.

SOC. And the things which are neither good nor evil, and which   468
partake sometimes of the nature of good and at other times of evil, or of neither, are such as sitting, walking, running, sailing; or, again, wood, stones, and the like: These are the things which you call neither good nor evil?

POL. Exactly so.

SOC. Are these indifferent things done for the sake of the good, or the good for the sake of the indifferent?

POL. Clearly, the indifferent for the sake of the good.   b

SOC. When we walk we walk for the sake of the good, and under the idea that it is better to walk, and when we stand we stand equally for the sake of the good?

POL. Yes.

SOC. And when we kill a man we kill him or exile him or despoil him of his goods, because, as we think, it will conduce to our good?

POL. Certainly.

SOC. Men who do any of these things do them for the sake of the good?

POL. Yes.

SOC. And did we not admit that in doing something for the sake of something else, we do not will those things which we do, but that   c
other thing for the sake of which we do them?

POL. Most true.

SOC. Then we do not will simply to kill a man or to exile him or to despoil him of his goods, but we will to do that which conduces to our good, and if the act is not conducive to our good we do not will it; for we will, as you say, that which is our good, but that which is neither good nor evil, or simply evil, we do not will. Why are you silent, Polus? Am I not right?

POL. You are right.

d   SOC. Hence we may infer, that if anyone, whether a tyrant or a rhetorician, kills another or exiles another or deprives him of his property, under the idea that the act is for his own interests when really it is not for his own interests, he may be said to do what seems best to him?

POL. Yes.

SOC. But does he do what he wills if he does what is evil? Why do you not answer?

POL. Well, I suppose not.

e   SOC. Then if great power is a good as you allow, will such man have great power in a state?

POL. He will not.

SOC. Then I was right in saying that a man may do what seems good to him in a state, and not have great power, and not do what he wills?

POL. As though you, Socrates, would not like to have the power of doing what seemed good to you in the state, rather than not; you would not be jealous when you saw any one killing or despoiling or imprisoning whom he pleased, Oh, no!

469   SOC. Justly or unjustly, do you mean?

POL. In either case is he not equally to be envied?

SOC. Forbear, Polus!

POL. Why 'forbear'?

SOC. Because you ought not to envy wretches who are not to be envied, but only to pity them.

POL. And are those of whom I spoke wretches?

SOC. Yes, certainly they are.

POL. And so you think that he who slays anyone whom he pleases, and justly slays him, is pitiable and wretched?

b   SOC. No, I do not say that of him: but neither do I think that he is to be envied.

POL. Were you not saying just now that he is wretched?

SOC. Yes, my friend, if he killed another unjustly, in which case he is also to be pitied; and he is not to be envied if he killed him justly.

POL. At any rate you will allow that he who is unjustly put to death is wretched, and to be pitied?

SOC. Not so much, Polus, as he who kills him, and not so much as he who is justly killed.

POL. How can that be, Socrates?

Soc. That may very well be, inasmuch as doing injustice is the greatest of evils.

POL. But is it the greatest? Is not suffering injustice a greater evil?

Soc. Certainly not.

POL. Then would you rather suffer than do injustice?   c

Soc. I should not like either, but if I must choose between them, I would rather suffer than do.

POL. Then you would not wish to be a tyrant?

Soc. Not if you mean by tyranny what I mean.

POL. I mean, as I said before, the power of doing whatever seems good to you in a state, killing, banishing, doing in all things as you like.

Soc. Well then, illustrious friend, when I have said my say, reply to   d
me. Suppose that I go into a crowded Agora, and take a dagger under my arm. Polus, I say to you, I have just acquired rare power, and become a tyrant; for if I think that any of these men whom you see ought to be put to death, the man whom I have a mind to kill is as good as dead; and if I am disposed to break his head or tear his garment, he will have his head broken or his garment torn in an instant. Such is my   e
great power in this city. And if you do not believe me, and I show you the dagger, you would probably reply: Socrates, in that sort of way any one may have great power—he may burn any house which he pleases, and the docks and triremes of the Athenians, and all their other vessels, whether public or private—but can you believe that this mere doing as you think best is great power?

POL. Certainly not such doing as this.

Soc. But can you tell me why you disapprove of such a power?   470

POL. I can.

Soc. Why then?

POL. Why, because he who did as you say would be certain to be punished.

Soc. And punishment is an evil?

POL. Certainly.

Soc. And you would admit once more, my good sir, that great power is a benefit to a man if his actions turn out to his advantage, and that this is the meaning of great power; and if not, then his power is an evil and is no power. But let us look at the matter in another way: do   b
we not acknowledge that the things of which we were speaking, the infliction of death, and exile, and the deprivation of property, are sometimes a good and sometimes not a good?

POL. Certainly.

Soc. About that you and I may be supposed to agree?

POL. Yes.

SOC. Tell me, then, when do you say that they are good and when that they are evil—what principle do you lay down?

POL. I would rather, Socrates, that you should answer as well as ask that question.

c   SOC. Well, Polus, since you would rather have the answer from me, I say that they are good when they are just, and evil when they are unjust.

POL. You are hard of refutation, Socrates, but might not a child refute that statement?

SOC. Then I shall be very grateful to the child, and equally grateful to you if you will refute me and deliver me from my foolishness. And I hope that refute me you will, and not weary of doing good to a friend.

d   POL. Yes, Socrates, and I need not go far or appeal to antiquity; events which happened only a few days ago are enough to refute you, and to prove that many men who do wrong are happy.

SOC. What events?

POL. You see, I presume, that Archelaus[2] the son of Perdiccas is now the ruler of Macedonia?

SOC. At any rate I hear that he is.

POL. And do you think that he is happy or miserable?

SOC. I cannot say, Polus, for I have never had any acquaintance with him.

e   POL. And cannot you tell at once, without having an acquaintance with him, whether a man is happy?

SOC. Most certainly not.

POL. Then clearly, Socrates, you would say that you did not even know whether the great king is a happy man?

SOC. And I would speak the truth; for I do not know how he stands in the matter of education and justice.

POL. What! and does all happiness consist of this?

SOC. Yes, indeed, Polus, that is my doctrine; the men and women who are gentle and good are also happy, as I maintain, and the unjust and evil are miserable.

471   POL. Then, according to your doctrine, the said Archelaus is miserable?

SOC. Yes, my friend, if he is wicked.

POL. That he is wicked I cannot deny; for he had no title at all to the throne which he now occupies, he being only the son of a woman who was the slave of Alcetas the brother of Perdiccas; he himself therefore in strict right was the slave of Alcetas; and if he had meant to do rightly he would have remained his slave, and then, according to your doctrine, he would have been happy. But now he is unspeakably miserable, for he has been guilty of the greatest crimes: in the first place **b** he invited his uncle and master, Alcetas, to come to him, under the pretence that he would restore to him the throne which Perdiccas has usurped, and after entertaining him and his son Alexander, who was his own cousin, and nearly of an age with him, and making them drunk, he threw them into a waggon and carried them off by night, and slew them, and got both of them out of the way; and when he had done all this wickedness he never discovered that he was the most miserable of all men, and was very far from repenting: shall I tell you how **c** he showed his remorse? he had a younger brother, a child of seven years old, who was the legitimate son of Perdiccas, and to him of right the kingdom belonged; Archelaus, however, had no mind to bring him up as he ought and restore the kingdom to him; that was not his notion of happiness; but not long afterwards he threw him into a well and drowned him, and declared to his mother Cleopatra that he had fallen in while running after a goose, and had been killed. And now as he is the greatest criminal of all the Macedonians, he may be supposed to be the most miserable and not the happiest of them, and I dare say that there **d** are many Athenians, and you would be at the head of them, who would rather be any other Macedonian than Archelaus!

Soc. I praised you at first, Polus, for being a rhetorician rather than a reasoner. And this, as I suppose, is the sort of argument with which you fancy that a child might refute me, and by which I stand refuted when I say that the unjust man is not happy. But, my good friend, where is the refutation? I cannot admit a word which you have been saying.

Pol. That is because you just will not; for you surely must think as **e** I do.

Soc. Not so, my simple friend, but because you will refute me after the manner which rhetoricians practise in courts of law. For there the one party think that they refute the other when they bring forward a number of witnesses of good repute in proof of their allegations, and their **472** adversary has only a single one or none at all. But this kind of proof is of no value where truth is the aim; a man may often be sworn down by a multitude of false witnesses who have a great air of respectability. And in this argument nearly every one, Athenian and stranger alike, would be on your side, if you should bring witnesses in disproof of my statement;— you may, if you will, summon Nicias* the son of Niceratus, and let his

---

*Athenian general of the Peloponnesian War who authored the unsuccessful peace treaty with Sparta of 421 B.C.E.; he died in the Sicilian expedition (see note 1 to *Ion*).

b brothers, who gave the row of tripods which stand in the precincts of Dionysus, come with him; or you may summon Aristocrates,* the son of Scellius, who is the giver of that famous offering which is at Delphi; summon, if you will, the whole house of Pericles, or any other great Athenian family whom you choose—they will all agree with you: I only am left alone and cannot agree, for you do not convince me, although you produce many false witnesses against me, in the hope of depriving me of my inheritance, which is the truth. But I consider that nothing

c worth speaking of will have been effected by me unless I make you the one witness of my words; nor by you, unless you make me the one witness of yours; no matter about the rest of the world. For there are two ways of refutation, one which is yours and that of the world in general, but mine is of another sort—let us compare them, and see in what they differ. For, indeed, we are at issue about matters which to know is honorable and not to know disgraceful; to know or not to know happiness and misery—that is the chief of them. And what knowledge can be no-

d bler? or what ignorance more disgraceful than this? And therefore I will begin by asking you whether you do not think that a man who is unjust and doing injustice can be happy, seeing that you think Archelaus unjust, and yet happy? May I assume this to be your opinion?

POL. Certainly.

SOC. But I say that this is an impossibility—here is one point about which we are at issue—very good. And do you mean to say also that if he meets with retribution and punishment he will still be happy?

POL. Certainly not; in that case he will be most miserable.

SOC. On the other hand, if the unjust be not punished, then, ac-

e cording to you, he will be happy?

POL. Yes.

SOC. But in my opinion, Polus, the unjust or doer of unjust actions is miserable in any case; more miserable, however, if he is not punished and does not meet with retribution, and less miserable if he is pun-

473 ished and meets with retribution at the hands of gods and men.

POL. You are maintaining a strange doctrine, Socrates.

SOC. I shall try to make you agree with me, my friend, for as a friend I regard you. Then these are the points at issue between us—are they not? I was saying that to do is worse than to suffer injustice?

POL. Exactly so.

SOC. And you said the opposite?

POL. Yes.

SOC. I said also that the wicked are miserable, and you refuted me?

---

*Athenian general and oligarchic politician.

POL. By Zeus, I did.

SOC. In your own opinion, Polus.   b

POL. Yes, and I rather suspect that I was in the right.

SOC. You further said that the wrong-doer is happy if he is unpunished?

POL. Certainly.

SOC. And I affirm that he is most miserable, and that those who are punished are less miserable—are you going to refute this proposition also?

POL. A proposition which is harder of refutation than the other, Socrates.

SOC. Say rather, Polus, impossible; for who can refute the truth?

POL. What do you mean? If a man is detected in an unjust attempt   c
to make himself a tyrant, and when detected is racked, mutilated, has his eyes burned out, and after having had all sorts of great injuries inflicted on him, and having seen his wife and children suffer the like, is at last impaled or tarred and burned alive, will he be happier than if he escape and become a tyrant, and continue all through life doing what he likes and holding the reins of government, the envy and admiration both of citizens and strangers? Is that the paradox which, as you say,   d
cannot be refuted?

SOC. There again, noble Polus, you are raising hobgoblins instead of refuting me; just now you were calling witnesses against me. But please to refresh my memory a little; did you say—'in an unjust attempt to make himself a tyrant'?

POL. Yes, I did.

SOC. Then I say that neither of them will be happier than the other; neither he who unjustly acquires a tyranny, nor he who suffers in the attempt, for of two miserables one cannot be the happier, but that he   e
who escapes and becomes a tyrant is the more miserable of the two. Do you laugh, Polus? Well, this is a new kind of refutation—when anyone says anything, instead of refuting him to laugh at him.

POL. But do you not think, Socrates, that you have been sufficiently refuted, when you say that which no human being will allow? Ask the company.

SOC. Polus, I am not a public man, and only last year, when my tribe were serving as Prytanes,* and it became my duty as their president to take the votes, there was a laugh at me, because I was unable to take   474
them. And as I failed then, you must not ask me to count the votes of the company now; but if, as I was saying, you have no better argument than

---

*Presidents of the Senate.

b   numbers, let me have a turn, and do you make trial of the sort of proof which, as I think, is required; for I shall produce one witness only of the truth of my words, and he is the person with whom I am arguing; his vote I know how to take; but with the many I have nothing to do, and do not even address myself to them. May I ask then whether you will answer in turn and have your words put to the proof? For I certainly think that I and you and every man do really believe that to do is a greater evil than to suffer injustice, and not to be punished than to be punished.

POL. And I should say neither I, nor any man: would you yourself, for example, suffer rather than do injustice?

SOC. Yes, and you, too; I or any man would.

POL. Quite the reverse; neither you, nor I, nor any man.

c   SOC. But will you answer?

POL. To be sure, I will; for I am curious to hear what you can possibly have to say.

SOC. Tell me, then, and you will know. Let us suppose that I am beginning at the beginning: which of the two, Polus, in your opinion, is the worst—to do injustice or to suffer?

POL. I should say that suffering was worst.

SOC. And which is the greater disgrace? Answer.

POL. To do.

SOC. And the greater disgrace is the greater evil?

POL. Certainly not.

d   SOC. I understand you to say, if I am not mistaken, that the honorable is not the same as the good, or the disgraceful as the evil?

POL. Certainly not.

SOC. Let me ask a question of you: When you speak of beautiful things, such as bodies, colors, figures, sounds, institutions, do you not call them beautiful in reference to some standard: bodies, for example, are beautiful in proportion as they are useful, or as the sight of them gives pleasure to the spectators. Can you give any other account of personal beauty?

e   POL. I cannot.

SOC. And you would say of figures or colors generally that they were beautiful, either by reason of the pleasure which they give, or of their use, or of both?

POL. Yes, I would.

SOC. And you would call sounds and music beautiful for the same reason?

POL. I would.

SOC. Laws and institutions also have no beauty in them except in so far as they are useful or pleasant or both?

475   POL. I think not.

Soc. And may not the same be said of the beauty of knowledge?

Pol. To be sure, Socrates; and I very much approve of your measuring beauty by the standard of pleasure and utility.

Soc. And deformity or disgrace may be equally measured by the opposite standard of pain and evil?

Pol. Certainly.

Soc. Then when of two beautiful things one exceeds in beauty, the measure of the excess is to be taken in one or both of these; that is to say, in pleasure or utility or both?

Pol. Very true.

Soc. And of two deformed things, that which exceeds in deformity   b
or disgrace, exceeds either in pain or evil—must it not be so?

Pol. Yes.

Soc. But then again, what was the observation which you just now made, about doing and suffering wrong? Did you not say that suffering wrong was more evil, and doing wrong more disgraceful?

Pol. I did.

Soc. Then, if doing wrong is more disgraceful than suffering, the more disgraceful must be more painful and must exceed in pain or in evil or both; does not that also follow?

Pol. Of course.

Soc. First, then, let us consider whether the doing of injustice ex-   c
ceeds the suffering in the consequent pain: Do the injurers suffer more than the injured?

Pol. No, Socrates; certainly not.

Soc. Then they do not exceed in pain?

Pol. No.

Soc. But if not in pain, then not in both?

Pol. Certainly not.

Soc. Then they can only exceed in the other?

Pol. Yes.

Soc. That is to say, in evil?

Pol. True.

Soc. Then doing injustice will have an excess of evil, and will therefore be a greater evil than suffering injustice?

Pol. Clearly.

Soc. But have not you and the world already agreed that to do in-   d
justice is more disgraceful than to suffer?

Pol. Yes.

Soc. And that is now discovered to be more evil?

Pol. True.

Soc. And would you prefer a greater evil or a greater dishonor to a less one? Answer, Polus, and fear not; for you will come to no harm if

you nobly resign yourself into the healing hand of the argument as to
e   a physician without shrinking, and either say 'Yes' or 'No' to me.

POL. I would say 'No.'

SOC. Would any other man prefer a greater to a lesser evil?

POL. No, not according to this way of putting the case, Socrates.

SOC. Then I said truly, Polus, that neither you, nor I, nor any man,
would rather do than suffer injustice; for to do injustice is the greater
evil of the two.

POL. That is the conclusion.

SOC. You see, Polus, when you compare the two kinds of refuta-
tions, how unlike they are. All men, with the exception of myself, are
of your way of thinking; but your single assent and witness are enough
476 for me—I have no need of any other. I take your vote, and do not care
about the rest. Enough of this, and now let us proceed to the next question, which is whether the greatest of evils to a guilty man is to suffer
punishment, as you supposed, or whether to escape punishment is not
a greater evil, as I supposed. Consider: You would say that to suffer punishment is another name for being justly corrected when you do
wrong?

POL. I would.

b   SOC. And would you not allow that all just things are honorable in
so far as they are just? Please reflect, and tell me your opinion.

POL. Yes, Socrates, I think that they are.

SOC. Consider again: Where there is an agent, must there not also
be a patient?

POL. I would say so.

SOC. And will not the patient suffer that which the agent does, and
will not the suffering have the quality of the action? I mean, for example, that if a man strikes, there must be something which is stricken?

POL. Yes.

c   SOC. And if the striker strikes violently or quickly, that which is
struck will be struck violently or quickly?

POL. True.

SOC. And the suffering to him who is stricken is of the same nature
as the act of him who strikes?

POL. Yes.

SOC. And if a man burns, there is something which is burned?

POL. Certainly.

SOC. And if he burns, in excess or so as to cause pain, the thing
burned will be burned in the same way?

POL. Truly.

SOC. And if he cuts, the same argument holds—there will be something cut?

POL. Yes.

SOC. And if the cutting is great or deep or such as will cause pain, *d* the cut will be of the same nature?

POL. That is evident.

SOC. Then you would agree generally to the universal proposition which I was just now asserting: that the affection of the patient answers to the act of the agent?

POL. I agree.

SOC. Then, as this is admitted, let me ask whether being punished is suffering or acting?

POL. Suffering, Socrates; there can be no doubt of that.

SOC. And suffering implies an agent?

POL. Certainly, Socrates; and he is the punisher.

SOC. And he who punishes rightly, punishes justly? *e*

POL. Yes.

SOC. And therefore he acts justly?

POL. Justly.

SOC. Then he who is punished and suffers retribution, suffers justly?

POL. That is evident.

SOC. And that which is just has been admitted to be honorable?

POL. Certainly.

SOC. Then the punisher does what is honorable, and the punished suffers what is honorable?

POL. True.

SOC. And if what is honorable, then what is good, for the honorable is either pleasant or useful?

477

POL. Certainly.

SOC. Then he who is punished suffers what is good?

POL. That is true.

SOC. Then he is benefited?

POL. Yes.

SOC. Do I understand you to mean what I mean by the term 'benefited'? I mean, that if he is justly punished his soul is improved.

POL. Surely.

SOC. Then he who is punished is delivered from the evil of his soul?

POL. Yes.

SOC. And is he not then delivered from the greatest evil? Look at the *b* matter in this way: In respect of a man's estate, do you see any greater evil than poverty?

POL. There is no greater evil.

SOC. Again, in a man's bodily frame, you would say that the evil is weakness and disease and deformity?

POL. I would.

SOC. And do you not imagine that the soul likewise has some evil of her own?

POL. Of course.

SOC. And this you would call injustice and ignorance and cowardice, and the like?

POL. Certainly.

c   SOC. So then, in mind, body, and estate, which are three, you have pointed out three corresponding evils—injustice, disease, poverty?

POL. True.

SOC. And which of the evils is the most disgraceful? Is not the most disgraceful of them injustice, and in general the evil of the soul?

POL. By far the most.

SOC. And if the most disgraceful, then also the worst?

POL. What do you mean, Socrates?

SOC. I mean to say that what is most disgraceful has been already admitted to be most painful or hurtful, or both.

POL. Certainly.

SOC. And now injustice and all evil in the soul has been admitted by
d   us to be most disgraceful?

POL. It has been admitted.

SOC. And most disgraceful either because most painful and causing excessive pain, or most hurtful, or both?

POL. Certainly.

SOC. And therefore to be unjust and intemperate, and cowardly and ignorant, is more painful than to be poor and sick?

POL. Nay, Socrates; the painfulness does not appear to me to follow from your premises.

SOC. Then, if, as you would argue, not more painful, the evil of the
e   soul is of all evils the most disgraceful; and the excess of disgrace must be caused by some preternatural greatness, or extraordinary hurtfulness of the evil.

POL. Clearly.

SOC. And that which exceeds most in hurtfulness will be the greatest of evils?

POL. Yes.

SOC. Then injustice and intemperance, and in general the depravity of the soul, are the greatest of evils!

POL. That is evident.

SOC. Now, what art is there which delivers us from poverty? Does not the art of making money?

POL. Yes.

SOC. And what art frees us from disease? Does not the art of medicine?

POL. Very true.

SOC. And what from vice and injustice? If you are not able to an-   478
swer at once, ask yourself whither we go with the sick, and to whom
we take them.

POL. To the physicians, Socrates.

SOC. And to whom do we go with the unjust and intemperate?

POL. To the judges, you mean.

SOC. . . . who are to punish them?

POL. Yes.

SOC. And do not those who rightly punish others, punish them in
accordance with a certain rule of justice?

POL. Clearly.

SOC. Then the art of money-making frees a man from poverty;   b
medicine from disease; and justice from intemperance and injustice?

POL. That is evident.

SOC. Which, then, is the best of these three?

POL. Will you enumerate them?

SOC. Money-making, medicine, and justice.

POL. Justice, Socrates, far excels the two others.

SOC. And justice, if the best, gives the greatest pleasure or advantage
or both?

POL. Yes.

SOC. But is the being healed a pleasant thing, and are those who are
being healed pleased?

POL. I think not.

SOC. A useful thing, then?

POL. Yes.   c

SOC. Yes, because the patient is delivered from a great evil; and this
is the advantage of enduring the pain—that you get well?

POL. Certainly.

SOC. And would he be the happier man in his bodily condition,
who is healed, or who never was out of health?

POL. Clearly he who was never out of health.

SOC. Yes; for happiness surely does not consist in being delivered
from evils, but in never having had them.

POL. True.

SOC. And suppose the case of two persons who have some evil in   d
their bodies, and that one of them is healed and delivered from evil,
and another is not healed, but retains the evil—which of them is the
most miserable?

POL. Clearly he who is not healed.

SOC. And was not punishment said by us to be a deliverance from
the greatest of evils, which is vice?

POL. True.

SOC. And justice punishes us, and makes us more just, and is the medicine of our vice?

POL. True.

SOC. He, then, has the first place in the scale of happiness who has never had vice in his soul; for this has been shown to be the greatest of

e evils.

POL. Clearly.

SOC. And he has the second place, who is delivered from vice?

POL. True.

SOC. That is to say, he who receives admonition and rebuke and punishment?

POL. Yes.

SOC. Then he lives worst, who, having been unjust, has no deliverance from injustice?

POL. Certainly.

479 SOC. That is, he lives worst who commits the greatest crimes, and who, being the most unjust of men, succeeds in escaping rebuke or correction or punishment; and this, as you say, has been accomplished by Archelaus and other tyrants and rhetoricians and potentates?

POL. True.

SOC. May not their way of proceeding, my friend, be compared to the conduct of a person who is afflicted with the worst of diseases and yet contrives not to pay the penalty to the physician for his sins against his constitution, and will not be cured, because, like a child, he is afraid

b of the pain of being burned or cut—is not that a parallel case?

POL. Yes, truly.

SOC. He would seem as if he did not know the nature of health and bodily vigour; and if we are right, Polus, in our previous conclusions, they are in a like case who strive to evade justice, which they see to be painful, but are blind to the advantage which ensues from it, not know-

c ing how far more miserable a companion a diseased soul is than a diseased body; a soul, I say, which is corrupt and unrighteous and unholy. And hence they do all they can to avoid punishment and to avoid being released from the greatest of evils; they provide themselves with money and friends, and cultivate to the utmost their powers of persuasion. But if we, Polus, are right, do you see what follows, or shall we draw out the consequences in form?

POL. If you want to.

SOC. Is it not a fact that injustice, and the doing of injustice, is the greatest of evils?

d POL. That is quite clear.

Soc. And, further, that to suffer punishment is the way to be released from this evil?

Pol. True.

Soc. And not to suffer, is to perpetuate the evil?

Pol. Yes.

Soc. To do wrong, then, is second only in the scale of evils; but to do wrong and not to be punished, is first and greatest of all?

Pol. That is true.

Soc. Well, and was not this the point in dispute, my friend? You   e
deemed Archelaus happy, because he was a very great criminal and unpunished? I, on the other hand, maintained that he, or any other like him, who has done wrong and has not been punished, is, and ought to be, the most miserable of all men; and that the doer of injustice is more miserable than the sufferer; and he who escapes punishment, more miserable than he who suffers. Was not that what I said?

Pol. Yes.

Soc. And it has been proved to be true?

Pol. Certainly.

Soc. Well, Polus, but if this is true, where is the great use of rheto-   480
ric? If we admit what has been just now said, every man ought in every way to guard himself against doing wrong, for he will thereby suffer great evil?

Pol. True.

Soc. And if he, or any one about whom he cares, does wrong, he ought of his own accord to go where he will be immediately punished; he will run to the judge, as he would to the physician, in order that the disease of injustice may not be rendered chronic and become the in-   b
curable cancer of the soul; must we not allow this consequence, Polus, if our former admissions are to stand? Is any other inference consistent with them?

Pol. To that, Socrates, there can be but one answer.

Soc. Then rhetoric is of no use to us, Polus, in helping a man to excuse his own injustice, or that of his parents or friends, or children or country; but it may be of use to anyone who holds that instead of   c
excusing he ought to accuse—himself above all, and in the next degree his family or any of his friends who may be doing wrong; he should bring to light the iniquity and not conceal it, that so the wrong-doer may suffer and be made whole; and he should even force himself and others not to shrink, but with closed eyes like brave men to let the physician operate with knife or searing iron, not regarding the pain, in the hope of attaining the good and the honorable; let him who has done things worthy of stripes, allow himself to be scourged, if of bonds,   d

to be bound, if of a fine, to be fined, if of exile, to be exiled, if of death, to die, himself being the first to accuse himself and his own relations, and using rhetoric to this end, that his and their unjust actions may be made manifest, and that they themselves may be delivered from injustice, which is the greatest evil. Then, Polus, rhetoric would indeed be useful. Do you say 'Yes' or 'No' to that?

e   POL. To me, Socrates, what you are saying appears absurd, though probably in agreement with your premises.

SOC. Is not this the conclusion, if the premises are not disproven?

POL. Yes; it certainly is.

SOC. And from the opposite point of view, if indeed it is our duty to harm another, whether an enemy or not (I except the case of self-defence—then I have to be upon my guard), and if my enemy injures 481 a third person, then in every sort of way, by word as well as deed, I should try to prevent his being punished, or appearing before the judge; and if he appears, I should contrive that he should escape, and not suffer punishment: if he has stolen a sum of money, let him keep what he has stolen and spend it on him and his, regardless of religion b   and justice; and if he has done things worthy of death, let him not die, but rather be immortal in his wickedness; or, if this is not possible, let him at any rate be allowed to live as long as he can. For such purposes, Polus, rhetoric may be useful, but is of small if of any use to him who is not intending to commit injustice; at least, there was no such use discovered by us in the previous discussion.

CAL. Tell me, Chaerephon, is Socrates in earnest, or is he joking?

CHAER. I should say, Callicles, that he is in most profound earnest; but you may as well ask him.

c   CAL. By the gods, and I will. Tell me, Socrates, are you in earnest, or only in jest? For if you are in earnest, and what you say is true, is not the whole of human life turned upside down; and are we not doing, as would appear, in everything the opposite of what we ought to be doing?

SOC. Callicles, if there were not some community of feelings among d   mankind, however varying in different persons—I mean to say, if every man's feelings were peculiar to himself and were not shared by the rest of his species—I do not see how we could ever communicate our impressions to one another. I make this remark because I perceive that you and I have a common feeling. For we are lovers both, and both of us have two loves apiece: I am the lover of Alcibiades, the son of Clinias, and of philosophy; and you of the Athenian people, and of Demus the son of Pyrilampes. Now, I observe that you, with all your cleverness, do not venture to contradict your favourite in any word or opinion of his; e   but as he changes you change, backwards and forwards. When the

Athenian people deny anything that you are saying in the assembly, you go over to their opinion; and you do the same with Demus, the fair young son of Pyrilampes. For you have not the power to resist the words and ideas of your loves; and if a person were to express surprise at the strangeness of what you say from time to time when under their influence, you would probably reply to him, if you were honest, that   482 you cannot help saying what your loves say unless they are prevented; and that you can only be silent when they are. Now you must understand that my words are an echo too, and therefore you need not wonder at me; but if you want to silence me, silence philosophy, who is my love, for she is always telling me what I am now telling you, my friend; neither is she capricious like my other love, for the son of Clinias says one thing today and another thing tomorrow, but philosophy always   b says the same. She is the teacher at whose words you are now wondering, and you have heard her yourself. Her you must refute, and either show, as I was saying, that to do injustice and to escape punishment is not the worst of all evils; or, if you leave her word unrefuted, by the dog the god of Egypt,* I declare, Callicles, that Callicles will never be at one with himself, but that his whole life will be a discord. And yet, my friend, I would rather that my lyre should be inharmonious, and that there should be no music in the chorus which I provided; aye, or   c that the whole world should be at odds with me, and oppose me, rather than that I myself should be at odds with myself, and contradict myself.

　　Cal. Socrates, you are a regular orator for the masses, and seem to be running riot in the argument. And now you are declaiming in this way because Polus has fallen into the same error himself of which he accused Gorgias: for he said that when Gorgias was asked by you   d whether, if someone came to him who wanted to learn rhetoric, and did not know justice, he would teach him justice, Gorgias in his modesty replied that he would, because he thought that mankind in general would be displeased if he answered 'No'; and then in consequence of this admission, Gorgias was compelled to contradict himself, that being just the sort of thing in which you delight. Whereupon Polus laughed at you deservedly, as I think; but now he has himself fallen into the same trap. I cannot say very much for his wit when he conceded to you that to do is more dishonorable than to suffer injustice, for this was   e the admission which led to his being entangled by you; and because he was too modest to say what he thought, he had his mouth stopped.

---

*The Egyptian god Anubis had a dog's head; Plato perhaps knew about Anubis from *Herodotus* 2.66–67.

For the truth is, Socrates, that you, who pretend to be engaged in the pursuit of truth, are appealing now to the popular and vulgar notions of right, which are not natural, but only conventional. Convention and nature are generally at variance with one another: and hence, if a per-

483 son is too modest to say what he thinks, he is compelled to contradict himself; and you, in your ingenuity perceiving the advantage to be thereby gained, slyly ask of him who is arguing conventionally a question which is to be determined by the rule of nature; and if he is talking of the rule of nature, you slip away to custom: as, for instance, you did in this very discussion about doing and suffering injustice. When Polus was speaking of the conventionally dishonorable, you assailed him from the point of view of nature; for by the rule of nature, to suffer injustice is the greater disgrace because the greater evil; but conventionally, to do evil is the more disgraceful. For the suffering of

b injustice is not the part of a man, but of a slave, who indeed had better die than live; since when he is wronged and trampled upon, he is unable to help himself, or any other about whom he cares. The reason, as I conceive, is that the makers of laws are the majority who are weak; and they make laws and distribute praises and censures with a view to

c themselves and to their own interests; and they terrify the stronger sort of men, and those who are able to get the better of them, in order that they may not get the better of them; and they say, that dishonesty is shameful and unjust; meaning, by the word injustice, the desire of a man to have more than his neighbours; for knowing their own inferiority, I suspect that they are too glad of equality. And therefore the endeavour to have more than the many, is conventionally said to be

d shameful and unjust, and is called injustice, whereas nature herself intimates that it is just for the better to have more than the worse, the more powerful than the weaker; and in many ways she shows, among men as well as among animals, and indeed among whole cities and races, that justice consists in the superior ruling over and having more

e than the inferior. For on what principle of justice did Xerxes invade Hellas, or his father the Scythians? (not to speak of numberless other examples). Nay, but these are the men who act according to nature; yes, by heaven, and according to the law of nature. Not, perhaps, according to that artificial law, which we invent and impose upon our fellows, of

484 whom we take the best and strongest from their youth upwards, and tame them like young lions, charming them with the sound of the voice, and saying to them, that with equality they must be content, and that the equal is the honorable and the just. But if there were a man who had sufficient force, he would shake off and break through, and escape from all this; he would trample under foot all our formulas and spells and charms, and all our laws which are against nature: the slave would rise in rebellion and be lord over us, and the light of natural jus- b tice would shine forth. And this I take to be the sentiment of Pindar, when he says in his poem, that

'Law is the king of all, of mortals as well as of immortals;'

this, as he says,

'Makes might to be right, doing violence with highest hand; as I infer from the deeds of Heracles, for without buying them—'*

—I do not remember the exact words, but the meaning is, that without buying them, and without their being given to him, he carried off c the oxen of Geryon, according to the law of natural right, and that the oxen and other possessions of the weaker and inferior properly belong to the stronger and superior. And this is true, as you may ascertain, if you will leave philosophy and go on to higher things: for philosophy, Socrates, if pursued in moderation and at the proper age, is an elegant accomplishment, but too much philosophy is the ruin of human life. Even if a man has good parts, still, if he carries philosophy into later life, he is necessarily ignorant of all those things which a gentleman d and a person of honor ought to know; he is inexperienced in the laws of the State, and in the language which ought to be used in the deal- ings of man with man, whether private or public, and utterly ignorant of the pleasures and desires of mankind and of human character in general. And people of this sort, when they betake themselves to poli- tics or business, are as ridiculous as I imagine the politicians to be, when they make their appearance in the arena of philosophy. For, as Eu- e ripides says,

'Every man shines in that and pursues that, and devotes the greatest por- tion of the day to that in which he most excels,'†

but anything in which he is inferior, he avoids and depreciates, and 485 praises the opposite from partiality to himself, and because he thinks

---

*This fragment from a lost poem by the Greek poet Pindar (c.522–c.438 B.C.E.) has been much discussed; I have kept Jowett's version.
†This fragment and the ones following in 486a–c are from Euripides' *Antiope*.

that he will thus praise himself. The true principle is to unite them. Philosophy, as a part of education, is an excellent thing, and there is no disgrace to a man while he is young in pursuing such a study; but when he is more advanced in years, the thing becomes ridiculous, and

b I feel towards philosophers as I do towards those who lisp and imitate children. For I love to see a little child, who is not of an age to speak plainly, lisping at his play; there is an appearance of grace and freedom in his utterance, which is natural to his childish years. But when I hear some small creature carefully articulating its words, I am offended; the sound is disagreeable, and has to my ears the twang of slavery. So when

c I hear a man lisping, or see him playing like a child, his behaviour appears to me ridiculous and unmanly and worthy of a beating. And I have the same feeling about students of philosophy; when I see a youth thus engaged, he appears to me to be in character, and becoming a man of liberal education, and him who neglects philosophy I regard

d as an inferior man, who will never aspire to anything great or noble. But if I see him continuing the study in later life, and not leaving off, I should like to beat him, Socrates; for, as I was saying, such a man, even though he has good natural parts, becomes effeminate. He flies from the busy centre and the market-place, in which, as the poet says,

e men become distinguished; he creeps into a corner for the rest of his life, and talks in a whisper with three or four admiring youths, but never speaks out like a freeman in a satisfactory manner. Now I, Socrates, am very well inclined towards you, and my feeling may be compared with that of Zethus towards Amphion, in the play of Euripides, whom I was mentioning just now: for I am disposed to say to you much what Zethus said to his brother, that you, Socrates, are careless about the things of which you ought to be careful; and that you

486   'Who have a soul so noble, are remarkable for a puerile exterior;
       Neither in a court of justice could you state a case, or give any reason or
          proof,
       Or offer valiant counsel on another's behalf.'

And you must not be offended, my dear Socrates, for I am speaking out of good-will towards you, if I ask whether you are not ashamed of being thus defenseless; which I affirm to be the condition not of you only but of all those who will carry the study of philosophy too far. For suppose that some one were to take you, or anyone of your sort, off to

b prison, declaring that you had done wrong when you had done no wrong, you must allow that you would not know what to do: there you would stand giddy and gaping, and not having a word to say; and when you went up before the Court, even if the accuser were a poor creature and not good for much, you would die if he were disposed to claim the penalty of death. And yet, Socrates, what is the value of

'An art which converts a man of sense into a fool,'

who is helpless, and has no power to save either himself or others? He is in the greatest danger and is going to be despoiled by his enemies of all his goods, and has to live, simply deprived of his rights of citizenship. He is a man who, if I may use the expression, may be punched with impunity. My good friend, take my advice, and refute no more:

'Learn the skills of business, and acquire the reputation of good sense.
But leave to others the niceties,'

whether they are to be described as follies or absurdities:

'For they will only
Give you poverty in your dwelling.'

Cease, then, emulating these paltry splitters of words, and emulate only the man of substance and honor, who is well to do.

Soc. If my soul, Callicles, were made of gold, should I not rejoice to discover one of those stones with which they test gold, and the very best possible one to which I might bring my soul; and if the stone and I agreed in approving of my soul's training, then I should know that I was in a satisfactory state, and that no other test was needed by me.

Cal. What is your meaning, Socrates?

Soc. I will tell you; I think that I have found in you the desired touchstone.

Cal. Why?

Soc. Because I am sure that if you agree with me in any of the opinions which my soul forms, I have at last found the truth indeed. For I consider that if a man is to make a complete trial of the good or evil of the soul, he ought to have three qualities—knowledge, good-will, outspokenness, which are all possessed by you. Many whom I meet are unable to make trial of me, because they are not wise as you are; others are wise, but they will not tell me the truth, because they have not the same interest in me which you have; and these two strangers, Gorgias and Polus, are undoubtedly wise men and my very good friends, but they are not outspoken enough, and they are too modest. Why, their modesty is so great that they are driven to contradict themselves, first one and then the other of them, in the face of a large company, on matters of the highest importance. But you have all the qualities in which

these others are deficient, having received an excellent education; to
c this many Athenians can testify. And you are my friend. Shall I tell you
why I think so? I know that you, Callicles, and Tisander* of Aphidnae,
and Andron† the son of Androtion, and Nausicydes‡ of the deme of
Cholarges, studied together: there were four of you, and I once heard
you advising with one another as to the extent to which the pursuit of
philosophy should be carried, and, as I know, you came to the conclu-
d sion that the study should not be pushed too much into detail. You
were cautioning one another not to be overwise; you were afraid that
too much wisdom might unconsciously to yourselves be the ruin of
you. And now when I hear you giving the same advice to me which
you then gave to your most intimate friends, I have a sufficient evidence of your real good-will to me. And of the frankness of your nature and freedom from modesty I am assured by yourself, and the
e assurance is confirmed by your last speech. Well then, the inference in
the present case clearly is, that if you agree with me in an argument
about any point, that point will have been sufficiently tested by us, and
will not require to be submitted to any further test. For you could not
have agreed with me, either from lack of knowledge or from super-
fluity of modesty, nor yet from a desire to deceive me, for you are my
friend, as you tell me yourself. And therefore when you and I are
agreed, the result will be the attainment of perfect truth. Now there is
no nobler enquiry, Callicles, than that which you censure me for making. What ought the character of a man to be, and what his pursuits,
and how far is he to go, both in maturer years and in youth? For be as-
488 sured that if I err in my own conduct I do not err intentionally, but
from ignorance. Do not then desist from advising me, now that you
have begun, until I have learned clearly what this is which I am to practise, and how I may acquire it. And if you find me assenting to your
words, and hereafter not doing that to which I assented, call me 'dolt,'
b and deem me unworthy of receiving further instruction. Once more,
then, tell me what you and Pindar mean by natural justice: Do you not
mean that the superior should take the property of the inferior by
force; that the better should rule the worse, the noble have more than
the mean? Am I not right in my recollection?

CAL. Yes; that is what I was saying, and so I still do.

c SOC. And do you mean by the better the same as the superior? for

---

*We know little of him, other than that he was a member of a wealthy family.
†Politician favorable to oligarchy and a friend of Callicles (see "Introduction" to *Gorgias*).
‡Greedy miller who became rich under the Thirty Tyrants (see "General Introduction,"
p. xvii).

I could not make out what you were saying at the time—whether you meant by the superior the stronger, and that the weaker must obey the stronger, as you seemed to imply when you said that great cities attack small ones in accordance with natural right, because they are superior and stronger, as though the superior and stronger and better were the same; or whether the better may be also the inferior and weaker, and   d
the superior the worse, or whether better is to be defined in the same way as superior: this is the point which I want to have cleared up. Are the superior and better and stronger the same or different?

CAL. I say unequivocally that they are the same.

SOC. Then the many are by nature superior to the one, against whom, as you were saying, they make the laws?

CAL. Certainly.

SOC. Then the laws of the many are the laws of the superior?

CAL. Very true.

SOC. Then they are the laws of the better; for the superior class are   e
far better, as you were saying?

CAL. Yes.

SOC. And since they are superior, the laws which are made by them are by nature good?

CAL. Yes.

SOC. And are not the many of opinion, as you were lately saying,   489
that justice is equality, and that to do is more disgraceful than to suffer injustice?—is that so or not? Answer, Callicles, and let no modesty be found to come in the way;* do the many think, or do they not think thus?—I must beg of you to answer, in order that if you agree with me I may fortify myself by the assent of so competent an authority.

CAL. Yes; the opinion of the many is what you say.

SOC. Then not only custom but nature also affirms that to do is more disgraceful than to suffer injustice, and that justice is equality; so   b
that you seem to have been wrong in your former assertion, when, accusing me, you said that nature and custom are opposed, and that I, knowing this, was dishonestly playing between them, appealing to custom when the argument is about nature, and to nature when the argument is about custom.

CAL. This man will never cease talking nonsense. At your age, Socrates, are you not ashamed to be catching at words and chuckling over some verbal slip? do you not see—have I not told you already, that by superior I mean better: do you imagine me to say, that if a rabble of   c

---

*Socrates thus deprives Callicles of the excuse he himself gave for Gorgias at 482d.

slaves and nondescripts, who are of no use except perhaps for their physical strength, get together, their very words are laws?

Soc. Ho! my philosopher, is that your line?

Cal. Certainly.

d Soc. I was thinking, Callicles, that something of the kind must have been in your mind, and that is why I repeated the question,—What is the superior? I wanted to know clearly what you meant; for you surely do not think that two men are better than one, or that your slaves are better than you because they are stronger? Then please begin again, and tell me who the better are, if they are not the stronger; and I will ask you, great Sir, to be a little milder in your instructions, or I shall have to run away from you.

e Cal. You are ironical.

Soc. No, by the hero Zethus, Callicles, by whose aid you were just now saying many ironical things against me, I am not:—tell me, then, whom you mean by the better?

Cal. I mean the more excellent.

Soc. Do you not see that you are yourself using words which have no meaning and that you are explaining nothing?—will you tell me whether you mean by the better and superior the wiser, or if not, whom?

490 Cal. Most assuredly, I do mean the wiser.

Soc. Then according to you, one wise man may often be superior to ten thousand fools, and he ought to rule them, and they ought to be his subjects, and he ought to have more than they should. This is what I believe that you mean (and you must not suppose that I am word-catching), if you allow that the one is superior to the ten thousand?

Cal. Yes; that is what I mean, and that is what I conceive to be natural justice—that the better and wiser should rule and have more than the inferior.

b Soc. Stop there, and let me ask you what you would say in this case: Let us suppose that we are all together as we are now; there are several of us, and we have a large common store of meats and drinks, and there are all sorts of persons in our company having various degrees of strength and weakness, and one of us, being a physician, is wiser in the matter of food than all the rest, and he is probably stronger than some and not so strong as others of us—will he not, being wiser, be also better than we are, and our superior in this matter of food?

Cal. Certainly.

c Soc. Either, then, he will have a larger share of the meats and drinks, because he is better, or he will have the distribution of all of them by reason of his authority, but he will not expend or make use of a larger share of them on his own person, or if he does, he will be punished; his share will exceed that of some, and be less than that of others, and if he be the weakest of all, he being the best of all will have the smallest share of all, Callicles: Am I not right, my friend?

CAL. You talk about meats and drinks and physicians and other non-   *d* sense; I am not speaking of them.

SOC. Well, but do you admit that the wiser is the better? Answer 'Yes' or 'No.'

CAL. Yes.

SOC. And ought not the better to have a larger share?

CAL. Not of meats and drinks.

SOC. I understand: then, perhaps, of coats—the skilfullest weaver ought to have the largest coat, and the greatest number of them, and go about clothed in the best and finest of them?

CAL. Coats now!

SOC. Then the skilfullest and best in making shoes ought to have the   *e* advantage in shoes; the shoemaker, clearly, should walk about in the largest shoes, and have the greatest number of them?

CAL. Shoes! What nonsense are you talking?

SOC. Or, if this is not your meaning, perhaps you would say that the wise and good and true farmer should actually have a larger share of seeds, and have as much seed as possible for his own land?

CAL. How you go on, always talking in the same way, Socrates!

SOC. Yes, Callicles, and also about the same things.   491

CAL. Yes, by the gods, you are literally always talking of cobblers and fullers and cooks and doctors, as if this had to do with our argument.

SOC. But why will you not tell me in what a man must be superior and wiser in order to claim a larger share; will you neither accept a suggestion, nor offer one?

CAL. I have already told you. In the first place, I mean by superiors not cobblers or cooks, but wise politicians who understand the ad-   *b* ministration of a state, and who are not only wise, but also valiant and able to carry out their designs, and not the men who faint from lack of spirit.

SOC. See now, most excellent Callicles, how different my charge against you is from that which you bring against me, for you reproach me with always saying the same; but I reproach you with never saying the same about the same things, for at one time you were defining the   *c* better and the superior to be the stronger, then again as the wiser, and now you bring forward a new notion; the superior and the better are now declared by you to be the more courageous: I wish, my good friend, that you would tell me, once and for all, whom you affirm to be the better and superior, and in what they are better?

CAL. I have already told you that I mean those who are wise and
d courageous in the administration of a state—they ought to be the
rulers of their states, and justice consists in their having more than
their subjects.

SOC. But whether rulers or subjects will they or will they not have
more than themselves, my friend?

CAL. What do you mean?

SOC. I mean that every man is his own ruler; but perhaps you think
that there is no necessity for him to rule himself; he is only required to
rule others?

CAL. What do you mean by his 'ruling over himself'?

SOC. A simple thing enough; just what is commonly said, that a
man should be temperate and master of himself, and ruler of his own
e pleasures and passions.

CAL. What innocence! you mean those fools—the temperate?

SOC. Certainly; anyone may know that to be my meaning.

CAL. Quite so, Socrates; and they are really fools, for how can a man
be happy who is the servant of anything? On the contrary, I plainly assert, that he who would truly live ought to allow his desires to wax to
the uttermost, and not to chastise them; but when they have grown
492 to their greatest he should have courage and intelligence to minister to
them and to satisfy all his longings. And this I affirm to be natural justice and nobility. To this however the many cannot attain; and they blame
the strong man because they are ashamed of their own weakness, which
they desire to conceal, and hence they say that intemperance is base. As
I have remarked already, they enslave the nobler natures, and being un-
b able to satisfy their pleasures, they praise temperance and justice out of
their own cowardice. For if a man had been originally the son of a king,
or had a nature capable of acquiring an empire or a tyranny or sovereignty, what could be more truly base or evil than temperance—to a
man like him, I say, who might freely be enjoying every good, and has
no one to stand in his way, and yet has admitted custom and reason and
c the opinion of other men to be lords over him? Must not he be in a miserable plight whom the reputation of justice and temperance hinders
from giving more to his friends than to his enemies, even if he were a
ruler in his city? Nay, Socrates, for you profess to be a votary of the truth,
and the truth is this: luxury and intemperance and licence, if they are
provided with means, are virtue and happiness; all the rest is a mere
babble, agreements contrary to nature, foolish talk of men, worthless.

d SOC. There is a noble freedom, Callicles, in your way of approaching the argument; for what you say is what the rest of the world think,
but do not like to say. And I must beg of you to persevere, so that the
true rule of human life may become manifest. Tell me, then: you say,

do you not, that in the rightly developed man the passions ought not to be controlled, but that we should let them grow to the utmost and somehow or other satisfy them, and that this is virtue?

CAL. Yes; I do.

SOC. Then those who want nothing are not truly said to be happy?

CAL. No indeed, for then stones and dead men would be the happiest of all.

SOC. But surely life according to your view is an awful thing; and indeed I think that Euripides may have been right in saying,

'Who knows if life be not death and death life;'

and that we are very likely dead; I have heard a philosopher say that at this moment we are actually dead, and that the body is our tomb, and that the part of the soul which is the seat of the desires is liable to be tossed about by words and blown up and down; and some ingenious person, probably a Sicilian or an Italian, playing with the word, invented a tale in which he called the soul—because of its believing and make-believe nature—a vessel;* and the ignorant he called the uninitiated or leaky, and the place in the souls of the uninitiated in which the desires are seated, being the intemperate and incontinent part, he compared to a vessel full of holes, because it can never be satisfied. He is not of your way of thinking, Callicles, for he declares, that of all the souls in Hades, meaning the invisible world, these uninitiated or leaky persons are the most miserable, and that they pour water into a vessel which is full of holes out of a colander which is similarly perforated. The colander, as my informer assures me, is the soul, and the soul which he compares to a colander is the soul of the ignorant, which is likewise full of holes, and therefore incontinent, owing to a bad memory and lack of faith. These notions are strange enough, but they show the principle which, if I can, I would like to prove to you; that you should change your mind, and, instead of the intemperate and insatiate life, choose that which is orderly and sufficient and has a due provision for daily needs. Do I make any impression on you, and are you coming over to the opinion that the orderly are happier than the intemperate? Or do I fail to persuade you, and, however many tales I rehearse to you, do you continue of the same opinion still?

CAL. The latter, Socrates, is more like the truth.

SOC. Well, I will tell you another image, which comes out of the

---

*Greek etymological pun with "believing" (*pithanon*), "make-believe" (*pistikon*), and "vessel" (*pithon*).

same school. Let me request you to consider how far you would accept this as an account of the two lives of the temperate and intemperate in a figure: there are two men, both of whom have a number of casks; the one man has his casks sound and full, one of wine, another of honey, and a third of milk, besides others filled with other liquids, and the streams which fill them are few and scanty, and he can only obtain them with a great deal of toil and difficulty; but when his casks are once filled he has no need to feed them any more, and has no further trouble with them or care about them. The other, in like manner, can procure streams, though not without difficulty; but his vessels are leaky and unsound, and night and day he is compelled to be filling them, and if he pauses for a moment, he is in an agony of pain. Such are their respective lives. Now would you say that the life of the intemperate is happier than that of the temperate? Do I not convince you that the opposite is the truth?

CAL. You do not convince me, Socrates, for the one who has filled himself has no longer any pleasure left; and this, as I was just now saying, is the life of a stone: he has neither joy nor sorrow after he is once filled; but the pleasure depends on the superabundance of the influx.

SOC. But the more you pour in, the greater the waste; and the holes must be large for the liquid to escape.

CAL. Certainly.

SOC. The life which you are now depicting is not that of a dead man, or of a stone, but of a cormorant; you mean that he is to be hungering and eating?

CAL. Yes.

SOC. And he is to be thirsting and drinking?

CAL. Yes, that is what I mean; he is to have all his desires about him, and to be able to live happily in the gratification of them.

SOC. Excellent; go on as you have begun, and have no shame; I, too, must disencumber myself of shame: and first, will you tell me whether you include itching and scratching, provided you have enough of them and pass your life in scratching, in your notion of happiness?

CAL. What a strange being you are, Socrates! a regular orator for the masses.

SOC. That was the reason, Callicles, why I scared Polus and Gorgias, until they were too modest to say what they thought; but you will not be too modest and will not be scared, for you are a brave man. And now, answer my question.

CAL. I answer, that even the scratcher would live pleasantly.

SOC. And if pleasantly, then also happily?

CAL. To be sure.

SOC. But what if the itching is not confined to the head? Shall I pursue the question? And here, Callicles, I would have you consider how you would reply if consequences are pressed upon you, especially if in the last resort you are asked, whether the life of a catamite is not terrible, foul, miserable? Or would you venture to say, that they too are happy, if they only get enough of what they want?

CAL. Are you not ashamed, Socrates, of introducing such topics into the argument?

SOC. Well, my fine friend, but am I the introducer of these topics, or he who says without any qualification that all who feel pleasure in whatever manner are happy, and who admits of no distinction between 495 good and bad pleasures? And I would still ask, whether you say that pleasure and good are the same, or whether there is some pleasure which is not a good?

CAL. Well, then, for the sake of consistency, I will say that they are the same.

SOC. You are breaking the original agreement, Callicles, and will no longer be a satisfactory companion in the search after truth, if you say what is contrary to your real opinion.

CAL. Why, that is what you are doing too, Socrates. b

SOC. Then we are both doing wrong. Still, my dear friend, I would ask you to consider whether pleasure, from whatever source derived, is the good; for, if this be true, then the disagreeable consequences which have been darkly intimated must follow, and many others.

CAL. That, Socrates, is only your opinion.

SOC. And do you, Callicles, seriously maintain what you are saying?

CAL. Indeed I do.

SOC. Then, as you are in earnest, shall we proceed with the argu- c
ment?

CAL. Absolutely.

SOC. Well, if you are willing to proceed, determine this question for me: there is something, I presume, which you would call knowledge?

CAL. There is.

SOC. And were you not saying just now, that some courage implied knowledge?

CAL. I was.

SOC. And you were speaking of courage and knowledge as two things different from one another?

CAL. Certainly I was.

SOC. And would you say that pleasure and knowledge are the same, or not the same?

CAL. Not the same, O man of wisdom. d

SOC. And would you say that courage differed from pleasure?

CAL. Certainly.

Soc. Well, then, let us remember that Callicles, the Acharnian, says that pleasure and good are the same; but that knowledge and courage are not the same, either with one another, or with the good.

CAL. And what does our friend Socrates, of Alopece, say—does he assent to this, or not?

e Soc. He does not assent; neither will Callicles, when he sees himself truly. You will admit, I suppose, that good and evil fortune are opposed to each other?

CAL. Yes.

Soc. And if they are opposed to each other, then, like health and disease, they exclude one another; a man cannot have them both, or be without them both, at the same time?

CAL. What do you mean?

Soc. Take the case of any bodily affection: a man may have the complaint in his eyes which is called ophthalmia?

CAL. To be sure.

496 Soc. But he surely cannot have the same eyes well and sound at the same time?

CAL. Certainly not.

Soc. And when he has got rid of his ophthalmia, has he got rid of the health of his eyes too? Is the final result, that he gets rid of them both together?

CAL. Certainly not.

b Soc. That would surely be marvellous and absurd?

CAL. Very.

Soc. I suppose that he is affected by them, and gets rid of them in turns?

CAL. Yes.

Soc. And he may have strength and weakness in the same way, by fits?

CAL. Yes.

Soc. Or swiftness and slowness?

CAL. Certainly.

Soc. And does he have and not have good and happiness, and their opposites, evil and misery, in a similar alternation?

CAL. Certainly he has.

c Soc. If then there is anything which a man has and has not at the same time, clearly that cannot be good and evil—do we agree? Please do not answer without consideration.

CAL. I entirely agree.

Soc. Go back now to our former admissions. Did you say that to hunger, I mean the mere state of hunger, was pleasant or painful?

CAL. I said painful, but that to eat when you are hungry is pleasant.

Soc. I know; but still the actual hunger is painful: am I not right?   *d*

Cal. Yes.

Soc. And thirst, too, is painful?

Cal. Yes, very.

Soc. Need I adduce any more instances, or would you agree that all wants or desires are painful?

Cal. I agree, and therefore you need not adduce any more instances.

Soc. Very good. And you would admit that to drink, when you are thirsty, is pleasant?

Cal. Yes.

Soc. And in the sentence which you have just uttered, the word 'thirsty' implies pain?

Cal. Yes.   *e*

Soc. And the word 'drinking' is expressive of pleasure, and of the satisfaction of the want?

Cal. Yes.

Soc. There is pleasure in drinking?

Cal. Certainly.

Soc. When you are thirsty?

Cal. Yes.

Soc. And in pain?

Cal. Yes.

Soc. Do you see the inference: that pleasure and pain are simultaneous, when you say that being thirsty, you drink? For are they not simultaneous, and do they not affect at the same time the same part, whether of the soul or the body? Which of them is affected cannot be supposed to be of any consequence: Is not this true?

Cal. It is.

Soc. You said also, that no man could have good and evil fortune at the same time?

Cal. Yes, I did.

Soc. But you admitted, that when in pain a man might also have   *497* pleasure?

Cal. Clearly.

Soc. Then pleasure is not the same as good fortune, or pain the same as evil fortune, and therefore the good is not the same as the pleasant?

Cal. I wish I knew, Socrates, what your quibbling means.

Soc. You know, Callicles, but you pretend not to know.

Cal. Go on! Why do you keep talking nonsense?   *b*

Soc. So that you know that you were right in taking me to task. Does not a man cease from his thirst and from his pleasure in drinking at the same time?

CAL. I do not understand what you are saying.

GOR. Nay, Callicles, answer, if only for our sakes; we would like to hear the argument out.

CAL. Yes, Gorgias, but I must complain of the habitual trifling of Socrates; he is always arguing about little and unworthy questions.

GOR. What matter? Your reputation, Callicles, is not at stake. Let Socrates argue in his own fashion.

c   CAL. Well, then, Socrates, you shall ask these little peddling questions, since Gorgias wishes to have them.

SOC. I envy you, Callicles, for having been initiated into the great mysteries before you were initiated into the lesser. I thought that this was not allowable. But to return to our argument: Does not a man cease from thirsting and from the pleasure of drinking at the same moment?

CAL. True.

SOC. And if he is hungry, or has any other desire, does he not cease from the desire and the pleasure at the same moment?

CAL. Very true.

d   SOC. Then he ceases from pain and pleasure at the same moment?

CAL. Yes.

SOC. But he does not cease from good and evil at the same moment, as you have admitted: do you still adhere to what you said?

CAL. Yes, I do; but what is the inference?

SOC. Why, my friend, the inference is that the good is not the same as the pleasant, or the evil the same as the painful; there is a cessation of pleasure and pain at the same moment; but not of good and evil, for they are different. How then can pleasure be the same as good, or pain

e   as evil? And I would have you look at the matter in another light, which could hardly, I think, have been considered by you when you identified them. Are not the good good because they have good present with them, as the beautiful are those who have beauty present with them?

CAL. Yes.

SOC. And do you call the fools and cowards good men? For you were saying just now that the courageous and the wise are the good—would you not say so?

CAL. Certainly.

SOC. And did you never see a foolish child rejoicing?

CAL. Yes, I have.

SOC. And a foolish man too?

CAL. Yes, certainly; but what is your drift?

498 SOC. Nothing particular, if you will only answer.

CAL. Yes, I have.

SOC. And did you ever see a sensible man rejoicing or sorrowing?

CAL. Yes.

Soc. Which rejoice and sorrow most—the wise or the foolish?

CAL. They are much upon a par, I think, in that respect.

Soc. Enough. And did you ever see a coward in battle?

CAL. To be sure.

Soc. And which rejoiced most at the departure of the enemy, the coward or the brave?

CAL. I should say 'most' of both; or at any rate, they rejoiced about equally.

Soc. No matter. Then the cowards, and not only the brave, rejoice?

CAL. Greatly.

Soc. And the foolish; so it would seem?

CAL. Yes.

Soc. And are only the cowards pained at the approach of their enemies, or are the brave also pained?

CAL. Both are pained.

Soc. And are they equally pained?

CAL. I should imagine that the cowards are more pained.

Soc. And are they not better pleased at the enemy's departure?

CAL. I dare say.

Soc. Then are the foolish and the wise and the cowards and the brave all pleased and pained, as you were saying, in nearly equal degree; but are the cowards more pleased and pained than the brave?

CAL. Yes.

Soc. But surely the wise and brave are the good, and the foolish and the cowardly are the bad?

CAL. Yes.

Soc. Then the good and the bad are pleased and pained in a nearly equal degree?

CAL. Yes.

Soc. Then are the good and bad good and bad in a nearly equal degree, or have the bad the advantage both in good and evil?

CAL. I really do not know what you mean.

Soc. Why, do you not remember saying that the good were good because good was present with them, and the evil because evil; and that pleasures were goods and pains evils?

CAL. Yes, I remember.

Soc. And are not these pleasures or goods present to those who rejoice—if they do rejoice?

CAL. Certainly.

Soc. Then those who rejoice are good when goods are present with them?

CAL. Yes.

Soc. And those who are in pain have evil or sorrow present with them?

Cal. Yes.

e Soc. And would you still say that the evil are evil by reason of the presence of evil?

Cal. I should.

Soc. Then those who rejoice are good, and those who are in pain evil?

Cal. Yes.

Soc. The degrees of good and evil vary with the degrees of pleasure and of pain?

Cal. Yes.

Soc. Have the wise man and the fool, the brave and the coward, joy and pain in nearly equal degrees, or would you say that the coward has more?

Cal. I should say that he has.

499 Soc. Help me then to draw out the conclusion which follows from our admissions; for it is good to repeat and review what is good twice and thrice over, as they say. Both the wise man and the brave man we allow to be good?

Cal. Yes.

Soc. And the foolish man and the coward to be evil?

Cal. Certainly.

Soc. And he who has joy is good?

Cal. Yes.

Soc. And he who is in pain is evil?

Cal. Certainly.

Soc. The good and evil both have joy and pain, but, perhaps, the evil has more of them?

Cal. Yes.

Soc. Then must we not infer, that the bad man is as good and bad b as the good, or, perhaps, even better? Is not this a further inference which follows equally with the preceding from the assertion that the good and the pleasant are the same?

Cal. I have been listening and making admissions to you, Socrates, and I remark that if a person grants you anything in play, you, like a child, want to keep hold and will not give it back. But do you really suppose that I or any other human being denies that some pleasures are good and others bad?

Soc. Alas, Callicles, how unfair you are! You certainly treat me as if c I were a child, sometimes saying one thing, and then another, as if you were meaning to deceive me. And yet I thought at first that you were my friend, and would not have deceived me if you could have helped.

But I see that I was mistaken; now I suppose that I must make the best of a bad business, as they said of old, and take what I can get out of you. Well, then, as I understand you to say, I may assume that some pleasures are good and others evil?

CAL. Yes.

SOC. The beneficial are good, and the hurtful are evil?

CAL. To be sure.

SOC. And the beneficial are those which do some good, and the hurtful are those which do some evil?

CAL. Yes.

SOC. Take, for example, the bodily pleasures of eating and drinking, which we were just now mentioning—you mean to say that those which promote health, or any other bodily excellence, are good, and their opposites evil?

CAL. Certainly.

SOC. And in the same way there are good pains and there are evil pains?

CAL. To be sure.

SOC. And ought we not to choose and use the good pleasures and pains?

CAL. Certainly.

SOC. But not the evil?

CAL. Clearly.

SOC. Because, if you remember, Polus and I have agreed that all our actions are to be done for the sake of the good; will you agree with us in saying that the good is the end of all our actions, and that all our actions are to be done for the sake of the good, and not the good for the sake of them? Will you add a third vote to our two?

CAL. I will.

SOC. Then pleasure, like everything else, is to be sought for the sake of that which is good, and not that which is good for the sake of pleasure?

CAL. To be sure.

SOC. But can every man choose what pleasures are good and what are evil, or must he have art or knowledge of them in detail?

CAL. He must have art.

SOC. Let me now remind you of what I was saying to Gorgias and Polus; I was saying, as you will not have forgotten, that there were some processes which aim only at pleasure, and know nothing of a better and worse, and there are other processes which know good and evil. And I considered that cookery, which I do not call an art, but only an experience, was of the former class, which is concerned with pleasure, and that the art of medicine was of the class which is concerned with the good. And now, by the god of friendship, I must beg you, Callicles,

c   not to jest, or to imagine that I am jesting with you; do not answer at random and contrary to your real opinion. You will observe that we are arguing about the way of human life; and to a man who has any sense at all, what question can be more serious than whether he should follow after that way of life to which you exhort me, and act what you call the manly part of speaking in the assembly, and cultivating rhetoric, and engaging in public affairs, according to the principles now in

d   vogue, or whether he should pursue the life of philosophy, and in what the latter way differs from the former? But perhaps we had better first try to distinguish them, as I did before, and when we have come to an agreement that they are distinct, we may proceed to consider in what way they differ from one another, and which of them we should choose. Perhaps, however, you do not even now understand what I mean?

CAL. No, I do not.

SOC. Then I will explain myself more clearly: you and I have agreed that there is such a thing as good, and that there is such a thing as pleasure, and that pleasure is not the same as good, and that the pursuit and process of acquisition of the one, that is pleasure, is different from the pursuit and process of acquisition of the other, which is good—I wish

e   that you would tell me whether you agree with me thus far or not.

CAL. I do.

SOC. Then I will proceed, and ask whether you also agree with me,

501   and whether you think that I spoke the truth when I further said to Gorgias and Polus that cookery in my opinion is only an experience, and not an art at all; and that whereas medicine is an art, and attends to the nature and constitution of the patient, and has principles of action and reason in each case, cookery in attending upon pleasure never regards either the nature or reason of that pleasure to which she devotes herself, but goes straight to her end, nor ever considers or calcu-

b   lates anything, but works by experience and routine, and just preserves the recollection of what she has usually done when producing pleasure. And first, I would have you consider whether I have proved what I was saying, and then whether there are not other similar processes which have to do with the soul—some of them processes of art, making a provision for the soul's highest interest—others despising the interest, and, as in the previous case, considering only the pleasure of the soul, and how this may be acquired, but not considering what pleasures are good or bad, and having no other aim but to afford gratifica-

c   tion, whether good or bad. In my opinion, Callicles, there are such processes, and this is the sort of thing which I term flattery, whether concerned with the body or the soul, or whenever employed with a view to pleasure and without any consideration of good and evil. And now I wish that you would tell me whether you agree with us in this notion, or whether you differ.

CAL. I do not differ; on the contrary, I agree; for in that way I shall soonest bring the argument to an end, and shall oblige my friend Gorgias.

SOC. And is this notion true of one soul, or of two or more?   d

CAL. Equally true of two or more.

SOC. Then a man may delight a whole assembly, and yet have no regard for their true interests?

CAL. Yes.

SOC. Can you tell me the pursuits which delight mankind—or rather, if you would prefer, let me ask, and you answer, which of them belong to the pleasurable class, and which of them not? In the first place, what   e
say you of flute-playing? Does not that appear to be an art which seeks only pleasure, Callicles, and thinks of nothing else?

CAL. I assent.

SOC. And is not the same true of all similar arts, as, for example, the art of playing the lyre at festivals?

CAL. Yes.

SOC. And what do you say of the choral art and of dithyrambic poetry*—are not they of the same nature? Do you imagine that Cinesias† the son of Meles cares about what will tend to the moral im-   502
provement of his hearers, or about what will give pleasure to the multitude?

CAL. There can be no mistake about Cinesias, Socrates.

SOC. And what do you say of his father, Meles the harp-player? Did he perform with any view to the good of his hearers? Could he be said to regard even their pleasure? For his singing was an infliction to his audience. And of harp-playing and dithyrambic poetry in general, what would you say? Have they not been invented wholly for the sake of pleasure?

CAL. That is my notion of them.

SOC. And as for the Muse of Tragedy, that solemn and august   b
personage—what are her aspirations? Is all her aim and desire only to give pleasure to the spectators, or does she fight against them and refuse to speak of their pleasant vices, and willingly proclaim in word and song truths welcome and unwelcome? Which in your judgment is her character?

---

*Narrative choral poems, originally in honor of Dionysus, the god of wine; in classical times, they seem to have become more artificial and concerned with rhythm so as to be "catchy."

†Author (fifth century B.C.E.) of dithyrambs, perhaps responsible for their degeneration.

CAL. There can be no doubt, Socrates, that Tragedy has her face turned towards pleasure and the gratification of the audience.

SOC. And is not that the sort of thing, Callicles, which we were just now describing as flattery?

CAL. Quite true.

SOC. Well now, suppose that we strip all poetry of song and rhythm and metre, there will remain speech?[3]

CAL. To be sure.

SOC. And this speech is addressed to a crowd of people?

CAL. Yes.

SOC. Then poetry is a sort of rhetoric?

CAL. True.

SOC. And do not the poets in the theatres seem to you to be rhetoricians?

CAL. Yes.

SOC. Then now we have discovered a sort of rhetoric which is addressed to a crowd of men, women, and children, freemen and slaves. And this is not much to our taste, for we have described it as having the nature of flattery.

CAL. Quite true.

SOC. Very good. And what do you say of that other rhetoric which addresses the Athenian assembly and the assemblies of freemen in other states? Do the rhetoricians appear to you always to aim at what is best, and do they seek to improve the citizens by their speeches, or are they too, like the rest of mankind, bent upon giving them pleasure, forgetting the public good in the thought of their own interest, playing with the people as with children, and trying to amuse them, but never considering whether they are better or worse for this?

CAL. I must distinguish. There are some who have a real care of the public in what they say, while others are such as you describe.

SOC. I am contented with the admission that rhetoric is of two sorts; one, which is mere flattery and disgraceful declamation; the other, which is noble and aims at the training and improvement of the souls of the citizens, and strives to say what is best, whether welcome or unwelcome, to the audience; but have you ever known such a rhetoric; or if you have, and can point out any rhetorician who is of this stamp, who is he?

CAL. But, indeed, I am afraid that I cannot tell you of any such among the orators who are at present living.

SOC. Well, then, can you mention anyone of a former generation, who may be said to have improved the Athenians, who found them worse and made them better, from the day that he began to make speeches? for, indeed, I do not know of such a man.

Cal. What! Did you never hear that Themistocles was a good man, and Cimon* and Miltiades† and Pericles, who is just lately dead, and whom you heard yourself?

Soc. Yes, Callicles, they were good men, if, as you said at first, true virtue consists only in the satisfaction of our own desires and those of others; but if not, and if, as we were afterwards compelled to acknowledge, the satisfaction of some desires makes us better, and of others, worse, and we ought to gratify the one and not the other, and there is an art in distinguishing them, can you tell me of any of these statesmen who did distinguish them?

Cal. No, indeed, I cannot.

Soc. Yet, surely, Callicles, if you look you will find one. Suppose that we just calmly consider whether any of these was such as I have described. Will not the good man, who says whatever he says with a view to the best, speak with a reference to some standard and not at random, just as all other artists, whether the painter, the builder, the shipwright, or any other look all of them to their own work, and do not select and apply at random what they apply, but strive to give a definite form to it? The artist disposes all things in order, and compels the one part to harmonize and accord with the other part, until he has constructed a regular and systematic whole; and this is true of all artists, and in the same way the trainers and physicians, of whom we spoke before, give order and regularity to the body; do you deny this?

Cal. No; I am ready to admit it.

Soc. Then the house in which order and regularity prevail is good; that in which there is disorder, evil?

Cal. Yes.

Soc. And the same is true of a ship?

Cal. Yes.

Soc. And the same may be said of the human body?

Cal. Yes.

Soc. And what would you say of the soul? Will the good soul be that in which disorder is prevalent, or that in which there is harmony and order?

Cal. The latter follows from our previous admissions.

Soc. What is the name which is given to the effect of harmony and order in the body?

---

*Famous Athenian politician and military leader; he was a rival of Themistocles (see footnote on p. 128).

†Military leader of shifting allegiance during the Persian Wars (see "General Introduction," p. xvii).

CAL. I suppose that you mean health and strength?

c   SOC. Yes, I do; and what is the name which you would give to the effect of harmony and order in the soul? Try and discover a name for this as well as for the other.

CAL. Why not give the name yourself, Socrates?

SOC. Well, if you had rather that I should, I will; and you shall say whether you agree with me, and if not, you shall refute and answer me. 'Healthy,' as I conceive, is the name which is given to the regular order of the body, whence comes health and every other bodily excellence: is that true or not?

CAL. True.

d   SOC. And 'lawful' and 'law' are the names which are given to the regular order and action of the soul, and these make men lawful and orderly. And so we have temperance and justice: have we not?

CAL. Granted.

SOC. And will not the true rhetorician who is honest and understands his art have his eye fixed upon these, in all the words which he addresses to the souls of men, and in all his actions, both in what he gives and in what he takes away? Will not his aim be to implant justice in the souls of his citizens and take away injustice, to implant temperance and take away intemperance, to implant every virtue and take away every vice? Do you not agree?

CAL. I agree.

SOC. For what use is there, Callicles, in giving to the body of a sick 505 man who is in a bad state of health a quantity of the most delightful food or drink or any other pleasant thing, which may be really as bad for him as if you gave him nothing, or even worse if rightly estimated. Is not that true?

CAL. I will not say 'No' to it.

SOC. For in my opinion there is no profit in a man's life if his body is in an evil plight—in that case his life also is evil: am I not right?

CAL. Yes.

SOC. When a man is in health the physicians will generally allow him to eat when he is hungry and drink when he is thirsty, and to satisfy his desires as he likes, but when he is sick they hardly suffer him to satisfy his desires at all: even you will admit that?

CAL. Yes.

b   SOC. And does not the same argument hold of the soul, my good sir? While it is in a bad state and is senseless and intemperate and unjust and unholy, its desires ought to be controlled, and it ought to be prevented from doing anything which does not tend to its own improvement.

CAL. Yes.

Soc. Such treatment will be better for the soul itself?

Cal. To be sure.

Soc. And to restrain it from its appetites is to chastise it?

Cal. Yes.

Soc. Then restraint or chastisement is better for the soul than intemperance or the absence of control, which you were just now preferring?

Cal. I do not understand you, Socrates, and I wish that you would ask someone who does.

Soc. Here is a gentleman who cannot endure to be improved or to subject himself to that very chastisement of which the argument speaks!

Cal. I do not heed a word of what you are saying, and have only answered hitherto out of civility to Gorgias.

Soc. What are we to do, then? Shall we break off in the middle?

Cal. Up to you.

Soc. Well, but people say that 'a tale should have a head and not break off in the middle,' and I should not like to have the argument going about without a head; please then go on a little longer, and put the head on.

Cal. How tyrannical you are, Socrates! I wish that you and your argument would rest, or that you would get someone else to argue with you.

Soc. But who else is willing? I want to finish the argument.

Cal. Cannot you finish without my help, either talking straight on, or questioning and answering yourself?

Soc. Must I then say with Epicharmus,* 'Two men spoke before, but now one shall be enough'? I suppose that there is absolutely no help. And if I am to carry on the enquiry by myself, I will first of all remark that not only I but all of us should have an ambition to know what is true and what is false in this matter, for the discovery of the truth is a common good. And now I will proceed to argue according to my own notion. But if any of you think that I arrive at conclusions which are untrue you must interpose and refute me, for I do not speak from any knowledge of what I am saying; I am an enquirer like yourselves, and therefore, if my opponent says anything which is of force, I shall be the first to agree with him. I am speaking on the supposition that the argument ought to be completed; but if you think otherwise let us leave off and go our ways.

Gor. I think, Socrates, that we should not go our ways until you

---

*Sicilian comic poet.

have completed the argument; and this appears to me to be the wish of the rest of the company; I myself should very much like to hear what more you have to say.

SOC. I too, Gorgias, should have liked to continue the argument with Callicles, and then I might have given him an 'Amphion' in return for his 'Zethus';[4] but since you, Callicles, are unwilling to con-

c   tinue, I hope that you will listen, and interrupt me if I seem to you to be in error. And if you refute me, I shall not be angry with you as you are with me, but I shall inscribe you as the greatest of benefactors on the tablets of my soul.

CAL. My good fellow, never mind me, but get on.

SOC. Listen to me, then, while I recapitulate the argument: Is the pleasant the same as the good? Not the same. Callicles and I are agreed about that. And is the pleasant to be pursued for the sake of the good? or the good for the sake of the pleasant? The pleasant is to be pursued for the sake of the good. And that is pleasant at the presence of which

d   we are pleased, and that is good at the presence of which we are good? To be sure. And we are good, and all good things whatever are good, when some virtue is present in us or them? That, Callicles, is my conviction. But the virtue of each thing, whether body or soul, instrument or creature, when given to them in the best way comes to them not by chance but as the result of the order and truth and art which are im-

e   parted to them: Am I not right? I maintain that I am. And is not the virtue of each thing dependent on order or arrangement? Yes, I say. And that which makes a thing good is the proper order inhering in each thing? Such is my view. And is not the soul which has an order of her own better than that which has no order? Certainly. And the soul which

507 has order is orderly? Of course. And that which is orderly is temperate? Assuredly. And the temperate soul is good? No other answer can I give, Callicles dear; have you any?

CAL. Go on, my good fellow.

SOC. Then I shall proceed to add that if the temperate soul is the good soul, the soul which is in the opposite condition, that is, the foolish and intemperate, is the bad soul. Very true.

And will not the temperate man do what is proper, both in rela-

b   tion to the gods and to men, for he would not be temperate if he did not? Certainly he will do what is proper. In his relation to other men he will do what is just, and in his relation to the gods he will do what is holy; and he who does what is just and holy must be just and holy? Very true. And must he not be courageous? For the duty of a temperate man is not to follow or to avoid what he ought not, but what he

c   ought, whether things or men or pleasures or pains, and patiently to endure when he ought; and therefore, Callicles, the temperate man, being, as we have described, also just and courageous and holy, cannot be other than a perfectly good man, nor can the good man do otherwise than well and perfectly whatever he does; and he who does well must of necessity be happy and blessed, and the evil man who does evil, miserable: now this latter is he whom you were applauding—the intemperate who is the opposite of the temperate. Such is my position, and these things I affirm to be true. And if they are true, then I further *d* affirm that he who desires to be happy must pursue and practise temperance and run away from intemperance as fast as his legs will carry him: he had better order his life so as not to need punishment; but if either he or any of his friends, whether private individual or city, are in need of punishment, then justice must be done and he must suffer punishment, if he is to be happy. This appears to me to be the aim which a man ought to have, and towards which he ought to direct all the energies both of himself and of the state, acting so that he may have temperance and justice present with him and be happy, not suffering his lusts to be unrestrained, and in the never-ending desire to satisfy them *e* leading a robber's life. Such a one is the friend neither of god nor man, for he is incapable of communion, and he who is incapable of communion is also incapable of friendship. And philosophers tell us, Callicles, that communion and friendship and orderliness and temperance *508* and justice bind together heaven and earth and gods and men, and that this universe is therefore called Cosmos or order, not disorder or misrule, my friend. But although you are a philosopher you seem to me never to have observed that geometrical equality is mighty, both among gods and men; you think that you ought to cultivate inequality or excess, and do not care about geometry. Well, then, either the principle that *b* the happy are made happy by the possession of justice and temperance, and the miserable miserable by the possession of vice, must be refuted, or, if it is granted, what will be the consequences? All the consequences which I drew before, Callicles, and about which you asked me whether I was in earnest when I said that a man ought to accuse himself and his son and his friend if he did anything wrong, and that to this end he should use his rhetoric—all those consequences are true. And that which you thought that Polus was led to admit out of modesty is true, namely that, to do injustice, if more disgraceful than to suffer, is in that *c* degree worse; and the other position, which, according to Polus, Gorgias admitted out of modesty, that he who would truly be a rhetorician ought to be just and have a knowledge of justice, has also turned out to be true.

And now, these things being as we have said, let us proceed in the next place to consider whether you are right in throwing in my teeth that I am unable to help myself or any of my friends or kinsmen, or to

save them in the extremity of danger, and that I am in the power of an-
d   other like an outlaw to whom anyone may do what he likes—he may
punch me, was the brave saying of yours, or take away my goods or
banish me, or even do his worst and kill me; a condition which, as you
say, is the height of disgrace. My answer to you is one which has been
already often repeated, but may as well be repeated once more. I tell
you, Callicles, that to be punched wrongfully is not the worst evil which
e   can befall a man, nor to have my purse or my body cut open, but that
to smite and slay me and mine wrongfully is far more disgraceful and
more evil; aye, and to despoil and enslave and pillage, or in any way at
all to wrong me and mine, is far more disgraceful and evil to the doer
509 of the wrong than to me who am the sufferer. These truths, which have
been already set forth as I state them in the previous discussion, would
seem now to have been fixed and riveted by us, if I may use an expression which is certainly bold, in words which are like bonds of iron
and adamant; and unless you or some other still more enterprising
hero shall break them, there is no possibility of denying what I say. For
my position has always been, that I myself am ignorant how these
b   things are, but that I have never met anyone who could say otherwise,
any more than you can, and not appear ridiculous. This is my position
still, and if what I am saying is true, and injustice is the greatest of evils
to the doer of injustice, and yet there is if possible a greater than this
greatest of evils, in an unjust man not suffering retribution, what is that
defense, the absence of which will make a man truly ridiculous? Must
not the defense be one which will avert the greatest of human evils? Is
not this the defense, the inability to provide which for self or family or
friends is the most disgraceful? And next will come that which is un-
c   able to avert the next greatest evil; thirdly that which is unable to avert
the third greatest evil; and so of other evils. As is the greatness of evil
so is the honor of being able to avert them in their several degrees, and
the disgrace of not being able to avert them. Am I not right, Callicles?

CAL. Quite right.

SOC. Seeing then that there are these two evils, the doing injustice
and the suffering injustice—and we affirm that to do injustice is a
d   greater, and to suffer injustice a lesser evil—by what devices can a man
succeed in obtaining the two advantages, the one of not doing and the
other of not suffering injustice? Must he have the power, or only the will
to obtain them? I mean to ask whether a man will escape injustice if he
has only the will to escape, or must he have provided himself with the
power?

CAL. He must have provided himself with the power; that is clear.

SOC. And what do you say of doing injustice? Is the will only sufficient, and will that prevent him from doing injustice, or must he have

provided himself with power and art; and if he has not studied and practised, will he be unjust still? Surely you might say, Callicles, whether you think that Polus and I were right or not in admitting the conclusion that no one does wrong voluntarily, but that all do wrong against their will?

CAL. Granted, Socrates. Press on.

510

SOC. Then, as would appear, power and art have to be provided in order that we may do no injustice?

CAL. Certainly.

SOC. And what art will protect us from suffering injustice, if not completely, yet as far as possible? I want to know whether you agree with me; for I think that such an art is the art of one who is either a ruler or even tyrant himself, or the equal and companion of the ruling power.

CAL. Well said, Socrates; and please observe how ready I am to praise you when you talk sense.

b

SOC. Think and tell me whether you would approve of another view of mine: to me every man appears to be most the friend of him who is most like him—like to like, as ancient sages say. Would you not agree to this?

CAL. I would.

SOC. But when the tyrant is rude and uneducated, he may be expected to fear anyone who is his superior in virtue, and will never be able to be perfectly friendly with him.

c

CAL. That is true.

SOC. Neither will he be the friend of anyone who is greatly his inferior, for the tyrant will despise him, and will never seriously regard him as a friend.

CAL. That again is true.

SOC. Then the only friend worth mentioning, whom the tyrant can have, will be one who is of the same character, and has the same likes and dislikes, and is at the same time willing to be subject and subservient to him; he is the man who will have power in the state, and no one will injure him with impunity—is not that so?

CAL. Yes.

d

SOC. And if a young man begins to ask how he may become great and formidable, this would seem to be the way—he will accustom himself, from his youth upward, to feel sorrow and joy on the same occasions as his master, and will contrive to be as like him as possible?

CAL. Yes.

SOC. And in this way he will have accomplished, as you and your friends would say, the end of becoming a great man and not suffering injury?

e

CAL. Very true.

SOC. But will he also escape from doing injury? Must not the very
511   opposite be true, if he is to be like the tyrant in his injustice, and to
have influence with him? Will he not rather contrive to do as much
wrong as possible, and not be punished?

CAL. True.

SOC. And by the imitation of his master and by the power which he
thus acquires will not his soul become bad and corrupted, and will not
this be the greatest evil to him?

CAL. You always contrive somehow or other, Socrates, to invert
everything: do you not know that he who imitates the tyrant will, if he
has a mind, kill the one who does not imitate him and take away his
goods?

b   SOC. Excellent Callicles, I am not deaf, and I have heard that a great
many times from you and from Polus and from nearly every man in the
city, but I wish that you would hear me too. I dare say that he will kill
him if he has a mind—the bad man will kill the good and true.

CAL. And is not that just the provoking thing?

SOC. Nay, not to a man of sense, as the argument shows: do you
think that all our cares should be directed to prolonging life to the ut-
c   termost, and to the study of those arts which secure us from danger
always; like that art of rhetoric which saves men in courts of law, and
which you advise me to cultivate?

CAL. Yes, truly, and very good advice it is.

SOC. Well, my friend, but what do you think of swimming; is that
an art of any great pretensions?

CAL. No, indeed.

SOC. And yet surely swimming saves a man from death, and there
d   are occasions on which he must know how to swim. And if you despise the swimmers, I will tell you of another and greater art, the art of
the pilot, who not only saves the souls of men, but also their bodies and
properties from the extremity of danger, just like rhetoric. Yet his art is
modest and unpresuming: it has no airs or pretences of doing anything
extraordinary, and, in return for the same salvation which is given by
the pleader, demands only two obols, if he brings us from Aegina to
Athens, or for the longer voyage from Pontus or Egypt, at the utmost
e   two drachmae, when he has saved, as I was just now saying, the passenger and his wife and children and goods, and safely disembarked
them at the Piraeus. This is the payment which he asks in return for so
great a boon; and he who is the master of the art, and has done all this,
gets out and walks about on the sea-shore by his ship in an unassum-
ing way. For he is able to reflect and is aware that he cannot tell which
of his fellow-passengers he has benefited, and which of them he has

injured in not allowing them to be drowned. He knows that they are just the same when he has disembarked them as when they embarked, and no better either in their bodies or in their souls; and he considers that if a man who is afflicted by great and incurable bodily diseases is only to be pitied for having escaped, and is in no way benefited by him in having been saved from drowning, much less he who has great and incurable diseases, not of the body, but of the soul, which is the more valuable part of him; neither is life worth having nor of any profit to the bad man, whether he is delivered from the sea, or the law-courts, or any other devourer; and so he reflects that such man had better not live, for he cannot live well.

And this is the reason why the pilot, although he is our saviour, is not usually conceited, any more than the engineer, who is not at all behind either the general, or the pilot, or anyone else, in his saving power, for he sometimes saves whole cities. Is there any comparison between him and the pleader? And if he were to talk, Callicles, in your grandiose style, he would bury you under a mountain of words, declaring and insisting that we ought all of us to be engine-makers, and that no other profession is worth thinking about; he would have plenty to say. Nevertheless you despise him and his art, and sneeringly call him an engine-maker, and you will not allow your daughters to marry his son, or marry your son to his daughters. And yet, on your principle, what justice or reason is there in your refusal? What right have you to despise the engine-maker, and the others whom I was just now mentioning? I know that you will say, 'I am better, and better born.' But if the better is not what I say, and virtue consists only in a man saving himself and his, whatever may be his character, then your censure of the engine-maker, and of the physician, and of the other arts of salvation, is ridiculous. My friend! I want you to see that the noble and the good may possibly be something different from saving and being saved. May not he who is truly a man cease to care about living a certain time?—he knows, as women say,* that no man can escape fate, and therefore he is not fond of life; he leaves all that with god, and considers in what way he can best spend his appointed term: whether by assimilating himself to the constitution under which he lives, as you at this moment have to consider how you may become as like as possible to the Athenian people, if you mean to be in their good graces, and to have power in the state; whereas I want you to think and see whether this is for the interest of either of us—I would not have us risk that which is dearest because of the acquisition of this power, like the Thessalian

512

b

c

d

e

513

---

*Why women? I have not found a satisfactory explanation.

b enchantresses, who, as they say, bring down the moon from heaven at the risk of their own perdition. But if you suppose that any man will show you the art of becoming great in the city, and yet not conforming yourself to the ways of the city, whether for better or worse, then I can only say that you are mistaken, Callicles; for he who would deserve to be the true natural friend of the Athenian people, aye, or of Pyrilampes' darling who is called after them, must be by nature like them, and not an imitator only. He, then, who will make you most like

c them, will make you as you desire, a statesman and orator: for every man is pleased when he is spoken to in his own language and spirit, and dislikes any other. But perhaps you, sweet Callicles, may be of another mind. What do you say?

CAL. Somehow or other your words, Socrates, always appear to me to be good words; and yet, like the rest of the world, I am not quite convinced by them.

SOC. The reason is, Callicles, that the love of people which abides in

d your soul is an adversary to me; but I dare say that if we recur to these same matters, and consider them more thoroughly, you may be convinced for all that. Please, then, remember that there are two processes of training all things, including body and soul; in the one, as we said, we treat them with a view to pleasure, and in the other with a view to the highest good, and then we do not indulge but resist them: was not that the distinction which we drew?

CAL. Very true.

SOC. And the one which had pleasure in view was just a vulgar flattery—was not that another of our conclusions?

e CAL. So be it, if you will.

SOC. And the other had in view the greatest improvement of that which was ministered to, whether body or soul?

CAL. Quite true.

SOC. And must we not have the same end in view in the treatment of our city and citizens? Must we not try and make them as good as

514 possible? For we have already discovered that there is no use in imparting to them any other good, unless the mind of those who are to have the good, whether money, or office, or any other sort of power, be gentle and good. Shall we say that?

CAL. Yes, certainly, if you like.

SOC. Well, then, if you and I, Callicles, were intending to set about some public business, and were advising one another to undertake

b buildings, such as walls, docks or temples of the largest size, ought we not to examine ourselves, first, as to whether we know or do not know the art of building, and who taught us?—would not that be necessary, Callicles?

CAL. True.

SOC. In the second place, we should have to consider whether we had ever constructed any private house, either of our own or for our friends, and whether this building of ours was a success or not; and if upon consideration we found that we had had good and eminent masters, and had been successful in constructing many fine buildings, not only with their assistance, but without them, by our own unaided skill—in that case prudence would not dissuade us from proceeding to the construction of public works. But if we had no master to show, and only a number of worthless buildings or none at all, then, surely, it would be ridiculous of us to attempt public works, or to advise one another to undertake them. Is not this true?

CAL. Certainly.

SOC. And does not the same hold in all other cases? If you and I were physicians, and were advising one another that we were competent to practise as state-physicians, should I not ask about you, and would you not ask about me: well, but how about Socrates himself, has he good health? and was anyone else ever known to be cured by him, whether slave or freeman? And I should make the same enquiries about you. And if we arrived at the conclusion that no one, whether citizen or stranger, man or woman, had ever been any the better for the medical skill of either of us, then, by heaven, Callicles, what an absurdity to think that we or any human being should be so silly as to set up as state-physicians and advise others like ourselves to do the same, without having first practised in private, whether successfully or not, and acquired experience of the art! Is not this, as they say, to begin with the big jar when you are learning the potter's art, which is a foolish thing?

CAL. True.

SOC. And now, my friend, as you are already beginning to be a public character, and are admonishing and reproaching me for not being one, suppose that we ask a few questions of one another. Tell me, then, Callicles, how about making any of the citizens better? Was there ever a man who was once vicious, or unjust, or intemperate, or foolish, and became by the help of Callicles good and noble? Was there ever such a man, whether citizen or stranger, slave or freeman? Tell me, Callicles, if a person were to ask these questions of you, what would you answer? Whom would you say that you had improved by your conversation? There may have been good deeds of this sort which were done by you as a private person, before you came forward in public. Why will you not answer?

CAL. You are contentious, Socrates.

SOC. Nay, I ask you, not from a love of contention, but because I really want to know in what way you think that affairs should be administered among us—whether, when you come to the administration of them, you have any other aim but the improvement of the citizens. Have we not already admitted many times over that such is the duty of a public man? We have surely said so; for if you will not answer for yourself I must answer for you. But if this is what the good man ought to effect for the benefit of his own state, allow me to recall to you the names of those whom you were just now mentioning, Pericles,

d   and Cimon, and Miltiades, and Themistocles, and ask whether you still think that they were good citizens.

CAL. I do.

Soc. But if they were good, then clearly each of them must have made the citizens better instead of worse?

CAL. Yes.

Soc. And, therefore, when Pericles first began to speak in the assembly, the Athenians were not so good as when he spoke last?

CAL. Very likely.

Soc. My friend, 'likely' is not the word; for if he was a good citizen, the inference is certain.

e   CAL. And what difference does that make?

Soc. None; only I would like further to know whether the Athenians are supposed to have been made better by Pericles, or, on the contrary, to have been corrupted by him; for I hear that he was the first who gave the people pay, and made them idle and cowardly, and encouraged them in the love of talk and of money.[5]

CAL. You heard that, Socrates, from the laconising set who bruise their ears.[6]

Soc. But what I am going to tell you now is not mere hearsay, but well known both to you and me: that at first, Pericles was glorious and

516   his character unimpeached by any verdict of the Athenians—this was during the time when they were not so good—yet afterwards, when they had been made good and gentle by him, at the very end of his life they convicted him of theft, and almost put him to death, clearly under the notion that he was a malefactor.

CAL. Well, but how does that prove Pericles' badness?

Soc. Why, surely you would say that he was a bad manager of asses or horses or oxen, who had received them originally neither kicking nor butting nor biting him, and implanted in them all these savage tricks? Would he not be a bad manager of any animals who received them gen-

b   tle, and made them fiercer than they were when he received them? What do you say?

CAL. I will do you the favour of saying 'yes.'

Soc. And will you also do me the favour of saying whether man is an animal?

CAL. Certainly he is.

SOC. And was not Pericles a shepherd of men?

CAL. Yes.

SOC. And if he was a good political shepherd, ought not the animals who were his subjects, as we were just now acknowledging, to have become more just, and not more unjust?   c

CAL. Quite true.

SOC. And are not just men gentle, as Homer says?—or are you of another mind?

CAL. I agree.

SOC. And yet he really did make them more savage than he received them, and their savageness was shown towards himself; which he must have been very far from desiring.

CAL. Do you want me to agree with you?

SOC. Yes, if I seem to you to speak the truth.

CAL. Granted then.

SOC. And if they were more savage, must they not have been more unjust and inferior?

CAL. Granted again.   d

SOC. Then upon this view, Pericles was not a good statesman?

CAL. That is, upon your view.

SOC. Nay, the view is yours, after what you have admitted. Take the case of Cimon again. Did not the very persons whom he was serving ostracize him, in order that they might not hear his voice for ten years? and they did just the same to Themistocles, adding the penalty of exile; and they voted that Miltiades, the hero of Marathon, should be thrown into the pit of death, and he was only saved by the Prytanis. And yet, if   e
they had been really good men, as you say, these things would never have happened to them. For the good charioteers are not those who at first keep their place, and then, when they have broken in their horses, and themselves become better charioteers, are thrown out—that is not the way either in charioteering or in any profession.—What do you think?

CAL. I would think not.

SOC. Well, but if so, the truth is as I have said already, that in the   517
Athenian State no one has ever shown himself to be a good statesman—you admitted that this was true of our present statesmen, but not true of former ones, and you preferred them to the others; yet they have turned out to be no better than our present ones; and therefore, if they were rhetoricians, they did not use the true art of rhetoric or of flattery, or they would not have fallen out of favour.

CAL. But surely, Socrates, no living man ever came near anyone of   b
them in his performances.

Soc. My dear friend, I say nothing against them regarded as the servants of the State; and I do think that they were certainly more serviceable than those who are living now, and better able to gratify the wishes of the State; but as to transforming those desires and not allowing them to have their way, and using the powers which they had, whether of persuasion or of force, in the improvement of their fellow-
c   citizens, which is the prime object of the truly good citizen, I do not see that in these respects they were at all superior to our present statesmen, although I do admit that they were more clever at providing ships and walls and docks, and all that. You and I have a ridiculous way, for during the whole time that we are arguing, we are always going round and round to the same point, and constantly misunderstanding one an-
d   other. If I am not mistaken, you have admitted and acknowledged more than once, that there are two kinds of operations which have to do with the body, and two which have to do with the soul: one of the two is ministerial, and if our bodies are hungry provides food for them, and if they are thirsty gives them drink, or if they are cold supplies them with garments, blankets, shoes, and all that they crave. I use the same images as before intentionally, in order that you may understand me better. The purveyor of the articles may provide them either whole-sale or retail, or he may be the maker of any of them—the baker, or
e   the cook, or the weaver, or the shoemaker, or the tanner; and in so doing, being such as he is, he is naturally supposed by himself and everyone to minister to the body. For none of them know that there is another art—an art of gymnastics and medicine which is the true minister of the body, and ought to be the mistress of all the rest, and to use their results according to the knowledge which she has and they have not, of the real good or bad effects of meats and drinks on the body. All
518 other arts which have to do with the body are servile and menial and illiberal; and gymnastics and medicine are, as they ought to be, their mistresses. Now, when I say that all this is equally true of the soul, you seem at first to know and understand and assent to my words, and then
b   a little while afterwards you come repeating: Has not the State had good and noble citizens? and when I ask you who they are, you reply, seemingly quite in earnest, as if I had asked who are or have been good trainers, and you had replied: Thearion, the baker, Mithoecus, who wrote the Sicilian cookery-book, Sarambus, the vintner: these are ministers of the body, first-rate in their art; for the first makes admirable loaves, the second excellent dishes, and the third fabulous wine. To me
c   these appear to be the exact parallel of the statesmen whom you mention. Now you would not be altogether pleased if I said to you: 'My friend, you know nothing of gymnastics; those of whom you are speaking to me are only the ministers and purveyors of luxury, who

have no good or noble notions of their art, and may very likely be filling and fattening men's bodies and gaining their approval, although
the result is that they lose their original flesh in the long run, and become thinner than they were before; and yet they, in their simplicity,
will not attribute their diseases and loss of flesh to their entertainers,
but when in later years the unhealthy surfeit brings the attendant   *d*
penalty of disease, he who happens to be near them at the time, and
offers them advice, is accused and blamed by them, and if they could
they would do him some harm, while they proceed to eulogize the
men who have been the real authors of the mischief'. And that, Callicles, is just what you are now doing. You praise the men who feasted   *e*
the citizens and satisfied their desires, and people say that they have
made the city great, not seeing that the swollen and ulcerated condition of the State is to be attributed to these elder statesmen; for they
have filled the city with harbors and docks and walls and revenues and
all that, and have left no room for justice and temperance. And when   519
the crisis of the disorder comes, the people will blame the advisers
of the hour, and applaud Themistocles and Cimon and Pericles, who
are the real authors of their calamities; and if you are not careful they *b*
may assail you and my friend Alcibiades, when they are losing not only
their new acquisitions, but also their original possessions; not that you
are the authors of these misfortunes of theirs, although you may perhaps be accessories to them. A great piece of work is always being
made, as I see and am told, now as of old, about our statesmen. When
the State treats any of them as malefactors, I observe that there is a
great uproar and indignation at the supposed wrong which is done to
them; 'after all their many services to the State, that they should unjustly perish'—so the tale runs. But the cry is all a lie; for no states- *c*
man ever could be unjustly put to death by the city of which he is
the head. The case of the professed statesman is, I believe, very much
like that of the professed sophist; for the sophists, although they are
wise men, are nevertheless guilty of a strange piece of folly: profess-
ing to be teachers of virtue, they will often accuse their disciples of
wronging them, and defrauding them of their pay, and showing no
gratitude for their services. Yet what can be more absurd than that men *d*
who have become just and good, and whose injustice has been taken
away from them, and who have had justice implanted in them by their
teachers, should act unjustly by reason of the injustice which is not in
them? Can anything be more irrational, my friends, than this? You,
Callicles, compel me to be an orator for the masses, because you will
not answer.

CAL. And you are the man who cannot speak unless there is someone to answer?

e   Soc. I guess I can; just now, at any rate, the speeches which I am making are long enough because you refuse to answer me. But I adjure you by the god of friendship, my good sir, do tell me whether there does not appear to you to be a great inconsistency in saying that you have made a man good, and then blaming him for being bad?

Cal. Yes, it appears so to me.

520   Soc. Do you never hear our professors of education speaking in this inconsistent manner?

Cal. Yes, but why talk of men who are good for nothing?

Soc. I would rather say, why talk of men who profess to be rulers, and declare that they are devoted to the improvement of the city, and nevertheless upon occasion declaim against the utter vileness of the city—do you think that there is any difference between one and the other? My good friend, the sophist and the rhetorician, as I was saying to Polus, are the same, or nearly the same; but you ignorantly fancy that rhetoric is a perfect thing, and sophistry a thing to be despised;

b   whereas the truth is that sophistry is as much superior to rhetoric as legislation is to the practice of law, or gymnastics to medicine. The orators and sophists, as I am inclined to think, are the only class who cannot complain of the mischief ensuing to themselves from that which they teach others, without in the same breath accusing themselves of having done no good to those whom they profess to benefit. Is not this a fact?

c   Cal. Certainly it is.

Soc. If they were right in saying that they make men better, then they are the only class who can afford to leave their remuneration to those who have been benefited by them. Whereas if a man has been benefited in any other way, if, for example, he has been taught to run by a trainer, he might possibly defraud him of his pay, if the trainer left the matter to him, and made no agreement with him that he should receive money as soon as he had given him the utmost speed; for not be-

d   cause of any deficiency of speed do men act unjustly, but by reason of injustice.

Cal. Very true.

Soc. And he who removes injustice can be in no danger of being treated unjustly: he alone can safely leave the fee to his pupils, if he be really able to make them good—am I not right?

Cal. Yes.

Soc. Then we have found the reason why there is no dishonor in a man receiving pay who is called in to advise about building or any other art?

e   Cal. Yes, we have found the reason.

Soc. But when the point is how a man may become best himself, and best govern his family and state, then to say that you will give no advice for free is held to be dishonorable?

CAL. True.

Soc. And why? Because only such benefits call forth a desire to requite them, and there is evidence that a benefit has been conferred when the benefactor receives a return; otherwise not. Is this true?

CAL. It is.

Soc. Then to which service of the State do you invite me? Determine for me. Am I to be the physician of the State who will strive and struggle to make the Athenians as good as possible; or am I to be the servant and flatterer of the State? Speak out, my good friend, freely and fairly as you did at first and ought to do again, and give me your entire mind.

CAL. I say then that you should be the servant of the State.

Soc. The flatterer? Well, sir, that is a noble invitation.

CAL. The Mysian,* Socrates, or what you please. For if you refuse, the consequences will be—

Soc. Do not repeat the old story—that he who likes will kill me and get my money; for then I shall have to repeat the old answer, that he will be a bad man and will kill the good, and that the money will be of no use to him, but that he will wrongly use that which he wrongly took, and if wrongly, basely, and if basely, hurtfully.

CAL. How confident you are, Socrates, that you will never come to harm! You seem to think that you are living in another country, and can never be brought into a court of justice, as you very likely may be brought by some miserable and mean person.

Soc. Then I must indeed be a fool, Callicles, if I do not know that in the Athenian State any man may suffer anything. And if I am brought to trial and incur the dangers of which you speak, he will be a villain who brings me to trial—of that I am very sure, for no good man would accuse the innocent. Nor shall I be surprised if I am put to death. Shall I tell you why I anticipate this?

CAL. By all means.

Soc. I think that I am the only or almost the only Athenian living who practises the true art of politics; I am the only politician of my time. Now, seeing that when I speak my words are not uttered with any view of gaining favour, and that I look to what is best and not to what is most pleasant, having no mind to use those arts and graces which you recommend, I shall have nothing to say in the justice court. And you might argue with me, as I was arguing with Polus—I shall be tried

---

*The insulting purpose is clear, but not the meaning; "low" or "coward" are possible.

just as a physician would be tried in a court of little boys at the indictment of the cook. What would he reply under such circumstances, if
someone were to accuse him, saying, 'O my boys, many evil things has
this man done to you: he is the death of you, especially of the younger
522 ones among you, cutting and burning and starving and suffocating
you, until you know not what to do; he gives you the bitterest potions,
and compels you to hunger and thirst. How unlike the variety of meats
and sweets on which I feasted you!' What do you suppose that the
physician would be able to reply when he found himself in such a
predicament? If he told the truth he could only say, 'All these evil
things, my boys, I did for your health,' and then would there not just
be a clamour among a jury like that? How they would cry out!

CAL. I dare say.

b   SOC. Would he not be utterly at a loss for a reply?

CAL. He certainly would.

SOC. And I too shall be treated in the same way, as I well know, if I
am brought before the court. For I shall not be able to rehearse to the
people the pleasures which I have procured for them, and which, although I am not disposed to envy either the procurers or enjoyers of
them, are deemed by them to be benefits and advantages. And if anyone says that I corrupt young men, and perplex their minds, or that I
speak evil of old men, and use bitter words towards them, whether in
c   private or public, it is useless for me to reply, as I truly might. 'Gentleman of the jury'—as your rhetoricians say—'All this I say and do
justly'—or anything else. So I'll take whatever comes to me as a result.

CAL. And do you think, Socrates, that a man who is so defenseless
is in a good position?

SOC. Yes, Callicles, if he has that defense, which as you have often
d   acknowledged he should have—if he be his own defense, and have
never said or done anything wrong, either in respect of gods or men;
this has been repeatedly acknowledged by us to be the best sort of defense. And if anyone could convict me of inability to defend myself or
others in this way, I would blush with shame, whether I was convicted
before many, or before a few, or by myself alone; and if I died from lack
of ability to do so, that would indeed grieve me. But if I died because
I have no powers of flattery or rhetoric, I am very sure that you would
e   not find me fretting about death. For no man who is not an utter fool
and coward is afraid of death itself, but he is afraid of doing wrong. For
to go to the world below having one's soul full of injustice is the last
and worst of all evils. And in proof of what I say, if you have no objection, I would like to tell you a story.

CAL. Very well, proceed; and then we will be done for good.

523   SOC. Listen, then, as storytellers say, to a very pretty tale, which I

dare say that you may be disposed to regard as a fable only, but which, as I believe, is a true tale, for I mean to speak the truth. Homer tells us how Zeus and Poseidon and Pluto divided the empire which they inherited from their father.[7] Now in the days of Cronos there existed a law respecting the destiny of man, which has always been, and still continues to be in heaven: the one who has lived all his life in justice and holiness shall go, when he is dead, to the Islands of the Blessed, and dwell there in perfect happiness out of the reach of evil; but he who has lived unjustly and impiously shall go to the house of vengeance and punishment, which is called Tartarus. And in the time of Cronos, and even quite lately in the reign of Zeus, the judgment was given on the very day on which the men were to die; the judges were alive, and the men were alive; and the consequence was that the judgments were not well given. Then Pluto and the authorities from the Islands of the Blessed came to Zeus, and said that the souls found their way to the wrong places. Zeus said: 'I shall put a stop to this; the judgments are not well given, because the persons who are judged have their clothes on, for they are alive; and there are many who, having evil souls, are apparelled in fair bodies, or encased in wealth or rank, and, when the day of judgment arrives, numerous witnesses come forward and testify on their behalf that they have lived righteously. The judges are awed by them, and they themselves too have their clothes on when judging; their eyes and ears and their whole bodies are interposed as a veil before their own souls. All this is a hindrance to them; there are the clothes of the judges and the clothes of the judged. What is to be done? I will tell you: in the first place, I will deprive men of the foreknowledge of death, which they possess at present—this power which they have Prometheus has already received my orders to take from them; in the second place, they shall be entirely stripped before they are judged, for they shall be judged when they are dead; and the judge too shall be naked, that is to say, dead—he with his naked soul shall pierce into the other naked souls; and they shall die suddenly and be deprived of all their kindred, and leave their brave attire strewn upon the earth—conducted in this manner, the judgment will be just. I knew all about the matter before any of you, and therefore I have made my sons judges; two from Asia, Minos and Rhadamanthus, and one from Europe, Aeacus. These, when they are dead, shall give judgment in the meadow at the parting of the ways, whence the two roads lead, one to the Islands of the Blessed, and the other to Tartarus. Rhadamanthus shall judge those who come from Asia, and Aeacus those who come from Europe. And to Minos I shall give the primacy, and he shall hold a court of appeal, in case either of the two others are in any doubt: then the judgment about the last journey of men will be as just as possible.'

b   From this tale, Callicles, which I have heard and believe, I draw the
following inferences: Death, if I am right, is in the first place the separation from one another of two things, soul and body; nothing else.
And, after they are separated, they retain their several natures, as in life;
the body keeps the same habit, and the results of treatment or accident
c   are distinctly visible in it: for example, the one who, by nature or training or both, was a tall man while he was alive, will remain as he was,
after he is dead; and the fat man will remain fat; and so on; and the
dead man who in life had a fancy to have flowing hair, will have flowing hair. And if he was marked with the whip and had the prints of the
scourge, or of wounds in him when he was alive, you might see the
same in the dead body; and if his limbs were broken or misshapen
d   when he was alive, the same appearance would be visible in the dead.
In a word, whatever was the habit of the body during life would be distinguishable after death, either perfectly, or in a great measure and for
a certain time. And I should imagine that this is equally true of the soul,
Callicles; when a man is stripped of the body, all the natural or acquired
affections of the soul are laid open to view. And when they come to the
e   judge, as those from Asia come to Rhadamanthus, he places them near
him and inspects them quite impartially, not knowing whose the soul
is: perhaps he may lay hands on the soul of the great king, or of some
other king or potentate, who has no soundness in him, but his soul is
marked with the whip, and is full of the prints and scars of perjuries
and crimes with which each action has stained him, and he is all
525 crooked with falsehood and imposture, and has no straightness, because he has lived without truth. Him Rhadamanthus beholds, full of
all deformity and disproportion, which is caused by licence and luxury
and insolence and incontinence, and despatches him ignominiously to
his prison, and there he undergoes the punishment which he deserves.
b   Now the proper office of punishment is twofold: he who is rightly
punished ought either to become better and profit by it, or he ought
to be made an example to his fellows, that they may see what he suffers, and fear and become better. Those who are improved when they
are punished by gods and men are those whose sins are curable; and
they are improved, as in this world so also in another, by pain and suffering; for there is no other way in which they can be delivered from
c   their evil. But they who have been guilty of the worst crimes, and are
incurable by reason of their crimes, are made examples; for, as they are
incurable, the time has passed at which they can receive any benefit.
They get no good themselves, but others get good when they behold
them enduring for ever the most terrible and painful and fearful
sufferings as the penalty of their sins—there they are, hanging up as

examples, in the prison-house of the world below, a spectacle and a warning to all unrighteous men who come thither. And among them, as I confidently affirm, will be found Archelaus, if Polus truly reports of him, and any other tyrant who is like him. Of these fearful examples, most, as I believe, are taken from the class of tyrants and kings and potentates and public men, for they are the authors of the greatest and most impious crimes, because they have the power. And Homer witnesses to the truth of this; for they are always kings and potentates whom he has described as suffering everlasting punishment in the world below: such were Tantalus and Sisyphus and Tityus.* But no one ever described Thersites,† or any private person who was a villain, as suffering everlasting punishment, or as incurable. For to commit the worst crimes, as I am inclined to think, was not in his power, and he was happier than those who had the power. No, Callicles, the very bad men come from the class of those who have power. And yet in that very class there may arise good men, and worthy of all admiration they are, for where there is great power to do wrong, to live and to die justly is a hard thing, and greatly to be praised, and few there are who attain to this. Such good and true men, however, there have been, and will be again, at Athens and in other states, who have fulfilled their trust righteously; and there is one who is quite famous all over the Greek world, Aristeides,‡ the son of Lysimachus. But, in general, great men are also bad, my friend.

As I was saying, Rhadamanthus, when he gets a soul of the bad kind, knows nothing about him, neither who he is, nor who his parents are; he knows only that he has got hold of a villain; seeing this, he stamps him as curable or incurable, and sends him away to Tartarus, whither he goes and receives his proper recompense. Or, again, he looks with admiration on the soul of some just one who has lived in holiness and truth; he may have been a private man or not; and I should say, Callicles, that he is most likely to have been a philosopher who has done his own work, and not troubled himself with the doings of other men in his lifetime; him Rhadamanthus sends to the Islands of the Blessed. Aeacus does the same; and they both have sceptres, and

---

*Tantalus: mythical king of Lydia, known for his great wealth and his offenses against the gods; Sisyphus: clever but wicked Corinthian king, eternally punished in Hades (*Odyssey* 11.593ff.); Tityus: a son of Earth (*Gaia*), punished in Hades for trying to rape Leto (mother of Artemis and Apollo).

†Ugliest of the Greeks at Troy; he reviles Agamemnon at *Iliad* 2.212ff.

‡Prominent general in the Persian Wars and framer of the Delian League (see "General Introduction," p. xvii).

d   judge; but Minos alone has a golden sceptre and is seated looking on, as Odysseus in Homer declares that he saw him:

'Holding a sceptre of gold, and giving laws to the dead.'*

Now I, Callicles, am persuaded of the truth of these things, and I consider how I shall present my soul whole and undefiled before the judge in that day. Renouncing the honours at which the world aims, I desire

e   only to know the truth, and to live as well as I can, and, when I die, to die as well as I can. And, to the utmost of my power, I exhort all other men to do the same. And, in return for your exhortation of me, I exhort you also to take part in the great combat, which is the combat of life, and greater than every other earthly conflict. And I retort your reproach of me, and say that you will not be able to help yourself when the day of trial and judgment, of which I was speaking, comes upon you; you will go before the judge, the son of Aegina, and, when he has

527   got you in his grip and is carrying you off, you will gape and your head will swim round, just as mine would in the courts of this world, and very likely someone will shamefully punch you, and put upon you any sort of insult.

Perhaps this may appear to you to be only an old wife's tale, which you will despise. And there might be reason in your despising such tales, if by searching we could find out anything better or truer: but

b   now you see that you and Polus and Gorgias, who are the three wisest of the Greeks of our day, are not able to show that we ought to live any life which does not profit in another world as well as in this. And of all that has been said, nothing remains unshaken but the saying that to do injustice is more to be avoided than to suffer injustice, and that the reality and not the appearance of virtue is to be followed above all things, as well in public as in private life; and that when anyone has been wrong in anything, he is to be chastised, and that the next best thing

c   to a man being just is that he should become just, and be chastised and punished; also that he should avoid all flattery of himself as well as of others, of the few or of the many: and rhetoric and any other art should be used by him, and all his actions should be done always, with a view to justice.

Follow me then, and I will lead you where you will be happy in life and after death, as the argument shows. And never mind if someone despises you as a fool, and insults you, if he likes; let him strike

d   you, by Zeus, and be of good cheer, and do not mind the insulting

---

Odyssey 11.569.

blow, for you will never come to any harm in the practice of virtue, if you are a really good and true man. When we have practised virtue together, we will apply ourselves to politics, if that seems desirable, or we will advise about whatever else may seem good to us, for we shall be better able to judge then. In our present condition we ought not to give ourselves airs, for even on the most important subjects we are always changing our minds; so utterly stupid are we! Let us, then, take the argument as our guide, which has revealed to us that the best way of life is to practice justice and every virtue in life and death. This way let us go; and in this exhort all men to follow, not in the way to which you trust and in which you exhort me to follow you; for that way, Callicles, is worthless.

PHAEDRUS

Introduction

THE THEMATIC UNITY OF *Phaedrus* has traditionally been difficult to appreciate, but it is clear that this is a dialogue about the power of language, and about the limitations of its rhetorical use and of writing in general. This conclusion is solidly backed up by the reference to the "garden of Adonis" (276b), a practice that consisted in planting seeds in small pots in order to test their strength, following which they were ritually disposed of by women, who threw them into a river. This is what happens, metaphorically speaking, to the speech about love written by the famous orator Lysias that Phaedrus, Socrates' young companion, carries with him. In contrast to written speeches, Socrates advocates planting the seeds of dialectic in the soul and letting them come to full fruition. This view is, of course, consistent with the fact that Socrates never wrote anything down. The question of why Plato wrote dialogues if he agreed with Socrates' view is often asked, and is answered in the dialogue, I believe, by the admission of philosophical rhetoric and the writing of reminders that will come in handy during "the forgetfulness of old age" (276d).

The following is a suggested outline of the dialogue:

- (227a–230e) Socrates and Phaedrus go for a walk outside the city wall. Phaedrus tells Socrates about a formidable speech by Lysias that he has just heard. Socrates notices that Phaedrus carries the written speech with him and asks him to read it to him at a pleasant spot by the river.

- (230e–234c) The speech of Lysias attempts to persuade the audience that it is better for a young man to yield to the sexual advances of another who is not in love with him than it is to yield to a lover. The reasons for this are: (a) the favors of the lover will cease once his desire is exhausted; (b) the lover will keep account of all the trouble he went into because of the beloved; (c) the lover will move on to a new beloved; (d) the lover does not act rationally; (e) there is a limited choice of lovers; (f) the lover is indiscreet and/or too obvious; (g) the lover is jealous; (h) the lover is not a friend; and (i) the lover does not point out or correct the flaws of the beloved. In contrast, the nonlover exhibits none of these problems, nor does he ask for too much.

- (234c–237b) Socrates says that he finds Lysias' speech repetitive and claims that it is possible to make Lysias' point better, drawing on his own inspiration. Covering his head, in order, he says, to avoid the embarrassment of looking at Phaedrus while he speaks, Socrates proceeds to deliver an improvement on Lysias' speech.

- (237b–241d) Socrates begins by enquiring about the subject matter—that is, the nature of love. He next claims that sexual love makes the lover seek pleasure instead of what is best, and as a result of this, the lover needs to make the beloved weaker, inferior, and dependent. Besides, when love fades, the lover loses his trust in the beloved, and the beloved finds himself in pursuit of the ex-lover.

- (241d–243e) Socrates claims to have realized that he has committed an offense against Love, and proceeds to issue now a speech in recantation.

- (243e–257b) Socrates' second speech is a long piece of which the main elements are: (a) that madness can be a good thing when it is a divine gift; (b) examples of good madness are prophecy, purification rituals, and possession by the Muses; (c) a discussion of the immortality of the soul, access to truth in the "other world," and classification of people, according to the degree of truth seen by their souls between successive reincarnations, in nine categories (the highest are the philosopher and the erotic lover, the lowest is the tyrant); (d) comparison of the soul to a charioteer that needs to manage two horses, one self-restrained and one "out of control"; (e) the fourth example of madness: falling in love by recognizing Beauty in the beloved; and (f) obvious benefits from yielding to this sort of lover.

- (257b–259d) Phaedrus acknowledges the superiority of Socrates' speech over that of Lysias. The discussion turns to the value of writing speeches, and the difference between good and bad ones.

- (259e–274b) In the ensuing discussion about rhetoric, Socrates makes a fundamental distinction between the purposes of conveying truth and of being persuasive. Knowing the truth requires the practice of philosophy, and rhetoric must be useful not only in court, but also in order to guide the souls of the listeners. Furthermore, in order for the philosophical method to be effective, it must proceed by "division" of things that differ very little, must include the study of nature, and must not lose sight of the audience that is being addressed by means of philosophical rhetoric.

- (274b–277a) Socrates turns next to the value of writing. According to a myth, writing was given, among other inventions, by the god Theuth to Thamus, king of Egypt. Thamus complained that writing would induce forgetfulness in people, and would make them believe that they know a lot while, in fact, they know nothing. Socrates then refers to writing as planting seeds in a garden of Adonis (see above in this introduction) and allows writing to be practiced only in order to keep reminders for the time when we are old and forgetful. In contrast, philosophical rhetoric "writes" the right way to knowledge in the soul of the listener.

- (277a–279c) In this last section, Socrates criticizes the practice of writing law or political documents, and defends philosophical writing. Finally, Phaedrus asks Socrates what to think about Isocrates (see "General Introduction," p. xxii). Socrates replies that he is "still young," but a very gifted writer and one of noble character who may well be drawn to write more important things.

PHAEDRUS

SOCRATES. My dear Phaedrus, where are you coming from, and where are you going?

PHAEDRUS. I come from Lysias the son of Cephalus,[1] and I am going to take a walk outside the wall, for I have been sitting with him the whole morning; and our common friend Acumenus* tells me that it is much more refreshing to walk in the open air than in the city streets.

SOC. There he is right. Lysias then, I suppose, was in town?

PHAEDR. Yes, he was staying with Epicrates,† here at the house of Morychus; that house which is near the temple of Olympian Zeus.

SOC. And how did he entertain you? Can I be wrong in supposing than Lysias gave you a feast of discourse?

PHAEDR. You shall hear, if you can spare time to accompany me.

SOC. And should I not deem the conversation of you and Lysias 'a thing of higher import,' as I may say in the words of Pindar, 'than any business'?

PHAEDR. Come along, then.

SOC. Tell me, then.

PHAEDR. My tale, Socrates, is one of your sort, for love was the theme which occupied us—after a fashion: Lysias has been writing about a fair youth who was being tempted, but not by a lover; and this was the point: he ingeniously proved that the non-lover should be accepted rather than the lover.

SOC. That is noble of him! I wish that he would say the poor man rather than the rich, and the old man rather than the young one; then he would meet the case of me and of many a man; his words would be quite refreshing, and he would be a public benefactor. For my part, I so long to hear his speech, that if you walk all the way to Megara, and when you have reached the wall come back, as Herodicus‡ recommends, without going in, I will keep you company.

PHAEDR. What do you mean, my good Socrates? How can you imag- ine that my unpracticed memory can do justice to an elaborate work, which the greatest rhetorician of the age spent a long time in composing? Indeed, I cannot; I would give a great deal if I could.

SOC. I believe that I know Phaedrus about as well as I know myself,

---

*Doctor and relative of Eryximachus (also a doctor, and a speaker in *Symposium*).
†Wealthy and persuasive orator of shifting political allegiance.
‡Medical man criticized by Socrates in *Republic* 406a–b.

and I am very sure that the speech of Lysias was repeated to him, not
b   once only, but again and again; he insisted on hearing it many times
over and Lysias was very willing to gratify him; at last, when nothing
else would do, he got hold of the book, and looked at what he most
wanted to see, this occupied him during the whole morning; then
when he was tired with sitting, he went out to take a walk, not until,
by the dog, as I believe, he had simply learned by heart the entire discourse, unless it was unusually long, and he went to a place outside the
wall in order to practice his lesson. There he saw a certain lover of discourse who had a similar weakness; he saw and rejoiced; now thought
he, 'I shall have a partner in my revels.' And he invited him to come and
c   walk with him. But when the lover of discourse begged that he would
repeat the tale, he gave himself airs and said, 'No, I cannot,' as if he
were indisposed; although, if the hearer had refused, he would sooner
or later have been compelled by him to listen whether he would or no.
Therefore, Phaedrus, bid him do at once what he will soon do whether
bidden or not.

PHAEDR. I see that you will not let me off until I speak in some fashion or other; verily therefore my best plan is to speak as I best can.

SOC. A very true remark, that of yours.

d   PHAEDR. I will do as I say; but believe me, Socrates, I did not learn
the very words—O no; nevertheless I have a general notion of what he
said, and will give you a summary of the points in which the lover differed from the non-lover. Let me begin at the beginning.

SOC. Yes, my sweet one; but you must first of all show what you
have in your left hand under your cloak, for that roll, as I suspect, is the
e   actual discourse. Now, much as I love you, I would not have you suppose that I am going to have your memory exercised at my expense, if
you have Lysias himself here.

229   PHAEDR. Enough; I see that I have no hope of practising my art upon
you. But if I am to read, where would you like to sit?

SOC. Let us turn aside and go by the Ilissus; we will sit down at
some quiet spot.

PHAEDR. I am fortunate in not having my sandals, and as you never
have any, I think that we may go along the brook and cool our feet in
the water; this will be the easiest way; at midday and in the summer it
is far from being unpleasant.

SOC. Lead on, and look out for a place in which we can sit down.

PHAEDR. Do you see the very tall plane-tree in the distance?

SOC. Yes.

b   PHAEDR. There are shade and gentle breezes, and grass on which we
may either sit or lie down.

SOC. Move forward.

PHAEDR. I should like to know, Socrates, whether the place is not somewhere here at which Boreas is said to have carried off Orithyia from the banks of the Ilissus?[2]

SOC. Such is the tradition.

PHAEDR. And is this the exact spot? The little stream is delightfully clear and bright; I can fancy that there might be maidens playing near.

SOC. I believe that the spot is not exactly here, but about a quarter   c
of a mile lower down, where you cross to the temple of Artemis, and there is, I think, some sort of an altar of Boreas at the place.

PHAEDR. I have never noticed it; but I beseech you to tell me, Socrates, do you believe this tale?

SOC. The wise are doubtful, and I should not be alone if, like them, I too doubted. I might have a rational explanation that Orithyia was playing with Pharmacia,* when a northern gust carried her over the neighbouring rocks; and this being the manner of her death, she was said to have been carried away by Boreas. There is a discrepancy, how-   d
ever, about the locality; according to another version of the story she was taken from Areopagus,† and not from this place. Now I quite acknowledge that these allegories are very nice, but he is not to be envied who has to invent them; much labour and ingenuity will be required of him; and when he has once begun, he must go on and rehabilitate Hippocentaurs and chimeras dire. Gorgons and winged steeds flow in apace, and numberless other inconceivable and porten-   e
tous natures. And if he is sceptical about them, and would like to reduce them one after another to the rules of probability, this sort of crude philosophy will take up a great deal of time. Now I have no leisure for such enquiries; shall I tell you why? I must first know myself, as the Delphian inscription says; to be curious about that which is   230
not my concern, while I am still in ignorance of my own self, would be ridiculous. And therefore I bid farewell to all this; the common opinion is enough for me. For, as I was saying, I want to know not about this, but about myself: am I a monster more complicated and swollen with passion than the serpent Typho,‡ or a creature of a gentler and simpler sort, to whom Nature has given a diviner and lowlier destiny? But let me ask you, friend: have we not reached the plane-tree to which you were conducting us?

PHAEDR. Yes, this is the tree.   b

---

*One of the nymphs Orithyia played with when Boreas kidnapped her, according to the myth (see endnote 2 to this dialogue).
†Hill in Athens northwest of the Acropolis, the seat of the Athenian Council.
‡Hesiod, *Theogony* 820ff.

Soc. By Hera, a fair resting place, full of summer sounds and scents. Here is this lofty and spreading plane-tree, and the agnus castus high and clustering, in the fullest blossom and the greatest fragrance; and the stream which flows beneath the plane-tree is deliciously cold to the feet. Judging from the ornaments and images, this must be a spot sa-

c   cred to Achelous* and the Nymphs. How delightful is the breeze—so very sweet; and there is a sound in the air shrill and summerlike which makes answer to the chorus of the cicadas. But the greatest charm of all is the grass, like a pillow gently sloping to the head. My dear Phaedrus, you have been an admirable guide.

PHAEDR. What an incomprehensible being you are, Socrates: when

d   you are in the country, as you say, you really are like some stranger who is led about by a guide. Do you ever cross the border? I rather think that you never venture even outside the gates.

Soc. Very true, my good friend; and I hope that you will excuse me when you hear the reason, which is, that I am a lover of knowledge, and the men who dwell in the city are my teachers, and not the trees or the country. Though I do indeed believe that you have found a spell with which to draw me out of the city into the country, like a hungry

e   cow before whom a bough or a bunch of fruit is waved. For only hold up before me in like manner a book, and you may lead me all round Attica, and over the wide world. And now having arrived, I intend to lie down, and do you choose any posture in which you can read best. Begin.

PHAEDR. Listen. 'You know how matters stand with me; and how, as

231   I conceive, this affair may be arranged for the advantage of both of us. And I maintain that I ought not to fail in my suit, because I am not your lover: for lovers repent of the kindnesses which they have shown when their passion ceases, but to the non-lovers who are free and not under any compulsion, no time of repentance ever comes; for they confer their benefits according to the measure of their ability, in the way which is most conducive to their own interest. Then again, lovers consider how by reason of their love they have neglected their own concerns and rendered service to others: and when to these benefits conferred they add on the troubles which they have endured, they

b   think that they have long ago made to the beloved a very ample return. But the non-lover has no such tormenting recollections; he has never neglected his affairs or quarrelled with his relations; he has no troubles to add up or excuse to invent; and being well rid of all these evils, why should he not freely do what will gratify the beloved? If you say that

---

*A river god.

the lover is more to be esteemed, because his love is thought to be c greater, for he is willing to say and do what is hateful to other men, in order to please his beloved—that, if true, is only a proof that he will prefer any future love to his present, and will injure his old love at the pleasure of the new. And how, in a matter of such infinite importance, can a man be right in trusting himself to one who is afflicted with a malady which no experienced person would attempt to cure, for the patient himself admits that he is not in his right mind, and acknowl- d edges that he is wrong in his mind, but says that he is unable to con- trol himself? And if he came to his right mind, would he ever imagine that the desires were good which he conceived when in his wrong mind? Once more, there are many more non-lovers than lovers; and if you choose the best of the lovers, you will not have many to choose from; but if from the non-lovers, the choice will be larger, and you will be far more likely to find among them a person who is worthy of your friendship. If public opinion be your dread, and you would avoid re- e proach, in all probability the lover, who is always thinking that other 232 men are as emulous of him as he is of them, will boast to someone of his successes, and make a show of them openly in the pride of his heart; he wants others to know that his labour has not been lost; but the non-lover is more his own master, and is desirous of solid good, and not of the opinion of mankind. Again, the lover may be generally noted or seen following the beloved (this is his regular occupation), and whenever they are observed to exchange two words they are sup- posed to meet about some affair of love either past or contemplated; b but when non-lovers meet, no one asks the reason why, because people know that talking to another is natural, whether friendship or mere plea- sure be the motive. Once more, if you fear the fickleness of friendship, consider that in any other case a quarrel might be a mutual calamity; but now, when you have given up what is most precious to you, you c will be the greater loser, and therefore, you will have more reason in being afraid of the lover, for his vexations are many, and he is always fancying that everyone is allied against him. Wherefore also he debars his beloved from society; he will not have you intimate with the wealthy, lest they should exceed him in wealth, or with men of educa- tion, lest they should be his superiors in understanding; and he is equally d afraid of anybody's influence who has any other advantage over him- self. If he can persuade you to break with them, you are left without a friend in the world; or if, out of a regard to your own interest, you have more sense than to comply with his desire, you will have to quarrel with him. But those who are non-lovers, and whose success in love is the reward of their merit, will not be jealous of the companions of their beloved, and will rather hate those who refuse to be his associates,

thinking that their favourite is slighted by the latter and benefited by
the former; for more love than hatred may be expected to come to him
out of his friendship with others. Many lovers too have loved the person of a youth before they knew his character or the rest of his per-
sonality; so that when their passion has passed away, there is no
knowing whether they will continue to be his friends; whereas, in the
case of non-lovers who were always friends, the friendship is not less-
ened by the favours granted; but the recollection of these remains with
them, and is a reminder of good things to come. Further, I say that you
are likely to be improved by me, whereas the lover will spoil you. For
they praise your words and actions in a wrong way; partly, because they
are afraid of offending you, and also, their judgment is weakened by
passion. Such are the feats which love exhibits; he makes things painful
to the disappointed which give no pain to others; he compels the successful lover to praise what ought not to give him pleasure, and therefore the beloved is to be pitied rather than envied. But if you listen to
me, in the first place, I, in my intercourse with you, shall not merely
regard present enjoyment, but also future advantage, being not mas-
tered by love, but my own master; nor for small causes taking violent
dislikes, but even when the cause is great, slowly laying up little
wrath—unintentional offences I shall forgive, and intentional ones I
shall try to prevent; and these are the marks of a friendship which will
last. Do you think that a lover only can be a firm friend? reflect—if this
were true, we should set small value on sons, or fathers, or mothers;
nor should we ever have loyal friends, for our love of them arises not
from passion, but from other associations. Further, if we ought to
shower favours on those who are the most eager suitors, on that principle, we ought always to do good, not to the most virtuous, but to the
most needy; for they are the persons who will be most relieved, and
will therefore be the most grateful; and when you make a feast you
should invite not your friend, but the beggar and the empty soul; for
they will love you, and attend you, and come about your doors, and
will be the best pleased, and the most grateful, and will invoke many a
blessing on your head. Yet surely you ought not to be granting favours
to those who besiege you with prayer, but to those who are best able
to reward you; nor to the lover only, but to those who are worthy of
love; nor to those who will enjoy the bloom of your youth, but to
those who will share their possessions with you in age; nor to those
who, having succeeded, will glory in their success to others, but to
those who will be modest and tell no tales; nor to those who care about
you for a moment only, but to those who will continue to be your
friends through life; nor to those who, when their passion is over, will

pick a quarrel with you, but rather to those who, when the charm of youth has left you, will show their own virtue. Remember what I have said; and consider yet this further point: friends admonish the lover under the idea that his way of life is bad, but no one of his kindred ever yet censured the non-lover, or thought that he was ill-advised about his own interests.

'Perhaps you will ask me whether I propose that you should indulge every non-lover. To which I reply that not even the lover would advise you to indulge all lovers, for the indiscriminate favour is less esteemed by the rational recipient, and less easily hidden by him who would escape the censure of the world. Now love ought to be for the advantage of both parties, and for the injury of neither.

'I believe that I have said enough; but if there is anything more which you desire or which in your opinion needs to be supplied, ask and I will answer.'

Now, Socrates, what do you think? Is not the discourse excellent, more especially in the matter of the language?

Soc. Yes, quite admirable; the effect on me was ravishing. And this I owe to you, Phaedrus, for I observed you while reading to be in an ecstasy, and thinking that you are more experienced in these matters than I am, I followed your example, and, like you, my divine darling, I became inspired with a frenzy.

Phaedr. Indeed, you are pleased to be merry.

Soc. Do you mean that I am not in earnest?

Phaedr. Now don't talk in that way, Socrates, but let me have your real opinion; I adjure you, by Zeus, the god of friendship to tell me whether you think that any Hellene could have said more or spoken better on the same subject.

Soc. Well, but are you and I expected to praise the sentiments of the author, or only the clearness, and roundness, and finish, and tournure of the language? As to the first I willingly submit to your better judgment, for I am not worthy to form an opinion, having only attended to the rhetorical manner; and I was doubting whether this could have been defended even by Lysias himself; I thought, please correct me if I am wrong, that he repeated himself two or three times, either from want of words or from want of pains; and also, he appeared to me ostentatiously to exult in showing how well he could say the same thing in two or three ways.

Phaedr. Nonsense, Socrates; what you call repetition was the especial merit of the speech; for he omitted no topic which the subject rightly allowed, and I do not think that anyone could have spoken better or more exhaustively.

Soc. There I cannot go along with you. Ancient sages, men and women, who have spoken and written of these things, would rise up in judgment against me, if out of complaisance I assented to you.

c   PHAEDR. Who are they, and where did you hear anything better than this?

Soc. I am sure that I must have heard; but at this moment I do not remember from whom; perhaps from Sappho the fair, or Anacreon the wise;* or, possibly, from a prose writer. Why do I say so? Why, because I perceive that my bosom is full, and that I could make another speech as good as that of Lysias, and different. Now I am certain that this is not

d   an invention of my own, who am well aware that I know nothing, and therefore I can only infer that I have been filled through the ears, like a pitcher, from the waters of another, though I have actually forgotten in my stupidity who was my informant.

PHAEDR. That is grand; never mind where you heard the discourse or from whom; let that be a mystery not to be divulged even at my earnest desire. Only, as you promise, make another and better oration, equal in length and entirely new, on the same subject; and I, like the

e   nine Archons,† will promise to set up a golden image at Delphi, not only of myself, but of you, and as large as life.

Soc. You are truly golden if you suppose me to mean that Lysias has altogether missed the mark, and that I can make a speech from which all his arguments are to be excluded. The worst of authors will say something which is to the point. Who, for example, could speak on this thesis of yours without praising the discretion of the non-lover and blaming the indiscretion of the lover? These are the commonplaces of

236 the subject which must come in (for what else is there to be said?) and must be allowed and excused; the only merit is in the arrangement of them, for there can be none in the invention; but when you leave the commonplaces, then there may be some originality.

PHAEDR. I admit that there is reason in what you say, and I too will be reasonable, and will allow you to start with the premiss that the lover

b   is more disordered in his wits than the non-lover; if in what remains you make a longer and better speech than Lysias, and use other arguments, then I say again, that a statue you shall have of beaten gold, and take your place by the colossal offerings of the Cypselids at Olympia.[3]

Soc. How profoundly in earnest is the lover, because to tease him I lay a finger upon his love! And so, Phaedrus, you really imagine that I am going to improve upon the ingenuity of Lysias?

---

*Both Sappho and Anacreon (sixth century B.C.E.) were famous for their love poetry.
†Chief magistrates in Athens.

PHAEDR. There I have you as you had me, and you must just speak
'as you best can.' Do not let us exchange 'you-toos' as in a farce, or   c
compel me to say to you as you said to me, 'I know Socrates as well as
I know myself, and he was wanting to speak, but he gave himself airs.'
Rather I would have you consider that from this place we stir not until
you have unbosomed yourself of the speech; for here are we all alone,
and I am stronger, remember, and younger than you: Wherefore go to   d
it, and do not compel me to use violence.

SOC. But, my sweet Phaedrus, how ridiculous it would be of me to
compete with Lysias in an extempore speech! He is a master in his art
and I am an untaught man.

PHAEDR. You see how matters stand; and therefore let there be no
more pretences; for, indeed, I know the word that is irresistible.

SOC. Then don't say it.

PHAEDR. Yes, but I will; and my word shall be an oath. 'I say, or
rather swear'—but what god will be witness of my oath?—'By this   e
plane-tree I swear, that unless you repeat the discourse here in the face
of this very plane-tree, I will never tell you another; never let you have
word of another!'

SOC. Villain! I am conquered; the poor lover of discourse has no
more to say.

PHAEDR. Then why are you still at your tricks?

SOC. I am not going to play tricks now that you have taken the oath,
for I cannot allow myself to be starved.

PHAEDR. Proceed.

SOC. Shall I tell you what I will do?   237

PHAEDR. What?

SOC. I will veil my face and gallop through the discourse as fast as
I can, for if I see you I shall feel ashamed and not know what to say.

PHAEDR. Only go on and you may do anything else which you
please.

SOC. Come, O ye Muses, melodious, as ye are called, whether you
have received this name from the character of your strains, or because
the Melians are a musical race, help, O help me in the tale which my
good friend here desires me to rehearse, in order that his friend whom   b
he always deemed wise may seem to him to be wiser than ever.

Once upon a time there was a fair boy, or, more properly speaking,
a youth; he was very fair and had a great many lovers; and there was
one special cunning one, who had persuaded the youth that he did not
love him, although he really loved him all the same; and one day when
he was paying his addresses to him, he used this very argument—that
he ought to accept the non-lover rather than the lover; his words were
as follows:—

c   'All good counsel begins in the same way; a man should know what he is advising about, or his counsel will all come to nought. But people imagine that they know about the nature of things, when they don't know about them, and, not having come to an understanding at first because they think that they know, they end, as might be expected, in contradicting one another and themselves. Now you and I must not be guilty of this fundamental error which we condemn in others; but as our question is whether the lover or non-lover is to be preferred, let us first of all agree in defining the nature and power of

d love, and then, keeping our eyes upon the definition and to this appealing, let us further enquire whether love brings advantage or disadvantage.

    'Everyone sees that love is a desire, and we know also that non-lovers desire the beautiful and good. Now in what way is the lover to be distinguished from the non-lover? Let us note that in every one of us there are two guiding and ruling principles which lead us whither they will; one is the natural desire of pleasure, the other is an acquired opinion which aspires after the best; and these two are sometimes in harmony and then again at war, and sometimes one, sometimes the

e other conquers. When opinion by the help of reason leads us to the best, the conquering principle is called temperance; but when desire, which is devoid of reason, rules in us and drags us to pleasure, that

238 power of misrule is called excess. Now excess has many names, and many members, and many forms, and any of these forms when very marked gives a name, neither honorable nor creditable, to the bearer of the name. The desire of eating, for example, which gets the better of

b the higher reason and the other desires, is called gluttony, and he who is possessed by it is called a glutton; the tyrannical desire of drink, which inclines the possessor of the desire to drink, has a name which is only too obvious, and there can be as little doubt by what name any other appetite of the same family would be called;—it will be the name of that which happens to be dominant. And now I think that you will perceive the drift of my discourse; but as every spoken word is in a manner plainer than the unspoken, I had better say further that the ir-

c rational desire which overcomes the tendency of opinion towards right, and is led away to the enjoyment of beauty, and especially of personal beauty, by the desires which are her own kindred—that supreme desire, I say, which by leading conquers and by the force of passion is reinforced, from this very force, receiving a name, is called love.'[4]

    And now, dear Phaedrus, I shall pause for an instant to ask whether you do not think me, as I appear to myself, inspired?

PHAEDR. Yes, Socrates, you seem to have a very unusual flow of words.

SOC. Listen to me, then, in silence; for surely the place is holy; so *d* that you must not wonder, if, as I proceed, I appear to be in a divine fury, for already I am getting into dithyrambics.*

PHAEDR. Nothing can be truer.

SOC. The responsibility rests with you. But hear what follows, and perhaps the fit may be averted; all is in their hands above. I will go on talking to my youth. Listen:

Thus, my friend, we have declared and defined the nature of the subject. Keeping the definition in view, let us now enquire what advantage or disadvantage is likely to ensue from the lover or the non- *e* lover to him who accepts their advances.

The one who is the victim of his passions and the slave of pleasure will of course desire to make his beloved as agreeable to himself as possible. Now to him who has a mind diseased anything is agreeable which is not opposed to him, but that which is equal or superior is hateful to him, and therefore the lover will not brook any superiority 239 or equality on the part of his beloved; he is always employed in reducing him to inferiority. And the ignorant is the inferior of the wise, the coward of the brave, the slow of speech of the speaker, the dull of the clever. These, and not these only, are the mental defects of the beloved; defects which, when implanted by nature, are necessarily a delight to the lover, and when not implanted, he must contrive to implant in him, if he would not be deprived of his fleeting joy. And therefore he cannot help being jealous, and will debar his beloved from the advan- *b* tages of society which would make a man of him, and especially from that society which would have given him wisdom, and thereby he cannot fail to do him great harm. That is to say, in his excessive fear lest he should come to be despised in his eyes he will be compelled to banish from him divine philosophy; and there is no greater injury which he can inflict upon him than this. He will contrive that his beloved shall be wholly ignorant, and in everything shall look to him; he is to be the delight of the lover's heart, and a curse to himself. Verily, a lover is a profitable guardian and associate for him in all that relates to his *c* mind.

Let us next see how his master, whose law of life is pleasure and not good, will keep and train the body of his servant. Will he not choose a beloved who is delicate rather than sturdy and strong? One brought up in shady bowers and not in the bright sun, a stranger to

---

*Narrative choral poems, originally in honor of Dionysus, the god of wine; in classical times, they seem to have become more artificial and concerned with rhythm so as to be "catchy."

manly exercises and the sweat of toil, accustomed only to a soft and
luxurious diet, instead of the hues of health having the colours of paint
and ornament, and the rest of a piece? Such a life anyone can imagine
d   and which I need not detail at length. But I may sum up all that I have to
say in a word, and move on. Such a person in war, or in any of the great
crises of life, will be the anxiety of his friends and also of his lover, and
certainly not the terror of his enemies; this nobody can deny.

And now let us tell what advantage or disadvantage the beloved
e   will receive from the guardianship and society of his lover in the matter of his property; this is the next point to be considered. The lover
will be the first to see what, indeed, will be sufficiently evident to all
240 men, that he desires above all things to deprive his beloved of his dearest and best and holiest possessions, father, mother, kindred, friends, of
all whom he thinks may be hinderers or reprovers of their most sweet
converse; he will even cast a jealous eye upon his gold and silver or
other property, because these make him a less easy prey, and when
caught less manageable; hence he is of necessity displeased at his possession of them and rejoices at their loss; and he would like him to be
wifeless, childless, homeless, as well; and the longer the better, for the
longer he is all this, the longer he will enjoy him.

There are some sort of animals, such as flatterers, who are danger-
b   ous and mischievous enough, and yet nature has mingled a temporary
pleasure and grace in their composition. You may say that a courtesan
is hurtful, and disapprove of such creatures and their practices, and yet
for the time they are very pleasant. But the lover is not only hurtful to
his love; he is also an extremely disagreeable companion. The old
c   proverb says that 'we find pleasure in our own age'; I suppose that
equality of years inclines them to the same pleasures, and similarity
begets friendship; yet you may have more than enough even of this;
and verily constraint is always said to be grievous. Now the lover is not
only unlike his beloved, but he forces himself upon him. For he is old
and his love is young, and neither day nor night will he leave him if he
can help; necessity and the sting of desire drive him on, and allure him
d   with the pleasure which he receives from seeing, hearing, touching,
perceiving him in every way. And therefore he is delighted to fasten
upon him and to minister to him. But what pleasure or consolation can
the beloved be receiving all this time? Must he not feel the extremity
of disgust when he looks at an old shrivelled face and the remainder to
match, which even in a description is disagreeable, and quite detestable
e   when he is forced into daily contact with his lover; moreover he is jeal-
ously watched and guarded against everything and everybody, and has
to hear misplaced and exaggerated praises of himself, and censures
equally inappropriate, which are intolerable when the man is sober,

and, besides being intolerable, are published all over the world in all their indelicacy and wearisomeness when he is drunk.

And not only while his love continues is he mischievous and unpleasant, but when his love ceases he becomes a perfidious enemy of him on whom he showered his oaths and prayers and promises, and 241 yet could hardly prevail upon him to tolerate the tedium of his company even from motives of interest. The hour of payment arrives, and now he is the servant of another master; instead of love and infatuation, wisdom and temperance are his bosom's lords; but the beloved has not discovered the change which has taken place in him, when he asks for a return and recalls to his recollection former sayings and doings; he believes himself to be speaking to the same person, and the other, not having the courage to confess the truth, and not knowing how to fulfil the oaths and promises which he made when under the b dominion of folly, and having now grown wise and temperate, does not want to do as he did or to be as he was before. And so he runs away and is constrained to be a defaulter; the oyster-shell has fallen with the other side uppermost[5]—he changes pursuit into flight, while the other is compelled to follow him with passion and imprecation not knowing c that he ought never from the first to have accepted a demented lover instead of a sensible non-lover; and that in making such a choice he was giving himself up to a faithless, morose, envious, disagreeable being, hurtful to his estate, hurtful to his bodily health, and still more hurtful to the cultivation of his mind, than which there neither is nor ever will be anything more honored in the eyes both of gods and men. Consider this, fair youth, and know that in the friendship of the lover there is no real kindness; he has an appetite and wants to feed upon you:

'As wolves love lambs so lovers love their loves.'* d

But I told you so, I am speaking in verse, and therefore I had better make an end; enough.

PHAEDR. I thought that you were only half-way and were going to make a similar speech about all the advantages of accepting the non-lover. Why do you not proceed?

Soc. Does not your simplicity observe that I have got out of e dithyrambics into epic, when only uttering a censure on the lover? And if I am to add the praises of the non-lover, what will become of me? Do you not perceive that I am already overtaken by the Nymphs to

---

*Possible allusion to *Iliad* 22.262–263.

whom you have mischievously exposed me? And therefore I will only add that the non-lover has all the advantages in which the lover is accused of being deficient. And now I will say no more; there has been 242 enough of both of them. Leaving the tale to its fate, I will cross the river and make the best of my way home, lest a worse thing be inflicted upon me by you.

PHAEDR. Not yet, Socrates; not until the heat of the day has passed; do you not see that the hour is almost noon? there is the midday sun standing still, as people say, in the meridian. Let us rather stay and talk over what has been said, and then return in the cool.

Soc. Your love of discourse, Phaedrus, is superhuman, simply marvellous, and I do not believe that there is any one of your contempo-b raries who has either made or in one way or another has compelled others to make an equal number of speeches. I would except Simmias* the Theban, but all the rest are far behind you. And now I do verily believe that you have been the cause of another.

PHAEDR. That is good news. But what do you mean?

c   Soc. I mean to say that as I was about to cross the stream the usual sign was given to me,—that sign which always forbids, but never bids, me to do anything which I am going to do; and I thought that I heard a voice saying in my ear that I had been guilty of impiety, and that I must not go away until I had made an atonement. Now I am a diviner, though not a very good one, but I have enough religion for my own use, as you might say of a bad writer—his writing is good enough for him; and I am beginning to see that I was in error. My friend, how prophetic is the human soul! At the time I had a sort of misgiving, and, d   like Ibycus,† 'I was troubled; I feared that I might be buying honor from men at the price of sinning against the gods.' Now I recognize my error.

PHAEDR. What error?

Soc. That was a dreadful speech which you brought with you, and you made me utter one as bad.

PHAEDR. How so?

Soc. It was foolish, I say, and to a certain extent, impious; can anything be more dreadful?

PHAEDR. Nothing, if the speech was really such as you describe.

---

*Follower of Socrates, perhaps a Pythagorean (see Xenophon, *Memorabilia* 1.2.48 and 3.11.17; Pythagoras was a sixth-century B.C.E. Greek philosopher and mathematician and an author of dialogues.

†Samian poet (sixth century B.C.E.) famous for his passionate love poetry (Samos is an island in the Aegean Sea).

Soc. Well, and is not Eros the son of Aphrodite, and a god?

Phaedr. So men say.

Soc. But that was not acknowledged by Lysias in his speech, nor by you in that other speech which you by a charm drew from my lips. For if Love be, as he surely is, a divinity, he cannot be evil. Yet this was the error of both the speeches. There was also a simplicity about them which was refreshing; having no truth or honesty in them, nevertheless they pretended to be something, hoping to succeed in deceiving the puppets of earth and gain celebrity among them. Wherefore I must have a purgation. And I think of an ancient purgation of mythological error which was devised, not by Homer, for he never had the wit to discover why he was blind, but by Stesichorus,* who was a philosopher and knew the reason why; and therefore, when he lost his eyes, for that was the penalty which was inflicted upon him for reviling the lovely Helen, he at once purged himself. And the purgation was a recantation, which began thus:

'False is that word of mine—the truth is that thou didst not embark in ships, nor ever go to the walls of Troy.'†

and when he had completed his poem, which is called 'the recantation,' immediately his sight returned to him. Now I will be wiser than either Stesichorus or Homer, in that I am going to make my recantation for reviling love before I suffer; and this I will attempt, not as before, veiled and ashamed, but with forehead bold and bare.

Phaedr. Nothing could be more agreeable to me than to hear you say so.

Soc. Only think, my good Phaedrus, what an utter want of delicacy was shown in the two discourses; I mean, in my own and in that which you recited out of the book. Would not anyone who was himself of a noble and gentle nature, and who loved or ever had loved a nature like his own, when we tell of the petty causes of lovers' jealousies, and of their exceeding animosities, and of the injuries which they do to their beloved, have imagined that our ideas of love were taken from some haunt of sailors to which good manners were unknown—he would certainly never have admitted the justice of our censure?

Phaedr. I dare say not, Socrates.

Soc. Therefore, because I blush at the thought of this person, and

---

*Another sixth-century B.C.E. author of lyric poetry and dithyrambs.

†Alternative version of the story in Homer's *Iliad* of Helen's abduction by the Trojan prince Paris, which brought on the Trojan War.

also because I am afraid of Love himself, I desire to wash the brine out of my ears with water from the spring; and I would counsel Lysias not to delay, but to write another discourse, which shall prove that 'all other things being equal' the lover ought to be accepted rather than the non-lover.

e   PHAEDR. Be assured that he shall. You shall speak the praises of the lover, and Lysias shall be compelled by me to write another discourse on the same theme.

SOC. You will be true to your nature in that, and therefore I believe you.

PHAEDR. Speak, and fear not.

SOC. But where is the fair youth whom I was addressing before, and who ought to listen now; lest, if he hear me not, he should accept a non-lover before he knows what he is doing?

PHAEDR. He is close at hand, and always at your service.

SOC. Know then, fair youth, that the former discourse was the
244   word of Phaedrus, the son of Pythokles, who dwells in the city of Myrrhina. And this which I am about to utter is the recantation of Stesichorus the son of Euphemus, who comes from the town of Himera,[6] and is to the following effect: 'I told a lie when I said that the beloved ought to accept the non-lover when he might have the lover, because the one is sane, and the other mad. It might be so if madness were simply an evil; but there is also a madness which is a divine gift, and the source of the chiefest blessings granted to men. For prophecy is a madness, and the prophetess at Delphi and the priestesses at Dodona
b   when out of their senses have conferred great benefits on the Greeks, both in public and private life, but when in their senses few or none. And I might also tell you how the Sibyl and other inspired persons have given to many an one many an intimation of the future which has saved them from falling. But it would be tedious to speak of what everyone knows.

There will be more reason in appealing to the ancient inventors of names, who would never have connected prophecy, which foretells the
c   future and is the noblest of arts, with madness,[7] or called them both by the same name, if they had deemed madness to be a disgrace or dishonor. They must have thought that there was an inspired madness which was a noble thing; for the two words, mantikē and manikē, are really the same, and the letter 'tau' is only a modern and tasteless insertion. And this is confirmed by the name which was given by them to the rational investigation of futurity, whether made by the help of birds or of other signs—this, for as much as it is an art which supplies from the reasoning faculty mind (nous) and information (historia) to

human thought (oiēsis), they originally termed oionoistikē, but the word has been lately altered and made sonorous by the modern intro- d duction of the letter omega (oionoistikē and oiōnistikē), and in proportion as prophecy (mantikē) is more perfect and august than augury, both in name and fact, in the same proportion, as the ancients testify, is madness superior to a sane mind, for the one is only of human, but the other of divine origin. Again, where plagues and mightiest woes have bred in certain families, owing to some ancient blood-guiltiness, there madness has entered with holy prayers and rites, and by inspired utterances found a way of deliverance for those who are in need; and he who has part in this gift, and is truly possessed and duly out of his e mind, is by the use of purifications and mysteries made whole and exempt from evil, future as well as present, and has a release from the calamity which was afflicting him. The third kind is the madness of 245 those who are possessed by the Muses; which taking hold of a delicate and virgin soul, and there inspiring frenzy, awakens lyrical and all other numbers; with these adorning the myriad actions of ancient heroes for the instruction of posterity. But he who, having no touch of the Muses' madness in his soul, comes to the door and thinks that he will get into the temple by the help of art—he, I say, and his poetry are not admitted; the sane man disappears and is nowhere when he enters into rivalry with the madman.

I might tell of many other noble deeds which have sprung from b inspired madness. And therefore, let no one frighten or flutter us by saying that the temperate friend is to be chosen rather than the inspired, but let him further show that love is not sent by the gods for any good to lover or beloved; if he can do so we will allow him to carry off the palm. And we, on our part, will prove in answer to him that the madness of love is the greatest of heaven's blessings, and the proof shall c be one which the wise will receive, and the witling disbelieve. But first of all, let us view the affections and actions of the soul divine and human, and try to ascertain the truth about them. The beginning of our proof is as follows:

The soul through all her being is immortal, for that which is ever in motion is immortal; but that which moves another and is moved by another, in ceasing to move ceases also to live. Only the self-moving, never leaving self, never ceases to move, and is the fountain and beginning of motion to all that moves besides. Now, the beginning is unbe- d gotten, for that which is begotten has a beginning; but the beginning is begotten of nothing, for if it were begotten of something, then the begotten would no longer be a beginning. But if unbegotten, it must also be indestructible; for if beginning were destroyed, there could be no beginning out of anything, nor anything out of a beginning; and all things must have a beginning. And therefore the self-moving is the beginning of motion; and this can neither be destroyed nor begotten, else the whole heavens and all creation would collapse and stand still, and never again have motion or birth. But if the self-moving is proved to be immortal, he who affirms that self-motion is the very idea and essence of the soul will not be put to confusion. For the body which is moved from without is soulless; but that which is moved from within has a soul, for such is the nature of the soul. But if this is true, must not the soul be the self-moving, and therefore of necessity unbegotten and immortal? Enough of the soul's immortality.

Of the nature of the soul, though her true form be ever a theme of large and more than mortal discourse, let me speak briefly, and in a figure. And let the figure be composite—a pair of winged horses and a charioteer. Now the winged horses and the charioteers of the gods are all of them noble and of noble descent, but those of other races are mixed; the human charioteer drives his in a pair; and one of them is noble and of noble breed, and the other is ignoble and of ignoble breed; and the driving of them of necessity gives a great deal of trouble to him.[8] I will endeavour to explain to you in what way the mortal differs from the immortal creature. The soul in her totality has the care of inanimate being everywhere, and traverses the whole heaven appearing in different forms: when perfect and fully winged it soars upward, and orders the whole world; whereas the imperfect soul, losing its wings and drooping in its flight at last settles on the solid ground—there, finding a home, it receives an earthly frame which appears to be self-moved, but is really moved by its power; and this composition of soul and body is called a living and mortal creature. For immortal no such union can be reasonably believed to be; although fancy, not having seen nor surely known the nature of god, may imagine an immortal creature having both a body and also a soul which are united throughout all time. Let that, however, be as god wills, and be spoken of acceptably to him. And now let us ask the reason why the soul loses her wings!

The wing is the corporeal element which is most akin to the divine, and which by nature tends to soar aloft and carry that which gravitates downwards into the upper region, which is the habitation of the gods. The divine is beauty, wisdom, goodness, and the like; and by these the wing of the soul is nourished, and grows apace; but when fed upon evil and foulness and the opposite of good, wastes and falls away. Zeus, the mighty lord, holding the reins of a winged chariot, leads the way in heaven, ordering all and taking care of all; and there follows him the array of gods and demi-gods, marshalled in eleven bands; Hestia alone abides at home in the house of heaven; of the rest they who are reckoned among the princely twelve march in their appointed order.* They see many blessed sights in the inner heaven, and there are many ways to and fro, along which the blessed gods are passing, every one doing his own work; he may follow who will and can, for jealousy has no place in the celestial choir. But when they go to banquet and festival, then they move up the steep to the top of the vault of heaven. The chariots of the gods in even poise, obeying the rein, glide rapidly; but the others labour, for the vicious steed goes **b** heavily, weighing down the charioteer to the earth when his steed has not been thoroughly trained: and this is the hour of agony and extremest conflict for the soul. For the immortals, when they are at the end of their course, go forth and stand upon the outside of heaven, and the revolution of the spheres carries them round, and they behold the things beyond. But of the heaven which is above the heavens, what **c** earthly poet ever did or ever will sing worthily? It is such as I will describe; for I must dare to speak the truth, when truth is my theme. There abides the very being with which true knowledge is concerned; the colourless, formless, intangible essence, visible only to mind, the pilot of the soul. The divine intelligence, being nurtured upon mind and pure knowledge, and the intelligence of every soul which is capa- **d** ble of receiving the food proper to it, rejoices at beholding reality, and once more gazing upon truth, is replenished and made glad, until the revolution of the worlds brings her round again to the same place. In the revolution she beholds justice, and temperance, and knowledge absolute, not in the form of generation or of relation, which men call ex- **e** istence, but knowledge absolute in existence absolute; and beholding the other true existences in like manner, and feasting upon them, she passes down into the interior of the heavens and returns home; and there the charioteer putting up his horses at the stall, gives them ambrosia to eat and nectar to drink.

Such is the life of the gods; but of other souls, that which follows **248** god best and is likest to him lifts the head of the charioteer into the outer world, and is carried round in the revolution, troubled indeed by the steeds, and with difficulty beholding true being; while another only rises and falls, and sees, and again fails to see by reason of the unruliness of the steeds. The rest of the souls are also longing after the upper world and they all follow, but not being strong enough they are carried round below the surface, plunging, treading on one another, **b**

---

*The twelve mythological Olympians on the Parthenon frieze are Aphrodite, Apollo, Ares, Artemis, Athena, Demeter, Dionysus, Hephaestus, Hera, Hermes, Poseidon, and Zeus.

each striving to be first; and there is confusion and perspiration and the extremity of effort; and many of them are lamed or have their wings broken through the ill-driving of the charioteers; and all of them after a fruitless toil, not having attained to the mysteries of true being, go away, and feed upon opinion. The reason why the souls exhibit this exceeding eagerness to behold the plain of truth is that pasturage is found
c there, which is suited to the highest part of the soul; and the wing on which the soul soars is nourished with this. And there is a law of Destiny, that the soul which attains any vision of truth in company with a god is preserved from harm until the next period,* and if attaining always is always unharmed. But when she is unable to follow, and fails to behold the truth, and through some ill-hap sinks beneath the double load of forgetfulness and vice, and her wings fall from her and she drops to the ground, then the law ordains that this soul shall at her first
d birth pass, not into any other animal, but only into man; and the soul which has seen most of truth shall come to the birth as a philosopher, or artist, or some musical and loving nature; that which has seen truth in the second degree shall be some righteous king or warrior chief; the soul which is of the third class shall be a politician, or economist, or trader; the fourth shall be a lover of gymnastic toils, or a physician; the fifth shall lead the life of a prophet or hierophant; to the sixth the char-
e acter of a poet or some other imitative artist will be assigned; to the seventh the life of an artisan or farmer; to the eighth that of a sophist or demagogue; to the ninth that of a tyrant; all these are states of probation, in which he who does righteously improves, and he who does unrighteously, deteriorates his lot.

Ten thousand years must elapse before the soul of each one can re-
249 turn to the place from whence it came, for she cannot grow its wings in less; only the soul of a philosopher, guileless and true, or the soul of a lover who is not devoid of philosophy, may acquire wings in the third of the recurring periods of a thousand years; and they who choose this life three times in succession have wings given them, and go away at the end of three thousand years. But the others receive judgment when they have completed their first life, and after the judgment they go, some of them to the houses of correction which are under the earth, and are punished; others to some place in heaven whither they are lightly borne by justice, and there they live in a manner worthy of the life which they
b led here when in the form of men. And at the end of the first thousand years the good souls and also the evil souls both come to draw lots and choose their second life, and they may take any which they please. The

---

*Between 3,000 and 10,000 years, as will become clear in the following sections.

soul of a man may pass into the life of a beast, or from the beast return again into the man. But the soul which has never seen the truth will not pass into the human form. For a man must have intelligence of universals, and be able to proceed from the many particulars of sense to one conception of reason—this is the recollection of those things which our soul once saw while following god—when regardless of that which we now call being it raised its head up towards the true being. And therefore the mind of the philosopher alone has wings; and this is just, for he is always, according to the measure of his abilities, clinging in recollection to things that are divine because god clings to them. And he who employs aright these memories is ever being initiated into perfect mysteries and alone becomes truly perfect. But, as he forgets earthly interests and is rapt in the divine, most people deem him mad, and rebuke him; they do not see that he is divinely inspired.

Thus far I have been speaking of the fourth and last kind of madness, which is imputed to him who, when he sees the beauty of earth, is transported with the recollection of the true beauty; he would like to fly away, but he cannot; he is like a bird fluttering and looking upward and careless of the world below; and he is therefore thought to be mad. And I have shown this of all inspirations to be the noblest and highest and the offspring of the highest to him who has or shares in it, and that he who loves the beautiful is called a lover because he partakes of it. For, as has been already said, every soul of man has in the way of nature beheld true being; this was the condition of her passing into the form of man. But all souls do not easily recall the things of the other world; they may have seen them for a short time only, or they may have been unfortunate in their earthly lot, and, having had their hearts turned to unrighteousness through some corrupting influence, they may have lost the memory of the holy things which once they saw. Few only retain an adequate remembrance of them; and they, when they behold here any image of that other world, are rapt in amazement; but they are ignorant of what this rapture means, because they do not clearly perceive. For there is no light of justice or temperance or any of the higher ideas which are precious to souls in the earthly copies of them: they are seen through a glass dimly; and there are few who, going to the images, behold in them the realities, and these only with difficulty. There was a time when with the rest of the happy band they saw beauty shining in brightness; we philosophers following in the train of Zeus, others in company with other gods; and then we beheld the beatific vision and were initiated into a mystery which may be truly called most blessed, celebrated by us in our state of innocence, before we had any experience of evils to come, when we were admitted to the sight of apparitions innocent and simple and calm and happy, which we beheld shining in pure light, pure ourselves and not yet enshrined in that living tomb which we carry about, now that we are imprisoned in the body, like an oyster in his shell. Let me linger over the memory of scenes which have passed away.

But of beauty, I repeat again that we saw her there shining in company with the celestial forms; and coming to earth we find her here too, shining in clearness through the clearest aperture of sense. For sight is the most piercing of our bodily senses; though not by that is wisdom seen; her loveliness would have been transporting if there had been a visible image of her, and the other ideas, if they had visible counterparts, would be equally lovely. But this is the privilege of beauty, that being the loveliest she is also the most palpable to sight. Now he who is not newly initiated or who has become corrupted, does not easily rise out of this world to the sight of true beauty in the other; he looks only at her earthly namesake, and instead of being awed at the sight of her, he is given over to pleasure, and like a brutish beast he rushes on to enjoy and beget; he consorts with wantonness, and is not afraid or ashamed of pursuing pleasure in violation of nature. But he whose initiation is recent, and who has been the spectator of many glories in the other world, is amazed when he sees anyone having a god-like face or form, which is the expression of divine beauty; and at first a shudder runs through him, and again the old awe steals over him; then looking upon the face of his beloved as of a god he reverences him, and if he were not afraid of being thought a downright madman, he would sacrifice to his beloved as to the image of a god; then while he gazes on him there is a sort of reaction, and the shudder passes into an unusual heat and perspiration; for, as he receives the effluence of beauty through the eyes, the wing moistens and he warms. And as he warms, the parts out of which the wing grew, and which had been hitherto closed and rigid, and had prevented the wing from shooting forth, are melted, and as nourishment streams upon him, the lower end of the wings begins to swell and grow from the root upwards; and the growth extends under the whole soul—for once the whole was winged. During this process the whole soul is all in a state of ebullition and effervescence,—which may be compared to the irritation and uneasiness in the gums at the time of cutting teeth,—bubbles up, and has a feeling of uneasiness and tickling; but when in like manner the soul is beginning to grow wings, the beauty of the beloved meets her eye and she receives the sensible warm motion of particles which flow towards her, therefore called emotion,* and is refreshed and warmed by

---

*One of Plato's far-fetched etymologies, intelligible only in Greek.

them, and then she ceases from her pain with joy. But when she is   *d*
parted from her beloved and her moisture fails, then the orifices of the
passage out of which the wing shoots dry up and close, and intercept
the germ of the wing; which, being shut up with the emotion, throb-
bing as with the pulsations of an artery, pricks the aperture which is
nearest, until at length the entire soul is pierced and maddened and
pained, and at the recollection of beauty is again delighted. And from
both of them together the soul is oppressed at the strangeness of its
condition, and is in a great strait and excitement, and in its madness   *e*
can neither sleep by night nor abide in its place by day. And wherever
it thinks that it will behold the beautiful one, thither in its desire it
runs. And when it has seen him, and bathed itself in the waters of
beauty, its constraint is loosened, and it is refreshed, and has no more
pangs and pains; and this is the sweetest of all pleasures at the time, and
is the reason why the soul of the lover will never forsake his beautiful   252
one, whom he esteems above all; he has forgotten mother and brethren
and companions, and he thinks nothing of the neglect and loss of his
property; the rules and proprieties of life, on which he formerly
prided himself, he now despises, and is ready to sleep like a servant,
wherever he is allowed, as near as he can to his desired one, who is the
object of his worship, and the physician who can alone assuage the greatness of his pain. And this state, my dear imaginary youth to whom I am   *b*
talking, is by men called love, and among the gods has a name which you,
in your simplicity, may be inclined to mock; there are two lines in the
apocryphal writings of Homer in which the name occurs. One of them is
rather outrageous, and not altogether metrical. They are as follows:

> 'Mortals call him fluttering love,
> But the immortals call him winged one,
> Because the growing of wings is a necessity to him.'

You may believe this, or not. At any rate the loves of lovers and their   *c*
causes are such as I have described.

Now the lover who is taken to be the attendant of Zeus is better
able to bear the winged god, and can endure a heavier burden; but the
attendants and companions of Ares, when under the influence of love,
if they fancy that they have been at all wronged, are ready to kill and
put an end to themselves and their beloved. And he who follows in the
train of any other god, while he is unspoiled and the impression lasts,   *d*
honors and imitates him, as far as he is able; and after the manner of
his god he behaves in his intercourse with his beloved and with the rest
of the world during the first period of his earthly existence. Everyone
chooses his love from the ranks of beauty according to his character,

and this he makes his god, and fashions and adorns as a sort of image
which he is to fall down and worship. The followers of Zeus desire that
their beloved should have a soul like him; and therefore they seek out
someone of a philosophical and imperial nature, and when they have
found him and loved him, they do all they can to confirm such a nature in him, and if they have no experience of such a disposition hitherto, they learn of anyone who can teach them, and follow themselves
in the same way. And they have less difficulty in finding the nature of
their own god in themselves, because they have been compelled to gaze
intensely on him; their recollection clings to him, and they become
possessed of him, and receive from him their character and disposition, so far as man can participate in god. The qualities of their god
they attribute to the beloved, wherefore they love him all the more, and
if, like the Bacchic Nymphs, they draw inspiration from Zeus, they
pour out their own fountain upon him, wanting to make him as like as
possible to their own god. But those who are the followers of Hera seek
a royal love, and when they have found him they do just the same with
him; and in like manner the followers of Apollo, and of every other god
walking in the ways of their god, seek a love who is to be made like
him whom they serve, and when they have found him, they themselves
imitate their god, and persuade their love to do the same, and educate
him into the manner and nature of the god as far as they each can; for
no feelings of envy or jealousy are entertained by them towards their
beloved, but they do their utmost to create in him the greatest likeness
of themselves and of the god whom they honor. So fair and blissful to
the beloved is the desire of the inspired lover, and the initiation of
which I speak into the mysteries of true love, if he is captured by the
lover and their purpose is effected. Now the beloved is taken captive in
the following manner:

As I said at the beginning of this tale, I divided each soul into
three—two horses and a charioteer; one of the horses was good and
the other bad: the division may remain, but I have not yet explained in
what the goodness or badness of either consists, and to that I will proceed. The right-hand horse is upright and cleanly made; he has a lofty
neck and an aquiline nose; his colour is white, and his eyes dark; he is
a lover of honor and modesty and temperance, and the follower of true
glory; he needs no touch of the whip, but is guided by word and admonition only. The other is a crooked lumbering animal, put together
at random; he has a short thick neck; he is flat-faced and of a dark
colour, with grey eyes and blood-red complexion; the mate of insolence and pride, shag-eared and deaf, hardly yielding to whip and spur.
Now when the charioteer beholds the vision of love, and has his whole
soul warmed through sense, and is full of the prickings and ticklings

of desire, the obedient steed, then as always under the government of   254
shame, refrains from leaping on the beloved; but the other, heedless of
the pricks and of the blows of the whip, plunges and runs away, giving
all manner of trouble to his companion and the charioteer, whom he
forces to approach the beloved and to remember the joys of love. They
at first indignantly oppose him and will not be urged on to do terrible   b
and unlawful deeds; but at last, when he persists in plaguing them, they
yield and agree to do as he bids them. And now they are at the spot and
behold the flashing beauty of the beloved; which when the charioteer
sees, his memory is carried to the true beauty, whom he beholds in
company with Modesty like an image placed upon a holy pedestal. He
sees her, but he is afraid and falls backwards in adoration, and by his   c
fall is compelled to pull back the reins with such violence as to bring
both the steeds on their haunches, the one willing and unresisting, the
unruly one very unwilling; and when they have gone back a little, the
one is overcome with shame and wonder, and his whole soul is bathed
in perspiration; the other, when the pain is over which the bridle and
the fall had given him, having with difficulty taken breath, is full of
wrath and reproaches, which he heaps upon the charioteer and his
fellow-steed, for want of courage and manhood, declaring that they
have been false to their agreement and guilty of desertion. Again they   d
refuse, and again he urges them on, and will scarcely yield to their
prayer that he would wait until another time. When the appointed hour
comes, they make as if they had forgotten, and he reminds them, fighting and neighing and dragging them on, until at length he, on the
same thoughts intent, forces them to draw near again. And when they
are near he stoops his head and puts up his tail, and takes the bit in his
teeth and pulls shamelessly. Then the charioteer is worse off than ever;
he falls back like a racer at the barrier, and with a still more violent   e
wrench drags the bit out of the teeth of the wild steed and covers his
abusive tongue and jaws with blood, and forces his legs and haunches
to the ground and punishes him sorely. And when this has happened several times and the villain has ceased from his wanton way, he is tamed
and humbled, and follows the will of the charioteer, and when he sees
the beautiful one he is ready to die of fear. And from that time forward
the soul of the lover follows the beloved in modesty and holy fear.

And so the beloved who, like a god, has received every true and   255
loyal service from his lover, not in pretence but in reality, being also
himself of a nature friendly to his admirer, if in former days he has
blushed to own his passion and turned away his lover, because his
youthful companions or others slanderously told him that he would be
disgraced, now as years advance, at the appointed age and time, is led
by necessity to get together with him. For fate which has ordained that   b

there shall be no friendship among the evil has also ordained that there shall ever be friendship among the good. And the beloved when he has received him into intimacy, is quite amazed at the good-will of the lover; he recognizes that the inspired friend is worth all other friends or kinsmen; they have nothing of friendship in them worthy to be compared with his. And when his feeling continues and he is nearer to him and embraces him, in gymnastic exercises and at other times of

c meeting, then the fountain of that stream, which Zeus when he was in love with Ganymede* named Desire, overflows upon the lover, and some enters into his soul, and some when he is filled flows out again; and as a breeze or an echo rebounds from the smooth rocks and returns whence it came, so does the stream of beauty, passing through the eyes which are the windows of the soul, come back to the beauti-

d ful one; there arriving and quickening the passages of the wings, watering them and inclining them to grow, and filling the soul of the beloved also with love. And thus he loves, but he knows not what; he does not understand and cannot explain his own state; he appears to have caught the infection of blindness from another; the lover is his mirror in whom he is beholding himself, but he is not aware of this. When he is with the lover, both cease from their pain, but when he is away then he longs as he is longed for, and has love's image, love for love lodging in his breast, which he calls and believes to be not love

e but friendship only, and his desire is as the desire of the other, but weaker; he wants to see him, touch him, kiss, embrace him, and probably not long afterwards his desire is accomplished. When they meet, the wanton steed of the lover has a word to say to the charioteer; he

256 would like to have a little pleasure in return for many pains, but the wanton steed of the beloved says not a word, for he is bursting with passion which he understands not; he throws his arms round the lover and embraces him as his dearest friend; and, when they are side by side, he is not in a state in which he can refuse the lover anything, if he asks him; although his fellow-steed and the charioteer oppose him with the arguments of shame and reason. After this their happiness depends upon their self-control; if the better elements of the mind which lead to order and philosophy prevail, then they pass their life here in

b happiness and harmony—masters of themselves and orderly—enslaving the vicious and emancipating the virtuous elements of the soul; and when the end comes, they are light and winged for flight, having conquered in one of the three heavenly or truly Olympian victories;[9] nor can human discipline or divine inspiration confer any greater blessing

---

*Young Trojan prince that Zeus kidnapped as a companion; see Iliad 20.231ff.

on man than this. If, on the other hand, they leave philosophy and lead
the lower life of ambition, then probably, after wine or in some other   c
careless hour, the two wanton animals take the two souls when off
their guard and bring them together, and they accomplish that desire
of their hearts which to the many is bliss; and this having once enjoyed
they continue to enjoy, yet rarely, because they have not the approval of
the whole soul. They too are dear, but not so dear to one another as the   d
others, either at the time of their love or afterwards. They consider that
they have given and taken from each other the most sacred pledges,
and they may not break them and fall into enmity. At last they pass out
of the body, unwinged, but eager to soar, and thus obtain no mean reward of love and madness. For those who have once begun the heaven-
ward pilgrimage may not go down again to darkness and the journey
beneath the earth, but they live in light always; happy companions in
their pilgrimage, and when the time comes at which they receive their   e
wings they have the same plumage because of their love.

Thus great are the heavenly blessings which the friendship of a
lover will confer upon you, my youth. Whereas the attachment of the
non-lover, which is alloyed with a worldly prudence and has worldly
and niggardly ways of doling out benefits, will breed in your soul those
vulgar qualities which the populace applaud, will send you bowling
round the earth during a period of nine thousand years, and leave you   257
a fool in the world below.

And thus, dear Eros, I have made and paid my recantation, as well
and as fairly as I could; more especially in the matter of the poetical figures which I was compelled to use, because Phaedrus would have
them. And now forgive the past and accept the present, and be gracious
and merciful to me, and do not in thine anger deprive me of sight, or
take from me the art of love which thou hast given me, but grant that
I may be yet more esteemed in the eyes of the fair. And if Phaedrus or
I myself said anything rude in our first speeches, blame Lysias, who is   b
the father of the brat, and let us have no more of his progeny; bid him
study philosophy, like his brother Polemarchus; and then his lover
Phaedrus will no longer halt between two opinions, but will dedicate
himself wholly to love and to philosophical discourses.

PHAEDR. I join in the prayer, Socrates, and say with you, if this be for
my good, may your words come to pass. But why did you make your
second oration so much finer than the first? I wonder why. And I think   c
that Lysias would appear tame in comparison, even if he were willing
to put another as fine and as long as yours into the field, which I doubt.
For quite lately one of your politicians was abusing him on this very
account; and called him a 'speech-writer' again and again. So that a
feeling of pride may probably induce him to give up writing speeches.

Soc. What a very amusing notion! But I think, my young man, that
d you are much mistaken about your friend if you imagine that he is
frightened at a little noise; and possibly, you think that his assailant was
in earnest?

PHAEDR. I thought, Socrates, that he was. And you are aware that the
greatest and most influential statesmen are ashamed of writing
speeches and leaving them in a written form, lest they should be called
Sophists by posterity.

Soc. You seem to be unaware, Phaedrus, that the 'Pleasant Bend' of
e the proverb is really the long arm of the Nile.[10] And you appear to be
equally unaware of the fact that this sweet elbow of theirs is also a long
arm. For there is nothing of which our great politicians are so fond as
of writing speeches and bequeathing them to posterity. And they add
their admirers' names at the top of the writing, out of gratitude to them.

258   PHAEDR. What do you mean? I do not understand.

Soc. Why, do you not know that when a politician writes, he begins with the names of his supporters?

PHAEDR. How so?

Soc. Why, he begins in this manner: 'The council, the people, or
both, decided, on the motion of a certain person,' who is our author;
and so putting on a serious face, he proceeds to display his own wisdom to his supporters in what is often a long and tedious composition.
Now what is that sort of thing but a regular piece of speech-writing?

b   PHAEDR. True.

Soc. And if the law is finally approved, then the author leaves the
theatre in high delight; but if the law is rejected and he is done out of
his speech-making, and not thought good enough to write, then he
and his party are in mourning.

PHAEDR. Very true.

Soc. So far are they from despising, or rather so highly do they
value the practice of writing.

PHAEDR. No doubt.

c   Soc. And when the king or orator is so powerful, as Lycurgus or
Solon or Darius were, that their speeches become immortal, is he not
thought by posterity, when they see his compositions, and does he not
think himself, while he is yet alive, to be a god?

PHAEDR. Very true.

Soc. Then do you think that anyone of this class, however ill-
disposed, would reproach Lysias with being an author?

PHAEDR. Not upon your view; for according to you he would be
casting a slur upon his own favourite pursuit.

d   Soc. Anyone may see that there is no disgrace in the mere fact of
writing speeches.

PHAEDR. Certainly not.

SOC. The disgrace begins when a man writes not well, but badly.

PHAEDR. Clearly.

SOC. And what is well and what is badly—need we ask Lysias, or any other poet or orator, who ever wrote or will write either a political or any other work, in metre or out of metre, poet or prose writer, to teach us this?

PHAEDR. Need we? What should a man live for if not for the pleasures of discourse? Surely not for the sake of bodily pleasures, which almost always have previous pain as a condition of them, and therefore are rightly called slavish.

SOC. There is time enough. And I believe that the grasshoppers chirruping after their manner in the heat of the sun over our heads are talking to one another and looking down at us. What would they say if they saw that we, like the many, are not conversing, but slumbering at mid-day, lulled by their voices, too indolent to think? Would they not have a right to laugh at us? They might imagine that we were slaves, who, coming to rest at a place of resort of theirs, like sheep lie asleep at noon around the well. But if they see us discoursing, and like Odysseus sailing past them, deaf to their siren voices, they may perhaps, out of respect, give us of the gifts which they receive from the gods in order that they may impart them to men.

PHAEDR. What gifts do you mean? I never heard of any.

SOC. A lover of music like yourself ought surely to have heard the story of the grasshoppers, who are said to have been human beings in an age before the Muses. And when the Muses came and song appeared they were ravished with delight; and singing always, never thought of eating and drinking, until at last in their forgetfulness they died. And now they live again in the grasshoppers; and this is the return which the Muses make to them—they neither hunger, nor thirst, but from the hour of their birth are always singing, and never eating or drinking; and when they die they go and inform the Muses in heaven who honors them on earth. They win the love of Terpsichore for the dancers by their report of them; of Erato for the lovers, and of the other Muses for those who do them honor, according to the several ways of honoring them; of Calliope the eldest Muse and of Urania who is next to her, for the philosophers, of whose music the grasshoppers make report to them; for these are the Muses who are chiefly concerned with heaven and thought, divine as well as human, and they have the sweetest utterance. For many reasons, then, we ought always to talk and not to sleep at mid-day.

PHAEDR. Let us talk.

SOC. Shall we discuss the rules of writing and speech as we were proposing?

PHAEDR. Very good.

SOC. In good speaking should not the mind of the speaker know the truth of the matter about which he is going to speak?

260   PHAEDR. And yet, Socrates, I have heard that he who would be an orator has nothing to do with true justice, but only with that which is likely to be approved by the many who sit in judgment; nor with the truly good or honorable, but only with opinion about them, and that from opinion comes persuasion, and not from the truth.

SOC. The words of the wise are not to be set aside; for there is probably something in them; and therefore the meaning of this saying is not hastily to be dismissed.

PHAEDR. Very true.

b   SOC. Let us put the matter thus: Suppose that I persuaded you to buy a horse and go to war. Neither of us knew what a horse was like, but I knew that you believed a horse to be of tame animals the one which has the longest ears.

PHAEDR. That would be ridiculous.

SOC. There is something more ridiculous coming: Suppose, further, that in sober earnest I, having persuaded you of this, went and composed a speech in honor of an ass, whom I entitled a horse, beginning: 'A noble animal and a most useful possession, especially in war, and

c   you may get on his back and fight, and he will carry baggage or anything.'

PHAEDR. How ridiculous!

SOC. Ridiculous! Yes; but is not even a ridiculous friend better than a cunning enemy?

PHAEDR. Certainly.

SOC. And when the orator instead of putting an ass in the place of a horse puts good for evil, being himself as ignorant of their true nature as the city on which he imposes is ignorant; and having studied the notions of the multitude, falsely persuades them not about 'the shadow of an ass,' which he confounds with a horse, but about good which he confounds with evil, what will be the harvest which rheto-

d   ric will be likely to gather after the sowing of that seed?

PHAEDR. The reverse of good.

SOC. But perhaps rhetoric has been getting too roughly handled by us, and she might answer: What amazing nonsense you are talking! As if I forced any man to learn to speak in ignorance of the truth! Whatever my advice may be worth, I should have told him to arrive at the truth first, and then come to me. At the same time I boldly assert that mere knowledge of the truth will not give you the art of persuasion.

e   PHAEDR. There is reason in the lady's defense of herself.

SOC. Quite true; if only the other arguments which remain to be brought up bear her witness that she is an art at all. But I seem to hear them arraying themselves on the opposite side, declaring that she speaks falsely, and that rhetoric is a mere routine and trick, not an art. To put it bluntly, there never is nor ever will be a real art of speaking which is divorced from the truth.

PHAEDR. And what are these arguments, Socrates? Bring them out so 261 that we may examine them.

SOC. Come out, fair children, and convince Phaedrus, who is the father of similar beauties, that he will never be able to speak about anything as he ought to speak unless he has a knowledge of philosophy. And let Phaedrus answer you.

PHAEDR. Put the question.

SOC. Is not rhetoric, taken generally, a universal art of enchanting the mind by arguments, which is practised not only in courts and public assemblies, but in private houses also, having to do with all matters, great as well as small, good and bad alike, and is in all equally right, b and equally to be esteemed—that is what you have heard?

PHAEDR. Nay, not exactly that; I should say rather that I have heard the art confined to speaking and writing in lawsuits, and to speaking in public assemblies—not extended farther.

SOC. Then I suppose that you have only heard of the rhetoric of Nestor and Odysseus, which they composed in their leisure hours when at Troy, and never of the rhetoric of Palamedes?[11]

PHAEDR. No more than of Nestor and Odysseus, unless Gorgias is c your Nestor, and Thrasymachus or Theodorus* your Odysseus.

SOC. Perhaps that is my meaning. But let us leave them. And do you tell me, instead, what are plaintiff and defendant doing in a law court—are they not contending?

PHAEDR. Exactly so.

SOC. About the just and unjust—that is the matter in dispute?

PHAEDR. Yes.

SOC. And a professor of the art will make the same thing appear to the same persons to be at one time just, at another time, if he is so in- d clined, to be unjust?

PHAEDR. Exactly.

SOC. And when he speaks in the assembly, he will make the same things seem good to the city at one time, and at another time the reverse of good?

PHAEDR. That is true.

---

*Thrasymachus: a Sophist, and the main interlocutor of Socrates in book I of *Republic*. Theodorus: not the mathematician of Plato's *Theaetetus*; on his thought, see 266e.

SOC. Have we not heard of the Eleatic Palamedes,* who has an art of speaking by which he makes the same things appear to his hearers like and unlike, one and many, at rest and in motion?

PHAEDR. Very true.

SOC. The art of disputation, then, is not confined to the courts and the assembly, but is one and the same in every use of language; this is the art, if there be such an art, which is able to find a likeness of everything to which a likeness can be found, and draws into the light of day the likenesses and disguises which are used by others?

PHAEDR. How do you mean?

SOC. Let me put the matter thus: When will there be more chance of deception—when the difference is large or small?

PHAEDR. When the difference is small.

SOC. And you will be less likely to be discovered in passing by degrees into the other extreme than when you go all at once?

PHAEDR. Of course.

SOC. He, then, who would deceive others, and not be deceived, must exactly know the real likenesses and differences of things?

PHAEDR. He must.

SOC. And if he is ignorant of the true nature of any subject, how can he detect the greater or less degree of likeness in other things to that of which by the hypothesis he is ignorant?

PHAEDR. He cannot.

SOC. And when men are deceived and their notions are at variance with realities, it is clear that the error slips in through resemblances?

PHAEDR. Yes, that is the way.

SOC. Then he who would be a master of the art must understand the real nature of everything; or he will never know either how to make the gradual departure from truth into the opposite of truth which is effected by the help of resemblances, or how to avoid it?

PHAEDR. He will not.

SOC. He then, who being ignorant of the truth aims at appearances, will only attain an art of rhetoric which is ridiculous and is not an art at all?

PHAEDR. That may be expected.

SOC. Shall I propose that we look for examples of art and want of art, according to our notion of them, in the speech of Lysias which you have in your hand, and in my own speech?

PHAEDR. Nothing could be better; and indeed I think that our previous argument has been too abstract and wanting in illustrations.

---

*Reference to the pre-Socratic philosopher Zeno of Elea.

Soc. Yes; and the two speeches happen to afford a very good ex-   *d*
ample of the way in which the speaker who knows the truth may, without any serious purpose, steal away the hearts of his hearers. This piece
of good-fortune I attribute to the local deities; and perhaps, the prophets
of the Muses who are singing over our heads may have imparted their
inspiration to me. For I do not imagine that I have any rhetorical art of
my own.

Phaedr. Granted; if you will only please get on.

Soc. Suppose that you read me the first words of Lysias' speech.

Phaedr. 'You know how matters stand with me, and how, as I con-   *e*
ceive, they might be arranged for our common interest; and I maintain
that I ought not to fail in my suit, because I am not your lover. For
lovers repent——'

Soc. Enough. Now, shall I point out the rhetorical error of those   263
words?

Phaedr. Yes.

Soc. Everyone is aware that about some things we are agreed,
whereas about other things we differ.

Phaedr. I think that I understand you; but will you explain yourself?

Soc. When anyone speaks of iron and silver, is not the same thing
present in the minds of all?

Phaedr. Certainly.

Soc. But when anyone speaks of justice and goodness we part company and are at odds with one another and with ourselves?

Phaedr. Precisely.

Soc. Then in some things we mean the same things, but not in   *b*
others?

Phaedr. That is true.

Soc. In which are we more likely to be deceived, and in which has
rhetoric the greater power?

Phaedr. Clearly, in the uncertain class.

Soc. Then the rhetorician ought to make a regular division, and acquire a distinct notion of both classes, as well of that in which the
many err, as of that in which they do not err?

Phaedr. He who made such a distinction would have an excellent   *c*
principle.

Soc. Yes; and in the next place he must have a keen eye for the observation of particulars in speaking, and not make a mistake about the
class to which they are to be referred.

Phaedr. Certainly.

Soc. Now to which class does love belong—to the debatable or to
the undisputed class?

Phaedr. To the debatable, clearly; for if not, do you think that Love would have allowed you to say as you did, that he is an evil both to the lover and the beloved, and also the greatest possible good?

d   Soc. That is extremely well put. But will you tell me whether I defined love at the beginning of my speech? for, having been in an ecstasy, I cannot well remember.

PHAEDR. Yes, indeed; that you did, absolutely.

Soc. Then I perceive that the Nymphs of Achelous and Pan* the son of Hermes, who inspired me, were far better rhetoricians than Lysias the son of Cephalus. Alas! how inferior to them he is! But perhaps I am mistaken; and Lysias at the commencement of his lover's speech did insist on our supposing Love to be something or other which he fancied him to be, and according to this model he fashioned e   and framed the remainder of his discourse. Suppose we read his beginning over again:

PHAEDR. If you please; but you will not find what you want.

Soc. Read, that I may have his exact words.

PHAEDR. 'You know how matters stand with me, and how, as I con-
264   ceive, they might be arranged for our common interest; and I maintain I ought not to fail in my suit because I am not your lover, for lovers repent of the kindnesses which they have shown, when their love is over.'

Soc. Here he appears to have done just the reverse of what he ought; for he has begun at the end, and is swimming on his back through the flood to the starting place. His address to the fair youth begins where the lover would have ended. Am I not right, sweet Phaedrus?

b   PHAEDR. Yes, indeed, Socrates; he does begin at the end.

Soc. Then as to the other topics—are they not thrown down anyhow? Is there any principle in them? Why should the next topic follow next in order, or any other topic? I cannot help fancying in my ignorance that he wrote off boldly just what came into his head, but I dare say that you would recognize a rhetorical necessity in the succession of the several parts of the composition?

c   PHAEDR. You have too good an opinion of me if you think that I have any such insight into his principles of composition.

Soc. At any rate, you will allow that every discourse ought to be a living creature, having a body of its own and a head and feet; there should be a middle, beginning, and end, adapted to one another and to the whole?

PHAEDR. Certainly.

---

*Half-man, half-goat in appearance; god of shepherds and other dwellers of the wild.

Soc. Can this be said of the discourse of Lysias? See whether you can find any more connection in his words than in the epitaph which is said by some to have been inscribed on the grave of Midas the Phrygian.*

PHAEDR. What is there remarkable in the epitaph?   *d*
Soc. It is as follows:—

> 'I am a maiden of bronze and lie on the tomb of Midas;
> So long as water flows and tall trees grow,
> So long here on this spot by his sad tomb abiding,
> I shall declare to passers-by that Midas sleeps below.'

Now in this rhyme whether a line comes first or comes last, as you will   *e*
perceive, makes no difference.

PHAEDR. You are making fun of that oration of ours.
Soc. Well, I will say no more about your friend's speech lest I should give offence to you; although I think that it might furnish many other examples of what a man ought rather to avoid. But I will proceed   265 to the other speech, which, as I think, is also suitable for students of rhetoric.

PHAEDR. In what way?
Soc. The two speeches, as you may remember, were unlike; the one argued that the lover and the other that the non-lover ought to be accepted.

PHAEDR. And very manfully.
Soc. You should rather say 'madly'; and madness was the argument of them, for, as I said, 'love is a madness.'

PHAEDR. Yes.
Soc. And of madness there were two kinds; one produced by human infirmity, the other was a divine release of the soul from the yoke of custom and convention.

PHAEDR. True.   *b*
Soc. The divine madness was subdivided into four kinds, prophetic, initiatory, poetic, erotic, having four gods presiding over them; the first was the inspiration of Apollo, the second that of Dionysus, the third that of the Muses, the fourth that of Aphrodite and Eros. In the description of the last kind of madness, which was also said to be the best, we spoke of the affection of love in a figure, into which we introduced a tolerably credible and possibly true though partly erring

---

*Legendary Phrygian king (eighth century B.C.E.).

myth, which was also a hymn in honor of Love, who is your lord and
c   also mine, Phaedrus, and the guardian of fair children, and to him we
sung the hymn in measured and solemn strain.

PHAEDR. I know that I had great pleasure in listening to you.

SOC. Let us take this instance and note how the transition was made
from blame to praise.

PHAEDR. What do you mean?

SOC. I mean to say that the composition was mostly playful. Yet in
these chance fancies of the hour were involved two principles of which
d   we should be too glad to have a clearer description if art could give
us one.

PHAEDR. What are they?

SOC. First, the comprehension of scattered particulars in one idea;
as in our definition of love, which whether true or false certainly gave
clearness and consistency to the discourse, the speaker should define
his several notions and so make his meaning clear.

PHAEDR. What is the other principle, Socrates?

e   SOC. The second principle is that of division into species according
to the natural formation, where the joint is, not breaking any part as a
266 bad carver might. Just as our two discourses, alike assumed, first of all,
a single form of unreason; and then, as the body which from being one
becomes double and may be divided into a left side and right side, each
having parts right and left of the same name—after this manner the
speaker proceeded to divide the parts of the left side and did not desist
until he found in them an evil or left-handed love which he justly reviled; and the other discourse leading us to the madness which lay on
the right side, found another love, also having the same name, but di-
b   vine, which the speaker held up before us and applauded and affirmed
to be the author of the greatest benefits.

PHAEDR. Most true.

SOC. I am myself a great lover of these processes of division and
generalization; they help me to speak and to think. And if I find any
man who is able to see 'a One and Many' in nature, him I follow, and
'walk in his footsteps as if he were a god.' And those who have this art,
c   I have hitherto been in the habit of calling dialecticians; but god knows
whether the name is right or not. And I should like to know what name
you would give to your or to Lysias' disciples, and whether this may
not be that famous art of rhetoric which Thrasymachus and others
teach and practise? Skilful speakers they are, and impart their skill to
any who is willing to make kings of them and to bring gifts to them.

PHAEDR. Yes, they are royal men; but their art is not the same with
the art of those whom you call, and rightly, in my opinion, dialecticians: Still we are in the dark about rhetoric.

Soc. What do you mean? The remains of it, if there be anything re- *d* maining which can be brought under rules of art, must be a fine thing; and, at any rate, is not to be despised by you and me. But how much is left?

PHAEDR. There is a great deal surely to be found in books of rhetoric?

Soc. Yes; thank you for reminding me: There is the exordium, showing how the speech should begin, if I remember rightly; that is what you mean—the niceties of the art?

PHAEDR. Yes. *e*

Soc. Then follows the statement of facts, and upon that witnesses; thirdly, proofs; fourthly, probabilities are to come; the great Byzantian word-maker also speaks, if I am not mistaken, of confirmation and further confirmation.

PHAEDR. You mean the excellent Theodorus.

Soc. Yes; and he tells how refutation or further refutation is to be *267* managed, whether in accusation or defence. I ought also to mention the illustrious Parian, Evenus,* who first invented insinuations and indirect praises; and also indirect censures, which according to some he put into verse to help the memory. But shall I 'to dumb forgetfulness consign' Tisias† and Gorgias, who are not ignorant that probability is superior to truth, and who by force of argument make the little appear great and the great little, disguise the new in old fashions and the old *b* in new fashions, and have discovered forms for everything, either short or going on to infinity. I remember Prodicus‡ laughing when I told him of this; he said that he had himself discovered the true rule of art, which was to be neither long nor short, but of a convenient length.

PHAEDR. Well done, Prodicus!

Soc. Then there is Hippias the gentleman from Elis,§ who probably agrees with him.

PHAEDR. Yes.

Soc. And there is also Polus,‖ who has treasuries of diplasiology and gnomology, and eikonology, and who teaches in them the names of *c* which Licymnius# made him a present; they were to give a polish.

---

*Minor Sophist who specialized in literary composition and invented rhetorical devices.
†Rhetorician from Sicily, whose teachings Gorgias of Leontini (see "General Introduction," p. xxi) may have followed.
‡Prodicus of Ceos was a well-known Sophist and diplomat, and a contemporary of Socrates.
§See "Introduction" to *Shorter Hippias*.
‖A master rhetorician (see "Introduction" to *Gorgias*).
#Rhetorician and author of dithyrambs.

PHAEDR. Had not Protagoras* something of the same sort?

SOC. Yes, rules of correct diction and many other fine precepts; for the 'sorrows of a poor old man,' or any other pathetic case, no one is better than the Chalcedonian giant;† he can put a whole company of people into a passion and out of one again by his mighty magic, and is first-rate at inventing or disposing of any sort of calumny on any grounds or none. All of them agree in asserting that a speech should end in a recapitulation, though they do not all agree to use the same word.

PHAEDR. You mean that there should be a summing up of the arguments in order to remind the hearers of them.

SOC. I have now said all that I have to say of the art of rhetoric: have you anything to add?

PHAEDR. Not much; nothing very important.

SOC. Leave the unimportant and let us bring the really important question into the light of day, which is: What power has this art of rhetoric, and when?

PHAEDR. A very great power in public meetings.

SOC. It has. But I should like to know whether you have the same feeling as I have about the rhetoricians? To me there seem to be a great many holes in their web.

PHAEDR. Give an example.

SOC. I will. Suppose a person comes to your friend Eryximachus,‡ or to his father Acumenus, and says to him: 'I know how to apply drugs which shall have either a heating or a cooling effect, and I can give a vomit and also a purge, and all that sort of thing; and knowing all this, as I do, I claim to be a physician and to make physicians by imparting this knowledge to others,'—what do you suppose that they would say?

PHAEDR. They would be sure to ask him whether he knew 'to whom' he would give his medicines, and 'when,' and 'how much.'

SOC. And suppose that he were to reply: 'No; I know nothing of all that; I expect the patient who consults me to be able to do these things for himself'?

PHAEDR. They would say in reply that he is a madman or a pedant who fancies that he is a physician because he has read something in a book, or has stumbled on a prescription or two, although he has no real understanding of the art of medicine.

SOC. And suppose a person were to come to Sophocles or Euripides and say that he knows how to make a very long speech about a small

---

*See "Introduction" to *Protagoras*.

†Reference to Thrasymachus of Chalcedon, the Sophist who engages Socrates in conversation in book 1 of *Republic*.

‡See "Introduction" to *Symposium*.

matter, and a short speech about a great matter, and also a sorrowful speech, or a terrible, or threatening speech, or any other kind of speech, and in teaching this fancies that he is teaching the art of tragedy—what would they do?

PHAEDR. They too would surely laugh at him if he fancies that tragedy is anything but the arranging of these elements in a manner which will be suitable to one another and to the whole.

SOC. But I do not suppose that they would be rude or abusive to him: Would they not treat him as a musician would a man who thinks that he is a harmonist because he knows how to pitch the highest and lowest note; happening to meet such a person he would not say to him savagely, 'Fool, you are mad!' But like a musician, in a gentle and harmonious tone of voice, he would answer: 'My good friend, he who would be a harmonist must certainly know this, and yet he may understand nothing of harmony if he has not got beyond your stage of knowledge, for you only know the preliminaries of harmony and not harmony itself.'

PHAEDR. Very true.

SOC. And will not Sophocles say to the display of the would-be tragedian, that this is not tragedy but the preliminaries of tragedy? and will not Acumenus say the same of medicine to the would-be physician?

PHAEDR. Quite true.

SOC. And if Adrastus* the mellifluous or Pericles heard of these wonderful arts, brachylogies and eikonologies and all the hard names which we have been endeavouring to draw into the light of day, what would they say? Instead of losing temper and applying uncomplimentary epithets, as you and I have been doing, to the authors of such an imaginary art, their superior wisdom would rather censure us, as well as them. 'Have a little patience, Phaedrus and Socrates, they would say; you should not be so angry with those who from some want of dialectical skill are unable to define the nature of rhetoric, and consequently suppose that they have found the art in the preliminary conditions of it, and when these have been taught by them to others, fancy that the whole art of rhetoric has been taught by them; but as to using the several instruments of the art effectively, or making the composition a whole—an application of it such as this is they regard as an easy thing which their disciples may make for themselves.'

PHAEDR. I quite admit, Socrates, that the art of rhetoric which these men teach and of which they write is such as you describe—there I

---

*Warrior featured in Euripides' *Suppliants*.

agree with you. But I still want to know where and how the true art of
d   rhetoric and persuasion is to be acquired.

Soc. The perfection which is required of the finished orator is, or
rather must be, like the perfection of anything else, partly given by nature, but may also be assisted by art. If you have the natural power and
add to it knowledge and practice, you will be a distinguished speaker;
if you fall short in either of these, you will be to that extent defective.
But the art, as far as there is an art, of rhetoric does not lie in the direction of Lysias or Thrasymachus.

Phaedr. In what direction then?

e   Soc. I conceive Pericles to have been the most accomplished of
rhetoricians.

Phaedr. How come?

Soc. All the great arts require discussion and high speculation about
270 the truths of nature; hence come loftiness of thought and completeness
of execution. And this, as I conceive, was the quality which in addition
to his natural gifts, Pericles acquired from his intercourse with
Anaxagoras whom he happened to know. He was thus imbued with the
higher philosophy, and attained the knowledge of Mind and the negative of Mind, which were favourite themes of Anaxagoras,* and applied
what suited his purpose to the art of speaking.

Phaedr. Explain.

b   Soc. Rhetoric is like medicine.

Phaedr. What do you mean?

Soc. Why, because medicine has to define the nature of the body
and rhetoric of the soul—if we would proceed, not empirically but scientifically, in the one case to impart health and strength by giving medicine and food, in the other to implant the conviction or virtue which
you desire, by the right application of words and training.

Phaedr. There, Socrates, I suspect that you are right.

c   Soc. And do you think that you can know the nature of the soul in-
telligently without knowing the nature of the whole?

Phaedr. Hippocrates the Asclepiad says that the nature even of the
body can only be understood as a whole.[12]

Soc. Yes, friend, and he was right; still, we ought not to be content
with the name of Hippocrates, but to examine and see whether his argument agrees with his conception of nature.

Phaedr. I agree.

Soc. Then consider what truth, as well as Hippocrates, says about
d   this or about any other nature. Ought we not to consider first whether

---

*Pre-Socratic philosopher (see "General Introduction," p. xxi).

that which we wish to learn and to teach is a simple or multiform thing, and if simple, then to enquire what power it has of acting or being acted upon in relation to other things, and if multiform, then to number the forms; and see first in the case of one of them, and then in the case of all of them, what is that power of acting or being acted upon which makes each and all of them to be what they are?

PHAEDR. You may very likely be right, Socrates.

SOC. The method which proceeds without analysis is like the groping of a blind man. Yet, surely, he who is an artist ought not to admit of a comparison with the blind, or deaf. The rhetorician, who teaches his pupil to speak scientifically, will particularly set forth the nature of that being to which he addresses his speeches; and this, I conceive, to be the soul.

PHAEDR. Certainly.

SOC. His whole effort is directed to the soul; for in that he seeks to produce conviction.

PHAEDR. Yes.

SOC. Then clearly, Thrasymachus or anyone else who teaches rhetoric in earnest will give an exact description of the nature of the soul; which will enable us to see whether it is single and same, or, like the body, multiform. That is what we should call showing the nature of the soul.

PHAEDR. Exactly.

SOC. He will explain, secondly, the mode in which it acts or is acted upon.

PHAEDR. True.

SOC. Thirdly, having classified men and speeches, and their kinds and affections, and adapted them to one another, he will tell the reasons of his arrangement, and show why one soul is persuaded by a particular form of argument, and another not.

PHAEDR. You have hit upon a very good way.

SOC. Yes, that is the true and only way in which any subject can be set forth or treated by rules of art, whether in speaking or writing. But the writers of the present day, at whose feet you have sat, craftily hide what they know quite well about the soul. Until they adopt our method of reading and writing, let us not admit that they write by rules of art?

PHAEDR. What is our method?

SOC. I cannot give you the exact details; but I should like to tell you generally, as far as is in my power, how a man ought to proceed according to rules of art.

PHAEDR. Let me hear.

SOC. Oratory is the art of enchanting the soul, and therefore he who would be an orator has to learn the differences of human souls—they are so many and of such a nature, and from them come the differences between man and man. Having proceeded thus far in his analysis, he will next divide speeches into their different classes:—'Such and such persons,' he will say, 'are affected by this or that kind of speech in this or that way,' and he will tell you why. The pupil must have a good theoretical notion of them first, and then he must have experience of them in actual life, and be able to follow them with all his senses about him, or he will never get beyond the precepts of his masters. But when he understands what persons are persuaded by what arguments, and sees the person about whom he was speaking in the abstract actually before him, and knows that it is he, and can say to himself, 'This is the man or this is the character who ought to have a certain argument applied to him in order to convince him of a certain opinion;'—he who knows all this, and knows also when he should speak and when he should refrain, and when he should use pithy sayings, pathetic appeals, sensational effects, and all the other modes of speech which he has learned; when, I say, he knows the times and seasons of all these things, then, and not till then, he is a perfect master of his art; but if he fails in any of these points, whether in speaking or teaching or writing them, and yet declares that he speaks by rules of art, he who says 'I don't believe you' has the better of him. Well, the teacher will say, is this, Phaedrus and Socrates, your account of the so-called art of rhetoric, or am I to look for another?

PHAEDR. He must take this, Socrates, for there is no possibility of another, and yet the creation of such an art is not easy.

Soc. Very true; and therefore let us consider this matter in every light, and see whether we cannot find a shorter and easier road; there is no use in taking a long rough round-about way if there be a shorter and easier one. And I wish that you would try and remember whether you have heard from Lysias or anyone else anything which might be of service to us.

PHAEDR. If trying would avail, then I might; but at the moment I can think of nothing.

Soc. Suppose I tell you something which somebody who knows told me.

PHAEDR. Certainly.

Soc. May not 'the wolf,' as the proverb says, 'claim a hearing'?*

PHAEDR. You be the wolf.

Soc. He will argue that there is no use in putting a solemn face on these matters, or in going round and round, until you arrive at first

---

*"May I play devil's advocate?" would be the English idiom.

principles; for, as I said at first, when the question is of justice and good, or is a question in which men are concerned who are just and good, either by nature or habit, he who would be a skilful rhetorician has no need of truth—for that in courts of law men literally care noth- e ing about truth, but only about persuasion: and this is based on prob- ability, to which he who would be a skilful orator should therefore give his whole attention. And they say also that there are cases in which the ac- tual facts, if they are improbable, ought to be withheld, and only the probabilities should be told either in accusation or defence, and that al- ways in speaking, the orator should keep probability in view, and say good-bye to the truth. And the observance of this principle throughout 273 a speech furnishes the whole art.

PHAEDR. That is what the professors of rhetoric do actually say, Socrates. I have not forgotten that we have quite briefly touched upon this matter already; with them the point is all-important.

SOC. I dare say that you are familiar with Tisias.* Does he not de- b fine probability to be that which the many think?

PHAEDR. Certainly, he does.

SOC. I believe that he has a clever and ingenious case of this sort: He supposes a feeble and valiant man to have assaulted a strong and cowardly one, and to have robbed him of his coat or of something or other; he is brought into court, and then Tisias says that both parties should tell lies: the coward should say that he was assaulted by more men than one; the other should prove that they were alone, and should c argue thus: 'How could a weak man like me have assaulted a strong man like him?' The complainant will not like to confess his own cow- ardice, and will therefore invent some other lie which his adversary will thus gain an opportunity of refuting. And there are other devices of the same kind which have a place in the system. Am I not right, Phaedrus?

PHAEDR. Certainly.

SOC. Bless me, what a wonderfully mysterious art is this which Tisias or some other gentleman, in whatever name or country he re- joices, has discovered. Shall we say a word to him or not?

PHAEDR. What shall we say to him? d

SOC. Let us tell him that, before he appeared, you and I were saying that the probability of which he speaks was engendered in the minds of the many by the likeness of the truth, and we had just been affirm- ing that he who knew the truth would always know best how to dis- cover the resemblances of the truth. If he has anything else to say about

---

*Rhetorician from Sicily (see footnote on p. 241).

the art of speaking we would hear him; but if not, we are satisfied with
our own view, that unless a man estimates the various characters of his
hearers and is able to divide all things into classes and to comprehend
e them under single ideas, he will never be a skilful rhetorician even within
the limits of human power. And this skill he will not attain without a
great deal of trouble, which a good man ought to undergo, not for the
sake of speaking and acting before men, but in order that he may be
able to say what is acceptable to god and always to act acceptably to
274 him as far as in him lies; for there is a saying of wiser men than ourselves, that a man of sense should not try to please his fellow-servants
(at least this should not be his first object) but his good and noble masters; and therefore if the way is long and circuitous, marvel not at this,
for, where the end is great, there we may take the longer road, but not
for lesser ends such as yours. Truly, the argument may say, Tisias, that if
you do not mind going so far, rhetoric has a fair beginning here.

PHAEDR. I think, Socrates, that this is admirable, if it were at all possible.

b SOC. But even to fail in an honourable object is honourable.

PHAEDR. True.

SOC. Enough appears to have been said by us of a true and false art
of speaking.

PHAEDR. Certainly.

SOC. But there is something yet to be said of propriety and impropriety of writing.

PHAEDR. Yes.

SOC. Do you know how you can speak or act about rhetoric in a
manner which will be acceptable to god?

PHAEDR. No, indeed. Do you?

c SOC. I have heard a tradition of the ancients, whether true or not
they only know; although if we had found the truth ourselves, do you
think that we should care much about the opinions of men?

PHAEDR. Your question needs no answer; but I wish that you would
tell me what you say that you have heard.

SOC. At the Egyptian city of Naucratis, there was a famous old god,
whose name was Theuth; the bird which is called the Ibis is sacred to
him, and he was the inventor of many arts, such as arithmetic and cal-
d culation and geometry and astronomy and draughts and dice, but his
great discovery was the use of letters. Now in those days the god
Thamus was the king of the whole country of Egypt; and he dwelt in
that great city of Upper Egypt which the Greeks call Egyptian Thebes,
and the god himself is called by them Ammon. To him came Theuth
and showed his inventions, desiring that the other Egyptians might
be allowed to have the benefit of them; he enumerated them, and
Thamus enquired about their several uses, and praised some of them

and censured others, as he approved or disapproved of them. It would   e
take a long time to repeat all that Thamus said to Theuth in praise or
blame of the various arts. But when they came to letters, This, said
Theuth, will make the Egyptians wiser and give them better memories;
it is a specific both for the memory and for the wit. Thamus replied: O
most ingenious Theuth, the parent or inventor of an art is not always
the best judge of the utility or inutility of his own inventions to their   275
users. And in this instance, you who are the father of letters, from a pa-
ternal love of your own children have been led to attribute to them a
quality which they cannot have; for this discovery of yours will create
forgetfulness in the learners' souls, because they will not use their
memories; they will trust the external written characters and not remember of themselves. The specific which you have discovered is an
aid not to memory, but to reminiscence, and you give your disciples
not truth, but only the semblance of truth; they will be hearers of many
things and will have learned nothing; they will appear to be omniscient   b
and will generally know nothing; they will be tiresome company, having the show of wisdom without the reality.

PHAEDR. Yes, Socrates, you can easily invent tales of Egypt, or of any
other country.

SOC. There was a tradition in the temple of Dodona that oaks first
gave prophetic utterances. The men of old, unlike in their simplicity to
young philosophy, deemed that if they heard the truth even from 'oak
or rock,' it was enough for them; whereas you seem to consider not
whether a thing is or is not true, but who the speaker is and from what   c
country the tale comes.

PHAEDR. I acknowledge the justice of your rebuke; and I think that
the Theban is right in his view about letters.

SOC. He would be a very simple person, and quite a stranger to the
oracles of Thamus or Ammon, who should leave in writing or receive
in writing any art under the idea that the written word would be intelligible or certain; or who deemed that writing was at all better than   d
knowledge and recollection of the same matters?

PHAEDR. That is most true.

SOC. I cannot help feeling, Phaedrus, that writing is unfortunately
like painting; for the creations of the painter have the attitude of life,
and yet if you ask them a question they preserve a solemn silence. And
the same may be said of speeches. You would imagine that they had intelligence, but if you want to know anything and put a question to one
of them, there is always one and the same answer. And when they have
been once written down they are tumbled about anywhere among   e
those who may or may not understand them, and know not to whom
they should reply, to whom not: and, if they are maltreated or abused,

they have no parent to protect them; and they cannot protect or defend themselves.

PHAEDR. That again is most true.

Soc. Is there not another kind of word or speech far better than this, and having far greater power—a son of the same family, but lawfully begotten?

PHAEDR. Whom do you mean, and what is his origin?

Soc. I mean an intelligent word graven in the soul of the learner, which can defend itself, and knows when to speak and when to be silent.

PHAEDR. You mean the living word of knowledge which has a soul, and of which the written word is properly no more than an image?

Soc. Yes, of course that is what I mean. And now may I be allowed to ask you a question: Would a farmer, who is a man of sense, take the seeds, which he values and which he wishes to bear fruit, and in sober seriousness plant them during the heat of summer, in some garden of Adonis,* in order to rejoice when he sees them in eight days appearing in beauty? at least he would do so, if at all, only for the sake of amusement and pastime. But when he is in earnest he sows in fitting soil, and practises farming, and is satisfied if in eight months the seeds which he has sown arrive at perfection?

PHAEDR. Yes, Socrates, that will be his way when he is in earnest; he will do the other, as you say, only in play.

Soc. And can we suppose that he who knows the just and good and honorable has less understanding than the farmer about his own seeds?

PHAEDR. Certainly not.

Soc. Then he will not seriously incline to 'write' his thoughts 'in water' with pen and ink, sowing words which can neither speak for themselves nor teach the truth adequately to others?

PHAEDR. No, that is not likely.

Soc. No, that is not likely—in the garden of letters he will sow and plant, but only for the sake of recreation and amusement; he will write them down as memorials to be treasured against the forgetfulness of old age, by himself, or by any other old man who is treading the same path. He will rejoice in beholding their tender growth; and while others are refreshing their souls with banqueting and the like, this will be the pastime in which his days are spent.

PHAEDR. A pastime, Socrates, as noble as the other is ignoble, the pastime of a man who can be amused by serious talk, and can discourse merrily about justice and the like.

---

*During the festival for Adonis, the strength of the seed was tested by planting it in small pots; the plants soon withered and were ritually disposed of by women.

Soc. True, Phaedrus. But far nobler is the serious pursuit of the dialectician, who, finding a congenial soul, by the help of science sows and plants therein words which are able to help themselves and him 277
who planted them, and are not unfruitful, but have in them a seed which others, brought up in different soils, render immortal, making the possessors of it happy to the utmost extent of human happiness.

PHAEDR. Far nobler, certainly.

Soc. And now, Phaedrus, having agreed upon the premises, we decide about the conclusion.

PHAEDR. About what conclusion?

Soc. About Lysias, whom we censured, and his art of writing, and his discourses, and the rhetorical skill or want of skill which was b
shown in them—these are the questions which we sought to determine, and they brought us to this point. And I think that we are now pretty well informed about what is artistic and what is not.

PHAEDR. Yes, I think so; but I wish that you would repeat what was said.

Soc. Until a man knows the truth of the several particulars of which he is writing or speaking, and is able to define them as they are, and, having defined them again, divide them until they can be no longer divided, and until in like manner he is able to discern the nature of the soul, and discover the different modes of discourse which are adapted to c
different natures, and to arrange and dispose them in such a way that the simple form of speech may be addressed to the simpler nature, and the complex and composite to the more complex nature—until he has accomplished all this, he will be unable to handle arguments according to rules of art, as far as their nature allows them to be subjected to art, either for the purpose of teaching or persuading; such is the view which is implied in the whole preceding argument.

PHAEDR. Yes, that was our view, certainly.

Soc. Secondly, as to the censure which was passed on the speaking d
or writing of discourses, and how they might be rightly or wrongly censured—did not our previous argument show—?

PHAEDR. Show what?

Soc. That whether Lysias or any other writer that ever was or will be, whether private man or statesman, proposes laws and so becomes the author of a political treatise, fancying that there is any great certainty and clearness in his performance, the fact of his so writing is only a disgrace to him, whatever men may say. For not to know the nature of justice and injustice, and good and evil, and not to be able to distinguish the dream from the reality, cannot in truth be otherwise e
than disgraceful to him, even with the applause of the whole mob.

PHAEDR. Certainly.

SOC. But he who thinks that in the written word there is necessarily much which is not serious, and that neither poetry nor prose, spoken or written, is of any great value, if, like the compositions of the
278 rhapsodes, they are only recited in order to be believed, and not with any view to criticism or instruction; and who thinks that even the best of writings are but a reminiscence of what we know, and that only in principles of justice and goodness and nobility taught and communicated orally for the sake of instruction and graven in the soul, which is the true way of writing, is there clearness and perfection and seriousness, and that such principles are a man's own and his legitimate offspring, being, in the first place, the word which he finds in his own bosom; and secondly, the brethren and descendants and relations of
b his others—and who cares for them and no others—this is the right sort of man; and you and I, Phaedrus, would pray that we may become like him.

PHAEDR. That is most assuredly my desire and prayer.

SOC. And now the play is played out; enough of rhetoric. Go and tell Lysias that to the fountain and school of the Nymphs we went
c down, and were bidden by them to convey a message to him and to other composers of speeches—to Homer and other writers of poems, whether set to music or not; and to Solon and others who have composed writings in the form of political discourses which they would term laws—to all of them we are to say that if their compositions are based on knowledge of the truth, and they can defend or prove them, when they are put to the test, by spoken arguments, which leave their writings poor in comparison of them, then they are to be called, not only poets, orators, legislators, but are worthy of a higher name, befitting the serious pursuit of their life.

PHAEDR. What name would you assign to them?

SOC. Wise, I may not call them; for that is a great name which belongs to god alone. Lovers of wisdom or philosophers is their modest and befitting title.

PHAEDR. Very suitable.

SOC. And he who cannot rise above his own compilations and compositions, which he has been long patching and piecing, adding some and taking away some, may be justly called poet or speech-maker or law-maker.

PHAEDR. Certainly.

SOC. Now go and tell this to your companion.

PHAEDR. But there is also a friend of yours who ought not to be forgotten.

SOC. Who is he?

PHAEDR. Isocrates* the fair: What message will you send to him, and   279
how shall we describe him?

SOC. Isocrates is still young, Phaedrus; but I am willing to hazard a
prophecy concerning him.

PHAEDR. What would you prophesy?

SOC. I think that he has a genius which soars above the orations of
Lysias, and that his character is cast in a finer mould. My impression of
him is that he will marvellously improve as he grows older, and that all
former rhetoricians will be as children in comparison of him. And I believe that he will not be satisfied with rhetoric, but that there is in him
a divine inspiration which will lead him to things higher still. For he
has an element of philosophy in his nature. This is the message of the   b
gods dwelling in this place, and which I will myself deliver to Isocrates,
who is my delight; and do you give the other to Lysias, who is yours.

PHAEDR. I will; and now, as the heat is abated, let us depart.

SOC. Should we not offer up a prayer first to the local deities?

PHAEDR. By all means.

SOC. Beloved Pan, and all ye other gods who haunt this place, give
me beauty in the inward soul; and may the outward and inward man   c
be at one. May I reckon the wise to be the wealthy, and may I have such
a quantity of gold as a temperate man and he only can bear and carry.
Anything more? The prayer, I think, is enough for me.

PHAEDR. Ask the same for me, for friends should have all things in
common.

SOC. Let us go.

---

*See "General Introduction," p. xxii.

III. THE PROSECUTION AND DEATH OF SOCRATES

———◆———

Euthyphro
Apology
Crito
Phaedo

EUTHYPHRO

Introduction

EUTHYPHRO WAS AN ATHENIAN prophet who ran a farm with his father on
the island of Naxos, on which the Athenians had instituted a coloniz-
ing presence. We know very little about him beyond that. From his appearance in *Cratylus* (396d; not included in this volume) we know that
he was probably in his mid-forties in *Euthyphro*, and that his father,
whom he is prosecuting on the charge of homicide (a religious crime
in Athens), must have been in his seventies, which means that his father was an almost exact contemporary of Socrates.

The conversation proceeds as follows:

- (2a–6e) Meeting at the court building entrance. Euthyphro is
  prosecuting his own father; Socrates is being prosecuted for (a)
  corrupting the young and (b) impiety. Socrates questions the
  holiness of Euthyphro's course of action. Euthyphro appeals to
  the Hesiodic myths of Zeus' imprisonment of his father Cronos,
  and of Cronos' castration of his father Uranus (*Theogony* 126ff.
  and 453ff.); Socrates rejects this justification and demands a rational definition of holiness.

- (7a–11a) After a preliminary discussion about the conflicting
  preferences of the different gods, Euthyphro defines holiness as
  that which all the gods agree to regard as acceptable. According
  to Socrates, this poses a problem: If holiness is determined by
  what the gods find acceptable, and what the gods find acceptable
  is determined by what is holy, the two cannot be the same, or
  else we have a circular definition.

- (11b–14a) Socrates proposes to attempt a definition of holiness
  as a form of justice, and asks to proceed along those lines. Euthyphro defines holiness as the form of justice that serves the
  gods and, more specifically, as the knowledge of the form of
  prayer and sacrifice that serves the gods; Socrates asks how
  prayer and sacrifice actually serve the gods.

- (14b–16a) Euthyphro rejects the notion that the gods have
  needs that must be met by men, and states that prayer and sacrifice are simply pleasing to the gods. The conversation has gone
  full circle. Socrates suggests starting all over again, but Euthyphro is out of time.

It would surely be wrong to take this dialogue as a proof of Socrates' atheism, and even more so of Plato's. Nevertheless, Socrates shows himself convinced of the circularity of the argument that predicates the moral goodness of human actions according to divine will.

EUTHYPHRO

EUTHYPHRO. Why have you left the Lyceum,* Socrates? and what are you doing in the Porch of the King Archon?† Surely you cannot be concerned in a suit before the King, like myself?

SOCRATES. Not in a suit, Euthyphro; public prosecution is the word which the Athenians use.

EUTH. What! I suppose that someone is prosecuting you, for I cannot believe that you are the prosecutor of another.

SOC. Certainly not.

EUTH. Then someone else is prosecuting you?

SOC. Yes.

EUTH. And who is he?

SOC. A young man who is little known, Euthyphro; and I hardly know him: his name is Meletus, and he is of the deme of Pitthis. Perhaps you may remember his appearance; he has a beak, long straight hair, and an unshapely beard.

EUTH. No, I do not remember him, Socrates. But what is the charge which he brings against you?

SOC. What is the charge? A very serious one, which shows a good deal of character in the young man, and for which he is certainly not to be despised. He says he knows how the youth are corrupted and who are their corruptors. I fancy that he must be a wise man, and seeing that I am the reverse of a wise man, he has found me out, and is going to accuse me of corrupting his young friends. And of this our mother the city is to be the judge. Of all our political men he is the only one who seems to me to begin in the right way, with the cultivation of virtue in youth; like a good farmer, he makes the young shoots his first care, and clears away us who destroy them. This is only the first step; he will afterwards attend to the elder branches; and if he goes on as he has begun, he will be a very great public benefactor.

EUTH. I hope that he may; but I rather fear, Socrates, that the opposite will turn out to be the truth. My opinion is that in attacking you he is simply aiming a blow at the foundation of the city. But in what way does he say that you corrupt the young?

SOC. He brings a wonderful accusation against me, which at first hearing excites surprise: he says that I am a poet or maker of gods, and

---

*Gymnasium that Socrates visited frequently.
†Religious crimes (including homicide, in Athens) were tried at this court.

that I invent new gods and deny the existence of old ones; there are the grounds of his indictment.

EUTH. I understand, Socrates; he means to attack you about the familiar sign which occasionally, as you say, comes to you. He thinks that you are a neologian, and he is going to have you up before the court c for this. He knows that such a charge is readily received by the world, as I myself know too well; for when I speak in the assembly about divine things, and foretell the future to them, they laugh at me and think me a madman. Yet every word that I say is true. But they are jealous of us all; we must be brave and take them on.

SOC. Their laughter, friend Euthyphro, is not a matter of much consequence. For a man may be thought wise; but the Athenians, I suspect, do not trouble themselves much about him until he begins to impart d his wisdom to others; and then for some reason or other, perhaps, as you say, from jealousy, they are angry.

EUTH. I am never likely to try their temper in this way.

SOC. I dare say not, for you are reserved in your behaviour, and seldom impart your wisdom. But I have a benevolent habit of pouring out myself to everybody, and would even pay for a listener, and I am afraid that the Athenians may think me too talkative. Now if, as I was saying, e they would only laugh at me, as you say that they laugh at you, the time might pass gaily enough in the court; but perhaps they may be in earnest, and then what the end will be you soothsayers only can predict.

EUTH. I dare say that the affair will end in nothing, Socrates, and that you will win your cause; and I think that I shall win my own.

SOC. And what is your suit, Euthyphro? are you the plaintiff or the defendant?

EUTH. I am the plaintiff.

SOC. Of whom?

4   EUTH. You will think me mad when I tell you.

SOC. Why, has the fugitive wings?

EUTH. Nay, he is not very volatile at his time of life.

SOC. Who is he?

EUTH. My father.

SOC. Your father! my good man?

EUTH. Yes.

SOC. And of what is he accused?

EUTH. Of murder, Socrates.

SOC. My goodness, Euthyphro! how little does the common herd know of the nature of right and truth. A man must be an extraordinary b man, and have made great strides in wisdom, before he could have seen his way to bring such an action.

EUTH. Indeed, Socrates, he must.

SOC. I suppose that the man whom your father murdered was one of your relatives—clearly he was; for if he had been a stranger you would never have thought of prosecuting him.

EUTH. I am amused, Socrates, at your making a distinction between one who is a relation and one who is not a relation; for surely the pollution is the same in either case, if you knowingly associate with the murderer when you ought to clear yourself and him by proceeding against him. The real question is whether the murdered man has been justly slain. If justly, then your duty is to let the matter alone; but if unjustly, then even if the murderer lives under the same roof with you and eats at the same table, proceed against him. Now the man who is dead was a poor dependant of mine who worked for us as a field labourer[1] on our farm in Naxos, and one day in a fit of drunken passion he got into a quarrel with one of our domestic servants and slew him. My father bound him hand and foot and threw him into a ditch, and then sent to Athens to ask of a diviner what he should do with him. Meanwhile he never attended to him and took no care about him, for he regarded him as a murderer; and thought that no great harm would be done even if he died. Now this was just what happened. For such was the effect of cold and hunger and chains upon him, that before the messenger returned from the diviner, he was dead. And my father and family are angry with me for taking the part of the murderer and prosecuting my father. They say that he did not kill him, and that if he did, the dead man was but a murderer, and I ought not to take any notice, for a son who prosecutes a father is impious. Which shows, Socrates, how little they know what the gods think about piety and impiety.

SOC. Good heavens, Euthyphro! and is your knowledge of religion and of things pious and impious so very exact, that, supposing the circumstances to be as you state them, you are not afraid lest you too may be doing an impious thing in bringing an action against your father?

EUTH. The best of Euthyphro, and that which distinguishes him, Socrates, from other men, is his exact knowledge of all such matters. What should I be good for without it?

SOC. Rare friend! I think that I cannot do better than be your disciple. Then before the trial with Meletus comes on I shall challenge him, and say that I have always had a great interest in religious questions, and now, as he charges me with rash imaginations and innovations in religion, I have become your disciple. You, Meletus, as I shall say to him, acknowledge Euthyphro to be a great theologian, and sound in his opinions; and if you approve of him you ought to approve of me, and not have me into court; but if you disapprove, you should begin by indicting him who is my teacher, and who will be the ruin, not of the young, but

of the old; that is to say, of myself whom he instructs, and of his old father whom he admonishes and chastises. And if Meletus refuses to listen
to me, but will go on, and will not shift the indictment from me to you,
I cannot do better than repeat this challenge in the court.

c   EUTH. Yes, indeed, Socrates; and if he attempts to indict me I am
mistaken if I do not find a flaw in him; the court shall have a great deal
more to say to him than to me.

SOC. And I, my dear friend, knowing this, am desirous of becoming your disciple. For I observe that no one appears to notice you—not
even this Meletus; but his sharp eyes have found me out at once, and
he has indicted me for impiety. And therefore, I beg you to tell me the
d   nature of piety and impiety, which you said that you knew so well, and
of murder, and of other offences against the gods. What are they? Is not
piety in every action always the same? and impiety, again—is it not always the opposite of piety, and also the same with itself, having, as
impiety, one notion which includes whatever is impious?

EUTH. To be sure, Socrates.

SOC. And what is piety, and what is impiety?

EUTH. Piety is doing as I am doing; that is to say, prosecuting any-
e   one who is guilty of murder, sacrilege, or of any similar crime whether
he be your father or mother, or whoever he may be —that makes no
difference; and not to prosecute them is impiety. And please consider,
Socrates, what a notable proof I will give you of the truth of my
words, a proof which I have already given to others:—of the principle,
I mean, that the impious, whoever he may be, ought not to go unpun-
6   ished. For do not men regard Zeus as the best and most righteous of
the gods?—and yet they admit that he bound his father (Cronos) because he wickedly devoured his sons, and that he too had punished his
own father (Uranus) for a similar reason, in a nameless manner.[2] And
yet when I proceed against my father, they are angry with me. So inconsistent are they in their way of talking when the gods are concerned, and when I am concerned.

SOC. May not this be the reason, Euthyphro, why I am charged with
impiety—that I cannot put up with these stories about the gods? and
therefore I suppose that people think me wrong. But, as you who are
well informed about them approve of them, I cannot do better than as-
b   sent to your superior wisdom. What else can I say, confessing as I do,
that I know nothing about them? Tell me, for the love of Zeus, whether
you really believe that they are true.

EUTH. Yes, Socrates; and things more wonderful still, of which the
world is ignorant.

SOC. And do you really believe that the gods fought with one another, and had dire quarrels, battles, and the like, as the poets say, and

as you may see represented in the works of great artists? The temples are full of them; and notably the robe of Athene, which is carried up to the Acropolis at the great Panathenaea,* is embroidered with them. Are all these tales of the gods true, Euthyphro?

EUTH. Yes, Socrates; and, as I was saying, I can tell you, if you would like to hear them, many other things about the gods which would quite amaze you.

SOC. I dare say; and you shall tell me them at some other time when I have leisure. But just at present I would rather hear from you a more precise answer, which you have not as yet given, my friend, to the question, What is 'piety'? When asked, you only replied, Doing as you do, charging your father with murder.

EUTH. And what I said was true, Socrates.

SOC. No doubt, Euthyphro; but you would admit that there are many other pious acts?

EUTH. There are.

SOC. Remember that I did not ask you to give me two or three examples of piety, but to explain the general idea which makes all pious things to be pious. Do you not recollect that there was one idea which made the impious impious, and the pious pious?

EUTH. I remember.

SOC. Tell me what is the nature of this idea, and then I shall have a standard to which I may look, and by which I may measure actions, whether yours or those of anyone else, and then I shall be able to say that such and such an action is pious, and such other impious.

EUTH. I will tell you, if you like.

SOC. I should very much like.

EUTH. Piety, then, is that which is dear to the gods, and impiety is that which is not dear to them.

SOC. Very good, Euthyphro; you have now given me the sort of answer which I wanted. But whether what you say is true or not I cannot yet tell, although I have no doubt that you will prove the truth of your words.

EUTH. Of course.

SOC. Come, then, and let us examine what we are saying. That thing or person which is dear to the gods is pious, and that thing or person which is hateful to the gods is impious, these two being the extreme opposites of one another. Was not that said?

EUTH. It was.

SOC. And well said?

---

*Yearly Athenian festival in honor of the goddess Athena.

b   EUTH. Yes, Socrates, I thought so; it was certainly said.

Soc. And further, Euthyphro, the gods were admitted to have enmities and hatreds and differences?

EUTH. Yes, that was also said.

Soc. And what sort of difference creates enmity and anger? Suppose for example that you and I, my good friend, differ about a calculation;
c   do differences of this sort make us enemies and set us at variance with one another? Do we not go at once to arithmetic, and put an end to them by a sum?

EUTH. True.

Soc. Or suppose that we differ about magnitudes, do we not quickly end the differences by measuring?

EUTH. Very true.

Soc. And we end a controversy about heavy and light by resorting to a weighing machine?

EUTH. To be sure.

Soc. But what differences are there which cannot be thus decided, and which therefore make us angry and set us at enmity with one another? I dare say the answer does not occur to you at the moment, and
d   therefore I will suggest that these enmities arise when the matters of difference are the just and unjust, good and evil, honourable and dishonourable. Are not these the points about which men differ, and about which when we are unable satisfactorily to decide our differences, you and I and all of us quarrel, when we do quarrel?

EUTH. Yes, Socrates, the nature of the differences about which we quarrel is such as you describe.

Soc. And the quarrels of the gods, noble Euthyphro, when they occur, are of a like nature?

EUTH. Certainly they are.

e   Soc. They have differences of opinion, as you say, about good—and evil, just and unjust, honourable and dishonourable: there would have been no quarrels among them, if there had been no such differences—would there now?

EUTH. You are quite right.

Soc. Does not every man love that which he deems noble and just and good, and hate the opposite of them?

EUTH. Very true.

Soc. But, as you say, the same things, are regarded by some as just and by others as unjust; about these they dispute; and so there arise
8   wars and fightings among them.

EUTH. Very true.

Soc. Then the same things are hated by the gods and loved by the gods, and are both hateful and dear to them?

EUTH. True.

SOC. And upon this view the same things, Euthyphro, will be pious and also impious?

EUTH. So I should suppose.

SOC. Then, my friend, I remark with surprise that you have not answered the question which I asked. For I certainly did not ask you to tell me what action is both pious and impious: but now it would seem that what is loved by the gods is also hated by them. And therefore, Euthyphro, in thus chastising your father you may very likely be doing what   b
is agreeable to Zeus but disagreeable to Cronos or Uranus, and what is acceptable to Hephaestus but unacceptable to Hera, and there may be other gods who have similar differences of opinion.

EUTH. But I believe, Socrates, that all the gods would be agreed as to the propriety of punishing a murderer: there would be no difference of opinion about that.

SOC. Well, but speaking of men, Euthyphro, did you ever hear any-   c
one arguing that a murderer or any sort of evil-doer ought to be let off?

EUTH. I should rather say that these are the questions which they are always arguing, especially in courts of law: they commit all sorts of crimes, and there is nothing which they will not do or say in their own defense.

SOC. But do they admit their guilt, Euthyphro, and yet say that they ought not to be punished?

EUTH. No; they do not.

SOC. Then there are some things which they do not venture to say and do: for they do not venture to argue that the guilty are to be unpunished, but they deny their guilt, do they not?   d

EUTH. Yes.

SOC. Then they do not argue that the evil-doer should not be punished, but they argue about who the evil-doer is, and what he did and when?

EUTH. True.

SOC. And the gods are in the same case, if as you assert they quarrel about just and unjust, and some of them say while others deny that injustice is done among them. For surely neither god nor man will ever   e
venture to say that the doer of injustice is not to be punished?

EUTH. That is true, Socrates, in the main.

SOC. But they take issue about the particulars—gods and men alike; and, if they dispute at all, they dispute about some act which is called in question, and which by some is affirmed to be just, by others to be unjust. Is not that true?

EUTH. Quite true.

SOC. Well then, my dear friend Euthyphro, do tell me, for my better   9 instruction and information, what proof have you that in the opinion of all the gods a servant who is guilty of murder, and is put in chains by the master of the dead man, and dies because he is put in chains before he who bound him can learn from the interpreters of the gods what he ought to do with him, dies unjustly; and that on behalf of such servant a son ought to proceed against his father and accuse him of

b   murder. How would you show that all the gods absolutely agree in approving of his act? Prove to me that they do, and I will applaud your wisdom as long as I live.

EUTH. It will be a difficult task; but I could make the matter very clear indeed to you.

SOC. I understand; you mean to say that I am not so quick of apprehension as the judges: for to them you will be sure to prove that the act is unjust, and hateful to the gods.

EUTH. Yes indeed, Socrates; at least if they listen to me.

c   SOC. But they will be sure to listen if they find that you are a good speaker. There was a notion that came into my mind while you were speaking; I said to myself: 'Well, and what if Euthyphro does prove to me that all the gods regarded the death of the servant as unjust, how do I know anything more of the nature of piety and impiety? for granting that this action may be hateful to the gods, still piety and impiety are not adequately defined by these distinctions, for that which is hateful to the gods has been shown to be also pleasing and dear to them.' And therefore, Euthyphro, I do not ask you to prove this; I will suppose, if you like, that all the gods condemn and abominate such an ac-

d   tion. But I will amend the definition so far as to say that what all the gods hate is impious, and what they love pious or holy; and what some of them love and others hate is both or neither. Shall this be our definition of piety and impiety?

EUTH. Why not, Socrates?

SOC. Why not! certainly, as far as I am concerned, Euthyphro, there is no reason why not. But whether this admission will greatly assist you in the task of instructing me as you promised, is a matter for you to consider.

e   EUTH. Yes, I should say that what all the gods love is pious and holy, and the opposite which they all hate, impious.

SOC. Ought we to enquire into the truth of this, Euthyphro, or simply to accept the mere statement on our own authority and that of others? What do you say?

EUTH. We should enquire; and I believe that the statement will stand the test of enquiry.

SOC. We shall know better, my good friend, in a little while. The point which I should first wish to understand is whether the pious or holy is beloved by the gods because it is holy, or holy because it is 10 beloved of the gods.

EUTH. I do not understand your meaning, Socrates.

Soc. I will endeavour to explain: we speak of carrying and we speak of being carried, of leading and being led, seeing and being seen. You know that in all such cases there is a difference, and you know also in what the difference lies?

EUTH. I think that I understand.

Soc. And is not that which is beloved distinct from that which loves?

EUTH. Certainly.

Soc. Well; and now tell me, is that which is carried in this state of b carrying because it is carried, or for some other reason?

EUTH. No; that is the reason.

Soc. And the same is true of what is led and of what is seen?

EUTH. True.

Soc. And a thing is not seen because it is visible, but conversely, visible because it is seen; nor is a thing led because it is in the state of being led, or carried because it is in the state of being carried, but the converse of this. And now I think, Euthyphro, that my meaning will be intelligible; and my meaning is, that any state of action or passion im- c plies previous action or passion. It does not become because it is becoming, but it is in a state of becoming because it becomes; neither does it suffer because it is in a state of suffering, but it is in a state of suffering because it suffers. Do you not agree?

EUTH. Yes.

Soc. Is not that which is loved in some state either of becoming or suffering?

EUTH. Yes.

Soc. And the same holds in the previous instances; the state of being loved follows the act of being loved, and not the act the state.

EUTH. Certainly.

Soc. And what do you say of piety, Euthyphro: is not piety, accord- d ing to your definition, loved by all the gods?

EUTH. Yes.

Soc. Because it is pious or holy, or for some other reason?

EUTH. No, that is the reason.

Soc. It is loved because it is holy, not holy because it is loved?

EUTH. Yes.

Soc. And that which is dear to the gods is loved by them, and is in a state to be loved by them because it is loved by them?

EUTH. Certainly.

Soc. Then that which is dear to the gods, Euthyphro, is not holy, nor is that which is holy loved by god, as you affirm; but they are two different things.

Euth. How do you mean, Socrates?

e   Soc. I mean to say that the holy has been acknowledged by us to be loved by god because it is holy, not to be holy because it is loved.

Euth. Yes.

Soc. But that which is dear to the gods is dear to them because it is loved by them, not loved by them because it is dear to them.

Euth. True.

Soc. But, friend Euthyphro, if that which is holy is the same with that which is dear to god, and is loved because it is holy, then that which is dear to god would have been loved as being dear to god; but

11   if that which is dear to god is dear to him because loved by him, then that which is holy would have been holy because loved by him. But now you see that the reverse is the case, and that they are quite different from one another. For one is of a kind to be loved because it is loved, and the other is loved because it is of a kind to be loved.[3] Thus you appear to me, Euthyphro, when I ask you what is the essence of holiness, to offer an attribute only, and not the essence—the attribute

b   of being loved by all the gods. But you still refuse to explain to me the nature of holiness. And therefore, if you please, I will ask you not to hide your treasure, but to tell me once more what holiness or piety really is, whether dear to the gods or not (for that is a matter about which we will not quarrel); and what is impiety?

Euth. I really do not know, Socrates, how to express what I mean. For somehow or other our arguments, on whatever ground we rest them, seem to turn round and walk away from us.

Soc. Your words, Euthyphro, are like the handiwork of my ancestor

c   Daedalus;* and if I were the sayer or propounder of them, you might say that my arguments walk away and will not remain fixed where they are placed because I am a descendant of his. But now, since these notions are your own, you must find some other joke, for they certainly, as you yourself allow, show an inclination to be on the move.

Euth. Nay, Socrates, I shall still say that you are the Daedalus who sets arguments in motion; not I, certainly, but you make them move or

d   go round, for they would never have stirred, as far as I am concerned.

Soc. Then I must be greater than Daedalus: for whereas he only made his own inventions to move, I move those of other people as well. And the beauty of it is, that I would rather not. For I would give

---

*Mythical craftsman of exceptional talent.

the wisdom of Daedalus, and the wealth of Tantalus,* to be able to de-   *e*
tain them and keep them fixed. But enough of this. As I perceive that
you are lazy, I will myself endeavor to show you how you might instruct me in the nature of piety; and I hope that you will not grudge
your labour. Tell me, then,—Is not that which is pious necessarily just?

EUTH. Yes.

SOC. And is, then, all which is just pious? or, is that which is pious
all just, but that which is just, only in part and not all, pious?   12

EUTH. I do not understand you, Socrates.

SOC. And yet I know that you are as much wiser than I am, as you
are younger. But, as I was saying, revered friend, the abundance of your
wisdom makes you lazy. Please exert yourself, for there is no real difficulty in understanding me. What I mean I may explain by an illustration of what I do not mean. The poet sings—

> 'Of Zeus, the author and creator of all these things,
>   You will not tell: for where there is fear there is also reverence.'†

Now I disagree with this poet. Shall I tell you in what respect?   *b*

EUTH. By all means.

SOC. I should not say that where there is fear there is also reverence;
for I am sure that many persons fear poverty and disease, and the like
evils, but I do not perceive that they reverence the objects of their fear.

EUTH. Very true.

SOC. But where there is reverence, there is fear; for he who has a
feeling of reverence and shame about the commission of any action,
fears and is afraid of an ill reputation.   *c*

EUTH. No doubt.

SOC. Then we are wrong in saying that where there is fear there is
also reverence; and we should say, where there is reverence there is also
fear. But there is not always reverence where there is fear; for fear is a
more extended notion, and reverence is a part of fear, just as the odd is
a part of number, and number is a more extended notion than the odd.
I suppose that you follow me now?

EUTH. Quite well.

SOC. That was the sort of question which I meant to raise when I   *d*
asked whether the just is always the pious, or the pious always the
just; and whether there may not be justice where there is not piety;

---

*Mythical king of Lydia, known for both his great wealth and his offenses against the
gods.

†An obscure fragment, perhaps by Stesinaos, whom some thought a relative of Homer.

for justice is the more extended notion of which piety is only a part. Do you dissent?

EUTH. No, I think that you are quite right.

SOC. Then, if piety is a part of justice, I suppose that we should enquire what part? If you had pursued the enquiry in the previous cases; for instance, if you had asked me what is an even number, and what part of number the even is, I should have had no difficulty in replying, a number which represents a figure having two equal sides. Do you not agree?

EUTH. Yes, I quite agree.

e   SOC. In like manner, I want you to tell me what part of justice is piety or holiness, that I may be able to tell Meletus not to do me injustice, or indict me for impiety, as I am now adequately instructed by you in the nature of piety or holiness, and their opposites.

EUTH. Piety or holiness, Socrates, appears to me to be that part of justice which attends to the gods, as there is the other part of justice which attends to men.

13   SOC. That is good, Euthyphro; yet still there is a small point about which I should like to have further information. What is the meaning of 'attention'? For attention can hardly be used in the same sense when applied to the gods as when applied to other things. For instance, horses are said to require attention, and not every person is able to attend to them, but only a person skilled in horsemanship. Is it not so?

EUTH. Certainly.

SOC. I should suppose that the art of horsemanship is the art of attending to horses?

EUTH. Yes.

SOC. Nor is everyone qualified to attend to dogs, but only the hunter?

EUTH. True.

SOC. And I should also conceive that the art of the hunter is the art
b   of attending to dogs?

EUTH. Yes.

SOC. As the art of the oxherd is the art of attending to oxen?

EUTH. Very true.

SOC. In like manner holiness or piety is the art of attending to the gods?—that would be your meaning, Euthyphro?

EUTH. Yes.

SOC. And is not attention always designed for the good or benefit of that to which the attention is given? As in the case of horses, you may observe that when attended to by the horseman's art they are benefited and improved, are they not?

EUTH. True.

Soc. As the dogs are benefited by the hunter's art, and the oxen by the art of the oxherd, and all other things are tended or attended for their good and not for harm?

Euth. Certainly, not for their harm.

Soc. But for their good?

Euth. Of course.

Soc. And does piety or holiness, which has been defined to be the art of attending to the gods, benefit or improve them? Would you say that when you do a holy act you make any of the gods better?

Euth. No, no; that was certainly not what I meant.

Soc. And I, Euthyphro, never supposed that you did. I asked you the question about the nature of the attention, because I thought that you did not.

Euth. You do me justice, Socrates; that is not the sort of attention which I mean.

Soc. Good: but I must still ask what is this attention to the gods which is called piety?

Euth. It is such, Socrates, as servants show to their masters.

Soc. I understand—a sort of ministration to the gods.

Euth. Exactly.

Soc. Medicine is also a sort of ministration or service, having in view the attainment of some object—would you not say of health?

Euth. I should.

Soc. Again, there is an art which ministers to the ship-builder with a view to the attainment of some result?

Euth. Yes, Socrates, with a view to the building of a ship.

Soc. As there is an art which ministers to the housebuilder with a view to the building of a house?

Euth. Yes.

Soc. And now tell me, my good friend, about the art which ministers to the gods: what work does that help to accomplish? For you must surely know if, as you say, you are of all men living the one who is best instructed in religion.

Euth. And I speak the truth, Socrates.

Soc. Tell me then, oh tell me—what is that fair work which the gods do by the help of our ministrations?

Euth. Many and fair, Socrates, are the works which they do.

Soc. Why, my friend, and so are those of a general. But the chief of them is easily told. Would you not say that victory in war is the chief of them?

Euth. Certainly.

Soc. Many and fair, too, are the works of the farmer, if I am not mistaken; but his chief work is the production of food from the earth?

EUTH. Exactly.

SOC. And of the many and fair things done by the gods, which is the chief or principal one?

b   EUTH. I have told you already, Socrates, that to learn all these things accurately will be very tiresome. Let me simply say that piety or holiness is learning how to please the gods in word and deed, by prayers and sacrifices. Such piety is the salvation of families and states, just as the impious, which is unpleasing to the gods, is their ruin and destruction.

SOC. I think that you could have answered in much fewer words the chief question which I asked, Euthyphro, if you had chosen. But I see

c   plainly that you are not disposed to instruct me—clearly not: else why, when we reached the point, did you turn aside? Had you only answered me I should have truly learned of you by this time the nature of piety. Now, as the asker of a question is necessarily dependent on the answerer, whither he leads I must follow; and can only ask again, what is the pious, and what is piety? Do you mean that they are a sort of science of praying and sacrificing?

EUTH. Yes, I do.

SOC. And sacrificing is giving to the gods, and prayer is asking of the gods?

EUTH. Yes, Socrates.

d   SOC. Upon this view, then, piety is a science of asking and giving?

EUTH. You understand me completely well, Socrates.

SOC. Yes, my friend; the reason is that I am desirous of your science, and give my mind to it, and therefore nothing which you say will be thrown away upon me. Please then to tell me, what is the nature of this service to the gods? Do you mean that we make requests and give gifts to them?

EUTH. Yes, I do.

SOC. Is not the right way of asking to ask of them what we want?

EUTH. Certainly.

e   SOC. And the right way of giving is to give them in return what they want of us. There would be no meaning in an art which gives to anyone that which he does not want.

EUTH. Very true, Socrates.

SOC. Then piety, Euthyphro, is an art which gods and men have of doing business with one another?

EUTH. That is an expression which you may use, if you like.

SOC. But I have no particular liking for anything but the truth. I wish, however, that you would tell me what benefit accrues to the gods from our gifts. There is no doubt about what they give to us; for there

15   is no good thing which they do not give; but how we can give any

good thing to them in return is far from being equally clear. If they give everything and we give nothing, that must be a transaction in which we have very greatly the advantage over them.

EUTH. And do you imagine, Socrates, that any benefit accrues to the gods from our gifts?

SOC. But if not, Euthyphro, what is the meaning of gifts which are conferred by us upon the gods?

EUTH. What else, but tributes of honor; and, as I was just now saying, what pleases them?

SOC. Piety, then, is pleasing to the gods, but not beneficial or dear to them? b

EUTH. I should say that nothing could be dearer.

SOC. Then once more the assertion is repeated that piety is dear to the gods?

EUTH. Certainly.

SOC. And when you say this, can you wonder at your words not standing firm, but walking away? Will you accuse me of being the Daedalus who makes them walk away, not perceiving that there is another and far greater artist than Daedalus who makes them go round in a circle, and he is yourself; for the argument, as you will perceive, c comes round to the same point. Were we not saying that the holy or pious was not the same with that which is loved by the gods? Have you forgotten?

EUTH. I quite remember.

SOC. And are you not saying that what is loved by the gods is holy; and is not this the same as what is dear to them—do you see?

EUTH. True.

SOC. Then either we were wrong in our former assertion; or, if we were right then, we are wrong now.

EUTH. One of the two must be true.

SOC. Then we must begin again and ask, What is piety? That is an enquiry which I shall never shrink from pursuing until I am satisfied; d and I entreat you not to scorn me, but to apply your mind to the utmost, and tell me the truth. For, if any man knows, you are the one; and therefore I must detain you, like Proteus,* until you tell. If you had not certainly known the nature of piety and impiety, I am confident that you would never, on behalf of a servant, have charged your aged father with murder. You would not have run such a risk of doing wrong in the sight of the gods, and you would have had too much respect for the opinions of men. I am sure, therefore, that you know the nature of

---

*Shape-shifting god of the sea who has knowledge of the future (*Odyssey* 4.382ff.).

e   piety and impiety. Speak out then, my dear Euthyphro, and do not hide
your knowledge.

EUTH. Another time, Socrates; for I am in a hurry, and must go now.

SOC. Alas! my companion, and will you leave me in despair? I was
hoping that you would instruct me in the nature of piety and impiety;
16   and then I might have cleared myself of Meletus and his indictment. I
would have told him that I had been enlightened by Euthyphro, and
had given up rash innovations and speculations, in which I indulged
only through ignorance, and that now I am about to lead a better life.

APOLOGY

Introduction

THE WORD "APOLOGY" IS a translation of the Greek *apologia*, which means "defense speech." I have decided to maintain the customary translation, but readers will soon realize that Socrates does anything but apologize in this work.

We must note that Socrates is not the only speaker in *Apology*. Even in this case, Plato makes use of the dialogue form and has the prosecutor Meletus reply to several of Socrates' questions (24d–27d), in a passage that Aristotle calls an example of the good use of interrogation (*Rhetoric* 1419a8). While cross-examination of witnesses had no place in Athenian procedure, either party could ask questions of the other, who was obliged by law to answer them.

Meletus is the primary prosecutor and acts, according to Socrates, "on behalf of the poets" (24a); he himself was probably not a poet, although his father, who was made fun of by the comic poets, may have been. At the time of the trial, Meletus is young and unknown (*Euthyphro* 2b; p. 259), but the brevity of his answers to Socrates' questions should not deceive us: He expresses very clearly the opinion that any staunch Athenian democrat would have held in this case.

A suggested outline of the contents of *Apology* is as follows:

- (17a–19a) Introduction and statement of the case. Socrates asks for permission to address the court in informal style and immediately begins to do so. Ignoring the court charges, he makes a distinction between the charges brought against him now and his longstanding unpopularity.

- (19a–24b) Socrates states as the reasons for his unpopularity the common practices of the pre-Socratics and the Sophists. He then denies teaching anything and claims that his questioning style and conversations were only an attempt to establish the truth of an oracle that singles him out as the wisest of men.

- (24b–28a) Socrates demonstrates how questioning works, by an interrogation of Meletus, in which he shows that: (a) following Meletus' logic, prosecution is entirely inappropriate in this case; and (b) the terms of the impiety charge in fact imply that he believes in the gods.

- (28a–35d) Socrates restates that his questioning duty derives from Apollo and says that he must attend to it rather than to the requests of the city. A divine sign stops him from taking part in public affairs. He also reminds the jurors of a few events in which he opposed unconstitutional action, although the people approved of such action. Finally, he criticizes Meletus for not producing witnesses and mentions his young followers in an attempt to show that his influence is not so pernicious after all. Last, he refuses to supplicate the jurors for a vote of acquittal, which was the common practice in Athens at that time.

- (35e–38b) A guilty verdict is returned, and the death penalty is proposed. Following Athenian procedure, Socrates must make a counter-proposal for a penalty. He restates his view of himself as a benefactor of Athens and claims that he should be dining at the public expense. Next, he rejects the possibility of prison or exile, and offers a small sum of money as a counter-penalty.

- (38c–42a) Socrates is given the death penalty by about two-thirds of the jurors. He prophesies that the city will be punished because of its wrong way of life, and he asks the question (that will be explored further in *Phaedo*) of what death means to humans.

APOLOGY

How you, Athenians, have been struck by the words of my accusers, I cannot tell; but I know that they almost made me forget that I was the accused—so persuasively did they speak; and yet they have hardly uttered a word of truth. But of the many falsehoods told by them, there was one which quite amazed me;—I mean when they said that you should be upon your guard and not allow yourselves to be deceived by the force of my eloquence. To say this, when they were certain to be detected as soon as I opened my lips and proved myself to be anything but a great speaker, did indeed appear to me most shameless—unless by the force of eloquence they mean the force of truth; for if such is their meaning, I admit that I am eloquent. But in how different a way from theirs! Well, as I was saying, they have scarcely spoken the truth at all; but from me you shall hear the whole truth: not, however, delivered after their manner in a set oration duly ornamented with words and phrases. No, by heaven! but I shall use the words and arguments which occur to me at the moment; for I am confident in the justice of what I say: at my time of life I ought not to be appearing before you, men of Athens, in the character of a juvenile orator—let no one expect it of me. And I must beg of you to grant me a favour:—If I defend myself in my accustomed manner, and you hear me using the words which I have been in the habit of using in the agora, at the tables of the money-changers, or anywhere else, I would ask you not to be surprised, and not to interrupt me on this account. For I am more than seventy years of age, and appearing now for the first time in a court of law, I am quite a stranger to the language of the place; and therefore I would have you regard me as if I were really a stranger, whom you would excuse if he spoke in his native tongue, and after the fashion of his country:—Am I making an unfair request of you? Never mind the manner, which may or may not be good; but think only of the truth of my words, and give heed to that: let the speaker speak truly and the judge decide justly.

First, I have to reply to the older charges and to my first accusers, and then I will go on to the later ones. For I have had many accusers for a long time who have accused me falsely to you during many years; and I am more afraid of them than of Anytus* and his associates, who are dangerous, too, in their own way. But far more dangerous are the others, who began when you were children, and took possession of

*Athenian general and possibly a Council member.

your minds with their falsehoods, telling of one Socrates, a wise man, who speculated about the heaven above, and searched into the earth beneath, and made the worse cause appear as the better one. The disseminators of this tale are the accusers whom I dread; for their hearers are apt to fancy that such enquirers do not believe in the existence of the gods. And they are many, and their charges against me are of ancient date, and they were made by them in the days when you were more impressionable than you are now—in childhood, or it may have been in youth—and the cause when heard went by default, for there was none to answer. And hardest of all, I do not know and cannot tell the names of my accusers; except for the comic poet.* All who from envy and malice have persuaded you—some of them having first convinced themselves—all this class of men are most difficult to deal with; for I cannot have them up here, and cross-examine them, and therefore I must simply fight with shadows in my own defense, and argue when there is no one who answers. I will ask you then to assume with me, as I was saying, that my opponents are of two kinds; one recent, the other ancient: and I hope that you will see the propriety of my answering the latter first, for these accusations you heard long before the others, and much more often.

Well, then, I must make my defense, and endeavor to clear away in a short time, a slander which has lasted a long time. May I succeed, if to succeed be for my good and yours, or likely to help me in my cause! The task is not an easy one; I quite understand the nature of it. And so leaving the event with god, in obedience to the law I will now make my defense.

I will begin at the beginning, and ask what is the accusation which has given rise to the slander of me, and in fact has encouraged Meletus to bring this charge against me. Well, what do the slanderers say? They shall be my prosecutors, and I will sum up their words in an affidavit: 'Socrates is an evil-doer, and a meddlesome person, who searches into things under the earth and in heaven, and he makes the worse appear the better cause; and he teaches the aforesaid doctrines to others.' Such is the nature of the accusation: it is just what you have yourselves seen in the comedy of Aristophanes, who has introduced a man whom he calls Socrates, going about and saying that he walks in air, and talking nonsense concerning matters of which I do not pretend to know anything at all—not that I mean to speak disparagingly of anyone who is a student of natural philosophy. I should be very sorry if Meletus could bring so grave a charge against me. But the simple truth is, Athenians,

---

*A clear allusion to Aristophanes, who pokes fun at Socrates in his play *Clouds* (225ff.).

that I have nothing to do with physical speculations. Very many of those here present are witnesses to the truth of this, and to them I appeal. Speak then, you who have heard me, and tell your neighbours whether any of you have ever known me hold forth about such matters. . . . You hear their answer. And from what they say of this part of the charge you will be able to judge the truth of the rest. *d*

As little foundation is there for the report that I am a teacher, and take money; this accusation has no more truth in it than the other. Although, if a man were really able to instruct mankind, receiving money *e* for giving instruction would, in my opinion, be an honor to him. There is Gorgias of Leontini, and Prodicus of Ceos, and Hippias of Elis, who go the round of the cities, and are able to persuade the young men to leave their own citizens by whom they might be taught for nothing, 20 and come to them whom they not only pay, but are thankful if they may be allowed to pay them.[1] There is at this time a Parian philosopher residing in Athens, of whom I have heard; and I came to hear of him in this way: I came across a man who has spent a fortune on the sophists, Callias,* the son of Hipponicus, and knowing that he had sons, I asked him: 'Callias, if your two sons were colts or calves, there would be no difficulty in finding someone to put in charge of them; we should hire a trainer of horses, or a farmer probably, who would improve and perfect them in their own proper virtue and excellence; but as they are *b* human beings, whom are you thinking of putting in charge of them? Is there anyone who understands human and political virtue? You must have thought about the matter, for you have sons; is there anyone?' 'There is,' he said. 'Who is he?' said I; 'and of what country? and what does he charge?' 'Evenus† the Parian,' he replied; 'he is the man, and his charge is five minae.' Happy is Evenus, I said to myself, if he really has this wisdom, and teaches at such a moderate charge. Had I the *c* same, I should have been very proud and conceited; but the truth is that I have no knowledge of the kind.

I dare say, Athenians, that someone among you will reply, 'Yes, Socrates, but what is the origin of these accusations which are brought against you; there must have been something strange which you have been doing? All these rumours and this talk about you would never have arisen if you had been like other men: tell us, then, what is the cause, for we would be sorry to judge you hastily.' I regard this as a fair *d* challenge, and I will endeavor to explain the reason why I am called wise and have such an evil fame. Listen then. Although some of you

---

*Very rich man, notorious for spending a lot of money on the fees charged by Sophists.
†Minor Sophist who specialized in literary composition and invented rhetorical devices.

may think that I am joking, I declare that I will tell you the entire truth. Men of Athens, this reputation of mine has come from a certain sort of wisdom which I possess. If you ask me what kind of wisdom, I reply, wisdom such as may perhaps be attained by man, for to that extent I am inclined to believe that I am wise; whereas the persons of whom I

e   was speaking have a superhuman wisdom, which I may fail to describe, because I do not have it myself; and he who says that I have it, speaks falsely, and slanders me. And here, men of Athens, I must beg you not to interrupt me, even if I seem to say something extravagant. For the word which I will speak is not mine. I will refer you to a witness who is worthy of credit; that witness shall be the god of Delphi—he will tell you about my wisdom, if I have any, and of what sort it is. You must have known Chaerephon;* he was a friend of mine, and also a friend

21   of yours, for he shared in the recent exile of the people, and returned with you. Chaerephon, as you know, was very impetuous in all his doings, and he went to Delphi and boldly asked the oracle to tell him whether—as I was saying, I must beg you not to interrupt—he asked the oracle to tell him whether anybody was wiser than I was, and the Pythian prophetess answered that there was no wiser man. Chaerephon himself is dead; but his brother, who is in court, will confirm the truth of what I am saying.

b   Why do I mention this? Because I am going to explain to you why I have such an evil reputation. When I heard the answer, I said to myself, What can the god mean? and what is the interpretation of his riddle? for I know that I have no wisdom, small or great. What then can he mean when he says that I am the wisest of men? And yet he is a god, and cannot lie; that would be against his nature. After long consideration, I thought of a method of trying the question. I reflected that if I

c   could only find a man wiser than myself, then I might go to the god with a refutation in my hand. I should say to him, 'Here is a man who is wiser than I am; but you said that I was the wisest.' Accordingly I went to one who had the reputation of wisdom, and observed him— his name I need not mention; he was a politician whom I selected for examination—and the result was as follows: When I began to talk with him, I could not help thinking that he was not really wise, although he was thought wise by many, and still wiser by himself; and thereupon I tried to explain to him that he thought himself wise, but was not re-

d   ally wise; and the consequence was that he hated me, and his enmity

---

*Close follower of Socrates whose interest in entomology is mocked by Aristophanes in Clouds 503 and Birds 1296, 1564.

was shared by several who were present and heard me. So I left him, saying to myself, as I went away: Although I do not suppose that either of us knows anything really beautiful and good, I am better off than he is, for he knows nothing, and thinks that he knows; I neither know nor think that I know. In this latter particular, then, I seem to have a slight advantage over him. Then I went to another who had still higher pretensions to wisdom, and my conclusion was exactly the same. Whereupon I made another enemy of him, and of many others besides him. *e*

Then I went to one man after another, being aware of the enmity which I provoked, and I lamented and feared this: But necessity was laid upon me—the word of god, I thought, ought to be considered first. And I said to myself, I must go to all who appear to know, and find out the meaning of the oracle. And I swear to you, Athenians, by the 22 dog I swear!—for I must tell you the truth—the result of my mission was just this: I found that the men most in repute were all but the most foolish; and that others less esteemed were really wiser and better. I will tell you the tale of my wanderings and of the 'Herculean' labours, as I may call them, which I endured only to find at last the oracle irrefutable. After the politicians, I went to the poets; tragic, dithyrambic, *b* and all sorts. And there, I said to myself, you will be instantly detected; now you will find out that you are more ignorant than they are. Accordingly, I took them some of the most elaborate passages in their own writings, and asked what was the meaning of them—thinking that they would teach me something. Will you believe me? I am almost ashamed to confess the truth, but I must say that there is hardly a person present who would not have talked better about their poetry than they did themselves. Then I knew that not by wisdom do poets write poetry, but by a sort of genius and inspiration; they are like diviners or *c* soothsayers who also say many fine things, but do not understand their meaning. The poets appeared to me to be much in the same case; and I further observed that upon the strength of their poetry they believed themselves to be the wisest of men in other things in which they were not wise. So I departed, thinking myself superior to them for the same reason that I was superior to the politicians.

At last I went to the artisans, for I was conscious that I knew nothing at all, as I may say, and I was sure that they knew many fine things; *d* and here I was not mistaken, for they did know many things of which I was ignorant, and in this they certainly were wiser than I was. But I observed that even the good artisans fell into the same error as the poets;—because they were good workmen they thought that they also knew all sorts of high matters, and this defect in them overshadowed their wisdom; and therefore I asked myself on behalf of the oracle, *e* whether I would like to be as I was, neither having their knowledge nor their ignorance, or like them in both; and I answered myself and the oracle that I was better off as I was.

23 This enquiry has led to my having many enemies of the worst and most dangerous kind, and has given occasion also to many calumnies. And I am called wise, for my hearers always imagine that I myself possess the wisdom which I find wanting in others: but the truth is, men of Athens, that god only is wise; and by his answer he intends to show that the wisdom of men is worth little or nothing; he is not speaking

b of Socrates, he is only using my name by way of illustration, as if he said, He, men, is the wisest, who, like Socrates, knows that his wisdom is in truth worth nothing. And so I go about the world, obedient to the god, and search and make enquiry into the wisdom of anyone, whether citizen or stranger, who appears to be wise; and if he is not wise, then in vindication of the oracle I show him that he is not wise; and my occupation quite absorbs me, and I have no time to give either to any public matter of interest or to any concern of my own, but I am

c in utter poverty by reason of my devotion to the god.

There is another thing:—young men of the richer classes, who have not much to do, come about me of their own accord; they like to hear the pretenders examined, and they often imitate me, and proceed to examine others; there are plenty of persons, as they quickly discover, who think that they know something, but really know little or nothing; and then those who are examined by them instead of being angry with

d themselves are angry with me: This confounded Socrates, they say; this villainous misleader of youth!—and then if somebody asks them, Why, what evil does he practise or teach? they do not know, and cannot tell; but in order that they may not appear to be at a loss, they repeat the ready-made charges which are used against all philosophers about teaching things up in the clouds and under the earth, and having no gods, and making the worse appear the better cause; for they do not like to confess that their pretence of knowledge has been detected—

e which is the truth; and as they are numerous and ambitious and energetic, and are drawn up in battle array and have persuasive tongues, they have filled your ears with their loud and inveterate calumnies. And this is the reason why my three accusers, Meletus and Anytus and Lycon,* have set upon me; Meletus, who has a quarrel with me on be-

24 half of the poets; Anytus, on behalf of the craftsmen and politicians; Lycon, on behalf of the rhetoricians: and as I said at the beginning, I cannot expect to get rid of such a mass of calumny all in a moment.

---

*Democratic politician of foreign origin and extravagant lifestyle.

And this, men of Athens, is the truth and the whole truth; I have concealed nothing, I have dissembled nothing. And yet, I know that my plainness of speech makes them hate me, and what is their hatred but a proof that I am speaking the truth?—Hence has arisen the prejudice against me; and this is the reason of it, as you will find out either in this or in any future enquiry.

I have said enough in my defence against the first class of my accusers; I turn to the second class. They are headed by Meletus, that good man and true lover of his country, as he calls himself. Against these, too, I must try to make a defence:—Let their affidavit be read; it contains something of this kind: It says that Socrates is a doer of evil, who corrupts the youth; and who does not believe in the gods of the state, but has other new divinities of his own. Such is the charge; and now let us examine the particular counts. He says that I am a doer of evil, and corrupt the youth; but I say, men of Athens, that Meletus is a doer of evil, in that he pretends to be in earnest when he is only in jest, and is so eager to bring men to trial from a pretended zeal and interest about matters in which he really never had the smallest interest. And the truth of this I will endeavour to prove to you.

Come hither, Meletus, and let me ask a question of you. You think a great deal about the improvement of youth?

Yes, I do.

Tell the judges, then, who is their improver; for you must know, as you have taken pains to discover their corruptor, and are citing and accusing me before them. Speak, then, and tell the judges who their improver is. Observe, Meletus, that you are silent, and have nothing to say. But is not this rather disgraceful, and a very considerable proof of what I was saying, that you have no interest in the matter? Speak up, friend, and tell us who their improver is.

The laws.

But that, my good sir, is not my meaning. I want to know who the person is, who, in the first place, knows the laws.

The judges, Socrates, who are present in court.

What, do you mean to say, Meletus, that they are able to instruct and improve youth?

Certainly they are.

What, all of them, or some only and not others?

All of them.

By the goddess Hera, that is good news! There are plenty of improvers, then. And what do you say of the audience,—do they improve them?

Yes, they do.

And the Council members?

Yes, the Council members improve them.

But perhaps the members of the assembly corrupt them?—or do they too improve them?

They improve them.

Then every Athenian improves and elevates them; all with the exception of myself; and I alone am their corruptor? Is that what you affirm?

That is what I stoutly affirm.

I am very unfortunate if you are right. But suppose I ask you a question: How about horses? Does one man do them harm and all the world good? Is not the exact opposite the truth? One man is able to do them good, or at least not many; the trainer of horses, that is to say, does them good, and others who have to do with them rather injure them? Is not that true, Meletus, of horses, or of any other animals? Most assuredly it is; whether you and Anytus say yes or no. Happy indeed would be the condition of youth if they had one corruptor only, and all the rest of the world were their improvers. But you, Meletus, have sufficiently shown that you never had a thought about the young: your carelessness is seen in your not caring about the very things which you bring against me.

And now, Meletus, I will ask you another question—by Zeus I will: Which is better, to live among bad citizens, or among good ones? Answer, friend, I say; the question is one which may be easily answered. Do not the good do their neighbours good, and the bad do them evil?

Certainly.

And is there anyone who would rather be injured than benefited by those who live with him? Answer, my good friend, the law requires you to answer—does anyone like to be injured?

Certainly not.

And when you accuse me of corrupting and deteriorating the youth, do you allege that I corrupt them intentionally or unintentionally?

Intentionally, I say.

But you have just admitted that the good do their neighbours good, and evil do them evil. Now, is that a truth which your superior wisdom has recognized thus early in life, and am I, at my age, in such darkness and ignorance as not to know that if a man with whom I have to live is corrupted by me, I am very likely to be harmed by him; and yet I corrupt him, and intentionally, too—so you say, although neither I nor any other human being is ever likely to be convinced by you. But either I do not corrupt them, or I corrupt them unintentionally; and on either view of the case you lie. If my offense is unintentional, the law has no cognizance of unintentional offenses: you ought to have taken me privately, and warned and admonished me; for if I had been better advised, I should have stopped doing what I only did unintentionally—no doubt I should; but you would have nothing to say to me and refused to teach me. And now you bring me up in this court, which is a place not of instruction, but of punishment.

It will be very clear to you, Athenians, as I was saying, that Meletus has no care at all, great or small, about the matter. But still I should like to know, Meletus, in what I am said to corrupt the young. I suppose you mean, as I infer from your indictment, that I teach them not to acknowledge the gods which the state acknowledges, but some other new divinities or spiritual agencies in their place. These are the lessons by which I corrupt the youth, as you say.

Yes, that I say emphatically.

Then, by the gods, Meletus, of whom we are speaking, tell me and the court, in somewhat plainer terms, what you mean! for I do not yet understand whether you affirm that I teach other men to acknowledge some gods, and therefore that I do believe in gods, and am not an entire atheist—this you do not lay to my charge,—but only you say that they are not the same gods which the city recognizes—the charge is that they are different gods. Or, do you mean that I am an atheist simply, and a teacher of atheism?

I mean the latter—that you are a complete atheist.

What an extraordinary statement! Why do you think so, Meletus? Do you mean that I do not believe in the godhead of the sun or moon, like other men?

I assure you, judges, that he does not: for he says that the sun is stone, and the moon earth.

Friend Meletus, you think that you are accusing Anaxagoras: and you have but a bad opinion of the judges, if you fancy them illiterate to such a degree as not to know that these doctrines are found in the books of Anaxagoras the Clazomenian, which are full of them.[2] And so, the youth are said to be taught them by Socrates, when there are not unfrequently exhibitions of them at the theatre (price of admission one drachma at the most); they might pay their money, and laugh at Socrates if he pretends to father these extraordinary views. And so, Meletus, you really think that I do not believe in any god?

I swear by Zeus that you believe absolutely in none at all.

Nobody will believe you, Meletus, and I am pretty sure that you do not believe yourself. I cannot help thinking, men of Athens, that Meletus is reckless and impudent, and that he has written this indictment in a spirit of mere wantonness and youthful bravado. Has he not compounded a riddle, thinking to try me? He said to himself: I shall see whether the wise Socrates will discover my facetious contradiction, or whether I shall be able to deceive him and the rest of them. For he certainly does appear to me to contradict himself in the indictment, which comes to saying that Socrates is guilty of not believing in the gods, and yet of believing in them—this is not like a person who is in earnest.

I should like you, men of Athens, to join me in examining what I conceive to be his inconsistency; and you, Meletus, answer. And I must

b remind the audience of my request that they would not make an uproar if I speak in my accustomed manner:

Did ever man, Meletus, believe in the existence of human things, and not of human beings? . . . I wish, men of Athens, that he would answer, and not be always making objections. Did ever any man believe in horsemanship, and not in horses? or in flute-playing, and not in flute-players? No, my friend; I will answer you and the court, as you refuse to answer for yourself. There is no man who ever did. But now

c please answer the next question: Can a man believe in spiritual and divine agencies, and not in spirits or demigods?

He cannot.

How lucky I am to have extracted that answer, thanks to the assistance of the court! But then you swear in the indictment that I teach and believe in divine or spiritual agencies (new or old, regardless); at any rate, I believe in spiritual agencies,—so you say and swear in the affidavit; and yet if I believe in divine beings, how can I help believing in spirits or demigods;—must I not? To be sure I must; and therefore I may assume that your silence gives consent. Now what are spirits or

d demigods? are they not either gods or the sons of gods?

Certainly they are.

But this is what I call the facetious riddle invented by you: the demigods or spirits are gods, and you say first that I do not believe in gods, and then again that I do believe in gods; that is, if I believe in demigods. For if the demigods are the illegitimate sons of gods, whether by the nymphs or by any other mothers, of whom they are said to be the sons—what human being will ever believe that there are

e no gods if they are the sons of gods? You might as well affirm the existence of mules, and deny that of horses and asses. Such nonsense, Meletus, could only have been intended by you to make trial of me. You have put this into the indictment because you had nothing real of which to accuse me. But no one who has a speck of understanding will ever be convinced by you that the same men can believe in divine and super-

28 human things, and yet not believe that there are gods and demigods and heroes.

I have said enough in answer to the charge of Meletus: any elaborate defence is unnecessary; but I know only too well how many are the enmities which I have incurred, and this is what will be my destruction

if I am destroyed; not Meletus, nor yet Anytus, but the envy and dis-
paragement of the world, which has been the death of many good
men, and will probably be the death of many more; there is no danger   b
of my being the last of them.

Someone will say: are you not ashamed, Socrates, of a course of life
which is likely to bring you to an untimely end? To him I may fairly
answer: there you are mistaken; a man who is good for anything ought
not to calculate the chance of living or dying; he ought only to consider whether in doing anything he is doing right or wrong—acting
the part of a good man or of a bad one. Whereas, in your view, the heroes who fell at Troy were not good for much, and the son of Thetis   c
above all, who altogether despised danger in comparison with disgrace; when he was so eager to slay Hector, his goddess mother said to
him that if he avenged his companion Patroclus and slew Hector, he
would die himself—'Fate,' she said, in these or similar words, 'waits
for you next after Hector;' he, receiving this warning, utterly despised
danger and death, and instead of fearing them, feared rather to live in
dishonour, and not to avenge his friend. 'Let me die forthwith,' he   d
replies, 'and be avenged of my enemy, rather than abide here by the
beaked ships, a laughing-stock and a burden of the earth.' Had Achilles
any thought of death and danger? For wherever a man's place is,
whether the place which he has chosen or that in which he has been
placed by a commander, there he ought to remain in the hour of danger; he should not think of death or of anything but of disgrace. This,
men of Athens, is a true saying.

Strange, indeed, would be my conduct, men of Athens, if I who,
when I was ordered by the generals whom you chose to command me   e
at Potidaea and Amphipolis and Delium,* remained where they placed
me, like any other man, facing death—if now, when, as I conceive and
imagine, god orders me to fulfil the philosopher's mission of searching into myself and other men, I were to desert my post through fear
of death, or any other fear; that would indeed be strange, and I might   29
justly be arraigned in court for denying the existence of the gods, if I
disobeyed the oracle because I was afraid of death, fancying that I was
wise when I was not. For the fear of death is indeed the pretence of wisdom, and not real wisdom, being a pretence of knowing the unknown;
and no one knows whether death, which men in their fear apprehend

---

*Cities of ancient Greece: Potidaea, in Macedonia, was the site of an intense battle in
432 B.C.E., just before the outbreak of the Peloponnesian War; fighting took place in Amphipolis, also in Macedonia, in 437 and 422 B.C.E. (Socrates was perhaps too old for the
latter); Delium, a seaport of central Greece, was the site of an Athenian defeat at the
hands of the Boeotians during the Peloponnesian War (Thucydides 4.91–96).

b to be the greatest evil, may not be the greatest good. Is not this ignorance of a disgraceful sort, the ignorance which is the conceit that man knows what he does not know? And in this respect only I believe myself to differ from men in general, and may perhaps claim to be wiser than they are:—that whereas I know but little of the world below, I do not suppose that I know: but I do know that injustice and disobedience

c to a superior, whether god or man, is evil and dishonourable, and I will never fear or avoid a possible good rather than a certain evil. And therefore if you let me go now, and are not convinced by Anytus, who said that since I had been prosecuted I must be put to death (or if not that I ought never to have been prosecuted at all); and that if I escape now, your sons will all be utterly ruined by listening to my words—if you say to me: Socrates, this time we will not mind Anytus, and you shall be let off, but upon one condition, that you are not to enquire and spec-

d ulate in this way any more, and that if you are caught doing so again you shall die; if this was the condition on which you let me go, I should reply: Men of Athens, I honour and love you; but I shall obey god rather than you, and while I have life and strength I shall never cease from the practice and teaching of philosophy, exhorting anyone whom I meet and saying to him after my manner: you, my friend— a citizen of the great, mighty and wise city of Athens—are you not

e ashamed of heaping up the greatest amount of money and honour and reputation, and caring so little about wisdom and truth and the greatest improvement of the soul, which you never regard or heed at all? And if the person with whom I am arguing, says: Yes, but I do care; then I do not leave him or let him go at once; but I proceed to interrogate and examine and cross-examine him, and if I think that he has no virtue in him, but only says that he has, I reproach him with un-

30 dervaluing the greater thing, and overvaluing the lesser one. And I shall repeat the same words to everyone whom I meet, young and old, citizen and alien, but especially to the citizens, inasmuch as they are my brethren. For know that this is the command of god; and I believe that no greater good has ever happened in the state than my service to the god. For I do nothing but go about persuading you all, old and young

b alike, not to take thought for your persons or your properties, but first and chiefly to care about the greatest improvement of the soul. I tell you that virtue is not given by money, but that from virtue comes money and every other good of man, public as well as private. This is my teaching, and if this is the doctrine which corrupts the youth, I am a mischievous person. But if anyone says that this is not my teaching, he is lying. Wherefore, men of Athens, I say to you: do as Anytus bids or not as Anytus bids, and either acquit me or not; whichever you do, under-

c stand that I shall never alter my ways, not even if I have to die many times.

Men of Athens, do not interrupt, but hear me; there was an understanding between us that you should hear me to the end: I have something more to say, at which you may be inclined to cry out; but I believe that to hear me will be good for you, and therefore I beg that you will not cry out. I would have you know, that if you kill someone like me, you will injure yourselves more than you will injure me. Nothing will injure me, not Meletus nor yet Anytus—they cannot, for *d* a bad man is not permitted to injure a better than himself. I do not deny that Anytus may, perhaps, kill me, or drive me into exile, or deprive me of civil rights; and he may imagine, and others may imagine, that he is inflicting a great injury: but there I do not agree, for the evil of doing as he is doing—attempting to end the life of another unjustly— is far greater.

And now, Athenians, I am not going to argue for my own sake, as you may think, but for yours, in order that you may not sin against the god by condemning me, who am his gift to you. For if you kill me you *e* will not easily find a successor to me, who, if I may use such a ludicrous figure of speech, am a sort of gadfly, given to the state by god; and the state is a great and noble steed who is tardy in his motions owing to his very size, and requires to be stirred into life. I am that gad- *31* fly which god has attached to the state, and all day long and in all places am always fastening upon you, arousing and persuading and reproaching you. You will not easily find another like me, and therefore I would advise you to spare me. I dare say that you may feel out of temper (like a person who is suddenly awakened from sleep), and you think that you might easily strike me dead as Anytus advises, and then you would sleep on for the remainder of your lives, unless god in his care of you sent you another gadfly. When I say that I am given to you by god, the proof of my mission is this: if I had been like other men, *b* I should not have neglected all my own concerns or patiently seen the neglect of them during all these years, and have been doing yours, coming to you individually like a father or elder brother, exhorting you to regard virtue; such conduct, I say, would be unlike human nature. If I had gained anything, or if my exhortations had been paid, there would have been some sense in my doing so; but now, as you will perceive, not even the impudence of my accusers dares to say that I have ever exacted or sought pay from anyone; of that they have no witness. *c* And I have a sufficient witness to the truth of what I say—my poverty.

Someone may wonder why I go about in private giving advice and busying myself with the concerns of others, but do not venture to come forward in public and advise the state. I will tell you why. You have heard me speak, at sundry times and in different places, of an oracle or sign which comes to me; it is the divinity which Meletus ridicules *d* in the indictment. This sign, which is a kind of voice, first began to come to me when I was a child; it always forbids but never commands me to do anything which I am going to do. This is what deters me from being a politician. And rightly so, I think. For I am certain, men of Athens, that if I had engaged in politics, I should have perished long ago, and

e   done no good either to you or to myself. And do not be offended at my telling you the truth: for the truth is that no man who goes to war with you or any other multitude, honestly striving against the many lawless

32   and unrighteous deeds which are done in a state, will save his life; he who will fight for the right, if he is to live even for a brief space, must have a private station and not a public one.

I can give you convincing evidence of what I say, not words only, but what you value far more—actions. Let me relate to you a passage of my own life which will prove to you that I would never yield to injustice because of any fear of death, even my own. I will tell you a tale of the courts, not very interesting perhaps, but nevertheless true. The

b   only office of state which I ever held, men of Athens, was that of Council member: the tribe Antiochis, which is my tribe, had the presidency at the trial of the generals who had not taken up the bodies of the slain after the battle of Arginusae;[3] and you proposed to try them in a body, contrary to law, as you all thought afterwards; but at the time I was the only one of the Prytanes who was opposed to the illegality, and I gave my vote against you; and when the orators threatened to impeach and arrest me, and you called and shouted, I made up my mind that I would

c   run the risk, having law and justice with me, rather than take part in your injustice because I feared imprisonment and death. This happened in the days of the democracy. But when the oligarchy of the Thirty* was in power, they sent for me and four others into the Rotunda,† and bade us bring Leon‡ the Salaminian from Salamis, as they wanted to put him to death. This was an example of the sort of commands which they were always giving with the view of implicating as many as pos-

d   sible in their crimes; and then I showed, not in word only but in deed, that, if I may be allowed to use such an expression, I did not give a damn about death, and that my great and only care was not to do an unrighteous or unholy thing. For the strong arm of that oppressive power did not frighten me into doing wrong; and when we came out of the Rotunda the other four went to Salamis and fetched Leon, but I went quietly home. For which I might have lost my life, had not the

---

*Thirty Tyrants (see "General Introduction," p. xviii).
†Headquarters of the Thirty; the building is known as Tholos.
‡Democratic Athenian citizen resident on the island of Salamis, who served Athens as a general.

power of the Thirty shortly afterwards come to an end. Many will wit-   e
ness to my words.

Now do you really imagine that I could have survived all these
years, if I had led a public life, supposing that like a good man I had always maintained the right and had made justice, as I ought, the first
thing? No indeed, men of Athens, neither I nor any other man. I have
been always the same in all my actions, public as well as private, and   33
never have I yielded any base compliance to those who are slanderously
termed my disciples, or to any other. Not that I have any regular disciples. But if anyone likes to come and hear me while I am pursuing my
mission, whether he be young or old, he is not excluded. Nor do I converse only with those who pay; but anyone, rich or poor, may ask and   b
answer me and listen to my words; and whether he turns out to be a
bad man or a good one, neither result can be justly imputed to me; for
I never taught or professed to teach him anything. And if anyone says
that he has ever learned or heard anything from me in private which
all the world has not heard, let me tell you that he is lying.

But I shall be asked: why do people delight in continually conversing with you? I have told you already, Athenians, the whole truth   c
about this matter: they like to hear the cross-examination of the pretenders to wisdom; there is amusement in it. Now this duty of cross-
examining other men has been imposed upon me by god; and has
been signified to me by oracles, visions, and in every way in which the
will of divine power was ever intimated to anyone. This is true, Athenians; or, if not true, would be soon refuted. If I am or have been cor-   d
rupting the youth, those of them who are now grown up and become
aware that I gave them bad advice in the days of their youth should
come forward as accusers, and take their revenge; or if they do not like
to come themselves, some of their relatives, fathers, brothers, or other
kinsmen, should say what evil their families have suffered at my hands.
Now is their time. Many of them I see in court. There is Crito, who is
of the same age and of the same deme as I am, and there is Critobulus   e
his son, whom I also see. Then again there is Lysanias of Sphettus, who
is the father of Aeschines—he is present; and also there is Antiphon of
Cephisus, who is the father of Epigenes; and there are the brothers of
several who have been associated with me. There is Nicostratus the son
of Theosdotides, and the brother of Theodotus (Theodotus himself is
dead, and therefore he, at any rate, will not seek to stop him); and there
is Paralus the son of Demodocus, who had a brother named Theages;
and Adeimantus the son of Ariston, whose brother Plato is present;[4]   34
and Aeantodorus, who is the brother of Apollodorus, whom I also see.
I might mention a great many others, some of whom Meletus should
have produced as witnesses in the course of his speech; and let him still

produce them, if he has forgotten—I will make way for him. And let him say, if he has any testimony of the sort which he can produce. Nay, Athenians, the very opposite is the truth. For all these are ready to witness on behalf of the corruptor, of the injurer of their kindred, as Meletus and Anytus call me; not the corrupted youth only—there might have been a motive for that—but their uncorrupted elder relatives. Why should they too support me with their testimony? Why, indeed, except for the sake of truth and justice, and because they know that I am speaking the truth, and that Meletus is a liar.

Well, Athenians, this and the like of this is all the defence which I have to offer. Yet a word more. Perhaps there may be someone who is offended by me, when he recalls how he himself on a similar, or even a less serious occasion, prayed and entreated the judges with many tears, and how he produced his children in court, which was a moving spectacle, together with a host of relations and friends; whereas I, who am probably in danger of my life, will do none of these things. The contrast may occur to his mind, and he may be set against me, and vote in anger because he is displeased at me on this account. Now if there be such a person among you,—I do not say that there is—to him I may fairly reply: My friend, I am a man, and like other men, a creature of flesh and blood, and not 'of wood or stone,' as Homer says,* and I have a family, yes, and sons, Athenians, three in number, one almost a man, and two others who are still young; and yet I will not bring any of them hither in order to petition you for an acquittal. And why not? Not from any self-assertion or want of respect for you. Whether I am or am not afraid of death is another question, of which I will not now speak. But, having regard for public opinion, I feel that such conduct would be discreditable to myself, and to you, and to the whole city. One who has reached my years, and who has a name for wisdom, ought not to demean himself. Whether this opinion of me be deserved or not, at any rate the world has decided that Socrates is in some way superior to other men. And if those among you who are said to be superior in wisdom and courage, and any other virtue, demean themselves in this way, how shameful is their conduct! I have seen men of reputation, when they have been condemned, behaving in the strangest manner: they seemed to fancy that they were going to suffer something dreadful if they died, and that they could be immortal if you only allowed them to live; and I think that such are a dishonour to the city, and that any stranger coming in would have said of them that the most eminent men of Athens, to whom the Athenians themselves

---

*Odyssey 19.163.

give honour and command, are no better than women. And I say that these things ought not to be done by those of us who have a reputation; and if they are done, you ought not to permit them; you ought rather to show that you are far more disposed to condemn the man who gets up a doleful scene and makes the city ridiculous, than him who holds his peace.

But, setting aside the question of public opinion, there seems to be something wrong in asking a favour of a judge, and thus procuring an acquittal, instead of informing and convincing him. For his duty is not to make a present of justice, but to give judgment; and he has sworn that he will judge according to the laws, and not according to his own good pleasure; and we ought not to encourage you, nor should you allow yourself to be encouraged, in this habit of perjury—there can be no piety in that. Do not then require me to do what I consider dishonourable and impious and wrong, especially now, when I am being tried for impiety on the indictment of Meletus. For if, men of Athens, by force of persuasion and entreaty I could overpower your oaths, then I should be teaching you to believe that there are no gods, and in defending should simply convict myself of the charge of not believing in them. But that is not so—far otherwise. For I do believe that there are gods, and in a sense higher than that in which any of my accusers believe in them. And to you and to god I commit my cause, to be determined by you as is best for you and me.

There are many reasons why I am not grieved, men of Athens, at the vote of condemnation. I expected it, and am only surprised that the votes are so nearly equal;[5] for I had thought that the majority against me would have been far larger; but now, had thirty votes gone over to the other side, I should have been acquitted. And I may say, I think, that I have escaped Meletus. I may say more; for without the assistance of Anytus and Lycon, anyone may see that he would not have had a fifth part of the votes, as the law requires, in which case he would have incurred a fine of a thousand drachmae.

And so he proposes death as the penalty. And what shall I propose on my part, men of Athens? Clearly that which is my due. And what is my due? What return shall be made to the man who has never had the wit to be idle during his whole life; but has been careless of what the many care for—wealth, and family interests, and military offices, and speaking in the assembly, and magistracies, and plots, and parties? Reflecting that I was really too honest a man to be a politician and live, I did not go where I could do no good to you or to myself; but where I could do the greatest good privately to every one of you, thither I went, and sought to persuade every man among you that he must look to

himself, and seek virtue and wisdom before he looks to his private interests, and look to the city itself before he looks to the interests of the
city; and that this should be the order which he observes in all his ac-
d   tions. What shall be done to such a man? Doubtless some good thing,
men of Athens, if he has his reward; and the good should be of a kind
suitable to him. What would be a reward suitable to a poor man who is
your benefactor, and who desires leisure in order to instruct you? There
can be no reward so fitting as maintenance in the Prytaneum,* men of
Athens, a reward which he deserves far more than the citizen who has
won the prize at Olympia in the horse or chariot race, whether the chariots were drawn by two horses or by many. For I am needy and he has
enough; and he only gives you the appearance of happiness, and I give
e   you the reality. And if I am to estimate the penalty fairly, I should say that
maintenance in the Prytaneum is the just return.

37   Perhaps you think that I am braving you in what I am saying now,
as in what I said before about the tears and prayers. But this is not so. I
speak rather because I am convinced that I never intentionally wronged
anyone, although I cannot convince you—the time has been too short;
if there were a law at Athens, as there is in other cities, that a capital
cause should not be decided in one day, then I believe that I should
b   have convinced you. But I cannot in a moment refute great slanders;
and, as I am convinced that I never wronged another, I will assuredly
not wrong myself. I will not say of myself that I deserve any evil, or
propose any penalty. Why should I? Because I am afraid of the penalty
of death which Meletus proposes? Since I do not know whether death
is a good or an evil, why should I propose a penalty which would cer-
c   tainly be an evil? Shall I say imprisonment? And why should I live in
prison, and be the slave of the magistrates of the year—of the Eleven?†
Or shall the penalty be a fine, and imprisonment until the fine is paid?
There is the same objection. I should have to lie in prison, for I have no
money, and cannot pay. And if I say exile (and this may possibly be the
penalty which you will affix), I must indeed be blinded by the love of
life, if I am so irrational as to expect that when you, who are my own
d   citizens, cannot endure my discourses and words, and have found them
so grievous and odious that you will have no more of them, others are
likely to endure me. No indeed, men of Athens, that is not very likely.
And what a life should I lead, at my age, wandering from city to city,
ever changing my place of exile, and always being driven out! For I am

---

*Dinner at this public building in the center of the city was offered to victors at the
Olympic and other games.
†Magistrates in charge of the penitentiary system.

quite sure that wherever I go, there, as here, the young men will flock to me; if I drive them away, their elders will drive me out at their request; and if I let them come, their fathers and friends will drive me out for their sakes.

Someone will say: Yes, Socrates, but cannot you hold your tongue, and then you may go into a foreign city, and no one will interfere with you? I have great difficulty in making you understand my answer to this. For if I tell you that to do as you say would be a disobedience to the god, and therefore that I cannot hold my tongue, you will not believe that I am serious; and if I say again that to discourse daily about virtue, and of those other things about which you hear me examining myself and others, is the greatest good of man, and that the unexamined life is not worth living, you are still less likely to believe me. Yet I say what is true, although a thing of which it is hard for me to persuade you. Also, I have never been accustomed to think that I deserve to suffer any harm. Had I money, I might have estimated the offence at what I was able to pay, and not have been much the worse. But I have none, and therefore I must ask you to proportion the fine to my means. Well, perhaps I could afford a mina, and therefore I propose that penalty: Plato, Crito, Critobulus, and Apollodorus, my friends here, bid me say thirty minae, and they will be the sureties. Let thirty minae be the penalty; for which sum they will be ample security to you.

Not much time will be gained, Athenians, in return for the evil name which you will get from the detractors of the city, who will say that you killed Socrates, a wise man; for they will call me wise, even though I am not wise, when they want to reproach you. If you had waited a little while, your desire would have been fulfilled in the course of nature. For I am far advanced in years, as you may perceive, and not far from death. I am speaking now not to all of you, but only to those who have condemned me to death. And I have another thing to say to them: you think that I was convicted because I had no words of the sort which would have procured my acquittal—I mean, if I had thought fit to leave nothing undone or unsaid. Not so; the deficiency which led to my conviction was not of words—certainly not. But I had not the boldness or impudence or inclination to address you as you would have liked me to do, weeping and wailing and lamenting, and saying and doing many things which you have been accustomed to hear from others, and which, as I maintain, are unworthy of me. I thought at the time that I ought not to do anything common or mean when in danger: nor do I now repent of the style of my defence; I would rather die having spoken after my manner, than live speaking in yours. For neither in war nor yet at law ought I or any man to use every way of escaping death.

Often in battle there can be no doubt that if a man will throw away his arms, and fall on his knees before his pursuers, he may escape death; and in other dangers there are other ways of escaping death, if a man is willing to say and do anything. The difficulty, my friends, is not to avoid death, but to avoid unrighteousness; for that runs faster than death.

b   I am old and move slowly, and the slower runner has overtaken me, and my accusers are keen and quick, and the faster runner, who is unrighteousness, has overtaken them. And now I depart hence condemned by you to suffer the penalty of death,—they too go their ways condemned by the truth to suffer the penalty of villainy and wrong; and I must abide by my award—let them abide by theirs. I suppose that these things may be regarded as fated, and I think that they are well.

c   And now, I would like to prophesy to you who have condemned me, for I am about to die, and in the hour of death men are gifted with prophetic power. I prophesy to you, my murderers, that immediately after my departure punishment far heavier than you have inflicted on me will surely await you. You have killed me because you wanted to escape the accuser, and not to give an account of your lives. But that will

d   not be as you suppose: far otherwise. For I say that there will be more accusers of you than there are now; accusers whom hitherto I have restrained: and as they are younger they will be more inconsiderate with you, and you will be more offended by them. If you think that by killing men you can prevent someone from censuring your evil lives, you are mistaken; that is not a way of escape which is either possible or honourable; the easiest and the noblest way is not to disable others, but to improve yourselves. This is the prophecy which I utter, before my departure, to the judges who have condemned me.

e   Friends, who would have acquitted me, I would like also to talk with you about the thing which has come to pass, while the magistrates are busy, and before I go to the place at which I must die. Stay then a little, for we may as well talk with one another while there is

40 time. You are my friends, and I should like to show you the meaning of this event which has happened to me. My judges—for you I may truly call judges—I should like to tell you of a wonderful circumstance. Hitherto the divine faculty of which the internal oracle is the source has constantly been in the habit of opposing me even about trifles, if I was going to make a slip or error in any matter; and now as you see there has come upon me that which may be thought, and is generally believed to be, the last and worst evil. But the oracle made no sign of

b   opposition, either when I was leaving my house in the morning, or when I was on my way to the court, or while I was speaking, at anything which I was going to say; and yet I have often been stopped in the middle of a speech, but now in nothing I either said or did touching the matter in hand has the oracle opposed me. What do I take to be the explanation of this silence? I will tell you. It is an intimation that what has happened to me is a good, and that those of us who think that death is an evil are in error. For the customary sign would surely have opposed me, had I been going to evil and not to good.

Let us reflect in another way, and we shall see that there is great reason to hope that death is a good; for one of two things are possible— either death is a state of nothingness and utter unconsciousness, or, as men say, there is a change and migration of the soul from this world to another. Now if you suppose that there is no consciousness, but a sleep like the sleep of the one who is undisturbed even by dreams, death will be an unspeakable gain. For if a person were to select the night in which his sleep was undisturbed even by dreams, and were to compare it with the other days and nights of his life, and then were to tell us how many days and nights he had passed in the course of his life better and more pleasantly than this one, I think that any man, I will not say a private man, but even the great king will not find many such days or nights, when compared with the others. Now if death were such, I say that to die is gain; for eternity is then only a single night. But if death is the journey to another place, and there, as men say, all the dead abide, what good, my friends and judges, can be greater than this? If indeed when the pilgrim arrives in the world below, he is delivered from the professors of justice in this world, and finds the true judges who are said to give judgment there, Minos and Rhadamanthus and Aeacus and Triptolemus, and other sons of god who were righteous in their own life, that pilgrimage will be worth making. What would not a man give if he might converse with Orpheus* and Musaeus† and Hesiod and Homer? Nay, if this be true, let me die again and again. I myself, too, shall have a wonderful interest in meeting and conversing there with Palamedes, and Ajax the son of Telamon, and any other ancient hero who has suffered death through an unjust judgment; there will be no small pleasure, as I think, in comparing my own sufferings with theirs. Above all, I shall then be able to continue my search into true and false knowledge; as in this world, so also in the next; and I shall find out who is wise, and who pretends to be wise, and is not. What would not a man give, judges, to be able to examine the leader of the great Trojan expedition; or Odysseus or Sisyphus,‡ or numberless

---

*Thracian of myth who sang so sweetly that he charmed trees and animals.
†Singer and priest often connected with Orpheus.
‡Clever but wicked Corinthian king who was eternally punished in Hades (*Odyssey* 11.593ff.).

others, men and women too! What infinite delight would there be in conversing with them and asking them questions! In another world they do not put a man to death for asking questions: assuredly not. For besides being happier than we are, they will be immortal, if what is said is true.

Wherefore, judges, be of good cheer about death, and know for certain that no evil can happen to a good man, either in life or after death. He and his are not neglected by the gods; nor has my own approaching end happened by mere chance. But I see clearly that the time had arrived when it was better for me to die and be released from trouble; wherefore the oracle gave no sign. For which reason, also, I am not angry with my condemners, or with my accusers; they have done me no harm, although they did not mean to do me any good; for this I may gently blame them.

Still I have a favour to ask of them. When my sons are grown up, I would ask you, my friends, to punish them; and I would have you trouble them, as I have troubled you, if they seem to care about riches, or anything, more than about virtue; or if they pretend to be something when they are really nothing, then reprove them, as I have reproved you, for not caring about that for which they ought to care, and thinking that they are something when they are really nothing. And if you do this, both I and my sons will have received justice at your hands.

The hour of departure has arrived, and we go our ways—I to die, and you to live. Which is better god only knows.

CRITO

Introduction

IN THIS SHORT DIALOGUE, Socrates' wealthy friend Crito, a man as old as Socrates who had made his money from agriculture, visits Socrates in prison (after bribing the prison guard) and invites him to escape.

The structure of the dialogue is rather simple:

- (43a–46a) Crito asks Socrates to accept his help and escape. His reasons are: Socrates' refusal is damaging to his friends' reputations; financial and other arrangements can be made; he is only helping his enemies against himself; he should think of his children; he should show courage and not let his own reputation and (again) that of his friends be ruined.

- (46b–50a) Socrates replies: One who is right matters more than many who are wrong—this is particularly true when the soul is concerned; one should never do wrong.

- (50a–53a) The laws of Athens are given a voice: Escaping would destroy the legal order of the city; and there is a "contract" between them and Socrates that he has entered into by remaining in the city all his life.

- (53b–54e) The laws go on: Escaping will stigmatize Socrates and his sons, no matter where he goes; it will also contradict his own views on morality and will jeopardize his position in the afterlife.

Socrates' refusal to accept Crito's escape plan has been very difficult to swallow for many scholars, but I believe it is in line with Plato's view of Socrates. As regards the "contract" between Socrates and the laws of Athens, one should notice how giving a voice to the laws of Athens avoids the problem of showing Socrates abiding by the majority view, whose counsel he deems of no consequence when faced with right individual action.

CRITO

SOCRATES. Why have you come at this hour, Crito? it must be quite early?

CRITO. Yes, certainly.

SOC. What is the exact time?

CR. The dawn is breaking.

SOC. I wonder how the keeper of the prison let you in.

CR. He knows me, because I come often, Socrates; moreover, I have done him a favour.

SOC. And have you only just arrived?

CR. No, I came some time ago.

SOC. Then why did you sit and say nothing, instead of awakening me at once? b

CR. I would not have liked, Socrates, to be in such great trouble and unrest myself, as you are—really I would not: I have been watching with amazement your peaceful slumbers; and for that reason I did not awake you, because I wished to minimize the pain. I have always thought you to be of a happy disposition; but never did I see anything like the easy, tranquil manner in which you bear this calamity.

SOC. Why, Crito, when a man has reached my age he ought not to fret at the approach of death.

CR. And yet other old men find themselves in similar misfortunes, c and age does not prevent them from fretting.

SOC. That is true. But you have not told me why you come at this early hour.

CR. I have come to bring you a message which is sad and painful; not, as I believe, to yourself, but to all of us who are your friends, and saddest of all to me.

SOC. What? Has the ship come from Delos, on the arrival of which I am to die?[1] d

CR. No, the ship has not actually arrived, but it will probably be here today, as people who have come from Sunium tell me that they left it there; therefore tomorrow, Socrates will be the last day of your life.

SOC. Very well, Crito; if such is the will of god, I am willing; but my belief is that there will be a delay of a day.

CR. Why do you think so? 44

SOC. I will tell you. I am to die on the day after the arrival of the ship.

CR. Yes; that is what the authorities say.

Soc. But I do not think that the ship will be here until tomorrow; this I infer from a vision which I had last night, or rather only just now, when you fortunately allowed me to sleep.

Cr. And what was the nature of the vision?

Soc. There appeared to me the likeness of a woman, fair and
b comely, clothed in bright garment, who called to me and said: Socrates,

'The third day hence to fertile Phthia shalt thou go.'*

Cr. What a singular dream, Socrates!

Soc. There can be no doubt about the meaning, Crito, I think.

Cr. Yes; the meaning is only too clear. But, oh! my dear Socrates, let me entreat you once more to take my advice and escape. For if you die I shall not only lose a friend who can never be replaced, but there is an- other evil: people who do not know you and me will believe that I might have saved you if I had been willing to give money, but that I did
c not care. Now, can there be a worse disgrace than this—that I should be thought to value money more than the life of a friend? For most people will not be persuaded that I wanted you to escape, and that you refused.

Soc. But why, my dear Crito, should we care about the opinion of most people? Good men, and they are the only persons who are worth considering, will think of these things truly as they occurred.

d Cr. But you see, Socrates, that the opinion of the majority must be regarded, for what is now happening shows that they can do the great- est evil to anyone who has lost their good opinion.

Soc. I only wish it were so, Crito; and that the many could do the greatest evil; for then they would also be able to do the greatest good— and what a fine thing this would be! But in reality they can do neither; for they cannot make a man either wise or foolish; and whatever they do is the result of chance.

e Cr. Well, I will not argue with you; but please tell me, Socrates, whether you are not acting out of regard for me and your other friends: are you not afraid that if you escape from prison we may get into trouble with the informers for having stolen you away, and lose ei- ther the whole or great part of our property; or that even a worse evil
45 may happen to us? Now, if you fear on our account, be at ease; for in order to save you, we ought surely to run this, or even a greater risk; be persuaded, then, and do as I say.

Soc. Yes, Crito, that is one fear I have, but by no means the only one.

---

*Iliad 9.363.

CR. Fear not—there are persons who are willing to get you out of prison at no great cost; and as for the informers, they are far from being exorbitant in their demands—a little money will satisfy them. My means, which are certainly ample, are at your service, and if you have a scruple about spending all mine, here are strangers who will give you the use of theirs; one of them, Simmias* the Theban, has brought a large sum of money for this very purpose; and Cebes† and many others are prepared to spend their money in helping you to escape. I say, therefore, do not hesitate on our account, and do not say, as you did in court,‡ that you will have difficulty in knowing what to do with yourself anywhere else. For men will love you in other places to which you may go, and not in Athens only; there are friends of mine in Thessaly, if you like to go to them, who will value and protect you, and no Thessalian will give you any trouble. Nor can I think that you are at all justified, Socrates, in betraying your own life when you might be saved; in acting thus you are playing into the hands of your enemies, who are hurrying on your destruction. And further I should say that you are deserting your own children; for you might bring them up and educate them; instead of which you go away and leave them, and they will have to take their chances; and if they do not meet with the usual fate of orphans, there will be small thanks to you. No man should bring children into the world who is unwilling to persevere to the end in their nurture and education. But you appear to be choosing the easier part, not the better and manlier, which would have been more becoming to one who professes to care for virtue in all his actions, like yourself. And indeed, I am ashamed not only of you, but of us who are your friends, when I reflect that the whole business will be attributed entirely to our want of courage. The trial should have never taken place, or might have been managed differently; this last act, or crowning folly, will seem to have occurred through our negligence and cowardice, who might have saved you, if we had been good for anything; and you might have saved yourself, for there was no difficulty at all. See now, Socrates, how sad and discreditable are the consequences, both to us and to you. Make up your mind then, or rather have your mind already made up, for the time of deliberation is over, and there is only one thing to be done, which must be

---

*Follower of Socrates, perhaps a Pythagorean (see Xenophon, *Memorabilia* 1.2.48 and 3.11.17; Pythagoras was a sixth-century B.C.E. Greek philosopher and mathematician) and author of dialogues.

†Also a follower of Socrates, and also perhaps a Pythagorean and author of dialogues, of which *Pinax* is extant.

‡See *Apology* 37c–d (p. 294).

done this very night, and if we delay at all will be no longer practicable or possible; I beseech you therefore, Socrates, be persuaded by me, and do as I say.

Soc. Dear Crito, your zeal is invaluable, if a right one; but if wrong, the greater the zeal the greater the danger; and therefore we ought to consider whether I shall or shall not do as you say. For I am and always have been one of those natures who must be guided by reason, whatever the reason may be which upon reflection appears to me the best; and now that this chance has befallen me, I cannot repudiate my own words: the principles which I have hitherto honored and revered I still honor, and unless we can at once find other and better principles, I am certain not to agree with you; no, not even if the power of the multitude could inflict many more imprisonments, confiscations, deaths, frightening us like children with hobgoblin terrors. What will be the fairest way of considering the question? Shall I return to your old argument about the opinions of men?—we were saying that some of them are to be taken into account, and others not. Now were we right in maintaining this before I was condemned? And has the argument which was once good now proved to be talk for the sake of talking—mere childish nonsense? That is what I want to consider with your help, Crito: whether, under my present circumstances, the argument appears to be in any way different or not; and whether it is to be allowed by me or disallowed. That argument, which, as I believe, is maintained by many persons of authority, was to the effect, as I was saying, that the opinions of some men are to be taken into account, and those of other men to be disregarded. Now you, Crito, are not going to die tomorrow—at least, there is no likelihood of that and therefore you are disinterested and not liable to be deceived by the circumstances in which you are placed. Tell me then, whether I am right in saying that some opinions, and the opinions of some men only, are to be valued, and that other opinions, and the opinions of other men, are not to be valued. I ask you whether I was right in maintaining this.

Cr. Certainly.

Soc. The good are to be regarded, and not the bad?

Cr. Yes.

Soc. And the opinions of the wise are good, and the opinions of the unwise are evil?

Cr. Certainly.

Soc. And what was said about another matter? Is the pupil who devotes himself to the practice of gymnastics supposed to attend to the praise and blame and opinion of every man, or of one man only—his physician or trainer, whoever he may be?

CR. Of one man only.

Soc. And he ought to fear the censure and welcome the praise of that one only, and not of most people?

CR. Clearly so.

Soc. And he ought to act and train, and eat and drink in the way which seems good to his single master who has understanding, rather than according to the opinion of all other men put together?

CR. True.

Soc. And if he disobeys and disregards the opinion and approval of   c
the one, and regards the opinion of the many who have no understanding, will he not suffer evil?

CR. Certainly he will.

Soc. And what will the evil be, whither tending and what affecting, in the disobedient person?

CR. Clearly, affecting the body; that is what is destroyed by the evil.

Soc. Very good; and is not this true, Crito, of other things which we need not separately enumerate? In questions of just and unjust, fair and foul, good and evil, which are the subjects of our present consultation, ought we to follow the opinion of the many and to fear them; or the opinion of the one man who has understanding? ought we not   d
to fear and reverence him more than all the rest of the world: and if we desert him shall we not destroy and injure that principle in us which may be assumed to be improved by justice and deteriorated by injustice; there is such a principle?

CR. Certainly there is, Socrates.

Soc. Take a parallel instance: if, acting under the advice of those who have no understanding, we destroy that which is improved by health and is deteriorated by disease, would life be worth having? And that which has been destroyed is—the body?   e

CR. Yes.

Soc. Could we live, having an evil and corrupted body?

CR. Certainly not.

Soc. And will life be worth having, if that higher part of man be destroyed, which is improved by justice and depraved by injustice? Do we suppose that principle, whatever it may be in man, which has to do   48
with justice and injustice, to be inferior to the body?

CR. Certainly not.

Soc. More honourable than the body?

CR. Far more.

Soc. Then, my friend, we must not regard what most people say of us: but what he, the one man who has understanding of just and unjust, will say, and what the truth will say. And therefore you begin in error when you advise that we should regard the opinion of the majority about just and unjust, good and evil, honourable and dishonourable.— 'Well,' someone will say, 'but the majority can kill us.'

b   CR. Yes, Socrates; that will clearly be the answer.

SOC. And it is true: but still I find with surprise that the old argument is unshaken as ever. And I should like to know whether I may say the same of another proposition—that not life, but a good life, is to be chiefly valued?

CR. Yes, that also remains unshaken.

SOC. And a good life is equivalent to a just and honourable one— that holds also?

CR. Yes, it does.

SOC. From these premises I proceed to argue the question whether I ought or ought not to try and escape without the consent of the Athe-
c nians: and if I am clearly right in escaping, then I will make the attempt; but if not, I will abstain. The other considerations which you mention, of money and loss of character and the duty of educating one's children, are, I fear, only the doctrines of the multitude, who would be as ready to restore people to life, if they were as able as they are to put them to death—and with as little reason. But now, since the argument has thus far prevailed, the only question which remains to be consid-
d ered is whether we shall do rightly either in escaping or in allowing others to aid in our escape and paying them in money and thanks, or whether in reality we shall not do rightly; and if the latter, then death or any other calamity which may ensue from my remaining here must not be factored into the calculation.

CR. I think that you are right, Socrates; how shall we proceed?

SOC. Let us consider the matter together, and do you either refute
e me if you can, and I will be convinced; or else cease, my dear friend, from repeating to me that I ought to escape against the wishes of the Athenians: for I highly value your attempts to persuade me to do so, but I may not be persuaded against my own better judgment. Now
49 please consider my first position, and try your best to answer me.

CR. I will.

SOC. Are we to say that we are never intentionally to do wrong, or that in one way we ought and in another we ought not to do wrong, or is doing wrong always evil and dishonourable, as I was just now saying, and as has been already acknowledged by us? Are all our former admissions which were made within a few days to be thrown away? And have we, at our age, been earnestly discoursing with one another
b all our life long only to discover that we are no better than children? Or, in spite of the opinion of the majority, and in spite of consequences, whether better or worse, shall we insist on the truth of what was then

said, that injustice is always an evil and dishonour to him who acts unjustly? Shall we say so or not?

CR. Yes.

Soc. Then we must do no wrong?

CR. Certainly not.

Soc. Nor when injured injure in return, as the many imagine; for
we must injure no one at all?

CR. Clearly not.   c

Soc. Again, Crito, may we do evil?

CR. Surely not, Socrates.

Soc. And what of doing evil in return for evil, which is the morality of the majority—is that just or not?

CR. Not just.

Soc. For doing evil to another is the same as injuring him?

CR. Very true.

Soc. Then we ought not to retaliate or render evil for evil to anyone, whatever evil we may have suffered from him. But I would have
you consider, Crito, whether you really mean what you are saying. For   d
this opinion has never been held, and never will be held, by any considerable number of persons; and those who are agreed and those who
are not agreed upon this point have no common ground, and can only
despise one another when they see how widely they differ. Tell me,
then, whether you agree with and assent to my first principle, that neither injury nor retaliation nor warding off evil by evil is ever right. And
shall that be the premiss of our argument? Or do you decline and dissent from this? For so I have always thought, and continue to think;   e
but, if you are of another opinion, let me hear what you have to say. If,
however, you remain of the same mind as formerly, I will proceed to
the next step.

CR. You may proceed, for I have not changed my mind.

Soc. Then I will go on to the next point, which may be put in the
form of a question: Ought a man to do what he admits to be right, or
ought he to betray the right?

CR. He ought to do what he thinks right.

Soc. But if this is true, what is the application? In leaving the prison
against the will of the Athenians, do I wrong any? or rather do I not   50
wrong those whom I ought least to wrong? Do I not desert the principles which were acknowledged by us to be just—what do you say?

CR. I cannot tell, Socrates; for I do not know.

Soc. Then consider the matter in this way:—Imagine that I am
about to play truant (you may call the proceeding by any name which
you like), and the laws and the government come and interrogate me:
'Tell us, Socrates,' they say; 'what are you about? are you not going by   b

an act of yours to overturn us—the laws, and the whole city as much as you can? Do you imagine that a state can subsist and not be overthrown, in which the decisions of law have no power, but are set aside and trampled upon by individuals?' What will be our answer, Crito, to these and the like words? Anyone, and especially a rhetorician, will have a good deal to say on behalf of the law which requires a sentence to be carried out. He will argue that this law should not be set aside; and shall we reply, 'Yes; but the city has injured us and given an unjust sentence.' Suppose I say that?

CR. Very good, Socrates.

SOC. 'And was that our agreement with you?' the law would answer; 'or were you to abide by the sentence of the city?' And if I were to express my astonishment at their words, the law would probably add: 'Answer, Socrates, instead of opening your eyes—you are in the habit of asking and answering questions. Tell us,—What complaint have you to make against us which justifies you in attempting to destroy us and the city? In the first place did we not bring you into existence? Your father married your mother by our aid and begat you. Say whether you have any objection to urge against those of us who regulate marriage?' None, I should reply. 'Or against those of us who after birth regulate the nurture and education of children, in which you also were trained? Were not the laws, which have the charge of education, right in commanding your father to train you in music and gymnastics?' Right, I should reply. 'Well then, since you were brought into the world and nurtured and educated by us, can you deny in the first place that you are our child and slave, as your fathers were before you? And if this is true you are not on equal terms with us; nor can you think that you have a right to do to us what we are doing to you. Would you have any right to strike or revile or do any other evil to your father or your master, if you had one, because you have been struck or reviled by him, or received some other evil at his hands?—you would not say this? And because we think right to destroy you, do you think that you have any right to destroy us in return, and your country as far as in you lies? Will you, professor of true virtue, pretend that you are justified in this? Has a philosopher like you failed to discover that our country is more to be valued and higher and holier far than mother or father or any ancestor, and more to be regarded in the eyes of the gods and of men of understanding? also to be soothed, and gently and reverently entreated when angry, even more than a father, and either to be persuaded, or if not persuaded, to be obeyed? And when we are punished by it, whether with imprisonment or stripes, the punishment is to be endured in silence; and if it leads us to wounds or death in battle, thither we follow as is right; neither may anyone yield or retreat or leave his rank, but whether in battle or in a court of law, or in any other place, he must do what his city and his country order him; or he must change their view of what is just: and if he may do no violence to his father or mother, much less may he do violence to his country.' What   *c* answer shall we make to this, Crito? Do the laws speak truly, or do they not?

CR. I think that they do.

SOC. Then the laws will say, 'Consider, Socrates, if we are speaking truly that in your present attempt you are going to do us an injury. For, having brought you into the world, and nurtured and educated you, and given you and every other citizen a share in every good which we   *d* had to give, we further proclaim to any Athenian by the liberty which we allow him, that if he does not like us when he has become of age and has seen the ways of the city, and made our acquaintance, he may go where he pleases and take his goods with him. None of us laws will forbid him or interfere with him. Anyone who does not like us and the city, and who wants to emigrate to a colony or to any other city, may   *e* go where he likes, retaining his property. But he who has experience of the manner in which we order justice and administer the city, and still remains, has entered into an implied contract that he will do as we command him. And he who disobeys us is, as we maintain, thrice wrong; first, because in disobeying us he is disobeying his parents; secondly, because we are the authors of his education; thirdly, because he has made an agreement with us that he will duly obey our commands;   52 and he neither obeys them nor convinces us that our commands are unjust; and we do not rudely impose them, but give him the alternative of obeying or convincing us; that is what we offer, and he does neither.

'These are the sort of accusations to which, as we were saying, you, Socrates, will be exposed if you accomplish your intentions; you, above all other Athenians.' Suppose now I ask, why I rather than anybody else? they will justly retort upon me that I above all other men have acknowl-   *b* edged the agreement. 'There is clear proof,' they will say, 'Socrates, that we and the city were not displeasing to you. Of all Athenians you have been the most constant resident in the city, which, as you never leave, you may be supposed to love. For you never went out of the city either to see the games, except once when you went to the Isthmus,* or to any other place unless when you were on military service; nor did you travel as other men do. Nor had you any curiosity to know other cities or their laws: your affections did not go beyond us and our city; we

---

*Reference to the Isthmian games held in the Isthmus of Corinth, which included chariot races, wrestling, etc.; some editors think that this passage was not included by Plato.

c   were your special favourites, and you acquiesced in our government of
you; and here in this city you begat your children, which is a proof of
your satisfaction. Moreover, you might in the course of the trial, if you
had liked, have fixed the penalty at banishment; the city which refuses
to let you go now would have let you go then. But you pretended that
you preferred death to exile, and that you were not unwilling to die.
And now you have forgotten these fine sentiments, and pay no respect
d   to us the laws, of whom you are the destroyer; and are doing what only
a miserable slave would do, running away and turning your back upon
the compacts and agreements which you made as a citizen. And first of
all answer this very question: Are we right in saying that you agreed to
be governed according to us in deed, and not in word only? Is that true
or not?' How shall we answer, Crito? Must we not assent?

CR. We cannot help it, Socrates.

Soc. Then will they not say: 'You, Socrates, are breaking the covenants
e   and agreements which you made with us at your leisure, not in any
haste or under any compulsion or deception, but after you have had
seventy years to think of them, during which time you were at liberty
to leave the city, if we were not to your mind, or if our covenants appeared to you to be unfair. You had your choice, and might have gone
either to Sparta or Crete, both which states are often praised by you for
53 their good government, or to some other Greek or foreign state. Whereas
you, above all other Athenians, seemed to be so fond of the city, or, in
other words, of us her laws (and who would care about a city which
has no laws?), that you never stirred out of her; the cripple, the blind,
the maimed were not more stationary in it than you were. And now
you run away and forsake your agreements. Not so, Socrates, if you will
take our advice; do not make yourself ridiculous by escaping out of the
city.

'For just consider, if you transgress and err in this sort of way,
b   what good will you do either to yourself or to your friends? That your
friends will be driven into exile and deprived of citizenship, or will
lose their property, is fairly certain; and you yourself, if you fly to one
of the neighbouring cities, as, for example, Thebes or Megara, both of
which are well governed, will come to them as an enemy, Socrates, and
their government will be against you, and all patriotic citizens will cast
an evil eye upon you as a subverter of the laws, and you will confirm
in the minds of the judges the justice of their own condemnation of
c   you. For he who is a corruptor of the laws is more than likely to be a
corruptor of the young and foolish portion of mankind. Will you then
flee from well-ordered cities and virtuous men? and is existence worth
having on these terms? Or will you go to them without shame, and talk

to them, Socrates? And what will you say to them? What you say here
about virtue and justice and institutions and laws being the best things
among men? Would that be decent of you? Surely not. But if you
go away from well-governed states to Crito's friends in Thessaly, where   *d*
there is great disorder and licence, they will be charmed to hear the tale
of your escape from prison, set off with ludicrous particulars of the
manner in which you were wrapped in a goatskin or some other disguise, and metamorphosed in the manner typical of runaways; but will
there be no one to remind you that in your old age you were not
ashamed to violate the most sacred laws from a miserable desire of a
little more life? Perhaps not, if you keep them in a good temper; but if   *e*
they are out of temper you will hear many degrading things; you will
live, but how?—as the flatterer of all men, and the servant of all men;
and doing what?—eating and drinking in Thessaly, having gone abroad
in order that you may get a dinner. And where will be your fine sentiments about justice and virtue? Say that you wish to live for the sake of   54
your children—you want to bring them up and educate them—will
you take them into Thessaly and deprive them of Athenian citizenship?
Is this the benefit which you will confer upon them? Or are you under
the impression that they will be better cared for and educated here if
you are still alive, although absent from them; for your friends will take
care of them? Do you fancy that if you are an inhabitant of Thessaly
they will take care of them, and if you are an inhabitant of the other
world that they will not take care of them? Nay; but if they who call
themselves friends are good for anything, they will—to be sure they   *b*
will.

'Listen, then, Socrates, to us who have brought you up. Think not
of life and children first, and of justice afterwards, but of justice first,
so that you may be justified before the princes of the world below. For
neither will you nor any that belong to you be happier or holier or
juster in this life, or happier in another, if you do as Crito bids. Now
you depart in innocence, a sufferer and not a doer of evil; a victim, not   *c*
of the laws but of men. But if you go forth, returning evil for evil, and
injury for injury, breaking the covenants and agreements which you
have made with us, and wronging those whom you ought least of all
to wrong, that is to say, yourself, your friends, your country, and us, we
shall be angry with you while you live, and our brethren, the laws in
the world below, will receive you as an enemy; for they will know that
you have done your best to destroy us. Listen, then, to us and not to   *d*
Crito.'

This, dear Crito, is the voice which I seem to hear murmuring in
my ears, like the sound of the flute in the ears of the mystic; that voice,

I say, is humming in my ears, and prevents me from hearing any other. And I know that anything more which you may say will be in vain. Yet speak, if you have anything to say.

Cr. I have nothing to say, Socrates.

e   Soc. Leave me then, Crito, to fulfil the will of god, and to follow whither he leads.

PHAEDO

Introduction

ALTHOUGH THIS DIALOGUE IS generally considered to be from the early period, it is easy to see an increase in complexity, in the number of speakers, in the narrative framework, and in the depth and intricacy of the arguments. It shows Plato reaching philosophical maturity and getting ready to explore questions in more depth.

Away from Athens, in Phlius, a village that sheltered a Pythagorean community (Pythagoras was a sixth century B.C.E. Greek philosopher and mathematician) and was strongly supportive of Sparta, Phaedo, a member of the Socratic circle, narrates Socrates' last hours and death in prison to Echecrates, a resident of Phlius. Within Phaedo's narrative, the conversation takes place between Socrates and four of his followers: the young men Simmias (who had come to Athens with money in order to help Socrates escape) and Cebes, both versed in Pythagorean thought, Phaedo himself, and Crito, whom we know from the eponymous dialogue. Apollodorus, also present, punctuates the beginning and the end of the dialogue with his wailing (59a, 117d). The prison guard is not identified.

Three topics mark this dialogue as crucial in the Platonic output: Socrates' theory of knowledge as recollection, the Ideas, and the immortality of the soul. The suggested structural outline is as follows:

- (57a–69e) Socrates' followers find him with his wife Xanthippe, and busy turning Aesop's fables into verse. Socrates says that the philosopher should welcome death; Cebes and Simmias object. Socrates explains that the philosopher will have access to true knowledge in the afterlife, unencumbered by the mortal body.

- (69e–72d) Cebes objects that there is no reason to assume there will be an afterlife at all. Socrates responds with an argument based on the existence of opposite things (for example, wet and dry). If being alive is the opposite of being dead, the argument goes, it must surely be possible to "be" dead. There are two logical problems that Plato leaves unexamined: (a) how can the soul be dead or alive, when it simply (by Socrates' own prior admission) becomes embodied or disembodied? and (b) how could a dead body change states and become alive?

- (72e–78a) The theory of knowledge as recollection is introduced in support of the immortality of the soul. A question is posed by Socrates: How can one have a concept of equality when there is no perfect equality among worldly things? No doubt, Socrates says, this is the result of our having known of perfect equality during a phase of our existence that is out of this world. Worldly things remind us of equality, but cannot teach it to us. The Ideas that we can know when out of this world are what the philosopher desires to know, and he can have access to them only when the mortal body has been left behind at death. Cebes demands further arguments.

- (78b–85e) Socrates presents the argument from affinity: The soul, especially when separated from the body, is more akin to immutable Ideas than to things, since it is also immutable and invisible. Socrates equates philosophy with a preparation for death. Simmias and Cebes object again. Simmias (following a Pythagorean doctrine) likens the soul to the right tuning of a lyre. Cebes appears by now convinced of the differences between soul and body, but is still unsure about whether the destruction of the body does not harm the soul as well.

- (85e–91c) Simmias elaborates further: The soul is the right relation of physical elements that make the lyre sound correctly. When the lyre is destroyed, is the soul not destroyed too? In posing this question, he departs from Pythagorean belief in an afterlife and challenges Socrates. Cebes tries to mediate: Can the soul be separate from the body but not everlasting? After all, the body changes and is constantly renewed; can the soul be immutable through life but disappear at death? At this point, Echecrates interrupts in order to support the theory of the soul as harmony and remark on the difficulty that Socrates is in at this point of the conversation narrated by Phaedo, who responds by narrating his own intervention in the conversation with Socrates. The exchange between Phaedo and Socrates has the effect of reinforcing the reliance on argument until the very end.

- (91c–95e) Socrates answers Simmias with four objections to the theory of the soul as harmony: (a) It is incompatible with the theory of knowledge as recollection; (b) it does not account for different levels of "tuning," while the soul is immutable; (c) it does not explain how the body can be in good shape and the soul "out of tune"; and (d) it is inconsistent with the principle of the soul as ruling the body. Cebes is impressed but still expects an answer to his own question. Socrates reminds the listeners (and us) of Cebes' position: The soul may well be long-lived and have existed before the body is born, yet it may die with it.

- (95e–102d) Socrates talks about his own research into the causes of coming-to-be and passing away, and comments on the work of the pre-Socratic Anaxagoras, who studied the physical world and posited Mind as its organizing principle, without explaining how the organization is in fact achieved. He next proceeds to establish that worldly things are what they are and receive their names by their participation in the Ideas—for example, a beautiful thing is beautiful because it participates in Beauty, not because of its physical attributes. Surprisingly (but perhaps only for a modern reader), neither his listeners nor Echecrates have any objection to this theory.

- (102d–107a) Socrates goes on to distinguish between what we may call the accidental and the essential properties of a thing. Afterward, he argues that certain things must participate in one of two opposite things, so that if they participate in the opposite, they must be destroyed or go away. The soul is one such thing: It brings life to the body it resides in, and cannot ever participate in death, or else it would be destroyed or would go away. Therefore, at death, since the soul cannot participate in it, it goes away.

- (107a–115a) Socrates relates a myth of the afterlife. It is, of course, a fanciful myth; we must notice that a very different future awaits the soul of the philosopher and that of the common man. This myth is elaborated further at the end of *Gorgias* and *Republic*.

- (115b-118a) Socrates drinks the hemlock and dies, in a very dramatic passage.

The argument for the immortality of the soul becomes a key piece for the understanding of Platonic ethics. The issue of the Ideas, which is intimated in the dialogue, is a very difficult topic that is further developed in *Republic* and *Parmenides* and has been discussed extensively by scholars. As for the theory of knowledge as recollection, it must be noted that Plato develops his epistemology further in the middle and late dialogues, especially in *Theaetetus* and *Sophist*.

PHAEDO

57

ECHECRATES. Were you yourself, Phaedo, in the prison with Socrates on the day he drank the poison?

PHAEDO. Yes, Echecrates, I was.

ECH. I would so like to hear about his death. What did he say in his last hours? We were informed that he died by taking poison, but no one knew anything more; for no Phliasian ever goes to Athens now, and it is a long time since any stranger from Athens has found his way hither; so we had no clear account.

PHAED. Did you not hear of the proceedings at the trial?

58

ECH. Yes; someone told us about the trial, and we could not understand why, having been condemned, he should not have been put to death immediately, but long afterwards. What was the reason for this?

PHAED. An accident, Echecrates: the stern of the ship which the Athenians send to Delos happened to have been crowned on the day before he was tried.

ECH. What is this ship?

PHAED. It is the ship in which, according to Athenian tradition, Theseus went to Crete when he took with him the fourteen youths, and was the saviour of them and of himself. And they are said to have vowed to Apollo at the time, that if they were saved they would send a yearly mission to Delos. Now this custom still continues, and the whole period of the voyage to and from Delos, beginning when the priest of Apollo crowns the stern of the ship, is a holy season, during which the city is not allowed to be polluted by public executions; and when the vessel is detained by contrary winds, the time spent in going and returning is very considerable. As I was saying, the ship was crowned on the day before the trial, and this was the reason why Socrates remained in prison and was not put to death until long after he was condemned.

ECH. What was the manner of his death, Phaedo? What was said or done? And which of his friends were with him? Or did the authorities forbid them to be present—so that he had no friends near him when he died?

PHAED. No; there were several of them with him.

ECH. If you have some time, please tell me what happened, as exactly as you can.

PHAED. I have nothing pressing to do, and will try to tell you as you wish. To be reminded of Socrates is always the greatest delight to me, whether I speak myself or hear another speak of him.

ECH. You will have listeners who are of the same mind with you, and I hope that you will be as exact as you can.

PHAED. I had a singular feeling at being in his company. For I could hardly believe that I was present at the death of a friend, and therefore I did not pity him, Echecrates; he died so fearlessly, and his words and bearing were so noble and gracious, that to me he appeared blessed. I thought that in going to the other world he could not be without a divine call, and that he would be happy, if any man ever was, when he arrived there; and therefore I did not pity him as might have seemed natural at such an hour. But I had not the pleasure which I usually feel in philosophical discourse (for philosophy was the theme of which we spoke). I was pleased, but in the pleasure there was also a strange admixture of pain; for I reflected that he was soon to die, and this double feeling was shared by us all; we were laughing and weeping by turns, especially the excitable Apollodorus—you know what he is like.

ECH. Yes.

PHAED. He was quite beside himself; and I and all of us were greatly moved.

ECH. Who were present?

PHAED. Of native Athenians there were, besides Apollodorus, Critobulus and his father Crito, Hermogenes, Epigenes, Aeschines, Antisthenes; likewise Ctesippus of the deme of Paeania, Menexenus, and some others. Plato was sick, I think.[1]

ECH. Were there any strangers?

PHAED. Yes, there were; Simmias the Theban, and Cebes, and Phaedondes; Euclid and Terpsion, who came from Megara.

ECH. And was Aristippus there, and Cleombrotus?

PHAED. No, they were said to be in Aegina.

ECH. Anyone else?

PHAED. I think that these were nearly all.

ECH. Well, and what did you talk about?

PHAED. I will begin at the beginning, and endeavor to repeat the entire conversation. On the previous days we had been in the habit of assembling early in the morning at the court in which the trial took place, which is not far from the prison. There we used to wait talking with one another until the doors were opened (they were not opened very early); then we went in and generally passed the day with Socrates. On the last morning we assembled earlier than usual, having heard on the day before when we left the prison in the evening that the sacred ship had come from Delos; and so we arranged to meet very early at the usual place. On our arrival the jailer who answered the door, instead of admitting us, came out and told us to stay until he called us.

'For the Eleven,'* he said, 'are now with Socrates; they are taking off his chains, and giving orders that he is to die today.' He soon returned and said that we might come in. On entering we found Socrates just re-   60 leased from chains, and Xanthippe,† whom you know, sitting by him, and holding his child in her arms. When she saw us she uttered a cry and said, as women do: 'Socrates, this is the last time that either you will converse with your friends, or they with you.' Socrates turned to Crito and said: 'Crito, let someone take her home.' Some of Crito's people accordingly led her away, crying out and beating herself. When she was gone, Socrates, sitting up on the couch, bent and rubbed his leg,   b saying, as he was rubbing: How singular is the thing called pleasure, and how curiously related to pain, which might be thought to be the opposite of it; for they are never present to a man at the same instant, and yet the one who pursues either is generally compelled to take the other too; their bodies are two, but they are joined by a single head. And I cannot help thinking that if Aesop had remembered them, he   c would have made a fable about god trying to reconcile their strife, and how, when he could not, he fastened their heads together; and this is the reason why when one comes the other follows: as I know by my own experience now, when after the pain in my leg which was caused by the chain pleasure seems to follow.

At this Cebes said: I am glad, Socrates, that you have mentioned the name of Aesop. For it reminds me of a question which has been asked   d by many, and was asked of me only the day before yesterday by Evenus‡ the poet—he will be sure to ask it again, and therefore if you would like me to have an answer ready for him, you may as well tell me what I should say to him: he wanted to know why you, who never before wrote a line of poetry, now that you are in prison are turning Aesop's fables§ into verse, and also composing that hymn in honour of Apollo.

Tell him, Cebes, he replied, the truth—that I had no intention of rivalling him or his poems; to do so, as I knew, would be no easy task. But I wanted to explore and comply with the meaning of certain dreams of mine. In the course of my life I have often had intimations in dreams 'that I should compose music.' The same dream came to me sometimes in one form, and sometimes in another, but always saying the same or nearly the same words: 'Cultivate and make music,' said the dream. And hitherto I had imagined that this was only intended to

---

*Magistrates in charge of the penitentiary system.
†Socrates' wife.
‡Minor Sophist who specialized in literary composition and invented rhetorical devices.
§Stories of speaking animals that illustrate moral points; we know nothing of Aesop.

61 exhort and encourage me in the study of philosophy, which has been
the pursuit of my life, and is the noblest and best of music. The dream
was bidding me do what I was already doing, in the same way that the
competitor in a race is bidden by the spectators to run when he is already running. But I was not certain of this; for the dream might have
meant music in the popular sense of the word, and being under sentence of death, and with the festival giving me a respite, I thought that
it would be safer for me to do as told, and, in obedience to the dream,
b to compose a few verses before I departed. First I made a hymn in honour of the god of the festival, and then considering that a poet, if he
is really to be a poet, should not only put together words, but should
invent stories, and that I have no invention, I took some fables of Aesop,
which I had ready at hand and which I knew—they were the first I
came upon—and turned them into verse. Tell this to Evenus, Cebes,
and bid him be of good cheer; say that I would have him come after
me if he were a wise man, and not tarry; and that today I am likely to
c be going, for the Athenians say that I must.

Simmias said: What a message for such a man! having been a frequent companion of his I should say that, as far as I know him, he will
never take your advice unless he is obliged.

Why, said Socrates, is not Evenus a philosopher?

I think that he is, said Simmias.

Then he, or any man who has the spirit of philosophy, will be
willing to die; but he will not take his own life, for that is held to be
unlawful.

Here he changed his position, and put his legs on the ground, and
d during the rest of the conversation he remained sitting.

Why do you say, enquired Cebes, that a man ought not to take his
own life, but that the philosopher will be ready to follow the dying?

Socrates replied: And have you, Cebes and Simmias, who are the
disciples of Philolaus,* never heard him speak of this?

His language was obscure, Socrates.

My words, too, are hearsay; but there is no reason why I should
not repeat what I have heard: and indeed, as I am going to another
e place, it is very appropriate for me to be thinking and talking of the nature of the pilgrimage which I am about to make. What else can I do
between now and sunset?

Then tell me, Socrates, why is suicide held to be unlawful? as I have
certainly heard Philolaus, about whom you were just now asking, affirm when he was staying with us at Thebes; and there are others who

---

*Famous Pythagorean (fifth century B.C.E.), resident of Thebes.

say the same, although I have never understood what was meant by any of them.

Do not lose heart, replied Socrates, and the day may come when you will understand. I suppose that you wonder why, when other things which are evil may be good at certain times and to certain persons, death is to be the only exception, and why, when a man is better dead, he is not permitted to be his own benefactor, but must wait for the hand of another.

Very true, said Cebes, laughing gently and speaking in his own dialect.

I admit the appearance of inconsistency in what I am saying; but there might not be any real inconsistency after all. There is a doctrine whispered in secret that man is a prisoner who has no right to open the door and run away; this is a great mystery which I do not quite understand. Yet I too believe that the gods are our guardians, and that we men are a possession of theirs. Do you not agree?

Yes, I quite agree, said Cebes.

And if one of your own possessions, an ox or an ass, for example, took the liberty of putting himself out of the way when you had given no intimation of your wish that he should die, would you not be angry with him, and would you not punish him if you could?

Certainly, replied Cebes.

Then, if we look at the matter thus, there may be reason in saying that a man should wait, and not take his own life until god summons him, as he is now summoning me.

Yes, Socrates, said Cebes, there seems to be truth in what you say. And yet how can you reconcile this seemingly true belief that god is our guardian and we his possessions, with the willingness to die which you were just now attributing to the philosopher? That the wisest of men should be willing to leave a service in which they are ruled by the gods who are the best of rulers, is not reasonable; for surely no wise man thinks that when set at liberty he can take better care of himself than the gods take of him. A fool may perhaps think so—he may argue that he had better run away from his master, not considering that his duty is to remain to the end, and not to run away from the good, and that there would be no sense in his running away. The wise man will want to be ever with him who is better than himself. Now this, Socrates, is the reverse of what was just now said; for upon this view the wise man should be sorry and the fool rejoice at dying.

The earnestness of Cebes seemed to please Socrates. Here, said he, turning to us, is a man who is always enquiring, and is not so easily convinced by the first thing he hears.

Certainly, added Simmias, the objection which he is now making does appear to me to have some force. For what can be the meaning of a truly wise man wanting to fly away and lightly leave a master who is better than himself? And I rather think that Cebes is referring to you; he thinks that you are too ready to leave us, and too ready to leave the gods whom you acknowledge to be our good masters.

b   Yes, replied Socrates; there is reason in what you say. And I ought to answer your indictment as if I were in a court.

We should like you to do so, said Simmias.

Then I must try to make a more successful defence before you than I did before the judges. For I am quite ready to admit, Simmias and Cebes, that I ought to be grieved at death, if I were not persuaded in the first place that I am going to other gods who are wise and good (of which I am as certain as I can be of any such matters), and secondly
c   (though I am not so sure of this last) to men departed, better than those whom I leave behind; and therefore I do not grieve as I might have done, for I have good hope that there is yet something remaining for the dead, and as has been said of old, some far better thing for the good than for the evil.

But do you mean to take away your thoughts with you, Socrates?
d   said Simmias. Will you not impart them to us?—for they are a benefit in which we too are entitled to share. Moreover, if you succeed in convincing us, that will be an answer to the charge against yourself.

I will do my best, replied Socrates. But you must first let me hear what Crito wants; he has long been wishing to say something to me.

Only this, Socrates, replied Crito: the attendant who is to give you the poison has been telling me, and he wants me to tell you, that you are not to talk much; talking, he says, increases heat, and this is apt to
e   interfere with the action of the poison; persons who excite themselves are sometimes obliged to take a second or even a third dose.

Then, said Socrates, let him mind his business and be prepared to give the poison twice or even thrice if necessary; that is all.

I knew quite well what you would say, replied Crito; but I was obliged to satisfy him.

Never mind him, he said.

And now, my judges, I desire to prove to you that the real philosopher has reason to be of good cheer when he is about to die, and that
64   after death he may hope to obtain the greatest good in the other world. And how this may be, Simmias and Cebes, I will endeavour to explain. For I deem that the true votary of philosophy is likely to be misunderstood by other men; they do not perceive that he is always pursuing death and dying; and if this be so, and he has had the desire of death all his life long, why when his time comes should he fret at what he has been always pursuing and desiring?

Simmias said laughingly: Though not in a laughing humour, you   b
have made me laugh, Socrates; for I cannot help thinking that the many
when they hear your words will say how truly you have described
philosophers, and our people at home will likewise say that the life which
philosophers desire is in reality death, and that they have found them
out to be deserving of the death which they desire.

And they are right, Simmias, in thinking so, with the exception of
the words 'they have found them out;' for they have not found out either what is the nature of that death which the true philosopher deserves, or how he deserves or desires death. But enough of them; let us   c
discuss the matter among ourselves. Do we believe that there is such a
thing as death?

To be sure, replied Simmias.

Is it not the separation of soul and body? And to be dead is the
completion of this; when the soul exists by itself, and is released from
the body and the body is released from the soul, what is this but death?

Just so, he replied.

There is another question, which will probably throw light on our   d
present enquiry if you and I can agree about it: Ought the philosopher
to care about the pleasures—if they are to be called pleasures—of eating and drinking?

Certainly not, answered Simmias.

And what about the pleasures of love—should he care for them?

By no means.

And will he think much of the other ways of indulging the body, for
example, the acquisition of costly garments, or sandals, or other adorn-
ments of the body? Instead of caring about them, does he not rather despise anything more than nature needs? What do you say?   e

I should say that the true philosopher would despise them.

Would you not say that he is entirely concerned with the soul and
not with the body? He would like, as far as he can, to get away from
the body and to turn to the soul.

Quite true.

In matters of this sort philosophers, above all other men, may be
observed in every sort of way to sever the soul from the body.   65

Very true.

Whereas, Simmias, the rest of the world is of the opinion that to
the one who has no sense of pleasure and no part in bodily pleasure,
life is not worth having; and that the one who is indifferent about them
is as good as dead.

That is also true.

What again shall we say of the actual acquisition of knowledge? Is
the body, if invited to share in the enquiry, a hinderer or a helper? I   b

mean to say, have sight and hearing any truth in them? Are they not, as the poets are always telling us, inaccurate witnesses? and yet, if even they are inaccurate and indistinct, what is to be said of the other senses?—for you will allow that they are the best of them?

Certainly, he replied.

Then when does the soul attain truth?—for in attempting to consider anything in company with the body, it is obviously deceived.

c   True.

Then must not clarity about things be revealed to it in thought, if at all?

Yes.

And thought is best when the mind is left alone and none of these things trouble it—neither sounds nor sights nor pain nor any pleasure, —when it takes leave of the body, and has as little as possible to do with it, when it has no bodily sense or desire?

Certainly.

d   And in this the philosopher's soul dishonours the body; his soul runs away from his body and desires to be alone and by herself?

That is true.

Well, but there is another thing, Simmias: Is there or is there not an absolute justice?

Assuredly there is.

And an absolute beauty and absolute good?

Of course.

But did you ever behold any of them with your eyes?

Certainly not.

Or did you ever reach them with any other bodily sense? and I speak not of these alone, but of absolute greatness, and health, and

e   strength, and of the essence of everything. Has the reality of them ever been perceived by you through the bodily organs? or rather, is not the nearest approach to knowledge made by the one who prepares himself to have the most exact conception of what he considers?

Certainly.

And he attains the purest knowledge of them who goes to each with the mind alone, not introducing or intruding in the act of thought sight or any other sense together with reason, but with the very light

66   of the mind in its own clearness searches into the very truth of each; he who has gotten rid, as far as he can, of eyes and ears and, so to speak, of the whole body, these being in his opinion distracting elements which, when they infect the soul, hinder it from acquiring truth and knowledge—who, if not he, is likely to attain the knowledge of true being?

What you say has a marvelous truth in it, Socrates, replied Simmias.

And when real philosophers consider all these things, will they not   b
be led to make a reflection which they will express in words like the
following? 'Have we not found,' they will say, 'a path of thought which
seems to bring us and our argument to the conclusion, that while we
are in the body, and while the soul is infected with the evils of the body,
our desire will not be satisfied? and our desire is of the truth. For the
body is a source of endless trouble to us by reason of the mere re-
quirement of food; and is liable also to diseases which overtake and im-   c
pede our search for true being: it fills us with loves, lusts, fears, fancies
of all kinds, and endless foolery; in fact, as men say, it takes away from
us the power of thinking at all. Whence come wars, and fightings, and
factions? whence but from the body and the lusts of the body? Wars are
occasioned by the love of money, and money has to be acquired for the   d
sake and in the service of the body; and by reason of all these impediments we have no time to give to philosophy; and, last and worst of all,
even if we are at leisure and betake ourselves to some speculation, the
body is always breaking in upon us, causing turmoil and confusion in
our enquiries, and so amazing us that we are prevented from seeing the
truth. It has been proved to us by experience that if we would have
pure knowledge of anything we must be rid of the body—the soul
alone must behold things in themselves: then we shall attain the wis-   e
dom we desire, and of which we say that we are lovers; not while we
live, but after death; for, while in company with the body, the soul cannot have pure knowledge, and one of two things follows: either knowledge is not to be attained at all, or only after death. For then, and not   67
till then, the soul will be parted from the body and exist alone. In this
present life, I reckon that we make the nearest approach to knowledge
when we have the least possible intercourse or communion with the
body, and are not burdened with our bodily nature, but keep ourselves
pure until the hour when god himself is pleased to release us. And thus
having gotten rid of the foolishness of the body we shall be pure and
converse with the pure, and know by ourselves the clear light every-   b
where, which is no other than the light of truth.' For the impure are
not permitted to approach the pure. These are the sort of words, Simmias, which the true lovers of knowledge cannot help saying to one
another, and thinking. You would agree; would you not?

Undoubtedly, Socrates.

But, my friend, if this is true, there is great reason to hope that,
going whither I go, when I have come to the end of my journey, I shall
attain what has been the pursuit of my life. And therefore I go on my   c
way rejoicing, and not only I, but every other man who believes that
his mind has been made pure and ready.

Certainly, replied Simmias.

And what is purification but the separation of the soul from the body, as I was saying before; the habit of the soul gathering and collecting herself into herself from all sides out of the body; the dwelling in her own place alone, as in another life, so also in this, as far as she
d can; the release of the soul from the chains of the body?

Very true, he said.

And this separation and release of the soul from the body is termed death?

To be sure, he said.

The true philosophers, and they only, are ever seeking to release the soul. Is not the separation and release of the soul from the body their especial study?

That is true.

Then, as I was saying at first, there would be a ridiculous contra-
e diction in men studying to live as nearly as they can in a state of death, and yet fretting when death comes upon them.

Clearly.

The true philosophers, Simmias, are always occupied in the practice of dying, wherefore also to them least of all men is death terrible. Look at the matter thus: if they have been in every way the enemies of the body, and want to be alone with the soul, when this desire of theirs is granted, how inconsistent would they be if they trembled and fretted, instead of rejoicing at their departure to that place where, when
68 they arrive, they hope to gain that which they desired in life—wisdom—and at the same time to be rid of the company of their enemy. Many men have been willing to go to the world below animated by the hope of seeing there an earthly love, or wife, or son, and conversing with them. Will the one who is a true lover of wisdom, and is strongly persuaded in like manner that only in the world below he
b can worthily enjoy it, still fret at death? Will he not depart with joy? Surely he will, my friend, if he is a true philosopher. For he will have a firm conviction that there, and there only, he can find wisdom in its purity. And if this is true, it would be very absurd, as I was saying, if he were afraid of death.

It would indeed, replied Simmias.

And when you see a man who is fretting at the approach of death, is not his reluctance a sufficient proof that he is not a lover of wisdom,
c but a lover of the body, and probably at the same time a lover of either money or power, or both?

Quite so, he replied.

And is not courage, Simmias, a quality which is specially characteristic of the philosopher?

Certainly.

There is also temperance, which even popularly is supposed to consist in the control and regulation of the passions, and in the sense of superiority to them—is not temperance a virtue belonging to those only who despise the body, and who pass their lives in philosophy?

Most assuredly. *d*

For the courage and temperance of other men, if you will consider them, are really a contradiction.

How so?

Well, he said, you are aware that death is regarded by men in general as a great evil.

Very true, he said.

And do not courageous men face death because they are afraid of yet greater evils?

That is quite true.

Then all but the philosophers are courageous only out of fear, and yet that a man should be courageous out of fear is surely a strange thing.

Very true. *e*

And are not the temperate exactly in the same case? They are temperate because they are intemperate—which might seem to be a contradiction, but is nevertheless the sort of thing which happens with this foolish temperance. For there are pleasures which they are afraid of losing; and in their desire to keep them, they abstain from some pleasures, because they are overcome by others; and although to be conquered by *69* pleasure is called by men intemperance, to them the conquest of pleasure consists in being conquered by pleasure. And that is what I mean by saying that, in a sense, they are made temperate through intemperance.

Such appears to be the case.

Yet the exchange of one fear or pleasure or pain for another fear or pleasure or pain, and of the greater for the less, as if they were coins, is not the exchange of virtue. O my blessed Simmias, is there not one true coin for which all things ought to be exchanged? That is wisdom; *b* only in exchange for this, and in company with this, is anything truly bought or sold, whether courage or temperance or justice. And is not all true virtue the companion of wisdom, no matter what fears or pleasures or other similar goods or evils may or may not attend her? But the virtue which is made up of these goods, when they are severed from wisdom and exchanged with one another, is a shadow of virtue only, there is no freedom or health or truth in it; but in the true ex- *c* change there is a riddance of all these things, and temperance, and justice, and courage, and wisdom itself are but the purgation of them. The founders of the mysteries would appear to have had a real meaning, and were not talking nonsense when they intimated in a riddle long ago that he who passes unsanctified and uninitiated into the world below will lie in the mud, but that he who arrives there after initiation and purification will dwell with the gods. For 'many,' as they say in the mysteries, 'are the thyrsus-bearers, but few are the mystics,'—

d meaning, as I interpret the words, 'the true philosophers.'² In the number of whom, during my whole life, I have been seeking, according to my ability, to find a place. Whether I have sought in a right way or not, and whether I have succeeded or not, I shall truly know in a little while, if god will, when I arrive in the other world—such is my belief. And therefore I maintain that I am right, Simmias and Cebes, in not grieving or fretting at parting from you and my masters in this world, for I believe that I shall equally find good masters and friends

e in another world. But most men do not believe this saying; if then I succeed in convincing you by my defence better than I did the Athenian judges, it will be well.

Cebes answered: I agree, Socrates, in the greater part of what you

70 say. But in what concerns the soul, men are apt to be incredulous; they fear that when it has left the body, its place may be nowhere, and that on the very day of death it may perish and come to an end—immediately on its release from the body, issuing forth dispersed like smoke or air and vanishing away into nothingness. If it could only be collected into itself after it has obtained release from the evils of which you were speaking, there would be good reason to hope, Socrates, that what you

b say is true. But surely it requires a great deal of argument and many proofs to show that when the man is dead his soul yet exists, and has any force or intelligence.

True, Cebes, said Socrates; may I suggest that we converse a little of the probabilities of these things?

For my part, said Cebes, I would greatly like to know your opinion about them.

I reckon, said Socrates, that no one who heard me now, not even

c if he were one of my old enemies, the comic poets, could accuse me of idle talking about matters in which I have no concern: If you please, then, we will proceed with the enquiry.

Suppose we consider the question whether the souls of men after death are or are not in the world below. There comes into my mind an ancient doctrine which affirms that they go from hence into the other world, and returning hither, are born again from the dead. Now if it were true that the living come from the dead, then our souls must exist in the other world, for if not, how could they have been born again?

d And this would be conclusive, if there were any real evidence that the living are only born from the dead; but if this is not so, then other arguments will have to be adduced.

Very true, replied Cebes.

Then let us consider the whole question, not in relation to man only, but in relation to animals generally, and to plants, and to everything of which there is generation, and the proof will be easier. Are not *e* all things which have opposites generated out of their opposites? I mean such things as good and evil, just and unjust, and innumerable other opposites which are generated out of opposites. I want to show that in all opposites there is of necessity a similar alternation; I mean, for example, that anything which becomes greater must become greater after being less.

True.

And that which becomes less must have been once greater and *71* then have become less.

Yes.

And the weaker is generated from the stronger, and the swifter from the slower.

Very true.

And the worse is from the better, and the more just is from the more unjust.

Of course.

And is this true of all opposites? and are we convinced that all of them are generated out of opposites?

Yes.

And in this universal opposition of all things, are there not also two intermediate processes which are always going on, from one to the other opposite, and back again; where there is a greater and a less there *b* is also an intermediate process of increase and diminution, and that which grows is said to wax, and that which decays to wane?

Yes, he said.

And there are many other processes, such as division and composition, cooling and heating, which equally involve a passage into and out of one another. And this necessarily holds of all opposites, even though not always expressed in words—they are really generated out of one another, and there is a passing or process from one to the other of them?

Very true, he replied.

Well, and is there not an opposite of life, as sleep is the opposite *c* of waking?

True, he said.

And what is it?

Death, he answered.

And these, if they are opposites, are generated the one from the other, and have their two intermediate processes also?

Of course.

Now, said Socrates, I will analyze one of the two pairs of opposites which I have mentioned to you, and also its intermediate processes, and you shall analyze the other to me. One of them I term sleep, the other waking. The state of sleep is opposed to the state of waking, and out of sleeping waking is generated, and out of waking, sleeping; and the process of generation is in the one case falling asleep, and in the other waking up. Do you agree?

I entirely agree.

Then, suppose that you analyze life and death to me in the same manner. Is not death opposed to life?

Yes.

And they are generated one from the other?

Yes.

What is generated from the living?

The dead.

And what from the dead?

I can only say in answer—the living.

Then the living, whether things or persons, Cebes, are generated from the dead?

That is clear, he replied.

Then the inference is that our souls exist in the world below?

That is true.

And one of the two processes or generations is visible—for surely the act of dying is visible?

Surely, he said.

What then is to be the result? Shall we exclude the opposite process? Shall we suppose nature to walk on one leg only? Must we not rather assign to death some corresponding process of generation?

Certainly, he replied.

And what is that process?

Return to life.

And return to life, if there were such a thing, is the birth of the dead into the world of the living?

Quite true.

Then here is a new way by which we arrive at the conclusion that the living come from the dead, just as the dead come from the living; and this, if true, affords a most certain proof that the souls of the dead exist in some place out of which they come again.

Yes, Socrates, he said; the conclusion seems to flow necessarily out of our previous admissions.

And that these admissions were not unfair, Cebes, he said, may be shown, I think, as follows: If generation were in a straight line only, and   b there were no compensation or circle in nature, no turn or return of elements into their opposites, then you would know that all things have the same form and pass into the same state, and there would be no more generation of them.

What do you mean? he said.

A simple thing enough, which I will illustrate by the case of sleep, he replied. You know that if there were no alternation of sleeping and   c waking, the tale of the sleeping Endymion* would in the end have no meaning, because all other things would be asleep too, and he would not be distinguishable from the rest. Or if there were composition only, and no division of substances, then Anaxagoras' "mixture of all things"³ would come again. And in like manner, my dear Cebes, if all things which partook of life were to die, and after they were dead remained in death, and did not come to life again, all would at last die, and nothing would be alive—what other result could there be? For if the living   d spring from any other things, and they too die, must not all things at last be swallowed up by death?

There is no escape, Socrates, said Cebes; to me your argument seems to be absolutely true.

Yes, he said, Cebes, it is and must be so, in my opinion; we have not been deluded in making these admissions. I am confident that there truly is such a thing as living again, and that the living spring from the dead, and that the souls of the dead are in existence.

Cebes added: Your favourite doctrine, Socrates, that knowledge is   e simply recollection, if true, also necessarily implies a previous time in which we have learned that which we now recollect. But this would be   73 impossible unless our soul had been in some place before existing in human form; here then is another proof of the soul's immortality.

But tell me, Cebes, said Simmias, interrupting, what arguments are there in favour of this doctrine of recollection? I am not quite sure that I remember them at the moment.

One excellent proof, said Cebes, is afforded by questions. If you put a question to a person in the right way, he will give a right answer, but how could he do this unless there were knowledge and right reason already in him? This is most clearly shown when he goes to make   b a diagram or anything of that sort.

But if, said Socrates, you are still incredulous, Simmias, I would ask you whether you may not agree with me when you look at the matter

---

*Mythical lover of the Moon, kept in eternal slumber.

in another way; I mean, if you are still incredulous as to whether knowledge is recollection.

Incredulous I am not, said Simmias; but I want to have this doctrine of recollection brought to my own recollection, and, from what Cebes has said, I am beginning to recollect and be convinced: but I should still like to hear what you were going to say.

c   This is what I would say, he replied: We should agree, if I am not mistaken, that what a man recollects he must have known at some previous time.

Very true.

And what is the nature of this knowledge or recollection? I mean, may a person who, having seen or heard or in any way perceived anything, knows not only that, but also has a conception of something else which is the subject, not of the same but of some other kind of knowledge, not be fairly said to recollect that of which he has the conception?

d   What do you mean?

I mean what I may illustrate by the following instance: The knowledge of a lyre is not the same as the knowledge of a man?

True.

And yet what is the feeling of lovers when they recognize a lyre, or a garment, or anything else which the beloved has been in the habit of using? Do not they, from knowing the lyre, form in the mind's eye an image of the youth to whom the lyre belongs? This is recollection. In like manner anyone who sees Simmias may remember Cebes; and there are endless examples of the same thing.

Endless, indeed, replied Simmias.

e   Recollection is most commonly a process of recovering that which has been already forgotten through time and inattention.

Very true, he said.

Well; and may you not also from seeing the picture of a house or a lyre remember a man? and from the picture of Simmias, may be led to remember Cebes?

True.

Or you may also be led to the recollection of Simmias himself?

74   Quite so.

And in all these cases, the recollection may be derived from things either like or unlike?

Yes.

And when the recollection is derived from like things, then another consideration is sure to arise, which is whether the likeness in any degree falls short or not of that which is recollected?

Very true, he said.

And shall we proceed a step further, and affirm that there is such a thing as equality, not of one piece of wood or stone with another, but that, over and above this, there is absolute equality? Shall we say so?

Say so, yes, replied Simmias, and swear to it, with all the confidence in life.

And do we know what that is?

To be sure, he said.

And whence did we obtain our knowledge? Did we not see equalities of material things, such as pieces of wood and stones, and gather from them the idea of an equality which is different from them? For you will acknowledge that there is a difference. Or look at the matter in another way:—Do not the same pieces of wood or stone appear at one time equal, and at another time unequal?

That is certain.

But do unequals ever become equal? or is the idea of equality the same as of inequality?

Impossible, Socrates.

Then these (so-called) equals are not the same with the idea of equality?

I should say, clearly not, Socrates.

And yet from these equals, although differing from the idea of equality, you conceived and attained that idea?

Very true, he said.

Which might be like, or might be unlike them?

Yes.

But that makes no difference: whenever from seeing one thing you conceived another, whether like or unlike, there must surely have been an act of recollection?

Very true.

But what would you say of equal portions of wood and stone, or other material equals? and what is the impression produced by them? Are they equals in the same sense in which absolute equality is equal? or do they fall short of this perfect equality in a measure?

Yes, he said, in a very great measure at that.

And must we not allow, that when I or anyone, looking at any object, observes that the thing which he sees aims at being some other thing, but falls short of, and cannot be, that other thing, but is inferior, the one who makes this observation must have had a previous knowledge of that to which the other, although similar, was inferior?

Certainly.

And has not this been our own case in the matter of equals and of absolute equality?

Precisely.

Then we must have known equality prior to the time when we first
75   saw the material equals, and reflected that all these apparent equals
strive to attain absolute equality, but fall short of it?

Very true.

And we recognize also that this absolute equality has only been
known, and can only be known, through the medium of sight or
touch, or of some other of the senses, which are all alike in this respect?

Yes, Socrates, as far as the argument is concerned, one of them is
the same as the other.

b   From the senses then is derived the knowledge that all sensible
things aim at an absolute equality of which they fall short?

Yes.

Then before we began to see or hear or perceive in any way, we
must have had a knowledge of absolute equality, or we could not have
referred to that standard the equals which are derived from the senses;
for to that they all aspire, and of that they fall short?

No other inference can be drawn.

And did we not see and hear and have the use of our other senses
as soon as we were born?

Certainly.

c   Then we must have acquired the knowledge of equality at some
previous time?

Yes.

That is to say, before we were born, I suppose?

True.

And if we acquired this knowledge before we were born, and were
born having the use of it, then we also knew before we were born and
at the instant of birth not only the equal or the greater or the less, but
all other ideas; for we are not speaking only of equality, but of beauty,
goodness, justice, holiness, and of all which we stamp with the name
d   of essence in the dialectical process, both when we ask and when we
answer questions. Of all this we may certainly affirm that we acquired
the knowledge before birth?

We may.

But if, after having acquired, we have not forgotten what in each
case we acquired, then we must always have come into life having
knowledge, and shall always continue to know as long as life lasts—for
knowing is the acquiring and retaining knowledge and not forgetting.
Is not forgetting, Simmias, just the losing of knowledge?

e   Quite true, Socrates.

But if the knowledge which we acquired before birth was lost by
us at birth, and if afterwards by the use of the senses we recovered what

we previously knew, will not the process which we call learning be a recovering of the knowledge which is natural to us, and may not this be rightly termed recollection?

Very true.

So much is clear—that when we perceive something, either by the 76 help of sight, or hearing, or some other sense, from that perception we are able to obtain a notion of some other thing like or unlike which is associated with it but has been forgotten. Whence, as I was saying, one of two alternatives follows: either we had this knowledge at birth, and continued to know through life; or, after birth, those who are said to learn only remember, and learning is simply recollection.

Yes, that is quite true, Socrates.

And which alternative, Simmias, do you prefer? Had we the knowledge at our birth, or did we recollect the things which we knew b previously to our birth?

I cannot decide at the moment.

At any rate you can decide whether he who has knowledge will or will not be able to render an account of his knowledge? What do you say?

Certainly, he will.

But do you think that every man is able to give an account of these very matters about which we are speaking?

I wish they could, Socrates, but I rather fear that tomorrow, at this time, there will no longer be anyone alive who is able to give an account of them as ought to be given.

Then you are not of the opinion, Simmias, that all men know these c things?

Certainly not.

They are in process of recollecting that which they learned before?

To be sure.

But when did our souls acquire this knowledge?—not since we were born as men?

Certainly not.

And therefore, previously?

Yes.

Then, Simmias, our souls must also have existed without bodies before they were in human form, and must have had intelligence.

Unless indeed you suppose, Socrates, that these notions are given us at the very moment of birth; for this is the only time which remains.

Yes, my friend, but if so, when do we lose them? for they are not d in us when we are born—that is admitted. Do we lose them at the moment of receiving them, or if not at what other time?

No, Socrates, I realize that I was unconsciously talking nonsense.

Then may we not say, Simmias, that if, as we are always repeating, there is an absolute beauty, and goodness, and an absolute essence of

e all things; and if to this, which is now discovered to have existed in our former state, we refer all our sensations, and with this compare them, finding these ideas to be pre-existent and our inborn possession, then our souls must have had a prior existence, or else, there would be no force in the argument? There is the same proof that these ideas must have existed before we were born, as that our souls existed before we were born; and if not the ideas, then not the souls.

Yes, Socrates; I am convinced that there is precisely the same ne-cessity for the one as for the other; and the argument retreats success-

77 fully to the position that the existence of the soul before birth cannot be separated from the existence of the essence of which you speak. For there is nothing which to my mind is so patent as that beauty, good-ness, and the other notions of which you were just now speaking, have a most real and absolute existence; and I am satisfied with the proof.

Well, but is Cebes equally satisfied? for I must convince him too.

I think, said Simmias, that Cebes is satisfied: although he is the most incredulous of mortals, yet I believe that he is sufficiently con-

b vinced of the existence of the soul before birth. But that after death the soul will continue to exist is not yet proven even to my own satisfac-tion. I cannot get rid of the feeling of the majority to which Cebes was referring—the feeling that when the man dies the soul will be dis-persed, and that this may be the extinction of it. For admitting that it may have been born elsewhere, and framed out of other elements, and was in existence before entering the human body, why after having en-tered in and gone out again may it not be destroyed and come to an end?

c Very true, Simmias, said Cebes; about half of what was required has been proven; to wit, that our souls existed before we were born: but that the soul exist after death as well as before birth is the other half of which the proof is still wanting, and has to be supplied; when that is given the demonstration will be complete.

But that proof, Simmias and Cebes, has been already given, said Socrates, if you put the two arguments together—I mean this and the former one, in which we admitted that everything living is born of the dead. For if the soul exists before birth, and in coming to life and

d being born can be born only from death and dying, must she not after death continue to exist, since she has to be born again?—Surely the proof which you desire has been already furnished. Still I suspect that you and Simmias would be glad to probe the argument further. Like children, you are haunted with a fear that when the soul leaves the body, the wind may really blow it away and scatter it, especially if a man should happen to die in a great storm and not when the sky is calm.

Cebes answered with a smile: Then, Socrates, you must argue us out of our fears—and yet, strictly speaking, they are not our fears, but there is a child within us to whom death is a sort of hobgoblin: him too we must persuade not to be afraid when he is alone in the dark.

Socrates said: Let the voice of the charmer be applied daily until you have charmed away the fear.

And where shall we find a good charmer of our fears, Socrates, when you are gone? 78

The Greek World, he replied, is a large place, Cebes, and has many good men, and there are many barbarian races: seek him among them all, far and wide, sparing neither pains nor money; for there is no better way of spending it. And you must seek among yourselves too; for you will not find others better able to make the search.

The search, replied Cebes, shall certainly be made. And now, if you please, let us return to the point of the argument at which we digressed. b

By all means, replied Socrates.

Very good.

Must we not, said Socrates, ask ourselves what it is that, as we imagine, is liable to be scattered, and about which we fear? and what again is that about which we have no fear? And then we may proceed further to enquire whether that which suffers dispersion is or is not the soul—our hopes and fears as to our own souls will turn upon the answers to these questions.

Very true, he said.

Now the compound or composite may be supposed to be naturally capable, as of being compounded, so also of being dissolved; but that which is uncompounded, and that only, must be, if anything is, indissoluble. c

Yes; I would think so, said Cebes.

And the uncompounded may be assumed to be the same and unchanging, whereas the compound is always changing and never the same.

I agree, he said.

Then now let us return to the previous discussion. Is that essence, which in the dialectical process we define as essence of existence— whether essence of equality, beauty, or anything else—are these essences, I say, liable at times to some degree of change? or are they each of them always what they are, having the same simple self-existent and unchanging forms, not admitting of variation at all, or in any way, or at any time? d

They must be always the same, Socrates, replied Cebes.

And what would you say of the many beautiful things—whether men or horses or garments or any other things which are named by the
e   same names—are they all unchanging and the same always, or quite the reverse? May they not rather be described as almost always changing and hardly ever equal, either to themselves or to one another?

The latter, replied Cebes; they are always in a state of change.

79   And these you can touch and see and perceive with the senses, but the unchanging things you can only perceive with the mind—they are invisible and are not seen?

That is very true, he said.

Well then, added Socrates, let us suppose that there are two sorts of existences—one seen, the other unseen.

Let us suppose that.

The seen is the changing, and the unseen is the unchanging?

All right.

b   And, further, is not one part of us body, another part soul?

To be sure.

And to which class is the body more alike and akin?

Clearly to the seen—no one can doubt that.

And is the soul seen or not seen?

Not by humans, Socrates.

And what we mean by 'seen' and 'not seen' is that which is or is not visible to the human eye?

Yes.

And is the soul seen or not seen?

Not seen.

Unseen then?

Yes.

Then the soul is more like the unseen, and the body like the seen?
c   That follows necessarily, Socrates.

And have we not been saying that the soul, when using the body as an instrument of perception, either through sight or hearing or some other sense (for the meaning of perceiving through the body is perceiving through the senses)—the soul too is then dragged by the body into the region of the changeable, and wanders and is confused; the world spins round it, and it is like a drunkard, when it comes in contact with change?

Very true.

d   But when returning into itself it reflects, then it passes into the other world, the region of purity, eternity, immortality, and unchangeableness, which are its kindred, and with them it ever lives, when it is by itself and is not hindered; then it ceases from its erring, and being with the unchanging is unchanging. And this state of the soul is called wisdom?

That is well and truly said, Socrates, he replied.

And to which class is the soul more nearly alike and akin, as far as may be inferred from this argument, as well as from the preceding one?

I think, Socrates, that, in the opinion of everyone who follows the argument, the soul will be infinitely more like the unchangeable—even the most stupid person will not deny that.

And the body is more like the changing?

Yes.

Yet once more consider the matter in another light: When the soul and the body are united, then nature orders the soul to rule and govern, and the body to obey and serve. Now which of these two functions is akin to the divine? and which to the mortal? Does not the divine appear to you to be that which naturally orders and rules, and the mortal to be that which is subject and servant?

Yes, it does.

And which does the soul resemble?

The soul resembles the divine, and the body the mortal—there can be no doubt of that, Socrates.

Then reflect, Cebes: of all which has been said is not this the conclusion, that the soul is the very likeness of the divine, immortal, intellectual, uniform, indissoluble, and unchangeable; and that the body is the very likeness of the human, mortal, unintellectual, multiform, dissoluble, and changeable? Can this, my dear Cebes, be denied?

It cannot.

But if it is true, then is not the body liable to speedy dissolution? and is not the soul almost or altogether indissoluble?

Certainly.

And do you further observe that, after a man is dead, the body or visible part of him, which is lying in the visible world and is called a corpse, and would naturally be dissolved and decomposed and dissipated, is not dissolved or decomposed at once, but may remain for some time, even for a long time, if the constitution is sound at the time of death, and the season of the year favourable? For the body when shrunk and embalmed, as they do in Egypt, may remain almost entire through infinite ages; and even in decay, there are still some parts, such as the bones and ligaments, which are practically indestructible. Do you agree?

Yes.

And is it likely that the soul, invisible, in passing to the place of the true Hades—which like it is invisible, pure, and noble—and on its way to the good and wise god, whither, god willing, my soul is also soon to go, will be blown away and destroyed immediately upon leaving the body, as most say? That can never be, my dear Simmias and Cebes. The truth is rather that the soul, which is pure at departing and draws no bodily taint, having never voluntarily during life had connection with the body, which it is always avoiding, follows its tendency and gathers into itself; for it has been a true disciple of philosophy, and therefore has in fact been always engaged in the practice of dying. For is not philosophy the study of death?

Certainly.

That soul, I say, itself invisible, departs to the invisible world—to the divine and immortal and rational; arriving there, it is secure of bliss and is released from the error and folly of men, their fears and wild passions and all other human ills, and forever dwells, as they say of the initiated, in company with the gods. Is not this true, Cebes?

Yes, said Cebes, beyond a doubt.

But the soul which has been polluted, and is impure at the time of her departure, and is the companion and servant of the body always, and is in love with and fascinated by the body and by the desires and pleasures of the body, until it is led to believe that the truth only exists in a bodily form, which a person may touch and see and taste, and use for sexual purposes—the soul, I mean, accustomed to hate and fear what is dark and invisible to the eyes, and can be attained only by philosophy; do you suppose that such a soul will depart pure and unalloyed?

Impossible, he replied.

It is held fast by the corporeal, which the continual association and constant care of the body have wrought into its nature.

Very true.

And this corporeal element, my friend, is heavy and weighty and earthy, and is that element of sight by which a soul is depressed and dragged down again into the visible world, because it is afraid of the invisible and of the world below—prowling about tombs and sepulchres, near which, as they tell us, are seen certain ghostly apparitions of souls which have not departed pure, but are clouded with the visible and therefore are seen.

That is very likely, Socrates.

Yes, that is very likely, Cebes; and these must be the souls, not of the good, but of the evil, which are compelled to wander about such places in payment of the penalty of their former evil way of life; and they continue to wander until through the craving after the corporeal which never leaves them, they are imprisoned finally in another body. And they may be supposed to find their prisons in the same natures which they have had in their former lives.

What natures do you mean, Socrates?

What I mean is that men who have followed after gluttony, wantonness, drunkenness, and have had no thought of avoiding them, 82 would pass into asses and animals of that sort. What do you think?

I think such an opinion to be exceedingly probable.

And those who have chosen injustice, tyranny, and violence, will pass into wolves, or into hawks and kites; whither else can we suppose them to go?

Yes, said Cebes; with such natures, beyond question.

And there is no difficulty, he said, in assigning to all of them places answering to their several propensities?

There is not, he said.

Some are happier than others; and the happiest both in themselves and in the place to which they go are those who have practised the civil and social virtues which are called temperance and justice, and are ac- b quired by habit and attention without philosophy and mind.

Why are they the happiest?

Because they may be expected to pass into some gentle and social kind which is like their own, such as bees or wasps or ants, or back again into human form, and just and moderate men may spring from them.

Very likely.

No one who has not studied philosophy and who is not entirely pure at the time of his departure is allowed to enter the company of the c gods, but the lover of knowledge only. And this is the reason, Simmias and Cebes, why the true votaries of philosophy abstain from all fleshly lusts, and hold out against them and refuse to give themselves up to them; not because they fear poverty or the ruin of their families, like the lovers of money and people in general; nor like the lovers of power and honour, because they dread the dishonour or disgrace of evil deeds.

No, Socrates, that would not become them, said Cebes.

No indeed, he replied; and therefore the ones who care at all for d their own souls and do not merely live moulding and fashioning the body say farewell to all this; they will not walk in the ways of the blind: and when philosophy offers them purification and release from evil, they feel that they ought not to resist its influence, and whither it leads they turn and follow.

What do you mean, Socrates?

I will tell you, he said. The lovers of knowledge are conscious that e the soul was simply fastened and glued to the body—until philosophy received it, it could only view real existence through the bars of a prison, not in and by itself; it was wallowing in the mire of every sort of ignorance, and by reason of lust had become the principal accomplice in its own captivity. This was its original state; and then, as I was saying, and as the lovers of knowledge are well aware, philosophy, seeing how terrible was its confinement, of which it was itself the cause, received and gently comforted it and sought to release it, pointing out that the eye and the ear and the other senses are full of deception, and persuading it to retire from them, and abstain from all but the necessary use, and be gathered up and collected into itself, bidding it trust in itself and its own direct apprehension of existence, and to mistrust whatever comes to it through other channels and is subject to variation; for such things are visible and tangible, but what it sees itself is intelligible and invisible. And the soul of the true philosopher thinks that it ought not to resist this deliverance, and therefore abstains from pleasures and desires and pains and fears, as far as it can; reflecting that when a man has great joys or sorrows or fears or desires, he suffers from them not merely the sort of evil which might be anticipated—as for example, the loss of his health or property which he has sacrificed to his lust—but the greatest and worst of all evils, and one of which he never thinks.

What is it, Socrates? said Cebes.

The evil is that when the feeling of pleasure or pain is most intense, every soul of man imagines the objects of this intense feeling to be then plainest and truest: but this is not so, they are really the things of sight.

Very true.

And is not this the state in which the soul is most trapped by the body?

How so?

Because each pleasure and pain is a sort of nail which nails and rivets the soul to the body, until it becomes like the body, and believes in the truth of what the body affirms to be true; and from agreeing with the body and having the same delights it is obliged to have the same habits and haunts, and is not likely ever to be pure upon departure to the underworld, but is always infected by the body; and so it sinks into another body and there germinates and grows, and has therefore no part in the communion of the divine, pure and simple.

Most true, Socrates, answered Cebes.

And this, Cebes, is the reason why the true lovers of knowledge are temperate and brave; and not for the reason which other people are.

Certainly not.

Of course not. The soul of a philosopher will reason in quite another way; it will not ask philosophy to release it in order to give itself again to pleasures and pains, doing a work only to be undone again, weaving instead of unweaving its Penelope's web. But it will calm passion, follow reason, and dwell in contemplation, beholding the true, the divine, the unopinable, and thence deriving nourishment. Thus it seeks to live while it lives, and after death it hopes to go to its own kindred and to that which is like it, and to be freed from human ills. Never fear, Simmias and Cebes, that a soul which has been thus nurtured and has had these pursuits, will upon departure from the body be scattered and blown away by the winds, be nowhere and nothing.

When Socrates finished speaking, for a considerable time there was silence; he himself appeared to be meditating, as most of us were, on what had been said; only Cebes and Simmias spoke a few words to one another. And Socrates observing them asked what they thought of the argument, and whether there was anything still pending? For, said he, there are many points still open to suspicion and attack, if anyone were disposed to sift the matter thoroughly. Should you be considering some other matter I say no more, but if you are still in doubt do not hesitate to say exactly what you think, and let us have anything better which you can suggest; and if you think that I can be of any use, allow me to help you.

Simmias said: I must confess, Socrates, that doubts did arise in our minds, and each of us was urging and inciting the other to put the question which we wanted to have answered but which neither of us liked to ask, fearing that our importunity might be troublesome at such a time.

Socrates replied with a smile: Simmias, what are you saying? I am not very likely to persuade other men that I do not regard my present situation as a misfortune, if I cannot even persuade you that I am no worse off now than at any other time in my life. Will you not allow that I have as much of the spirit of prophecy in me as a swan? For they, when they realize that they are about to die, having sung all their life, sing then more lustily than ever, rejoicing in the thought that they are about to go away to the god whose ministers they are. But men, because they are themselves afraid of death, slanderously affirm of the swans that they sing a lament at the last, not considering that no bird sings when cold, or hungry, or in pain, not even the nightingale, nor the swallow, nor yet the hoopoe, which are said indeed to tune a lay of sorrow, although I do not believe this to be true of them any more than of the swans. But because they are sacred to Apollo, they have the gift of prophecy, and anticipate the good things of another world; wherefore they sing and rejoice in that day more than they ever did before. I too, believing myself to be the consecrated servant of the same god, and the fellow-servant of the swans, and thinking that I have received from my master gifts of prophecy which are not inferior to theirs, would not go out of life less merrily than the swans. Never mind then, if this is your only objection, but speak and ask anything you like, while the Eleven allow.

c   Very good, Socrates, said Simmias; then I will tell you my difficulty, and Cebes will tell you his. I feel myself (and I daresay that you have the same feeling) how hard or rather impossible is the attainment of any certainty about questions such as these in the present life. And yet I should deem him a coward who did not prove what is said about them to the uttermost, or whose heart failed him before he had examined them on every side. For he should persevere until he has achieved one of two things: either he should discover, or be taught the truth d about them; or, if this is impossible, I would have him take the best and most irrefutable of human theories, and let this be the raft upon which he sails through life—not without risk, as I admit, if he cannot find some word of god which will more surely and safely carry him. And now, as you bid me, I will venture to question you, and then I shall not have to reproach myself later for not having said what I thought. For when I consider the matter, either alone or with Cebes, the argument does certainly appear to me, Socrates, to be not sufficient.

e   Socrates answered: I dare say, my friend, that you may be right, but I should like to know in what respect the argument is insufficient.

Simmias replied. Suppose a person uses the same argument about 86 harmony and the lyre; might he not say that harmony is a thing invisible, incorporeal, perfect, divine, existing in the lyre which is harmonized, but that the lyre and the strings are matter and material, composite, earthy, and akin to mortality? And when someone breaks the lyre, or cuts and rends the strings, then he who takes this view would argue as you do, and on the same analogy, that the harmony survives and has not perished—you cannot imagine, he would say, that the lyre without the strings, and the broken strings themselves which are b mortal remain, and yet that the harmony, which is of heavenly and immortal nature and kindred, has perished—perished before the mortal. The harmony must still be somewhere, and the wood and strings will decay before anything can happen to that. The thought, Socrates, must have occurred to your own mind that such is our conception of the soul; and that when the body is in a manner strung and held together by the elements of hot and cold, wet and dry, then the soul is the harc mony or proportionate mixture of them. But if so, whenever the strings of the body are unduly loosened or overstrained through disease or other injury, then the soul, though most divine, like other harmonies of music or of works of art, of course perishes at once; although the material remains of the body may last for a considerable d time, until they are either decayed or burnt. And if anyone maintains that the soul, being the harmony of the elements of the body, is first to perish in that which is called death, how shall we answer him?

Socrates looked fixedly at us as he used to, and said with a smile: Simmias has reason on his side; and why does not one of you who is better able than myself answer him? for there is force in his attack upon me. But perhaps, before we answer him, we should also hear what Cebes has to say, so that we may gain time for reflection, and when they have both spoken, we may either assent to them, if there is truth in what they say, or if not, we will maintain our position. Please tell me then, Cebes, he said, what was the difficulty which troubled you?   *e*

Cebes said: I will tell you. My feeling is that the argument is where it was, and open to the same objections as before; for I am ready to admit that the existence of the soul before entering into the bodily   87 form has been very ingeniously, and, if I may say so, quite sufficiently proven; but the existence of the soul after death is still, in my judgment, unproven. Now my objection is not the same as that of Simmias; for I am not disposed to deny that the soul is stronger and more lasting than the body, being of the opinion that in all such respects the soul excels the body by far. Well then, says the argument to me, why do you remain unconvinced? When you see that the weaker continues in existence after the person is dead, will you not admit that the more lasting   *b* must also survive during the same period of time? Now I will ask you to consider whether the objection, which, like Simmias, I will express in a simile, has any weight. The analogy which I will adduce is that of an old weaver, who dies, and after his death somebody says: He is not dead, he must be alive; see, there is the coat which he himself wove and wore, and which remains whole and undecayed. And then he proceeds to ask someone who is incredulous, whether a person lasts longer, or   *c* the coat which is in use and wear; and when he is answered that a person lasts far longer, thinks that he has thus certainly demonstrated the survival of the person, who is the more lasting, because the less lasting remains. But that, Simmias, as I would beg you to remark, is a mistake; anyone can see that he who talks thus is talking nonsense. For the truth is that this weaver, having woven and worn many such coats, outlived   *d* several of them, and was outlived by the last; but a person is not therefore proved to be slighter and weaker than a coat. Now the relation of the body to the soul may be expressed in a similar manner; and anyone may very fairly say in like manner that the soul is lasting, and the body weak and short-lived in comparison. He may argue in like manner that every soul wears out many bodies, especially if a person lives many years. While he is alive the body deliquesces and decays, and the soul always weaves another garment and repairs the waste. But of   *e* course, whenever the soul perishes, it must have on its last garment, and this will survive it; and then at length, when the soul is dead, the body will show its native weakness, and quickly decompose and pass away. I would therefore rather not rely on the argument from superior 88 strength to prove the continued existence of the soul after death. For granting even more than you affirm to be possible, and acknowledging not only that the soul existed before birth, but also that the souls of some exist, and will continue to exist after death, and will be born and die again, and that there is a natural strength in the soul which will hold out and be born many times, nevertheless we may be still inclined to think that it will weary in the labours of successive births, and may at last succumb in one of her deaths and utterly perish; and this death b and dissolution of the body which brings destruction to the soul may be unknown to any of us, for none of us can have had any experience of it: and if so, then I maintain that the one who is confident about death has but a foolish confidence, unless he is able to prove that the soul is altogether immortal and imperishable. But if he cannot prove the soul's immortality, the one who is about to die will always have reason to fear that when the body is disunited, the soul may also utterly perish.

c   All of us, as we afterwards remarked to one another, had an unpleasant feeling at hearing what they said. Although we had been so firmly convinced before, now to have our faith shaken seemed to introduce confusion and uncertainty, not only about the previous argument, but about any future one; either we were incapable of forming a judgment, or there were no grounds of belief.

        ECH. There I agree with you—by heaven I do, Phaedo, and when d you were speaking, I was beginning to ask myself the same question: What argument can I ever trust again? For what could be more convincing than the argument of Socrates, which has now fallen into discredit? That the soul is a harmony is a doctrine which has always had a wonderful attraction for me, and, when mentioned, came back to me at once, as my own original conviction. And now I must begin again and find another argument which will assure me that when the man is dead the soul survives. Tell me, I implore you, how did Socrates proceed? e Did he appear to share the unpleasant feeling which you mention? or did he calmly meet the attack? And did he answer forcibly or feebly? Narrate what happened as exactly as you can.

        PHAED. Often, Echecrates, I have wondered at Socrates, but never 89 more than on that occasion. That he should be able to answer was nothing, but what astonished me was, first, the gentle and pleasant and approving manner in which he received the words of the young men, and then his quick sense of the wound which had been inflicted by the argument, and the readiness with which he healed it. He might be compared to a general rallying his defeated and broken army, urging them to accompany him and return to the field of argument.

ECH. Tell me how.

PHAED. You shall hear, for I was close to him on his right hand, seated on a sort of stool, and he on a couch which was a good deal higher. He stroked my head, and pressed the hair upon my neck—he had a way of playing with my hair—and then he said: tomorrow, Phaedo, I suppose that these fair locks of yours will be severed.

Yes, Socrates, I suppose that they will, I replied.

Not so, if you will take my advice.

What shall I do with them? I said.

Today, he replied, and not tomorrow, if this argument dies and we cannot bring it to life again, you and I will both shave our locks: and if I were you, and the argument got away from me, and I could not hold my ground against Simmias and Cebes, I would myself take an oath, like the Argives, not to wear hair any more until I had renewed the conflict and defeated them.

Yes, I said; but Heracles himself is said not to be a match for two.

Summon me then, he said, and I will be your Iolaus until the sun goes down.

I summon you rather, I rejoined, not as Heracles summoning Iolaus, but as Iolaus might summon Heracles.

That will do as well, he said. But first let us take care that we avoid a danger.

Of what nature? I said.

Lest we become misologists,* he replied: no worse thing can happen to a man than this. For as there are misanthropists or haters of people, there are also misologists or haters of argument, and both spring from the same cause, which is ignorance of the world. Misanthropy arises out of the too great confidence of inexperience; you trust a man and think him altogether true and sound and faithful, and then in a little while he turns out to be false and knavish; and then another and another, and when this has happened several times to a man, especially when it happens among those whom he deems to be his own most trusted and familiar friends, and he has often quarrelled with them, he at last hates everyone, and believes that no one has any good in him at all. You must have observed this trait of character?

I have.

And is not the feeling discreditable? Is it not obvious that such a one having to deal with other men was clearly without any experience

---

*Literally, talk-haters.

90   of human nature? For experience would have taught him the true state
      of the case: that few are the good and few the evil, and that the great
      majority are in the interval between them.

      What do you mean? I said.

      I mean, he replied, as you might say of the very large and very
      small—that nothing is more uncommon than a very large or very small
      man; and this applies generally to all extremes, whether of great and
      small, or swift and slow, or fair and foul, or black and white: and whether
      the instances you select be men or dogs or anything else, few are the
      extremes, but many are in the mean between them. Did you never ob-
      serve this?

      Yes, I said, I have.

b   And do you not imagine, he said, that if there were a competition
      in evil, the worst would be found to be very few?

      Yes, that is very likely, I said.

      Yes, indeed, he replied; although in this respect arguments are un-
      like men—there I was led on by you to say more than I had intended;
      but the point of comparison was that when a simple man who has no
      skill in dialectics believes an argument to be true which he afterwards
      imagines to be false, whether really false or not, and then another and
      another, he has no longer any faith left, and great disputers, as you
c   know, come to think at last that they have grown to be the wisest of
      mankind; for they alone perceive the utter unsoundness and instability
      of all arguments, or indeed, of all things, which, like the currents in the
      Euripus, are going up and down in never-ceasing ebb and flow.

      That is quite true, I said.

      Yes, Phaedo, he replied, and how pitiful, if there be such a thing as
d   truth or certainty or possibility of knowledge, that a man should have
      lighted upon some argument or other which at first seemed true and
      then turned out to be false, and instead of blaming himself and his own
      want of wit, because he is annoyed, should at last be too glad to trans-
      fer the blame from himself to arguments in general: and for ever after-
      wards should hate and revile them, and lose truth and the knowledge
      of realities.

      Yes indeed, I said; that is very pitiful.

      Let us then, in the first place, he said, be careful of allowing or of
e   admitting into our souls the notion that there is no health or sound-
      ness in any arguments at all. Rather say that we have not yet attained to
      soundness in ourselves, and that we must struggle bravely and do our
      best to gain health of mind—you and all other men having regard to
      the whole of your future life, and I myself in the prospect of death. For
91   at this moment I realize that I have not the temper of a philosopher;

like most people, I am only a partisan. Now the partisan, when he is engaged in a dispute, cares nothing about the rights of the question, but is anxious only to convince his hearers of his own assertions. And the difference between him and me at the present moment is merely this—that whereas he seeks to convince his hearers that what he says is true, I am rather seeking to convince myself; to convince my hearers is a secondary matter with me. See how much I gain by the argument: if b what I say is true, then I do well to be persuaded of the truth; but if there were nothing after death, still, during the short time that remains, I shall not distress my friends with lamentations, and my ignorance will not last, but will die with me, and therefore no harm will be done. This is the state of mind, Simmias and Cebes, in which I approach the argument. And I would ask you to be thinking of the truth and not of c Socrates: agree with me, if I seem to you to be speaking the truth; if not, withstand me with all your might, in order that I may not deceive you as well as myself in my enthusiasm, and like the bee, leave my sting in you before I die.

Now let us proceed, he said. First of all let me be sure that I have in my mind what you were saying. Simmias, if I remember rightly, has fears and misgivings whether the soul, although a fairer and diviner thing than the body, being as it is in the form of harmony, may not per- d ish first. On the other hand, Cebes appeared to grant that the soul was more lasting than the body, but he said that no one could know whether the soul, after having worn out many bodies, might not perish itself and leave its last body behind; and that this is death, which is the destruction not of the body but of the soul, for in the body the work of destruction is always going on. Are not these, Simmias and Cebes, the points which we have to consider?

They both agreed to this statement of them. e

He proceeded: And did you deny the force of the whole preceding argument, or of a part only?

Of a part only, they replied.

And what did you think, he said, of that part of the argument in which we said that knowledge was recollection, and hence inferred that the soul must have previously existed somewhere else before it was 92 enclosed in the body?

Cebes said that he had been wonderfully impressed by that part of the argument, and that his conviction remained absolutely unshaken. Simmias agreed, and added that he himself could hardly imagine the possibility of his ever thinking differently.

But, rejoined Socrates, you will have to think differently, my Theban friend, if you still maintain that harmony is a compound, and that

b   the soul is a harmony which is made out of strings set in the frame of
the body; for you will surely never allow yourself to say that a harmony
is prior to the elements which compose it.

Never, Socrates.

But do you not see that this is what you imply when you say that
the soul existed before it took human form and body, and was made
up of elements which as yet had no existence? For harmony is not like
the soul, as you suppose; but first the lyre, and the strings, and the sounds
c   exist in a state of discord, and then harmony is made last of all, and
perishes first. And how can such a notion of the soul agree with the
other?

It cannot, replied Simmias.

And yet, he said, there surely ought to be harmony in a discourse
of which harmony is the theme?

There ought, replied Simmias.

But there is no harmony, he said, in the two propositions that
knowledge is recollection, and that the soul is a harmony. Which of
them will you retain?

d   I think, he replied, that I have a much stronger faith, Socrates, in
the first of the two, which has been fully demonstrated to me, than in
the latter, which has not been demonstrated at all, but rests only on
probable and plausible grounds, and is therefore believed by common
people. I know too well that these arguments from probabilities are
impostors, and unless great caution is observed in the use of them,
they are apt to be deceptive—in geometry, and in other things too. But
the doctrine of knowledge and recollection has been proven to me on
trustworthy grounds: and the proof was that the soul must have existed before it came into the body, because to it belongs the essence of
e   which the very name implies existence. Having, as I am convinced,
rightly accepted this conclusion, and on sufficient grounds, I must, as
I suppose, cease to argue or allow others to argue that the soul is a
harmony.

Let me put the matter, Simmias, he said, in another perspective: Do
93   you imagine that a harmony or any other composition can be in a state
other than that of the elements, out of which it is compounded?

Certainly not.

Or do or suffer anything other than they do or suffer?

He agreed.

Then a harmony does not, properly speaking, lead the parts or elements which make up the harmony, but only follows them.

He assented.

For harmony cannot possibly have any motion, or sound, or other
quality which is opposed to its parts.

That would be impossible, he replied.

And does not the nature of every harmony depend upon the manner in which the elements are harmonized?

I do not understand you, he said.

I mean to say that a harmony admits of degrees, and is more of a **b** harmony, and more completely a harmony, when more truly and fully harmonized, to any extent which is possible; and less of a harmony, and less completely a harmony, when less truly and fully harmonized.

True.

But does the soul admit of degrees? or is one soul in the very least degree more or less, or more or less completely, a soul than another?

Not in the least.

Yet surely of two souls, one is said to have intelligence and virtue, and to be good, and the other to have folly and vice, and to be an evil **c** soul: and this is said truly?

Yes, truly.

But what will those who maintain the soul to be a harmony say of this presence of virtue and vice in the soul?—will they say that here is another harmony, and another discord, and that the virtuous soul is harmonized, and itself being a harmony has another harmony within it, and that the vicious soul is inharmonical and has no harmony within it?

I cannot tell, replied Simmias; but I suppose that something of the sort would be asserted by those who say that the soul is a harmony.

And we have already admitted that no soul is more a soul than an- **d** other; which is equivalent to admitting that harmony is not more or less harmony, or more or less completely a harmony?

Quite true.

And that which is not more or less a harmony is not more or less harmonized?

True.

And that which is not more or less harmonized cannot have more or less of harmony, but only an equal harmony?

Yes.

Then one soul not being more or less absolutely a soul than an- **e** other, is not more or less harmonized?

Exactly.

And therefore it has neither more nor less of discord, nor yet of harmony?

It has not.

And having neither more nor less of harmony or of discord, one soul has no more vice or virtue than another, if vice is discord and virtue harmony?

Not at all.

94   Or speaking more correctly, Simmias, the soul, if it is a harmony,
will never have any vice; because a harmony, being absolutely a harmony, has no part in the inharmonical.

No.

And therefore a soul which is absolutely a soul has no vice?

How can it, if the previous argument holds?

Then, if all souls are equally by their nature souls, all souls of all
living creatures will be equally good?

I agree with you, Socrates, he said.

b   And can all this be true? he said; for these are the consequences
which seem to follow from the assumption that the soul is a harmony?

It cannot be true.

Once more, he said, what ruler is there of the elements of human
nature other than the soul, and especially the wise soul? Do you know
of any?

Indeed, I do not.

And is the soul in agreement with the affections of the body? or is
it at variance with them? For example, when the body is hot and thirsty,
does not the soul incline us against drinking? and when the body is
hungry, against eating? And this is only one instance out of a million of

c   the opposition of the soul to the things of the body.

Very true.

But we have already acknowledged that the soul, being a harmony,
can never utter a note at variance with the tensions and relaxations and
vibrations and other affections of the strings out of which it is composed; it can only follow, but cannot lead them?

It must be so, he replied.

And yet do we not now discover the soul to be doing the exact
opposite—leading the elements of which it is believed to be composed;
almost always opposing and coercing them in all sorts of ways through-

d   out life, sometimes more violently with the pains of medicine and gymnastic; then again more gently; now threatening, now admonishing the
desires, passions, fears, as if talking to a thing which is not itself, as
Homer in the *Odyssey* represents Odysseus doing in the words—

> 'He beat his breast, and thus reproached his heart:
> Endure, my heart; far worse hast thou endured!'*

Do you think that Homer wrote this under the idea that the soul is a
harmony capable of being led by the affections of the body, and not

---

*Odyssey 20.17–18.

rather of a nature which should lead and master them—itself a far diviner thing than any harmony?

Yes, Socrates, I quite think so.

Then, my friend, we can never be right in saying that the soul is a **95** harmony, for we should contradict the divine Homer, and contradict ourselves.

True, he said.

Thus much, said Socrates, of Harmonia, your Theban goddess, who has graciously yielded to us; but what shall I say, Cebes, to her husband Cadmus, and how shall I make peace with him?

I think that you will discover a way of propitiating him, said Cebes; I am sure that you have put the argument with Harmonia in a manner that I could never have expected. For when Simmias was mentioning **b** his difficulty, I quite imagined that no answer could be given to him, and therefore I was surprised at finding that his argument could not sustain the first onset of yours, and not impossibly the other, whom you call Cadmus, may share a similar fate.

My good friend, said Socrates, let us not boast, lest some evil eye should put to flight the words which I am about to speak. That, however, may be left in the hands of those above; while I draw near in Homeric fashion, and try the mettle of your words. Here lies the point: You want to have it proven to you that the soul is imperishable and im- **c** mortal, and the philosopher who is confident in death appears to you to have but a vain and foolish confidence, if he believes that he will fare better in the world below than one who has led another sort of life, unless he can prove this; and you say that the demonstration of the strength and divinity of the soul, and of her existence prior to our becoming men, does not necessarily imply her immortality. Admitting the soul to be long-lived, and to have known and done much in a former state, still it is not on that account immortal; and its entrance into **d** the human form may be a sort of disease which is the beginning of dissolution, and may at last, after the toils of life are over, end in that which is called death. And whether the soul enters into the body once only or many times, does not, as you say, make any difference in the fears of individuals. For any man who is not devoid of sense, must fear, if he has no knowledge and can give no account of the soul's immor- **e** tality. This, or something like this, I suspect to be your notion, Cebes; and I designedly recur to it in order that nothing may escape us, and that you may, if you wish, add or subtract anything.

As far as I see at present, said Cebes, I have nothing to add or subtract: I mean what you say I mean.

Socrates paused awhile, and seemed to be absorbed in reflection. At length he said: You are raising a tremendous question, Cebes, involving **96** the whole nature of generation and corruption, about which, if you like, I will give you my own experience; and if anything which I say is likely to avail towards the solution of your difficulty you may make use of it.

I should very much like, said Cebes, to hear what you have to say.

Then I will tell you, said Socrates. When I was young, Cebes, I had a prodigious desire to know that branch of enquiry which is called the investigation of nature; to know the causes of things, and why a thing is and is created or destroyed appeared to me to be a lofty profession; b and I was always agitating myself with the consideration of questions such as these: Is the growth of animals the result of some decay which the hot and cold principle contracts, as some have said? Is the blood the element with which we think, or the air, or the fire? or perhaps nothing of the kind—but the brain may be the originating power of the perceptions of hearing and sight and smell, and memory and opinion may come from them, and science may be based on memory and opinion when they have become fixed. And then I went on to examine the c corruption of them, and then to the things of heaven and earth, and at last I concluded myself to be utterly and absolutely incapable of these enquiries, as I will satisfactorily prove to you. For I was fascinated by them to such a degree that my eyes grew blind to things which I had seemed to myself, and also to others, to know quite well; I forgot what I had before thought self-evident truths; e.g., that the growth of man is d the result of eating and drinking; for when by the digestion of food flesh is added to flesh and bone to bone, and whenever there is an aggregation of congenial elements, the lesser bulk becomes larger and the small man great. Was not that a reasonable notion?

Yes, said Cebes, I think so.

Well; let me tell you something more. There was a time when I thought that I understood the meaning of greater and less pretty well; and when I saw a great man standing by a little one, I fancied that one was taller than the other by a head; or one horse would appear to e be greater than another horse: and still more clearly did I seem to perceive that ten is two more than eight, and that two cubits are more than one, because two is the double of one.

And what is now your notion of such matters? said Cebes.

I would be far from thinking, he replied, that I knew the cause of any of them, by heaven I would; for I cannot satisfy myself that, when 97 one is added to one, the one to which the addition is made becomes two, or that the two units added together make two by reason of the addition. I cannot understand how, when separated from the other, each of them was one and not two, and now, when they are brought together, the mere juxtaposition or meeting of them should be the cause

of their becoming two: neither can I understand how the division of
one is the way to make two; for then a different cause would produce   b
the same effect, as in the former instance the addition and juxtaposition of one to one was the cause of two, in this the separation and sub-
traction of one from the other would be the cause. Nor am I any longer
satisfied that I understand the reason why one or anything else is either
generated or destroyed or is at all, but I have in my mind some confused notion of a new method, and can never admit the other.

Then I heard someone reading, as he said, from a book of Anaxago-   c
ras, that Mind was the organizer and cause of all, and I was delighted
at this notion, which appeared quite admirable, and I said to myself: If
Mind is the organizer, Mind will organize all for the best, and put each
particular in the best place; and I argued that if anyone desired to find
out the cause of the generation or destruction or existence of anything,
he must find out what state of being or doing or suffering was best   d
for that thing, and therefore a man had only to consider the best for
himself and others, and then he would also know the worse, since the
same science comprehended both. And I rejoiced to think that I had
found in Anaxagoras a teacher of the causes of existence such as I desired,
and I imagined that he would tell me first whether the earth is flat or   e
round; and whichever was true, he would proceed to explain the cause
and the necessity of this being so, and then he would teach me the nature of the best and show that this was best; and if he said that the
earth was in the centre, he would further explain that this position
was the best, and I should be satisfied with the explanation given, and
not want any other sort of cause. And I thought that I would then go   98
on and ask him about the sun and moon and stars, and that he would
explain to me their comparative swiftness, and their returnings and
various states, active and passive, and how all of them were for the   b
best. For I could not imagine that when he spoke of mind as their organizer, he would give any other account of their being as they are,
except that this was best; and I thought that when he had explained to
me in detail the cause of each and all, he would go on to explain to
me what was best for each and what was good for all. These hopes I
would not have sold for a large sum of money, and I seized the books
and read them as fast as I could in my eagerness to know the better
and the worse.

What expectations I had formed, and how grievously was I disappointed! As I proceeded, I found my philosopher altogether forsaking
mind or any other principle of order, but having recourse to air, and   c
ether, and water, and other eccentricities. I might compare him to a
person who began by maintaining generally that mind is the cause of
the actions of Socrates, but who, when he endeavoured to explain the

causes of my several actions in detail, went on to show that I sit here because my body is made up of bones and muscles; and the bones, as he would say, are hard and have joints which divide them, and the mus-
d   cles are elastic, and they cover the bones, which have also a covering or environment of flesh and skin which contains them; and as the bones are lifted at their joints by the contraction or relaxation of the muscles, I am able to bend my limbs, and this is why I am sitting here in a curved posture—that is what he would say; and he would have a sim-ilar explanation of my talking to you, which he would attribute to sound, and air, and hearing, and he would assign ten thousand other causes of the same sort, forgetting to mention the true cause, which is,
e   that the Athenians have thought fit to condemn me, and accordingly I have thought it better and more right to remain here and undergo my
99 sentence; for I am inclined to think that I would have gone off long ago to Megara or Boeotia—by the dog, I would—if I had been moved only by my idea of what was best, and if I had not chosen the better and no-bler part, instead of playing truant and running away, of enduring any punishment which the city inflicts. There is surely a strange confusion of causes and conditions in all this. It may be said, indeed, that with-out bones and muscles and the other parts of the body I cannot exe-cute my purposes. But to say that I do as I do because of them, and that this is the way in which mind acts, and not from the choice of the best,
b   is a very careless and idle mode of speaking. I wonder that they cannot distinguish the cause from the condition, which the many, feeling about in the dark, are always mistaking and misnaming. And thus one man makes a vortex all round and steadies the earth by the heaven; another
c   gives the air as a support to the earth, which is a sort of broad trough. Any power which in arranging them as they are arranges them for the best never enters into their minds; and instead of finding any superior strength in it, they rather expect to discover another Atlas* of the world who is stronger and more everlasting and more containing than the good; of the obligatory and containing power of the good they think nothing; and yet this is the principle which I would like to learn, if anyone would teach me. But as I have failed either to discover myself, or to learn of anyone else, the nature of the best, I will exhibit to you,
d   Cebes, if you like, what I have found to be the second best mode of en-quiring into the cause.

I would very much like to hear, he replied.

I thought that as I had failed in the contemplation of true existence,

---

*The point is that only extremely simple-minded people would really believe in Atlas, the mythical Titan forced to hold the world on his shoulders.

I ought to be careful that I did not lose the eye of my soul; as people may injure their bodily eye by observing and gazing on the sun during an eclipse, unless they take the precaution of only looking at the image reflected in the water, or in some similar medium. So in my own case,   e
I was afraid that my soul might be blinded altogether if I looked at things with my eyes or tried to apprehend them by the help of the senses. And I thought that I had better have recourse to reasoning and seek the truth of things there. The simile is not perfect—for I am very   100
far from admitting that the one who contemplates existences through the medium of thought, sees them through "images" any more than the one who considers them in action and operation. However, this was the method which I adopted: I first assumed some principle which I judged to be the strongest, and then I affirmed as true whatever seemed to agree with this, whether relating to the cause or to anything else; and that which disagreed I regarded as untrue. But I should like to explain my meaning more clearly, since I do not think that you understand me yet.

No indeed, replied Cebes, not very well.

There is nothing new, he said, in what I am about to tell you; but   b
only what I have been always and everywhere repeating in the previous discussion and on other occasions: I want to show you the nature of that cause which has occupied my thoughts. I shall have to go back to those familiar words which are in everyone's mouth, and first of all assume that there is an absolute beauty and goodness and greatness, and the like; grant me this, and I hope to be able to show you the nature of the cause, and to prove the immortality of the soul.

Cebes said: You may proceed at once with the proof, for I grant you   c
this.

Well, he said, see whether you agree with me in the next step; if there were anything beautiful other than absolute beauty, it can be beautiful only in so far as it partakes of absolute beauty—and I should say the same of everything. Do you agree in this notion of the cause?

Yes, he said, I agree.

I know nothing and can understand nothing of any other of those wise causes which are alleged; and if a person says to me that the bloom of color, or form, or any such thing is a source of beauty, I leave all that,   d
which is only confusing to me, and simply and singly, and perhaps foolishly, hold and am assured in my own mind that nothing makes a thing beautiful but the presence and participation of beauty in whatever way or manner obtained; for as to the manner I am uncertain, but I stoutly contend that by beauty all beautiful things become beautiful.   e
This appears to me to be the safest answer which I can give, either to myself or to another, and to this I cling, in the persuasion that this

principle will never be overthrown, and that to myself or to anyone who asks the question, I may safely reply that by beauty beautiful things become beautiful. Do you not agree with me?

I do.

And that by greatness only great things become great and the greater even greater, and by smallness the less become less?

True.

101 Then if a person were to remark that A is taller by a head than B, and B shorter by a head than A, you would refuse to admit his statement, and would stoutly contend that what you mean is only that the greater is greater by, and by reason of, greatness, and the less is less only by, and by reason of, smallness; and thus you would avoid the danger of saying that the greater is greater and the less less by the measure of the head, which is the same in both, and would also avoid the monstrous absurdity of supposing that the greater man is greater by reason
b of the head, which is small. You would be afraid to draw such an inference, would you not?

Indeed, I would, said Cebes, laughing.

In like manner you would be afraid to say that ten exceeded eight by, and by reason of, two; but would say by, and by reason of, number; or you would say that two cubits exceed one cubit not by a half, but by magnitude?—for there is the same room for error in all these cases.

Very true, he said.

Again, would you not be cautious to affirm that the addition of
c one to one, or the division of one, is the cause of two? And you would loudly asseverate that you know of no way in which anything comes into existence except by participation in its own proper essence, and consequently, as far as you know, the only cause of two is the participation in duality—this is the way to make two, and the participation in one is the way to make one. You would say: I will let alone puzzles of division and addition—wiser heads than mine may answer them; inexperienced as I am, and ready to start, as the proverb says, at my own
d shadow, I cannot afford to give up the sure ground of a principle. And if anyone assails you there, you would not mind him, or answer him until you had seen whether the consequences which follow agree with one another or not, and when you are further required to give an explanation of this principle, you would go on to assume a higher principle, and a higher, until you found a resting-place in the best of the higher; but you would not confuse the principle and the consequences in your reasoning, like those who make contradiction their business—
e at least if you wanted to discover real existence. Not that this confusion matters to them, who never care or think about the matter at all, for they have the wit to be well pleased with themselves however great may

be the turmoil of their ideas. But you, if you are a philosopher, will cer- 102
tainly do as I say.

What you say is most true, said Simmias and Cebes, both speaking
at once.

ECH. Yes, Phaedo; and I do not wonder at their assenting. Anyone
with the least sense will acknowledge the wonderful clearness of
Socrates' reasoning.

PHAED. Certainly, Echecrates; and such was the feeling of the whole
company at the time.

ECH. Yes, and equally of ourselves, who were not of the company,
and are now listening to your recital. What happened next?

PHAED. After all this had been admitted, and they had agreed that b
ideas exist, and that other things participate in them and derive their
names from them, Socrates, if I remember rightly, said:

This is your way of speaking; and yet when you say that Simmias
is larger than Socrates and shorter than Phaedo, do you not predicate
of Simmias both largeness and smallness?

Yes, I do.

But still you allow that Simmias does not really surpass Socrates, as
the words may seem to imply, because he is Simmias, but by reason of
the size which he has; just as Simmias does not surpass Socrates be- c
cause he is Simmias, any more than because Socrates is Socrates, but
because he has smallness when compared with the largeness of Simmias?

True.

And if Phaedo surpasses him in size, this is not because Phaedo is
Phaedo, but because Phaedo has largeness relatively to Simmias, who is
comparatively smaller?

That is true.

And therefore Simmias is said to be large, and is also said to be
small, because he is in a mean between them, exceeding the smallness
of the one by his largeness, and allowing the largeness of the other to d
surpass his own smallness. He added, laughing, I am speaking like a
treatise, but I believe that what I am saying is true.

Simmias assented.

I speak as I do because I want you to agree with me in thinking,
not only that absolute largeness will never be large and also small, but
that largeness in us or in the concrete will never admit the small or
admit of being surpassed: instead of this, one of two things will happen, either the larger will fly or retire before the opposite, which is the e
smaller, or at the approach of the smaller, it has already ceased to exist;
but will not, if allowing or admitting of smallness, be changed by that;
even as I, having received and admitted smallness when compared with

Simmias, remain just as I was, and am the same small person. And as the idea of largeness cannot condescend ever to be or become small, in like manner the smallness in us cannot be or become large; nor can any
103 other opposite which remains the same ever be or become its own opposite, but either passes away or perishes in the change.

That, replied Cebes, is quite my notion.

Hereupon one of the company, though I do not exactly remember which of them, said: In heaven's name, is not this the direct contrary of what was admitted before—that out of the larger came the smaller and out of the small the larger, and that opposites were simply generated from opposites; now this principle seems to be utterly denied!

Socrates inclined his head to the speaker and listened. I like your
b courage, he said, in reminding us of this. But you do not observe that there is a difference in the two cases. For then we were speaking of opposites in the concrete, and now of the essential opposite which, as is affirmed, neither in us nor in nature can ever be at variance with itself: then, my friend, we were speaking of things in which opposites are inherent and which are called after them, but now about the opposites which are inherent in them and which give their name to them; and
c these essential opposites will never, as we maintain, admit of generation into or out of one another. At the same time, turning to Cebes, he said: Are you at all disconcerted, Cebes, at our friend's objection?

Not now, said Cebes; and yet I cannot deny that many things disturb me.

Then we are agreed after all, said Socrates, that the opposite will never in any case be opposed to itself?

To that we are quite agreed, he replied.

Yet once more let me ask you to consider the question from another point of view, and see whether you agree with me: There is a thing which you term heat, and another thing which you term cold?

Certainly.

But are they the same as fire and snow?
d Most assuredly not.

Heat is a thing different from fire, and cold is not the same as snow?

Agreed.

And yet you will surely admit that when snow, as was before said, is under the influence of heat, they will not remain snow and heat; but at the advance of the heat, the snow will either retire or perish?

Very true, he replied.

And the fire too at the advance of the cold will either retire or perish; and when the fire is under the influence of the cold, they will not remain as before, fire and cold.

That is true, he said.   e

And in some cases the name of the idea is not only attached to the
idea in an eternal connection, but anything else which, not being the
idea, has the form of the idea, may also lay claim to it. I will try to
make this clearer by an example: the odd number is always called by
the name of odd, is it not?

Very true.

But is this the only thing which is called odd? Are there not other
things which have their own name, and yet are called odd, because,   104
although not the same as oddness, they are never without oddness?—
that is what I mean to ask—whether numbers such as the number
three are not of the class of odd. And there are many other examples:
would you not say, for example, that three may be called by its proper
name, and also be called odd, which is not the same with three? and
this may be said not only of three but also of five, and of every alter-   b
nate number—each of them without being oddness is odd; and in the
same way two and four, and the other series of alternate numbers, are
even, without being evenness. Do you agree?

Of course.

Then now mark the point at which I am aiming:—not only do essential opposites exclude one another, but also concrete things, which,
although not in themselves opposed, contain opposites; these, I say, likewise reject the idea which is opposed to what is contained in them, and
when it approaches them they either perish or withdraw. For example: c
will not the number three endure annihilation or anything sooner than
be converted into an even number, while remaining three?

Very true, said Cebes.

And yet, he said, the number two is certainly not opposed to the
number three?

It is not.

Then not only do opposite ideas repel the advance of one another,
but also there are other natures which repel the approach of opposites.

Very true, he said.

Suppose, he said, that we endeavour, if possible, to determine what
these are.

By all means.

Are they not, Cebes, such as compel the things of which they have   d
possession, not only to take their own form, but also the form of some
opposite?

What do you mean?

I mean, as I was just now saying, and as I am sure that you know,
that those things which are possessed by the number three must not
only be three in number, but must also be odd.

Quite true.

And on this oddness, of which the number three has the impress,
e the opposite idea will never intrude?

No.

And this impress was given by the odd principle?

Yes.

And to the odd is opposed the even?

True.

Then the idea of the even number will never arrive at three?

No.

Then three has no part in the even?

None.

Then the triad or number three is uneven?

Very true.

To return then to my distinction of natures which are not opposed,
and yet do not admit opposites—as, in the instance given, three, although not opposed to the even, does not any the more admit of the
105 even, but always brings the opposite into play on the other side; or as two
does not receive the odd, or fire the cold—from these examples (and
there are many more of them) perhaps you may be able to arrive at the
general conclusion, that not only opposites will not receive opposites,
but also that nothing which brings the opposite will admit the opposite
of that which it brings, in that to which it is brought. And here let me
recapitulate—for there is no harm in repetition. The number five will not
admit the nature of the even, any more than ten, which is the double of
five, will admit the nature of the odd. The double has another opposite,
b and is not strictly opposed to the odd, but nevertheless rejects the odd altogether. Nor again will parts in the ratio 3:2, nor any fraction in which
there is a half, nor again in which there is a third, admit the notion of the
whole, although they are not opposed to the whole: You agree?

Yes, he said, I entirely agree and go along with you in that.

Now, he said, let us begin again; and do not answer my question
in the words in which I ask it: let me have not the old safe answer of
which I spoke at first, but another equally safe, of which the truth will
be inferred by you from what has just been said. I mean that if any one
asks you 'what that is, of which the inherence makes the body hot,' you
c will reply not heat (this is what I call the safe and stupid answer), but
fire, a far superior answer, which we are now in a condition to give. Or
if any one asks you 'why a body is diseased,' you will not say from disease, but from fever; and instead of saying that oddness is the cause of
odd numbers, you will say that the monad is the cause of them: and so
of things in general, as I dare say that you will understand sufficiently
without my adducing any further examples.

Yes, he said, I quite understand you.

Tell me, then, what is that of which the inherence will render the body alive?

The soul, he replied.

And is this always the case? *d*

Yes, he said, of course.

Then whatever the soul possesses, to that she comes bearing life?

Yes, certainly.

And is there any opposite to life?

There is, he said.

And what is that?

Death.

Then the soul, as has been acknowledged, will never receive the opposite of what she brings.

Impossible, replied Cebes.

And now, he said, what did we just now call that principle which repels the even?

The odd.

And that principle which repels the musical or the just?

The unmusical, he said, and the unjust. *e*

And what do we call that principle which does not admit of death?

The immortal, he said.

And does the soul admit of death?

No.

Then the soul is immortal?

Yes, he said.

And may we say that this has been proven?

Yes, abundantly proven, Socrates, he replied.

Supposing that the odd were imperishable, must not three be im- *106* perishable?

Of course.

And if that which is cold were imperishable, when the warm principle came attacking the snow, must not the snow have retired whole and unmelted—for it could never have perished, nor could it have remained and admitted the heat?

True, he said.

Again, if the uncooling or warm principle were imperishable, the fire when assailed by cold would not have perished or have been extinguished, but would have gone away unaffected?

Certainly, he said.

And the same may be said of the immortal: if the immortal is also *b* imperishable, the soul when attacked by death cannot perish; for the preceding argument shows that the soul will not admit of death, or ever be dead, any more than three or the odd number will admit of the even, or fire, or the heat in the fire, of the cold. Yet a person may say: 'But although the odd will not become even at the approach of the even, why may not the odd perish and the even take the place of the

c   odd?' Now to him who makes this objection, we cannot answer that the odd principle is imperishable; for this has not been acknowledged, but if this had been acknowledged, there would have been no difficulty in contending that at the approach of the even the odd principle and the number three took their departure; and the same argument would have held good of fire and heat and anything else.

Very true.

And the same may be said of the immortal: if the immortal is also imperishable, then the soul will be imperishable as well as immortal;

d   but if not, some other proof of her imperishableness will have to be given.

No other proof is needed, he said; for if the immortal, being eternal, is liable to perish, then nothing is imperishable.

Yes, replied Socrates, and yet all men will agree that god, and the essential form of life, and the immortal in general, will never perish.

Yes, he said—that is true; and what is more, gods, if I am not mistaken, as well as men.

e   Seeing then that the immortal is indestructible, must not the soul, if it is immortal, be also imperishable?

Most certainly.

Then when death attacks a man, his mortal part may be supposed to die, but the immortal retires at the approach of death and is preserved safe and sound?

True.

Then, Cebes, beyond question, the soul is immortal and imperish-
107   able, and our souls will truly exist in another world!

I am convinced, Socrates, said Cebes, and have nothing more to object; but if my friend Simmias, or anyone else, has any further objection to make, he had better speak out, and not keep silent, since I do not know to what other season he can defer the discussion, if there is anything which he wants to say or hear.

But I have nothing more to say, replied Simmias; nor can I see any reason for doubt after what has been said. But I still feel and cannot help feeling uncertain in my own mind, when I think of the greatness

b   of the subject and the feebleness of man.

Yes, Simmias, replied Socrates, that is well said: and I may add that first principles, even if they appear certain, should be carefully considered; and when they are satisfactorily ascertained, then, with a sort of hesitating confidence in human reason, you may, I think, follow the course of the argument; and if that is plain and clear, there will be no need for any further enquiry.

Very true.

But then, my friends, he said, if the soul is really immortal, what care should be taken of it, not only in respect of the share of time which is called life, but of eternity! And the danger of neglecting it from this point of view does indeed appear to be awful. If death had only been the end of all, the wicked would have had a good bargain in dying, for they would have been happily rid not only of their body, but of their own evil together with their souls. But now, inasmuch as the soul is manifestly immortal, there is no release or salvation from evil except the attainment of the highest virtue and wisdom. For the soul when on its progress to the underworld takes nothing with it but nurture and education; and these are said greatly to benefit or greatly to injure the departed, at the very beginning of his journey.

For after death, as they say, the spirit of each individual, to whom he belonged in life, leads him to a certain place in which the dead are gathered together, whence after judgment has been given they pass into the underworld, following the guide, who is appointed to conduct them from this world to the other: and when they have received their due there and remained their time, another guide brings them back again after many revolutions of ages. Now this way to the other world is not, as Aeschylus makes Telephus* say, a single and straight path—if that were so no guide would be needed, for no one could miss it; but there are many forks in the road, and windings, as I infer from the rites and sacrifices which are offered to the gods below in places where three ways meet on earth. The wise and orderly soul follows the straight path and is conscious of its surroundings; but the soul which desires the body, and which, as I was relating before, has long been fluttering about the lifeless frame and the world of sight, is after many struggles and many sufferings carried away with violence and differently by its attendant spirit; and when it arrives at the place where the other souls are gathered, if it is impure and has done impure deeds, whether foul murders or other crimes which are the brothers of these, and the works of brothers in crime—from that soul every one flees and turns away; no one will be its companion, no one its guide; it wanders alone in extremity of evil until certain times are fulfilled, and when they are fulfilled, it is borne irresistibly to its own fitting habitation; as every pure and just soul which has passed through life in the company and under the guidance of the gods has also its own proper home.

---

*Arcadian hero (raised by deer in the myth) who led the Greeks to Troy.

Now the earth has different wonderful regions, and is indeed in nature and extent very unlike the notions of geographers, as I believe on the authority of a certain person.

d   What do you mean, Socrates? said Simmias. I have myself heard many descriptions of the earth, but I do not know, and I would very much like to know, in which of these you put faith.

And I, Simmias, replied Socrates, if I had the art of Glaucus* would tell you; although I know not that the art of Glaucus could prove the truth of my tale, which I myself would never be able to prove, and even if I could, I fear, Simmias, that my life would come to an end before the argument was completed. I may describe to you, however, the form
e   and regions of the earth according to my conception of them.

That, said Simmias, will be enough.

Well then, he said, my conviction is that the earth is a round body in the centre of the heavens, and therefore has no need of air or of any
109 similar force to be a support, but is kept there and hindered from falling or inclining any way by the equability of the surrounding heaven and by her own equipoise. For that which, being in equipoise, is in the centre of that which is equably diffused, will not incline any way in any degree but will always remain in the same state and not deviate. This is my first notion.

Which is surely a correct one, said Simmias.

I further believe that the earth is very vast, and that we who dwell
b in the region extending from the river Phasis† to the Pillars of Heracles‡ inhabit a small portion only about the sea, like ants or frogs about a marsh, and that there are other inhabitants of many other like places; for everywhere on the face of the earth there are hollows of various forms and sizes, into which the water and the mist and the lower air collect. But the true earth is pure and situated in the pure heaven—
c there are the stars also; and it is the heaven which is commonly spoken of as the ether, and of which our own earth is the sediment gathering in the hollows beneath. But we who live in these hollows are deceived into the notion that we are dwelling above on the surface of the earth; which is just as if a creature who was at the bottom of the sea were to fancy that he was on the surface of the water, and that the sea was the heaven through which he saw the sun and the other stars, he having
d never come to the surface by reason of his feebleness and sluggishness,

---

*Perhaps a rhapsode (reciter of epic poems); his skill is often referred to as exemplary.
†River east of the Black Sea; that is, the eastern end of the Greek world.
‡Or Pillars of Hercules; promontories on the Strait of Gibraltar; that is, the western end of the Greek world.

and having never lifted up his head and seen, nor ever heard from one who had seen, how much purer and fairer the world above is than his own. And such is exactly our case: for we are dwelling in a hollow of the earth, and fancy that we are on the surface; and the air we call heaven, in which we imagine that the stars move. But the fact is that owing to our feebleness and sluggishness we are prevented from reaching the surface of the air: for if any man could arrive at the exterior limit, or take the wings of a bird and come to the top, then like a fish who puts his head out of the water and sees this world, he would see a world beyond; and, if the nature of man could sustain the sight, he would acknowledge that this other world was the place of the true heaven and the true light and the true earth. For our earth, and the stones, and the entire region which surrounds us, are spoilt and corroded, as in the sea all things are corroded by the brine, neither is there any noble or perfect growth, but caverns only, and sand, and an endless slough of mud; and even the shore is not to be compared to the fairer sights of this world. And still less is our world to be compared with the other. Of that upper earth which is under the heaven, I can tell you a charming tale, Simmias, which is well worth hearing.

And we, Socrates, replied Simmias, shall be charmed to listen to you.

The tale, my friend, he said, is as follows: In the first place, the earth, when looked at from above, is in appearance streaked like one of those balls which have leather coverings in twelve pieces, and is decked with various colors, of which the colors used by painters on earth are in a manner samples. But there the whole earth is made up of them, and they are far brighter and clearer than ours; there is a purple of wonderful lustre, also the radiance of gold, and the white which is in the earth is whiter than any chalk or snow. Of these and other colors the earth is made up, and they are more in number and fairer than the eye of man has ever seen; the very hollows (of which I was speaking) filled with air and water have a color of their own, and are seen like light gleaming amid the diversity of the other colors, so that the whole presents a single and continuous appearance of variety in unity. And in this fair region everything that grows—trees, and flowers, and fruits—are in a like degree fairer than any here; and there are hills, having stones in them in a like degree smoother, and more transparent, and fairer in color than our highly valued emeralds and sardonyxes and jaspers, and other gems, which are but minute fragments of them: for there all the stones are like our precious stones, and fairer still. The reason is that they are pure, and not, like our precious stones, infected or corroded by the corrupt briny elements which coagulate among us, and which breed foulness and disease both in earth and stones, as well

as in animals and plants. They are the jewels of the upper earth, which also shines with gold and silver and the like, and they are set in the
111 light of day and are large and abundant and in all places, making the earth a sight to gladden the beholder's eye. And there are animals and people, some in a middle region, others dwelling about the air as we dwell about the sea; others in islands which the air flows round, near the continent; and in a word, the air is used by them as the water and
b the sea are by us, and the ether is to them what the air is to us. Moreover, their seasons are so temperate that they have no disease, and live much longer than we do, and have sight and hearing and smell, and all the other senses in far greater perfection, in the same proportion that air is purer than water or the ether than air. Also they have temples and sacred places in which the gods really dwell, and they hear their voices
c and receive their answers, and are conscious of them and converse with them; and they see the sun, moon, and stars as they truly are, and their other blessedness is of a piece with this.

Such is the nature of the whole earth, and of the things which are around the earth; and there are different regions in the hollows on the face of the globe everywhere, some of them deeper and more extended than the one we inhabit, others deeper but with a narrower opening
d than ours, and some shallower and also wider. All have numerous perforations, and there are passages broad and narrow in the interior of the earth, connecting them with one another; and there flows out of and into them, as into basins, a vast tide of water, and huge subterranean streams of perennial rivers, and springs hot and cold, and a great
e fire, and great rivers of fire, and streams of liquid mud, thin or thick (like the rivers of mud in Sicily, and the lava streams which follow them), and the regions about which they happen to flow are filled up with them. And there is a swinging or see-saw in the interior of the earth which moves all this up and down, and is due to the following cause: there is a chasm which is the vastest of them all, and pierces
112 right through the whole earth; this is that chasm which Homer describes in the words:

'Far off, where is the inmost depth beneath the earth;'*

and which he in other places, and many other poets, have called Tartarus. And the see-saw is caused by the streams flowing into and out of this chasm, and they each have the nature of the soil through which
b they flow. And the reason why the streams are always flowing in and

---

*Iliad 8.14.

out, is that the watery element has no bed or bottom, but is swinging and surging up and down, and the surrounding wind and air do the same; they follow the water up and down, hither and thither, over the earth—just as in the act of respiration the air is always in process of inhalation and exhalation—; and the wind swinging with the water in and out produces fearful and irresistible blasts: when the waters retire with a rush into the lower parts of the earth, as they are called, they flow through the earth in those regions, and fill them up like water raised by a pump, and then when they leave those regions and rush back hither, they again fill the hollows here, and when these are filled, flow through subterranean channels and find their way to their several places, forming seas, and lakes, and rivers, and springs. Thence they again enter the earth, some of them making a long circuit into many lands, others going to a few places and not so distant; and again fall into Tartarus, some at a point a good deal lower than that at which they rose, and others not much lower, but all in some degree lower than the point from which they came. And some burst forth again on the opposite side, and some on the same side, and some wind round the earth with one or many folds like the coils of a serpent, and descend as far as they can, but always return and fall into the chasm. The rivers flowing in either direction can descend only to the centre and no further, for opposite to the rivers is a precipice.

Now these rivers are many, and mighty, and different, and there are four principal ones, of which the greatest and outermost is that called Oceanus, which flows round the earth in a circle; and in the opposite direction flows Acheron, which passes under the earth through desert places into the Acherusian lake: this is the lake to the shores of which the souls of the many go when they are dead, and after waiting an appointed time, which is to some a longer and to some a shorter time, they are sent back to be born again as animals. The third river passes out between the two, and near the place of outlet pours into a vast region of fire, and forms a lake larger than the Mediterranean Sea, boiling with water and mud; and proceeding muddy and turbid, and winding about the earth, comes, among other places, to the extremities of the Acherusian lake, but mingles not with the waters of the lake, and after making many coils about the earth plunges into Tartarus at a deeper level. This is that Pyriphlegethon, as the stream is called, which throws up jets of fire in different parts of the earth. The fourth river goes out on the opposite side, and falls first of all into a wild and savage region, which is all of a dark blue colour, like lapis lazuli; and this is that river which is called the Stygian river, and falls into and forms the Lake Styx, and after falling into the lake and receiving strange powers in the waters, passes under the earth, winding round in the opposite direction, and comes near the Acherusian lake from the opposite side to Pyriphlegethon. And the water of this river too mingles with no other, but flows round in a circle and falls into Tartarus over against Pyriphlegethon; and the name of the river, as the poets say, is Cocytus.

d   Such is the nature of the other world; and when the dead arrive at the place to which the spirit of each severally guides them, first of all, they have sentence passed upon them, as to whether they have lived well and piously or not. And those who appear to have lived neither well nor badly, go to the river Acheron, and embarking in any vessels which they may find, are carried in them to the lake, and there they dwell and are purified of their evil deeds, and having suffered the penalty for the wrongs which they have done to others, they are absolved, and receive the rewards of their good deeds, each of them according to his deserts.

e   But those who appear to be incurable by reason of the greatness of their crimes—who have committed many and terrible deeds of sacrilege, murders foul and violent, or the like—such are hurled into Tartarus which is their suitable destiny, and they never come out. Those again who have committed crimes, which, although great, are not irremediable—who in a moment of anger, for example, have done some violence to a father or a mother, and have repented for the remainder

114 of their lives, or who have taken the life of another under the like extenuating circumstances—these are plunged into Tartarus, the pains of which they are compelled to undergo for a year, but at the end of the year the wave casts them forth—mere homicides by way of Cocytus, parricides and matricides by Pyriphlegethon—and they are borne to the Acherusian lake, and there they lift up their voices and call upon the victims whom they have slain or wronged, to have pity on them, and

b   to be kind to them, and let them come out into the lake. If they prevail, they come forth and cease from their troubles; if not, they are carried back again into Tartarus and from thence into the rivers unceasingly, until they obtain mercy from those whom they have wronged: for that is the sentence inflicted upon them by their judges. Those too who have been pre-eminent for holiness of life are released from this earthly prison, and go to their pure home which is above,

c   and dwell in the purer earth; and of these, such as have duly purified themselves with philosophy live henceforth altogether without the body, in mansions fairer still, which may not be described, and of which the time would fail me to tell.

Wherefore, Simmias, seeing all these things, what ought not we to do in order to obtain virtue and wisdom in this life? Fair is the prize, and the hope great!

d   A man of sense ought not to say, nor will I be very confident, that the description which I have given of the soul and her mansions is exactly true. But I do say that, inasmuch as the soul is shown to be immortal, he may venture to think, not improperly or unworthily, that something of the kind is true. The venture is a glorious one, and he ought to comfort himself with words like these, which is the reason why I lengthen out the tale. Wherefore, I say, let a man be of good cheer about his soul, who having cast away the pleasures and ornaments of the body as alien to him and working harm rather than good, has sought after the pleasures of knowledge; and has arrayed the soul, not in some foreign attire, but in her own proper jewels: temperance, justice, courage, nobility, and truth—in these adorned it is ready to go on its journey to the underworld, when the hour comes. You, Simmias and Cebes, and all other men, will depart at some time or other. Me already, as a tragic poet would say, the voice of fate calls. Soon I must drink the poison; and I think I had better take a bath first, in order that the women may not have the trouble of washing my dead body.

When he finished speaking, Crito said: Have you any commands for us, Socrates—anything to say about your children, or any other matter in which we can serve you?

Nothing particular, Crito, he replied: only, as I have always told you, take care of yourselves; that is a service which you may be ever rendering to me and mine and to all of us, whether you promise to do so or not. But if you have no thought for yourselves, and care not to walk according to the rule which I have prescribed for you now and earlier, however much you may profess or promise at the moment, it will be of no avail.

We will do our best, said Crito: And in what way shall we bury you?

In any way you like; but get hold of me, and take care that I do not run away! Then he turned to us, and added with a smile: I cannot make Crito believe that I am the same Socrates who has been talking and conducting the argument; he fancies that I am the other Socrates whom he will soon see, a dead body; he asks how shall he bury me. And though I have spoken many words in the endeavour to show that when I have drunk the poison I shall leave you and go to the joys of the Blessed, these words of mine, with which I was comforting you and myself, have had, I realize, no effect on Crito. And therefore I want you to be surety for me to him now, as at the trial he was surety to the judges for me: but let the promise be of another sort; for he was surety for me to the judges that I would remain, and you must be my surety to him that I shall not remain, but go away and depart; and then he will suffer less at my death, and not be grieved when he sees my body being burned or buried. I would not have him be sorry at my hard lot, or say at the burial, "Thus we lay out Socrates" or "Thus we follow him to the grave

or bury him"; for false words are not only evil in themselves, but they infect the soul with evil. Be of good cheer then, my dear Crito, and say
116 that you are burying my body only, and do with that whatever is usual, and what you think best.

When he had spoken these words, he arose and went into a chamber to bathe; Crito followed him and told us to wait. So we remained behind, talking and thinking of the subject of discourse, and also of the greatness of our sorrow; he was like a father of whom we were being bereaved, and we were about to pass the rest of our lives as orphans. When he had taken the bath his children were brought to him (he had
b two young sons and an elder one); the women of his family also came, and he talked to them and gave them a few directions in the presence of Crito; then he dismissed them and returned to us.

Now the hour of sunset was near, for a good deal of time had passed while he was inside. When he came out, he sat down with us again after his bath, but not much was said. Soon the guard, who was
c the servant of the Eleven, entered and stood by him, saying: to you, Socrates, whom I know to be the noblest and gentlest and best of all who ever came to this place, I will not impute the angry feelings of other men, who rage and swear at me, when, in obedience to the authorities, I bid them drink the poison; indeed, I am sure that you will not be angry with me; for others, as you are aware, and not I, are to
d blame. And so fare you well, and try to bear lightly what must be—you know my errand. Then bursting into tears he turned away and went out.

Socrates looked at him and said: I return your good wishes, and will do as you bid. Then turning to us, he said: how charming the man is; since I have been in prison he has always been coming to see me, and at times he would talk to me, and was as good to me as could be, and now see how generously he is sad on my account. We must do as he says, Crito; let the cup be brought, if the poison is prepared. If not, let the attendant prepare some.

e Yet, said Crito, the sun is still upon the hill-tops, and I know that many have taken the draught late, and after the announcement has been made to him, he has eaten and drunk, and enjoyed the society of his beloved; do not hurry, there is time enough.

Socrates said: Yes, Crito, and they of whom you speak are right in so acting, for they think that they will gain by the delay; but I am right in not following their example, for I do not think that I should gain any-
117 thing by drinking the poison a little later; I could only be ridiculous in my own eyes for sparing and saving a life which is already forfeit. Please then to do as I say, and do not refuse me.

Crito made a sign to the servant, who was standing by; and he

went out, and having been absent for some time, returned with the
guard carrying the cup of poison. Socrates said: You, my good friend,
who are experienced in these matters, shall give me directions how I
am to proceed. The man answered: You have only to walk about until   b
your legs are heavy, and then to lie down, and the poison will act. At
the same time he handed the cup to Socrates, who in the easiest and
gentlest manner, without the least fear or change of colour or feature,
looking at the man with all his eyes, Echecrates, as his manner was,
took the cup and said: What do you say about making a libation out of
this cup to any god? May I, or not? The man answered: We only prepare, Socrates, just so much as we deem enough. I understand, he said: c
but I may and must ask the gods to prosper my journey from this to
the other world; so be it according to my prayer. Then raising the cup
to his lips, quite readily and cheerfully he drank the poison. And hitherto most of us had been able to control our sorrow; but now when we
saw him drinking, and saw too that he had finished the draught, we
could no longer forbear, and in spite of myself my own tears were flowing fast; so that I covered my face and wept, not for him, but at the
thought of my own calamity in having to part from such a friend. Nor
was I the first; for Crito, when he found himself unable to restrain his   d
tears, had got up, and I followed; and at that moment, Apollodorus,
who had been weeping all the time, broke out in a loud and passionate cry which made cowards of us all. Socrates alone retained his calm-
ness: What is this strange outcry? he said. I sent away the women
mainly in order that they might not misbehave in this way, for I have
been told that a man should die in peace. Be quiet then, and have pa-   e
tience. When we heard his words we were ashamed, and refrained our
tears; he walked about until, as he said, his legs began to fail, and then
he lay on his back, according to the directions, and the man who gave
him the poison now and then looked at his feet and legs; after a while
he pressed his foot hard, and asked him if he could feel; he said no;   118
then his leg, and so upwards and upwards, and showed us that he was
cold and stiff. And he felt them himself, and said: when the poison
reaches the heart, that will be the end. He was beginning to grow cold
about the groin, when he uncovered his face, for he had covered himself up, and said—they were his last words—: Crito, I owe a cock to Asclepius;[4] will you remember to pay the debt? The debt shall be paid,
said Crito; is there anything else? There was no answer to this question.
In a minute or two a movement was heard, and the attendants uncovered him; his eyes were set, and Crito closed his eyes and mouth.

Such was the end, Echecrates, of our friend, concerning whom I
may truly say that of all the men of his time whom I have known, he
was the wisest and justest and best.

IV. VIRTUE, POLITICS, AND LAW-MAKING

Protagoras
Statesman
Laws I–III

PROTAGORAS

Introduction

THE CONVERSATION OF *PROTAGORAS* takes place at the house of Callias, a wealthy Athenian who was known to spend large sums of money in fees charged by the Sophists. Several of them are present: Prodicus of Ceos, Hippias of Elis (on both of whom see "General Introduction," p. xxi), and perhaps the most celebrated of all the Sophists, Protagoras of Abdera. Protagoras was the author of works on grammar and rhetoric, and he might have been commissioned by Pericles to draft a constitution for the Greek colony of Thurii (modern Sibari, in the south of Italy). Also present are Critias, a cousin of Plato's mother and one of the Thirty Tyrants, and Alcibiades (see "Introduction" to *Symposium*).

The conversation takes place in the following stages:

- (309a–310a) Socrates narrates to a nameless companion his encounter with Protagoras, whom they agree to call "the wisest of all living men" (309d).

- (310a–314c) Socrates clarifies that it was his friend Hippocrates who asked him for an introduction to Protagoras, and that Hippocrates was unable to state what he expected to learn from him, other than how to be an effective speaker. Socrates considers that to be an inadequate definition of Sophists, since it does not differentiate them from other experts.

- (314c–320c) At Callias' house, Socrates asks Protagoras what he will teach Hippocrates. Protagoras puts forward success in public and private life as the outcome of his teachings. This, Socrates thinks, means that Protagoras claims to teach men how to be good citizens, to which Protagoras agrees. But Socrates disbelieves the claim, for two reasons: (a) Athenians believe that nobody is an expert in policy; and (b) even those who are good citizens have proved to be unable to teach their own sons to follow suit.

- (320c–328d) Protagoras replies to both objections in two steps. First, he tells the story of Prometheus and Epimetheus, in which Prometheus gave men the technical skill to produce fire, following which men developed by themselves the skills of articulated speech, house-building, and agriculture. Later in the same story, Zeus sent Hermes to give all men a share in the sense of justice, which men are aware of and try to teach and promote. Next,

Protagoras explains that much effort is indeed spent in teaching children, but that becoming a truly excellent citizen requires natural talent and a good, specialized teacher, which he claims to be.

- (328d–332a) Socrates asks Protagoras whether different virtues add up to excellence or if they are all one and the same. Protagoras' view is that there are different virtues. Socrates disagrees. Protagoras objects, but no final decision can be made on this point.

- (332a–338e) Socrates argues that wisdom and justice are nothing but soundness of mind. Protagoras interrupts the argument and states that goodness is a very complex notion and depends on the relation of different elements, and that the good for one can be bad for another. Socrates objects to this mode of discussion and asks to proceed by questions and answers.

- (338e–348c) The discussion continues with the analysis of a poem by Simonides about the truly good man that only shows that criticism of poetry can lead to no conclusion. Socrates and Protagoras are back where they started.

- (348c–351e) Protagoras states that there are different virtues; some (wisdom, soundness of mind, justice) are alike, but courage is different. Socrates argues that courage is identical to wisdom. Protagoras objects by elaborating on the difference between daring and courage. Socrates changes topics from courage to pleasure.

- (352a–357e) Socrates states his conviction that when one is sure about what is right, the pursuit of pleasure will not stand in the way of doing it. Yielding to pleasure is nothing but a miscalculation of the consequences of our actions.

- (358a–361d) Turning to courage again, Socrates forces Protagoras to agree that cowards are also nothing but men in error. Hence courage and knowledge are indeed one. Socrates then summarizes the course of the argument and reaches the conclusion that if all virtues are one, and they are knowledge, they can be taught (as Protagoras has claimed), since knowledge can be taught. On the other hand, this position is in contradiction with Protagoras' first statement that there are different virtues. Socrates proposes to continue the discussion.

- (361d–362a) Protagoras says farewell, praising Socrates for his wisdom and promising to be available to continue the discussion some other time. Socrates says that it is also time for him to go.

Protagoras' relativism about what is good (332a–338e) was very problematic for Socrates and for Plato, since it means both a diametrical opposition to Platonic epistemology and a strong philosophical argument in favor of deliberative democracy. The question is explored further in *Theaetetus* (not included in this volume), in which Socrates conjures up Protagoras in order to examine his views about what constitutes knowledge. The lack of extant works by Protagoras is particularly debilitating for a correct assessment of the teachings and the actual relevance of the Sophists in classical Athens.

PROTAGORAS

COMPANION. Where do you come from, Socrates? And yet I need hardly ask the question, for I know that you have been in chase of the fair Alcibiades. I saw him the day before yesterday; and he had got a beard like a man; he is a man, as I may tell you in your ear. But I thought that he was still very charming.

SOCRATES. What of his beard? Are you not of Homer's opinion, who says

> 'Youth is most charming when the beard first appears'?*

And that is now the charm of Alcibiades.

COM. Well, and how do matters proceed? Have you been visiting him, and was he gracious to you?

SOC. Yes, I thought that he was very gracious; and especially today, for I have just come from him, and he has been helping me in an argument. But shall I tell you a strange thing? I paid no attention to him, and several times I quite forgot that he was present.

COM. What is the meaning of this? Has anything happened between you and him? For surely you cannot have discovered a fairer love than he is; certainly not in this city of Athens.

SOC. Yes, much fairer.

COM. What do you mean—a local or a foreigner?

SOC. A foreigner.

COM. Where from?

SOC. From Abdera.

COM. And is this stranger really in your opinion a fairer love than the son of Clinias?

SOC. And is not the wiser always the fairer, sweet friend?

COM. But have you really met, Socrates, with some wise one?

SOC. Say rather, with the wisest of all living men, if you are willing to accord that title to Protagoras.

COM. What! Is Protagoras in Athens?

SOC. Yes; he has been here two days.

COM. And do you just come from an interview with him?

SOC. Yes; and I have heard and said many things.

309

b

c

d

310

---

*Iliad 24.348; Odyssey 10.279.

381

COM. Then, if you have no engagement, suppose that you sit down and tell me what passed, and my attendant here shall give up his place to you.

Soc. To be sure; and I shall be grateful to you for listening.

COM. Thank you, too, for telling us.

Soc. That is thank you twice over. Listen then.

b   Last night, or rather very early this morning, Hippocrates, the son of Apollodorus and the brother of Phason, gave a tremendous thump with his staff at my door; someone opened to him, and he came rushing in and bawled out: Socrates, are you awake or asleep?

I knew his voice, and said: Hippocrates, is that you? do you bring any news?

Good news, he said; nothing but good.

Delightful, I said; but what is the news? and why have you come hither at this unearthly hour?

He drew nearer to me and said: Protagoras is here.

Yes, I replied; he came two days ago: have you only just heard of his arrival?

Yes, by the gods, he said; but not until yesterday evening.

c   At the same time he felt for the truckle-bed, and sat down at my feet, and then he said: Yesterday quite late in the evening, on my return from Oenoe whither I had gone in pursuit of my runaway slave Satyrus, as I meant to have told you, if some other matter had not come in the way; on my return, when we had had supper and were about to retire to rest, my brother said to me: Protagoras is here. I was going to you at once, and then I thought that the night was far spent. But the mo-
d   ment sleep left me after my fatigue, I got up and came hither direct.

I, who knew the very courageous madness of the man, said: What is the matter? Has Protagoras robbed you of anything?

He replied, laughing: Yes, indeed he has, Socrates, of the wisdom which he keeps from me.

But, surely, I said, if you give him money, and make friends with him, he will make you as wise as he is himself.

Would to heaven, he replied, that this were the case! He might take
e   all that I have, and all that my friends have, if he pleased. But that is why I have come to you now, in order that you may speak to him on my behalf; for I am young, and I have never seen nor heard him (when he
311 visited Athens before I was but a child); all men praise him, Socrates; he is reputed to be the most accomplished of speakers. There is no reason why we should not go to him at once, and then we shall find him at home. He lodges, as I hear, with Callias the son of Hipponicus: let us start.

I replied: Not yet, my good friend; the hour is too early. But let us rise and take a turn in the court and wait about there until daybreak; when the day breaks, then we will go. For Protagoras is generally at home, and we shall be sure to find him; never fear.

Upon this we got up and walked about in the court, and I thought that I would make trial of the strength of his resolution. So I examined him and put questions to him. Tell me, Hippocrates, I said, as you are going to Protagoras, and will be paying your money to him, what is he to whom you are going? and what will he make of you? If, for example, you had thought of going to Hippocrates of Cos, the Asclepiad, and were about to give him your money, and someone had said to you: You are paying money to your namesake Hippocrates, Hippocrates; tell me, what is he that you give him money? How would you have answered?

I should say, he replied, that I gave money to him as a physician.

And what will he make of you?

A physician, he said.

And if you were resolved to go to Polycleitus* the Argive, or Pheidias† the Athenian, and were intending to give them money, and someone had asked you: What are Polycleitus and Pheidias? and why do you give them this money?—how would you have answered?

I should have answered, that they were statuaries.

And what will they make of you?

A statuary, of course.

Well now, I said, you and I are going to Protagoras, and we are ready to pay him money on your behalf. If our own means are sufficient, and we can gain him with these, we shall be only too glad; but if not, then we are to spend the money of your friends as well. Now suppose that while we are thus enthusiastically pursuing our object someone were to say to us: Tell me, Socrates, and you Hippocrates, what is Protagoras, and why are you going to pay him money,—how should we answer? I know that Pheidias is a sculptor, and that Homer is a poet; but what appellation is given to Protagoras? how is he designated?

They call him a Sophist, Socrates, he replied.

Then we are going to pay our money to him in the character of a Sophist?

Certainly.

But suppose a person were to ask this further question: And how about yourself? What will Protagoras make of you, if you go to see him?

---

*Sculptor from Argos (fifth century B.C.E.); author of treatises on sculpture.

†Athenian sculptor (fifth century B.C.E.); he ran a building project in the Athenian Acropolis under Pericles (see footnote on p. 41).

He answered, with a blush upon his face (for the day was just beginning to dawn, so that I could see him): Unless this differs in some way from the former instances, I suppose that he will make a Sophist of me.

By the gods, I said, and are you not ashamed at having to appear before the Greeks in the character of a Sophist?

Indeed, Socrates, to confess the truth, I am.

But you should not assume, Hippocrates, that the instruction of Protagoras is of this nature: may you not learn of him in the same way that you learned the arts of the grammarian, or musician, or trainer, not with the view of making any of them a profession, but only as a part of education, and because a private gentleman and freeman ought to know them?

Just so, he said; and that, in my opinion, is a far truer account of the teaching of Protagoras.

I said: I wonder whether you know what you are doing?

And what am I doing?

You are going to commit your soul to the care of a man whom you call a Sophist. And yet I hardly think that you know what a Sophist is; and if not, then you do not even know to whom you are committing your soul and whether the thing to which you commit yourself is good or evil.

I certainly think that I do know, he replied.

Then tell me, what do you imagine that he is?

I take him to be one who knows wise things, he replied, as his name implies.

And might you not, I said, affirm this of the painter and of the carpenter also: Do not they, too, know wise things? But suppose a person were to ask us: In what are the painters wise? We should answer: In what relates to the making of likenesses, and similarly of other things. And if he were further to ask: What is the wisdom of the Sophist, and what is the manufacture over which he presides?—how should we answer him?

How should we answer him, Socrates? What other answer could there be but that he presides over the art which makes men eloquent?

Yes, I replied, that is very likely true, but not enough; for in the answer a further question is involved: Of what does the Sophist make a man talk eloquently? The player on the lyre may be supposed to make a man talk eloquently about that which he makes him understand, that is about playing the lyre. Is not that true?

Yes.

Then about what does the Sophist make him eloquent? Must not he make him eloquent in that which he understands?

Yes, that may be assumed.

And what is that which the Sophist knows and makes his disciple know?

Indeed, he said, I cannot tell.

Then I proceeded to say: Well, but are you aware of the danger   313
which you are incurring? If you were going to commit your body to
someone, who might do good or harm to it, would you not carefully
consider and ask the opinion of your friends and kindred, and deliberate many days as to whether you should give him the care of your
body? But when the soul is in question, which you hold to be of far
more value than the body, and upon the good or evil of which depends
the well-being of your all, about this you never consulted either with
your father or with your brother or with anyone of us who are your   b
companions. But no sooner does this foreigner appear, than you instantly commit your soul to his keeping. In the evening, as you say, you
hear of him, and in the morning you go to him, never deliberating or
taking the opinion of anyone as to whether you ought to intrust yourself to him or not; you have quite made up your mind that you will at
all hazards be a pupil of Protagoras, and are prepared to expend all the
property of yourself and of your friends in carrying out at any price
this determination, although, as you admit, you do not know him, and
have never spoken with him: and you call him a Sophist, but are man-   c
ifestly ignorant of what a Sophist is; and yet you are going to commit
yourself to his keeping.

When he heard me say this, he replied: No other inference,
Socrates, can be drawn from your words.

I proceeded: Is not a Sophist, Hippocrates, one who deals wholesale
or retail in the food of the soul? To me that appears to be his nature.

And what, Socrates, is the food of the soul?

Surely, I said, knowledge is the food of the soul; and we must take
care, my friend, that the Sophist does not deceive us when he praises
what he sells, like the dealers wholesale or retail who sell the food of   d
the body; for they praise indiscriminately all their goods, without knowing what are really beneficial or hurtful: neither do their customers
know, with the exception of any trainer or physician who may happen
to buy them. In like manner those who carry about the wares of
knowledge, and make the round of the cities, and sell or retail them to
any customer who is in want of them, praise them all alike; though I
should not wonder, my friend, if many of them were really ignorant of
their effect upon the soul; and their customers equally ignorant, unless   e
he who buys of them happens to be a physician of the soul. If, therefore, you have understanding of what is good and evil, you may safely
buy knowledge of Protagoras or of anyone; but if not, then, my friend,   314

pause, and do not hazard your dearest interests at a game of chance. For there is far greater peril in buying knowledge than in buying meat and drink: the one you purchase of the wholesale or retail dealer, and carry them away in other vessels, and before you receive them into the body as food, you may deposit them at home and call in any experienced friend who knows what is good to be eaten or drunk, and what not, and how much, and when; and then the danger of purchasing them is

b   not great. But you cannot buy the wares of knowledge and carry them away in another vessel; when you have paid for them you must receive them into the soul and go your way, either greatly harmed or greatly benefited; and therefore we should deliberate and take counsel with our elders; for we are still young—too young to determine such a matter. And now let us go, as we were intending, and hear Protagoras; and when we have heard what he has to say, we may take counsel of others; for not only

c   is Protagoras at the house of Callias, but there is Hippias of Elis, and, if I am not mistaken, Prodicus of Ceos, and several other wise men.

      To this we agreed, and proceeded on our way until we reached the vestibule of the house; and there we stopped in order to conclude a discussion which had arisen between us as we were going along; and

d   we stood talking in the vestibule until we had finished and come to an understanding. And I think that the door-keeper, who was a eunuch, and who was probably annoyed at the great number of the Sophists, must have heard us talking. At any rate, when we knocked at the door, and he opened and saw us, he grumbled: 'Sophists—he is busy'; and instantly gave the door a hearty bang with both his hands. Again we knocked, and he answered without opening: 'Did you not hear me say that he is busy, fellows?' 'But, my friend,' I said, 'you need not be alarmed; for we are not Sophists, and we are not here to see Callias, but

e   we want to see Protagoras; and I must request you to announce us.' At last, after a good deal of difficulty, the man was persuaded to open the door.

      When we entered, we found Protagoras taking a walk in the cloister; and next to him, on one side, were walking Callias, the son of Hipponicus, and Paralus, the son of Pericles, who, on the mother's side, is his half-brother, and Charmides, the son of Glaucon. On the other side

315   of him were Xanthippus, the other son of Pericles, Philippides, the son of Philomelus; also Antimoerus of Mende, who of all the disciples of Protagoras is the most famous, and intends to make sophistry his profession. A train of listeners followed him;[1] the greater part of them appeared to be foreigners, whom Protagoras had brought with him out of the various cities visited by him in his journeys, he, like Orpheus,* attracting

---

*Thracian of myth who sang so sweetly that he charmed trees and animals.

them by his voice, and they following. I should mention also that there   b
were some Athenians in the company. Nothing delighted me more than
the precision of their movements: they never got into his way at all; but
when he and those who were with him turned back, the band of listeners parted regularly on either side; he was always in front, and they
wheeled round and took their places behind him in perfect order.

After him, as Homer says, 'I lifted up my eyes and saw'* Hippias
the Elean sitting in the opposite cloister on a chair of state, and around   c
him were seated on benches Eryximachus,† the son of Acumenus, and
Phaedrus‡ the Myrrhinusian, and Andron§ the son of Androtion, and
there were strangers whom he had brought with him from his native
city of Elis, and some others: they were putting to Hippias certain
physical and astronomical questions, and he, from the chair, was determining their several questions to them, and discoursing of them.

Also, 'my eyes beheld Tantalus;'‖ for Prodicus the Cean was at Athens;   d
he had been lodged in a room which, in the days of Hipponicus, was
a storehouse; but, as the house was full, Callias had cleared this out and
made the room into a guest-chamber. Now Prodicus was still in bed,
wrapped up in sheepskins and bedclothes, of which there seemed to
be a great heap; and there was sitting by him on the couches near, Pau-
sanias# of the deme of Cerameis, and with Pausanias was a youth quite
young, who is certainly remarkable for his good looks, and, if I am not   e
mistaken, is also of a fair and gentle nature. I thought that I heard him
called Agathon,** and my suspicion is that he is the beloved of Pausanias. There was this youth, and also there were the two Adeimantuses,
one the son of Cepis, and the other of Leucolophides,†† and some others. I was very anxious to hear what Prodicus was saying, for he seems
to me to be an all-wise and inspired man; but I was not able to get into   316
the inner circle, and his fine deep voice made an echo in the room
which rendered his words inaudible.

No sooner had we entered than there followed us Alcibiades the
beautiful, as you say, and I believe you; and also Critias the son of
Callaeschrus.

Odyssey 11.601ff.
†See "Introduction" to *Symposium*.
‡See "Introduction" to *Phaedrus*.
§Politician favorable to oligarchy; friend of Callicles (see "Introduction" to *Gorgias*).
‖*Odyssey* 11.582.
#See "Introduction" to *Symposium*.
**See "Introduction" to *Symposium*.
††Neither Adeimantus is Plato's brother or nephew of the same name: The son of Cepis
followed Prodicus; the son of Leucolophides was a general.

On entering we stopped a little, in order to look about us, and then
b   walked up to Protagoras, and I said: Protagoras, my friend Hippocrates
and I have come to see you.

Do you wish, he said, to speak with me alone, or in the presence
of the company?

Whichever you please, I said; you shall determine when you have
heard the purpose of our visit.

And what is your purpose? he said.

I must explain, I said, that my friend Hippocrates is a native Athenian; he is the son of Apollodorus, and of a great and prosperous house,
and he is himself in natural ability quite a match for anybody of his
c   own age. I believe that he aspires to political eminence; and this he
thinks that conversation with you is most likely to procure for him. And
now you can determine whether you would wish to speak to him of
your teaching alone or in the presence of the company.

Thank you, Socrates, for your consideration of me. For certainly a
stranger finding his way into great cities, and persuading the flower of
the youth in them to leave the company of their kinsmen or any other
acquaintances, old or young, and live with him, under the idea that
d   they will be improved by his conversation, ought to be very cautious;
great jealousies are aroused by his proceedings, and he is the subject of
many enmities and conspiracies. Now the art of the Sophist is, as I believe, of great antiquity; but in ancient times those who practised it,
fearing this odium, veiled and disguised themselves under various
names, some under that of poets, as Homer, Hesiod, and Simonides,*
some, of his hierophants and prophets, as Orpheus and Musaeus,† and
some, as I observe, even under the name of gym-masters, like Iccus of
Tarentum, or the more recently celebrated Herodicus, now of Selym-
e   bria and formerly of Megara, who is a first-rate Sophist. Your own
Agathocles‡ pretended to be a musician, but was really an eminent
Sophist; also Pythocleides§ the Cean; and there were many others; and
all of them, as I was saying, adopted these arts as veils or disguises be-
317   cause they were afraid of the odium which they would incur. But that
is not my way, for I do not believe that they effected their purpose,
which was to deceive the government, who were not blinded by them;
and as to the people, they have no understanding, and only repeat what
their rulers are pleased to tell them. Now to run away, and to be caught
in running away, is the very height of folly, and also greatly increases

---

*Lyric poet (sixth and fifth centuries B.C.E.).

†Singer and priest often connected with Orpheus.

‡A Sophist, otherwise unknown to us.

§Musician associated with Sophocles and Pericles (see footnote on p. 41).

the exasperation of mankind; for they regard him who runs away as a   b
rogue, in addition to any other objections which they have to him; and
therefore I take an entirely opposite course, and acknowledge myself to
be a Sophist and instructor of mankind; such an open acknowledgment
appears to me to be a better sort of caution than concealment. Nor do
I neglect other precautions, and therefore I hope, as I may say, by the
favor of heaven that no harm will come of the acknowledgment that I am
a Sophist. And I have been now many years in the profession—for all my   c
years when added up are many: there is no one here present of whom I
might not be the father. Wherefore I should much prefer conversing with
you, if you want to speak with me, in the presence of the company.

As I suspected that he would like to have a little display and glorification in the presence of Prodicus and Hippias, and would gladly
show us to them in the light of his admirers, I said: But why should we   d
not summon Prodicus and Hippias and their friends to hear us?

Very good, he said.

Suppose, said Callias, that we hold a council in which you may sit
and discuss. This was agreed upon, and great delight was felt at the
prospect of hearing wise men talk; we ourselves took the chairs and
benches, and arranged them by Hippias, where the other benches had
been already placed. Meanwhile Callias and Alcibiades got Prodicus out   e
of bed and brought in him and his companions.

When we were all seated, Protagoras said: Now that the company
are assembled, Socrates, tell me about the young man of whom you were   318
just now speaking.

I replied: I will begin again at the same point, Protagoras, and tell
you once more the purport of my visit: this is my friend Hippocrates,
who is desirous of making your acquaintance; he would like to know
what will happen to him if he associates with you. I have no more to say.

Protagoras answered: Young man, if you associate with me, on the
very first day you will return home a better man than you came, and
better on the second day than on the first, and better every day than
you were on the day before.

When I heard this, I said: Protagoras, I do not at all wonder at hear-   b
ing you say this; even at your age, and with all your wisdom, if anyone
were to teach you what you did not know before, you would become
better, no doubt: but please to answer in a different way—I will explain
how by an example. Let me suppose that Hippocrates, instead of desiring your acquaintance, wished to become acquainted with the young
man Zeuxippus* of Heraclea, who has lately been in Athens, and he

_____

*A painting teacher.

had come to him as he has come to you, and had heard him say, as he
c   has heard you say, that every day he would grow and become better if he
associated with him: and then suppose that he were to ask him, 'In
what shall I become better, and in what shall I grow?'—Zeuxippus
would answer, 'In painting.' And suppose that he went to Orthagoras*
the Theban, and heard him say the same thing, and asked him, 'In what
shall I become better day by day?' He would reply, 'In flute-playing.' Now
d   I want you to make the same sort of answer to this young man and to
me, who am asking questions on his account. When you say that on the
first day on which he associates with you he will return home a better
man, and on every day will grow in like manner, in what, Protagoras,
will he be better? and about what?

When Protagoras heard me say this, he replied: You ask questions
fairly, and I like to answer a question which is fairly put. If Hippocrates
comes to me he will not experience the sort of drudgery with which
e   other Sophists are in the habit of insulting their pupils; who, when they
have just escaped from the arts, are taken and driven back into them by
these teachers, and made to learn calculation, and astronomy, and geometry, and music (he gave a look at Hippias as he said this); but if he
comes to me, he will learn that which he comes to learn. And this is
prudence in affairs private as well as public; he will learn to order his
own house in the best manner, and he will be able to speak and act for
the best in the affairs of the state.

319   Do I understand you, I said, and is your meaning that you teach
the art of politics, and that you promise to make men good citizens?

That, Socrates, is exactly the profession which I make.

Then, I said, you do indeed possess a noble art, if there is no mistake about this; for I will freely confess to you, Protagoras, that I have
a doubt whether this art is capable of being taught, and yet I do not
b   know how to disbelieve your assertion. I ought to tell you why I am of
the opinion that this art cannot be taught or communicated by man to
man. I say that the Athenians are an understanding people, and indeed
they are esteemed to be such by the other Greeks. Now I observe that
when we are met together in the assembly, and the matter in hand relates to building, the builders are summoned as advisers; when the
question is one of ship-building, then the ship-builders; and the like of
c   other arts which they think capable of being taught and learned. And if
some person offers to give them advice who is not supposed by them
to have any skill in the art, even though he were good-looking, and
rich, and noble, they will not listen to him, but laugh and hoot at him,

---

*He taught the art of playing the flute (*aulos*).

until either he is clamoured down or retires of himself; if he persist, he is dragged away or put out by the constables at the command of the prytanes. This is their way of behaving about professors of the arts. But when the question is an affair of state, then everybody is free to have a *d* say—carpenter, tinker, cobbler, sailor, passenger; rich and poor, high and low—anyone who likes gets up, and no one reproaches him, as in the former case, with not having learned, and having no teacher, and yet giving advice; evidently because they are under the impression that this sort of knowledge cannot be taught. And not only is this true of the *e* state, but of individuals; the best and wisest of our citizens are unable to impart their political wisdom to others: as for example, Pericles, the 320 father of these young men, who gave them excellent instruction in all that could be learned from masters, in his own department of politics neither taught them, nor gave them teachers; but they were allowed to wander at their own free will in a sort of hope that they would light upon virtue of their own accord. Or take another example: there was Clinias the younger brother of our friend Alcibiades, of whom this very same Pericles was the guardian; and he being in fact under the apprehension that Clinias would be corrupted by Alcibiades, took him away, and placed him in the house of Ariphron* to be educated; but before six months had elapsed, Ariphron sent him back, not knowing what to *b* do with him. And I could mention numberless other instances of persons who were good themselves, and never yet made anyone else good, whether friend or stranger. Now I, Protagoras, having these examples before me, am inclined to think that virtue cannot be taught. But then again, when I listen to your words, I waver; and am disposed to think that there must be something in what you say, because I know that you have great experience, learning, and ingenuity. I wish that you would, if possible, show me a little more clearly that virtue can be taught. *c* Will you be so good?

That I will, Socrates, and gladly. What would you like? Shall I, as an elder, speak to you as younger men in an apologue or myth, or shall I argue out the question?

To this several of the company answered that he should choose for himself.

Well, then, he said, I think that the myth will be more interesting.

Once upon a time there were gods only, and no mortal creatures. *d* But when the time came that these also should be created, the gods fashioned them out of earth and fire and various mixtures of both elements in the interior of the earth; and when they were about to bring

---

*Pericles' brother.

them into the light of day, they ordered Prometheus and Epimetheus[2] to equip them, and to distribute to them severally their proper qualities. Epimetheus said to Prometheus: 'Let me distribute, and do you inspect.' This was agreed, and Epimetheus made the distribution. There

e were some to whom he gave strength without swiftness, while he equipped the weaker with swiftness; some he armed, and others he left unarmed; and devised for the latter some other means of preservation, making some large, and having their size as a protection, and others

321 small, whose nature was to fly in the air or burrow in the ground; this was to be their way of escape. Thus he compensated them with a view to preventing any race from becoming extinct. And when he had provided against their destruction by one another, he contrived also a means of protecting them against the seasons of heaven; clothing them with close hair and thick skins sufficient to defend them against the winter cold and able to resist the summer heat, so that they might have a natural bed of their own when they wanted to rest; also he furnished

b them with hoofs and hair and hard and callous skins under their feet. Then he gave them varieties of food—herb of the soil to some, to others fruits of trees, and to others roots, and to some again he gave other animals as food. And some he made to have few young ones, while those who were their prey were very prolific; and in this manner the race was preserved. Thus did Epimetheus, who, not being very wise,

c forgot that he had distributed among the brute animals all the qualities which he had to give, and when he came to man, who was still unprovided, he was terribly perplexed. Now while he was in this perplexity, Prometheus came to inspect the distribution, and he found that the other animals were suitably furnished, but that man alone was naked and shoeless, and had neither bed nor arms of defence. The appointed hour was approaching when man in his turn was to go forth into the light of day; and Prometheus, not knowing how he could devise his salvation, stole the mechanical arts of Hephaestus and Athene,

d and fire with them (they could neither have been acquired nor used without fire), and gave them to man. Thus man had the wisdom necessary to the support of life, but political wisdom he had not; for that was in the keeping of Zeus, and the power of Prometheus did not extend to entering into the citadel of heaven, where Zeus dwelt, who moreover had terrible sentinels; but he did enter by stealth into the

e common workshop of Athene and Hephaestus, in which they used to practise their favourite arts, and carried off Hephaestus' art of working by fire, and also the art of Athene, and gave them to man. And in this way man was supplied with the means of life. Prometheus is said to have been afterwards prosecuted for theft, owing to the blunder of Epimetheus.

Now man, having a share of the divine attributes, was at first the 322
only one of the animals who had any gods, because he alone was of
their kindred; and he would raise altars and images of them. He was
not long in inventing articulate speech and names; and he also constructed houses and clothes and shoes and beds, and drew sustenance
from the earth. Thus provided, mankind at first lived dispersed, and
there were no cities. But the consequence was that they were destroyed b
by the wild beasts, for they were utterly weak in comparison to them,
and their art was only sufficient to provide them with the means of life,
but did not enable them to carry on war against the animals: food they
had, but not as yet the art of government, of which the art of war is a
part. After a while the desire of self-preservation gathered them into
cities; but when they were gathered together, having no art of government, they treated one another badly, and were again in a process of
dispersion and destruction. Zeus feared that the entire race would be c
exterminated, and so he sent Hermes to them, bearing reverence and
justice to be the ordering principles of cities and the bonds of friendship and conciliation. Hermes asked Zeus how he should impart justice
and reverence among men: Should he distribute them as the arts are
distributed; that is to say, to a favoured few only, one skilled individual
having enough of medicine or of any other art for many unskilled
ones? 'Shall this be the manner in which I am to distribute justice and
reverence among men, or shall I give them to all?' 'To all,' said Zeus; 'I d
should like them all to have a share; for cities cannot exist, if a few only
share in the virtues, as in the arts. And further, make a law by my order,
that he who has no part in reverence and justice shall be put to death,
for he is a plague of the state.'

And this is the reason, Socrates, why the Athenians and mankind in
general, when the question relates to carpentering or any other mechanical art, allow but a few to share in their deliberations; and when
anyone else interferes, then, as you say, they object, if he is not of the e
favoured few; which, as I reply, is very natural. But when they meet to
deliberate about political virtue, which proceeds only by way of justice 323
and wisdom, they are patient enough with any man who speaks of
them, as is also natural, because they think that every man ought to
share in this sort of virtue, and that states could not exist if this were
otherwise. I have explained to you, Socrates, the reason of this phenomenon.

And, in order that you may not suppose yourself to be deceived in
thinking that all men regard every man as having a share of justice or
honesty and of every other political virtue, let me give you a further
proof, which is this. In other cases, as you are aware, if a man says that
he is a good flute-player, or skilful in any other art in which he has no

b   skill, people either laugh at him or are angry with him, and his relations think that he is mad and go and admonish him; but when honesty is in question, or some other political virtue, even if they know
that he is dishonest, yet, if the man comes publicly forward and tells the
truth about his dishonesty, then, what in the other case was held by
them to be good sense, they now deem to be madness. They say that
all men ought to profess honesty whether they are honest or not, and
that a man is out of his mind who says anything else. Their notion is
c   that a man must have some degree of honesty; and that if he has none
at all he ought not to be in the world.

I have been showing that they are right in admitting every man as
a counsellor about this sort of virtue, as they are of the opinion that
every man is a partaker of it. And I will now endeavour to show further
that they do not conceive this virtue to be given by nature, or to grow
spontaneously, but to be a thing which may be taught; and which
comes to a man by taking pains. No one would instruct, no one would
d   rebuke, or be angry with those whose calamities they suppose to be
due to nature or chance; they do not try to punish or to prevent them
from being what they are; they do but pity them. Who is so foolish as
to chastise or instruct the ugly, or the diminutive, or the feeble? And for
this reason. Because he knows that good and evil of this kind is the
e   work of nature and of chance; whereas if a man is wanting in those
good qualities which are attained by study and exercise and teaching,
and has only the contrary evil qualities, other men are angry with him,
324 and punish and reprove him—of these evil qualities one is impiety, another injustice, and they may be described generally as the very opposite of political virtue. In such cases any man will be angry with
another, and reprimand him, clearly because he thinks that by study
and learning, the virtue in which the other is deficient may be acquired. If you will think, Socrates, of the nature of punishment, you
will see at once that in the opinion of mankind virtue may be acquired;
no one punishes the evil-doer under the notion, or for the reason, that
b   he has done wrong,—only the unreasonable fury of a beast acts in that
manner. But he who desires to inflict rational punishment does not retaliate for a past wrong which cannot be undone; he has regard to the
future, and is desirous that the man who is punished, and he who sees
him punished, may be deterred from doing wrong again. He punishes
for the sake of prevention, thereby clearly implying that virtue is capable of being taught. This is the notion of all who retaliate upon others
c   either privately or publicly. And the Athenians, too, your own citizens,
like other men, punish and take vengeance on all whom they regard as
evil-doers; and hence, we may infer them to be among those who think
that virtue may be acquired and taught. Thus far, Socrates, I have shown

you clearly enough, if I am not mistaken, that your countrymen are right in admitting the tinker and the cobbler to advise about politics, and also that they deem virtue to be capable of being taught and acquired.   d

There yet remains one difficulty which has been raised by you about the sons of good men. What is the reason why good men teach their sons the knowledge which is gained from teachers, and make them wise in that, but do nothing towards improving them in the virtues which distinguish themselves? And here, Socrates, I will leave the apologue and resume the argument. Please consider: Is there or is there not a quality of which all the citizens must be partakers, if there is to be a city at all? In the answer to this question is contained the only solution   e of your difficulty; there is no other. For if there be any such quality, and this quality or unity is not the art of the carpenter, or the smith, or the potter, but justice and temperance and holiness and, in a word, manly   325 virtue—if this is the quality of which all men must be partakers, and which is the very condition of their learning or doing anything else, and if he who is wanting in this, whether he be a child only or a grown-up man or woman, must be taught and punished, until by punishment he becomes better, and he who rebels against instruction and punishment is either exiled or condemned to death under the idea that   b he is incurable—if what I am saying is true, that good men have their sons taught other things and not this, do consider how extraordinary their conduct would appear to be. For we have shown that they think virtue capable of being taught and cultivated both in private and public; and, notwithstanding, they have their sons taught lesser matters, ignorance of which does not involve the punishment of death: but   c greater things, of which the ignorance may cause death and exile to those who have no training or knowledge of them—aye, and confiscation as well as death, and, in a word, may be the ruin of families—those things, I say, they are supposed not to teach them, not to take the utmost care that they should learn. How improbable is this, Socrates!

Education and admonition commence in the first years of childhood, and last to the very end of life. Mother and nurse and father and   d tutor are vying with one another about the improvement of the child as soon as ever he is able to understand what is being said to him: he cannot say or do anything without their setting forth to him that this is just and that is unjust; this is honourable, that is dishonourable; this is holy, that is unholy; do this and abstain from that. And if he obeys, well and good; if not, he is straightened by threats and blows, like a piece of bent or warped wood. At a later stage they send him to teachers, and enjoin them to see to his manners even more than to his reading and music; and the teachers do as they are desired. And when the boy   e has learned his letters and is beginning to understand what is written, as

326 before he understood only what was spoken, they put into his hands the works of great poets, which he reads sitting on a bench at school; in these are contained many admonitions, and many tales, and praises, and encomia of ancient famous men, which he is required to learn by heart, in order that he may imitate or emulate them and desire to become like them. Then, again, the teachers of the lyre take similar care that their young disciple is temperate and gets into no mischief; and when they have taught him the use of the lyre, they introduce him to

b the poems of other excellent poets, who are the lyric poets; and these they set to music, and make their harmonies and rhythms quite familiar to the children's souls, in order that they may learn to be more gentle, and harmonious, and rhythmical, and so more fitted for speech and action; for the life of man in every part has need of harmony and rhythm. Then they send them to the master of gymnastic, in order that their bodies may better minister to the virtuous mind, and that they

c may not be compelled through bodily weakness to play the coward in war or on any other occasion. This is what is done by those who have the means, and those who have the means are the rich; their children begin to go to school soonest and leave off latest. When they are finished with masters, the state again compels them to learn the laws, and

d live after the pattern which they furnish, and not after their own fancies; and just as in learning to write, the writing-master first draws lines with a style for the use of the young beginner, and gives him the tablet and makes him follow the lines, so the city draws the laws, which were the invention of good lawgivers living in the olden time; these are given to the young man, in order to guide him in his conduct whether he is commanding or obeying; and he who transgresses them is to be

e corrected, or, in other words, called to account, which is a term used not only in your country, but also in many others, seeing that justice calls men to account. Now when there is all this care about virtue private and public, why, Socrates, do you still wonder and doubt whether virtue can be taught? Cease to wonder, for the opposite would be far more surprising.

But why then do the sons of good fathers often turn out badly? There is nothing very surprising in this; for, as I have been saying, the existence of a state implies that virtue is not any man's private posses-

327 sion. If so—and nothing can be truer—then I will further ask you to imagine, as an illustration, some other pursuit or branch of knowledge which may be assumed equally to be the condition of the existence of a state. Suppose that there could be no state unless we were all flute-players, as far as each had the capacity, and everybody was freely teaching everybody the art, both in private and public, and reproving the bad player as freely and openly as every man now teaches justice and

the laws, not concealing them as he would conceal the other arts, but   b
imparting them—for all of us have a mutual interest in the justice and
virtue of one another, and this is the reason why every one is so ready
to teach justice and the laws; suppose, I say, that there were the same
readiness and liberality among us in teaching one another flute-playing,
do you imagine, Socrates, that the sons of good flute-players would be
more likely to be good than the sons of bad ones? I think not. Would
not their sons grow up to be distinguished or undistinguished according to their own natural capacities as flute-players, and the son of a
good player would often turn out to be a bad one, and the son of a bad   c
player to be a good one, and all flute-players would be good enough in
comparison of those who were ignorant and unacquainted with the art
of flute-playing? In like manner I would have you consider that he who
appears to you to be the worst of those who have been brought up in
laws and humanities, would appear to be a just man and a master of
justice if he were to be compared with men who had no education, or
courts of justice, or laws, or any restraints upon them which compelled   d
them to practise virtue—with the savages, for example, whom the poet
Pherecrates* exhibited on the stage at the last year's Lenaean festival. If
you were living among men such as the man-haters in his Chorus, you
would be only too glad to meet with Eurybates and Phrynondas,† and
you would sorrowfully long to revisit the rascality of this part of the
world. And you, Socrates, are discontented, and why? Because all men   e
are teachers of virtue, each one according to his ability; and you say,
Where are the teachers? You might as well ask, Who teaches Greek? For   328
of that too there will not be any teachers found. Or you might ask, Who
is to teach the sons of our artisans this same art which they have
learned of their fathers? He and his fellow-workmen have taught them
to the best of their ability, but who will carry them further in their arts?
And you would certainly have a difficulty, Socrates, in finding a teacher
of them; but there would be no difficulty in finding a teacher of those
who are wholly ignorant. And this is true of virtue or of anything else;
if a man is better able than we are to promote virtue ever so little, we
must be content with the result. A teacher of this sort I believe myself   b
to be, and above all other men to have the knowledge which makes a
man noble and good; and I give my pupils their money's worth, and
even more, as they themselves confess. And therefore I have introduced
the following mode of payment: When a man has been my pupil, if
he likes he pays my price, but there is no compulsion; and if he does
not like, he has only to go into a temple and take an oath of the value

---

*Athenian comic poet (fifth century B.C.E.).
†The mention of Eurybates and Phrynondas is like saying "viciousness itself."

c   of the instructions, and he pays no more than he declares to be their value.

Such is my story, Socrates, and such is the argument by which I endeavour to show that virtue may be taught, and that this is the opinion of the Athenians. And I have also attempted to show that you are not to wonder at good fathers having bad sons, or at good sons having bad fathers, of which the sons of Polycleitus afford an example, who are the companions of our friends here, Paralus and Xanthippus, but are nothing in comparison with their father; and this is true of the sons of many other artists. As yet I ought not to say the same of Paralus and

d   Xanthippus themselves, for they are young and there is still hope of them.

Protagoras ended, and in my ear

> 'So charming left his voice, that I the while
> Thought him still speaking; still stood fixed to hear.'*

At length, when the truth dawned upon me, that he had really finished, not without difficulty I began to collect myself, and looking at Hippocrates, I said to him: Son of Apollodorus, how deeply grateful I am to you for having brought me hither; I would not have missed the

e   speech of Protagoras for a great deal. For I used to imagine that no human care could make men good; but I know better now. Yet I have still one very small difficulty which I am sure that Protagoras will easily explain, as he has already explained so much. If a man were to go

329 and consult Pericles or any of our great speakers about these matters, he might perhaps hear as fine a discourse; but then when one has a question to ask of any of them, like books, they can neither answer nor ask; and if anyone challenges the least particular of their speech, they go ringing on in a long harangue, like brazen pots, which when they are struck continue to sound unless some one puts his hand upon

b   them; whereas our friend Protagoras can not only make a good speech, as he has already shown, but when he is asked a question he can answer briefly; and when he asks he will wait and hear the answer; this is a very rare gift. Now I, Protagoras, want to ask of you a little question, which if you will only answer, I shall be quite satisfied. You were saying that virtue can be taught; that I will take upon your authority, and there is no one to whom I am more ready to trust. But I marvel at

c   one thing about which I should like to have my mind set at rest. You

---

*The English poet John Milton (1608–1674) borrowed these lines for the beginning of book 8 of *Paradise Lost*.

were speaking of Zeus sending justice and reverence to men; and several times while you were speaking, justice, and temperance, and holiness, and all these qualities, were described by you as if together they made up virtue. Now I want you to tell me truly whether virtue is one whole, of which justice and temperance and holiness are parts; or whether all these are only the names of one and the same thing: that is the doubt which still lingers in my mind.

There is no difficulty, Socrates, in answering that the qualities of which you are speaking are the parts of virtue which is one.

And are they parts, I said, in the same sense in which mouth, nose, and eyes, and ears, are the parts of a face; or are they like the parts of gold, which differ from the whole and from one another only in being larger or smaller?

I should say that they differed, Socrates, in the first way; they are related to one another as the parts of a face are related to the whole face.

And do men have some one part and some another part of virtue? Or if a man has one part, must he also have all the others?

By no means, he said; for many a man is brave and not just, or just and not wise.

You would not deny, then, that courage and wisdom are also parts of virtue?

Most undoubtedly they are, he answered; and wisdom is the noblest of the parts.

And they are all different from one another? I said.

Yes.

And has each of them a distinct function like the parts of the face; the eye, for example, is not like the ear, and has not the same functions; and the other parts are none of them like one another, either in their functions, or in any other way? I want to know whether the comparison holds concerning the parts of virtue. Do they also differ from one another in themselves and in their functions? For that is clearly what the simile would imply.

Yes, Socrates, you are right in supposing that they differ.

Then, I said, no other part of virtue is like knowledge, or like justice, or like courage, or like temperance, or like holiness?

No, he answered.

Well then, I said, suppose that you and I enquire into their natures. And first, you would agree with me that justice is of the nature of a thing, would you not? That is my opinion: would it not be yours also?

Mine also, he said.

And suppose that someone were to ask us, 'Protagoras, and you, Socrates, what about this thing which you were calling justice, is it

just or unjust?' and I were to answer, 'Just': would you vote with me
or against me?

With you, he said.

Thereupon I should answer to him who asked me, that justice is of
the nature of the just: would not you?

d   Yes, he said.

And suppose that he went on to say: 'Well now, is there also such
a thing as holiness?'; we should answer, 'Yes,' if I am not mistaken?

Yes, he said.

Which you would also acknowledge to be a thing—should we not
say so?

He assented.

'And is this a sort of thing which is of the nature of the holy, or of
the nature of the unholy?' I should be angry at his putting such a question, and should say, 'Peace, man; nothing can be holy if holiness is not
e   holy.' What would you say? Would you not answer in the same way?

Certainly, he said.

And then after this suppose that he came and asked us, 'What were
you saying just now? Perhaps I may not have heard you rightly, but you
seemed to me to be saying that the parts of virtue were not the same
331 as one another.' I should reply, 'You certainly heard that said, but not,
as you imagine, by me; for I only asked the question; Protagoras gave
the answer.' And suppose that he turned to you and said, 'Is this true,
Protagoras? do you maintain that one part of virtue is unlike another,
and is this your position?'—how would you answer him?

I could not help acknowledging the truth of what he said, Socrates.

Well then, Protagoras, we will assume this; and now supposing
that he proceeded to say further, 'Then holiness is not of the nature of
justice, nor justice of the nature of holiness, but of the nature of un-
holiness; and holiness is of the nature of the not just, and therefore of
the unjust, and the unjust is the unholy:' how shall we answer him? I
b   should certainly answer him on my own behalf that justice is holy, and
that holiness is just; and I would say in like manner on your behalf also,
if you would allow me, that justice is either the same with holiness, or
very nearly the same; and above all I would assert that justice is like holiness and holiness is like justice; and I wish that you would tell me
whether I may be permitted to give this answer on your behalf, and
whether you would agree with me.

He replied, I cannot simply agree, Socrates, to the proposition that
c   justice is holy and that holiness is just, for there appears to me to be a
difference between them. But what matter? if you please I please; and
let us assume, if you will, that justice is holy, and that holiness is just.

Pardon me, I replied; I do not want this 'if you wish' or 'if you will' sort of conclusion to be proven, but I want you and me to be proven: I mean to say that the conclusion will be best proven if there is no 'if.'   *d*

Well, he said, I admit that justice bears a resemblance to holiness, for there is always some point of view in which everything is like every other thing; white is in a certain way like black, and hard is like soft, and the most extreme opposites have some qualities in common; even the parts of the face which, as we were saying before, are distinct and have different functions, are still in a certain point of view similar, and one of them is like another. And you may prove that they are like one another on the same principle that all things are like one another; and   *e* yet things which are like in some particular ought not to be called alike, nor things which are unlike in some particular, however slight, unlike.

And do you think, I said in a tone of surprise, that justice and holiness have but a small degree of likeness?

Certainly not; but my view still differs from yours.

Well, I said, as you appear to have a difficulty about this, let us take   332 another of the examples which you mentioned instead. Do you admit the existence of folly?

I do.

And is not wisdom the very opposite of folly?

That is true, he said.

And when men act rightly and advantageously they seem to you to be temperate?

Yes, he said.

And temperance makes them temperate?   *b*

Certainly.

And they who do not act rightly act foolishly, and in acting thus are not temperate?

I agree, he said.

Then to act foolishly is the opposite of acting temperately?

He assented.

And foolish actions are done by folly, and temperate actions by temperance?

He agreed.

And that is done strongly which is done by strength, and that which is weakly done, by weakness?

He assented.

And that which is done with swiftness is done swiftly, and that which is done with slowness, slowly?

He assented again.   *c*

And that which is done in the same manner, is done by the same; and that which is done in an opposite manner by the opposite?

He agreed.

Once more, I said, is there anything beautiful?

Yes.

To which the only opposite is the ugly?

There is no other.

And is there anything good?

There is.

To which the only opposite is the evil?

There is no other.

And there is the acute in sound?

True.

To which the only opposite is the grave?

There is no other, he said, but that.

Then every opposite has one opposite only and no more?

He assented.

d   Then now, I said, let us recapitulate our admissions. First of all we admitted that everything has one opposite and not more than one?

We did so.

And we admitted also that what was done in opposite ways was done by opposites?

Yes.

And that which was done foolishly, as we further admitted, was done in the opposite way to that which was done temperately?

Yes.

And that which was done temperately was done by temperance, and that which was done foolishly by folly?

He agreed.

e   And that which is done in opposite ways is done by opposites?

Yes.

And one thing is done by temperance, and quite another thing by folly?

Yes.

And in opposite ways?

Certainly.

And therefore by opposites: then folly is the opposite of temperance?

Clearly.

And do you remember that folly has already been acknowledged by us to be the opposite of wisdom?

He assented.

And we said that everything has only one opposite?

Yes.

333   Then, Protagoras, which of the two assertions shall we renounce?

One says that everything has but one opposite; the other that wisdom is distinct from temperance, and that both of them are parts of virtue; and that they are not only distinct, but dissimilar, both in themselves and in their functions, like the parts of a face. Which of these two assertions shall we renounce? For both of them together are certainly not in harmony; they do not accord or agree: for how can they be said to agree if everything is assumed to have only one opposite and not more than one, and yet folly, which is one, has clearly the two opposites—wisdom and temperance? Is not that true, Protagoras? What else would you say?

He assented, but with great reluctance.

Then temperance and wisdom are the same, as before justice and holiness appeared to us to be nearly the same. And now, Protagoras, I said, we must finish the enquiry, and not give up. Do you think that an unjust man can be temperate in his injustice?

I should be ashamed, Socrates, he said, to acknowledge this which nevertheless many may be found to assert.

And shall I argue with them or with you? I replied.

I would rather, he said, that you should argue with the many first, if you will.

Whichever you please, if you will only answer me and say whether you are of their opinion or not. My object is to test the validity of the argument; and yet the result may be that I who ask and you who answer may both be put on trial.

Protagoras at first made a show of refusing, as he said that the argument was unpleasant; at length, he consented to answer.

Now then, I said, begin at the beginning and answer me. You think that some men are temperate, and yet unjust?

Yes, he said; let that be admitted.

And temperance is good sense?

Yes.

And good sense is good counsel in doing injustice?
Granted.

If they succeed, I said, or if they do not succeed?
If they succeed.

And you would admit the existence of goods?
Yes.

And is the good that which is expedient for man?

Yes, indeed, he said: and there are some things which may be inexpedient, and yet I call them good.

I thought that Protagoras was getting ruffled and excited; he seemed to be setting himself in an attitude of war. Seeing this, I minded my business, and gently said:

334   When you say, Protagoras, that things inexpedient are good, do
you mean inexpedient for man only, or inexpedient altogether? and do
you call the latter good?

Certainly not the last, he replied; for I know of many things—
meats, drinks, medicines, and ten thousand other things, which are inexpedient for man, and some which are expedient; and some which
are neither expedient nor inexpedient for man, but only for horses; and
some for oxen only, and some for dogs; and some for no animals, but
only for trees; and some for the roots of trees and not for their branches,
as for example, manure, which is a good thing when laid about the
b   roots of a tree, but utterly destructive if thrown upon the shoots and
young branches; or I may instance olive oil, which is mischievous to
all plants, and generally most injurious to the hair of every animal with
the exception of man, but beneficial to human hair and to the human
body generally; and even in this application (so various and changeable
is the nature of the benefit), that which is the greatest good to the out-
c   ward parts of a man, is a very great evil to his inward parts: and for this
reason physicians always forbid their patients the use of oil in their
food, except in very small quantities, just enough to extinguish the disagreeable sensation of smell in meats and sauces.

When he had given this answer, the company cheered him. And I
said: Protagoras, I have a wretched memory, and when anyone makes
a long speech to me I never remember what he is talking about. As
d   then, if I had been deaf, and you were going to converse with me, you
would have had to raise your voice; so now, having such a bad memory, I will ask you to cut your answers shorter, if you would take me
with you.

What do you mean? he said: how am I to shorten my answers?
shall I make them too short?

Certainly not, I said.

But short enough?

e   Yes, I said.

Shall I answer what appears to me to be short enough, or what appears to you to be short enough?

I have heard, I said, that you can speak and teach others to speak
about the same things at such length that words never seemed to fail,
or with such brevity that no one could use fewer of them. Please therefore, if you talk with me, to adopt the latter or more compendious
335 method.

Socrates, he replied, many a battle of words have I fought, and if I
had followed the method of disputation which my adversaries desired,
as you want me to do, I should have been no better than another, and
the name of Protagoras would have been nowhere.

I saw that he was not satisfied with his previous answers, and that he would not play the part of answerer any more if he could help it; and I considered that there was no call upon me to continue the conversation; so I said: Protagoras, I do not wish to force the conversation upon you if you had rather not, but when you are willing to argue with me in such a way that I can follow you, then I will argue with you. Now you, as is said of you by others and as you say of yourself, are able to have discussions in shorter forms of speech as well as in longer, for you are a master of wisdom; but I cannot manage these long speeches: I only wish that I could. You, on the other hand, who are capable of either, ought to speak shorter as I beg you, and then we might converse. But I see that you are disinclined, and as I have an engagement which will prevent my staying to hear you at greater length (for I have to be in another place), I will depart; although I should have liked to have heard you.

Thus I spoke, and was rising from my seat, when Callias seized me by the right hand, and in his left hand caught hold of this old cloak of mine. He said: We cannot let you go, Socrates, for if you leave us there will be an end of our discussions: I must therefore beg you to remain, as there is nothing in the world that I should like better than to hear you and Protagoras discourse. Do not deny the company this pleasure.

Now I had got up, and was in the act of departure. Son of Hipponicus, I replied, I have always admired, and do now heartily applaud and love your philosophical spirit, and I would gladly comply with your request, if I could. But the truth is that I cannot. And what you ask is as great an impossibility to me as if you bade me run a race with Crison* of Himera, when in his prime, or with someone of the long or day-course runners. To such a request I should reply that I would like to ask the same of my own legs; but they refuse to comply. And therefore if you want to see Crison and me in the same stadium, you must bid him slacken his speed to mine, for I cannot run quickly, and he can run slowly. And in like manner if you want to hear me and Protagoras discoursing, you must ask him to shorten his answers, and keep to the point, as he did at first; if not, how can there be any discussion? For discussion is one thing, and making an oration is quite another, in my humble opinion.

But you see, Socrates, said Callias, that Protagoras may fairly claim to speak in his own way, just as you claim to speak in yours.

Here Alcibiades interposed, and said: That, Callias, is not a true statement of the case. For our friend Socrates admits that he cannot

---

*Sicilian athlete famous for his running speed.

make a speech—in this he yields the palm to Protagoras: but I should
c be greatly surprised if he yielded to any living man in the power of
holding and apprehending an argument. Now if Protagoras will make
a similar admission, and confess that he is inferior to Socrates in argu-
mentative skill, that is enough for Socrates; but if he claims a superiority in argument as well, let him ask and answer—not, when a question
d is asked, slipping away from the point, and instead of answering, making a speech at such length that most of his hearers forget the question
at issue (not that Socrates is likely to forget—I will be bound for that,
although he may pretend in fun that he has a bad memory). And
Socrates appears to me to be more in the right than Protagoras; that is
my view, and every man ought to say what he thinks.

When Alcibiades finished speaking, someone—Critias, I believe—
went on to say: Prodicus and Hippias, Callias appears to me to be a par-
e tisan of Protagoras: and this led Alcibiades, who loves opposition, to
take the other side. But we should not be partisans either of Socrates or
of Protagoras; let us rather unite in entreating both of them not to
break up the discussion.

337 Prodicus added: That, Critias, seems to me to be well said, for
those who are present at such discussions ought to be impartial hearers of both the speakers; remembering, however, that impartiality is not
the same as equality, for both sides should be impartially heard, and yet
an equal merit should not be assigned to both of them; but to the wiser
a higher merit should be given, and a lower one to the less wise. And
I as well as Critias would beg you, Protagoras and Socrates, to grant our
b request, which is, that you will argue with one another and not wrangle; for friends argue with friends out of goodwill, but only adversaries
and enemies wrangle. And then our meeting will be delightful; for in
this way you, who are the speakers, will be most likely to win esteem,
and not praise only, among us who are your audience; for esteem is a
sincere conviction of the hearers' souls, but praise is often an insincere
expression of men uttering falsehoods contrary to their conviction.
c And thus we the hearers will be gratified and not pleased; for gratification is of the mind when receiving wisdom and knowledge, but pleasure is of the body when eating or experiencing some other bodily
delight. Thus spoke Prodicus, and many of the company applauded his
words.

Hippias the sage spoke next. He said: All of you who are present I
reckon to be kinsmen and friends and fellow-citizens, by nature and
d not by law; for by nature like is akin to like, whereas law is the tyrant
of mankind, and often compels us to do many things which are against
nature. How great would be the disgrace then, if we, who know the nature of things, and are the wisest of the Greeks, and as such have met

together in this city, which is the metropolis of wisdom, and in the greatest and most glorious house of this city, should have nothing to show worthy of this height of dignity, but should only quarrel with   e
one another like the meanest of mankind! I do pray and advise you, Protagoras, and you, Socrates, to agree upon a compromise. Let us be your peacemakers. And do not, Socrates, aim at this precise and extreme brevity in discourse, if Protagoras objects, but loosen and let go the reins of speech, so that your words may be grander and more be-   338
coming. Neither do you, Protagoras, go forth on the gale with every sail set out of sight of land into an ocean of words, but let there be a mean observed by both of you. Do as I say. And let me also persuade you to choose an arbiter or overseer or president; he will keep watch over your words and will prescribe their proper length.   b

This proposal was received by the company with universal approval; Callias said that he would not let me off, and they begged me to choose an arbiter. But I said that to choose an umpire of discourse would be unseemly; for if the person chosen was inferior, then the inferior or worse ought not to preside over the better; or if he was equal, neither would that be well; for he who is our equal will do as we do,   c
and what will be the use of choosing him? And if you say, 'Let us have a better then,'—to that I answer that you cannot have any one who is wiser than Protagoras. And if you choose another who is not really better, and whom you only say is better, to put another over him as though he were an inferior person would be an unworthy reflection on him; not that, as far as I am concerned, any reflection is of much consequence to me. Let me tell you then what I will do in order that the conversation and discussion may go on as you desire. If Protagoras is not   d
disposed to answer, let him ask and I will answer; and I will endeavour to show at the same time how, as I maintain, he ought to answer: and when I have answered as many questions as he likes to ask, let him in like manner answer me; and if he seems to be not very ready at answering the precise question asked of him, you and I will unite in entreating him, as you entreated me, not to spoil the discussion. And this will require no special arbiter—all of you shall be arbiters.   e

This was generally approved, and Protagoras, though very much against his will, was obliged to agree that he would ask questions; and when he had put a sufficient number of them, that he would answer in his turn those which he was asked in short replies. He began to put his questions as follows:—

I am of the opinion, Socrates, he said, that skill in poetry is the principal part of education; and this I conceive to be the power of   339
knowing what compositions of the poets are correct, and what are not, and how they are to be distinguished, and of explaining when asked

the reason of the difference. And I propose to transfer the question which you and I have been discussing to the domain of poetry; we will speak as before of virtue, but in reference to a passage of a poet. Now Simonides says to Scopas the son of Creon* the Thessalian:—

b   'Hardly on the one hand can a man become truly good, built four-
        square in hands and feet and mind, a work without a flaw.'†

Do you know the poem? or shall I repeat the whole?

There is no need, I said; for I am perfectly well acquainted with the ode; I have made a careful study of it.

Very well, he said. And do you think that the ode is a good com-position, and true?

Yes, I said, both good and true.

But if there is a contradiction, can the composition be good or true?

No, not in that case, I replied.

And is there not a contradiction? he asked. Reflect.

c   Well, my friend, I have reflected enough.

And does not the poet proceed to say, 'I do not agree with the word of Pittacus,‡ albeit the utterance of a wise man: Hardly can a man be good?' Now you will observe that this is said by the same poet.

I know.

And do you think, he said, that the two sayings are consistent?

Yes, I said, I think so (at the same time I could not help fearing that there might be something in what he said). Do you think otherwise?

d   Why, he said, how can he be consistent in both? First of all, premis-ing as his own thought, 'Hardly can a man become truly good;' and then a little further on in the poem, forgetting, and blaming Pittacus and refusing to agree with him, when he says, 'Hardly can a man be good,' which is the very same thing. And yet when he blames him who says the same with himself, he blames himself; so that he must be wrong either in his first or his second assertion.

e   Many of the audience cheered and applauded this. And I felt at first giddy and faint, as if I had received a blow from the hand of an expert boxer, when I heard his words and the sound of the cheering; and to

---

*This ruler of Thessaly (region of ancient Greece) often hosted the lyric poet Simonides and had him write poems in his honor.

†The poem has not survived other than in Plato.

‡Ruler (seventh century B.C.E.) of the Greek island of Lesbos, counted as one of the Seven Sages (see 343a).

confess the truth, I wanted to get time to think what the meaning of the poet really was. So I turned to Prodicus and called him. Prodicus, I said, Simonides is a countryman of yours, and you ought to come to his aid. I must appeal to you, like the river Scamander in Homer, who, 340 when beleaguered by Achilles, summons the Simoïs to aid him, saying:

'Brother dear, let us both together stay the force of the hero.'*

And I summon you, for I am afraid that Protagoras will make an end of Simonides. Now is the time to rehabilitate Simonides, by the application of your philosophy of synonyms, which enables you to distinguish 'will' and 'wish,' and make other charming distinctions like those which you drew just now. I would like to know whether you b would agree with me; for I am of the opinion that there is no contradiction in the words of Simonides. First of all I wish that you would say whether, in your opinion, Prodicus, 'being' is the same as 'becoming.'[3]

Not the same, certainly, replied Prodicus.

Did not Simonides first set forth, as his own view, that 'Hardly can a man become truly good'?

Quite right, said Prodicus. c

And then he blames Pittacus, not, as Protagoras imagines, for repeating that which he says himself, but for saying something different from himself. Pittacus does not say as Simonides says, that hardly can a man become good, but hardly can a man be good: and our friend Prodicus would maintain that being, Protagoras, is not the same as becoming; and if they are not the same, then Simonides is not inconsistent with himself. I dare say that Prodicus and many others would say, d as Hesiod says,

'On the one hand, hardly can a man become good,
For the gods have made virtue the reward of toil;
But on the other hand, when you have climbed the height,
Then, to retain virtue, however difficult the acquisition, is easy.'[†]

Prodicus heard and approved; but Protagoras said: Your correction, Socrates, involves a greater error than is contained in the sentence which you are correcting.

Alas! I said, Protagoras; then I am a sorry physician, and do but aggravate a disorder which I am seeking to cure. e

---

*Iliad 21.308.
†Works and Days 264ff.

Such is the fact, he said.

How so? I asked.

The poet, he replied, could never have made such a mistake as to say that virtue, which in the opinion of all men is the hardest of all things, can be easily retained.

Well, I said, and how fortunate are we in having Prodicus among us, at the right moment; for he has a wisdom, Protagoras, which, as I 341 imagine, is more than human and of very ancient date, and may be as old as Simonides or even older. Learned as you are in many things, you appear to know nothing of this; but I know, for I am a disciple of his. And now, if I am not mistaken, you do not understand the word 'hard' in the sense which Simonides intended; and I must correct you, as Prodicus corrects me when I use the word 'awful' as a term of praise. b If I say that Protagoras or anyone else is an 'awfully' wise man, he asks me if I am not ashamed of calling that which is good 'awful'; and then he explains to me that the term 'awful' is always taken in a bad sense, and that no one speaks of being 'awfully' healthy or wealthy, or 'awful' peace, but of 'awful' disease, 'awful' war, 'awful' poverty, meaning by the term 'awful,' evil. And I think that Simonides and his countrymen the Ceans, when they spoke of 'hard' meant 'evil,' or something which you do not understand. Let us ask Prodicus, for he ought to be able to answer questions about the dialect of Simonides. What did he mean, c Prodicus, by the term 'hard'?

Evil, said Prodicus.

And therefore, I said, Prodicus, he blames Pittacus for saying, 'Hard is the good,' just as if that were equivalent to saying, Evil is the good.

Yes, he said, that was certainly his meaning; and he is twitting Pittacus with ignorance of the use of terms, which is natural in a Lesbian who has been accustomed to speak a barbarous language.

Do you hear, Protagoras, I asked, what our friend Prodicus is say- d ing? And have you an answer for him?

You are entirely mistaken, Prodicus, said Protagoras; and I know very well that Simonides in using the word 'hard' meant what all of us mean, not evil, but that which is not easy—that which takes a great deal of trouble: of this I am positive.

I said: I also incline to believe, Protagoras, that this was the meaning of Simonides, of which our friend Prodicus was very well aware, but he thought that he would make fun, and see if you could maintain your thesis; for that Simonides could never have meant the other is e clearly proved by the context, in which he says that god only has this gift. Now he cannot surely mean to say that to be good is evil, when he afterwards proceeds to say that god only has this gift, and that this is the attribute of him and of no other. For if this is his meaning, Prod-

icus would impute to Simonides a character of recklessness which is
very unlike his countrymen. And I should like to tell you, I said, what 342
I imagine to be the real meaning of Simonides in this poem, if you will
test what, in your way of speaking, would be called my skill in poetry;
or if you would rather, I will be the listener.

To this proposal Protagoras replied: As you please; and Hippias,
Prodicus, and the others told me by all means to do as I proposed.

Then, I said, I will endeavour to explain to you my opinion about
this poem of Simonides. There is a very ancient philosophy which is
more cultivated in Crete and Sparta than in any other part of the Greek b
world, and there are more philosophers in those countries than anywhere else in the world. This, however, is a secret which the Spartans
deny; and they pretend to be ignorant, just because they do not wish
to have it thought that they rule the world by wisdom, like the Sophists
of whom Protagoras was speaking, and not by valor of arms; considering that if the reason of their superiority were disclosed, all men would
be practising their wisdom. And this secret of theirs has never been discovered by the imitators of Spartan fashions in other cities, who go
about with their ears bruised in imitation of them, and have the caes- c
tus* bound on their arms, and are always in training, and wear short
cloaks; for they imagine that these are the practices which have enabled
the Spartans to conquer the other Greeks. Now when the Spartans want
to unbend and hold free conversation with their wise men, and are no
longer satisfied with mere secret intercourse, they drive out all these la-
conizers, and any other foreigners who may happen to be in their
country, and they hold a philosophical debate unknown to strangers;
and they themselves forbid their young men to go out into other
cities—in this they are like the Cretans—in order that they may not un- d
learn the lessons which they have taught them. And in Sparta and Crete
not only men but also women have a pride in their high cultivation.
And hereby you may know that I am right in attributing to the Spartans this excellence in philosophy and speculation: If a man converses
with the most ordinary Spartan, he will find him seldom good for
much in general conversation, but at any point in the discourse he will e
be darting out some notable saying, terse and full of meaning, with un-
erring aim; and the person with whom he is talking seems to be like a
child in his hands. And many of our own age and of former ages have
noted that the true Spartan type of character has the love of philosophy
even stronger than the love of gymnastics; they are conscious that only
a perfectly educated man is capable of uttering such expressions. Such 343

*A covering for the hands of boxers.

were Thales of Miletus, and Pittacus of Mitylene, and Bias of Priene, and our own Solon, and Cleobulus the Lindian, and Myson the Chenian; and seventh in the catalogue of wise men was the Spartan Chilo.* All these were lovers and emulators and disciples of the culture of the Spartans, and anyone may perceive that their wisdom was of this character: consisting of short memorable sentences, which they severally uttered.

b And they met together and dedicated in the temple of Apollo at Delphi, as the first-fruits of their wisdom, the far-famed inscriptions, which are in all men's mouths,—'Know thyself,' and 'Nothing too much.'

Why do I say all this? I am explaining that this Spartan brevity was the style of primitive philosophy. Now there was a saying of Pittacus which was privately circulated and received the approbation of the wise, 'Hard is it to be good.' And Simonides, who was ambitious of the

c fame of wisdom, was aware that if he could overthrow this saying, then, as if he had won a victory over some famous athlete, he would carry off the palm among his contemporaries. And if I am not mistaken, he composed the entire poem with the secret intention of damaging Pittacus and his saying.

Let us all unite in examining his words, and see whether I am speaking the truth. Simonides must have been a lunatic, if, in the very first words of the poem, wanting to say only that to become good is

d hard, he inserted, 'on the one hand'⁴ ['on the one hand to become good is hard']; there would be no reason for this, unless you suppose him to speak with a hostile reference to the words of Pittacus. Pittacus is saying 'Hard is it to be good,' and he, in refutation of this thesis, rejoins that the truly hard thing, Pittacus, is to become good, not joining 'truly' with 'good,' but with 'hard.' Not that the hard thing is to be

e truly good, as though there were some truly good men, and there were others who were good but not truly good (this would be a very simple observation, and quite unworthy of Simonides); but you must suppose him to make a trajection of the word 'truly,' construing the saying of Pittacus thus (and let us imagine Pittacus to be speaking and Si-

344 monides answering him): 'My friends,' says Pittacus, 'hard is it to be good,' and Simonides answers, 'In that, Pittacus, you are mistaken; the difficulty is not to be good, but on the one hand, to become good, four-square in hands and feet and mind, without a flaw—that is hard truly.' This way of reading the passage accounts for the insertion of 'on the one hand,' and for the position at the end of the clause of the word 'truly,' and all that follows shows this to be the meaning. A great deal

b might be said in praise of the details of the poem, which is a charming

---

*The Seven Sages, according to Socrates; all were wise men and lawmakers.

piece of workmanship, and very finished, but such minutiae would be tedious. I would like, however, to point out the general intention of the poem, which is certainly designed in every part to be a refutation of the saying of Pittacus. For he speaks in what follows a little further on as if he meant to argue that although there is a difficulty in becoming good, yet this is possible for a time, and only for a time. But having become good, to remain in a good state and be good, as you, Pittacus, affirm, is not possible, and is not granted to man; god only has this blessing; 'but man cannot help being bad when the force of circumstances overpowers him.' Now whom does the force of circumstance overpower in the command of a vessel? Not the private individual, for he is always overpowered; and as one who is already prostrate cannot be overthrown, and only he who is standing upright but not he who is prostrate can be laid prostrate, so the force of circumstances can only overpower him who, at some time or other, has resources, and not him who is at all times helpless. The descent of a great storm may make the pilot helpless, or the severity of the season the farmer or the physician; for the good may become bad, as another poet witnesses:

'The good are sometimes good and sometimes bad.'

But the bad does not become bad; he is always bad. So that when the force of circumstances overpowers the man of resources and skill and virtue, then he cannot help being bad. And you, Pittacus, are saying, 'Hard is it to be good.' Now there is a difficulty in becoming good; and yet this is possible: but to be good is an impossibility,

'For he who does well is the good man, and he who does ill is the bad.'

But what sort of doing is good in letters? and what sort of doing makes a man good in letters? Clearly the knowing of them. And what sort of well-doing makes a man a good physician? Clearly the knowledge of the art of healing the sick. 'But he who does ill is the bad.' Now who becomes a bad physician? Clearly he who is in the first place a physician, and in the second place a good physician; for he may become a bad one also: but none of us unskilled individuals can by any amount of doing ill become physicians, any more than we can become carpenters or anything of that sort; and he who by doing ill cannot become a physician at all, clearly cannot become a bad physician. In like manner the good may become deteriorated by time, or toil, or disease, or other accident (the only real doing ill is to be deprived of knowledge), but the bad man will never become bad, for he is always bad; and if he were to become bad, he must previously have been good.

c   Thus the words of the poem tend to show that on the one hand a man cannot be continuously good, but that he may become good and may also become bad; and again that

> 'They are the best for the longest time whom the gods love.'

All this relates to Pittacus, as is further proved by the sequel. For he adds:

> 'Therefore I will not throw away my span of life to no purpose in searching after the impossible, hoping in vain to find a perfectly fault-less man among those who partake of the fruit of the broad-bosomed earth: if I find him, I will send you word.'

d   (This is the vehement way in which he pursues his attack upon Pitta-cus throughout the whole poem):

> 'But him who does no evil, voluntarily I praise and love—not even the gods war against necessity.'

All this has a similar drift, for Simonides was not so ignorant as to say that he praised those who did no evil voluntarily, as though there were some who did evil voluntarily. For no wise man, as I believe, will allow that any human being errs voluntarily, or voluntarily does evil

e   and dishonourable actions; but they are very well aware that all who do evil and dishonourable things do them against their will. And Si-monides never says that he praises him who does no evil voluntarily; the word 'voluntarily' applies to himself. For he was under the im-pression that a good man might often compel himself to befriend and

346   praise another; and that there might be an involuntary love, such as a man might feel to an unnatural father or mother, or country, or the like. Now bad men, when their parents or country have any defects, look on them with malignant joy, and find fault with them and expose and denounce them to others, under the idea that the rest of mankind will be less likely to take themselves to task and accuse them of neg-lect; and they blame their defects far more than they deserve, in order that the odium which is necessarily incurred by them may be in-creased: but the good man dissembles his feelings, and constrains

b   himself to praise them; and if they have wronged him and he is angry, he pacifies his anger and is reconciled, and compels himself to love and praise his own flesh and blood. And Simonides, as is probable, considered that he himself had often had to praise and magnify a tyrant or the like, much against his will, and he also wishes to imply to Pittacus that he does not censure him because he tries to find fault in others:

> 'For I am satisfied,' he says, 'when a man is neither bad nor very stupid; and when he knows justice (which is the health of states), and is of sound mind, I will find no fault with him, for I am not given to finding fault, and there are innumerable fools'

(implying that if he delighted in censure he might have abundant opportunity of finding fault).

> 'All things are good with which evil is unmingled.'

In these latter words he does not mean to say that all things are good which have no evil in them, as you might say 'All things are white which have no black in them,' for that would be ridiculous; but he means to say that he accepts and finds no fault with the moderate or intermediate state.

> ['I do not hope,' he says, 'to find a perfectly blameless man among those who partake of the fruits of the broad-bosomed earth (if I find him, I will send you word); in this sense I praise no man. But he who is moderately good, and does no evil, is good enough for me, who love and approve every one']

(and here observe that he uses a Lesbian word, [approve], because he is addressing Pittacus,—

> 'Who love and *approve* every one *voluntarily*, who does no evil':

and that the stop should be put after 'voluntarily'); 'but there are some whom I involuntarily praise and love. And you, Pittacus, I would never have blamed, if you had spoken what was moderately good and true; but I do blame you because, putting on the appearance of truth, you are speaking falsely about the highest matters.'—And this, I said, Prodicus and Protagoras, I take to be the meaning of Simonides in this poem.

Hippias said: I think, Socrates, that you have given a very good explanation of the poem; but I have also an excellent interpretation of my own which I will propose to you, if you will allow me.

Nay, Hippias, said Alcibiades; not now, but at some other time. At present we must abide by the compact which was made between Socrates and Protagoras, to the effect that as long as Protagoras is willing to ask, Socrates should answer; or that if he would rather answer, then that Socrates should ask.

I said: I wish Protagoras either to ask or answer as he is inclined;
c but I would rather have done with poems and odes, if he does not object, and come back to the question about which I was asking you at first, Protagoras, and by your help make an end of that. The talk about the poets seems to me like a commonplace entertainment to which a vulgar company have recourse; who, because they are not able to converse or amuse one another, while they are drinking, with the sound of
d their own voices and conversation, by reason of their stupidity, raise the price of flute-girls in the market, hiring for a great sum the voice of a flute instead of their own breath, to be the medium of intercourse among them: but where the company are real gentlemen and men of education, you will see no flute-girls, nor dancing-girls, nor harp-girls; and they have no nonsense or games, but are contented with one another's conversation, of which their own voices are the medium, and which they carry on by turns and in an orderly manner, even though
e they are very liberal in their potations.[5] A company like this of ours, and men such as we profess to be, do not require the help of another's voice, or of the poets whom you cannot interrogate about the meaning of what they are saying; people who cite them declaring, some that the poet has one meaning, and others that he has another, and the point which is in dispute can never be decided. This sort of entertainment they decline, and prefer to talk with one another, and put one another
348 to the proof in conversation. And these are the models which I desire that you and I should imitate. Leaving the poets, and keeping to ourselves, let us try the mettle of one another and make proof of the truth in conversation. If you have a mind to ask, I am ready to answer; or if you would rather, you answer, and give me the opportunity of resuming and completing our unfinished argument.

b I made these and some similar observations; but Protagoras would not distinctly say which he would do. Thereupon Alcibiades turned to Callias, and said: Do you think, Callias, that Protagoras is fair in refusing to say whether he will or will not answer? for I certainly think that he is unfair; he ought either to proceed with the argument, or distinctly to refuse to proceed, so that we may know his intention; then Socrates will be able to discourse with someone else, and the rest of the company will be free to talk with one another.

c I think that Protagoras was really made ashamed by these words of Alcibiades, and when the prayers of Callias and the company were superadded, he was at last induced to argue, and said that I might ask and he would answer.

So I said: Do not imagine, Protagoras, that I have any other interest in asking questions of you but that of clearing up my own difficulties. For I think that Homer was very right in saying that

'When two go together, one sees before the other,'*   d

for all men who have a companion are readier in deed, word, or thought; but if a man

'Sees a thing when he is alone,'

he goes about straightway seeking until he finds someone to whom he may show his discoveries, and who may confirm him in them. And I would rather hold discourse with you than with anyone, because I think that no man has a better understanding of most things which a   e
good man may be expected to understand, and in particular of virtue. For who is there, but you, who not only claim to be a good man and a gentleman, for many are this, and yet have not the power of making others good—whereas you are not only good yourself, but also the cause of goodness in others. Moreover, such confidence have you in yourself, that although other Sophists conceal their profession, you proclaim in the face of the Greeks that you are a Sophist or teacher of virtue and education, and are the first who demanded pay in return.   349
How then can I do otherwise than invite you to the examination of these subjects, and ask questions and consult with you? I must, indeed. And I should like once more to have my memory refreshed by you about the questions which I was asking you at first, and also to have your help in considering them. If I am not mistaken the question was   b
this: Are wisdom and temperance and courage and justice and holiness five names of the same thing? or has each of the names a separate underlying essence and corresponding thing having a peculiar function, no one of them being like any other of them? And you replied that the five names were not the names of the same thing, but that each of them   c
had a separate object, and that all these objects were parts of virtue, not in the same way that the parts of gold are like each other and the whole of which they are parts, but as the parts of the face are unlike the whole of which they are parts and one another, and have each of them a distinct function. I should like to know whether this is still your opinion; or if not, I will ask you to define your meaning, and I shall not take you to task if you now make a different statement. For I dare say that you   d
may have said what you did only in order to make trial of me.

---

*Iliad 10.224.

I answer, Socrates, he said, that all these qualities are parts of virtue, and that four out of the five are to some extent similar, and that the fifth of them, which is courage, is very different from the other four, as I prove in this way: You may observe that many men are utterly unrighteous, unholy, intemperate, ignorant, who are nevertheless remarkable for their courage.

e   Stop, I said; I would like to think about that. When you speak of brave men, do you mean the confident, or another sort of nature?

Yes, he said; I mean the impetuous, ready to go at that which others are afraid to approach.

In the next place, you would affirm virtue to be a good thing, of which good thing you assert yourself to be a teacher.

Yes, he said; I should say the best of all things, if I am in my right mind.

And is it partly good and partly bad, I said, or wholly good?

Wholly good, and in the highest degree.

Tell me then; who are they who have confidence when diving into
350 a well?

I should say, the divers.

And the reason of this is that they have knowledge?

Yes, that is the reason.

And who have confidence when fighting on horseback—the skilled horseman or the unskilled?

The skilled.

And who when fighting with light shields—the peltasts* or the nonpeltasts?

The peltasts. And that is true of all other things, he said, if that is your point: those who have knowledge are more confident than those
b   who have no knowledge, and they are more confident after they have learned than before.

And have you not seen persons utterly ignorant, I said, of these things, and yet confident about them?

Yes, he said, I have seen such persons far too confident.

And are not these confident persons also courageous?

In that case, he replied, courage would be a base thing, for the men of whom we are speaking are surely madmen.

Then who are the courageous? Are they not the confident?

Yes, he said; to that statement I adhere.

c   And those, I said, who are thus confident without knowledge are really not courageous, but mad; and in that case the wisest are also the

---

*Light infantry who carried a crescent-shaped wicker shield.

most confident, and being the most confident are also the bravest, and upon that view wisdom would be courage.

Nay, Socrates, he replied, you are mistaken in your remembrance of what was said by me. When you asked me, I certainly did say that the courageous are the confident; but I was never asked whether the confident are the courageous; if you had asked me, I should have answered, 'Not all of them:' and what I did answer you have not proved *d* to be false, although you proceeded to show that those who have knowledge are more courageous than they were before they had knowledge, and more courageous than others who have no knowledge, and were then led on to think that courage is the same as wisdom. But in this way of arguing you might come to imagine that strength is wisdom. You might begin by asking whether the strong are able, and I *e* should say 'Yes;' and then whether those who know how to wrestle are not more able to wrestle than those who do not know how to wrestle, and more able after than before they had learned, and I should assent. And when I had admitted this, you might use my admissions in such a way as to prove that upon my view wisdom is strength; whereas in that case I should not have admitted, any more than in the other, that the able are strong, although I have admitted that the strong are able. *351* For there is a difference between ability and strength; the former is given by knowledge as well as by madness or rage, but strength comes from nature and a healthy state of the body. And in like manner I say of confidence and courage, that they are not the same; and I argue that the courageous are confident, but not all the confident courageous. For confidence may be given to men by art, and also, like ability, by mad- *b* ness and rage; but courage comes to them from nature and the healthy state of the soul.

I said: You would admit, Protagoras, that some men live well and others ill?

He assented.

And do you think that a man lives well who lives in pain and grief?

He does not.

But if he lives pleasantly to the end of his life, will he not in that case have lived well?

He will.

Then to live pleasantly is a good, and to live unpleasantly an evil? *c*

Yes, he said, if the pleasure be good and honourable.

And do you, Protagoras, like the rest of the world, call some pleasant things evil and some painful things good?—for I am rather disposed to say that things are good in as far as they are pleasant, if they have no consequences of another sort, and in as far as they are painful they are bad.

I do not know, Socrates, he said, whether I can venture to assert in that unqualified manner that the pleasant is the good and the painful the evil. Having regard not only to my present answer, but also to the whole of my life, I shall be safer, if I am not mistaken, in saying that there are some pleasant things which are not good, and that there are some painful things which are good, and some which are not good, and that there are some which are neither good nor evil.

e   And you would call pleasant, I said, the things which participate in pleasure or create pleasure?

Certainly, he said.

Then my meaning is, that in as far as they are pleasant they are good; and my question would imply that pleasure is a good in itself.

According to your favourite mode of speech, Socrates, 'let us reflect about this,' he said; and if the reflection is to the point, and the result proves that pleasure and good are really the same, then we will agree; but if not, then we will argue.

And would you wish to begin the enquiry? I said; or shall I begin?

You ought to take the lead, he said; for you are the author of the discussion.

352   May I employ an illustration? I said. Suppose someone is enquiring into the health or some other bodily quality of another: he looks at his face and at the tips of his fingers, and then he says, 'Uncover your chest and back to me so that I may have a better view': —that is the sort of thing which I desire in this speculation. Having seen what your opinion is about good and pleasure, I am minded to say to you: Un-
b   cover your mind to me, Protagoras, and reveal your opinion about knowledge, so that I may know whether you agree with the rest of the world. Now the rest of the world are of the opinion that knowledge is a principle not of strength, or of rule, or of command: their notion is that a man may have knowledge, and yet that the knowledge which is in him may be overmastered by anger, or pleasure, or pain, or love, or perhaps by fear, just as if knowledge were a slave, and might be dragged
c   about. Now is that your view? or do you think that knowledge is a noble and commanding thing, which cannot be overcome, and will not allow a man, if he only knows the difference of good and evil, to do anything which is contrary to knowledge, but that wisdom will have strength to help him?

d   I agree with you, Socrates, said Protagoras; and not only so, but I, above all other men, am bound to say that wisdom and knowledge are the highest of human things.

Good, I said, and true. But are you aware that the majority of the world are of another mind; and that men are commonly supposed to know the things which are best, and not to do them when they might?

And most persons whom I have asked the reason of this have said that when men act contrary to knowledge they are overcome by pain, or pleasure, or some of those affections which I was just now mentioning.   e

Yes, Socrates, he replied; and that is not the only point about which mankind are in error.

Suppose, then, that you and I endeavour to instruct and inform them what is the nature of this affection which they call 'being overcome by pleasure,' and which they affirm to be the reason why they do   353 not always do what is best. When we say to them: Friends, you are mistaken, and are saying what is not true, they would probably reply: Socrates and Protagoras, if this affection of the soul is not to be called 'being overcome by pleasure,' pray, what is it, and by what name would you describe it?

But why, Socrates, should we trouble ourselves about the opinion of the many, who just say anything that happens to occur to them?

I believe, I said, that they may be of use in helping us to discover   b how courage is related to the other parts of virtue. If you are disposed to abide by our agreement, that I should show the way in which, as I think, our recent difficulty is most likely to be cleared up, do follow; but if not, never mind.

You are quite right, he said; and I would have you proceed as you have begun.

Well then, I said, let me suppose that they repeat their question,   c What account do you give of that which, in our way of speaking, is termed 'being overcome by pleasure'? I should answer thus: Listen, and Protagoras and I will endeavour to show you. When men are overcome by eating and drinking and other sensual desires which are pleasant, and they, knowing them to be evil, nevertheless indulge in them, would you not say that they were overcome by pleasure? They will not deny this. And suppose that you and I were to go on and ask them again: 'In what way do you say that they are evil, in that they are pleasant and   d give pleasure at the moment, or because they cause disease and poverty and other like evils in the future? Would they still be evil, if they had no attendant evil consequences, simply because they give the consciousness of pleasure of whatever nature?' Would they not answer that they are not evil on account of the pleasure which is immediately given by them, but   e on account of the after consequences—diseases and the like?

I believe, said Protagoras, that the world in general would answer as you do.

And in causing diseases do they not cause pain? and in causing poverty do they not cause pain; they would agree to that also, if I am not mistaken?

Protagoras assented.

Then I should say to them, in my name and yours: Do you think them evil for any other reason, except because they end in pain and rob 354 us of other pleasures: there again they would agree?

Both of us thought that they would.

And then I should take the question from the opposite point of view, and say: 'Friends, when you speak of goods being painful, do you not mean remedial goods, such as gymnastic exercises, and military service, and the physician's use of burning, cutting, drugging, and starving? Are these the things which are good but painful?'—they would assent to me?

He agreed.

b   'And do you call them good because they occasion the greatest im-mediate suffering and pain; or because, afterwards, they bring health and improvement of the bodily condition and the salvation of states and power over others and wealth?'—they would agree to the latter al-ternative, if I am not mistaken?

He assented.

'Are these things good for any other reason except that they end in c pleasure, and get rid of and avert pain? Are you looking to any other standard but pleasure and pain when you call them good?'—they would acknowledge that they were not?

I think so, said Protagoras.

'And do you not pursue pleasure as a good, and avoid pain as an evil?'

He assented.

'Then you think that pain is an evil and pleasure is a good: and even pleasure you deem an evil, when it robs you of greater pleasures d than it gives, or causes pains greater than the pleasure. If, however, you call pleasure an evil in relation to some other end or standard, you will be able to show us that standard. But you have none to show.'

I do not think that they have, said Protagoras.

'And have you not a similar way of speaking about pain? You call pain a good when it takes away greater pains than those which it has, or gives pleasures greater than the pains: then if you have some stan-dard other than pleasure and pain to which you refer when you call ac-e tual pain a good, you can show what that is. But you cannot.'

True, said Protagoras.

Suppose again, I said, that the world says to me: 'Why do you spend many words and speak in many ways on this subject?' Excuse me, friends, I should reply; but in the first place there is a difficulty in explaining the meaning of the expression 'overcome by pleasure'; and the whole argument turns upon this. And even now, if you see any pos-355 sible way in which evil can be explained as other than pain, or good as other than pleasure, you may still retract. Are you satisfied, then, at having a life of pleasure which is without pain? If you are, and if you are unable to show any good or evil which does not end in pleasure and pain, hear the consequences: If what you say is true, then the argument is absurd which affirms that a man often does evil knowingly, when he might abstain, because he is seduced and overpowered by pleasure; or *b* again, when you say that a man knowingly refuses to do what is good because he is overcome at the moment by pleasure. And that this is ridiculous will be evident if only we give up the use of various names, such as pleasant and painful, and good and evil. As there are two things, let us call them by two names—first, good and evil, and then pleasant *c* and painful. Assuming this, let us go on to say that a man does evil knowing that he does evil. But someone will ask, Why? Because he is overcome, is the first answer. And by what is he overcome? the enquirer will proceed to ask. And we shall not be able to reply, 'By pleasure,' for the name of pleasure has been exchanged for that of good. In our answer, then, we shall only say that he is overcome. 'By what?' he will reiterate. By the good, we shall have to reply; indeed we shall. Nay, but our questioner will rejoin with a laugh, if he be one of the swaggering *d* sort, 'That is too ridiculous, that a man should do what he knows to be evil when he ought not, because he is overcome by good. Is that, he will ask, because the good was worthy or not worthy of conquering the evil'? And in answer to that we shall clearly reply, Because it was not worthy; for if it had been worthy, then he who, as we say, was overcome by pleasure, would not have been wrong. 'But how,' he will reply, 'can the good be unworthy of the evil, or the evil of the good'? Is not *e* the real explanation that they are out of proportion to one another, either as greater and smaller, or more and fewer? This we cannot deny. And when you speak of being overcome—'What do you mean,' he will say, 'but that you choose the greater evil in exchange for the lesser good'? Admitted. And now substitute the names of pleasure and pain for good and evil, and say, not as before, that a man does what is evil *356* knowingly, but that he does what is painful knowingly, and because he is overcome by pleasure, which is unworthy to overcome. What measure is there of the relations of pleasure to pain other than excess and defect, which means that they become greater and smaller, and more and fewer, and differ in degree? For if anyone says: 'Yes, Socrates, but immediate pleasure differs widely from future pleasure and pain,' to that I would reply: And do they differ in anything but in pleasure and *b* pain? There can be no other measure of them. Like a skilful weigher, put into the balance the pleasures and the pains, and their nearness and distance, and weigh them, and then say which outweighs the other. If you weigh pleasures against pleasures, you of course take the more and

greater; or if you weigh pains against pains, you take the fewer and the less; or if pleasures against pains, then you choose that course of action in which the painful is exceeded by the pleasant, whether the distant by the near or the near by the distant; and you avoid that course of ac-
c   tion in which the pleasant is exceeded by the painful. Would you not admit, my friends, that this is true? I am confident that they cannot deny this.

He agreed with me.

Well then, I shall say, if you agree so far, be so good as to answer me a question: Do not the same magnitudes appear larger to your sight when near, and smaller when at a distance? They will acknowledge that.
d   And the same holds of thickness and number; also sounds, which are in themselves equal, are greater when near, and lesser when at a distance. They will grant that also. Now suppose happiness to consist in doing or choosing the greater, and in not doing or in avoiding the less, what would be the saving principle of human life? Would not the art of measuring be the saving principle; or would the power of appearance? Is not the latter that deceiving art which makes us wander up and down and take the things at one time of which we repent at another, both in our actions and in our choice of things great and small? But the art of measurement would do away with the effect of appearances, and, show-ing the truth, would teach the soul at last to find rest in the truth, and
e   would thus save our life. Would not mankind generally acknowledge that the art which accomplishes this result is the art of measurement?

Yes, he said, the art of measurement.

Suppose, again, the salvation of human life to depend on the choice of odd and even, and on the knowledge of when a man ought to choose the greater or less, either in reference to themselves or to each other, and
357   whether near or at a distance; what would be the saving principle of our lives? Would it not be knowledge?—a knowledge of measuring, when the question is one of excess and defect, and a knowledge of number, when the question is of odd and even? The world will assent, will they not?

Protagoras himself thought that they would.

Well then, my friends, I say to them; seeing that the salvation of human life has been found to consist in the right choice of pleasures
b   and pains, in the choice of the more and the fewer, and the greater and the less, and the nearer and remoter, must not this measuring be a con-sideration of their excess and defect and equality in relation to each other?

This is undeniably true.

And this, as possessing measure, must undeniably also be an art and science?

They will agree, he said.

The nature of that art or science will be a matter of future consideration; but the existence of such a science furnishes a demonstrative answer to the question which you asked of me and Protagoras. At the time when you asked the question, if you remember, both of us were   c
agreeing that there was nothing mightier than knowledge, and that knowledge, in whatever existing, must have the advantage over pleasure and all other things; and then you said that pleasure often got the advantage even over a man who has knowledge; and we refused to allow this, and you rejoined: Protagoras and Socrates, what is the meaning of being overcome by pleasure if not this?—tell us what you   d
call such a state. If we had immediately and at the time answered 'Ignorance,' you would have laughed at us. But now, in laughing at us, you will be laughing at yourselves: for you also admitted that men err in their choice of pleasures and pains; that is, in their choice of good and evil, from lack of knowledge; and you admitted further, that they err, not only from lack of knowledge in general, but of that particular knowledge which is called measuring. And you are also aware that the erring act which is done without knowledge is done in ignorance.   e
This, therefore, is the meaning of being overcome by pleasure; ignorance, and that the greatest. And our friends Protagoras and Prodicus and Hippias declare that they are the physicians of ignorance; but you, who are under the mistaken impression that ignorance is not the cause, and that the art of which I am speaking cannot be taught, neither go yourselves, nor send your children, to the Sophists, who are the teachers of these things—you take care of your money and give them none; and the result is, that you are the worse off both in public and private life. Let us suppose this to be our answer to the world in general: And now I should like to ask you, Hippias, and you, Prodicus, as well as Protagoras (for the argument is to be yours as well as ours), whether you   358
think that I am speaking the truth or not?

They all thought that what I said was entirely true.

Then you agree, I said, that the pleasant is the good, and the painful evil. And here I would beg my friend Prodicus not to introduce his distinction of names, whether he is disposed to say pleasurable, de-   b
lightful, joyful. However, by whatever name he prefers to call them, I will ask you, most excellent Prodicus, to answer in my sense of the words.

Prodicus laughed and assented, as did the others.

Then, my friends, what do you say to this? Are not all actions honorable and useful, of which the tendency is to make life painless and pleasant? The honorable work is also useful and good?

This was admitted.

Then, I said, if the pleasant is the good, nobody does anything
c under the idea or conviction that some other thing would be better and
is also attainable, when he might do the better. And this inferiority of
a man to himself is merely ignorance, as the superiority of a man to
himself is wisdom.

They all assented.

And is not ignorance the having a false opinion and being deceived
about important matters?

To this also they unanimously assented.

Then, I said, no man voluntarily pursues evil, or that which he
d thinks to be evil. To prefer evil to good is not in human nature; and when
a man is compelled to choose one of two evils, no one will choose the
greater when he may have the less.

All of us agreed to every word of this.

Well, I said, there is a certain thing called fear or terror; and here,
Prodicus, I would particularly like to know whether you would agree
with me in defining this fear or terror as expectation of evil.

e Protagoras and Hippias agreed, but Prodicus said that this was fear
and not terror.

Never mind, Prodicus, I said; but let me ask whether, if our former
assertions are true, a man will pursue that which he fears when he is
not compelled? Would not this be in flat contradiction to the admission
which has been already made, that he thinks the things which he fears
to be evil; and no one will pursue or voluntarily accept that which he
thinks to be evil?

That also was universally admitted.

359 Then, I said, these, Hippias and Prodicus, are our premises; and I
would beg Protagoras to explain to us how he can be right in what he
said at first. I do not mean in what he said quite at first, for his first
statement, as you may remember, was that whereas there were five
parts of virtue none of them was like any other of them; each of them
had a separate function. To this, however, I am not referring, but to the
assertion which he afterwards made that of the five virtues four were
b nearly akin to each other, but that the fifth, which was courage, differed
greatly from the others. And of this he gave me the following proof. He
said: You will find, Socrates, that some of the most impious, and unrighteous, and intemperate, and ignorant of men are among the most
courageous; which proves that courage is very different from the other
parts of virtue. I was surprised at his saying this at the time, and I am
still more surprised now that I have discussed the matter with you. So
I asked him whether by the brave he meant the confident. Yes, he
c replied, and the impetuous or goers. (You may remember, Protagoras,
that this was your answer.)

He assented.

Well then, I said, tell us against what are the courageous ready to go—against the same dangers as the cowards?

No, he answered.

Then against something different?

Yes, he said.

Then do cowards go where there is safety, and the courageous where there is danger?

Yes, Socrates, so men say.

Very true, I said. But I want to know against what do you say that *d* the courageous are ready to go—against dangers, believing them to be dangers, or not against dangers?

No, said he; the former case has been proved by you in the previous argument to be impossible.

That, again, I replied, is quite true. And if this has been rightly proven, then no one goes to meet what he thinks to be dangers, since the want of self-control, which makes men rush into dangers, has been shown to be ignorance.

He assented.

And yet the courageous man and the coward alike go to meet that about which they are confident; so that, in this point of view, the cow- *e* ardly and the courageous go to meet the same things.

And yet, Socrates, said Protagoras, that to which the coward goes is the opposite of that to which the courageous goes; the one, for example, is ready to go to battle, and the other is not ready.

And is going to battle honorable or disgraceful? I said.

Honorable, he replied.

And if honorable, then already admitted by us to be good; for all honorable actions we have admitted to be good.

That is true; and to that opinion I shall always adhere.

True, I said. But which of the two are they who, as you say, are un- *360* willing to go to war, which is a good and honorable thing?

The cowards, he replied.

And what is good and honorable, I said, is also pleasant?

It has certainly been acknowledged to be so, he replied.

And do the cowards knowingly refuse to go to the nobler, and pleasanter, and better?

The admission of that, he replied, would belie our former admissions.

But does not the courageous man also go to meet the better, and pleasanter, and nobler?

That must be admitted.

And the courageous man has no base fear or base confidence?   *b*

True, he replied.

And if not base, then honorable?

He admitted this.

And if honorable, then good?

Yes.

But the fear and confidence of the coward or foolhardy or madman, on the contrary, are base?

He assented.

And these base fears and confidences originate in ignorance and uninstructedness?

c   True, he said.

Then as to the motive from which the cowards act, do you call it cowardice or courage?

I should say cowardice, he replied.

And have they not been shown to be cowards through their ignorance of dangers?

Assuredly, he said.

And because of that ignorance they are cowards?

He assented.

And the reason why they are cowards is admitted by you to be cowardice?

He again assented.

Then the ignorance of what is and is not dangerous is cowardice?

He nodded assent.

But surely courage, I said, is opposed to cowardice?

d   Yes.

Then the wisdom which knows what are and are not dangers is opposed to the ignorance of them?

To that again he nodded assent.

And the ignorance of them is cowardice?

To that he very reluctantly nodded assent.

And the knowledge of that which is and is not dangerous is courage, and is opposed to the ignorance of these things?

At this point he would no longer nod assent, but was silent.

And why, I said, do you neither assent nor dissent, Protagoras?

Finish the argument by yourself, he said.

e   I only want to ask one more question, I said. I want to know whether you still think that there are men who are most ignorant and yet most courageous?

You seem to have a great ambition to make me answer, Socrates, and therefore I will gratify you, and say, that this appears to me to be impossible consistently with the argument.

My only object, I said, in continuing the discussion, has been the

desire to ascertain the nature and relations of virtue; for if this were
clear, I am very sure that the other controversy which has been carried   361
on at great length by both of us—you affirming and I denying that virtue
can be taught—would also become clear. The result of our discussion
appears to me to be singular. For if the argument had a human voice,
that voice would be heard laughing at us and saying: 'Protagoras and
Socrates, you are a pair of fools; there you are, Socrates, who were say-   b
ing that virtue cannot be taught, contradicting yourself now by your
attempt to prove that all things are knowledge, including justice, and
temperance, and courage, which tends to show that virtue can certainly
be taught; for if virtue were other than knowledge, as Protagoras attempted to prove, then clearly virtue cannot be taught; but if virtue is
entirely knowledge, as you are seeking to show, then I cannot but suppose that virtue is capable of being taught. Protagoras, on the other
hand, who started by saying that it might be taught, is now eager to   c
prove it to be anything rather than knowledge; and if this is true, it
must be quite incapable of being taught.' Now I, Protagoras, perceiving
this terrible confusion of our ideas, have a great desire that they be
cleared up. And I would like to carry on the discussion until we ascertain what virtue is, and whether it is capable of being taught or not,
lest haply Epimetheus should trip us up and deceive us in the argu-   d
ment, as he forgot us in the story; I prefer your Prometheus to your
Epimetheus, for of him I make use, whenever I am busy about these
questions, in Promethean care of my own life. And if you have no objection, as I said at first, I should like to have your help in the enquiry.

Protagoras replied: Socrates, I am not of a base nature, and I am the
last man in the world to be envious. I cannot but applaud your energy   e
and your conduct of an argument. As I have often said, I admire you
above all men whom I know, and far above all men of your age; I believe that you will become very eminent in philosophy. Let us come
back to the subject at some future time; at present we had better turn
to something else.

By all means, I said, if that is your wish; for I too ought long since
to have kept the engagement of which I spoke before, and only tarried   362
because I could not refuse the request of the noble Callias. So the conversation ended, and we went our way.

STATESMAN

Introduction

THE CONVERSATION OF STATESMAN is of a piece with those of Theaetetus and Sophist, in which Plato enters into very thorough epistemological discussions. Nevertheless, I think Statesman can be read on its own. Major changes have taken place from the dramatic conventions of the early and middle dialogues: Socrates is now merely an onlooker, and the conversation takes place mainly between a nameless Visitor from Elea and a young member of Plato's Academy who happens to be called Socrates, although he is not a relative of his famous namesake. Theodorus of Cyrene, a mathematician and a friend of the Sophist Protagoras of Abdera, also speaks briefly in the dialogue; he is the man who has introduced Socrates to the Visitor from Elea, and who is keeping account of the three explanations that have been promised to Socrates: those of the Sophist (given in Sophist, not included in this volume), the statesman (given in this dialogue), and the philosopher (which is not explicitly given anywhere).

The following is a suggested outline of the dialogue:

- (257a–258a) Socrates asks the Visitor to proceed with a definition of the statesman, with Young Socrates as an interlocutor, to which Young Socrates agrees.

- (258b–268d) As a first definition, statecraft is the art practiced by kings, statesmen, slave masters, and heads of households. It is an applied cognitive science that issues directives based on self-control and can be also practiced by advisers without real power over living creatures. The classification of living creatures follows by division, and statecraft comes to be defined as the rule over creatures that are tame, land-based, hornless, do not mix with other species, walk on two legs, and have no feathers. But this definition is not sufficiently clear, because tradesmen, farmers, and doctors may also exercise care over living creatures so defined.

- (268d–274d) Man's life on earth is subject to a cycle of two alternating ages: in the age of Cronos, a god takes care of the universe and of men and other creatures. There is no need for toil, war, or politics. Men are born fully grown up from the earth and return to the earth as small children, in order to give birth to future generations. In contrast with the age of Cronos, the current age of Zeus, the one we live in, is marked by strife and forgetfulness of divine guidance. It also is made to seem unending, although it is really not so.

- (274e–277a) Clearly, then, the right definition of the statesman must take into account the age we live in. The true statesman is not just a caretaker, but is truly concerned with the welfare and development of the herd. This means that the true statesman cannot be a tyrant, but must be accepted by the subjects. Still, the Visitor from Elea is not satisfied with this second definition, either.

- (277a–279a) This passage begins the long search for a third and final definition that takes up the rest of the dialogue. The procedure to be followed is searching for a good example of what we want to define. An example, in this sense, is a thing that we know and that contains the same elements as the thing we want to define.

- (279b–283b) The example chosen is weaving, which must be differentiated from manufacturing or other skills aimed at separating wool, like carding, as well as from ancillary skills that furnish tools to the weaver.

- (283b–287b) Are we taking too long? How do we measure the length of the right argument? Even philosophers do not always know how to do that. The right length is the one that achieves the performance we are looking for.

- (287b–303b) Following the example of weaving, the statesman requires some people to perform ancillary functions: (a) producers; (b) servants and merchants; and (c) heralds, prophets, and priests. We must not rely on imitative constitutions (enumerated later at 300e–303b) but must seek the true art of statecraft, in which no laws are required and the commands of the statesman are obeyed as those of the doctor. But there are very few of these statesmen. Are laws really not required (Young Socrates asks)? Law is too rigid to be suitable for all situations and cannot substitute for true statecraft. But law can be used as a second-best solution in the absence of the true statesman, much as a doctor's prescriptions are written down for the time while he is not at the side of the patient. But, again, in the presence of a true statesman, law must give way to him. The imitative constitutions are classified as the rule of one, a few, or many; each of these in turn can be subjected or not to the rule of law. The imitative constitutions subjected to a rule of law, the rule of one (kingship) among them, are to be preferred. But if there is no rule of law, the rule of many (democracy) is likely to cause the least harm.

- (303b–311c) In order to bring to an end the definition of the statesman, the differences from his ancillary personnel (orators, generals, and judges) must be spelled out. Although they have specialized skills that the statesman does not possess, they are all totally subordinated to him. Other than that, what is it exactly that the statesman does? His task is to weave the different forces that reside in different groups of people, which can be separated into two main groups: the aggressive members of a polity and the quiet ones. A key to this process is the right educational system, which makes children grow up strong but pliable enough to the requirements of society. Those who do not pass the test may be turned into slaves, while those who pass it become raw material for the statesman to weave the web of the polity. Ultimately, all citizens will share the same values and be married for the right reasons, in order to beget a well-balanced offspring (not because of money or personal affinity). Public offices should be filled also with a mind to achieving a balanced mixture of drive and self-control.

STATESMAN

SOCRATES. I owe you many thanks, indeed, Theodorus, for the acquaintance both of Theaetetus* and of the Stranger.

THEODORUS. And in a little while, Socrates, you will owe me three times as many, when they have completed for you the delineation of the Statesman and of the Philosopher, as well as of the Sophist.

SOC. Sophist, statesman, philosopher! O my dear Theodorus, do my ears truly witness that this is the estimate formed of them by the great calculator and geometrician?

THEOD. What do you mean, Socrates?

SOC. I mean that you rate them all at the same value, whereas they are really separated by an interval, which no geometrical ratio can express.

THEOD. By Ammon, the god of Cyrene, Socrates, that is a very fair hit; and shows that you have not forgotten your geometry. I will retaliate on you at some other time, but I must now ask the Stranger, who will not, I hope, tire of his goodness to us, to proceed either with the Statesman or with the Philosopher, whichever he prefers.

STRANGER. That is my duty, Theodorus; having begun I must go on, and not leave the work unfinished. But what shall be done with Theaetetus?

THEOD. In what respect?

STR. Shall we relieve him, and take his companion, the Young Socrates, instead of him? What do you advise?

THEOD. Yes, give the other a turn, as you propose. The young always do better when they have intervals of rest.

SOC. I think, Stranger, that both of them may be said to be in some way related to me; for the one, as you affirm, has the cut of my ugly face, and the other is called by my name. And we should always be on the look-out to recognize a kinsman by the style of his conversation. I myself was discoursing with Theaetetus yesterday, and I have just been listening to his answers; my namesake I have not yet examined, but I must. Another time will do for me; today let him answer you.

STR. Very good. Young Socrates, do you hear what the elder Socrates is proposing?

YOUNG SOCRATES. I do.

STR. And do you agree to his proposal?

Y. SOC. Certainly.

*Mathematician and follower of Socrates; a speaker in Plato's *Theaetetus* and *Sophist*.

b   STR. As you do not object, still less can I. After the Sophist, then, I think that the Statesman naturally follows next in the order of enquiry. Please say whether he, too, should be ranked among those who have science.

Y. Soc. Yes.

STR. Then the sciences must be divided as before?

Y. Soc. I dare say.

STR. But yet the division will not be the same?

Y. Soc. How then?

c   STR. They will be divided at some other point.

Y. Soc. Maybe so.

STR. Where shall we discover the path of the Statesman? We must find and separate off, and set our seal upon this, and we will set the mark of another class upon all the other diverging paths. Thus the soul will conceive of all kinds of knowledge under two classes.*

Y. Soc. To find the path is your business, Stranger, and not mine.

d   STR. Yes, Socrates, but the discovery, when once made, must be yours as well as mine.

Y. Soc. Very good.

STR. Well, are not arithmetic and certain other kindred arts, merely abstract knowledge, wholly separated from action?

Y. Soc. True.

STR. But in the art of carpentry and all other manual crafts, the knowledge of the workman is merged with his work; he not only knows,

e   but he also makes things which previously did not exist.

Y. Soc. Certainly.

STR. Then let us divide sciences in general into those which are practical and those which are purely intellectual.

Y. Soc. Let us assume these two divisions of science, which is one whole.

STR. And are 'statesman,' 'king,' 'master,' or 'householder,' one and the same; or is there a science or art answering to each of these names? Or rather, allow me to put the matter in another way.

259   Y. Soc. Let me hear.

STR. If anyone who is in a private station has the skill to advise one of the public physicians, must not he also be called a physician?

Y. Soc. Yes.

STR. And if anyone who is in a private station is able to advise the ruler of a country, may not he be said to have the knowledge which the ruler himself ought to have?

---

*That is, statecraft and what is not statecraft.

Y. Soc. True.

Str. But surely the science of a true king is royal science?   b

Y. Soc. Yes.

Str. And will not he who possesses this knowledge, whether he happens to be a ruler or a private man, when regarded only in reference to his art, be truly called 'royal'?

Y. Soc. He certainly ought to be.

Str. And the householder and master are the same?

Y. Soc. Of course.

Str. Again, a large household may be compared to a small State:— will they differ at all, as far as government is concerned?

Y. Soc. They will not.

Str. Then, returning to the point which we were just now discussing, do we not clearly see that there is one science of all of them; and this science may be called either royal or political or economical; we will not quarrel with anyone about the name.   c

Y. Soc. Certainly not.

Str. This, too, is evident, that the king cannot do much with his hands, or with his whole body, towards the maintenance of his empire, compared with what he does by the intelligence and strength of his mind.

Y. Soc. Clearly not.

Str. Then, shall we say that the king has a greater affinity to knowledge than to manual arts and to practical life in general?   d

Y. Soc. Certainly he has.

Str. Then we may put all together as one and the same—statesmanship and the statesman—the kingly science and the king.

Y. Soc. Clearly.

Str. And now we shall only be proceeding in due order if we go on to divide the sphere of knowledge?

Y. Soc. Very good.

Str. Think whether you can find any joint or parting in knowledge.

Y. Soc. Tell me of what sort.

Str. Such as this: You may remember that we made an art of calculation?   e

Y. Soc. Yes.

Str. Which was, unmistakably, one of the arts of knowledge?

Y. Soc. Certainly.

Str. And to this art of calculation which discerns the differences of numbers shall we assign any other function except to pass judgment on their differences?

Y. Soc. How could we?

Str. You know that the master-builder does not work himself, but is the ruler of workmen?

Y. Soc. Yes.

Str. He contributes knowledge, not manual labour?

Y. Soc. True.

Str. And may therefore be justly said to share in theoretical science?

Y. Soc. Quite true.

Str. But he ought not, like the calculator, to regard his functions as at an end when he has formed a judgment; he must assign to the individual workmen their appropriate task until they have completed the work.

Y. Soc. True.

Str. Are not all such sciences, no less than arithmetic and like, subjects of pure knowledge; and is not the difference between the two classes, that the one sort has the power of judging only, and the other of ruling as well?

Y. Soc. That is evident.

Str. May we not very properly say that of all knowledge there are two divisions—one which rules, and the other which judges?

Y. Soc. I should think so.

Str. And when men have anything to do in common, that they should be of one mind is surely a desirable thing?

Y. Soc. Very true.

Str. Then while we are at unity among ourselves, we need not mind about the fancies of others?

Y. Soc. Certainly not.

Str. And now, in which of these divisions shall we place the king? Is he a judge and a kind of spectator? Or shall we assign to him the art of command—for he is a ruler?

Y. Soc. The latter, clearly.

Str. Then we must see whether there is any mark of division in the art of command too. I am inclined to think that there is a distinction similar to that of manufacturer and retail dealer, which parts off the king from the herald.

Y. Soc. How is this?

Str. Why, does not the retailer receive and sell over again the productions of others, which have been sold before?

Y. Soc. Certainly he does.

Str. And is not the herald under command, and does he not receive orders, and in his turn give them to others?

Y. Soc. Very true.

Str. Then shall we mingle the kingly art in the same class with the art of the herald, the interpreter, the boatswain, the prophet, and the numerous kindred arts which exercise command; or, as in the preceding comparison we spoke of manufacturers, or sellers for themselves, and of retailers—seeing, too, that the class of supreme rulers, or rulers for themselves, is almost nameless—shall we make a word following the same analogy, and refer kings to a supreme or ruling-for-self science, leaving the rest to receive a name from someone else? For we are seeking the ruler; and our enquiry is not concerned with him who is not a ruler.

Y. Soc. Very good.

Str. Thus a very fair distinction has been attained between the man 261 who gives his own commands, and him who gives another's. And now let us see if the power of the former allows any further division.

Y. Soc. By all means.

Str. I think that it does; please assist me in making the division.

Y. Soc. At what point?

Str. May not all rulers be supposed to command for the sake of pro- b ducing something?

Y. Soc. Certainly.

Str. Nor is there any difficulty in dividing the things produced into two classes.

Y. Soc. How would you divide them?

Str. Of the whole class, some have life and some are without life.

Y. Soc. True.

Str. And by the help of this distinction we may make, if we please, a subdivision of the section of knowledge which commands.

Y. Soc. At what point?

Str. One part may be set over the production of lifeless, the other of living things; and in this way the whole will be divided. c

Y. Soc. Certainly.

Str. That division, then, is complete; and now we may leave one half, and take up the other; which may also be divided into two.

Y. Soc. Which of the two halves do you mean?

Str. Of course that which exercises command about living things. For, surely, the royal science is not like that of a master-workman, a science presiding over lifeless objects; the king has a nobler function, which is the management and control of living beings. d

Y. Soc. True.

Str. And the breeding and tending of living beings may be observed to be sometimes a tending of the individual; in other cases, a common care of creatures in flocks?

Y. Soc. True.

Str. But the statesman is not a tender of individuals—not like the driver or groom of a single ox or horse; he is rather to be compared with the keeper of a drove of horses or oxen.

Y. Soc. Yes, I see, thanks to you.

e   STR. Shall we call this art of tending many animals together, the art
of managing a herd, or the art of collective management?

Y. SOC. No matter; whichever suggests itself to us in the course of
conversation.

STR. Very good, Socrates; and, if you continue to be not too particular about names, you will be all the richer in wisdom when you are
262   an old man. And now, as you say, leaving the discussion of the name—
can you see a way in which a person, by showing the art of herding to
be of two kinds, may cause that which is now sought amongst twice
the number of things, to be then sought amongst half that number?

Y. SOC. I will try; there appears to me to be one management of men
and another of beasts.

STR. You have certainly divided them in a most straightforward and
manly style; but you have fallen into an error which hereafter I think
that we had better avoid.

Y. SOC. What is the error?

STR. I think that we had better not cut off a single small portion
b   which is not a species, from many larger portions; the part should be
a species. To separate off at once the subject of investigation is a most
excellent plan, if only the separation be rightly made; you were under
the impression that you were right, because you saw that you would
come to man; and this led you to hasten the steps. But you should not
chip off too small a piece, my friend; the safer way is to cut through
the middle; which is also the more likely way of finding classes. Atten-
c   tion to this principle makes all the difference in a process of enquiry.

Y. SOC. What do you mean, Stranger?

STR. I will endeavour to speak more plainly out of love to your
good character, Socrates; and, although I cannot at present entirely explain myself, I will try, as we proceed, to make my meaning a little
clearer.

Y. SOC. What was the error of which, as you say, we were guilty in
our recent division?

STR. The error was just as if someone who wanted to divide the
d   human race, were to divide them after the fashion which prevails in
this part of the world; here they cut off the Hellenes as one species, and
all the other species of mankind, which are innumerable, and have no
ties or common language, they include under the single name of 'barbarians,' and because they have one name they are supposed to be of
one species also. Or suppose that in dividing numbers you were to cut
e   off 10,000 from all the rest, and make of it one species, comprehending the rest under another separate name; you might say that here too
was a single class, because you had given it a single name. However, you
would make a much better and more equal and logical classification of

numbers, if you divided them into odd and even; or of the human species, if you divided them into male and female; and only separated off Lydians or Phrygians, or any other tribe, and arrayed them against the rest of the world, when you could no longer make a division into parts which were also classes.

263

Y. Soc. Very true; but I wish that this distinction between a part and a class could still be made somewhat plainer.

Str. Socrates, you are imposing upon me a very difficult task. We have already digressed further from our original intention than we ought, and you would have us wander still further away. We must now return to our subject; hereafter, when there is a leisure hour, we will follow up the other track; at the same time, I wish you to guard against imagining that you ever heard me declare—

b

Y. Soc. What?

Str. That a class and a part are distinct.

Y. Soc. What did I hear, then?

Str. That a class is necessarily a part, but there is no similar necessity that a part should be a class; that is the view which I should always wish you to attribute to me, Socrates.

Y. Soc. All right.

Str. There is another thing which I should like to know.

c

Y. Soc. What is it?

Str. The point at which we digressed; for, if I am not mistaken, the exact place was at the question, 'Where would you divide the management of herds?' To this you appeared too ready to answer that there were two species of animals; man being one, and all beasts together the other.

Y. Soc. True.

Str. I thought that in taking away a part, you imagined that the remainder formed a class, because a you were able to call them by the common name of beasts.

d

Y. Soc. That again is true.

Str. Suppose now, most courageous of dialecticians, that some wise and understanding creature, such as a crane is reputed to be, were, in imitation of you, to make a similar division, and set up cranes against all other animals to their own special glorification, at the same time jumbling together all the others, including man, under the appellation of beasts, here would be the sort of error which we must try to avoid.

e

Y. Soc. How can we be safe?

Str. If we do not divide the whole class of animals, we shall be less likely to fall into that error.

Y. Soc. Let us not.

Str. Yet, there lay the source of error in our former division.

Y. Soc. How?

STR. You remember how that part of the art of knowledge which was concerned with command had to do with the rearing of living creatures—I mean, with animals in herds?

Y. Soc. Yes.

264   STR. In that case, there was already implied a division of all animals into tame and wild; those whose nature can be tamed are called tame, and those which cannot be tamed are called wild.

Y. Soc. True.

STR. And the political science of which we are in search is and was always concerned with tame animals, and is also confined to gregarious animals.

Y. Soc. Yes.

STR. But then we ought not to divide, as we did, taking the whole class at once. Neither let us be in too great haste to arrive quickly at the
b   political science; for this mistake has already brought upon us the misfortune of which the proverb speaks.

Y. Soc. What misfortune?

STR. The misfortune of too much haste, which is too little speed.

Y. Soc. And all the better, Stranger; we got what we deserved.

STR. Very well: Let us then begin again, and endeavour to divide the collective rearing of animals; for probably the completion of the argument will best show what you are so anxious to know. Tell me, then—

Y. Soc. What?

STR. Have you ever heard, as you very likely may—for I do not sup-
c   pose that you ever actually visited them—of the preserves of fishes in the Nile, and in the ponds of the Great King; or you may have seen similar preserves in wells at home?

Y. Soc. Yes, to be sure, I have seen them, and I have often heard the others described.

STR. And you may have heard also, and may have been assured by report, although you have not travelled in those regions, of nurseries of geese and cranes in the plains of Thessaly?

Y. Soc. Certainly.

d   STR. I asked you, because here is a new division of the management of herds, into the management of land and of water herds.

Y. Soc. There is.

STR. And do you agree that we ought to divide the collective rearing of herds into two corresponding parts, the one the rearing of water, and the other the rearing of land herds?

Y. Soc. Yes.

STR. There is surely no need to ask which of these two contains the
e   royal art, for it is evident to everybody.

Y. Soc. Certainly.

STR. Anyone can divide the herds which feed on dry land?

Y. Soc. How would you divide them?

STR. I should distinguish between those which fly and those which walk.

Y. Soc. Most true.

STR. And where shall we look for the political animal? Might not an idiot, so to speak, know that he is a pedestrian?

Y. Soc. Certainly.

STR. The art of managing the walking animal has to be further divided, just as you might halve an even number.

Y. Soc. Clearly.

STR. Let me note that here appear in view two ways to that part or 265 class which the argument aims at reaching: the one a speedier way, which cuts off a small portion and leaves a large; the other agrees better with the principle which we were laying down, that as far as we can we should divide in the middle; but it is longer. We can take either of them, whichever we please.

Y. Soc. Cannot we have both ways?

STR. Together? What a thing to ask! but, if you take them in turn, you clearly may.

Y. Soc. Then I should like to have them in turn. b

STR. There will be no difficulty, as we are near the end; if we had been at the beginning, or in the middle, I should have demurred to your request; but now, in accordance with your desire, let us begin with the longer way; while we are fresh, we shall get on better. And now attend to the division.

Y. Soc. Let me hear.

STR. The tame walking herding animals are distributed by nature into two classes.

Y. Soc. Upon what principle?

STR. The one grows horns; and the other is without horns.

Y. Soc. Clearly. c

STR. Suppose that you divide the science which manages pedestrian animals into two corresponding parts, and define them; for if you try to invent names for them, you will find the intricacy too great.

Y. Soc. How must I speak of them, then?

STR. In this way: let the science of managing pedestrian animals be divided into two parts, and one part assigned to the horned herd, and the other to the herd that has no horns.

Y. Soc. All that you say has been abundantly proved, and may there- d fore be assumed.

STR. The king is clearly the shepherd of a herd without horns.

Y. Soc. That is evident.

STR. Shall we break up this hornless herd into sections, and endeavour to assign to him what is his?

Y. Soc. By all means.

STR. Shall we distinguish them by their having or not having cloven feet, or by their mixing or not mixing the breed? You know what I mean.

Y. Soc. What?

e   STR. I mean that horses and asses naturally breed from one another.

Y. Soc. Yes.

STR. But the remainder of the hornless herd of tame animals will not mix the breed.

Y. Soc. Very true.

STR. And of which has the Statesman charge, of the mixed or of the unmixed race?

Y. Soc. Clearly of the unmixed.

STR. I suppose that we must divide this again as before.

Y. Soc. We must.

266   STR. Every tame and herding animal has now been split up, with the exception of two species; for I hardly think that dogs should be reckoned among gregarious animals.

Y. Soc. Certainly not; but how shall we divide the two remaining species?

STR. There is a measure of difference which may be appropriately employed by you and Theaetetus, who are students of geometry.

Y. Soc. What is that?

STR. The diagonal; and, again, the diagonal of a diagonal.

Y. Soc. What do you mean?

b   STR. How does man walk, but as a diagonal, or the power of two feet?[1]

Y. Soc. Just so.

STR. And the power of the remaining kind, being the power of twice two feet, may be said to be the diagonal of our diagonal.

Y. Soc. Certainly; and now I think that I pretty nearly understand you.

c   STR. In these divisions, Socrates, I see we have come to a very funny point.

Y. Soc. What is it?

STR. Human beings have come out in the same class with the noblest and most easy-going of creation and have been running a race with them.[2]

Y. Soc. I remark that very singular coincidence.

STR. And would you not expect the slowest to arrive last?

Y. Soc. Indeed I should.

Str. And there is a still more ridiculous consequence, that the king is found running about with the herd, and in close competition with the swineherd, who of all mankind is most of an adept at the easy life.   d

Y. Soc. Certainly.

Str. Then here, Socrates, is still clearer evidence of the truth of what was said in the enquiry about the Sophist.

Y. Soc. What?

Str. That the dialectical method has no respect for people, and does not set the great above the small, but always arrives in her own way at the truest result.

Y. Soc. Clearly.

Str. And now, I will not wait for you to ask me, but will of my own accord take you by the shorter road to the definition of a king.   e

Y. Soc. By all means.

Str. We should have begun at first by dividing land animals into biped and quadruped; and since the winged herd, and that alone, comes out in the same class with man, we should divide bipeds into those which have feathers and those which have not, and when they have been divided, and the art of the management of mankind is brought to light, the time will have come to produce our Statesman and ruler, and set him like a charioteer in his place, and hand over to him the reins of state, for that too is a vocation which belongs to him.

Y. Soc. Very good; you have paid me the debt—I mean, you have   267 completed the argument; and I suppose that you added the digression by way of interest.

Str. Then, let us go back to the beginning, and join the links, which together make the definition of the name of the Statesman's art.

Y. Soc. By all means.

Str. The science of pure knowledge had, as we said originally, a part which was the science of rule or command, and from this was derived another part, which was called command-for-self, on the analogy of selling-for-self; an important section of this was the management of living things, and this again was further limited to the management of   b them in herds, and again in herds of pedestrian animals. The chief division of the latter was the art of managing pedestrian animals which are without horns; this again has a part which can only be comprehended under one term by joining together three names—shepherding   c pure-bred animals. The only further subdivision is the art of man-herding—this has to do with bipeds, and is what we were seeking after, and have now found, being at once the royal and political.

Y. Soc. To be sure.

STR. And do you think, Socrates, that we really have done as you say?

Y. SOC. What?

STR. Do you think, I mean, that we have really fulfilled our intention? There has been a sort of discussion, and yet the investigation
d seems to me not to be perfectly worked out: this is where the enquiry fails.

Y. SOC. I do not understand.

STR. I will try to make the thought, which is at this moment present in my mind, clearer to us both.

Y. SOC. Let me hear.

STR. There were many arts of shepherding, and one of them was the political, which had the charge of one particular herd?

Y. SOC. Yes.

STR. And this the argument defined to be the art of rearing, not horses or other brutes, but the art of rearing man collectively?

Y. SOC. True.

e STR. Note, however, a difference which distinguishes the king from all other shepherds.

Y. SOC. To what do you refer?

STR. I want to ask, whether any one of the other herdsmen has a rival who professes and claims to share with him in the management of the herd?

Y. SOC. What do you mean?

STR. I mean to say that merchants, farmers, providers of food, and also training-masters and physicians, will all contend with the herdsmen of humanity, whom we call Statesmen, declaring that they them-
268 selves have the care of rearing or managing mankind, and that they rear not only the common herd, but also the rulers themselves.

Y. SOC. Are they not right in saying so?

STR. Very likely they may be, and we will consider their claim. But we are certain of this: no one will raise a similar claim against the herdsman, who is allowed on all hands to be the sole and only feeder and physician of his herd; he is also their matchmaker and midwife—no
b one else knows that department of science. And he is their merry-maker and musician, as far as their nature is susceptible of such influences, and no one can console and soothe his own herd better than he can, either with the natural tones of his voice or with instruments. And the same may be said of tenders of animals in general.

Y. SOC. Very true.

STR. But if this is as you say, can our argument about the king be
c true and unimpeachable? Were we right in selecting him out of many other claimants to be the shepherd and rearer of the human flock?

Y. SOC. Surely not.

STR. Had we not reason just now* to apprehend that although we may have described a sort of royal form, we have not as yet accurately worked out the true image of the Statesman, and that we cannot reveal him as he truly is in his own nature, until we have disengaged and separated him from those who hang about him and claim to share in his prerogatives?

Y. Soc. Very true.   d

STR. And that, Socrates, is what we must do, if we are not to bring disgrace upon the argument at its close.

Y. Soc. We must certainly avoid that.

STR. Then let us make a new beginning, and travel by a different road.

Y. Soc. What road?

STR. I think that we may have a little amusement; there is a famous tale, of which a good portion may with advantage be interwoven, and   e
then we may resume our series of divisions, and proceed in the old path until we arrive at the desired summit. Shall we do as I say?

Y. Soc. By all means.

STR. Listen, then, to a tale which a child would love to hear; and you are not too old for childish amusement.

Y. Soc. Let me hear.

STR. There did really happen, and will again happen, like many other events of which ancient tradition has preserved the record, the portent which is traditionally said to have occurred in the quarrel of Atreus and Thyestes. You have heard, no doubt, and remember what they say happened at that time?

Y. Soc. I suppose you mean the sign of the golden lamb.[3]

STR. No, not that but another part of the story, which tells how the   269
sun and the stars once rose in the west, and set in the east, and that the god reversed their motion, and gave them that which they now have as a testimony to the right of Atreus.

Y. Soc. Yes; there is that legend also.

STR. Again, we have been often told of the reign of Cronos.

Y. Soc. Yes, very often.   b

STR. Did you ever hear that the men of former times were earth-born, and not begotten of one another?

Soc. Yes, that is another old tradition.

STR. All these stories, and a million others which are still more wonderful, have a common origin; many of them have been lost in the lapse of ages, or are repeated only in a disconnected form; but the origin

---

*In 267c–d, above.

of them is what no one has told, and may as well be told now; for the
c   tale is suited to throw light on the nature of the king.

SOC. Very good; and I hope that you will give the whole story, and
leave out nothing.

STR. Listen, then. There is a time when god himself guides and
helps to roll the world in its course; and there is a time, on the completion of a certain cycle, when he lets go, and the world being a living creature, and having originally received intelligence from its
d   author and creator, turns about and by an inherent necessity revolves
in the opposite direction.

Y. SOC. Why is that?

STR. Why, because only the most divine things of all remain ever
unchanged and the same, and body is not included in this class. Heaven
and the universe, as we have termed them, although they have been endowed by the creator with many glories, partake of bodily nature, and
therefore cannot be entirely free from perturbation. But their motion
e   is, as far as possible, single and in the same place, and of the same kind;
and is therefore only subject to a reversal, which is the least alteration
possible. For the lord of all moving things is alone able to move of himself; and to think that he moves them at one time in one direction and
at another time in another is blasphemy. Hence we must not say that
the world is either self-moved always, or all made to go round by god
270 in two opposite courses; or that two gods, having opposite purposes,
make it move round. But as I have already said (and this is the only remaining alternative) the world is guided at one time by an external
power which is divine and receives fresh life and immortality from the
renewing hand of the creator, and again, when let go, moves spontaneously, being set free at such a time as to have, during infinite cycles
of years, a reverse movement: this is due to its perfect balance, to its
vast size, and to the fact that it turns on the smallest pivot.

b   Y. SOC. Your account of the world seems to be very reasonable indeed.

STR. Let us now reflect and try to gather from what has been said
the nature of the phenomenon which we affirmed to be the cause of
all these wonders. It is this.

Y. SOC. What?

STR. The reversal which takes place from time to time of the motion of the universe.

Y. SOC. How is that the cause?

c   STR. Of all changes of the heavenly motions, we may consider this
to be the greatest and most complete.

Y. SOC. I should imagine so.

STR. And it may be supposed to result in the greatest changes to the
human beings who are the inhabitants of the world at the time.

Y. Soc. Such changes would naturally occur.

Str. And living things, as we know, survive with difficulty great and serious changes of many different kinds when they come upon them at once.

Y. Soc. Very true.

Str. Hence there necessarily occurs a great destruction of them, which extends also to the life of man; few survivors of the race are left, and those who remain become the subjects of several novel and remarkable phenomena, and of one in particular, which takes place at the time when the transition is made to the cycle opposite to that in which we are now living.

Y. Soc. What is it?

Str. The life of all animals first came to a standstill, and the mortal nature ceased to be or look older, and was then reversed and grew young and delicate; the white locks of the aged darkened again, and the cheeks of the bearded man became smooth, and recovered their former bloom; the bodies of youths in their prime grew softer and smaller, continually by day and night returning and becoming assimilated to the nature of a newly-born child in mind as well as body; in the succeeding stage they wasted away and wholly disappeared. And the bodies of those who died by violence at that time quickly passed through the like changes, and in a few days were no more seen.

Y. Soc. Then how, Stranger, were living things created in those days; and in what way were they begotten of one another?

Str. It is evident, Socrates, that there was no such thing in the then order of nature as the procreation of animals from one another; the earth-born race, of which we hear in story, was the one which existed in those days—they rose again from the ground; and of this tradition, which is now-a-days often unduly discredited, our ancestors, who were nearest in point of time to the end of the last period and came into being at the beginning of this, are to us the heralds. And mark how consistent the sequel of the tale is; after the return of age to youth, follows the return of the dead, who are lying in the earth, to life; simultaneously with the reversal of the world the wheel of their generation has been turned back, and they are put together and rise and live in the opposite order, unless god has carried any of them away to some other lot. According to this tradition they of necessity sprang from the earth and have the name of earth-born, and so the above legend clings to them.

Y. Soc. Certainly that is quite consistent with what has preceded; but tell me, was the life which you said existed in the reign of Cronos in that cycle of the world, or in this? For the change in the course of the stars and the sun must have occurred in both.

d   STR. I see that you are into the story; no, that blessed and spontaneous life does not belong to the present cycle of the world, but to the
previous one, in which god superintended the whole revolution of the
universe; and the several parts of the universe were distributed under
the rule of certain inferior deities, as is the way in some places still.
There were demigods, who were the shepherds of the various species
and herds of animals, and each one was in all respects sufficient for
those of whom he was the shepherd; neither was there any violence,
e   or devouring of one another, or war or quarrel among them; and I
might tell of countless other blessings, which belonged to that dispensation. The reason why the life of man was, as tradition says, spontaneous, is as follows: In those days god himself was their shepherd, and
ruled over them, just as man, who is by comparison a divine being,
still rules over the lower animals. Under him there were no forms of
272   government or separate possession of women and children; for all men
rose again from the earth, having no memory of the past. And although
they had nothing of this sort, the earth gave them fruits in abundance,
which grew on trees and shrubs unbidden, and were not planted by
the hand of man. And they dwelt naked, and mostly in the open air, for
the temperature of their seasons was mild; and they had no beds, but
b   lay on soft couches of grass, which grew plentifully out of the earth.
Such was the life of man in the days of Cronos, Socrates; the character
of our present life, which is said to be under Zeus, you know from
your own experience. Can you, and will you, determine which of them
you deem the happier?

Y. Soc. Impossible.

STR. Then shall I determine for you as well as I can?

Y. Soc. By all means.

STR. Suppose that the nurslings of Cronos, having this boundless
leisure, and the power of conversing not only with men, but also with
c   beasts, had used all these advantages with a view to philosophy, conversing with the beasts as well as with one another, and learning of
every nature which was gifted with any special power, and was able to
contribute some special experience to the store of wisdom, there
would be no difficulty in deciding that they would be a thousand times
happier than the men of our own day. Or, again, if they had merely
eaten and drunk until they were full, and told stories to one another
and to the animals—such stories as are now attributed to them—
d   in this case also, as I should imagine, the answer would be easy. But until
some satisfactory witness can be found of the love of that age for knowledge and discussion, we had better let the matter drop, and give the
reason why we have unearthed this tale, and then we shall be able to
get on. In the fulness of time, when the change was to take place, and

the earth-born race had all perished, and every soul had completed its e
proper cycle of births and been sown in the earth her appointed number
of times, the pilot of the universe let the helm go, and retired to his
place of view; and then fate and innate desire reversed the motion of
the world. Then also all the inferior deities who share the rule of the
supreme power, being informed of what was happening, let go the
parts of the world which were under their control. And the world turn- 273
ing round with a sudden shock, being impelled in an opposite direction from beginning to end, was shaken by a mighty earthquake, which
wrought a destruction of all manner of animals. Afterwards, when sufficient time had elapsed, the tumult and confusion and earthquake
ceased, and the universe, once more at peace, attained to a calm, and
settled down into its own orderly and accustomed course, having the
charge and rule of itself and of all the creatures which are contained in b
it, and executing, as far as it remembered them, the instructions of its
father and creator, more precisely at first, but afterwards with less ex-
actness. The reason of the falling off was the admixture of matter in it;
this was inherent in the primal nature, which was full of disorder, until
attaining to the present order. From god, the constructor, the world received all that is good in it, but from a previous state came elements of
evil and unrighteousness, which, thence derived, first of all passed into c
the world, and were then transmitted to the living things. While the
world was aided by the pilot in nurturing the living things, the evil was
small, and great the good which it produced, but after the separation,
when the world was let go, at first all proceeded well enough; but, as
time went on, there was more and more forgetting, and the old discord d
again held sway and burst forth in full glory; and at last small was the
good, and great was the admixture of evil, and there was a danger of
universal ruin to the world, and to the things contained in it. Wherefore god, the orderer of all, in his tender care, seeing that the world was
in great straits, and fearing that all might be dissolved in the storm and
disappear in infinite chaos, again seated himself at the helm; and bringing back the elements which had fallen into dissolution and disorder
to the motion which had prevailed under his dispensation, he set them
in order and restored them, and made the world imperishable and im- e
mortal. And this is the whole tale, of which the first part will suffice to
illustrate the nature of the king. For when the world turned towards the
present cycle of generation, the age of man again stood still, and a
change opposite to the previous one was the result. The small creatures
which had almost disappeared grew in stature, and the newly-born
children of the earth became grey and died and sank into the earth again. 274
All things changed, imitating and following the condition of the universe, and of necessity agreeing with that in their mode of conception

and generation and nurture; for no living thing was any longer allowed to come into being in the earth through the agency of other creative beings, but as the world was ordained to be the lord of his own progress, in like manner the parts were ordained to grow and generate and give nourishment, as far as they could, of themselves, impelled by

b   a similar movement. And so we have arrived at the real end of this discourse; for although there might be much to tell of the lower animals, and of the condition out of which they changed and of the causes of the change, about men there is not much, and that little is more to the purpose. Deprived of the care of god, who had possessed and tended them, they were left helpless and defenseless, and were torn in pieces by the beasts, who were naturally fierce and had now grown wild. And

c   in the first ages they were still without skill or resource; the food which once grew spontaneously had failed, and as yet they knew not how to procure it, because they had never felt the pressure of necessity. For all these reasons they were in a great strait; wherefore also the gifts spoken of in the old tradition were imparted to man by the gods, together with so much teaching and education as was indispensable; fire was given to them by Prometheus, the arts by Hephaestus and his fellow-

d   worker, Athene, seeds and plants by others. From these is derived all that has helped to frame human life; since the care of the gods, as I was saying, had now failed men, and they had to order their course of life for themselves, and were their own masters, just like the universe whom they imitate and follow, ever changing, as he changes, and ever living and growing, at one time in one manner, and at another time in an-

e   other. Enough of the story, which may be of use in showing us how greatly we erred in the delineation of the king and the statesman in our previous discourse.

Y. Soc. What was this great error of which you speak?

Str. There were two; the first a lesser one, the other was an error on a much larger and grander scale.

Y. Soc. What do you mean?

275   Str. I mean to say that when we were asked about a king and Statesman of the present cycle and generation, we told of a shepherd of a human flock who belonged to the other cycle, and of one who was a god when he ought to have been a man; and this was a great error. Again, we declared him to be the ruler of the entire State, without explaining how: this was not the whole truth, nor very intelligible; but still it was true, and therefore the second error was not so great as the first.

Y. Soc. Very good.

Str. Before we can expect to have a perfect description of the Statesman we must define the nature of his office.

Y. Soc. Certainly.

Str. And the myth was introduced in order to show, not only that   b
all others are rivals of the true shepherd who is the object of our search,
but in order that we might have a clearer view of him who is alone
worthy to receive this appellation, because he alone of shepherds and
herdsmen, according to the image which we have employed, has the
care of human beings.

Y. Soc. Very true.

Str. And I cannot help thinking, Socrates, that the form of the divine shepherd is even higher than that of a king; whereas the statesmen   c
who are now on earth seem to be much more like their subjects in
character, and much more nearly to partake of their breeding and education.

Y. Soc. Certainly.

Str. Still they must be investigated all the same, to see whether, like
the divine shepherd, they are above their subjects or on a level with
them.

Y. Soc. Of course.

Str. To resume: Do you remember that we spoke of an art of self-
command as part of the rule over living things, not singly but collectively, which we called the art of rearing a herd?   d

Y. Soc. Yes, I remember.

Str. There, somewhere, lay our error; for we never included or
mentioned the Statesman; and we did not observe that he had no place
in our nomenclature.

Y. Soc. How was that?

Str. All other herdsmen 'rear' their herds, but this is not a suitable
term to apply to the Statesman; we should use a name which is common to them all.   e

Y. Soc. True, if there be such a name.

Str. Why, is not 'care' of herds applicable to all? For this implies no
feeding, or any special duty; if we say either 'tending' the herds, or
'managing' the herds, or 'having the care' of them, the same word will
include all, and then we may wrap up the Statesman with the rest, as
the argument seems to require.

Y. Soc. Quite right; but how shall we take the next step in the divi-   276
sion?

Str. As before we divided the art of 'rearing' herds accordingly as
they were land or water herds, winged and wingless, mixing or not
mixing the breed, horned and hornless, so we may divide by these
same differences the 'tending' of herds, comprehending in our definition the kingship of today and the rule of Cronos.

Y. Soc. That is clear; but I still ask what is to follow.

STR. If the word had been 'managing' herds, instead of feeding or
b rearing them, no one would have argued that there was no care of men
in the case of the politician, although it was justly contended that there
was no human art of feeding them which was worthy of the name, or
at least, if there were, many a man had a prior and greater right to share
in such an art than any king.

Y. Soc. True.

STR. But no other art or science will have a prior or better right
than the royal science to care for human society and to rule over men
c in general.

Y. Soc. Quite true.

STR. In the next place, Socrates, we must surely notice that a great
error was committed at the end of our analysis.

Y. Soc. What was it?

STR. Why, supposing we were ever so sure that there is such an art
as the art of rearing or feeding bipeds, there was no reason why we
should call this the royal or political art, as though there were no more
to be said.

Y. Soc. Certainly not.

STR. Our first duty, as we were saying, was to remodel the name, so
d as to have the notion of care rather than of feeding, and then to divide,
for there may be still considerable divisions.

Y. Soc. How can they be made?

STR. First, by separating the divine shepherd from the human
guardian or manager.

Y. Soc. True.

STR. And the art of management which is assigned to man would
again have to be subdivided.

Y. Soc. On what principle?

STR. On the principle of voluntary and compulsory.

Y. Soc. Why?

e STR. Because, if I am not mistaken, there has been an error here; for
our simplicity led us to rank king and tyrant together, whereas they are
utterly distinct, like their modes of government.

Y. Soc. True.

STR. Then, now, as I said, let us make the correction and divide human
care into two parts, on the principle of voluntary and compulsory.

Y. Soc. Certainly.

STR. And if we call the management of violent rulers tyranny, and
the voluntary management of herds of voluntary bipeds politics, may
we not further assert that he who has this latter art of management is
the true king and Statesman?

Y. Soc. I think, Stranger, that we have now completed the account of 277 the Statesman.

Str. I wish we had, Socrates, but I have to satisfy myself as well as you; and in my judgment the figure of the king is not yet perfected; like statuaries who, in their too great haste, having overdone the several parts of their work, lose time in cutting them down, so too we, b partly out of haste, partly out of a magnanimous desire to expose our former error, and also because we imagined that a king required grand illustrations, have taken up a marvellous lump of fable, and have been obliged to use more than was necessary. This made us discourse at large, and, nevertheless, the story never came to an end. And our discussion might be compared to a picture of some living being which had been fairly drawn in outline, but had not yet attained the life and clearness c which is given by the blending of colours. Now to intelligent persons a living being had better be delineated by language and discourse than by any painting or work of art: to the duller sort by works of art.

Y. Soc. Very true; but what is the imperfection which still remains? I wish that you would tell me.

Str. The higher ideas, my dear friend, can hardly be set forth ex- d cept through the medium of examples; every man seems to know all things in a dreamy sort of way, and then again to wake up and to know nothing.

Y. Soc. What do you mean?

Str. I fear that I have been unfortunate in raising a question about our experience of knowledge.

Y. Soc. Why so?

Str. Why, because my 'example' requires the assistance of another example.

Y. Soc. Proceed; you need not fear that I shall tire. e

Str. I will proceed, finding, as I do, such a ready listener in you: when children are beginning to know their letters—

Y. Soc. What are you going to say?

Str. That they distinguish the several letters well enough in very short and easy syllables, and are able to tell them correctly. 278

Y. Soc. Certainly.

Str. Whereas in other syllables they do not recognize them, and think and speak falsely of them.

Y. Soc. Very true.

Str. Will not the best and easiest way of bringing them to a knowledge of what they do not as yet know be—

Y. Soc. Be what?

Str. To refer them first of all to cases in which they judge correctly

about the letters in question, and then to compare these with the cases
b in which they do not as yet know, and to show them that the letters are
the same, and have the same character in both combinations, until all
cases in which they are right have been placed side by side with all cases
in which they are wrong. In this way they have examples, and are made
to learn that each letter in every combination is always the same and
c not another, and is always called by the same name.

Y. Soc. Certainly.

STR. Are not examples formed in this manner? We take a thing and
compare it with another distinct instance of the same thing, of which
we have a right conception, and out of the comparison there arises one
true notion, which includes both of them.

Y. Soc. Exactly.

d STR. Can we wonder, then, that the soul has the same uncertainty
about the alphabet of things, and sometimes and in some cases is firmly
fixed by the truth in each particular, and then, again, in other cases is
altogether at sea; having somehow or other a correct notion of combinations; but when the elements are transferred into the long and difficult language (syllables) of facts, is again ignorant of them?

Y. Soc. There is nothing wonderful in that.

STR. Could anyone, my friend, who began with false opinion ever
e expect to arrive even at a small portion of truth and to attain wisdom?

Y. Soc. Hardly.

STR. Then you and I will not be far wrong in trying to see the
nature of example in general in a small and particular instance; afterwards from lesser things we intend to pass to the royal class, which is
the highest form of the same nature, and endeavour to discover by
rules of art what the management of cities is; and then the dream will
become a reality to us.

Y. Soc. Excellent plan.

279 STR. Then, once more, let us resume the previous argument, and as
there were innumerable rivals of the royal race who claim to have the
care of States, let us part them all off, and leave him alone; and, as I was
saying, a model or example of this process has first to be framed.

Y. Soc. Exactly.

STR. What model is there which is small, and yet has any analogy
b with the political occupation? Suppose, Socrates, that if we have no other
example at hand, we choose weaving, or, more precisely, weaving of
wool—this will be quite enough, without taking the whole of weaving, to illustrate our meaning?

Y. Soc. Certainly.

STR. Why should we not apply to weaving the same processes of division and subdivision which we have already applied to other classes,

going once more as rapidly as we can through all the steps until we come   c
to that which is needed for our purpose?

Y. Soc. How do you mean?

Str. I shall reply by actually performing the process.

Y. Soc. Very good.

Str. All things which we make or acquire are either creative or preventive; of the preventive class are antidotes, divine and human, and also
defenses; and defenses are either military weapons or protections; and   d
protections are veils, and also shields against heat and cold, and shields
against heat and cold are shelters and coverings; and coverings are blankets and garments; and garments are some of them in one piece, and
others are made in several parts; and of these latter some are stitched,
others are fastened and not stitched; and of the not stitched, some are
made of the sinews of plants, and some of hair; and of these, again, some   e
are cemented with water and earth, and others are fastened together by
themselves. And these last defenses and coverings which are fastened
together by themselves are called clothes, and the art which superin-
tends them we may call, from the nature of the operation, the art of
clothing, just as before the art of the Statesman was derived from the   280
State; and may we not say that the art of weaving, at least that largest
portion of it which was concerned with the making of clothes, differs
only in name from this art of clothing, in the same way that, in the previous case, the royal science differed from the political?

Y. Soc. Most true.

Str. In the next place, let us observe that the art of weaving clothes,
which an incompetent person might fancy to have been sufficiently de-   b
scribed, has been separated off from several others which are of the
same family, but not from the co-operative arts.

Y. Soc. And which are the kindred arts?

Str. I see that I have not taken you with me. So I think that we had
better go backwards, starting from the end. We just now parted off
from the weaving of clothes, the making of blankets, which differ from
each other in that one is put under and the other is put around! and
these are what I termed kindred arts.

Y. Soc. I understand.

Str. And we have subtracted the manufacture of all articles made of   c
flax and cords, and all that we just now metaphorically termed the
sinews of plants, and we have also separated off the process of felting
and the putting together of materials by stitching and sewing, of which
the most important part is the cobbler's art.

Y. Soc. Precisely.

Str. Then we separated off the tanner's art, which prepared coverings
in entire pieces, and the art of sheltering, and subtracted the various arts

of making water-tight which are employed in building, and in general
d in carpentry, and in other crafts, and all such arts as furnish impediments to thieving and acts of violence, and are concerned with making
the lids of boxes and the fixing of doors, being divisions of the art of
joining; and we also cut off the manufacture of arms, which is a section of the great and manifold art of making defenses; and we originally began by parting off the whole of the magic art which is concerned
e with antidotes, and have left, as would appear, the very art of which we
were in search, the art of protection against winter cold, which fabri-
cates woollen defenses, and has the name of weaving.

Y. Soc. Very true.

281   STR. Yes, my boy, but that is not all; for the first process to which the
material is subjected is the opposite of weaving.

Y. Soc. How so?

STR. Weaving is a sort of uniting?

Y. Soc. Yes.

STR. But the first process is a separation of the clotted and matted
fibres?

Y. Soc. What do you mean?

STR. I mean the work of the carder's art; for we cannot say that carding is weaving, or that the carder is a weaver.

Y. Soc. Certainly not.

STR. Again, if a person were to say that the art of making the warp
and the woof was the art of weaving, he would say what was paradox-
b ical and false.

Y. Soc. To be sure.

STR. Shall we say that the whole art of the fuller or of the mender
has nothing to do with the care and treatment of clothes, or are we to
regard all these as arts of weaving?

Y. Soc. Certainly not.

STR. And yet surely all these arts will maintain that they are concerned with the treatment and production of clothes; they will dispute
the exclusive prerogative of weaving, and though assigning a larger
sphere to that, will still reserve a considerable field for themselves.

c   Y. Soc. Very true.

STR. Besides these, there are the arts which make tools and instruments of weaving, and which will claim at least to be co-operative
causes in every work of the weaver.

Y. Soc. Most true.

STR. Well, then, suppose that we define weaving, or rather that part
of it which has been selected by us, to be the greatest and noblest of arts
d which are concerned with woollen garments—shall we be right? Is not

the definition, although true, wanting in clearness and completeness; for do not all those other arts require to be first cleared away?

Y. Soc. True.

Str. Then the next thing will be to separate them, in order that the argument may proceed in a regular manner?

Y. Soc. By all means.

Str. Let us consider, in the first place, that there are two kinds of arts entering into everything which we do.

Y. Soc. What are they?

Str. The one kind is the conditional or co-operative, the other the principal cause.

Y. Soc. What do you mean?

Str. The arts which do not manufacture the actual thing, but which furnish the necessary tools for the manufacture, without which the several arts could not fulfil their appointed work, are co-operative; but those which make the things themselves are causal.

Y. Soc. A very reasonable distinction.

Str. Thus the arts which make spindles, combs, and other instruments of the production of clothes, may be called co-operative, and those which treat and fabricate the things themselves, causal.

Y. Soc. Very true.

Str. The arts of washing and mending, and the other preparatory arts which belong to the causal class, and form a division of the great art of adornment, may be all comprehended under what we call the fuller's art.

Y. Soc. Very good.

Str. Carding and spinning threads and all the parts of the process which are concerned with the actual manufacture of a woollen garment form a single art, which is one of those universally acknowledged,— the art of working in wool.

Y. Soc. To be sure.

Str. Of working in wool, again, there are two divisions, and both these are parts of two arts at once.

Y. Soc. How is that?

Str. Carding and one half of the use of the comb, and the other processes of wool-working which separate the composite, may be classed together as belonging both to the art of wool-working, and also to one of the two great arts which are of universal application—the art of composition and the art of division.

Y. Soc. Yes.

Str. To the latter belong carding and the other processes of which I was just now speaking; the art of discernment or division in wool and yarn, which is effected in one manner with the comb and in another with the hands, is variously described under all the names which I just now mentioned.

Y. Soc. Very true.

Str. Again, let us take some process of wool-working which is also a portion of the art of composition, and, dismissing the elements of division which we found there, make two halves, one on the principle of composition, and the other on the principle of division.

Y. Soc. All right.

Str. And once more, Socrates, we must divide the part which be-
d longs at once both to wool-working and composition, if we are ever to discover satisfactorily the aforesaid art of weaving.

Y. Soc. We must.

Str. Yes, certainly, and let us call one part of the art the art of twisting threads, the other the art of combining them.

Y. Soc. Do I understand you, in speaking of twisting, to be referring to manufacture of the warp?

Str. Yes, and of the woof too; how, if not by twisting, is the woof made?

Y. Soc. There is no other way.

e Str. Then suppose that you define the warp and the woof, for I think that the definition will be of use to you.

Y. Soc. How shall I define them?

Str. Thus: a piece of carded wool which is drawn out lengthwise and breadthwise is said to be pulled out.

Y. Soc. Yes.

Str. And the wool thus prepared, when twisted by the spindle, and made into a firm thread, is called the warp, and the art which regulates these operations the art of spinning the warp.

Y. Soc. True.

Str. And the threads which are more loosely spun, having a softness proportioned to the intertexture of the warp and to the degree of
283 force used in dressing the cloth—the threads which are thus spun are called the woof, and the art which is set over them may be called the art of spinning the woof.

Y. Soc. Very true.

Str. And, now, there can be no mistake about the nature of the part of weaving which we have undertaken to define. For when that part of the art of composition which is employed in the working of wool forms a web by the regular intertexture of warp and woof, the entire woven substance is called by us a woollen garment, and the art which presides over this is the art of weaving.

Y. Soc. Very true.

STR. But why did we not say at once that weaving is the art of en- b
twining warp and woof, instead of making a long and useless circuit?

Y. SOC. I thought, Stranger, that there was nothing useless in what
was said.

STR. Very likely, but you may not always think so, my sweet friend;
and in case any feeling of dissatisfaction should hereafter arise in your
mind, as it very well may, let me lay down a principle which will apply c
to arguments in general.

Y. SOC. Proceed.

STR. Let us begin by considering the whole nature of excess and defect, and then we shall have a rational ground on which we may praise
or blame too much length or too much shortness in discussions of this
kind.

Y. SOC. Let us do so.

STR. The points on which I think that we ought to dwell are the
following—

Y. SOC. What?

STR. Length and shortness, excess and defect; with all of these the d
art of measurement is conversant.

Y. SOC. Yes.

STR. And the art of measurement has to be divided into two parts,
with a view to our present purpose.

Y. SOC. Where would you make the division?

STR. Thus: I would make two parts, one having regard to the rela-
tivity of greatness and smallness to each other; and there is another,
without which the existence of production would be impossible.

Y. SOC. What do you mean?

STR. Do you not think that it is only natural for the greater to be
called greater with reference to the less alone, and the less less with reference to the greater alone?   e

Y. SOC. Yes.

STR. Well, but is there not also something exceeding and exceeded
by the principle of the mean, both in speech and action, and is not this
a reality, and the chief mark of difference between good and bad men?

Y. SOC. Plainly.

STR. Then we must suppose that the great and small exist and are
discerned in both these ways, and not, as we were saying before, only
relatively to one another, but there must also be another comparison of
them with the mean or ideal standard; would you like to hear the reason why?

Y. SOC. Certainly.

STR. If we assume the greater to exist only in relation to the less, 284
there will never be any comparison of either with the mean.

Y. Soc. True.

Str. And would not this doctrine be the ruin of all the arts and their creations; would not the art of the Statesman and the aforesaid art of weaving disappear? For all these arts are on the watch against excess and defect, not as unrealities, but as real evils, which occasion a difficulty in action; and the excellence of beauty of every work of art is due
b to this observance of measure.

Y. Soc. Certainly.

Str. But if the science of the Statesman disappears, the search for the royal science will be impossible.

Y. Soc. Very true.

Str. Well, then, as in the case of the Sophist we extorted the inference that not-being had an existence, because here was the point at which the argument eluded our grasp, so in this we must endeavour to show that the greater and less are not only to be measured with one
c another, but also have to do with the production of the mean; for if this is not admitted, neither a statesman nor any other man of action can be an undisputed master of his science.

Y. Soc. Yes, we must certainly do again what we did then.

Str. But this, Socrates, is a greater work than the other, of which we only too well remember the length. I think, however, that we may fairly assume something of this sort—

Y. Soc. What?

d Str. That we shall some day require this notion of a mean with a view to the demonstration of absolute truth; meanwhile, the argument that the very existence of the arts must be held to depend on the possibility of measuring more or less, not only with one another, but also with a view to the attainment of the mean, seems to afford a grand support and satisfactory proof of the doctrine which we are maintaining; for if there are arts, there is a standard of measure, and if there is a standard of measure, there are arts; but if either is wanting, there is neither.

e Y. Soc. True; and what is the next step?

Str. The next step clearly is to divide the art of measurement into two parts, as we have said already, and to place in the one part all the arts which measure number, length, depth, breadth, swiftness with their opposites; and to have another part in which they are measured with the mean, and the fit, and the opportune, and the due, and with all those words, in short, which denote a mean or standard removed from the extremes.

Y. Soc. Here are two vast divisions, embracing two very different spheres.

285 Str. There are many accomplished men, Socrates, who say, believing themselves to speak wisely, that the art of measurement is universal, and

has to do with all things. And this means what we are now saying; for all things which come within the province of art do certainly in some sense partake of measure. But these persons, because they are not accustomed to distinguish things according to real classes, jumble together two widely different things, in relation to one another, and to a standard, under the idea that they are the same, and also fall into the converse error of dividing other things not according to their real parts. Whereas the right way is, if a man has first seen the unity of things, to go on with the enquiry and not desist until he has found all the differences contained in it which form distinct classes; nor again should he be able to rest contented with the manifold diversities which are seen in a multitude of things until he has comprehended all of them that have any affinity within the bounds of one similarity and embraced them within the reality of a single kind. But we have said enough on this, and also of excess and defect; we have only to bear in mind that two divisions of the art of measurement have been discovered which are concerned with them, and not forget what they are.

Y. Soc. We will not forget.

Str. And now that this discussion is completed, let us go on to consider another question, which concerns not this argument only but the conduct of such arguments in general.

Y. Soc. What is this new question?

Str. Take the case of a child who is engaged in learning his letters: when he is asked what letters make up a word, should we say that the question is intended to improve his grammatical knowledge of that particular word, or of all words?

Y. Soc. Clearly, in order that he may have a better knowledge of all words.

Str. And is our enquiry about the Statesman intended only to improve our knowledge of politics, or our power of reasoning generally?

Y. Soc. Clearly, as in the former example, the purpose is general.

Str. Still less would any rational man seek to analyse the notion of weaving for its own sake. But people seem to forget that some things have sensible images, which are readily known, and can be easily pointed out when any one desires to answer an enquirer without any trouble or argument; whereas the greatest and highest truths have no outward image of themselves visible to man, which he who wishes to satisfy the soul of the enquirer can adapt to the eye of sense, and therefore we ought to train ourselves to give and accept a rational account of them; for immaterial things, which are the noblest and greatest, are shown only in thought and idea, and in no other way, and all that we are now saying is said for the sake of them. It is easier, however, to discuss with the mind on small matters than on great.

Y. Soc. Very good.

Str. Let us call to mind the bearing of all this.

Y. Soc. What is it?

Str. I wanted to get rid of any impression of tediousness which we may have experienced in the discussion about weaving, and the reversal of the universe, and in the discussion concerning the Sophist and the being of not-being. I know that they were felt to be too long, and c I reproached myself with this, fearing that they might be not only tedious but irrelevant; and all that I have now said is only designed to prevent the recurrence of any such disagreeable things in the future.

Y. Soc. Very good. Will you proceed?

Str. Then I would like to observe that you and I, remembering what has been said, should praise or blame the length or shortness of discussions, not by comparing them with one another, but with what d is fitting, having regard to the part of measurement, which, as we said, was to be borne in mind.

Y. Soc. Very true.

Str. And yet, not everything is to be judged even with a view to what is fitting; for we should only want such a length as is suited to give pleasure, if at all, as a secondary matter; and reason tells us, that we should be contented to make the ease or rapidity of an enquiry, not our first, but our second object; the first and highest of all being to assert the great method of division according to species—whether the e discourse be shorter or longer is not the point. No offence should be taken at length, but the longer and shorter are to be employed indifferently, according to which of them is better calculated to sharpen the wits of the auditors. Reason would also say to him who censures the length of discourses on such occasions and cannot away with their circumlocution, that he should not be in such a hurry to have done with 287 them, when he can only complain that they are tedious, but he should prove that if they had been shorter they would have made those who took part in them better dialecticians, and more capable of expressing the truth of things; about any other praise and blame, he need not trouble himself—he should pretend not to hear them. But we have had b enough of this, as you will probably agree with me in thinking. Let us return to our Statesman, and apply to his case the aforesaid example of weaving.

Y. Soc. Very good; let us do as you say.

Str. The art of the king has been separated from the similar arts of shepherds, and, indeed, from all those which have to do with herds at all. There still remain, however, of the causal and co-operative arts those which are immediately concerned with States, and which must first be distinguished from one another.

Y. Soc. Very good.

Str. You know that these arts cannot easily be divided into two c halves; the reason will be very evident as we proceed.

Y. Soc. Then we had better do so.

Str. We must carve them like a victim into members or limbs, since we cannot bisect them. For we certainly should divide everything into as few parts as possible.

Y. Soc. What is to be done in this case?

Str. What we did in the example of weaving—all those arts which furnish the tools were regarded by us as co-operative.

Y. Soc. Yes.

Str. So now, and with still more reason, all arts which make any d implement in a State, whether great or small, may be regarded by us as co-operative, for without them neither State nor Statesmanship would be possible; and yet we are not inclined to say that any of them is a product of the kingly art.

Y. Soc. No, indeed.

Str. The task of separating this class from others is not an easy one; for there is plausibility in saying that anything in the world is the in- strument of doing something. But there is another class of possessions in a city, of which I have a word to say. e

Y. Soc. What class do you mean?

Str. A class which may be described as not having this power; that is to say, not like an instrument, framed for production, but designed for the preservation of that which is produced.

Y. Soc. To what do you refer?

Str. To the class of vessels, as they are comprehensively termed, which are constructed for the preservation of things moist and dry, of things prepared in the fire or out of the fire; this is a very large class, 288 and has, if I am not mistaken, literally nothing to do with the royal art of which we are in search.

Y. Soc. Certainly not.

Str. There is also a third class of possessions to be noted, different from these and very extensive, moving or resting on land or water, honourable and also dishonourable. The whole of this class has one name, because it is intended to be sat upon, being always a seat for something.

Y. Soc. What is it?

Str. A vehicle, which is certainly not the work of the Statesman, but of the carpenter, potter, and coppersmith.

Y. Soc. I understand. b

Str. And is there not a fourth class which is again different, and in which most of the things formerly mentioned are contained—every kind of dress, most sorts of arms, walls and enclosures, whether of earth or stone, and lots of other things, all of which being made for the sake of defense, may be truly called defenses, and are for the most part to be regarded as the work of the builder or of the weaver, rather than of the Statesman.

c   Y. Soc. Certainly.

Str. Shall we add a fifth class, of ornamentation and drawing, and of the imitations produced by drawing and music, which are designed for amusement only, and may be fairly comprehended under one name?

Y. Soc. What is it?

Str. "Entertainment" is the name.

Y. Soc. Certainly.

Str. That one name may be fitly predicated of all of them, for none

d   of these things have a serious purpose—amusement is their sole aim.

Y. Soc. That again I understand.

Str. Then there is a class which provides materials for all these, out of which and in which the arts already mentioned fabricate their works—this manifold class, I say, which is the creation and offspring of many other arts, may I not rank sixth?

Y. Soc. What do you mean?

Str. I am referring to gold, silver, and other metals, and all that

e   wood-cutting and shearing of every sort provides for the art of carpentry and plaiting; and there is the process of barking and stripping the cuticle of plants, and the tanner's art, which strips off the skins of animals, and other similar arts which manufacture corks and papyri and cords, and provide for the manufacture of composite species out of simple kinds—the whole class may be termed the primitive and simple possession of man, and with this the kingly science has no concern at all.

Y. Soc. True.

289   Str. The provision of food and of all other things which mingle their particles with the particles of the human body, and minister to the body, will form a seventh class, which may be called by the general term of nourishment, unless you have any better name to offer. This, however, appertains rather to the farmer, huntsman, trainer, doctor, cook, and is not to be assigned to the Statesman's art.

Y. Soc. Certainly not.

Str. These seven classes include nearly every description of prop-

b   erty, with the exception of tame animals. Consider—there was the original material, which ought to have been placed first; next come instruments, vessels, vehicles, defenses, entertainment, nourishment; small things, which may be included under one of these—for example, coins, seals and stamps—are omitted, for they have not in them the character of any larger kind which includes them; but some of them may, with a little forcing, be placed among ornaments, and others may be made to harmonize with the class of implements. The art of herding, which has been already divided into parts, will include all property in tame animals, except slaves.

Y. Soc. Very true.

Str. The class of slaves and ministers only remains, and I suspect that in this the real aspirants for the throne, who are the rivals of the king in the formation of the political web, will be discovered; just as spinners, carders, and the rest of them, were the rivals of the weaver. All the others, who were termed co-operators, have been got rid of among the occupations already mentioned, and separated from the royal and political science.

Y. Soc. I agree.

Str. Let us go a little nearer, in order that we may be more certain of the complexion of this remaining class.

Y. Soc. Let us do so.

Str. We shall find from our present point of view that the greatest servants are in a case and condition which is the reverse of what we anticipated.

Y. Soc. Who are they?

Str. Those who have been purchased, and have so become possessions; these are unmistakably slaves, and certainly do not claim royal science.

Y. Soc. Certainly not.

Str. Again, freemen who of their own accord become the servants of the other classes in a State, and who exchange and equalise the products of farming and the other arts, some sitting in the market-place, others going from city to city by land or sea, and giving money in exchange for money or for other productions—the money-changer, the merchant, the ship-owner, the retailer, will not put in any claim to statecraft or politics?

Y. Soc. No; unless, indeed, to the politics of commerce.

Str. But surely men whom we see acting as hirelings and serfs, and too happy to turn their hand to anything, will not profess to share in royal science?

Y. Soc. Certainly not.

Str. But what would you say of some other serviceable officials?

Y. Soc. Who are they, and what services do they perform?

Str. There are heralds, and scribes perfected by practice, and others who have great skill in various sorts of business connected with the government of states—what shall we call them?

Y. Soc. They are the officials, and servants of the rulers, as you just now called them, but not themselves rulers.

STR. There may be something strange in any servant pretending to
c   be a ruler, and yet I do not think that I could have been dreaming when
I imagined that the principal claimants to political science would be
found somewhere in this neighbourhood.

Y. Soc. Very true.

STR. Well, let us draw nearer, and try the claims of some who have
not yet been tested; in the first place, there are diviners, who have a
portion of servile or ministerial science, and are thought to be the interpreters of the gods to men.

Y. Soc. True.

d   STR. There is also the priestly class, who, as the law declares, know
how to give the gods gifts from men in the form of sacrifices which
are acceptable to them, and to ask on our behalf blessings in return from
them. Now both these are branches of the servile or ministerial art.

Y. Soc. Yes, clearly.

STR. And here I think that we seem to be getting on the right track;
for the priest and the diviner are swollen with pride and prerogative,
e   and they create an awful impression of themselves by the magnitude of
their enterprises; in Egypt, the king himself is not allowed to reign, unless he has priestly powers, and if he should be of another class and has
thrust himself in, he must get enrolled in the priesthood. In many parts
of the Greek world, the duty of offering the most solemn propitiatory
sacrifices is assigned to the highest magistracies, and here, at Athens, the
most solemn and national of the ancient sacrifices are supposed to be
celebrated by him who has been chosen by lot to be the King Archon.

Y. Soc. Precisely.

291   STR. But who are these other kings and priests elected by lot who
now come into view followed by their retainers and a vast throng, as
the former class disappears and the scene changes?

Y. Soc. Whom can you mean?

STR. They are a strange crew.

Y. Soc. Why strange?

STR. A minute ago I thought that they were animals of every tribe;
for many of them are like lions and centaurs, and many more like satyrs
b   and such weak and shifty creatures—Protean shapes quickly changing
into one another's forms and natures; and now, Socrates, I begin to see
who they are.

Y. Soc. Who are they? You seem to be gazing on some strange vision.

STR. Yes; everyone looks strange when you do not know him; and
just now I myself fell into this mistake—at first sight, coming suddenly
c   upon him, I did not recognize the politician and his troop.

Y. Soc. Who is he?

STR. The chief of Sophists and most accomplished of wizards, who must at any cost be separated from the true king or Statesman, if we are ever to see daylight in the present enquiry.

Y. Soc. That is a hope not lightly to be renounced.

Str. Never, if I can help it; and, first, let me ask you a question.

Y. Soc. What?

Str. Is not monarchy a recognized form of government?   d

Y. Soc. Yes.

Str. And, after monarchy, next in order comes the government of the few?

Y. Soc. Of course.

Str. Is not the third form of government the rule of the multitude, which is called by the name of democracy?

Y. Soc. Certainly.

Str. And do not these three expand in a manner into five, producing out of themselves two other names?

Y. Soc. What are they?

Str. There is a criterion of voluntary and involuntary, poverty and   e riches, law and the absence of law, which men now-a-days apply to them; the two first they subdivide accordingly, and ascribe to monarchy two forms and two corresponding names, royalty and tyranny.

Y. Soc. Very true.

Str. And the government of the few they distinguish by the names of aristocracy and oligarchy.

Y. Soc. Certainly.

Str. Democracy alone, whether rigidly observing the laws or not,   292 and whether the multitude rule over the men of property with their consent or against their consent, always in ordinary language has the same name.

Y. Soc. True.

Str. But do you suppose that any form of government which is defined by these characteristics of the one, the few, or the many, of poverty or wealth, of voluntary or compulsory submission, of written law or the absence of law, can be a right one?

Y. Soc. Why not?   b

Str. Reflect; and follow me.

Y. Soc. In what direction?

Str. Shall we abide by what we said at first, or shall we retract our words?

Y. Soc. To what do you refer?

Str. If I am not mistaken, we said that royal power was a science?

Y. Soc. Yes.

Str. And a science of a peculiar kind, which was selected out of the rest as having a character which is at once judicial and authoritative?

Y. Soc. Yes.

c Str. And there was one kind of authority over lifeless things and another over living things; and so we proceeded in the division step by step up to this point, not losing the idea of science, but unable as yet to determine the nature of the particular science?

Y. Soc. True.

Str. Hence we are led to observe that the distinguishing principle of the State cannot be the few or many, the voluntary or involuntary, poverty or riches; but some notion of science must enter into it, if we are to be consistent with what has preceded.

d Y. Soc. And we must be consistent.

Str. Well, then, in which of these various forms of States may the science of government, which is among the greatest of all sciences and most difficult to acquire, be supposed to reside? That we must discover, and then we shall see who are the false politicians who pretend to be politicians but are not, although they persuade many, and shall separate them from the wise king.

Y. Soc. That, as the argument has already intimated, will be our duty.

e Str. Do you think that the multitude in a State can attain political science?

Y. Soc. Impossible.

Str. But, perhaps, in a city of a thousand men, there would be a hundred, or say fifty, who could?

Y. Soc. In that case political science would certainly be the easiest of all sciences; there could not be found in a city of that number as many really first-rate draught-players, if judged by the standard of the rest of the Greek world, and there would certainly not be as many kings. For kings we may truly call those who possess royal science, whether they rule or not, as was shown in the previous argument.

293 Str. Thank you for reminding me; and the consequence is that any true form of government can only be supposed to be the government of one, two, or, at any rate, a few.

Y. Soc. Certainly.

Str. And these, whether they rule with the will, or against the will, of their subjects, with written laws or without written laws, and whether they are poor or rich, and whatever be the nature of their rule, must be supposed, according to our present view, to rule on some scientific

b principle; just as the physician, whether he cures us against our will or with our will, and whatever be his mode of treatment—incision, burning, or the infliction of some other pain—whether he practises out of a book or not out of a book, and whether he be rich or poor, whether he purges or reduces in some other way, or even fattens his patients, is a physician all the same, so long as he exercises authority over them according to rules of art, if he only does them good and heals and saves them. And this we lay down to be the only proper test of the art of medicine, or of any other art of command.

Y. Soc. Quite true.

Str. Then that can be the only true form of government in which the governors are really found to possess science, and are not mere pretenders, whether they rule according to law or without law, over willing or unwilling subjects, and are rich or poor themselves—none of these things can with any propriety be included in the notion of the ruler.

Y. Soc. No.

Str. And whether with a view to the public good they purge the State by killing some, or exiling some; whether they reduce the size of the body corporate by sending out from the hive swarms of citizens, or, by introducing persons from without, increase it; while they act according to the rules of wisdom and justice, and use their power with a view to the general security and improvement, the city over which they rule, and which has these characteristics, may be described as the only true State. All other governments are not genuine or real, but only imitations of this, and some of them are better and some of them are worse; the better are said to be well governed, but they are mere imitations, like the others.

Y. Soc. I agree, Stranger, in the greater part of what you say; but as to their ruling without laws—the expression has a harsh sound.

Str. You have been too quick for me, Socrates; I was just going to ask you whether you objected to any of my statements. And now I see that we shall have to consider this notion of there being good government without laws.

Y. Soc. Certainly.

Str. There can be no doubt that legislation is in a manner the business of a king, and yet the best thing of all is not that the law should rule, but that a man should rule, supposing him to have wisdom and royal power. Do you see why this is?

Y. Soc. Why?

Str. Because the law does not perfectly comprehend what is noblest and most just for all and therefore cannot enforce what is best. The differences of men and actions, and the endless irregular movements of human things, do not admit of any universal and simple rule. And no art whatsoever can lay down a rule which will last for all time.

Y. Soc. Of course not.

Str. But the law is always striving to make one; like an obstinate and ignorant tyrant, who will not allow anything to be done contrary to his appointment, or any question to be asked—not even in sudden changes of circumstances, when something happens to be better than what he commanded for someone.

Y. Soc. Certainly; the law treats us all precisely in the manner which you describe.

Str. A perfectly simple principle can never be applied to a state of things which is the reverse of simple.

Y. Soc. True.

Str. Then if the law is not the perfection of right, why are we com-
d pelled to make laws at all? The reason of this has next to be investigated.

Y. Soc. Certainly.

Str. Let me ask, whether you have not meetings for gymnastic contests in your city, such as there are in other cities, at which men compete in running, wrestling, and the like?

Y. Soc. Yes; they are very common among us.

Str. And what are the rules which are enforced on their pupils by professional trainers or by others having similar authority? Can you remember?

Y. Soc. To what do you refer?

Str. The training-masters do not issue minute rules for individuals, or give every individual what is exactly suited to his constitution; they think that they ought to go more roughly to work, and to prescribe
e generally the regimen which will benefit the majority.

Y. Soc. Very true.

Str. And therefore they assign equal amounts of exercise to them all; they send them forth together, and let them rest together from their running, wrestling, or whatever the form of bodily exercise may be.

Y. Soc. True.

295 Str. And now observe that the legislator who has to preside over the herd, and to enforce justice in their dealings with one another, will not be able, in enacting for the general good, to provide exactly what is suitable for each particular case.

Y. Soc. He cannot be expected to do so.

Str. He will lay down laws in a general form for the majority, roughly meeting the cases of individuals; and some of them he will deliver in writing, and others will be unwritten; and these last will be traditional customs of the country.

Y. Soc. He will be right.

Str. Yes, quite right; for how can he sit at every man's side all through his life, prescribing for him the exact particulars of his duty?
b Who, Socrates, would be equal to such a task? No one who really had

the royal science, if he had been able to do this, would have imposed upon himself the restriction of a written law.

Y. Soc. So I should infer from what has now been said.

Str. Or rather, my good friend, from what is going to be said.

Y. Soc. And what is that?

Str. Let us put to ourselves the case of a physician, or trainer, who is about to go into a far country, and is expecting to be a long time away   c
from his patients—thinking that his instructions will not be remembered unless they are written down, he will leave notes of them for the use of his pupils or patients.

Y. Soc. True.

Str. But what would you say, if he came back sooner than he had intended, and, owing to an unexpected change of the winds or other celestial influences, something else happened to be better for them—would he not venture to suggest this new remedy, although not contemplated in his former prescription? Would he persist in observing   d
the original law, neither himself giving any new commandments, nor the patient daring to do otherwise than was prescribed, under the idea that this course only was healthy and medicinal, all others noxious and heterodox? Viewed in the light of science and true art, would not all such enactments be utterly ridiculous?   e

Y. Soc. Utterly.

Str. And if he who gave laws, written or unwritten, determining what was good or bad, honourable or dishonourable, just or unjust, to the tribes of men who flock together in their several cities, and are governed in accordance with them; if, I say, the wise legislator were sud-   296
denly to come again, or another like him, is he to be prohibited from changing them? Would not this prohibition be in reality quite as ridiculous as the other?

Y. Soc. Certainly.

Str. Do you know a plausible saying of the common people which is in point?

Y. Soc. I do not recall what you mean at the moment.

Str. They say that if anyone knows how the ancient laws may be improved, he must first persuade his own State of the improvement, and then he may legislate, but not otherwise.

Y. Soc. And are they not right?

Str. Perhaps. But supposing that he does use some gentle violence   b
for their good, what is this violence to be called? Or rather, before you answer, let me ask the same question in reference to our previous instances.

Y. Soc. What do you mean?

Str. Suppose that a skilful physician has a patient, of whatever sex

or age, whom he compels against his will to do something for his good which is contrary to the written rules; what is this compulsion to be called? Would you ever dream of calling it a violation of the art, or a breach of the laws of health? Nothing could be more unjust than for the
c patient to whom such violence is applied, to charge the physician who practises the violence with wanting skill or aggravating his disease.

Y. Soc. Most true.

Str. In the political art error is not called disease, but evil, or disgrace, or injustice.

Y. Soc. Quite true.

Str. And when the citizen, contrary to law and custom, is com-
d pelled to do what is juster and better and nobler than he did before, the last and most absurd thing which he could say about such violence is that he has incurred disgrace or evil or injustice at the hands of those who compelled him.

Y. Soc. Very true.

Str. And shall we say that the violence, if exercised by a rich man,
e is just, and if by a poor man, unjust? May not any man, rich or poor, with or without laws, with the will of the citizens or against the will of the citizens, do what is for their interest? Is not this the true principle of government, according to which the wise and good man will
297 order the affairs of his subjects? As the pilot, by watching continually over the interests of the ship and of the crew—not by laying down rules, but by making his art a law—preserves the lives of his fellow-sailors, even so, and in the same way, may there not be a true form of polity created by those who are able to govern in a similar spirit, and who show a strength of art which is superior to the law? Nor can wise rulers ever err while they, observing the one great rule of distributing
b justice to the citizens with intelligence and skill, are able to preserve them, and, as far as may be, to make them better from being worse.

Y. Soc. No one can deny what has been now said.

Str. Neither, if you consider, can anyone deny the other statement.

Y. Sec. What was it?

Str. We said that no great number of persons, whoever they may be, can attain political knowledge, or order a State wisely, but that the
c true government is to be found in a small body, or in an individual, and that other States are but imitations of this, as we said a little while ago, some for the better and some for the worse.

Y. Soc. What do you mean? I cannot have understood your previous remark about imitations.

Str. And yet the mere suggestion which I hastily threw out is highly important, even if we leave the question where it is, and do not seek by
d the discussion of it to expose the error which prevails in this matter.

Y. Soc. What do you mean?

STR. The idea which has to be grasped by us is not easy or familiar; but we may attempt to express it thus: Supposing the government of which I have been speaking to be the only true model, then the others must use the written laws of this—in no other way can they be saved; they will have to do what is now generally approved, although not the best thing in the world.

Y. Soc. What is this?

STR. No citizen should do anything contrary to the laws, and any infringement of them should be punished with death and the most extreme penalties; and this is very right and good when regarded as the second best thing, if you set aside the first, of which I was just now speaking. Shall I explain the nature of what I call the second best?

Y. Soc. By all means.

STR. I must again have recourse to my favourite images; through them, and them alone, can I describe kings and rulers.

Y. Soc. What images?

STR. The noble pilot and the wise physician, who 'is worth many another man'—in the similitude of these let us endeavour to discover some image of the king.

Y. Soc. What sort of an image?

STR. Well, such as this: Every man will reflect that he suffers strange things at the hands of both of them; the physician saves any whom he wishes to save, and any whom he wishes to maltreat he maltreats—cutting or burning them, and at the same time requiring them to bring him payments, which are a sort of tribute, of which little or nothing is spent upon the sick man, and the greater part is consumed by him and his domestics; and the finale is that he receives money from the relations of the sick man or from some enemy of his, and puts him to death. And the pilots of ships are guilty of numberless evil deeds of the same kind; they intentionally play false and leave you ashore when the hour of sailing arrives; or they cause mishaps at sea and cast away their freight; and are guilty of other rogueries. Now suppose that we, bearing all this in mind, were to determine, after consideration, that neither of these arts shall any longer be allowed to exercise absolute control either over freemen or over slaves, but that we will summon an assembly either of all the people, or of the rich only, so that anybody who likes, whatever may be his calling, or even if he has no calling, may offer an opinion either about seamanship or about diseases—whether as to the manner in which physic or surgical instruments are to be applied to the patient, or again about the vessels and the nautical implements which are required in navigation, and how to meet the dangers of winds and waves which are incidental to the voyage, how to behave when encountering pirates, and what is to be done with the old-fashioned galleys, if they have to fight with others of a similar build—and that, whatever shall be decreed by the multitude on these points, upon the advice of persons skilled or unskilled, shall be written

e down on triangular tablets and columns, or enacted although unwritten to be national customs; and that in all future time vessels shall be navigated and remedies administered to the patient after this fashion.

Y. Soc. What a strange notion!

Str. Suppose further that the pilots and physicians are appointed annually, either out of the rich, or out of the whole people, and that they are elected by lot; and that after their election they navigate vessels and heal the sick according to the written rules.

Y. Soc. This is only getting worse.

Str. Now hear what follows: When the year of office has expired, the pilot or physician has to come before a court of review, in which

299 the judges are either selected from the wealthy classes or chosen by lot out of the whole people; anybody who pleases may be their accuser, and may lay to their charge that during the past year they have not navigated their vessels or healed their patients according to the letter of the law and the ancient customs of their ancestors; and if either of them is condemned, some of the judges must fix what he is to suffer or pay.

b Y. Soc. He who is willing to take a command under such conditions deserves to suffer any penalty.

Str. Yet, once more, we shall have to enact that if anyone is detected enquiring into piloting and navigation, or into health and the true nature of medicine, or about the winds, or other conditions of the atmosphere, contrary to the written rules, and has any ingenious notions about such matters, he is not to be called a pilot or physician, but a cloudy prating sophist; further, on the ground that he is a corrupter of the young, who would persuade them to follow the art of medicine or

c piloting in an unlawful manner, and to exercise an arbitrary rule over their patients or ships, anyone who is qualified by law may inform against him, and indict him in some court, and then if he is found to be persuading any, whether young or old, to act contrary to the written law, he is to be punished with the utmost rigour; for no one should presume to be wiser than the laws; and as touching healing and health

d and piloting and navigation, the nature of them is known to all, for anybody may learn the written laws and the national customs. If such were the mode of procedure, Socrates, about these sciences and about generalship, and any branch of hunting, or about painting or imitation in general, or carpentry, or any sort of handicraft, or farming, or planting, or if we were to see an art of rearing horses, or tending herds, or divination, or any ministerial service, or draught-playing, or any science conversant with number, whether simple or square or cube, or comprising motion—I say, if all these things were done in this way according to written regulations, and not according to art, what would be the result?

Y. Soc. All the arts would utterly perish, and could never be recovered, because enquiry would be unlawful. And human life, which is bad enough already, would then become utterly unendurable.

Str. But what, if while compelling all these operations to be regulated by written law, we were to appoint as the guardian of the laws someone elected by a show of hands, or by lot, and he caring nothing about the laws, were to act contrary to them from motives of interest or favour, and without knowledge—would not this be a still worse evil than the former?

Y. Soc. Very true.

Str. To go against the laws, which are based upon long experience, and the wisdom of counsellors who have graciously recommended them and persuaded the multitude to pass them, would be a far greater and more ruinous error than any adherence to written law?

Y. Soc. Certainly.

Str. Therefore, as there is a danger of this, the next best thing in legislating is not to allow either the individual or the multitude to break the law in any respect whatever.

Y. Soc. True.

Str. The laws would be copies of the true particulars of action as far as they admit of being written down from the lips of those who have knowledge?

Y. Soc. Certainly they would.

Str. And, as we were saying, he who has knowledge and is a true Statesman, will do many things within his own sphere of action by his art without regard to the laws, when he is of opinion that something other than that which he has written down and enjoined to be observed during his absence would be better.

Y. Soc. Yes, we said so.

Str. And any individual or any number of men, having fixed laws, in acting contrary to them with a view to something better, would only be acting, as far as they are able, like the true Statesman?

Y. Soc. Certainly.

Str. If they had no knowledge of what they were doing, they would imitate the truth, and they would always imitate ill; but if they had knowledge, the imitation would be the perfect truth, and an imitation no longer.

Y. Soc. Quite true.

Str. And the principle that no great number of men are able to acquire a knowledge of any art has been already admitted by us.

Y. Soc. Yes, it has.

Str. Then the royal or political art, if there be such an art, will never be attained either by the wealthy or by the other mob.

Y. Soc. Impossible.

301 Str. Then the nearest approach which these lower forms of government can ever make to the true government of the one scientific ruler is to do nothing contrary to their own written laws and national customs.

Y. Soc. Very good.

Str. When the rich imitate the true form, such a government is called aristocracy; and when they are regardless of the laws, oligarchy.

Y. Soc. True.

b Str. Or again, when an individual rules according to law in imitation of him who knows, we call him a king; and if he rules according to law, we give him the same name, whether he rules with opinion or with knowledge.

Y. Soc. To be sure.

Str. And when an individual truly possessing knowledge rules, his name will surely be the same—he will be called a king; and thus all the names of governments, as they are now reckoned, become only five.*

Y. Soc. That is true.

c Str. And when an individual ruler governs neither by law nor by custom, but following in the steps of the true man of science pretends that he can only act for the best by violating the laws, while in reality appetite and ignorance are the motives of the imitation, may not such a one be called a tyrant?

Y. Soc. Certainly.

Str. And this we believe to be the origin of the tyrant and the king, of oligarchies, and aristocracies, and democracies—because men are offended at the one monarch, and can never be made to believe that d anyone can be worthy of such authority, or is able and willing in the spirit of virtue and knowledge to act justly and holily to all; they fancy that he will be a despot who will wrong and harm and slay whom he

---

*Jowett's translation of this clause reads: "and thus the five names of governments, as they are now reckoned, become one." I have altered Jowett's "five" to "all," and "one" to "only five," following the latest Oxford Greek text without the transposition to 301c.7–8 after the five names themselves. In doing this I follow L. Brisson and J. F. Pradeau, Platon: Le Politique. Paris, 2003, note 344.

pleases of us; for if there could be such a despot as we describe, they would acknowledge that we ought to be too glad to have him, and that he alone would be the happy ruler of a true and perfect State.

Y. Soc. To be sure.

Str. But then, as the State is not like a beehive, and has no natural head who is at once recognized to be the superior both in body and in e
mind, mankind are obliged to meet and make laws, and endeavour to approach as nearly as they can to the true form of government.

Y. Soc. True.

Str. And when the foundation of politics is in the letter only and in custom, and knowledge is divorced from action, can we wonder, Socrates, at the miseries which there are, and always will be, in States? Any other art, built on such a foundation and thus conducted, would ruin all that it touched. Ought we not rather to wonder at the natural 302
strength of the political bond? For States have endured all this, for time immemorial, and yet some of them still remain and are not over-thrown, though many of them, like ships at sea, founder from time to time, and perish and have perished and will hereafter perish, through the badness of their pilots and crews, who have the worst sort of ig-norance of the highest truths—I mean to say, that they are wholly un- b
acquainted with politics, of which, above all other sciences, they believe themselves to have acquired the most perfect knowledge.

Y. Soc. Very true.

Str. Then the question arises: which of these untrue forms of gov-ernment is the least oppressive to their subjects, though they are all op-pressive; and which is the worst of them? Here is a consideration which is beside our present purpose, and yet having regard to the whole it seems to influence all our actions: We must examine it.

Y. Soc. Yes, we must.

Str. You may say that of the three forms, the same is at once the hard- c
est and the easiest.

Y. Soc. What do you mean?

Str. I am speaking of the three forms of government, which I men-tioned at the beginning of this discussion—monarchy, the rule of the few, and the rule of the many.

Y. Soc. True.

Str. If we divide each of these we shall have six, from which the true one may be distinguished as a seventh.

Y. Soc. How would you make the division?

Str. Monarchy divides into royalty and tyranny; the rule of the few d
into aristocracy, which has an auspicious name, and oligarchy; and democracy or the rule of the many, which before was one, must now be divided.

Y. Soc. On what principle of division?

e   Str. On the same principle as before, although the name is now discovered to have a twofold meaning. For the distinction of ruling with law or without law, applies to this as well as to the rest.

Y. Soc. Yes.

Str. The division made no difference when we were looking for the perfect State, as we showed before. But now that this has been separated off, and, as we said, the others alone are left for us, the principle of law and the absence of law will bisect them all.

Y. Soc. That would seem to follow, from what has been said.

Str. Then monarchy, when bound by good prescriptions or laws, is the best of all the six, and when lawless is the most bitter and oppressive to the subject.

Y. Soc. True.

303   Str. The government of the few, which is intermediate between that of the one and many, is also intermediate in good and evil; but the government of the many is in every respect weak and unable to do either any great good or any great evil, when compared with the others, because the offices are too minutely subdivided and too many hold them. And this therefore is the worst of all lawful governments, and the best of all lawless ones. If they are all without the restraints of law, democracy is the form in which to live is best; if they are well ordered, then this is the last which you should choose, as royalty, the first form, is the best, with the exception of the seventh, for that excels them all, and is among States what god is among men.

b

Y. Soc. You are quite right, and we should choose that above all.

Str. The members of all these States, with the exception of the one which has knowledge, may be set aside as being not Statesmen but partisans—upholders of the most monstrous idols, and themselves idols; and, being the greatest imitators and magicians, they are also the greatest of Sophists.

c

Y. Soc. The name of Sophist after many windings in the argument appears to have been most justly fixed upon the politicians, as they are termed.

Str. And so our satyric drama has been played out; and the troop of Centaurs and Satyrs, however unwilling to leave the stage, have at last been separated from the political science.

d

Y. Soc. I see.

Str. There remain, however, natures still more troublesome, because they are more nearly akin to the king, and more difficult to discern; the examination of them may be compared to the process of refining gold.

Y. Soc. What is your meaning?

STR. The workmen begin by sifting away the earth and stones and the like; there remain in a confused mass the valuable elements akin to gold, which can only be separated by fire—copper, silver, and other *e* precious metals; these are at last refined away by the use of tests, until the gold is left quite pure.

Y. SOC. Yes, that is the way in which these things are said to be done.

STR. In like manner, all alien and uncongenial matter has been separated from political science, and what is precious and of a kindred nature has been left; there remain the nobler arts of the general and the judge, and the higher sort of oratory which is an ally of the royal art, 304 and persuades men to do justice, and assists in guiding the helm of States. How can we best clear away all these, leaving him whom we seek alone and unalloyed?

Y. SOC. That is obviously what has in some way to be attempted.

STR. If the attempt is all that is wanting, he shall certainly be brought to light; and I think that the illustration of music may assist in exhibiting him. Please answer me a question.

Y. SOC. What question?

STR. There is such a thing as learning music or handicraft arts in *b* general?

Y. SOC. There is.

STR. And is there any higher art or science, having power to decide which of these arts are and are not to be learned—what do you say?

Y. SOC. I should answer that there is.

STR. And do we acknowledge this science to be different from the others?

Y. SOC. Yes.

STR. And ought the other sciences to be superior to this, or no single science to any other? Or ought this science to be the overseer and *c* governor of all the others?

Y. SOC. The latter.

STR. You mean to say that the science which judges whether we ought to learn or not, must be superior to the science which is learned or which teaches?

Y. SOC. Far superior.

STR. And the science which determines whether we ought to persuade or not, must be superior to the science which is able to persuade?

Y. SOC. Of course.

STR. Very good; and to what science do we assign the power of persuading a multitude by a pleasing tale and not by teaching? *d*

Y. SOC. That power, I think, must clearly be assigned to rhetoric.

STR. And to what science do we give the power of determining whether we are to employ persuasion or force towards anyone, or to refrain altogether?

Y. Soc. To that science which governs the arts of speech and persuasion.

STR. Which, if I am not mistaken, will be politics?

Y. Soc. Exactly.

e   STR. Rhetoric seems to be quickly distinguished from politics, being a different species, yet ministering to it.

Y. Soc. Yes.

STR. But what would you think of another sort of power or science?

Y. Soc. What science?

STR. The science which has to do with military operations against our enemies—is that to be regarded as a science or not?

Y. Soc. How can generalship and military tactics be regarded as other than a science?

STR. And is the art which is able and knows how to advise when we are to go to war, or to make peace, the same as this or different?

Y. Soc. If we are to be consistent, we must say different.

305   STR. And we must also suppose that this rules the other, if we are not to give up our former notion?

Y. Soc. True.

STR. And, considering how great and terrible the whole art of war is, can we imagine any which is superior to it but the truly royal?

Y. Soc. No other.

STR. The art of the general is only ministerial, and therefore not political?

Y. Soc. Exactly.

b   STR. Once more let us consider the nature of the righteous judge.

Y. Soc. By all means.

STR. Does he do anything but decide the dealings of men with one another to be just or unjust in accordance with the standard which he receives from the king and legislator, showing his own peculiar virtue only in this: that he is not perverted by gifts, or fears, or pity, or by any

c   sort of favour or enmity, into deciding the suits of men with one another contrary to the appointment of the legislator?

Y. Soc. No; his office is such as you describe.

STR. Then the inference is that the power of the judge is not royal, but only the power of a guardian of the law which ministers to the royal power?

Y. Soc. True.

STR. The review of all these sciences shows that none of them is po-

d   litical or royal. For the truly royal ought not itself to act, but to rule over those who are able to act; the king ought to know what is and what is not a fitting opportunity for taking the initiative in matters of the greatest importance, whilst others should execute his orders.

Y. Soc. True.

Str. And, therefore, the arts which we have described, as they have no authority over themselves or one another, but are each of them concerned with some special action of their own, have, as they ought to have, special names corresponding to their several actions.

Y. Soc. I agree.

Str. And the science which is over them all, and has charge of the laws, and of all matters affecting the State, and truly weaves them all into one, if we would describe under a name characteristic of their common nature, most truly we may call politics.

Y. Soc. Exactly so.

Str. Then, now that we have discovered the various classes in a State, shall I analyze politics after the pattern which weaving supplied?

Y. Soc. I greatly wish that you would.

Str. Then I must describe the nature of the royal web, and show how the various threads are woven into one piece.

Y. Soc. Clearly.

Str. A task has to be accomplished, which, although difficult, appears to be necessary.

Y. Soc. Certainly the attempt must be made.

Str. To assume that one part of virtue differs in kind from another is a position easily assailable by contentious disputants, who appeal to popular opinion.

Y. Soc. I do not understand.

Str. Let me put the matter in another way: I suppose that you would consider courage to be a part of virtue?

Y. Soc. Certainly I should.

Str. And you would think temperance to be different from courage; and likewise to be a part of virtue?

Y. Soc. True.

Str. I shall venture to put forward a strange theory about them.

Y. Soc. What is it?

Str. That they are two principles which thoroughly hate one another and are antagonistic throughout a great part of nature.

Y. Soc. How singular!

Str. Yes very—for all the parts of virtue are commonly said to be friendly to one another.

Y. Soc. Yes.

Str. Then let us carefully investigate whether this is universally true, or whether there are not parts of virtue which are at war with their kindred in some respect.

Y. Soc. Tell me how we shall consider that question.

Str. We must extend our enquiry to all those things which we consider beautiful and at the same time place in two opposite classes.

Y. Soc. Explain; what are they?

Str. Acuteness and quickness, whether in body or soul or in the production of sound, and the imitations of them which painting and music supply, you must have praised yourself before now, or been present when others praised them.

Y. Soc. Certainly.

Str. And do you remember the terms in which they are praised?

Y. Soc. I do not.

Str. I wonder whether I can explain to you in words the thought which is passing in my mind.

Y. Soc. Why not?

Str. You fancy that this is all so easy: Well, let us consider these notions with reference to the opposite classes of action under which they fall. When we praise quickness and energy and acuteness, whether of mind or body or sound, we express our praise of the quality which we admire by one word, and that one word is manliness or courage.

Y. Soc. How?

Str. We speak of an action as energetic and brave, quick and manly, and vigorous too; and when we apply the name of which I speak as the common attribute of all these natures, we certainly praise them.

Y. Soc. True.

Str. And do we not often praise the quiet strain of action also?

Y. Soc. To be sure.

Str. And do we not then say the opposite of what we said of the other?

Y. Soc. How do you mean?

Str. We exclaim: How calm! How temperate! in admiration of the slow and quiet working of the intellect, and of steadiness and gentleness in action, of smoothness and depth of voice, and of all rhythmical movement and of music in general, when these have a proper solemnity. Of all such actions we predicate not courage, but a name indicative of order.

Y. Soc. Very true.

Str. But when, on the other hand, either of these is out of place, the names of either are changed into terms of censure.

Y. Soc. How so?

Str. Too great sharpness or quickness or hardness is termed violence or madness; too great slowness or gentleness is called cowardice or sluggishness; and we may observe, that for the most part these qualities, and the temperance and manliness of the opposite characters, are arrayed as enemies on opposite sides, and do not mingle with one another in their respective actions; and if we pursue the enquiry, we shall find that men who have these different qualities of mind differ from one another.

Y. Soc. In what respect?

Str. In respect of all the qualities which I mentioned, and very likely   d
of many others. According to their respective affinities to either class of actions they distribute praise and blame—praise to the actions which are akin to their own, blame to those of the opposite party—and out of this many quarrels and occasions of quarrel arise among them.

Y. Soc. True.

Str. The difference between the two classes is often a trivial concern; but in a state, and when affecting really important matters, becomes of all disorders the most hateful.

Y. Soc. To what do you refer?

Str. To nothing short of the whole regulation of human life. For   e
the orderly class are always ready to lead a peaceful life, quietly doing their own business; this is their manner of behaving with all men at home, and they are equally ready to find some way of keeping the peace with foreign States. And on account of this fondness of theirs for peace, which is often out of season where their influence prevails, they become by degrees unwarlike, and bring up their young men to be like themselves; they are at the mercy of their enemies; whence in a few years they and their children and the whole city often pass imperceptibly from the condition of freemen into that of slaves.

Y. Soc. What a cruel fate!   308

Str. And now think of what happens with the more courageous natures. Are they not always inciting their country to go to war, owing to their excessive love of the military life? They raise up enemies against themselves many and mighty, and either utterly ruin their native-land or enslave and subject it to its foes.

Y. Soc. That, again, is true.

Str. Must we not admit, then, that where these two classes exist, they always feel the greatest antipathy and antagonism towards one another?

Y. Soc. We cannot deny it.   b

Str. And returning to the enquiry with which we began, have we not found that considerable portions of virtue are at variance with one another, and give rise to a similar opposition in the characters who are endowed with them?

Y. Soc. True.

Str. Let us consider a further point.

Y. Soc. What is it?

c   STR. I want to know whether any constructive art will make any, even the most trivial thing, out of bad and good materials indifferently, if this can be helped? Does not all art rather reject the bad as far as possible, and accept the good and fit materials, and from these elements, whether like or unlike, gathering them all into one, work out some nature or idea?

Y. Soc. To be sure.

d   STR. Then the true and natural art of statesmanship will never allow any State to be formed by a combination of good and bad men, if this can be avoided; but will begin by testing human natures in play, and after testing them, will entrust them to proper teachers who are the ministers of her purposes—she will herself give orders, and maintain authority; just as the art of weaving continually gives orders and maintains authority over the carders and all the others who prepare the material for the work, commanding the subsidiary arts to execute the

e   works which she deems necessary for making the web.

Y. Soc. Quite true.

STR. In like manner, the royal science appears to me to be the mistress of all lawful educators and instructors, and having this queenly power, will not permit them to train men in what will produce characters unsuited to the political constitution which she desires to create, but only in what will produce suitable ones. Those which have no share of manliness and temperance, or any other virtuous inclination, and, from the necessity of an evil nature, are violently carried away to godlessness and insolence and injustice, she gets rid of by death and exile, and punishes them with the greatest of disgraces.

Y. Soc. That is commonly said.

309   STR. But those who are wallowing in ignorance and baseness she bows under the yoke of slavery.

Y. Soc. Quite right.

STR. The rest of the citizens, out of whom, if they have education,

b   something noble may be made, and who are capable of being united by the Statesman, the kingly art blends and weaves together; taking on the one hand those whose natures tend rather to courage, which is the stronger element and may be regarded as the warp, and on the other hand those which incline to order and gentleness, and which are represented in the figure as spun thick and soft, after the manner of the woof—these, which are naturally opposed, she seeks to bind and weave together in the following manner:

Y. Soc. In what manner?

c   STR. First of all, she takes the eternal element of the soul and binds it with a divine cord, to which it is akin, and then the animal nature, and binds that with human cords.

Y. Soc. I do not understand what you mean.

Str. The meaning is that the opinion about the honorable and the just and good and their opposites, which is true and confirmed by reason, is a divine principle, and when implanted in the soul, is implanted, as I maintain, in a nature of heavenly birth.

Y. Soc. Yes; what else should it be?

Str. Only the Statesman and the good legislator, having the inspiration of the royal muse, can implant this opinion, and he, only in the rightly educated, whom we were just now describing.

Y. Soc. Likely enough.

Str. But him who cannot, we will not designate by any of the names which are the subject of the present enquiry.

Y. Soc. Very right.

Str. The courageous soul when attaining this truth becomes civilized, and rendered more capable of partaking of justice; but when not partaking, is inclined to brutality. Is not that true?

Y. Soc. Certainly.

Str. And again, the peaceful and orderly nature, if sharing in these opinions, becomes temperate and wise, as far as this may be in a State, but if not, deservedly obtains the ignominious name of silliness.

Y. Soc. Quite true.

Str. Can we say that such a connection as this will lastingly unite the evil with one another or with the good, or that any science would seriously think of using a bond of this kind to join such materials?

Y. Soc. Impossible.

Str. But in those who were originally of a noble nature, and who have been nurtured in noble ways, and in those only, may we not say that union is implanted by law, and that this is the medicine which art prescribes for them, and of all the bonds which unite the dissimilar and contrary parts of virtue is not this, as I was saying, the divinest?

Y. Soc. Very true.

Str. Where this divine bond exists there is no difficulty in imagining, or when you have imagined, in creating the other bonds, which are human only.

Y. Soc. How is that, and what bonds do you mean?

Str. Rights of intermarriage, and ties which are formed between States by giving and taking children in marriage, or between individuals by private betrothals and espousals. For most persons form marriage connections without due regard to what is best for the procreation of children.

Y. Soc. In what way?

Str. They seek after wealth and power, which in matrimony are objects not worthy even of a serious censure.

Y. Soc. There is no need to consider them at all.

c   Str. More reason is there to consider the practice of those who make family their chief aim, and to indicate their error.

Y. Soc. Quite true.

Str. They act on no true principle at all; they seek their ease and receive with open arms those who are like themselves, and hate those who are unlike them, being too much influenced by feelings of dislike.

Y. Soc. How so?

Str. The quiet orderly class seek for natures like their own, and as far as they can they marry and give in marriage exclusively in this class,

d   and the courageous do the same; they seek natures like their own, whereas they should both do precisely the opposite.

Y. Soc. How and why is that?

Str. Because courage, when untempered by the gentler nature during many generations, may at first bloom and strengthen, but at last bursts forth into downright madness.

Y. Soc. Very likely.

Str. And then, again, the soul which is too full of modesty and has

e   no element of courage in many successive generations, is apt to grow too indolent, and at last to become utterly paralyzed and useless.

Y. Soc. That, again, is quite likely.

Str. It was of these bonds I said that there would be no difficulty in creating them, if only both classes originally held the same opinion about the honourable and good—indeed, in this single work, the whole process of royal weaving is comprised—never to allow temperate natures to be separated from the brave, but to weave them together, like the warp and the woof, by common sentiments and honours and rep-

311   utation, and by the giving of pledges to one another; and out of them forming one smooth and even web, to entrust to them the offices of State.

Y. Soc. How do you mean?

Str. Where one officer only is needed, you must choose a ruler who has both these qualities—when many, you must mingle some of each, for the temperate ruler is very careful and just and safe, but is wanting in thoroughness and drive.

Y. Soc. Certainly, that is very true.

b   Str. The character of the courageous, on the other hand, falls short of the former in justice and caution, but has the power of action in a remarkable degree, and where either of these two qualities is wanting, there cities cannot altogether prosper either in their public or private life.

Y. Soc. Certainly they cannot.

STR. This then we declare to be the completion of the web of political action, which is created by a direct intertexture of the brave and temperate natures, whenever the royal science has drawn the two minds into communion with one another by unanimity and friendship, and having perfected the noblest and best of all the webs which political life admits. Enfolding therein all other inhabitants of cities—whether slaves or freemen—binds them in one fabric and governs and presides over them. So far as to be happy is vouchsafed to a city, in no particular fails to secure their happiness.

Y. Soc. Your picture, Stranger, of the king and Statesman, no less than of the Sophist, is quite perfect.

LAWS

Introduction

THE CHANGES IN PLATO'S narrative strategies and philosophical style that
are apparent between the early and late periods (for example, between
Laches and *Statesman*) come to a startling new level in *Laws*. In Plato's last
dialogue, not only do we not know any of the speakers, but we have
also left Athens in order to witness a conversation that takes place along
a country road on the island of Crete. The speakers are a nameless
Athenian Visitor, a Cretan by the name of Cleinias (unusual for a Cretan),
and a Spartan called Megillus. The last of the three may have been a former peace commissioner to Athens in 417–410 B.C.E., although the
evidence is far from conclusive.

Surprises do not stop there: Although the writing of laws was included by Socrates among the philosophically inadmissible kinds of
writing (*Phaedrus* 277d; p. 251), that seems to be exactly what Plato does
in this dialogue, his longest, in which he sets out the provisions of an
ideal legal code in extreme detail. Something has happened in between
the two dialogues: *Laws* may well have been Plato's last attempt to link
his philosophy with reality, and a declaration of how he thought a polity
should actually be organized and why. We find much that one could expect, such as borrowings from the Spartan legal system, side by side
with statements like the rejection of homosexuality (636d) that are
hard to reconcile with the treatment of homoeroticism in *Symposium* or
Phaedrus.

All the above, together with the fact that the Greek of *Laws* is much
harder to read than that of most other dialogues, has caused Plato's last
work to be neglected and even poked fun at since antiquity. Nevertheless, it is undoubtedly Plato's philosophical testament, and as such it
deserves careful study. Only the first three books, which do not yet
enter into the details of the legal code, are included here.

A suggested outline of the contents of the first three books is as
follows:

- (624a–632d) The Athenian Visitor enquires about the origin of
  Cretan and Spartan laws. Both claim divine origin for their laws,
  and the Athenian proposes that they spend their time discussing
  legislation, since they will be walking a long distance to the cave
  of Zeus in Mount Ida (where Zeus handed down laws to Minos)
  along a country road on a midsummer day. According to the

Athenian, the purpose of a good legal system should be not just to make sure that the citizens excel in the battlefield; it also should enable them to conduct their lives happily and justly.

- (632d–636e) The Athenian proposes to discuss courage as an example of virtue, which must include fighting not only fear and pain but also desires and pleasures. The discussion of legislation, which must be reserved to old and experienced men, begins with the question of the proper regulation of pleasure.

- (636e–641d) Given that neither the Cretan nor the Spartan system is particularly adept at regulating pleasure, the Athenian refers to the practice of drinking parties, common in Athens (see "Introduction" to *Symposium*), and implies that their proper conduct is a significant contribution to the education of the citizens.

- (641e–645c) Both Megillus and Cleinias reveal their ties with Athens and show themselves ready to listen however long the Athenian wishes to speak. The Athenian then distinguishes between education in different skills and education in virtue, which must include developing expertise in dealing with pleasure by managing the opposing forces that lead the individual toward virtue or vice. The law is a means to that end, whether it comes from a god or from a man.

- (645c–650b) Drinking parties, according to the Athenian, are educational because they intensify pleasure and pain, while weakening memory and thought, thereby providing a safe testing ground for virtue.

- (652a–655c) The Athenian discusses the role of the arts in education, which is understood as the correct management of pleasure and pain. Plato's basic assumption is that the representation of human actions in any artistic work triggers an imitative response in the audience. Therefore, it is imperative that good conduct be portrayed in a positive light and evil conduct in a negative one.

- (655c–660d) Pleasure is not an adequate criterion for judging the quality of art. The practice of artistic censorship in Egypt is brought up as an example of a way to stick to traditional form and content in artistic works, and as an achievement in legislation. Nevertheless, the Athenian admits that it is not possible to suppress creativity entirely in the Greek context; therefore, the judgment of the quality of different artistic productions must be reserved for experienced old men.

- (660d–664b) The objection (recurring in Plato) of Cleinias and Megillus is that evil people can be happy. The answer this time is not a refutation by the Athenian, but simply a statement that the gods surely mean to make just men happier than unjust ones, and therefore the educational system should make sure that children learn that unjust behavior does not lead to happiness.

- (664b–671a) The performance of poetic works is divided in three choruses: one of children, dedicated to the Muses; one of people under thirty, dedicated to Apollo; and one whose members are between thirty and sixty, dedicated to Dionysus. People over sixty will not sing, but will instead tell edifying stories. The innovative trend of splitting music into three parts (song, dance, and accompaniment) is strongly attacked.

- (671a–674c) The subject of drinking parties is taken up again. As it turns out, singing and dancing amount to education as a whole, and the chorus dedicated to Dionysus is therefore the main body of citizens responsible for such education. It follows that the proper regulation of drinking is essential for the polity.

- (676a–689e) The Athenian tells the story of mankind, starting with a flood that left a few survivors and finishing in the narrative present. The story has, of course, no historical value, but only serves the purpose of examining all the known political systems and determining their respective advantages and disadvantages. The story traces the development of autocracy, followed by the origins of legislation as a compromise between the ancestral laws of different communities, the story of Troy, and the history of the Dorian League, which failed, according to the Athenian, because it was entered into only for military purposes.

- (689e–698a) The story continues with Sparta's success, which is due to the Spartans' respect for proper titles of authority, which they vested in twenty-eight elders who had the same authority as the king, and in five annually elected officials (the ephors) who controlled the conduct of the king, in addition to their administrative and judicial duties. In contrast, the Persian monarchy failed because the king's unrestrained desire for power and pleasure was not checked by anyone.

- (698a–701d) Athenian democracy, the Athenian Visitor continues, sprang from a spirit of solidarity that was gained thanks to their single-handed opposition to Xerxes' invading army, but the system later became flawed by the opposite defect to that of the Persian monarchy, namely an excess of freedom in the citizens and a disregard for proper titles of authority (for example, old age, money, birth, and citizenship status).

- (701d–702e) The Athenian recapitulates. A good lawgiver should frame his laws with regard to three things: the freedom, unity, and wisdom of those for whom he legislates. The ideal state would be somewhere between the unbridled Persian autocracy and the excessively loose Athenian democracy. How would one go about legislating in detail from these premises? The Cretan Cleinias has an answer: He has just been appointed, with nine other men from Cnossos, to draft laws for the new colony of Magnesia, to be founded on the island. Therefore, he will be delighted to enlist the help of the Athenian and the Spartan in order to talk about what the ideal code for the colony might be, borrowing from existing laws of other states as needed.

LAWS

BOOK I

ATHENIAN STRANGER. Tell me, Strangers, is a god or some man supposed to be the author of your laws?   624

CLEINIAS. A god, Stranger; in very truth a god: among us Cretans he is said to have been Zeus, but in Sparta, whence our friend here comes, I believe they would say that Apollo is their lawgiver: would they not, Megillus?

MEGILLUS. Certainly.

ATH. And do you, Cleinias, believe, as Homer tells,* that every ninth   b
year Minos went to converse with his Olympian lord, and was inspired by him to make laws for your cities?

CLE. Yes, that is our tradition; and there was Rhadamanthus, a brother of his, with whose name you are familiar; he is reputed to have been the justest of men, and we Cretans are of opinion that he earned this reputation from his righteous administration of justice when he   625
was alive.[1]

ATH. Yes, and a noble reputation it was, worthy of a son of Zeus. As you and Megillus have been trained in these institutions, I dare say that you will not be unwilling to give an account of your government and laws; on our way we can pass the time pleasantly in talking about them, for I am told that the distance from Cnossos to the cave and temple of   b
Zeus is considerable; and doubtless there are shady places under the lofty trees, which will protect us from this scorching sun. Being no longer young, we may often stop to rest beneath them, and get over the whole journey without difficulty, beguiling the time by conversation.

CLE. Yes, Stranger, and if we proceed onward we shall come to   c
groves of cypresses, which are of rare height and beauty, and there are green meadows, in which we may repose and converse.

ATH. Very good.

CLE. Very good, indeed; and still better when we see them; let us move on cheerily.

ATH. I am willing. And first, I want to know why the law has ordained that you shall have common meals and gymnastic exercises, and wear arms.

CLE. I think, Stranger, that the aim of our institutions is easily intelligible to anyone. Look at the character of our country: Crete is not   d

---

*Perhaps a far-fetched interpretation of *Odyssey* 19.178–179.

like Thessaly, a large plain; for this reason they have horsemen in Thessaly, and we have runners—the inequality of the ground in our country is more adapted to locomotion on foot; but then, if you have runners you must have light arms; no one can carry a heavy weight when running, and bows and arrows are convenient because they are light. Now all these regulations have been made with a view to war, and the legislator appears to me to have looked to this in all his arrangements. The common meals, if I am not mistaken, were instituted by him for a similar reason, because he saw that while they are in the field the citizens are by the nature of the case compelled to take their meals together for the sake of mutual protection. He seems to me to have thought the world foolish in not understanding that all men are always at war with one another; and if in war there ought to be common meals and certain persons regularly appointed under others to protect an army, they should be continued in peace. For what men in general term peace would be said by him to be only a name; in reality every city is in a natural state of war with every other, not indeed proclaimed by heralds, but everlasting. And if you look closely, you will find that this was the intention of the Cretan legislator; all institutions, private as well as public, were arranged by him with a view to war; in giving them he was under the impression that no possessions or institutions are of any value to the one who is defeated in battle; for all the good things of the conquered pass into the hands of the conquerors.

ATH. You appear to me, Stranger, to have been thoroughly trained in the Cretan institutions, and to be well informed about them; will you tell me a little more explicitly what is the principle of government which you would lay down? You seem to imagine that a well-governed state ought to be so ordered as to conquer all other states in war; am I right in supposing this to be your meaning?

CLE. Certainly; and our Spartan friend, if I am not mistaken, will agree with me.

MEG. Why, my good friend, how could any Spartan say anything else?

ATH. And is what you say applicable only to states, or also to villages?

CLE. To both alike.

ATH. The case is the same?

CLE. Yes.

ATH. And in the village will there be the same war of family against family, and of individual against individual?

CLE. The same.

ATH. And should each man conceive himself to be his own enemy:—what shall we say?

CLE. Athenian Stranger—inhabitant of Attica I will not call you, for you seem to deserve rather to be named after the goddess herself, because you go back to first principles—you have thrown a light upon the argument, and will now be better able to understand what I was just saying: All men are publicly one another's enemies, and each man privately his own.

ATH. My good sir, what do you mean?   e

CLE. There is a victory and defeat—the first and best of victories, the lowest and worst of defeats—which each man gains or sustains at the hands, not of another, but of himself; this shows that there is a war against ourselves going on within every one of us.

ATH. Let us now reverse the order of the argument. Seeing that every individual is either his own superior or his own inferior, may we   627 say that there is the same principle in the house, the village, and the state?

CLE. You mean that in each of them there is a principle of superiority or inferiority to self?

ATH. Yes.

CLE. You are quite right in asking the question, for there certainly is such a principle, and above all in states; and the state in which the better citizens win a victory over the mob and over the inferior classes may be truly said to be better than itself, and may be justly praised, where such a victory is gained, or censured in the opposite case.

ATH. Whether the better is ever really conquered by the worse is a   b question which requires more discussion, and may be therefore left for the present. But I now quite understand your meaning when you say that citizens who are of the same race and live in the same cities may unjustly conspire, and having the superiority in numbers may overcome and enslave the few just; and when they prevail, the state may be truly called its own inferior and therefore bad; and when they are defeated, its own superior and therefore good.

CLE. Your remark, Stranger, is a paradox, and yet we cannot possibly deny it.   c

ATH. Here is another case for consideration: in a family there may be several brothers, who are the offspring of a single pair; very possibly the majority of them may be unjust, and the just may be in a minority.

CLE. Very possibly.

ATH. And you and I ought not to raise a question of words as to whether this family and household are rightly said to be superior when   d they conquer, and inferior when they are conquered; for we are not now considering what may or may not be the proper or customary way of speaking, but we are considering the natural principles of right and wrong in laws.

CLE. What you say, Stranger, is most true.

MEG. Quite excellent, in my opinion, as far as we have gone.

ATH. Again; might there not be a judge over these brethren, of whom we were speaking?

CLE. Certainly.

e   ATH. Now, which would be the better judge, one who destroyed the bad and appointed the good to govern themselves, or one who, while allowing the good to govern, let the bad live, and made them
628 voluntarily submit? Or third, I suppose, in the scale of excellence might be placed a judge, who, finding the family distracted, not only did not destroy anyone, but reconciled them to one another for ever after, and gave them laws which they mutually observed, and was able to keep them friends.

CLE. The last would be by far the best sort of judge and legislator.

ATH. And yet the aim of all the laws which he gave would be the reverse of war.

CLE. Very true.

ATH. And will he who constitutes the state and orders the life of
b   man have in view external war, or that kind of internecine war called civil—which no one, if he could prevent, would like to have occurring in his own state; and when occurring, everyone would wish to be rid of as soon as possible?

CLE. He would have the latter chiefly in view.

ATH. And would he prefer that this civil war should be terminated by the destruction of one of the parties, and by the victory of the other, or that peace and friendship should be re-established, and that, being reconciled, they should give their attention to foreign enemies?

c   CLE. Everyone would desire the latter in the case of his own state.

ATH. And would not that also be the desire of the legislator?

CLE. Certainly.

ATH. And would not everyone always make laws for the sake of the best?

CLE. To be sure.

ATH. But war, whether external or civil, is not the best, and the need of either is to be deprecated; but peace with one another, and good
d   will, are best. Nor is the victory of the state over itself to be regarded as a really good thing, but as a necessity; a man might as well say that the body was in the best state when sick and purged by medicine, forgetting that there is also a state of the body which needs no purge. And in like manner no one can be a true statesman, whether he aims at the happiness of the individual or state, who looks only, or first of all, to external warfare; nor will he ever be a sound legislator who orders
e   peace for the sake of war, and not war for the sake of peace.

CLE. I suppose that there is truth, Stranger, in that remark of yours; and yet I am greatly mistaken if war is not the entire aim and object of our own institutions, and also of the Spartan ones.

ATH. I dare say; but there is no reason why we should rudely quarrel with one another about your legislators, instead of gently questioning them, seeing that both we and they are equally in earnest. Please follow me and the argument closely. First I will put forward Tyrtaeus, an Athenian by birth, but also a Spartan citizen,[2] who of all men was most eager about war. He says:

> 'I sing not, I care not, about any man,   b

even if he were the richest of men, and possessed every good (and then he gives a whole list of them), if he is not at all times a brave warrior.' I imagine that you, too, must have heard his poems; our Spartan friend has probably heard more than enough of them.

MEG. Very true.

CLE. And they have found their way from Sparta to Crete.

ATH. Come now and let us all join in asking this question of Tyrtaeus: Most divine poet, we will say to him, the excellent praise which you have bestowed on those who excel in war sufficiently proves that   c
you are wise and good, and I and Megillus and Cleinias of Cnossos do, I believe, entirely agree with you. But we should like to be quite sure that we are speaking of the same men; tell us, then, do you agree with us in thinking that there are two kinds of war; or what would you say? A far inferior man to Tyrtaeus would have no difficulty in replying   d
quite truly, that war is of two kinds—one which is universally called civil war, and is, as we were just now saying, of all wars the worst; the other, as we should all admit, in which we fall out with other nations who are of a different race, is a far milder form of warfare.

CLE. Certainly, far milder.

ATH. Well, now, when you praise and blame war in this high-flown strain, whom are you praising or blaming, and to which kind of war are you referring? I suppose that you must mean foreign war, if I am   e
to judge from expressions of yours in which you say that you abominate those

> 'Who refuse to look upon fields of blood, and will not draw near and
>   strike at their enemies.'

And we shall naturally go on to say to him: You, Tyrtaeus, as it seems, praise those who distinguish themselves in external and foreign war; and he must admit this.

CLE. Evidently.

630   ATH. They are good; but we say that there are still better men whose virtue is displayed in the greatest of all battles. And we too have a poet whom we summon as a witness, Theognis,* citizen of Megara in Sicily:

> 'Cyrnus,' he says, 'he who is faithful in a civil broil is worth his weight in gold and silver.'

And such a man is far better, as we affirm, than the other in a more
b   difficult kind of war, much in the same degree as justice and temperance and wisdom, when united with courage, are better than courage only; for a man cannot be faithful and good in civil strife without having all virtue. But in the war of which Tyrtaeus speaks, many a mercenary soldier will take his stand and be ready to die at his post, and yet they are generally and almost without exception insolent, unjust, vio-
c   lent men, and the most senseless of human beings. You will ask what the conclusion is, and what I am seeking to prove: I maintain that the divine legislator of Crete, like any other who is worthy of consideration, will always and above all things in making laws have regard to the greatest virtue; which, according to Theognis, is loyalty in the hour of danger, and may be truly called perfect justice. Whereas that virtue which Tyrtaeus highly praises is well enough, and was praised by the
d   poet at the right time, yet in place and dignity may be said to be only fourth-rate.

CLE. Stranger, we are degrading our inspired lawgiver to a rank which is far beneath him.

ATH. Nay, I think that we degrade not him but ourselves, if we imagine that Lycurgus and Minos laid down laws both in Sparta and Crete mainly with a view to war.

CLE. What ought we to say then?

ATH. What truth and what justice require of us, if I am not mis-
e   taken, when speaking on behalf of divine excellence: that the legislator when making his laws had in view not a part only, and this the lowest part of virtue, but all virtue, and that he devised classes of laws answering to the kinds of virtue; not in the way in which modern inventors of laws make the classes, for they only investigate and offer laws whenever a want is felt, and one man has a class of laws about allotments and heiresses, another about assaults; others about a myriad
631   other such matters. But we maintain that the right way of examining laws is to proceed as we have now done, and I admired the spirit of

---

*Poet of the seventh and sixth centuries B.C.E.

your exposition; for you were quite right in beginning with virtue, and saying that this was the aim of the giver of the law, but I thought that you went wrong when you added that all his legislation had a view only to a part, and the least part of virtue, and this called forth my subsequent remarks. Will you allow me then to explain how I should have liked to have heard you expound the matter?

CLE. By all means.

ATH. You ought to have said, my dear sir: The Cretan laws are with reason famous among the Greeks; for they fulfil the object of laws, which is to make those who use them happy; and they confer every sort of good. Now goods are of two kinds: there are human and there are divine goods, and the human ones depend upon the divine; and the state which attains the greater, at the same time acquires the less, or, not having the greater, has neither. Of the lesser goods the first is health, the second beauty, the third strength, including swiftness in running and bodily agility generally, and the fourth is wealth, not the blind god, but one who is keen of sight, if only he has wisdom for his companion. For wisdom is chief and leader of the divine class of goods, and next follows temperance; and from the union of these two with courage springs justice, and fourth in the scale of virtue is courage. All these naturally take precedence of the other goods, and this is the order in which the legislator must place them, and after them he will enjoin the rest of his regulations on the citizens with a view to these, the human looking to the divine, and the divine looking to their leader mind. Some of his regulations will relate to contracts of marriage which they make one with another, and then to the procreation and education of children, both male and female; the duty of the lawgiver will be to take charge of his citizens, in youth and age, and at every time of life, and to give them punishments and rewards; and in reference to all their intercourse with one another, he ought to consider their pains and pleasures and desires, and the vehemence of all their passions; he should keep a watch over them, and blame and praise them rightly by the mouth of the laws themselves. Also with regard to anger and terror, and the other perturbations of the soul, which arise out of misfortune, and the deliverances from them which prosperity brings, and the experiences which come to men in diseases, or in war, or poverty, or the opposite of these; in all these states he should determine and teach what is the good and evil of the condition of each. In the next place, the legislator has to be careful how the citizens make their money and in what way they spend it, and to have an eye to their mutual contracts and dissolutions of contracts, whether voluntary or involuntary: he should see how they order all this, and consider where justice as well as injustice is found or is wanting in their several dealings

with one another; and honour those who obey the law, and impose
c   fixed penalties on those who disobey, until the round of civil life is
ended, and the time has come for the consideration of the proper funeral rites and honours of the dead. And the lawgiver, reviewing his
work, will appoint guardians to preside over these things—some who
walk by intelligence, others by true opinion only, and then mind will
bind together all his regulations and show them to be in harmony with
temperance and justice, and not with wealth or ambition. This is the
d   spirit in which I was and am desirous that you should pursue the subject. I want to know the nature of all these things, and how they are
arranged in the laws of Zeus, as they are termed, and in those of the
Pythian Apollo, which Minos and Lycurgus gave; and how the order of
them is discovered to the eyes of the one who has experience in laws
gained either by study or habit, although they are far from being self-
evident to the rest of mankind like ourselves.

CLE. How shall we proceed, Stranger?

e   ATH. I think that we must begin again as before, and first consider
the habit of courage; and then we will go on and discuss another and
then another form of virtue, if you please. In this way we shall have a
model of the whole; and with these and similar discourses we will beguile the way. And when we have gone through all the virtues, we will
show, by the grace of God, that the institutions of which I was speaking look to virtue.

633   MEG. Very good; suppose that you first criticize this praiser of Zeus
and the laws of Crete.

ATH. I will try to criticize you and myself, as well as him, for the
argument is a common concern. Tell me, were not first the common
meals, and secondly the gymnasia, invented by your legislator with a
view to war?

MEG. Yes.

ATH. And what comes third, and what fourth? For that, I think, is
the sort of enumeration which ought to be made of the remaining
parts of virtue, no matter whether you call them parts or what their
name is, provided the meaning is clear.

b   MEG. Then I, or any other Spartan, would reply that hunting is third
in order.

ATH. Let us see if we can discover what comes fourth and fifth.

MEG. I think that I can get as far as the fourth head, which is the
frequent endurance of pain, exhibited among us Spartans in certain
hand-to-hand fights; also in stealing with the prospect of getting a
c   good beating; there is, too, the so-called Crypteia, or secret service, in
which wonderful endurance is shown—our people wander over the

whole country by day and by night, and even in winter have not a shoe to their foot, and are without beds to lie upon, and have to attend upon themselves. Marvellous, too, is the endurance which our citizens show in their naked exercises, contending against the violent summer heat; and there are many similar practices, to speak of which in detail would be endless.

ATH. Excellent, my Spartan sir. But how ought we to define courage? Is it to be regarded only as a combat against fears and pains, or also *d* against desires and pleasures, and against flatteries, which exercise such a tremendous power that they make the hearts even of respectable citizens to melt like wax?

MEG. I should say the latter.

ATH. In what preceded, as you will remember, our friend from Cnossos was speaking of a man or a city being inferior to themselves— were you not, Cleinias?

CLE. I was.

ATH. Now, which is in the truest sense inferior, the man who is *e* overcome by pleasure or by pain?

CLE. I should say the man who is overcome by pleasure; for all men deem him to be inferior in a more disgraceful sense than the other who is overcome by pain.

ATH. But surely the lawgivers of Crete and Sparta have not legislated for a courage which is lame of one leg, able only to meet attacks which 634 come from the left, but impotent against the insidious flatteries which come from the right?

CLE. I agree.

ATH. Then let me once more ask what institutions have you in either of your states which give a taste of pleasures, and do not avoid them any more than they avoid pains; but which set a person in the midst of them, and compel or induce him by the prospect of reward to *b* overcome. Where is a regulation about pleasure similar to that about pain to be found in your laws? Tell me what there is of this nature among you: What is there which makes your citizen equally brave against pleasure and pain, conquering what they ought to conquer, and superior to the enemies who are most dangerous and nearest home?

MEG. I was able to tell you, Stranger, many laws which were directed *c* against pain; but I do not know that I can point out any great or obvious examples of similar institutions which are concerned with pleasure; there are some lesser provisions, however, which I might mention.

CLE. Neither can I show anything of that sort which is at all equally prominent in the Cretan laws.

ATH. No wonder, my dear friends; and if, as is very likely, in our search after the true and good, one of us may have to censure the laws of the others, we must not be offended, but take kindly what another says.

CLE. You are quite right, Athenian Stranger, and we will do as you say.

d   ATH. At our time of life, Cleinias, there should be no feeling of irritation.

CLE. Certainly not.

ATH. I will not at present determine whether he who censures the Cretan or Spartan polities is right or wrong. But I believe that I can tell better than either of you what the many say about them. For assuming that you have reasonably good laws, one of the best of them will be the

e   law forbidding any young men to enquire which of them are right or wrong; but with one mouth and one voice they must all agree that the laws are all good, for they came from god; and any one who says the contrary is not to be listened to. But an old man who remarks any defect in your laws may communicate his observation to a ruler or to an equal in years when no young man is present.

635   CLE. Exactly so, Stranger; and like a diviner, although not there at the time, you seem to me quite to have hit the meaning of the legislator, and to say what is most true.

ATH. As there are no young men present, and the legislator has given old men free licence, there will be no impropriety in our discussing these very matters now that we are alone.

CLE. True. And therefore you may be as free as you like in your censure of our laws, for there is no discredit in knowing what is wrong;

b   he who receives what is said in a generous and friendly spirit will be all the better for it.

ATH. Very good; however, I am not going to say anything against your laws until to the best of my ability I have examined them, but I am going to raise doubts about them. For you are the only people known to us, whether Greek or barbarian, whom the legislator commanded to eschew all great pleasures and amusements and never to touch them; whereas in the matter of pains or fears, which we have just

c   been discussing, he thought that they who from infancy had always avoided pains and fears and sorrows, when they were compelled to face them would run away from those who were hardened in them, and would become their subjects. Now the legislator ought to have considered that this was equally true of pleasure; he should have said to himself, that if our citizens are from their youth upward unacquainted with the greatest pleasures, and unused to endure amid the temptations of pleasure, and are not disciplined to refrain from all things evil, the

d   sweet feeling of pleasure will overcome them just as fear would overcome the former class; and in another, and even a worse manner, they

will be the slaves of those who are able to endure amid pleasures, and
have had the opportunity of enjoying them, they being often the worst
of mankind. One half of their souls will be a slave, the other half free;
and they will not be worthy to be called in the true sense men and
freemen. Tell me whether you assent to my words?

CLE. On first hearing, what you say appears to be the truth; but to   *e*
be hasty in coming to a conclusion about such important matters
would be very childish and simple.

ATH. Suppose, Cleinias and Megillus, that we consider the virtue
which follows next of those which we intended to discuss (for after
courage comes temperance), what institutions shall we find relating to
temperance, either in Crete or Sparta, which, like your military institutions, differ from those of any ordinary state?

MEG. That is not an easy question to answer; still I should say that   636
the common meals and gymnastic exercises have been excellently devised for the promotion both of temperance and courage.

ATH. There seems to be a difficulty, sir, with regard to states, in
making words and facts coincide so that there can be no dispute about
them. As in the human body, the regimen which does good in one way
does harm in another; and we can hardly say that any one course of
treatment is adapted to a particular constitution. Now the gymnasia   *b*
and common meals do a great deal of good, and yet they are a source
of evil in civil troubles as shown in the case of the Milesian, and Boeo-
tian, and Thurian youth, among whom these institutions seem always
to have had a tendency to degrade the ancient and natural custom of
love below the level, not only of man, but of the beasts. The charge may
be fairly brought against your cities above all others, and is true also of   *c*
most other states which especially cultivate gymnastics. Whether such
matters are to be regarded jestingly or seriously, I think that the pleasure is to be deemed natural which arises out of the intercourse between men and women; but the intercourse of men with men, or of
women with women, is contrary to nature, and the bold attempt was
originally due to unbridled lust. The Cretans are always accused of hav-   *d*
ing invented the story of Ganymede and Zeus because they wanted to
justify themselves in the enjoyment of unnatural pleasures by the practice of the god whom they believe to have been their lawgiver.* Leaving
the story, we may observe that any speculation about laws turns almost
entirely on pleasure and pain, both in states and in individuals: these are

---

*The condemnation of homosexuality in this passage is striking (see "Introduction" to
Laws I–III). Ganymede was a young Trojan prince whom Zeus kidnapped as a companion; see *Iliad* 20.231ff.

two fountains which nature lets flow, and he who draws from them
e where and when, and as much as he ought, is happy; and this holds of
men and animals—of individuals as well as states; and he who indulges
in them ignorantly and at the wrong time, is the reverse of happy.

MEG. I admit, Stranger, that your words are well spoken, and I
hardly know what to say in answer to you; but still I think that the Spartan lawgiver was quite right in forbidding pleasure. Of the Cretan laws,
637 I shall leave the defense to my friend from Cnossos. But the laws of
Sparta, in as far as they relate to pleasure, appear to me to be the best
in the world; for that which leads mankind in general into the wildest
pleasure and licence, and every other folly, the law has clean driven out;
and neither in the country nor in towns which are under the control
of Sparta will you find revelries and the many incitements of every kind
b of pleasure which accompany them; and anyone who meets a drunken
and disorderly person will immediately have him most severely punished, and will not let him off on any pretence, not even at the time of
a Dionysiac festival; although I have remarked that this may happen at
your performances 'on the cart,' as they are called; and among our Tar-
entine colonists I have seen the whole city drunk at a Dionysiac festival; but nothing of the sort happens among us.

c ATH. My Spartan sir, these festivities are praiseworthy where there
is a spirit of endurance, but are very senseless when they are under no
regulations. In order to retaliate, an Athenian has only to point out the
licence which exists among your women.[3] To all such accusations,
whether they are brought against the Tarentines, or us, or you, there is
one answer which exonerates the practice in question from impropriety. When a stranger expresses wonder at the singularity of what he
sees, any inhabitant will naturally answer him: Wonder not, stranger;
this is our custom, and you may very likely have some other custom
about the same things. Now we are speaking, my friends, not about
d men in general, but about the merits and defects of the lawgivers themselves. Let us then discourse a little more at length about intoxication,
which is a very important subject, and will seriously test the discrimination of the legislator. I am not speaking of drinking, or not drinking,
wine at all, but of intoxication. Are we to follow the custom of the Scythians, and Persians, and Carthaginians, and Celts, and Iberians, and Thra-
e cians, who are all warlike nations, or that of your countrymen, for they,
as you say, altogether abstain? But the Scythians and Thracians, both
men and women, drink unmixed wine, which they pour on their garments, and this they think a happy and glorious institution. The Persians,
again, are much given to other practices of luxury which you reject, but
they have more moderation in them than the Thracians and Scythians.

MEG. We have only to take arms into our hands, and we send all   638
these nations flying before us.

ATH. Nay, my good friend, do not say that; there have been, as there
always will be, flights and pursuits of which no account can be given,
and therefore we cannot say that victory or defeat in battle affords more
than a doubtful proof of the goodness or badness of institutions. For
when the greater states conquer and enslave the lesser, as the Syracu-   b
sans have done the Locrians, who appear to be the best-governed people in their part of the world, or as the Athenians have done the Ceans
(and there are many other instances of the same sort of thing), all this
is not to the point; let us endeavour rather to form a conclusion about
each institution in itself and say nothing, at present, of victories and
defeats. Let us only say that such and such a custom is honorable, and
another not. And first permit me to tell you how good and bad are to
be estimated in reference to these very matters.

MEG. How?

ATH. All those who are ready at a moment's notice to praise or cen-   c
sure any practice under discussion, seem to me to proceed in a wrong
way. Let me give you an illustration of what I mean: You may suppose
a person to be praising wheat as a good kind of food, whereupon another person instantly blames wheat, without ever enquiring into its
effect or use, or in what way, or to whom, or with what, or in what
state and how, wheat is to be given. That is just what we are doing in   d
this discussion. At the very mention of the word intoxication, one side
is ready with their praises and the other with their censures; which is
absurd. For either side adduce their witnesses and approvers, and some
of us think that we speak with authority because we have many witnesses; and others because they see those who abstain conquering in
battle, and this again is disputed by us. Now I cannot say that I shall be   e
satisfied, if we go on discussing each of the remaining laws in the same
way. And about this very point of intoxication I should like to speak in
another way, which I hold to be the right one; for if number is to be
the criterion, are there not myriads upon myriads of nations ready to
dispute the point with you, who are only two cities?

MEG. I shall gladly welcome any method of enquiry which is right.   639

ATH. Let me put the matter thus: Suppose a person praises the keeping of goats, and the creatures themselves as capital things to have, and
then someone who had seen goats feeding without a goatherd in cultivated spots, and doing mischief, were to censure a goat or any other
animal who has no keeper, or a bad keeper—would there be any sense
or justice in such censure?

MEG. Certainly not.

b   *ATH.* Does a captain require only to have nautical knowledge in order to be a good captain, whether he gets sea-sick or not? What do you say?

    MEG. I say that he is not a good captain if, although he has nautical skill, he is liable to sea-sickness.

    ATH. And what would you say of the commander of an army? Will he be able to command merely because he has military skill if he be a coward, who, when danger comes, is sick and drunk with fear?

    MEG. Impossible.

    ATH. And what if besides being a coward he has no skill?

    MEG. He is a miserable fellow, not fit to be a commander of men, but only of weak women.

c   *ATH.* And what would you say of someone who blames or praises any sort of meeting which is intended by nature to have a ruler, and is well enough when under his presidency? The critic, however, has never seen the society meeting together at an orderly feast under the control of a president, but always without a ruler or with a bad one. When observers of this class praise or blame such meetings, are we to suppose that what they say is of any value?

d   *MEG.* Certainly not, if they have never seen or been present at such a meeting when rightly ordered.

    ATH. Reflect; may not banqueters and banquets be said to constitute a kind of meeting?

    MEG. Of course.

    ATH. And did anyone ever see this sort of convivial meeting rightly ordered? Of course you two will answer that you have never seen them at all, because they are not customary or lawful in your country; but I have come across many of them in many different places, and moreover I have made enquiries about them wherever I went, and never did

e I see or hear of anything of the kind which was carried on altogether rightly; in some few particulars they might be right, but in general they were utterly wrong.

    CLE. What do you mean, Stranger, by this remark? Explain. For we, as you say, from our inexperience in such matters, might very likely not know, even if they came in our way, what was right or wrong in such societies.

640   *ATH.* Likely enough; then let me try to be your instructor. You would acknowledge, would you not, that in all gatherings of mankind, of whatever sort, there ought to be a leader?

    CLE. Certainly I should.

    ATH. And we were saying just now, that when men are at war the leader ought to be a brave man?

    CLE. We were.

ATH. The brave man is less likely than the coward to be disturbed by fears?

CLE. That again is true.

ATH. And if there were a possibility of having a general of an army b
who was absolutely fearless and imperturbable, should we not by all means appoint him?

CLE. Assuredly.

ATH. Now, however, we are speaking not of a general who is to command an army, when foe meets foe in time of war, but of one who is to regulate meetings of another sort, when friend meets friend in time of peace.

CLE. True.

ATH. And that sort of meeting, if attended with drunkenness, is apt c
to be unquiet.

CLE. Certainly; the reverse of quiet.

ATH. In the first place, then, the revelers as well as the soldiers will require a ruler?

CLE. To be sure; no men more so.

ATH. And we ought, if possible, to provide them with a quiet ruler?

CLE. Of course.

ATH. And he should be a man who understands society; for his duty d
is to preserve the friendly feelings which exist among the company at the time, and to increase them for the future by his use of the occasion.

CLE. Very true.

ATH. Must we not appoint a sober, wise man to be our master of the revels? For if the ruler of drinkers is himself young and drunken, and not over-wise, only by some special good fortune will he be saved from doing some great evil.

CLE. It will be by a singular good fortune that he is saved.

ATH. Now suppose such associations to be framed in the best way possible in states, and that someone blames the very fact of their e
existence—he may very likely be right. But if he blames a practice which he only sees very much mismanaged, he shows in the first place that he is not aware of the mismanagement, and also not aware that everything done in this way will turn out to be wrong, because it is done without the superintendence of a sober ruler. Do you not see that a drunken pilot or a drunken ruler of any sort will ruin ship, chariot, 641
army—anything, in short, of which he has the direction?

CLE. The last remark is very true, Stranger; and I see quite clearly the advantage of an army having a good leader—he will give victory in war to his followers, which is a very great advantage; and so of other things. But I do not see any similar advantage which either individuals

b   or states gain from the good management of a feast; and I want you to
    tell me what great good will be effected, supposing that this drinking
    regulation is duly established.

    ATH. If you mean to ask what great good accrues to the state from
    the right training of a single youth, or of a single chorus—when the
    question is put in that form, we cannot deny that the good is not very
    great in any particular instance. But if you ask what is the good of ed-
c   ucation in general, the answer is easy: education makes good men, and
    good men act nobly, and conquer their enemies in battle, because they
    are good. Education certainly gives victory, although victory sometimes
    produces forgetfulness of education; for many have grown insolent
    from victory in war, and this insolence has engendered in them innu-
    merable evils; and many a victory has been and will be suicidal to the
    victors; but education is never suicidal.

    CLE. You seem to imply, my friend, that convivial meetings, when
d   rightly ordered, are an important element of education.

    ATH. Certainly I do.

    CLE. And can you show that what you have been saying is true?

    ATH. To be absolutely sure of the truth of matters concerning which
    there are many opinions is an attribute of the gods not given to hu-
    mans, my good man; but I shall be very happy to tell you what I think,
    especially as we are now proposing to enter on a discussion concern-
    ing laws and constitutions.

    CLE. Your opinion, Stranger, about the questions which are now
e   being raised, is precisely what we want to hear.

    ATH. Very good; I will try to find a way of explaining my meaning,
    and you will do your best to understand me. But first let me make an
    apology. The Athenian citizen is reputed among all the Greeks to be a
    great talker, whereas Sparta is renowned for brevity, and the Cretans
642 have more wit than words. Now I am afraid of appearing to elicit a very
    long discourse out of very small materials. For drinking indeed may ap-
    pear to be a slight matter, and yet is one which cannot be rightly or-
    dered according to nature, without correct principles of music; these
    are necessary to any clear or satisfactory treatment of the subject, and
b   music again runs up into education generally, and there is much to be
    said about all this. What would you say then to leaving these matters for
    the present, and passing on to some other question of law?

    MEG. Athenian Stranger, let me tell you what perhaps you do not
    know, that our family is the proxenus of your state. I imagine that from
    their earliest youth all boys, when they are told that they are the prox-
    eni of a particular state, feel kindly towards their second country; and
    this has certainly been my own feeling. I can well remember from the
c   days of my boyhood, how, when any Spartans praised or blamed the

Athenians, they used to say to me: 'See, Megillus, how ill or how well,' as the case might be, 'has your state treated us.' Having always had to fight your battles against detractors when I heard you assailed, I became warmly attached to you. And I always like to hear the Athenian dialect; the common saying is quite true, that a good Athenian is more than ordinarily good, for he is the only man who is freely and genuinely good by the divine inspiration of his own nature, and is not *d* manufactured. Therefore be assured that I shall like to hear you say whatever you have to say.

CLE. Yes, Stranger; and when you have heard me speak, say boldly what is in your thoughts. Let me remind you of a tie which unites you to Crete. You must have heard here the story of the prophet Epimenides, who was of my family, and came to Athens ten years before the Persian war, in accordance with the response of the Oracle, and offered certain sacrifices which the god commanded. The Athenians were at that time in dread of the Persian invasion; and he said that for ten *e* years they would not come, and that when they came, they would go away again without accomplishing any of their objects, and would suffer more evil than they inflicted. At that time my forefathers formed ties of hospitality with you; so ancient is the friendship which I and my parents have had for you.

ATH. You seem to be quite ready to listen; and I am also ready to 643 perform as much as I can of an almost impossible task, which I will nevertheless attempt. At the outset of the discussion, let me define the nature and power of education; for this is the way by which our argument must travel onwards to the god.

CLE. Let us proceed, if you please.

ATH. Well, then, if I tell you what are my notions of education, will *b* you consider whether they satisfy you?

CLE. Let us hear.

ATH. According to my view, any one who would be good at anything must practise that thing from his youth upwards, both in sport and earnest, in its several branches: for example, he who is to be a good builder, should play at building children's houses; he who is to be a good farmer, at tilling the ground; and those who have the care of their *c* education should provide them when young with mimic tools. They should learn beforehand the knowledge which they will afterwards require for their art. For example, the future carpenter should learn to measure or apply the line in play; and the future warrior should learn riding, or some other exercise, for amusement, and the teacher should endeavour to direct the children's inclinations and pleasures, by the help of amusements, to their final aim in life. The most important part *d* of education is right training in the nursery. The soul of the child in his play should be guided to the love of that sort of excellence in which when he grows up to manhood he will have to be perfected. Do you agree with me thus far?

CLE. Certainly.

ATH. Then let us not leave the meaning of education ambiguous or ill-defined. At present, when we speak in terms of praise or blame about the bringing-up of each person, we call one man educated and another uneducated, although the uneducated man may be sometimes very well educated for the calling of a retail trader, or of a captain of a ship, and the like. For we are not speaking of education in this narrower sense, but of that other education in virtue from youth upwards, which makes a man eagerly pursue the ideal perfection of citizenship, and teaches him how rightly to rule and how to obey. This is the only education which, upon our view, deserves the name; that other sort of training, which aims at the acquisition of wealth or bodily strength, or mere cleverness apart from intelligence and justice, is mean and illiberal, and is not worthy to be called education at all. But let us not quarrel with one another about a word, provided that the proposition which has just been granted holds good: to wit, that those who are rightly educated generally become good men. Neither must we cast a slight upon education, which is the first and fairest thing that the best of men can ever have, and which, though liable to take a wrong direction, is capable of reformation. And this work of reformation is the great business of every man while he lives.

CLE. Very true; we entirely agree with you.

ATH. And we agreed before that they are good men who are able to rule themselves, and bad men who are not.

CLE. You are quite right.

ATH. Let me now proceed, if I can, to clear up the subject a little further by an illustration which I will offer you.

CLE. Proceed.

ATH. Do we not consider each of ourselves to be one?

CLE. We do.

ATH. And each one of us has in his bosom two counsellors, both foolish and also antagonistic; of which we call the one pleasure, and the other pain.

CLE. Exactly.

ATH. Also there are opinions about the future, which have the general name of expectations; and the specific name of fear, when the expectation is of pain; and of hope, when of pleasure; and further, there is reflection about the good or evil of them, and this, when embodied in a decree by the State, is called Law.

CLE. I am hardly able to follow you; proceed, however, as if I were.

Meg. Same here.

Ath. Let us look at the matter thus: May we not conceive each of us living beings to be a puppet of the gods, either their plaything only, or created with a purpose—which of the two we cannot certainly know? But we do know that these affections in us are like cords and strings,   *e* which pull us different and opposite ways, and to opposite actions; and herein lies the difference between virtue and vice. According to the argument there is one among these cords which every man ought to grasp and never let go, but to pull with it against all the rest; and this is the sacred and golden cord of reason, called by us the common law   645 of the State; there are others which are hard and of iron, but this one is soft because golden; and there are several other kinds. Now we ought always to co-operate with the lead of the best, which is law. For inasmuch as reason is beautiful and gentle, and not violent, her rule must have ministers in order to help the golden principle in vanquishing the other principles. And thus the moral of the tale about our being pup-   *b* pets will not have been lost, and the meaning of the expression 'superior or inferior to a man's self' will become clearer; the individual, attaining to right reason in this matter of pulling the strings of the puppet, should live according to its rule; the city, receiving the same from some god or from one who has knowledge of these things, should embody it in a law, to be her guide in her dealings with herself and with   *c* other states. In this way virtue and vice will be more clearly distinguished by us. And when they have become clearer, education and other institutions will in like manner become clearer; and in particular that question of convivial entertainment, which may seem, perhaps, to have been a very trifling matter, and to have taken a great many more words than were necessary.

Cle. Perhaps, however, the theme may turn out not to be unworthy of the length of discourse.

Ath. Very good; let us proceed with any enquiry which really bears on our present object.

Cle. Proceed.

Ath. Suppose that we give this puppet of ours drink—what will be   *d* the effect on him?

Cle. Having what in view do you ask that question?

Ath. Nothing as yet; but I ask generally, when the puppet is brought to the drink, what sort of result is likely to follow? I will endeavour to explain my meaning more clearly; what I am now asking is this: Does the drinking of wine heighten and increase pleasures and pains, and passions and loves?

Cle. Very greatly.

Ath. And are perception and memory, and opinion and prudence,   *e* heightened and increased? Do not these qualities entirely desert a man if he becomes saturated with drink?

CLE. Yes, they entirely desert him.

ATH. Does he not return to the state of soul in which he was when a young child?

CLE. He does.

ATH. Then at that time he will have the least control over himself?

CLE. Yes.

646

ATH. And will he not be in a most wretched plight?

CLE. Indeed he will be.

ATH. Then not only an old man but also a drunkard becomes a second time a child?

CLE. Well said, Stranger.

ATH. Is there any argument which will prove to us that we ought to encourage the taste for drinking instead of doing all we can to avoid it?

CLE. I suppose that there is; you, at any rate, were just now saying that you were ready to maintain such a doctrine.

b   ATH. True, I was; and I am ready still, seeing that you have both declared that you are anxious to hear me.

CLE. To be sure we are, if only for the strangeness of the paradox, which asserts that a man ought of his own accord to plunge into utter degradation.

ATH. Are you speaking of the soul?

CLE. Yes.

ATH. And what would you say about the body, my friend? Are you

c   not surprised at anyone of his own accord bringing upon himself deformity, leanness, ugliness, decrepitude?

CLE. Certainly.

ATH. Yet when a man goes of his own accord to a doctor's shop, and takes medicine, is he not quite aware that soon, and for many days afterwards, he will be in a state of body which he would die rather than accept as the permanent condition of his life? Are not those who train in gymnasia, at first beginning reduced to a state of weakness?

CLE. Yes, all that is well known.

ATH. Also that they go of their own accord for the sake of the subsequent benefit?

d   CLE. Very well put.

ATH. And we may conceive this to be true in the same way of other practices?

CLE. Certainly.

ATH. And the same view may be taken of the pastime of drinking wine, if we are right in supposing that the same good effect follows?

CLE. To be sure.

ATH. If such convivialities should turn out to have any advantage equal in importance to that of gymnastic, they are in their very nature to be preferred to mere bodily exercise, inasmuch as they have no accompaniment of pain.

CLE. True; but I hardly think that we shall be able to discover any e such benefits to be derived from them.

ATH. That is just what we must endeavour to show. Let me ask you a question: Do we not distinguish two kinds of fear, which are very different?

CLE. What are they?

ATH. There is the fear of expected evil.

CLE. Yes.

ATH. And there is the fear of an evil reputation; we are afraid of being thought evil, because we do or say some dishonorable thing, 647 which fear we and all men term shame.

CLE. Certainly.

ATH. These are the two fears, as I called them; one of which is the opposite of pain and other fears, and the opposite also of the greatest and most numerous sort of pleasures.

CLE. Very true.

ATH. And does not the legislator, and everyone who is good for anything, hold this fear in the greatest honor? This is what he terms reverence, and the confidence which is the reverse of this he terms b insolence; and the latter he always deems to be a very great evil both in private and in public life.

CLE. True.

ATH. Does not this kind of fear preserve us in many important ways? What is there which so surely gives victory and safety in war? For there are two things which give victory—confidence before enemies, and fear of disgrace before friends.

CLE. Yes.

ATH. Then each of us should be fearless and also fearful; and why we should be either has now been determined. c

CLE. Certainly.

ATH. And when we want to make anyone fearless, we and the law bring him face to face with many fears.

CLE. Clearly.

ATH. And when we want to make him rightly fearful, must we not introduce him to shameless pleasures, and train him to take up arms against them, and to overcome them? Or does this principle apply to d courage only, and must he who would be perfect in valor fight against and overcome his own natural character—since if he is unpracticed and inexperienced in such conflicts, he will not be half the man which he might have been—and are we to suppose that with temperance it is otherwise, and that he who has never fought with the shameless and unrighteous temptations of his pleasures and lusts, and conquered them, in earnest and in play, by word, deed, and act, will still be perfectly temperate?

CLE. A most unlikely supposition.

ATH. Suppose that some god had given a fear-potion to men, and that the more a man drank of this the more he regarded himself at every draught as a child of misfortune, and that he feared everything happening or about to happen to him; and that at last the most courageous of men utterly lost his presence of mind for a time, and only came to himself again when he had slept off the influence of the draught.

CLE. But has such a draught, Stranger, ever really been known among men?

ATH. No; but, if there had been, might not such a draught have been of use to the legislator as a test of courage? Might we not go and say to him: 'Legislator, whether you are legislating for the Cretan, or for any other State, would you not like to have a touchstone of the courage and cowardice of your citizens?'

CLE. 'I would,' will be the answer of everyone.

ATH. 'And you would rather have a touchstone in which there is no risk and no great danger than the reverse?'

CLE. In that proposition everyone may safely agree.

ATH. 'And in order to make use of the draught, you would lead them amid these imaginary terrors, and test them, when the affection of fear was working upon them, and compel them to be fearless, exhorting and admonishing them; and also honoring them, but dishonoring any one who will not be persuaded by you to be in all respects such as you command him; and if he underwent the trial well and manfully, you would let him go unscathed; but if badly, you would inflict a punishment upon him? Or would you abstain from using the potion altogether, although you have no reason for abstaining?'

CLE. He would be certain, Stranger, to use the potion.

ATH. This would be a mode of testing and training which would be wonderfully easy in comparison with those now in use, and might be applied to a single person, or to a few, or indeed to any number; and he would do well who provided himself with the potion only, rather than with any number of other things, whether he preferred to be by himself in solitude, and there contend with his fears, because he was ashamed to be seen by the eye of man until he was perfect; or trusting to the force of his own nature and habits, and believing that he had been already disciplined sufficiently, he did not hesitate to train himself in company with any number of others, and display his power in conquering

the irresistible change effected by the draught—his virtue being such
that he never in any instance fell into any great unseemliness, but was   e
always himself, and left off before he arrived at the last cup, fearing that
he, like all other men, might be overcome by the potion.

CLE. Yes, Stranger, in that last case, too, he might equally show his
self-control.

ATH. Let us return to the lawgiver, and say to him: 'Well, lawgiver,   649
there is certainly no such fear-potion which man has either received
from the gods or himself discovered; for witchcraft has no place at our
board. But is there any potion which might serve as a test of overbold-
ness and excessive and indiscreet boasting?'

CLE. I suppose that he will say, 'Yes,' meaning that wine is such a
potion.

ATH. Is not the effect of this quite the opposite of the effect of the
other? When a man drinks wine he begins to be better pleased with   b
himself, and the more he drinks the more he is filled full of brave
hopes, and conceit of his power, and at last the string of his tongue
is loosened, and, fancying himself wise, he is brimming over with
lawlessness, and has no more fear or respect, and is ready to do or say
anything.

CLE. I think that everyone will admit the truth of your description.

MEG. Certainly.

ATH. Now, let us remember, as we were saying, that there are two
things which should be cultivated in the soul: first, the greatest courage;   c
secondly, the greatest fear.

CLE. Which you said to be characteristic of reverence, if I am not
mistaken.

ATH. Thank you for reminding me. But now, as the habit of courage
and fearlessness is to be trained amid fears, let us consider whether the
opposite quality is not also to be trained among opposites.

CLE. That is probably the case.

ATH. There are times and seasons at which we are by nature more
than commonly valiant and bold; now we ought to train ourselves on
these occasions to be as free from impudence and shamelessness as   d
possible, and to be afraid to say or suffer or do anything that is base.

CLE. True.

ATH. Are not the moments in which we are apt to be bold and
shameless such as these: when we are under the influence of anger,
love, pride, ignorance, avarice, cowardice? or when wealth, beauty,
strength, and all the intoxicating workings of pleasure madden us?
What is better adapted than the festive use of wine, in the first place to
test, and in the second place to train the character of a man, if care be   e
taken in the use of it? What is there cheaper, or more innocent? For do

but consider which is the greater risk: Would you rather test a man of a morose and savage nature, which is the source of a myriad acts of in-
650 justice, by making bargains with him at a risk to yourself, or by having him as a companion at the festival of Dionysus? Or would you, if you wanted to apply a touchstone to a man who is prone to sex, entrust your wife, or your sons, or daughters to him, putting your dearest at risk in order to have a view of the condition of his soul? I might mention numberless cases in which the advantage would be manifest of getting to know a character in sport, and without paying dearly for ex-
b perience. And I do not believe that either a Cretan, or any other man, will doubt that such a test is a fair test. It is also safer, cheaper, and speedier than any other.

CLE. That is certainly true.

ATH. And this knowledge of the natures and habits of men's souls will be of the greatest use in that art which has the management of them; and that art, if I am not mistaken, is politics.

CLE. Exactly so.

BOOK II

652 ATHENIAN STRANGER. AND now we have to consider whether the insight into human nature is the only benefit derived from well-ordered drinking, or whether there are not other advantages great and much to be desired. The argument seems to imply that there are. But how and in
b what way these are to be attained, will have to be considered attentively, or we may be entangled in error.

CLEINIAS. Proceed.

ATH. Let me once more recall our doctrine of right education;
653 which, if I am not mistaken, depends on the due regulation of convivial intercourse.

CLE. You talk rather grandly.

ATH. Pleasure and pain I maintain to be the first perceptions of children, and I say that they are the forms under which virtue and vice are originally present to them. As to wisdom and true and fixed opinions, happy is the man who acquires them, even when declining in years; and we may say that he who possesses them, and the blessings which are
b contained in them, is a perfect man. Now I mean by education that training which is given by suitable habits to the first instincts of virtue in children; when pleasure, and friendship, and pain, and hatred, are rightly implanted in souls not yet capable of understanding their nature, and who find them, after they have attained reason, to be in harmony with her. This harmony of the soul, taken as a whole, is virtue;

but the particular training in respect of pleasure and pain, which leads   *c*
you always to hate what you ought to hate, and love what you ought
to love from the beginning of life to the end, may be separated off; and,
in my view, will be rightly called education.

CLE. I think, Stranger, that you are quite right in all that you have
said and are saying about education.

ATH. I am glad to hear that you agree with me; for, indeed, the discipline of pleasure and pain which, when rightly ordered, is a principle of education, has been often relaxed and corrupted in human life.   *d*
And the gods, pitying the toils which our race is born to undergo, have
appointed holy festivals, wherein men alternate rest with labour; and
have given them the Muses and Apollo, the leader of the Muses, and
Dionysus, to be companions in their revels, that they may improve their
education by taking part in the festivals of the gods, and with their
help. I should like to know whether a common saying is in our opinion true to nature or not. For men say that the young of all creatures
cannot be quiet in their bodies or in their voices; they are always want-   *e*
ing to move and cry out; some leaping and skipping, and overflowing
with sportiveness and delight at something, others uttering all sorts of
cries. But, whereas the animals have no perception of order or disorder
in their movements, that is, of rhythm or harmony, as they are called,
to us, the gods, who, as we say, have been appointed to be our com-   654
panions in the dance, have given the pleasurable sense of harmony and
rhythm; and so they stir us into life, and we follow them, joining hands
together in dances and songs; and these they call choruses, which is a
term naturally expressive of cheerfulness. Shall we begin, then, with the
acknowledgment that education is first given through Apollo and the
Muses? What do you say?

CLE. I assent.

ATH. And the uneducated is he who has not been trained in the
chorus, and the educated is he who has been well trained?   *b*

CLE. Certainly.

ATH. And the chorus is made up of two parts, dance and song?

CLE. True.

ATH. Then he who is well educated will be able to sing and dance
well?

CLE. I suppose that he will.

ATH. Let us see; what are we saying?

CLE. What?

ATH. He sings well and dances well; now must we add that he sings   *c*
what is good and dances what is good?

CLE. Let us make the addition.

ATH. We will suppose that he knows the good to be good, and the bad to be bad, and makes use of them accordingly: which now is the better trained in dancing and music—he who is able to move his body and to use his voice in what is understood to be the right manner, but

d   has no delight in good or hatred of evil; or he who is incorrect in gesture and voice, but is right in his sense of pleasure and pain, and welcomes what is good, and is offended at what is evil?

CLE. There is a great difference, Stranger, in the two kinds of education.

ATH. If we three know what is good in song and dance, then we truly know also who is educated and who is uneducated; but if not, then we certainly shall not know wherein lies the safeguard of education,

e   and whether there is any or not.

CLE. True.

ATH. Let us follow the scent like hounds, and go in pursuit of beauty of figure, and melody, and song, and dance; if these escape us, there will be no use in talking about true education, whether Greek or barbarian.

CLE. Yes.

ATH. And what is beauty of figure, or beautiful melody? When a

655 manly soul is in trouble, and when a cowardly soul is in similar case, are they likely to use the same figures and gestures, or to give utterance to the same sounds?

CLE. How can they, when the very colors of their faces differ?

ATH. Good, my friend; I may observe, however, in passing, that in music there certainly are figures and there are melodies. And music is concerned with harmony and rhythm, so that you may speak of a melody or figure having good rhythm or good harmony—the term is correct enough; but to speak metaphorically of a melody or figure having a 'good color,' as the masters of choruses do, is not allowable, although you can speak of the melodies or figures of the brave and the

b   coward, praising the one and censuring the other. Not to be tedious, let us say that the figures and melodies which are expressive of virtue of soul or body, or of images of virtue, are without exception good, and those which are expressive of vice are the reverse of good.

CLE. Your suggestion is excellent; let us say that these things are so.

ATH. Once more, are all of us equally delighted with every sort of

c   dance?

CLE. Far otherwise.

ATH. What, then, leads us astray? Are beautiful things not the same to us all, or are they the same in themselves, but not in our opinion of them? For no one will admit that forms of vice in the dance are more beautiful than forms of virtue, or that he himself delights in the forms of vice, and others in a muse of another character. And yet most per-

d   sons say that the excellence of music is to give pleasure to our souls.

But this is intolerable and blasphemous; there is, however, a much more plausible account of the delusion.

CLE. What?

ATH. The adaptation of art to the characters of men. Choral movements are imitations of manners occurring in various actions, fortunes, dispositions; each particular is imitated, and those to whom the words, or songs, or dances are suited, either by nature or habit or both, cannot help feeling pleasure in them and applauding them, and calling them beautiful. But those whose natures, or ways, or habits are unsuited to them, cannot delight in them or applaud them, and they call them base. There are others, again, whose natures are right and their habits wrong, or whose habits are right and their natures wrong, and they praise one thing, but are pleased at another. For they say that all these imitations are pleasant, but not good. And in the presence of those whom they think wise, they are ashamed of dancing and singing in the baser manner, or of deliberately lending any countenance to such proceedings; and yet, they have a secret pleasure in them.

CLE. Very true.

ATH. And is any harm done to the lover of vicious dances or songs, or any good done to the approver of the opposite sort of pleasure?

CLE. I think that there is.

ATH. 'I think' is not the word, but I would say, rather, 'I am certain.' For must they not have the same effect as when a man associates with bad characters, whom he likes and approves rather than dislikes, and only censures playfully because he has a suspicion of his own badness? In that case, he who takes pleasure in them will surely become like those in whom he takes pleasure, even though he is ashamed to praise them. And what greater good or evil can any destiny ever make us undergo?

CLE. I know of none.

ATH. Then in a city which has good laws, or in future ages is to have them, bearing in mind the instruction and amusement which are given by music, can we suppose that the poets are to be allowed to teach in the dance anything which they themselves like, in the way of rhythm, or melody, or words, to the young children of any well-conditioned parents? Is the poet to train his choruses as he pleases, without reference to virtue or vice?

CLE. That is surely quite unreasonable, and is not to be thought of.

ATH. And yet he may do this in almost any state with the exception of Egypt.

CLE. And what are the laws about music and dancing in Egypt?

ATH. You will wonder when I tell you: Long ago they appear to have recognized the very principle of which we are now speaking—that their young citizens must be habituated to forms and strains of virtue.

These they fixed, and exhibited the patterns of them in their temples;
e   and no painter or artist is allowed to innovate upon them, or to leave
the traditional forms and invent new ones. To this day, no alteration is
allowed either in these arts, or in music at all. And you will find that
their works of art are painted or moulded in the same forms which they
657 had ten thousand years ago—this is literally true and no exaggeration
—their ancient paintings and sculptures are no better or worse than the
work of today, but are made with just the same skill.

CLE. How extraordinary!

ATH. I should rather say, 'How statesmanlike, how worthy of a legislator!' I know that other things in Egypt are not so well. But what I
am telling you about music is true and deserving of consideration, because it shows that a lawgiver may institute melodies which have a natural truth and correctness without any fear of failure. To do this, however,
must be the work of god, or of a divine person; in Egypt they have a
tradition that their ancient chants which have been preserved for so
b   many ages are the composition of the goddess Isis. And therefore, as I
was saying, if a person can only find in any way the natural melodies,
he may confidently embody them in a fixed and legal form. For the love
of novelty which arises out of pleasure in the new and weariness of the
old, has not strength enough to corrupt the consecrated song and
dance, under the plea that they have become antiquated. At any rate,
they are far from being corrupted in Egypt.

c   CLE. Your arguments seem to prove your point.

ATH. May we not confidently say that the true use of music and of
choral festivities is as follows: We rejoice when we think that we prosper, and again we think that we prosper when we rejoice?

CLE. Exactly.

ATH. And when rejoicing in our good fortune, we are unable to be
still?

CLE. True.

d   ATH. Our young men break forth into dancing and singing, and we
who are their elders deem that we are fulfilling our part in life when
we look on at them. Having lost our agility, we delight in their sports
and merry-making, because we love to think of our former selves; and
gladly institute contests for those who are able to awaken in us the
memory of our youth.

CLE. Very true.

e   ATH. Is it altogether unmeaning to say, as the common people do
about festivals, that he should be judged the wisest of men, and the
winner of the palm, who gives us the greatest amount of pleasure and
mirth? For on such occasions, and when mirth is the order of the day,
658 ought not he to be honored most, and, as I was saying, bear the palm,

who gives most mirth to the greatest number? Now is this a true way of speaking or of acting?

CLE. Possibly.

ATH. My dear friend, let us distinguish between different cases, and not be hasty in forming a judgment; one way of considering the question will be to imagine a festival at which there are entertainments of all sorts, including gymnastic, musical, and equestrian contests: the citizens are assembled; prizes are offered, and proclamation is made that anyone who likes may enter the lists, and that he is to bear the palm who gives the most pleasure to the spectators—there is to be no regulation about the manner how; but he who is most successful in giving pleasure is to be crowned victor, and deemed to be the pleasantest of the candidates. What is likely to be the result of such a proclamation?

CLE. In what respect?

ATH. There would be various exhibitions: one man, like Homer, will exhibit a rhapsody, another a performance on the lute; one will have a tragedy, and another a comedy. Nor would there be anything astonishing in someone imagining that he could gain the prize by exhibiting a puppet-show. Suppose these competitors to meet, and not these only, but innumerable others as well—can you tell me who ought to be the victor?

CLE. I do not see how anyone can answer you, or pretend to know, unless he has heard with his own ears the several competitors; the question is absurd.

ATH. Well, then, if neither of you can answer, shall I answer this question which you deem so absurd?

CLE. By all means.

ATH. If very small children are to determine the question, they will decide for the puppet-show.

CLE. Of course.

ATH. The older children will be advocates of comedy; educated women, and young men, and people in general, will favour tragedy.

CLE. Very likely.

ATH. And I believe that we old men would have the greatest pleasure in hearing a rhapsode recite well the *Iliad* and *Odyssey*, or one of the Hesiodic poems, and would award the victory to him. But, who would really be the victor?—that is the question.

CLE. Yes.

ATH. Clearly you and I will have to declare that those whom we old men judge victors ought to win; for our ways are far and away better than any which at present exist anywhere in the world.

CLE. Certainly.

ATH. Thus far I too should agree with the many that the excellence

of music is to be measured by pleasure. But the pleasure must not be that of chance persons; the fairest music is that which delights the best
659 and best educated, and especially that which delights the one man who is pre-eminent in virtue and education. And therefore the judges must be men of character, for they will require both wisdom and courage; the true judge must not draw his inspiration from the theatre, nor ought he to be unnerved by the clamour of the many and his own incapacity; nor again, knowing the truth, ought he through cowardice and unmanliness carelessly to deliver a lying judgment, with the very same lips which have just appealed to the gods before he judged. He is
b sitting not as the disciple of the theatre, but, in his proper place, as their instructor, and he ought to be the enemy of all pandering to the pleasure of the spectators. The ancient and common custom of the Greek world, which still prevails in Italy and Sicily, did certainly leave the judgment to the body of spectators, who determined the victor by show of hands. But this custom has been the destruction of the poets; for they are now in the habit of composing with a view to please the bad taste of their judges, and the result is that the spectators instruct
c themselves—it has also been the ruin of the theatre; they ought to be having characters put before them better than their own, and so receiving a higher pleasure, but now by their own act the opposite result follows. What inference is to be drawn from all this? Shall I tell you?

CLE. What?

d   ATH. The inference at which we arrive for the third or fourth time is that education is the constraining and directing of youth towards that right reason, which the law affirms, and which the experience of the eldest and best has agreed to be truly right. In order, then, that the soul of the child may not be habituated to feel joy and sorrow in a manner at variance with the law, and those who obey the law, but may rather follow the law and rejoice and sorrow at the same things as the aged— in order, I say, to produce this effect, chants appear to have been invented, which really enchant, and are designed to implant that harmony
e of which we speak. And, because the mind of the child is incapable of enduring serious training, they are called plays and songs, and are performed in play; just as when men are sick and ailing in their bod-
660 ies, their attendants give them wholesome diet in pleasant meats and drinks, but unwholesome diet in disagreeable things, in order that they may learn, as they ought, to like the one and dislike the other. Similarly, the true legislator will persuade, and, if he cannot persuade, will compel the poet to express, as he ought, by fair and noble words, in his rhythms, the figures, and in his melodies, the music of temperate and brave and in every way good men.

b   CLE. But do you really imagine, Stranger, that this is the way in

which poets generally compose in States at the present day? As far as I can observe, except among us and the Spartans, there are no regulations like those of which you speak; in other places novelties are always being introduced in dancing and in music, generally not under the authority of any law, but at the instigation of lawless pleasures; and these pleasures are so far from being the same, as you describe the Egyptian   c
to be, or having the same principles, that they are never the same.

ATH. Most true, Cleinias; and I daresay that I may have expressed myself obscurely, and so led you to imagine that I was speaking of some really existing state of things, whereas I was only saying what regulations I would like to have about music; and hence there occurred a misapprehension on your part. For when evils are far gone and irremediable, the task of censuring them is never pleasant, although at   d
times necessary. But as we do not really differ, will you let me ask you whether you consider such institutions to be more prevalent among the Cretans and Spartans than among the other Greeks?

CLE. Certainly they are.

ATH. And if they were extended to the other Greeks, would it be an improvement on the present state of things?

CLE. A very great improvement, if the customs which prevail among them were such as prevail among us and the Spartans, and such as you were just now saying ought to prevail.

ATH. Let us see whether we understand one another: Are not the principles of education and music which prevail among you as follows: e
you compel your poets to say that the good man, if he be temperate and just, is fortunate and happy; and this whether he is great and strong or small and weak, and whether rich or poor; on the other hand, if he has a wealth passing that of Cinyras* or Midas,† and is unjust, he is wretched and lives in misery? As the poet says, and with truth: I sing not, I care not about him who accomplishes all noble things, not having justice; let him who 'draws near and stretches out his hand against his enemies be a just man.' But if he is unjust, I would not have him 'look calmly upon bloody death,' nor 'surpass in swiftness the Thracian   661
Boreas,'‡ and let no other thing that is called good ever be his. For the goods of which the many speak are not really good: First in the catalogue is placed health, beauty next, wealth third; and then innumerable others, as for example to have a keen eye or a quick ear, and in general   b
to have the senses perfect; or, again, to be a tyrant and do as you like;

---

*Mythical king of Cyprus.
†Mythical king of Phrygia, known for his golden touch.
‡God of the North Wind.

and the final consummation of happiness is to have acquired all these things, and when you have acquired them to become at once immortal. But you and I say that, while to the just and holy all these things are the best of possessions, to the unjust they are all, including even health, c the greatest of evils. For in truth, to have sight, and hearing, and the use of the senses, or to live at all without justice and virtue, even though rich in all the so-called goods of fortune, is the greatest of evils, if life be immortal; but not great, if the bad man lives only a very short time. These are the truths which, if I am not mistaken, you will persuade or compel our poets to utter with suitable accompaniments of harmony d and rhythm, and in these they must train up your youth. Am I not right? For I plainly declare that evils as they are termed are goods to the unjust, and only evils to the just, and that goods are truly good to the good, but evil to the evil. Let me ask again: Are you and I agreed about this?

CLE. I think that we partly agree and partly do not.

ATH. When a man has health and wealth and a tyranny which lasts, and when he is pre-eminent in strength and courage, and has the gift e of immortality, and none of the so-called evils which counter-balance these goods, but only the injustice and insolence of his own nature— of such a man you are, I suspect, unwilling to believe that he is miserable rather than happy.

CLE. That is quite true.

ATH. Once more: Suppose that he is valiant and strong, and handsome and rich, and does throughout his whole life whatever he likes; 662 still, if he is unrighteous and insolent, would not both of you agree that he will of necessity live basely? You will surely grant so much?

CLE. Certainly.

ATH. And an evil life too?

CLE. I am not equally disposed to grant that.

ATH. Will he not live painfully and to his own disadvantage?

CLE. How can I possibly say so?

b ATH. How! May heaven make us to be of one mind, for now we are of two. To me, dear Cleinias, the truth of what I am saying is as plain as the fact that Crete is an island. And, if I were a lawgiver, I would try to make the poets and all the citizens speak in this strain; and I would inflict the heaviest penalties on anyone in all the land who should dare to say that there are bad men who lead pleasant lives, or that the prof- c itable and gainful is one thing, and the just another; and there are many other matters about which I would make my citizens speak in a manner different from the Cretans and Spartans of this age, and I may say, indeed, from the world in general. For tell me, my good friends, by Zeus

and Apollo tell me, if I were to ask these same gods who were your legislators: 'Is not the most just life also the pleasantest, or are there two   *d*
lives, one of which is the justest and the other the pleasantest?' and
they were to reply that there are two; and thereupon I proceeded to ask:
'Which are the happier—those who lead the justest, or those who lead
the pleasantest life?' and they replied, 'Those who lead the pleasantest,'
that would be a very strange answer, which I would not like to put
into the mouth of the gods. The words will come with more propriety
from the lips of fathers and legislators, and therefore I will repeat my
former questions to one of them, and suppose him to say again that he
who leads the pleasantest life is the happiest. And to that I rejoin: 'Father,
did you not wish me to live as happily as possible? And yet you also never
ceased telling me that I should live as justly as possible.' Now, here the
giver of the rule, whether legislator or father, will be in a dilemma, and
will in vain endeavour to be consistent with himself. But if he were to
declare that the justest life is also the happiest, every one hearing him   663
would enquire, if I am not mistaken, what is that good and noble principle in life which the law approves, and which is superior to pleasure.
For what good can the just man have which is separated from pleasure?
Shall we say that glory and fame, coming from gods and men, though
good and noble, are nevertheless unpleasant, and infamy pleasant? Certainly not, sweet legislator. Or shall we say that the not-doing of wrong
and there being no wrong done is good and honorable, although there
is no pleasure in it, and that the doing wrong is pleasant, but evil and
base?

CLE. Impossible.

ATH. The view which identifies the pleasant and the just and the   *b*
good and the noble has an excellent moral and religious tendency. And
the opposite view is most at variance with the designs of the legislator,
and is, in his opinion, infamous; for no one, if he can help it, will be
persuaded to do what gives him more pain than pleasure. But as distant prospects are apt to make us dizzy, especially in childhood, the legislator will try to purge away the darkness and exhibit the truth; he will   *c*
persuade the citizens, in some way or other, by customs and praises
and words, that just and unjust are shadows only, and that injustice,
which seems opposed to justice, when contemplated by the unjust and
evil man, appears pleasant and the just most unpleasant; but that from
the just man's point of view, the very opposite is the appearance of
both of them.

CLE. True.

ATH. And which may be supposed to be the truer judgment—that
of the inferior or of the better soul?

d   CLE. Surely, that of the better soul.

ATH. Then the unjust life must not only be more base and depraved, but also more unpleasant than the just and holy life?

CLE. That seems to be implied in the present argument.

ATH. And even supposing this were otherwise, and not as the argument has proven, still the lawgiver, who is worth anything, if he ever ventures to tell a lie to the young for their good, could not invent a more useful lie than this, or one which will have a better effect in mak-
e   ing them do what is right, not on compulsion but voluntarily.

CLE. Truth, Stranger, is a noble and lasting thing, but a thing of which men are hard to be persuaded.

ATH. And yet the story of the Sidonian Cadmus,* which is so improbable, has been readily believed, and also innumerable other tales.

CLE. What is that story?

ATH. The story of armed men springing up after the sowing of teeth, which the legislator may take as a proof that he can persuade the
664   minds of the young of anything; so that he has only to reflect and find out what belief will be of the greatest public advantage, and then use all his efforts to make the whole community utter one and the same word in their songs and tales and discourses all their life long. But if you do not agree with me, there is no reason why you should not argue on the other side.

b   CLE. I do not see that any argument can fairly be raised by either of us against what you are now saying.

ATH. The next suggestion which I have to offer is that all our three choruses shall sing to the young and tender souls of children, reciting in their strains all the noble thoughts of which we have already spoken, or are about to speak; and the sum of them shall be, that the life which
c   is deemed by the gods to be the happiest is also the best; we shall affirm this to be a most certain truth; and the minds of our young disciples will be more likely to receive these words of ours than any others which we might address to them.

CLE. I assent to what you say.

ATH. First will enter in their natural order the sacred choir composed of children, which is to sing lustily the heaven-taught lay to the whole city. Next will follow the choir of young men under the age of
d   thirty, who will call upon the god Paean to testify to the truth of their words, and will pray him to be gracious to the youth and to turn their hearts. Thirdly, the choir of elder men, who are from thirty to sixty

---

*In the foundational myth of Thebes, Cadmus sows the teeth of a dragon, from which warriors spring up.

years of age, will also sing. There remain those who are too old to sing, and they will tell stories, illustrating the same virtues, as with the voice of an oracle.

CLE. Who are those who compose the third choir, Stranger? for I do not clearly understand what you mean to say about them.

ATH. And yet almost all that I have been saying has been said with a view to them.

CLE. Will you try to be a little plainer?

ATH. I was speaking at the commencement of our discourse, as you will remember, of the fiery nature of young creatures. I said that they were unable to keep quiet either in limb or voice, and that they called out and jumped about in a disorderly manner; and that no other animal attained to any perception of order, but man only. Now the order of motion is called rhythm, and the order of the voice, in which high and low are duly mingled, is called harmony; and both together are termed choral song. And I said that the gods had pity on us, and gave us Apollo and the Muses to be our playfellows and leaders in the dance; and Dionysus, as I daresay that you will remember, was the third.

CLE. I quite remember.

ATH. Thus far I have spoken of the chorus of Apollo and the Muses, and I have still to speak of the remaining chorus, which is that of Dionysus.

CLE. How is that arranged? There is something strange, at any rate on first hearing, in a Dionysiac chorus of old men, if you really mean that those who are above thirty, and may be fifty, or from fifty to sixty years of age, are to dance in his honour.

ATH. Very true; and therefore it must be shown that there is good reason for the proposal.

CLE. Certainly.

ATH. Are we agreed thus far?

CLE. About what?

ATH. That every man and boy, slave and free, both sexes, and the whole city, should never cease charming themselves with the strains of which we have spoken; and that there should be every sort of change and variation of them in order to take away the effect of sameness, so that the singers may always receive pleasure from their hymns, and may never weary of them?

CLE. Everyone will agree.

ATH. Where, then, will that best part of our city which, by reason of age and intelligence, has the greatest influence, sing these fairest of strains, which are to do so much good? Shall we be so foolish as to let them off who would give us the most beautiful and also the most useful of songs?

CLE. But, says the argument, we cannot let them off.

ATH. Then how can we carry out our purpose with decorum? Will this be the way?

CLE. Will what be the way?

ATH. When a man is advancing in years, he is afraid and reluctant
e to sing; he has no pleasure in his own performances. If compulsion is used, he will be more and more ashamed, the older and more discreet he grows; is not this true?

CLE. Certainly.

ATH. Well, and will he not be yet more ashamed if he has to stand up and sing in the theatre to a mixed audience? Moreover, when he is required to do so, like the other choirs who contend for prizes and have been trained under a singing master, if he is pinched and hungry,
666 he will certainly have a feeling of shame and discomfort which will make him very unwilling to exhibit.

CLE. No doubt.

ATH. How, then, shall we reassure him, and get him to sing? Shall we begin by enacting that boys shall not taste wine at all until they are eighteen years of age; we will tell them that fire must not be poured upon fire, whether in the body or in the soul, until they begin to go to work—this is a precaution which has to be taken against the excitableness of youth. Afterwards they may taste wine in moderation up to the age of thirty, but while a man is young he should abstain altogether
b from intoxication and from excess of wine; when, at length, he has reached forty years, after dinner at a public mess, he may invite not only the other gods, but Dionysus above all, to the mystery and festivity of the elder men, making use of the wine which he has given men to lighten the sourness of old age; so that in age we may renew our youth, and forget our sorrows; and also in order that the nature of the
c soul, like iron melted in the fire, may become softer and so more impressible. In the first place, will not anyone who is thus mellowed be more ready and less ashamed to sing—I do not say before a large audience, but before a moderate company; nor yet among strangers, but among his familiars, and, as we have often said, to chant, and to enchant?

CLE. He will be far more ready.

ATH. There will be no impropriety in our using such a method of
d persuading them to join with us in song.

CLE. None at all.

ATH. And what strain will they sing, and what Muse will they hymn? The strain should clearly be one suitable to them.

CLE. Certainly.

ATH. And what strain is suitable for heroes? Shall they sing a choral strain?

CLE. Truly, Stranger, we of Crete and Sparta know no strain other than that which we have learnt and been accustomed to sing in our chorus.

ATH. Of course not; for you have never acquired the knowledge of the most beautiful kind of song. Your military way of life is modelled after the camp, and is not like that of dwellers in cities; you have your young men herding and feeding together like young colts. No one takes his own individual colt and drags him away from his fellows against his will, raging and foaming, and gives him a groom to attend to him alone, and trains and rubs him down privately, and gives him the qualities in education which will make him not only a good soldier, but also a governor of a state and of cities. Such a man, as we said at first, would be a greater warrior than he of whom Tyrtaeus sings; and he would honor courage everywhere, but always as the fourth, and not as the first part of virtue, either in individuals or states.

CLE. Once more, Stranger, I must complain that you depreciate our lawgivers.

ATH. Not intentionally, if at all, my good friend; but whither the argument leads, thither let us follow; for if there is indeed some strain of song more beautiful than that of the choruses or the public theatres, I should like to impart it to those who, as we say, are ashamed of these, and want to have the best.

CLE. Certainly.

ATH. When things have an accompanying charm, either the best thing in them is this very charm, or there is some rightness or utility possessed by them; for example, I should say that eating and drinking, and the use of food in general, have an accompanying charm which we call pleasure; the rightness and utility is just the healthfulness of the things served up to us, which is their true rightness.

CLE. Just so.

ATH. Thus, too, I should say that learning has a certain accompanying charm which is the pleasure; but that the right and the profitable, the good and the noble, are qualities which the truth gives to it.

CLE. Exactly.

ATH. And so in the imitative arts, if they succeed in making likenesses, and are accompanied by pleasure, may not their works be said to have a charm?

CLE. Yes.

ATH. But equal proportions, whether of quality or quantity, and not pleasure, speaking generally, would give them truth or rightness.

CLE. Yes.

ATH. Then only what makes or furnishes no utility or hurt or truth or likeness can be rightly judged by the standard of pleasure, since it exists solely for the sake of the accompanying charm; and the term 'pleasure' is most appropriately applied to it when these other qualities are absent.

CLE. You are speaking of harmless pleasure, are you not?

ATH. Yes; and this I term amusement, when doing neither harm nor good in any degree worth speaking of.

CLE. Very true.

ATH. Then, if such are our principles, we must assert that imitation is not to be judged by pleasure and false opinion; and this is true of all equality, for the equal is not equal or the symmetrical symmetrical because somebody thinks or likes something, but they are to be judged by the standard of truth, and by no other whatever.

CLE. Quite true.

668   ATH. Do we not regard all music as representative and imitative?

CLE. Certainly.

ATH. Then, when anyone says that music is to be judged by pleasure, his doctrine cannot be admitted; and if there be any music of which pleasure is the criterion, such music is not to be sought out or b deemed to have any real excellence, but only that other kind of music which is an imitation of the good.

CLE. Very true.

ATH. And those who seek the best kind of song and music ought not to seek what is pleasant, but what is true; and the truth of imitation consists, as we were saying, in rendering the thing imitated according to quantity and quality.

CLE. Certainly.

ATH. And every one will admit that musical compositions are all c imitative and representative. Will not poets and spectators and actors all agree in this?

CLE. They will.

ATH. Surely then he who would judge correctly must know what each composition is; for if he does not know what is the character and meaning of the piece, and what it represents, he will never discern whether the intention is true or false.

CLE. Certainly not.

d   ATH. And will he who does not know what is true be able to distinguish what is good and bad? My statement is not very clear; but perhaps you will understand me better if I put the matter in another way.

CLE. How?

ATH. There are countless likenesses of objects of sight?

CLE. Yes.

ATH. And can he who does not know what the exact object is which is imitated, ever know whether the resemblance is truthfully executed? I mean, for example, whether a statue has the proportions of a body, *e* and the true situation of the parts; what those proportions are, and how the parts fit into one another in due order; also their colors and conformations, or whether this is all confused in the execution: do you think that anyone can know about this, who does not know what the living thing is that has been imitated?

CLE. Impossible.

ATH. But even if we know that the thing pictured or sculptured is a man, who has received at the hand of the artist all his proper parts and *669* colors and shapes, must we not also know whether the work is beautiful or in any respect deficient in beauty?

CLE. If this were not required, Stranger, we should all of us be judges of beauty.

ATH. Very true; and may we not say that in everything imitated, whether in drawing, music, or any other art, he who is to be a competent judge must possess three things—he must know, in the first place, of what the imitation is; secondly, he must know how correctly; *b* and thirdly, how well executed in words and melodies and rhythms?

CLE. Certainly.

ATH. Then let us not fail to discuss the peculiar difficulty of music. Music is more celebrated than any other kind of imitation, and therefore requires the greatest care of them all. For if a man makes a mistake here, he may do himself the greatest injury by welcoming evil dispositions, and the mistake may be very difficult to discern, because the *c* poets are artists very inferior in character to the Muses themselves, who would never fall into the monstrous error of assigning to the words of men the gestures and songs of women; nor after combining the melodies with the gestures of freemen would they add on the rhythms of slaves and men of the baser sort; nor, beginning with the rhythms and gestures of freemen, would they assign to them a melody or words which are of an opposite character; nor would they mix up the voices and sounds of animals and of men and instruments, and every other sort of *d* noise, as if they were all one. But human poets are fond of introducing this sort of inconsistent mixture, and so make themselves ridiculous in the eyes of those who, as Orpheus says, 'are ripe for true pleasure.' The experienced see all this confusion, and yet the poets go on and make still further havoc by separating the rhythm and the figure of the dance from the melody, setting bare words to metre, and also separating the melody and the rhythm from the words, using the lyre or the flute alone. For when there are no words, it is very difficult to rec- *e* ognize the meaning of the harmony and rhythm, or to see that any

worthy object is imitated by them. And we must acknowledge that all this sort of thing, which aims only at swiftness and smoothness and a brutish noise, and uses the flute and the lyre not as the mere accompa-
670   niments of the dance and song, is exceedingly coarse and tasteless. The use of either instrument, when unaccompanied, leads to every sort of irregularity and trickery. This is all rational enough. But we are considering not how those, who are from thirty to fifty years of age, and may be over fifty, are not to use the Muses, but how they are to use them. And the considerations which we have urged seem to show in what way these fifty-year-olds who are to sing may be expected to be better
b   trained. For they need to have a quick perception and knowledge of harmonies and rhythms; otherwise, how can they ever know whether a melody would be rightly sung to the Dorian mode, or to the rhythm which the poet has assigned to it?

CLE. Clearly they cannot.

ATH. The mob is ridiculous in imagining that they know what is in proper harmony and rhythm, and what is not, when they can only be
c   made to sing and step in rhythm by force; it never occurs to them that they are ignorant of what they are doing. Now every melody is right when it has suitable harmony and rhythm, and wrong when unsuitable.

CLE. That is most certain.

ATH. But can a man who does not know a thing, as we were saying, know that the thing is right?

CLE. Impossible.

d   ATH. Then now, as would appear, we are making the discovery that our newly-appointed chorus members, whom we hereby invite and, although they are their own masters, compel to sing, must be educated to such an extent as to be able to follow the steps of the rhythm and the notes of the song, so that they may know the harmonies and rhythms, and be able to select what are suitable for men of their age and character to sing, and may sing them, and have innocent pleasure from their
e   own performance, and also lead younger men to welcome with dutiful delight good dispositions. Having such training, they will attain a more accurate knowledge than falls to the lot of the common people, or even of the poets themselves. For the poet need not know the third point, that is to say whether the imitation is good or not, though he can hardly help knowing the laws of melody and rhythm. But the aged
671   chorus must know all the three, so that they may choose the best, and that which is nearest to the best; for otherwise they will never be able to charm the souls of young men in the way of virtue. And now the original design of the argument which was intended to bring eloquent

aid to the chorus of Dionysus has been accomplished to the best of our ability, and let us see whether we were right: I should imagine that a drinking assembly is likely to become more and more tumultuous as the drinking goes on; this, as we were saying at first, will certainly be the case. *b*

CLE. Certainly.

ATH. Every man has a more than natural elevation; his heart is glad within him, and he will say anything and will be restrained by nobody at such a time; he fancies that he is able to rule over himself and all mankind.

CLE. Quite true.

ATH. Were we not saying that on such occasions the souls of the drinkers become like iron heated in the fire, and grow softer and younger, and are easily moulded by him who knows how to educate and fashion them, just as when they were young, and that this fash- *c* ioner of them is the same who prescribed for them in the days of their youth, that is to say the good legislator; and that he ought to enact laws of the banquet, which, when a man is confident, bold, and impudent, and unwilling to wait his turn and have his share of silence and speech, and drinking and music, will change his character into the opposite— such laws as will infuse into him a just and noble fear, which will take *d* up arms at the approach of insolence, being that divine fear which we have called reverence and shame?

CLE. True.

ATH. And the guardians of these laws and fellow-workers with them are the calm and sober generals of the drinkers; and without their help there is greater difficulty in fighting against drink than in fighting against enemies when the commander of an army is not himself calm; and he who is unwilling to obey them and the command- ers of Dionysiac feasts who are more than sixty years of age, shall *e* suffer a disgrace as great as he who disobeys military leaders, or even greater.

CLE. Right.

ATH. If, then, drinking and amusement were regulated in this way, would not the companions of our revels be improved? they would part better friends than they were, and not, as now, enemies. Their whole *672* intercourse would be regulated by law and observant of it, and the sober would be the leaders of the drunken.

CLE. I think so too, if drinking were regulated as you propose.

ATH. Let us not then simply censure the gift of Dionysus as bad and unfit to be received into the State. For wine has many excellences, and one pre-eminent one, about which there is a difficulty in speaking to b   the many, from a fear of their misconceiving and misunderstanding what is said.

CLE. To what do you refer?

ATH. There is a tradition or story, which has somehow crept about the world, that Dionysus was robbed of his wits by his stepmother Hera, and that out of revenge he inspires Bacchic furies and dancing madnesses in others; for which reason he gave men wine. Such traditions concerning the gods I leave to those who think that they may be

c   safely uttered; I only know that no animal at birth is mature or perfect in intelligences; in the intermediate period, in which he has not yet acquired his own proper sense, he rages and roars and jumps around without rhyme or reason; and this, as you will remember, has been already said by us to be the origin of music and gymnastic.

CLE. To be sure, I remember.

d   ATH. And did we not say that the sense of harmony and rhythm sprang from this beginning among men, and that Apollo and the Muses and Dionysus were the gods whom we had to thank for them?

CLE. Certainly.

ATH. The other story implied that wine was given to man out of revenge, and in order to make him mad; but our present doctrine, on the contrary, is, that wine was given him as a balm, and in order to implant modesty in the soul, and health and strength in the body.

CLE. That, Stranger, is precisely what was said.

e   ATH. Then half the subject may now be considered to have been discussed; shall we proceed to the consideration of the other half?

CLE. What is the other half, and how do you divide the subject?

ATH. The whole choral art is also in our view the whole of education; and, of this art, rhythms and harmonies form the part which has to do with the voice.

CLE. Yes.

ATH. The movement of the body has rhythm in common with the movement of the voice, but gesture is peculiar to it, whereas song is simply the movement of the voice.

CLE. Most true.

673   ATH. And the sound of the voice which reaches and educates the soul, we have ventured to term music.

CLE. We were right.

ATH. And the movement of the body, when regarded as an amusement, we termed dancing; but when extended and pursued with a view to the excellence of the body, this scientific training may be called gymnastics.

CLE. Exactly.

b   ATH. Music, which was one half of the choral art, may be said to have been completely discussed. Shall we proceed to the other half or not? What would you like?

CLE. My good friend, when you are talking with a Cretan and Spartan, and we have discussed music and not gymnastic, what answer are either of us likely to make to such an enquiry?

ATH. An answer is contained in your question; I understand and accept what you say not only as an answer, but also as a command to proceed with gymnastics.   *c*

CLE. You quite understand me; do as you say.

ATH. I will; and there will not be any difficulty in speaking intelligibly to you about a subject with which both of you are far more familiar than with music.

CLE. There will not.

ATH. Is not the origin of gymnastics, too, to be sought in the tendency to rapid motion which exists in all animals; man, as we were   *d* saying, having attained the sense of rhythm, created and invented dancing; and melody arousing and awakening rhythm, both united formed the choral art?

CLE. Very true.

ATH. And one part of this subject has been already discussed by us, and there still remains another to be discussed?

CLE. Exactly.

ATH. I have first a final word to add to my discourse about drink, if   *e* you will allow me to do so.

CLE. What more have you to say?

ATH. I should say that if a city seriously means to adopt the practice of drinking under due regulation and with a view to the enforcement of temperance, and in like manner, and on the same principle, will allow other pleasures, designing to gain the victory over them—in this way all of them may be used. But if the State makes drinking an amusement only, and whoever likes may drink whenever he likes, and with whom he likes, and add to this any other indulgences, I shall never   674 agree or allow that this city or this man should practise drinking. I would go farther than the Cretans and Spartans, and am disposed rather to the law of the Carthaginians, that no one while he is on a campaign should be allowed to taste wine at all, but that he should drink water during all that time, and that in the city no slave, male or female, should ever drink wine; and that no magistrates should drink during   *b* their year of office, nor should pilots of vessels or judges while on duty taste wine at all, nor anyone who is going to hold a consultation about any matter of importance; nor in the day-time at all, unless in consequence of exercise or as medicine; nor again at night, when any one, either man or woman, is minded to get children. There are numberless c   other cases also in which those who have good sense and good laws ought not to drink wine, so that if what I say is true, no city will need many vineyards. Their farming and their way of life in general will follow an appointed order, and their cultivation of the vine will be the most limited and the least common of their employments. And this, Stranger, shall be the crown of my discourse about wine, if you agree.

CLE. Excellent. We agree.

BOOK III

676   ATHENIAN STRANGER. ENOUGH of this. What, then, is to be regarded as the origin of government? Will not a man be able to judge of it best from a point of view in which he may behold the progress of states and their transitions to good or evil?

CLEINIAS. What do you mean?

b   ATH. I mean that he might watch them from the point of view of time, and observe the changes which take place in them during infinite ages.

CLE. How so?

ATH. Why, do you think that you can reckon the time which has elapsed since cities first existed and men were citizens of them?

CLE. Hardly.

ATH. But you are sure that it must be vast and incalculable?

CLE. Certainly.

ATH. And have not thousands and thousands of cities come into
c   being during this period and as many perished? And has not each of them had every form of government many times over, now growing larger, now smaller, and again improving or declining?

CLE. To be sure.

ATH. Let us endeavour to ascertain the cause of these changes; for that will probably explain the first origin and development of forms of government.

CLE. Very good. You shall endeavour to impart your thoughts to us, and we will make an effort to understand you.

677   ATH. Do you believe that there is any truth in ancient traditions?

CLE. What traditions?

ATH. The traditions about the many destructions of mankind which have been occasioned by floods and pestilences, and in many other ways, and of the survival of a remnant?

CLE. Everyone is disposed to believe them.

ATH. Let us consider one of them, that which was caused by the famous flood.

CLE. What are we to observe about it?

ATH. I mean to say that those who then escaped would only be hill b
shepherds—small sparks of the human race preserved on the tops of mountains.

CLE. Clearly.

ATH. Such survivors would necessarily be unacquainted with the arts and the various devices which are suggested to the dwellers in cities by interest or ambition, and with all the wrongs which they contrive against one another.

CLE. Very true.

ATH. Let us suppose, then, that the cities in the plain and on the sea- c
coast were utterly destroyed at that time.

CLE. All right, let us suppose it.

ATH. Would not all implements have then perished and every other excellent invention of political or any other sort of wisdom have utterly disappeared?

CLE. Why, yes, my friend; and if things had always continued as they are at present ordered, how could any discovery have ever been made even in the least particular? For it is evident that the arts were unknown during millions of years. And no more than a thousand or two thousand years d
have elapsed since the discoveries of Daedalus, Orpheus and Palamedes[4]—since Marsyas and Olympus invented music, and Amphion the lyre—not to speak of numberless other inventions which are but of yesterday.

ATH. Have you forgotten, Cleinias, the name of a friend who is really of yesterday?

CLE. I suppose that you mean Epimenides.[*]

ATH. The same, my friend; he does indeed far overleap the heads of e
all mankind by his invention; for he carried out in practice, as you declare, what old Hesiod only preached.[†]

CLE. Yes, according to our tradition.

ATH. After the great destruction, may we not suppose that the state of man was something of this sort: In the beginning of things there was a fearful illimitable desert and a vast expanse of land; a herd or two of oxen would be the only survivors of the animal world; and there might be a few goats, these too hardly enough to maintain the shep- 678
herds who tended them?

---

*Cretan philosopher.
†*Works and Days* 40–41.

CLE. True.

ATH. And of cities or governments or legislation, about which we are now talking, do you suppose that they could have any recollection at all?

CLE. None whatever.

ATH. And out of this state of things has there not sprung all that we now are and have: cities and governments, and arts and laws, and a great deal of vice and a great deal of virtue?

CLE. What do you mean?

b   ATH. Why, my good friend, how can we possibly suppose that those who knew nothing of all the good and evil of cities could have attained their full development, whether of virtue or of vice?

CLE. I understand your meaning, and you are quite right.

ATH. But, as time advanced and the race multiplied, the world came to be what the world is.

CLE. Very true.

ATH. Doubtless the change was not made all in a moment, but little by little, during a very long period of time.

c   CLE. A highly probable supposition.

ATH. At first, they would have a natural fear ringing in their ears which would prevent their descending from the heights into the plain.

CLE. Of course.

ATH. The fewness of the survivors at that time would have made them all the more desirous of seeing one another; but then the means of travelling either by land or sea had been almost entirely lost, as I may say, with the loss of the arts, and there was great difficulty in getting at

d   one another; for iron and brass and all metals were jumbled together and had disappeared in the chaos; nor was there any possibility of extracting ore from them; and they had scarcely any means of felling timber. Even if you suppose that some implements might have been preserved in the mountains, they must quickly have worn out and vanished, and there would be no more of them until the art of metallurgy had again revived.

CLE. There could not have been.

ATH. In how many generations would this be attained?

e   CLE. Clearly, not for many generations.

ATH. During this period, and for some time afterwards, all the arts which require iron and brass and the like would disappear.

CLE. Certainly.

ATH. Faction and war would also have died out in those days, and for many reasons.

CLE. How would that be?

ATH. In the first place, the desolation of these primitive men would create in them a feeling of affection and good-will towards one another; and, secondly, they would have no occasion to quarrel about their subsistence, for they would have pasture in abundance, except just at first, and in some particular cases; and from their pasture-land they would obtain the greater part of their food in a primitive age, having plenty of milk and flesh; moreover they would procure other food by hunting, not to be despised either in quantity or quality. They would also have abundance of clothing, and bedding, and dwellings, and utensils either capable of standing on the fire or not; for the plastic and weaving arts do not require any use of iron: and god has given these two arts to man in order to provide him with all such things, so that, when reduced to the last extremity, the human race may still grow and increase. Hence in those days mankind were not very poor; nor was poverty a cause of difference among them. Rich they could not have been, having neither gold nor silver; such at that time was their condition. And the community which has neither poverty nor riches will always have the noblest principles; in it there is no insolence or injustice, nor, again, are there any contentions or envyings. And therefore they were good, and also because they were what is called simple-minded; and when they were told about good and evil, they in their simplicity believed what they heard to be the very truth and practiced it. No one had the wit to suspect another of a falsehood, as men do now; but what they heard about gods and men they believed to be true, and lived accordingly; therefore they were in all respects such as we have described them.

CLE. That quite accords with my views, and with those of my friend here.

ATH. Would not many generations living on in a simple manner, although ruder, perhaps, and more ignorant of the arts generally, and in particular of those of land or naval warfare, and likewise of other arts, termed in cities legal practices and party conflicts, and including all conceivable ways of hurting one another in word and deed (although inferior to those who lived before the flood, or to the men of our day in these respects); would they not, I say, be simpler and more manly, and also more temperate and altogether more just? The reason has been already explained.

CLE. You are right.

ATH. I should wish you to understand that what has preceded and what is about to follow has been, and will be said, with the intention of explaining what need the men of that time had of laws, and who was their lawgiver.

CLE. And thus far what you have said has been very well said.

ATH. They could hardly have wanted lawgivers as yet; nothing of that sort was likely to have existed in their days, for they had no letters at this early period; they lived by habit and the customs of their ancestors, as they are called.

CLE. Probably.

ATH. But there was already existing a form of government which, if b I am not mistaken, is generally termed a lordship, and this still remains in many places, both among Greeks and barbarians, and is the government which is declared by Homer to have prevailed among the Cyclopes:

'They have neither councils nor judgments, but they dwell in hollow caves on the tops of high mountains, and every one gives law to his wife c and children, and they do not busy themselves about one another.'*

CLE. That seems to be a charming poet of yours; I have read some other verses of his, which are very clever; but I do not know much of him, for foreign poets are very little read among the Cretans.

d MEGILLUS. But they are in Sparta, and he appears to be the prince of them all; the manner of life, however, which he describes is not Spartan, but rather Ionian, and he seems quite to confirm what you are saying, when he traces up the ancient state of mankind by the help of tradition to barbarism.

ATH. Yes, he does confirm it; and we may accept his testimony of the fact that such forms of government sometimes arise.

CLE. We may.

ATH. And were not such states composed of men who had been dispersed in single habitations and families by the poverty which attended the devastations; and did not the eldest then rule among them, e because with them government originated in the authority of a father and a mother, whom, like a flock of birds, they followed, forming one troop under the patriarchal rule and sovereignty of their parents, which of all sovereignties is the most just?

CLE. Very true.

ATH. After this they came together in greater numbers, and in-
681 creased the size of their cities, and betook themselves to farming, first of all at the foot of the mountains, and made enclosures of loose walls and works of defense, in order to keep off wild beasts; thus creating a single large and common habitation.

---

*Odyssey 9.112ff.

CLE. Yes; at least we may suppose so.

ATH. There is another thing which would probably have happened.

CLE. What?

ATH. When these larger habitations grew up out of the lesser original ones, each of the lesser ones would survive in the larger; every family would be under the rule of the eldest, and, owing to their separation from one another, would have peculiar customs in things divine and human, which they would have received from their several parents who had educated them; and these customs would incline them to order, when the parents had the element of order in their nature, and to courage, when they had the element of courage. And they would naturally stamp upon their children, and upon their children's children, their own likings; and, as we are saying, they would find their way into the larger society, having already their own peculiar laws. b

CLE. Certainly.

ATH. And every man surely likes his own laws best, and the laws of others not so well. c

CLE. True.

ATH. Then now we seem to have stumbled upon the beginnings of legislation.

CLE. Exactly.

ATH. The next step will be that these persons who have met together will select some arbiters, who will review the laws of all of them, and will publicly present such as they approve to the chiefs who lead the tribes, and who are in a manner their kings, allowing them to choose those which they think best. These persons will themselves be called legislators, and will appoint the magistrates, framing some sort of aristocracy, or perhaps monarchy, out of the lordships, and in this altered state of the government they will live. d

CLE. Yes, that would be the natural order of things.

ATH. Then, now let us speak of a third form of government, in which all other forms and conditions of polities and cities concur.

CLE. What is that? e

ATH. The form which in fact Homer indicates as following the second. This third form arose when, as he says, Dardanus founded Dardania:

'For not as yet had the holy Ilium been built on the plain to be a city of speaking men; but they were still dwelling at the foot of many-fountained Ida.'*

---

*Iliad 20.216ff.

682   For indeed, in these verses, and in what he said of the Cyclopes, he speaks the words of god and nature; for poets are a divine race and often in their strains, by the aid of the Muses and the Graces, they attain truth.

CLE. Yes.

ATH. Then now let us proceed with the rest of our tale, which will probably be found to illustrate in some degree our proposed design. Shall we do so?

b   CLE. By all means.

ATH. Ilium was built, when they had descended from the mountain, in a large and fair plain, on a sort of low hill, watered by many rivers descending from Ida.

CLE. Such is the tradition.

ATH. And we must suppose this event to have taken place many ages after the flood?

CLE. We must indeed.

ATH. A marvellous forgetfulness of the former destruction would

c   appear to have come over them, when they placed their town right under numerous streams flowing from the heights, trusting their security to not very high hills, either.

CLE. There must have been a long interval, clearly.

ATH. And, as population increased, many other cities would begin to be inhabited.

CLE. Doubtless.

d   ATH. Those cities made war against Troy—by sea as well as land— for at that time men were ceasing to be afraid of the sea.

CLE. Clearly.

ATH. The Achaeans remained ten years, and overthrew Troy.

CLE. True.

ATH. And during the ten years in which the Achaeans were besieging Ilium, the homes of the besiegers were falling into an evil plight. Their youth revolted; and when the soldiers returned to their own

e   cities and families, they did not receive them properly, as they ought to have done; numerous deaths, murders, exiles, were the consequence. The exiles came again, under a new name, no longer Achaeans, but Dorians—a name which they derived from Dorieus; for it was he who gathered them together. The rest of the story is told by you Spartans as part of the history of Sparta.[5]

MEG. To be sure.

ATH. Thus, after digressing from the original subject of laws into music and drinking-bouts, the argument has, providentially, come back to the same point, and presents to us another handle. For we have

reached the settlement of Sparta; which, as you truly say, is in laws and 683
in institutions the sister of Crete. And we are all the better for the digression, because we have gone through various governments and settlements, and have been present at the foundation of a first, second, and
third state, succeeding one another over a very long time. And now
there appears on the horizon a fourth state or nation which was once
in process of settlement and has continued settled to this day. If, out of b
all this, we are able to discern what is well or badly settled, and what
laws are the salvation and what are the destruction of cities, and what
changes would make a state happy, Megillus and Cleinias, we may now
begin again, unless we have some fault to find with the previous discussion.

MEG. If some god, Stranger, would promise us that our new enquiry about legislation would be as good and full as the present, I c
would go a great way to hear such another, and would think that a day
as long as this—and we are now toward the middle of the longest day
of the year—was too short for the discussion.

ATH. Then I suppose that we must consider this subject?

MEG. Certainly.

ATH. Let us place ourselves in thought at the moment when Sparta
and Argos and Messene and the rest of the Peloponnesus were all in d
complete subjection, Megillus, to your ancestors; for afterwards, as the
legend informs us, they divided their army into three portions, and settled three cities, Argos, Messene, Sparta.

MEG. True.

ATH. Temenus was the king of Argos, Cresphontes of Messene, Procles and Eurysthenes of Sparta.

MEG. Certainly.

ATH. To these kings all the men of that day made oath that they
would assist them, if anyone subverted their kingdom. e

MEG. True.

ATH. But can a kingship be destroyed, or was any other form of government ever destroyed, by any but the rulers themselves? No indeed,
by Zeus. Have we already forgotten what was said a little while ago?

MEG. No.

ATH. And may we not now further confirm what was then said? For
we have come upon facts which have brought us back again to the
same principle; so that, in resuming the discussion, we shall not be enquiring about an empty theory, but about events which actually hap- 684
pened. The case was as follows: Three royal heroes made oath to three
cities which were under a kingly government, and the cities to the
kings, that both rulers and subjects should govern and be governed

according to the laws which were common to all of them. The rulers promised that, as time and the race went forward, they would not make their rule more arbitrary; and the subjects said that if the rulers observed these conditions, they would never subvert or permit others to subvert those kingdoms; the kings were to assist kings and peoples when injured, and the peoples were to assist peoples and kings in like manner. Is not this the fact?

MEG. Yes.

ATH. And the three states to whom these laws were given, whether their kings or any others were the authors of them, had therefore the greatest security for the maintenance of their constitutions?

MEG. What security?

ATH. That the other two states were always to come to the rescue against a rebellious third.

MEG. True.

ATH. Many persons say that legislators ought to impose such laws as the mass of the people will be ready to receive; but this is just as if one were to command gymnastic masters or physicians to treat or cure their pupils or patients in an agreeable manner.

MEG. Exactly.

ATH. Whereas the physician may often be only too happy if he can restore health, and make the body whole, without any very great infliction of pain.

MEG. Certainly.

ATH. There was also another advantage possessed by the men of that day, which greatly lightened the task of passing laws.

MEG. What advantage?

ATH. The legislators of that day, when they equalized property, escaped the great accusation which generally arises in legislation, if a person attempts to disturb the possession of land, or to abolish debts, because he sees that without this reform there can never be any real equality. Now, in general, when the legislator attempts to make a new settlement of such matters, everyone meets him with the cry, that 'he is not to disturb vested interests'—declaring with imprecations that he is introducing agrarian laws and cancelling of debts, until a man is at his wits' end; whereas no one could quarrel with the Dorians for distributing the land—there was nothing to hinder them; and as for debts, they had none which were considerable or of old standing.

MEG. Very true.

ATH. But then, my good friends, why did the settlement and legislation of their country turn out so badly?

MEG. How do you mean; and why do you blame them?   685

ATH. There were three kingdoms, and of these, two quickly corrupted their original constitution and laws, and the only one which remained was the Spartan.

MEG. The question which you ask is not easily answered.

ATH. And yet must be answered when we are enquiring about laws, this being our old man's sober game of play, whereby we beguile the   b
way, as I was saying when we first set out on our journey.

MEG. Certainly; and we must find out why this was.

ATH. What laws are more worthy of our attention than those which have regulated such cities? or what settlements or states are greater or more famous?

MEG. I know of none.

ATH. Can we doubt that your ancestors intended these institutions not only for the protection of the Peloponnesus, but of all the Greeks,   c
in case they were attacked by the barbarians? For the inhabitants of the region about Ilium, when they provoked by their insolence the Trojan war, relied upon the power of the Assyrians and the Empire of Ninus, which still existed and had a great prestige; the people of those days fearing the united Assyrian Empire just as we now fear the Great King.   d
And the second capture of Troy was a serious offence against them, because Troy was a portion of the Assyrian Empire. To meet the danger the single army was distributed between three cities by the royal brothers, sons of Heracles—a fair device, as it seemed, and a far better arrangement than the expedition against Troy. For, firstly, the people of that day had, as they thought, in the Heraclidae better leaders than the Pelopidae; in the next place, they considered that their army was   e
superior in valor to that which went against Troy; for, although the latter conquered the Trojans, they were themselves conquered by the Heraclidae—Achaeans by Dorians. May we not suppose that this was the intention with which the men of those days framed the constitutions of their states?

MEG. Quite true.

ATH. And would not men who had shared with one another many   686
dangers, and were governed by a single race of royal brothers, and had taken the advice of oracles, and in particular of the Delphian Apollo, be likely to think that such states would be firmly and lastingly established?

MEG. Of course they would.

ATH. Yet these institutions, of which such great expectations were entertained, seem to have all rapidly vanished away; with the exception, as I was saying, of that small part of them which existed in your land.

b   And this third part has never to this day ceased warring against the two
others; whereas, if the original idea had been carried out, and they had
agreed to be one, their power would have been invincible in war.

MEG. No doubt.

ATH. But what was the ruin of this glorious confederacy? Here is a
subject well worthy of consideration.

MEG. Certainly, no one will ever find more striking instances of laws
c   or governments being the salvation or destruction of great and noble
interests, than are here presented to his view.

ATH. Then now we seem to have happily arrived at a real and important question.

MEG. Very true.

ATH. Did you never remark, sage friend, that all men, and we ourselves at this moment, often fancy that they see some beautiful thing
d   which might have effected wonders if anyone had only known how to
make a right use of it in some way; and yet this mode of looking at
things may turn out after all to be a mistake, and not according to nature, either in our own case or in any other?

MEG. To what are you referring, and what do you mean?

ATH. I was thinking of my own admiration of the aforesaid Hera-
cleid expedition, which was so noble, and might have had such wonderful results for the Greeks, if only rightly used; and I was just laughing
at myself.

e   MEG. But were you not right and wise in speaking as you did, and
we in assenting to you?

ATH. Perhaps; and yet I cannot help observing that anyone who sees
anything great or powerful, immediately has the feeling that 'If the
owner only knew how to use his great and noble possession, how
happy would he be, and what great results would he achieve!'

687   MEG. And would he not be justified?

ATH. Reflect; in what point of view does this sort of praise appear
just? First, in reference to the question in hand: If the then command-
ers had known how to arrange their army properly, how would they
have attained success? Would not this have been the way? They would
have bound them all firmly together and preserved them for ever, giving them freedom and dominion at pleasure, combined with the power
b   of doing in the whole world, Greek and barbarian, whatever they and
their descendants desired. What other aim would they have had?

MEG. Very good.

ATH. Suppose anyone were in the same way to express his admiration at the sight of great wealth or family honor, or the like; he would
praise them under the idea that through them he would attain either
all or the greater and chief part of what he desires.

MEG. He would.

ATH. Well, now, and does not the argument show that there is one   c
common desire of all mankind?

MEG. What is it?

ATH. The desire which a man has, that all things, if possible—at any
rate, things human—may come to pass in accordance with his soul's
desire.

MEG. Certainly.

ATH. And having this desire always, and at every time of life, in
youth, in manhood, in age, he cannot help always praying for the fulfilment of it.

MEG. No doubt.

ATH. And we join in the prayers of our friends, and ask for them   d
what they ask for themselves.

MEG. We do.

ATH. Dear is the son to the father—the younger to the elder.

MEG. Of course.

ATH. And yet the son often prays to obtain things which the father
prays that he may not obtain.

MEG. When the son is young and foolish, you mean?

ATH. Yes; or when the father, in the dotage of age or the heat of
youth, having no sense of right and justice, prays with fervour, under   e
the influence of feelings akin to those of Theseus when he cursed the
unfortunate Hippolytus,* do you imagine that the son, having a sense of
right and justice, will join in his father's prayers?

MEG. I understand you to mean that a man should not desire or be
in a hurry to have all things according to his wish, for his wish may be
at variance with his reason. But every state and every individual ought
to pray and strive for wisdom.   688

ATH. Yes; and I remember, and you will remember, what I said at
first, that a statesman and legislator ought to ordain laws with a view
to wisdom; while you were arguing that the good lawgiver ought to
order all with a view to war. And to this I replied that there were four
virtues, but that upon your view one of them only was the aim of legislation; whereas you ought to regard all virtue, and especially that   b
which comes first, and is the leader of all the rest—I mean wisdom and
mind and opinion, having affection and desire in their train. And now
the argument returns to the same point, and I say once more, in jest if

---

*Theseus prayed for his son Hippolytus' death when his wife (and Hippolytus' step-
mother), Phaedra, falsely accused Hippolytus of trying to have sex with her, when in
fact he had refused her own sexual advances.

you like, or in earnest if you like, that the prayer of a fool is full of danger, being likely to end in the opposite of what he desires. And if you

c would rather receive my words in earnest, I am willing that you should; and you will find, I suspect, as I have said already, that not cowardice was the cause of the ruin of the Dorian kings and of their whole design, nor ignorance of military matters, either on the part of the rulers or of their subjects; but their misfortunes were due to their general degeneracy, and especially to their ignorance of the most important human affairs. That was then, and is still, and always will be the

d case, as I will endeavour, if you will allow me, to make out and demonstrate as well as I am able to you who are my friends, in the course of the argument.

CLE. Pray go on, Stranger; compliments are troublesome, but we will show, not in word but in deed, how greatly we prize your words, for we will give them our best attention; and that is the way in which a freeman best shows his approval or disapproval.

e MEG. Excellent, Cleinias; let us do as you say.

CLE. By all means, if heaven wills. Go on.

ATH. Well, then, proceeding in the same train of thought, I say that the greatest ignorance was the ruin of the Dorian power, and that now, as then, ignorance is ruin. And if this be true, the legislator must endeavour to implant wisdom in states, and banish ignorance to the utmost of his power.

CLE. That is evident.

689 ATH. Then now consider what is really the greatest ignorance. I should like to know whether you and Megillus would agree with me in what I am about to say; for my opinion is——

CLE. What?

ATH. That the greatest ignorance is when a man hates that which he nevertheless thinks to be good and noble, and loves and embraces that which he knows to be unrighteous and evil. This disagreement between the sense of pleasure and the judgment of reason in the soul is, in my opinion, the worst ignorance; and also the greatest,

b because it affects the great mass of the human soul; for the principle which feels pleasure and pain in the individual is like the mass or populace in a state. And when the soul is opposed to knowledge, or opinion, or reason, which are her natural lords, that I call folly, just as in the state, when the multitude refuses to obey their rulers and the laws; or, again, in the individual, when fair reasonings have their habitation in the soul and yet do no good, but rather the reverse of

c good. All these cases I term the worst ignorance, whether in individuals or in states. You will understand, Stranger, that I am speaking

of something which is very different from the ignorance of handi-
craftsmen.

CLE. Yes, my friend, we understand and agree.

ATH. Let us, then, in the first place declare and affirm that the citizen who does not know these things ought never to have any kind of
authority entrusted to him: he must be stigmatized as ignorant, even
though he be versed in calculation and skilled in all sorts of accomplishments, and feats of mental dexterity; and the opposite are to be   d
called wise, even though, in the words of the proverb, they know neither how to read nor how to swim; and to them, as to men of sense,
authority is to be committed. For, my friends, how can there be the
least shadow of wisdom when there is no harmony? There is none; but
the noblest and greatest of harmonies may be truly said to be the greatest wisdom; and of this he is a partaker who lives according to reason;
whereas he who is devoid of reason is the destroyer of his house and
the very opposite of a savior of the state: he is utterly ignorant of po-   e
litical wisdom. Let this, then, as I was saying, be laid down by us.

CLE. Let it be so laid down.

ATH. I suppose that there must be rulers and subjects in states?

CLE. Certainly.

ATH. And what are the principles on which men rule and obey in   690
cities, whether great or small, and similarly in families? What are they,
and how many in number? Is there not one claim of authority which
is always just—that of fathers and mothers and in general of progeni-
tors to rule over their offspring?

CLE. There is.

ATH. Next follows the principle that the noble should rule over the
ignoble; and, thirdly, that the elder should rule and the younger obey?

CLE. To be sure.

ATH. And, fourthly, that slaves should be ruled, and their masters   b
rule?

CLE. Of course.

ATH. Fifthly, if I am not mistaken, comes the principle that the
stronger shall rule, and the weaker be ruled?

CLE. That is a rule not to be disobeyed.

ATH. Yes, and a rule which prevails very widely among all creatures, and is according to nature, as the Theban poet Pindar once said;
and the sixth principle, and the greatest of all, is, that the wise should
lead and command, and the ignorant follow and obey; and yet, O thou   c
most wise Pindar, as I should reply to him, this surely is not contrary
to nature, but according to nature, being the rule of law over willing
subjects, and not a rule of compulsion.

CLE. Most true.

ATH. There is a seventh kind of rule which is awarded by lot, and is dear to the gods and a token of good fortune: he on whom the lot falls is a ruler, and he who fails in obtaining the lot goes away and is the subject; and this we affirm to be quite just.

CLE. Certainly.

d ATH. 'Then now,' as we say playfully to any of those who lightly undertake the making of laws, 'you see, legislator, the principles of government, how many they are, and that they are naturally opposed to each other. There we have discovered a fountain-head of seditions, to which you must attend. And, first, we will ask you to consider with us how and in what respect the kings of Argos and Messene violated these our maxims, and ruined themselves and the great and famous Greek e power of the olden time. Was it because they did not know how wisely Hesiod spoke when he said that the half is often more than the whole? His meaning was that when to take the whole would be dangerous, and to take the half would be the safe and moderate course, then the moderate or better was more than the immoderate or worse.'

CLE. Very true.

ATH. And may we suppose this immoderate spirit to be more fatal when found among kings than when among peoples?

691 CLE. The probability is that ignorance will be a disorder especially prevalent among kings, because they lead a proud and luxurious life.

ATH. Is it not palpable that the chief aim of the kings of that time was to get the better of the established laws, and that they were not in harmony with the principles which they had agreed to observe by word and oath? This want of harmony may have had the appearance of wisdom, but was really, as we assert, the greatest ignorance, and utterly overthrew the whole empire by dissonance and harsh discord.

CLE. Very likely.

b ATH. Good; and what measures ought the legislator to have then taken in order to avert this calamity? Truly there is no great wisdom in knowing, and no great difficulty in telling, after the evil has happened; but to have foreseen the remedy at the time would have taken a much wiser head than ours.

MEG. What do you mean?

ATH. Anyone who looks at what has occurred with you Spartans, Megillus, may easily know and may easily say what ought to have been done at that time.

MEG. Speak a little more clearly.

ATH. Nothing can be clearer than the observation which I am about to make.

MEG. What is it?

ATH. That if anyone gives too great a power to anything, too large   c
a sail to a vessel, too much food to the body, too much authority to the
mind, and does not observe the mean, everything is overthrown, and,
in the wantonness of excess runs in the one case to disorders, and in
the other to injustice, which is the child of excess. I mean to say, my
dear friends, that there is no soul of man, young and irresponsible, who
will be able to sustain the temptation of arbitrary power—no one who   d
will not, under such circumstances, become filled with folly, that worst
of diseases, and be hated by his nearest and dearest friends: When this
happens his kingdom is undermined, and all his power vanishes from
him. And great legislators who know the mean should take heed of the
danger. As far as we can guess at this distance of time, what happened
was as follows:

MEG. What?

ATH. A god, who watched over Sparta, seeing into the future, gave
you two families of kings instead of one; and thus brought you more   e
within the limits of moderation. In the next place, some human wisdom mingled with divine power, observing that the constitution of
your government was still feverish and excited, tempered your inborn
strength and pride of birth with the moderation which comes of age,
making the power of your twenty-eight elders equal with that of the   692
kings in the most important matters. But your third savior, perceiving
that your government was still swelling and foaming, and desirous to
impose a curb upon it, instituted the Ephors, whose power he made to
resemble that of magistrates elected by lot; and by this arrangement the
kingly office, being compounded of the right elements and duly mod-
erated, was preserved, and was the means of preserving all the rest.
Since, if there had been only the original legislators, Temenus, Cre-   b
sphontes, and their contemporaries, as far as they were concerned not
even the portion of Aristodemus* would have been preserved; for they
had no proper experience in legislation, or they would surely not have
imagined that oaths would moderate a youthful spirit invested with a
power which might be converted into a tyranny. Now that god has instructed us what sort of government would have been or will be lasting,
there is no wisdom, as I have already said, in judging after the event;   c
there is no difficulty in learning from an example which has already occurred. But if anyone could have foreseen all this at the time, and had
been able to moderate the government of the three kingdoms and unite

---

*The Athenian means Sparta, won by Aristodemus after he sacrificed his daughter; his
sons Eurysthenes and Procles were the first Spartan kings.

them into one, he might have saved all the excellent institutions which were then conceived; and no Persian or any other armament would have dared to attack us, or would have regarded the Greek world as a power to be despised.

CLE. True.

d　ATH. There was small credit to us, Cleinias, in defeating them; and the discredit was, not that the conquerors did not win glorious victories both by land and sea, but what, in my opinion, brought discredit was, first of all, the circumstance that of the three cities one only fought on behalf of the Greeks, and the two others were so utterly useless that the one was waging a mighty war against Sparta, and was thus preventing her from rendering assistance, while the city of Argos, which

e　had the precedence at the time of the distribution, when asked to aid in repelling the barbarian, would not answer to the call, or give aid. Many things might be told about the Greeks in connection with that war which are far from honorable; nor, indeed, can we rightly say that the Greeks repelled the invader; for the truth is, that unless the Atheni-

693　ans and Spartans, acting in concert, had warded off the impending yoke, all the tribes of the Greek world would have been fused in a chaos of mingling with one another, of barbarians mingling with Greeks, and Greeks with barbarians; just as nations who are now subject to the Persian power, owing to unnatural separations and combinations of them, are dispersed and scattered, and live miserably. These, Cleinias and Megillus, are the reproaches which we have to make against statesmen and legislators, as they are called, past and

b　present, if we would analyze the causes of their failure, and find out what else might have been done. We said, for instance, just now, that there ought to be no great and unmixed powers; and this was under the idea that a state ought to be free and wise and harmonious, and that a legislator ought to legislate with a view to this end. Nor is there any reason to be surprised at our continually proposing aims for the leg-

c　islator which appear not to be always the same; but we should consider when we say that temperance is to be the aim, or wisdom is to be the aim, or friendship is to be the aim, that all these aims are really the same; and if so a variety in the modes of expression ought not to disturb us.

CLE. Let us resume the argument in that spirit. And now, speaking of friendship and wisdom and freedom, I wish that you would tell me at what, in your opinion, the legislator should aim.

d　ATH. Hear me, then: there are two mother forms of states from which the rest may be truly said to be derived; one of them may be called monarchy and the other democracy: The Persians have the highest form of the one, and we of the other; almost all the rest, as I was saying, are variations of these. Now, if you are to have liberty and the combination of friendship with wisdom, you must have both these forms of government in a measure; the argument emphatically declares that no city can be well governed which is not made up of both.

CLE. Impossible.

ATH. Neither the one, if it is exclusively and excessively attached to monarchy, nor the other, if it is similarly attached to freedom, observes moderation; but your states, the Spartan and Cretan, have more of it; and the same was the case with the Athenians and Persians of old time, but now they have less. Shall I tell you why?

CLE. By all means, if it will tend to elucidate our subject.

ATH. Hear, then: There was a time when the Persians had more of the state which is a mean between slavery and freedom. In the reign of Cyrus they were freemen and also lords of many others: the rulers gave a share of freedom to the subjects, and being treated as equals, the soldiers were on better terms with their generals, and showed themselves more ready in the hour of danger. And if there was any wise man among them, who was able to give good counsel, he imparted his wisdom to the public; for the king was not jealous, but allowed him full liberty of speech, and gave honour to those who could advise him in any matter. And the nation waxed in all respects, because there was freedom and friendship and communion of mind among them.

CLE. That certainly appears to have been the case.

ATH. How, then, was this advantage lost under Cambyses, and again recovered under Darius? Shall I try to divine?

CLE. The enquiry, no doubt, has a bearing upon our subject.

ATH. I imagine that Cyrus, though a great and patriotic general, had never given his mind to education, and never attended to the order of his household.

CLE. What makes you say so?

ATH. I think that from his youth upwards he was a soldier, and entrusted the education of his children to the women; and they brought them up from their childhood as the favourites of fortune, who were blessed already, and needed no more blessings. They thought that they were happy enough, and that no one should be allowed to oppose them in any way, and they compelled everyone to praise all that they said or did. This was how they brought them up.

CLE. A splendid education truly!

ATH. Such as women were likely to give them, and especially

princesses who had recently grown rich, and in the absence of the men, too, who were occupied in wars and dangers, and had no time to look after them.

CLE. What would you expect?

ATH. Their father had possessions of cattle and sheep, and many
695 herds of men and other animals; but he did not consider that those to whom he was about to make them over were not trained in his own calling, which was Persian; for the Persians are shepherds—sons of a rugged land, which is a stern mother, and well fitted to produce a sturdy race able to live in the open air and go without sleep, and also to fight, if fighting is required. He did not observe that his sons were trained differently; through the so-called blessing of being royal they were educated in the Median fashion by women and eunuchs,
b which led to their becoming such as people do become when they are brought up unreproved. And so, after the death of Cyrus, his sons, in the fulness of luxury and licence, took the kingdom, and first one slew the other because he could not endure a rival; and, afterwards, the slayer himself, mad with wine and brutality, lost his kingdom through the Medes and the Eunuch, as they called him, who despised the folly of Cambyses.

c CLE. So runs the tale, and such probably were the facts.

ATH. Yes; and the tradition says that the empire came back to the Persians, through Darius and the seven chiefs.

CLE. True.

ATH. Let us note the rest of the story. Observe that Darius was not the son of a king, and had not received a luxurious education. When he came to the throne, being one of the seven, he divided the country
d into seven portions, and of this arrangement there are some shadowy traces still remaining; he made laws upon the principle of introducing universal equality in the order of the state, and he embodied in his laws the settlement of the tribute which Cyrus promised, thus creating a feeling of friendship and community among all the Persians, and attaching the people to him with money and gifts. Hence his armies cheerfully acquired for him countries as large as those which Cyrus had left behind him. Darius was succeeded by his son Xerxes; and he
e again was brought up in the royal and luxurious fashion. Might we not most justly say: 'O Darius, how came you to bring up Xerxes in the same way in which Cyrus brought up Cambyses, and not to see his fatal mistake?' For Xerxes, being the creation of the same education, met with much the same fortune as Cambyses; and from that time until now there has never been a really great king among the Persians, although they are all called Great. And their degeneracy is not to be attributed to chance, as I maintain; the reason is rather the evil life which

is generally led by the sons of very rich and royal persons; for never 696
will boy or man, young or old, excel in virtue, who has been thus educated. And this, I say, is what the legislator has to consider, and what
at the present moment has to be considered by us. Justly may you, Spartans, be praised, in that you do not give special honor or a special education to wealth rather than to poverty, or to a royal rather than to a b
private station, where the divine and inspired lawgiver has not originally commanded them to be given. For no man ought to have pre-
eminent honor in a state because he surpasses others in wealth, any
more than because he is swift of foot or fair or strong, unless he has
some virtue in him; nor even if he has virtue, unless he has this particular virtue of temperance.

MEG. What do you mean, Stranger?

ATH. I suppose that courage is a part of virtue?

MEG. To be sure.

ATH. Then, now hear and judge for yourself: Would you like to have
for a fellow-lodger or neighbour a very courageous man, who had no
control ever himself?

MEG. Heaven forbid! c

ATH. Or an artist, who was clever in his profession, but a rogue?

MEG. Certainly not.

ATH. And surely justice does not grow apart from temperance?

MEG. Impossible.

ATH. Any more than our model wise man, whom we exhibited as
having his pleasures and pains in accordance with and corresponding
to true reason, can be intemperate?

MEG. No.

ATH. There is a further consideration relating to the due and undue d
award of honors in states.

MEG. What is it?

ATH. I should like to know whether temperance without the other
virtues, existing alone in the soul of man, is rightly to be praised or
blamed?

MEG. I cannot tell.

ATH. And that is the best answer; for whichever alternative you had
chosen, I think that you would have gone wrong.

MEG. I am fortunate.

ATH. Very good; a quality, which is a mere appendage of things
which can be praised or blamed, does not deserve an expression of e
opinion, but is best passed over in silence.

MEG. You are speaking of temperance?

ATH. Yes; but of the other virtues, that which having this appendage
is also most beneficial, will be most deserving of honor, and next that

which is beneficial in the next degree; and so each of them will be rightly honored according to a regular order.

MEG. True.

697   ATH. And ought not the legislator to determine these classes?

MEG. Certainly he should.

ATH. Suppose that we leave to him the arrangement of details. But the general division of laws according to their importance into a first and second and third class, we who are lovers of law may make ourselves.

MEG. Very good.

b   ATH. We maintain, then, that a state which would be safe and happy, as far as the nature of man allows, must and ought to distribute honor and dishonor in the right way. And the right way is to place the goods of the soul first and highest in the scale, always assuming temperance to be the condition of them; and to assign the second place to the goods of the body; and the third place to money and property. And if

c   any legislator or state departs from this rule by giving money the place of honor, or in any way preferring that which is really last, may we not say that he or the state is doing an unholy and unpatriotic thing?

MEG. Yes; let that be plainly declared.

ATH. The consideration of the Persian governments led us thus far to enlarge. We remarked that the Persians grew worse and worse. And we affirm the reason of this to have been that they too much dimin-

d   ished the freedom of the people, and introduced too much of despo-tism, and so destroyed friendship and community of feeling. And when there is an end of these, no longer do the governors govern on behalf of their subjects or of the people, but on behalf of themselves; and if they think that they can gain ever so small an advantage for themselves, they devastate cities, and send fire and desolation among friendly races. And as they hate ruthlessly and horribly, so are they hated; and when they want the people to fight for them, they find no community of

e   feeling or willingness to risk their lives on their behalf; their untold myriads are useless to them on the field of battle, and they think that their salvation depends on the employment of mercenaries and strangers whom they hire, as if they were in want of more men. And they can-not help being stupid, since they proclaim by their actions that the or-

698   dinary distinctions of right and wrong which are made in a state are a trifle, when compared with gold and silver.

MEG. Quite true.

ATH. And now enough of the Persians, and their present maladmin-istration of their government, which is owing to the excess of slavery and despotism among them.

MEG. Good.

ATH. Next, we must pass in review the government of Attica in like   b
manner, and from this show that entire freedom and the absence of all
superior authority is not by any means so good as government by others when properly limited, which was our ancient Athenian constitution at the time when the Persians made their attack on the Greeks, or,
speaking more correctly, on the whole continent of Europe. There
were four classes, arranged according to a property census, and reverence was our queen and mistress, and made us willing to live in obedience to the laws which then prevailed. Also the vastness of the
Persian armament, both by sea and on land, caused a helpless terror,
which made us more and more the servants of our rulers and of the   c
laws; and for all these reasons an exceeding harmony prevailed among
us. About ten years before the naval engagement at Salamis, Datis
came, leading a Persian host by command of Darius, which was ex-
pressly directed against the Athenians and Eretrians, having orders to
carry them away captive; and these orders he was to execute under
pain of death. Now Datis and his myriads soon became complete mas-   d
ters of Eretria, and he sent a terrifying report to Athens that no Eretrian
had escaped him; for the soldiers of Datis had joined hands and netted
the whole of Eretria. And this report, whether well or ill founded, was
terrible to all the Greeks, and above all to the Athenians, and they dis-
patched embassies in all directions, but no one was willing to come to
their relief, with the exception of the Spartans; and they, either because   e
they were detained by the Messenian war, which was then going on,
or for some other reason of which we are not told, came a day too late
for the battle of Marathon. After a while, the news arrived of mighty
preparations being made, and innumerable threats came from the king.
Then, as time went on, a rumour reached us that Darius had died, and
that his son, who was young and hot-headed, had come to the throne   699
and was persisting in his design. The Athenians were under the impression that the whole expedition was directed against them, in consequence of the battle of Marathon; and hearing of the bridge over the
Hellespont, and the canal of Athos, and the host of ships, considering
that there was no salvation for them either by land or by sea, for there
was no one to help them, and remembering that in the first expedition, when the Persians destroyed Eretria, no one came to their help,
or would risk the danger of an alliance with them, they thought that
this would happen again, at least on land; nor, when they looked to the   b
sea, could they harbor any hope of salvation; for they were attacked by
a thousand vessels and more. One chance of safety remained, slight indeed and desperate, but their only one. They saw that on the former

occasion they had gained a seemingly impossible victory, and borne up by this hope, they found that their only refuge was in themselves

c and in the gods. All these things created in them the spirit of friendship; there was the fear of the moment, and there was that higher fear, which they had acquired by obedience to their ancient laws, and which I have several times in the preceding discourse called reverence, of which the good man ought to be a willing servant, and of which the coward is independent and fearless. If this fear had not possessed them, they would never have met the enemy, or defended their temples and sepulchres and their country, and everything that was near

d and dear to them, as they did; but little by little they would have been all scattered and dispersed.

MEG. Your words, Athenian, are quite true, and worthy of yourself and of your country.

ATH. They are true, Megillus; and to you, who have inherited the virtues of your ancestors, I may properly speak of the actions of that

e day. And I would wish you and Cleinias to consider whether my words have not also a bearing on legislation; for I am not discoursing only for the pleasure of talking, but for the argument's sake. Please remark that the experience both of ourselves and the Persians was, in a certain sense, the same; for as they led their people into utter servitude, so we too led ours into all freedom. And now, how shall we proceed? for I would like you to observe that our previous arguments have a good deal to say for themselves.

700 MEG. True; but I wish that you would give us a fuller explanation.

ATH. I will. Under the ancient laws, my friends, the people was not as now the master, but rather the willing servant of the laws.

MEG. What laws do you mean?

ATH. In the first place, let us speak of the laws about music—that is to say, such music as then existed—in order that we may trace the growth of the excess of freedom from the beginning. Now music was

b early divided among us into certain kinds and manners. One sort consisted of prayers to the gods, which were called hymns; and there was another and opposite sort called lamentations, and another termed paeans, and another, celebrating the birth of Dionysus, called, I believe, 'dithyrambs.' And they used the actual word 'laws,'[6] for another kind of song; and to this they added the term 'citharoedic.' All these and others were duly distinguished, nor were the performers allowed to confuse

c one style of music with another. And the authority which determined and gave judgment, and punished the disobedient, was not expressed in a hiss, nor in the most unmusical shouts of the multitude, as in our days, nor in applause and clapping of hands. But the directors of public instruction insisted that the spectators should listen in silence to the end; and boys and their tutors, and the multitude in general, were kept quiet by a hint from a stick. Such was the good order which the multitude were willing to observe; they would never have dared to give judgment by noisy cries. And then, as time went on, the poets themselves introduced the reign of vulgar and lawless innovation. They were men of genius, but they had no perception of what is just and lawful in music; raging like Bacchanals and possessed with inordinate delights —mingling lamentations with hymns, and paeans with dithyrambs; imitating the sounds of the flute on the lyre, and making one general confusion; ignorantly affirming that music has no truth, and, whether good or bad, can only be judged rightly by the pleasure of the hearer. And by composing such licentious works, and adding to them words as licentious, they have inspired the multitude with lawlessness and boldness, and made them fancy that they can judge for themselves about melody and song. And in this way the theatres from being mute have become vocal, as though they had understanding of good and bad in music and poetry; and instead of an aristocracy, an evil sort of theatrocracy has grown up. For if the democracy which judged had only consisted of educated persons, no fatal harm would have been done; but in music there first arose the universal conceit of omniscience and general lawlessness; freedom came following afterwards, and men, fancying that they knew what they did not know, had no longer any fear, and the absence of fear begets shamelessness. For what is this shamelessness, which is so evil a thing, but the insolent refusal to regard the opinion of the better by reason of an over-daring sort of liberty?

MEG. Very true.

ATH. Consequent upon this freedom comes the other freedom, of disobedience to rulers; and then the attempt to escape the control and exhortation of father, mother, elders, and when near the end, the control of the laws also; and at the very end there is the contempt of oaths and pledges, and no regard at all for the gods—herein they exhibit and imitate the old so-called Titanic nature, and come to the same point as the Titans, leading a life of endless evils.* But why have I said all this? I ask, because the argument ought to be pulled up from time to time, and not be allowed to run away, but held with bit and bridle, and then we shall not, as the proverb says, fall off our ass. Let

*The Titans are offspring of Heaven and Earth; they fought against Zeus and lost, for which they were punished. See Hesiod's *Theogony* 131ff., 207–210, 450ff., and 629ff.

d   us then once more ask the question: To what end has all this been said?

     MEG. Very good.

     ATH. This, then, has been said for the sake——

     MEG. Of what?

     ATH. We were maintaining that the lawgiver ought to have three things in view: first, that the city for which he legislates should be free; and secondly, be at unity with herself; and thirdly, should have understanding; these were our principles, were they not?

     MEG. Certainly.

e   ATH. With a view to this we selected two kinds of government, the one the most despotic, and the other the most free; and now we are considering which of them is the right form: we took a mean in both cases, of despotism in the one, and of liberty in the other, and we saw that in a mean they attained their perfection; but that when they were carried to the extreme of either, slavery or licence, neither party were the gainers.

702   MEG. Very true.

     ATH. And that was our reason for considering the settlement of the Dorian army, and of the city built by Dardanus at the foot of the mountains, and the removal of cities to the seashore, and of our mention of the first men, who were the survivors of the flood. And all that was previously said about music and drinking, and what preceded, was said with the view of seeing how a state might be best adminis-

b   tered, and how an individual might best order his own life. And now, Megillus and Cleinias, how can we put to the proof the value of our words?

     CLE. Stranger, I think that I see how a proof of their value may be obtained. This discussion of ours appears to me to have been singularly

c   fortunate, and just what I at this moment want; most auspiciously have you and my friend Megillus come in my way. For I will tell you what has happened to me; and I regard the coincidence as a sort of omen. The greater part of Crete is going to send out a colony, and they have entrusted the management of the affair to Cnossos; and the government of Cnossos to me and nine others. And they desire us to give them any laws which we please, whether taken from the Cretan model or

d   from any other; and they do not mind about their being foreign if they are better. Grant me then this favour, which will also be a gain to yourselves: Let us make a selection from what has been said, and then let us imagine a State of which we will suppose ourselves to be the original founders. Thus we shall proceed with our enquiry, and, at the same time, I may have the use of the framework which you are constructing, for the city which is in contemplation.

ATH. Good news, Cleinias; if Megillus has no objection, you may be sure that I will do all in my power to please you.

CLE. Thank you.

MEG. And so will I.

CLE. Excellent; let us try to found the State in words first.[7] e

ENDNOTES

Ion

1. (p. 5) *the Sicilian expedition*: During the Peloponnesian War between Athens and Sparta (431–404 B.C.E.), Athens sent an armada to attack the city of Syracuse (the most important city in Sicily) in 413; the Athenian forces were wiped out in this battle, which was a turning point of the war.

2. (p. 7) *as good ideas about Homer as I have, or as many*: On the basis of Ion and other evidence from Plato, it would seem that rhapsodes did not only sing the poems, but also lectured on them to a variety of audiences. Given the importance of Homer as a reference for historical, moral, and political education, this seems entirely plausible.

3. (p. 11) *Corybantian revelers when they dance are not in their right mind*: Corybantians were named after the nature spirits Corybantes; they worshiped Cybele (a nature goddess) and Dionysus (god of wine) with plenty of wine, dance, and sex.

Shorter Hippias

1. (p. 24) *in the passage called the Prayers*: Homeric poems were not divided into books until the second century; the lines Hippias refers to are Iliad 9.308–313.

Laches

1. (p. 49) *but in the true Greek mode, which is the Dorian, and no other*: We know little about what Greek music sounded like. The different musical modes seem to have varied at least in harmony. Plato was not the only one who thought that listening to different musical modes—musical styles, we would perhaps say today—had a strong influence on one's character. On this question in Plato, see also *Republic* 400a–c and 424c.

Symposium

1. (p. 69) *one of my acquaintances, . . . calling out playfully in the distance, said: Apollodorus, Phalerian, halt!*: It is hard to see why this is "playful," although several explanations have been given; luckily the point is not crucial. If pressed, I would side with Jowett: The Greek words for Phalerian (*phalēreus*) and "bald-head" (*phalēris*) would have sounded very similar when shouted at some distance.

2. (p. 70) *let us change the proverb to say: 'To the feasts of the good the good unbidden go'*: The real proverb is "To the feasts of the worst men, the good unbidden go." The change is possible because Agathon means "good" in Greek. For the Homeric allusions that follow in 174c–d, see *Iliad* 2.408, 10.227, and 17.587.

3. (p. 78) *the love of Aristogeiton and the constancy of Harmodius had a strength which undid their power*: Harmodius and Aristogeiton were lovers who tried to end Hippias' tyrannical rule of Athens by assassinating his brother, Hipparchus, in 514 B.C.E. Although their attempt failed, they were hailed as victorious when Hippias fell three years later (see *Thucydides* 6.54–59).

4. (p. 84) *Should they kill them and annihilate the race with thunderbolts, as they had done with the giants*: See *Iliad* 5.385 and *Odyssey* 12.308. The struggle, in which Zeus makes use of the thunderbolt, was often represented in Attic pottery. Still, Plato seems to take a leap here by comparing men to giants; but the leap may not be that great—Homer says the Laestrygones are between men and giants (see *Odyssey* 10.118–120).

5. (p. 85) *they sowed the seed no longer as hitherto like grasshoppers in the ground*: Plato may have been thinking of cicadas, some species of which lay eggs into the ground by means of a long ovipositor (see Dover, ed., *Plato: Symposium*, Cambridge: Cambridge University Press, 1980, p. 117; see "For Further Reading").

6. (p. 89) *even the god of war . . . is the captive and Love is the Lord, for love, the love of Aphrodite, masters him, as the tale runs*: The reference is to the myth of Aphrodite seducing Ares, the god of war. In the story, as told in *Odyssey* 8.266–366, Aphrodite's husband, Hephaestus, rigs the bed in such a way that the adulterous lovers find themselves fettered to it when they awake from their postcoital slumber—a cautionary tale, if ever there was one.

7. (p. 107) *as the proverb says, 'there is truth in wine,' whether with boys, or without them*: The original proverb literally said "wine and children are true" (*oinos kai paides alētheis*), meaning, of course, that children and drunkards tell the truth. But the Greek word *paides* also means "slaves"; Kenneth Dover conjectures in the work cited in note 5 above (p. 169) that a derivative proverb may have emerged to the effect that drunkards tell the truth when there are no slaves around. If so, Alcibiades may be giving the original proverb a second twist here, because of the presence of slaves, which we know about from 218b.

Gorgias

1. (p. 133) *Athens, which is the most free-spoken state in the Greek World:* Freedom of speech was a treasured element of Athenian democracy. Notice that Socrates will show later in the dialogue that persuasive speakers do not really speak freely, and that sticking to truly free speech may sometimes pit the speaker against the majority.

2. (p. 142) *Archelaus:* This tyrant of Macedonia (a region of ancient Greece) was evil incarnate, and yet many Athenians (including leading poets like Euripides and Agathon) accepted his hospitality, perhaps to escape the roughness of life in wartime Athens. Archelaus was even praised publicly as an ally of Athens for "doing what he could," as we know from an inscription.

3. (p. 176) *suppose that we strip all poetry of song and rhythm and metre, there will remain speech?:* This way of putting the question is not Plato's—Gorgias had asked it earlier (*Defense of Helen* 9), in order to downgrade poetry in favor of rhetoric, just as Socrates here downgrades poetry in favor of philosophy. Aristotle addresses this question again, from a new angle, in *Poetics* 1447a22–b2ff.

4. (p. 180) *I . . . should have liked to continue the argument with Callicles, and then I might have given him an 'Amphion' in return for his 'Zethus':* This passage refers back to 485e. Socrates' strategy is to remind Gorgias that it is Callicles' fault if the argument does not come to closure; Callicles falls for it easily when he hears the names of Euripides' characters that he himself had brought up in order to belittle Socrates.

5. (p. 188) *I hear that [Pericles] was the first who gave the people pay, and made them idle and cowardly, and encouraged them in the love of talk and of money:* Pericles, an extremely influential Athenian statesman of the fifth century B.C.E., was the leader of the city at the start of the Peloponnesian War. The allusion is to Pericles' instituting pay for jury duty, and perhaps also for active military service and attendance at Council meetings. Critics of the system said it made people idle, since they could make money by serving in the popular courts (Aristophanes' *Wasps* features a "juryaddict"). Socrates' mention of cowardice is harder to explain; perhaps Plato has in mind the employment by Pericles of mercenary troops.

6. (p. 188) *the laconising set who bruise their ears:* "Laconize" means to be in favor of the Spartan way of life. The reference is to young oligarchic politicians who advertised their ideas by the practice of boxing, which

was considered typically Spartan. Some of them may well have been in Socrates' circle—notice that Socrates does not comment on their opinions but puts forward his own instead in 516.

7. (p. 195) *Homer tells us how Zeus and Poseidon and Pluto divided the empire which they inherited from their father:* See Iliad 15.187ff. The story that follows is the simplest, and perhaps earliest, of Plato's eschatological myths (those that deal with the ultimate purpose or destiny of humanity). Homer is brought in as an authority, but the elements of the myth are mostly not Homeric.

Phaedrus

1. (p. 205) *I come from Lysias the son of Cephalus:* Lysias is the famous orator, and Cephalus is the businessman of the Piraeus, owner of a shield factory, at whose house the conversation of Republic takes place.

2. (p. 207) *Boreas is said to have carried off Orithyia from the banks of the Ilissus?:* The North Wind (Boreas) kidnapped Orithyia, daughter of the Athenian king Erechtheus, while she played with the nymphs by this river.

3. (p. 212) *colossal offerings of the Cypselids at Olympia:* The Cypselids were Corinthian rulers (seventh century B.C.E.) of renowned wealth, descendants of Cypselus. One of their offerings at Olympia was an ornate chest of cedar-wood; the legend went that Cypselus' mother, Labda, had hidden him in a chest when he was a child, in order to save him from death at the hands of murderous aristocrats (the Bacchiadae).

4. (p. 214) *which by leading conquers and by the force of passion is reinforced, from this very force, receiving a name, is called love:* This is one of Plato's far-fetched etymologies, of which we can also find a number in Athenian rhetoric. The Greek words involved are erōs (love) and rhōmē (force). We must bear in mind that these etymological games were common in rhetoric, and that language is the true topic of the dialogue.

5. (p. 217) *the oyster-shell has fallen with the other side uppermost:* The image is that of a game of tag, played with an oyster shell that falls to the ground after being thrown up in the air—dark side up, one party pursues; light side up, the other one does.

6. (p. 220) *the recantation of Stesichorus the son of Euphemus, who comes from the town of Himera:* The lyric poet Stesichorus (sixth century B.C.E.) is the author of a famous palinode (literally, "song of retraction") in which he denies the story of the abduction of Helen.

7. (p. 220) *ancient inventors of names, who would never have connected prophecy, which foretells the future and is the noblest of arts, with madness:* The claim is based on etymology that is, again, fanciful. The Greek word for prophecy is mantikē; the one for madness is manikē. The rest of this passage (244c) continues in the same vein.

8. (p. 222) *the human charioteer drives his in a pair; and one of them is noble and of noble breed, and the other is ignoble and of ignoble breed; and the driving of them of necessity gives a great deal of trouble to him:* The image of the charioteer is common in Greek erotic poetry and art; it is a powerful metaphor of control. In Plato, compare the image of a charioteer as a metaphor of control with Plato's tripartite structure of the soul in *Republic* 434d–441c.

9. (p. 230) *having conquered in one of the three heavenly or truly Olympian victories:* An Olympic wrestling match required three throws to win (see Aeschylus, *Eumenides* 589). There may be also a reference here to the three recurring periods of a thousand years in 249a (p. 224).

10. (p. 232) *the 'Pleasant Bend' of the proverb is really the long arm of the Nile:* This expression has been much discussed since antiquity, and some scholars have tried to excise the clause from the Greek text. Others have tried to see in it a term of endearment addressed to Phaedrus. I think it belongs here, but with the sense that something called by a name means exactly the opposite. This, however, requires some additional explanation: What does the Nile have to do with this? Hackforth (*Plato: Phaedrus*, pp. 113–114) says that a bend in that river that lengthened the voyage had come to be known as a Pleasant Bend, a name that indicates the opposite of what is meant.

11. (p. 235) *you have only heard of the rhetoric of Nestor and Odysseus, which they composed in their leisure hours when at Troy, and never of the rhetoric of Palamedes?:* Palamedes is not in Homer's account of the Trojan War, but he is legendary for tricking Odysseus into joining the Trojan expedition (if so, he was more cunning than cunning itself), which is why Plato brings him up.

12. (p. 244) *Hippocrates the Asclepiad says that the nature even of the body can only be understood as a whole:* Hippocrates of Cos was a contemporary of Socrates and, like any doctor, was said to be a descendant of the legendary Greek physician Asclepius, so there is not much in calling him Asclepiad. On the other hand, Phaedrus' attribution of holistic views to Hippocrates is at odds with the extant Hippocratic writings.

Euthyphro

1. (p. 261) *a poor dependant of mine who worked for us as a field labourer:* The man is not a slave, whose death would have been of no consequence. Thetes (paid laborers) were the lowest rank of society, but their killing would nevertheless entail pollution (*miasma*) that would cause legal and religious remedies to come into play.

2. (p. 262) *Zeus . . . bound his father (Cronos) because he wickedly devoured his sons, and that he too had punished his own father (Uranus) for a similar reason, in a nameless manner:* Euthyphro refers to well-known stories, told by Hesiod in *Theogony* 126ff. and 453ff. From inside Earth (Gaia), Cronos (Time) castrates Uranus (Sky) as the only means to stop him from constant sexual activity with Gaia, who is then finally free to deliver her offspring to the world. Before the castration of Uranus, the world has no Cronos—that is, it is Time-less.

3. (p. 268) *For one is of a kind to be loved because it is loved, and the other is loved because it is of a kind to be loved:* The Greek is clearer than the English. The first kind of things Socrates talks about are the ones dear to god (*theopiles*); the second are the holy (*hosion*). It is perhaps easier to understand the argument if one keeps in mind that Athenian religion involved a highly ritualized set of practices but no reference to sacred scripture, at least in the sense of the word in later Western religion.

Apology

1. (p. 279) *Gorgias, . . . Prodicus, . . . and Hippias . . . persuade the young men to leave their own citizens by whom they might be taught for nothing, and come to them whom they not only pay, but are thankful if they may be allowed to pay them:* We must notice, however, that Socrates is remiss in taking up the issue of fees explicitly with the Sophists themselves in the dialogues. On Gorgias of Leontini, see "Introduction" to *Gorgias.* Gorgias, Prodicus, and Hippias were among the most famous Sophists. Notice that Protagoras (see "Introduction" to *Protagoras*) is left out.

2. (p. 285) *he says that the sun is stone, and the moon earth. . . . in the books of Anaxagoras the Clazomenian, which are full of them:* The pre-Socratic philosopher Anaxagoras is famous for having said that the sun was a large burning rock, and the moon a cold one that shone by reflecting the sun's light. Not bad, we might say, for the fifth century B.C.E., but the Athenians thought otherwise. There is some evidence that Anaxagoras was prosecuted for impiety, although this has not been ascertained by scholars.

3. (p. 290) *the trial of the generals who had not taken up the bodies of the slain after the battle of Arginusae:* Arginusae, a group of small islands off Lesbos in the Aegean Sea, was the site of a sea battle fought in 406 B.C.E., during the Peloponnesian War; the Athenians won, but a storm made it impossible for them to recover the bodies of their dead. The generals were prosecuted for it, although the process was later deemed illegal. The details of the whole case are unclear. See Xenophon, *Hellenica* 1.7.4ff.

4. (p. 291) *There is Crito, . . . whose brother Plato is present*: The enumeration of citizens of good standing may be meant to help Socrates' defense against the charge of corrupting the young. Plato, who was less than thirty years of age at the time of Socrates' trial, is mentioned in this dialogue here and at 38b; the only other dialogue in which Plato is mentioned is *Phaedo* (59b).

5. (p. 293) *the vote of condemnation. I . . . am only surprised that the votes are so nearly equal*: The total number of jurors must have been 500 or 501, with 280 votes against Socrates and 220 or 221 to acquit. Sixty votes in 500 is 12 percent; the margin is not all that narrow.

Crito

1. (p. 301) *Has the ship come from Delos, on the arrival of which I am to die?*: The Athenians sent a ceremonial boat to Delos every year in order to commemorate Theseus' victory over the Minotaur, a victory that is symbolic of the victory over the mythical Cretan king Minos. Socrates' execution was delayed, exceptionally, for this reason alone.

Phaedo

1. (p. 318) *Plato was sick, I think*: Other than *Apology* 34a and 38b, this is the only mention of Plato in the dialogues. Of course we cannot be sure about the excuse that Plato gives himself through Phaedo's vague words.

2. (p. 328) *For 'many,' as they say in the mysteries, 'are the thyrsus-bearers, but few are the mystics,'—meaning, as I interpret the words, 'the true philosophers'*: "Thyrsus-bearers" are followers of Dionysus (a thyrsus is a staff entwined with vines). Dionysiac ritual involved plenty of dance, wine, and sex; philosophy does not (at least for Plato). The point holds only because Socrates ascribes an aspect of initiation to philosophical activity, which would separate true philosophers from Sophist wannabes.

3. (p. 331) *Anaxagoras' 'mixture of all things'*: In the view of the pre-Socratic philosopher Anaxagoras, the beginning of all things is an undifferentiated chaos, which starts being separated into different things by the action of Mind (see 97c).

4. (p. 373) *I owe a cock to Asclepius*: Sick people went to the temples of Asclepius, god of medicine and healing, with the hope of receiving a cure in their dreams; the ritual involved the sacrifice of a cock to the god. This sentence has been much discussed. I think it signals that

Socrates has found a "cure" for death in the theory of the immortality of the soul.

Protagoras

1. (p. 386) *A train of listeners followed him*: Protagoras' cloud of listeners is unusually distinguished: Callias' mother was Pericles' ex-wife, Charmides is Plato's maternal uncle, and Philippides is a member of a high-ranking Athenian family. Later, in 315b, the Greek suggests comparison of this gathering with a theatrical chorus.

2. (p. 392) *Prometheus and Epimetheus*: The name Prometheus can be translated as "Forethought" and Epimetheus as "Afterthought," which enhances the meaning of the passage.

3. (p. 409) *'being' is the same as 'becoming'*: There is less of an overlap in meaning between these two verbs in English than in Greek, where the question is perhaps more pressing in its formulation.

4. (p. 412) *'on the one hand'*: As in English, a Greek sentence that contains "on the one hand" (*men*) is almost always balanced by another that contains "on the other hand" (*de*). Note, however, that *men* can also be used on its own for emphasis; it is clear from the beginning that the passage is open to interpretation, but that the answer may not be conclusive.

5. (p. 416) *they have no nonsense or games, . . . even though they are very liberal in their potations*: Other than the drinking, the setting for this dialogue is that of Plato's *Symposium*. Also, all the characters of *Symposium*, except Aristophanes, are present in this dialogue. This may be more than coincidence, but I have not found a fully satisfactory explanation.

Statesman

1. (p. 444) *How does man walk, but as a diagonal, or the power of two feet?*: The reference is to the diagonal of a square with sides measuring one foot; by the Pythagorean theorem, the diagonal is the square root of the sum of two sides—that is, the square root of two. In Plato, the Greek word *dunamis* means both "power" and "square root." The procedure has a scientific ring to it but does not yield good results, as is immediately seen (see note below).

2. (p. 444) *Human beings have come out in the same class with the noblest and most easygoing of creation, and have been running a race with them*: The general consensus is that pigs are meant here. The laughable consequence is that, by the

application of the "power" rule (see note above), pigs would run faster than humans.

3. (p. 447) *the sign of the golden lamb:* According to myth, Atreus and his brother Thyestes competed for the throne of Mycenae, who would be given to the one who had a golden lamb grow in his flocks. Hermes gave the golden lamb to Atreus, but Thyestes persuaded Atreus' wife Aerope to deliver the golden lamb to him. Zeus would not allow Thyestes' trickery, and caused the sun and the stars to change their courses, after which the throne finally went to Atreus.

Laws I–III

1. (p. 495) *Rhadamanthus . . . earned this reputation from his righteous administration of justice when he was alive:* Rhadamanthus, the son of Zeus, is known to us from *Odyssey* 5.564 and, with special reference to his fairness, from Pindar's *Olympian* 2.75 and *Pythian* 2.7. No reference is made here, though, to his role as a judge of the dead in *Gorgias* 526b (p. 197).

2. (p. 499) *Tyrtaeus, an Athenian by birth, but also a Spartan citizen:* Tyrtaeus was a seventh-century B.C.E. poet. The poem the Athenian goes on to quote is known to us from other sources. The first line is quoted correctly, but we should notice that wealth, which the Athenian lists preeminently here, comes only fourth in the poem, after running speed, strength, and looks. There seems to have been a considerable change in people's conceptions about what is most desirable in life between Tyrtaeus' and Plato's days.

3. (p. 506) *an Athenian has only to point out the licence which exists among your women:* This is a commonplace in the Greek world, beginning with the Spartan Helen, wife of Menelaus. Interestingly, Spartan women were lucky by reference to other women (in Athens, for example), in that they could own land and receive inheritance.

4. (p. 539) *the discoveries of Daedalus, Orpheus and Palamedes:* Daedalus was a mythical craftsman who constructed automata, wings for men, and the labyrinth that housed the Minotaur; Orpheus is the Thracian who could charm animals with his song; and Palamedes is credited in legend with the invention of the alphabet.

5. (p. 544) *The rest of the story is told by you Spartans as part of the history of Sparta:* There is no basis in historiography or myth for Plato's account of the Dorian invasion; for all we know, the Dorians were not Achaeans. The Athenian's only "evidence" is the name Dorieus, carried by the Spartan who tried to establish colonies first in Libya and later in Sicily, where he was killed by the Phoenicians toward the end of the sixth century B.C.E.

6. (p. 560) *the actual word 'laws'*: The Greek word *nomos* can mean both "law" and "musical mode." Plato will continue playing on this double meaning of the word in other parts of *Laws*. Perhaps the most significant instance of that play is 722 in book 4, where he puts forward the need for explanatory preambles to the provisions of the legal code, in parallel to the need for preludes in musical compositions.

7. (p. 563) *let us try to found the State in words first*: This is the task to which the Athenian turns in the remaining nine books of *Laws*, going into extraordinary detail about what is the proper way to organize society and why. The dialogue, of course, remains a purely literary creation; the provisions of its legal code were never enforced.

INSPIRED BY
PLATO AND HIS DIALOGUES

The Academy

Around 387 B.C.E. Plato founded an institution, which became known as the Academy, to teach young students, disseminate his thought, and improve society. Built on a plot of land on the outskirts of Athens, near the grove of the hero Academus, it lasted for centuries and became a model for higher learning and a precursor of the modern university. No records exist regarding its exact teachings, but it is believed that mathematics, biology, geometry, astronomy, political theory, and philosophy were among the subjects taught. Math and science seem to have been particularly important; according to legend, the inscription over the entrance read, "Let no man ignorant of geometry enter here."

Plato's student Aristotle (c.384–322 B.C.E.) entered the Academy when he was around seventeen and remained for twenty years, until Plato's death, when control of the Academy went to Plato's nephew Speusippus. Aristotle left Athens for a number of years. In 335 B.C.E. he returned and formed his own school, the Lyceum—also known as the Peripatetic School because Aristotle often conducted discussions while walking around a covered walkway.

Over the next millennium the Academy absorbed new philosophies and altered its direction of thought. After Plato's death it was marked for a time by a tendency toward Skepticism, a mode of thought made popular by Pyrrho (c.360–272 B.C.E.). Skepticism holds that sensory limitations and the flawed nature of comprehension make it impossible to know anything with certainty. Arcesilaus (c.316–241 B.C.E.) and Carneades (c.214–129 B.C.E.), whose philosophies had strong skeptic influences, were notable teachers at the Academy.

A stricter interpretation of Plato in the Academy began around 100 B.C.E., but it was Plotinus (c.205–270 C.E.) who was most influential in the return to a pure Platonism. Attempting to purge Platonic teaching of the Skepticism and Stoicism that had infiltrated it, Plotinus, who founded a school in Rome, developed what scholars now call Neoplatonism. Neoplatonic thought focuses on a central, ideal form from which all earthly forms emanate, based on Plato's earlier development of the idea of forms, or ideas, in his dialogue *Republic*. Among Plotinus's many adherents, Plutarch the Younger (c.350–433 C.E.) brought these ideas to Athens and became the first great teacher of Neoplatonism at the Academy.

The last great teacher of Plato's thought in antiquity was Proclus (c.410–485 C.E.), whose commentary on *Republic* survives today. Proclus studied at the Academy under Plutarch the Younger and pursued Neoplatonic ideas; he eventually became head of the Academy, a position he held until his death. A string of good but unremarkable leaders succeeded Proclus after his death. Around 529 C.E. the Byzantine emperor Justinian (c.483–565 C.E.) forbade the teaching of philosophy in Athens, calling the practice pagan, and forced the Academy to close its doors. Many Platonists fled to Asia Minor, which explains the abundance of Arabic translations of Greek work. Plato would be severely neglected in Europe throughout the Dark Ages.

Humanism and the Renaissance

Strong Platonic thought reemerged in Europe—to incalculable influence —a thousand years after the Academy closed its doors. In fifteenth-century Italy, a return to the study of Plato was significant in inspiring the Renaissance, the period that succeeded the Middle Ages and marked the beginning in the Western world of modern thought and advances in art, literature, philosophy, science, and religion.

Foremost among patrons of the arts during the Renaissance was Cosimo de' Medici (1389–1464), ruler of Florence and one of Europe's wealthiest men. In 1439 a Neoplatonist from Byzantium named Gemisthus Pletho (c.1355–1452) visited Italy and inspired Medici to found an Academy in Florence for the study of Platonic ideas. Medici arranged for young Marsilio Ficino (1433–1499) to be instructed in Greek philosophy. Ficino, who became the leader of the new Academy, translated the works of Plato and Plotinus into Latin and was influential in spreading Neoplatonic ideas in Europe.

At that time Neoplatonism was less an organized school of thought and study, as it had been in Greece, and more a loose way of considering man's relationship to the world and to ideal forms, especially beauty and God. Yet Neoplatonism managed to influence every artistic and academic discipline in Renaissance Europe. It was closely tied with humanism, the return to Classical, or Greek, ways of thinking. Among humanistic concerns were faith in the dignity, power, and capability of man, and an interest in the human ability to comprehend the ideal forms first identified in *Republic*. Many scholars consider the Italian poet Petrarch (1304–1374) to be the first humanist. In the Renaissance the humanistic and Neoplatonic concern with ideal forms merged with Christianity; many thinkers associated God with the ideal forms central to these modes of thought.

Sandro Botticelli's The Birth of Venus

Many scholars consider the Renaissance masterpiece *The Birth of Venus* (c.1485–1486), by Sandro Botticelli (1445–1510), to be the visual epitome of Neoplatonism. Botticelli took as his subject the mythical birth of the goddess Venus, who entered the world from the sea, nude and fully grown. In the painting, Venus floats calmly on a giant scallop shell over the blue waters, her eyes cool and her figure relaxed. The drape of her elegant, long tresses protects her modesty, and flowers fall from the sky in tribute. On one side of the painting, Zephyr, the west wind, blows Venus to shore, while on the other side a nymph waits on the sand, ready to cloak the goddess in a flowing red cape. Her serene, blank gaze suggests her power over man and her distance from earthly troubles. The painting's smooth, supple figures testify to the beauty in the human form. As the image of perfect love, Venus corresponds to the ideal forms that are central to Neoplatonic thought.

The Birth of Venus was commissioned by Lorenzo de' Medici (1449–1492); also known as Lorenzo the Magnificent, he was the son and successor of Piero de' Medici and the grandson of Cosimo. The painting now hangs in the Uffizi Gallery in Florence.

Raphael's The School of Athens

The best-known depiction of a large gathering of Greek intellectuals is *The School of Athens* (1510), by Raphael (1483–1520). This magnificent, complex painting presents an assembly of more than fifty famous thinkers, debating in harmoniously arranged groups under the arch of a vast Greek building. Nearby statues of Apollo and Minerva overlook their animated discussions. At the center of the painting, Plato, clutching his *Timaeus*, gestures toward the sky, to abstracted, ideal matters, while Aristotle grips his *Ethics* and points directly ahead, to earthly concerns. Other thinkers include Pythagoras, kneeling over a tome of his own, and Socrates, lecturing to a group of young students. Golden light floods the arena. Colorful, bright, and gorgeous in its deft arrangement of figures, *The School of Athens* exemplifies Raphael's reverence for the Greeks, which was shared by most of his contemporaries. Originally commissioned by Pope Julius II to decorate his palace in the Vatican, the painting remains in Rome and hangs today in the Sistine Chapel.

COMMENTS & QUESTIONS

In this section, we aim to provide the reader with an array of perspectives on the text, as well as questions that challenge those perspectives. The commentary has been culled from criticism of later generations and appreciations written throughout the work's history. Following the commentary, a series of questions seeks to filter Essential Dialogues of Plato through a variety of points of view and bring about a richer understanding of these enduring works.

Comments

PLUTARCH

[Cicero] said of Aristotle that he was a river of flowing gold, and of the dialogues of Plato that, if it were in the nature of God to converse in human words, this would be how He would do it.

—"Cicero" (about 100 C.E.), in *Plutarch: Fall of the Roman Republic*, translated by Rex Warner (1958)

SAINT AUGUSTINE

As [Plato] had a peculiar love for his master Socrates, he made him the speaker in all his dialogues, putting into his mouth whatever he had learned, either from others, or from the efforts of his own powerful intellect, tempering even his moral disputations with the grace and politeness of the Socratic style. And, as the study of wisdom consists in action and contemplation, so that one part of it may be called active, and the other contemplative—the active part having reference to the conduct of life, that is, to the regulation of morals, and the contemplative part to the investigation into the causes of nature and into pure truth—Socrates is said to have excelled in the active part of that study, while Pythagoras gave more attention to its contemplative part, on which he brought to bear all the force of his great intellect. To Plato is given the praise of having perfected philosophy by combining both parts into one. He then divides it into three parts—the first moral, which is chiefly occupied with action; the second natural, of which the object is contemplation; and the third rational, which discriminates between the true and the false. And though this last is necessary both to action and contemplation, it is contemplation, nevertheless, which lays peculiar claim to the office of investigating the nature of truth.

—from *De Civitate Dei* (A.D. 413–426);
translated by Marcus Dods, in *The City of God* (1872)

IMMANUEL KANT

From the way in which Plato uses the term *idea*, it is easy to see that he meant by it something which not only was never borrowed from the senses, but which even far transcends the concepts of the understanding, with which Aristotle occupied himself, there being nothing in experience corresponding to the ideas. With him the ideas are archetypes of things themselves, not only, like the categories, keys to possible experiences. According to his opinion they flowed out from the highest reason, which however exists no longer in its original state, but has to recall, with difficulty, the old but now very obscure ideas, which it does by means of reminiscence, commonly called philosophy. I shall not enter here on any literary discussions in order to determine the exact meaning which the sublime philosopher himself connected with that expression. I shall only remark, that it is by no means unusual, in ordinary conversations, as well as in written works, that by carefully comparing the thoughts uttered by an author on his own subject, we succeed in understanding him better than he understood himself, because he did not sufficiently define his concept, and thus not only spoke, but sometimes even thought, in opposition to his own intentions.

Plato knew very well that our faculty of knowledge was filled with a much higher craving than merely to spell out phenomena according to a synthetical unity, and thus to read and understand them as experience. He knew that our reason, if left to itself, tries to soar up to knowledge to which no object that experience may give can ever correspond; but which nevertheless is real, and by no means a mere cobweb of the brain.

Plato discovered his ideas principally in what is practical, that is, in what depends on freedom, which again belongs to a class of knowledge which is a peculiar product of reason. He who would derive the concept of virtue from experience, and would change what at best could only serve as an example or an imperfect illustration, into a type and a source of knowledge (as many have really done), would indeed transform virtue into an equivocal phantom, changing according to times and circumstances, and utterly useless to serve as a rule. Everybody can surely perceive that, when a person is held up to us as a model of virtue, we have always in our own mind the true original with which we compare this so-called model, and estimate it accordingly. The true original is the idea of virtue, in regard to which all possible objects of experience may serve as examples (proofs of the practicability, in a certain degree, of that which is required by the concept of reason), but never as archetypes. That no man can ever act up to the pure idea of virtue does not in the least prove the chimerical nature of that concept; for every judgment as to the moral worth or unworth of actions is possible by means of that idea only, which forms, therefore, the necessary foundation for every approach to moral perfection, however far the impediments inherent in human nature, to the extent of which it is difficult to determine, may keep us removed from it.

—from *Kritik der Reinen* Vernunft (1781);
translated by Max Muller, *Critique of Pure Reason* (1881)

GEORG WILHELM FRIEDRICH HEGEL

The development of philosophic science as science, and, further, the progress from the Socratic point of view to the scientific, begins with Plato and is completed by Aristotle. They of all others deserve to be called teachers of the human race. . . .

Plato is one of those world-famed individuals, his philosophy one of those world-renowned creations, whose influence, as regards the culture and development of the mind, has from its commencement down to the present time been all-important. For what is peculiar in the philosophy of Plato is its application to the intellectual and supersensuous world, and its elevation of consciousness, and is brought into consciousness; just as, on the other hand, consciousness obtains a foothold on the soil of the other. The Christian religion has certainly adopted the lofty principle that man's inner and spiritual nature is his true nature, and takes it as its universal principle, though interpreting it in its own way as man's inclination for holiness; but Plato and his philosophy had the greatest share in obtaining for Christianity its rational organization, and in bringing it into the kingdom of the supernatural, for it was Plato who made the first advance in this direction. . . .

Since Philosophy in its ultimate essence is one and the same, every succeeding philosopher will and must take up into his own, all philosophies that went before, and what falls specially to him is their further development. Philosophy is not a thing apart, like a work of art; though even in a work of art it is the skill which the artist learns from others that he puts into practice. What is original in the artist is his conception as a whole, and the intelligent use of the means already at his command; there may occur to him in working an endless variety of ideas and discoveries of his own. But Philosophy has one thought, one reality, as its foundation; and nothing can be put in the place of the true knowledge of this already attained; it must of necessity make itself evident in later developments. Therefore . . . Plato's Dialogues are not to be considered as if their aim were to put forward a variety of philosophies, nor as if Plato's were an eclectic philosophy derived from them; it forms rather the knot in which these abstract and one-sided principles have become truly united in a concrete fashion. . . . Such points of union, in which the true is concrete, must occur in the on-ward course of philosophical development. The concrete is the unity of diverse determinations and principles; these, in order to be perfected, in order to come definitely before the consciousness, must first of all be presented separately. Thereby they of course acquire an aspect of one-sidedness in comparison with the higher principle which follows: this, nevertheless, does not annihilate them, nor even leave them where they were, but takes them up into itself as moments. Thus in Plato's philosophy we see all manner of philosophic teaching from earlier times absorbed into a deeper principle, and therein united. It is in this way that Plato's philosophy shows itself to be a totality of ideas: there-fore, as the result, the principles of others are comprehended in itself. Frequently Plato does nothing more than explain the doctrines of ear-lier philosophers; and the only particular feature in his representation of them is that their scope is extended.

—from *Vorlesungen über die Geschichte der Philosophie* (1833–1836); translated by E. S. Haldane and Frances H. Simson in *Lectures on the History of Philosophy* (1892–1896)

JOHN STUART MILL

The enemy against whom Plato really fought, and the warfare against whom was the incessant occupation of the greater part of his life and writings, was not Sophistry, either in the ancient or the modern sense of the term, but Commonplace. It was the acceptance of traditional opinions and current sentiments as an ultimate fact; and bandying of the abstract terms which express approbation and disapprobation, de-sire and aversion, admiration and disgust, as if they had a meaning thoroughly understood and universally assented to. The men of his day (like those of ours) thought that they knew what Good and Evil, Just and Unjust, Honourable and Shameful, were, because they could use the words glibly, and affirm them of this and of that, in agreement with existing custom. But what the property was, which these several in-stances possessed in common, justifying the application of the term, nobody had considered; neither the Sophists, nor the rhetoricians, nor the statesmen, nor any of those who set themselves up or were set up by others as wise. Yet whoever could not answer this question was wandering in darkness; had no standard by which his judgments were regulated, and which kept them consistent with one another; no rule which he knew, and could stand by, for the guidance of his life. Not knowing what Justice and Virtue are, it was impossible to be just and virtuous; not knowing what Good is, we not only fail to reach it, but are certain to embrace Evil instead. Such a condition, to any one capable of thought, made life not worth having. The grand business of human intellect ought to consist in subjecting these general terms to the most rigorous scrutiny, and bringing to light the ideas that lie at the bottom of them. Even if this cannot be done, and real knowledge can be attained, it is already no small benefit to expel the false opinion of knowledge; to make men conscious of their ignorance of the things most needful to be known, fill them with shame and uneasiness at their own state, and rouse a pungent internal stimulus, summoning up all their mental energies to attack these greatest of all problems, and never rest until, as far as possible, the true solutions are reached. This is Plato's notion of the condition of the human mind in his time, and of what philosophy could do to help it; and any one who does not think the description applicable, with slight modifications, to the majority even of educated minds in our own and in all times known to us, certainly has not brought either the teachers or the practical men of any time to the Platonic test.

The sole means by which, in Plato's opinion, the minds of men can be delivered from this intolerable state, and put in the way of obtaining the real knowledge which has power to make them wise and virtuous, is what he terms Dialectics; and the philosopher, as conceived by him, is almost synonymous with the Dialectician. What Plato understood by this name consisted of two parts. One is, testing every opinion by a negative scrutiny, eliciting every objection or difficulty that could be raised against it, and demanding, before it was adopted, that they should be successfully met. This could only be done effectually by way of oral discussion; pressing the respondent by questions, to which he was generally unable to make replies that were not in contradiction either to admitted fact, or to his own original hypothesis. This cross-examination is the Sokratic Elenchus; which, wielded by a master such as Sokrates was, and as we can ourselves appreciate in Plato, no mere appearance of knowledge without the reality was able to resist. Its pressure was certain, in an honest mind, to dissipate the false opinion of knowledge, and make the confuted respondent sensible of his own ignorance, while it at once helped and stimulated him to the mental effort by which alone that ignorance could be exchanged for knowledge. Dialectics, thus understood, is one branch of an art which is a main portion of the Art of Living—that of not believing except on sufficient evidence; its function being that of compelling a man to put his belief into precise terms, and take a defensible position against all the objections that can be made to it. The other, or positive arm of Plato's dialectics, of which he and Sokrates may be regarded as the originators, is the direct search for the common feature of things that are classed together, or, in other words, for the meaning of the class-name. It comprehends the logical processes of Definition and Division or Classification; the theory and systematic employment of which were a new thing in Plato's day: indeed Aristotle says that the former of the operations was first introduced by Sokrates. They are indissolubly connected, Division being, as Plato inculcates, the only road to Definition. To find what a thing is, it is necessary to set out from Being in general, or from some large and known Kind which includes the thing sought—to dismember the kind into its component parts, and these into others, each division being, if possible, only into two members (an anticipation of Ramus and Bentham), marking at each stage the distinctive feature which differentiates one member from the other. By the time we have divided down to the thing of which we are in quest, we have remarked its points of agreement with all the things to which it is allied, and the points that constitute its differences from them; and are thus enabled to produce a definition of it, which is a compendium of its whole nature.

—from the *Edinburgh Review* (April 1866)

WALTER PATER

Like all masters of literature, Plato has of course varied excellences; but perhaps none of them has won for him a larger number of friendly readers than this impress of visible reality. For him, truly (as he supposed the highest sort of knowledge must of necessity be) all knowledge was like knowing a *person*. The Dialogue itself, being, as it is, the special creation of his literary art, becomes in his hands, and by his masterly conduct of it, like a single living person; so comprehensive a sense does he bring to bear upon it of the slowly-developing physiognomy of the thing—its organic structure, its symmetry and expression —combining all the various, disparate subjects of *The Republic*, for example, into a manageable whole, so entirely that, looking back, one fancies this long dialogue of at least three hundred pages might have occupied, perhaps an afternoon.

—from *Plato and Platonism* (1893)

WILLIAM HAMMOND

By his translation Jowett has raised Plato to the rank of an English classic.

—from the *Philosophical Review* (July 1893)

ALFRED NORTH WHITEHEAD

The safest general characterization of the European philosophical tradition is that it consists of a series of footnotes to Plato.

—from *Process and Reality* (1929)

BERTRAND RUSSELL

It must be admitted that, unless words, to some extent, had fixed meanings, discourse would be impossible. Here again, however, it is easy to be too absolute. Words do change their meanings; take, for example, the word "idea." It is only by a considerable process of education that we learn to give to this word something like the meaning which Plato gave to it. It is necessary that the changes in the meanings of words should be slower than the changes that the words describe; but it is not necessary that there should be *no* changes in the meanings of words. Perhaps this does not apply to the abstract words of logic and mathematics, but these words, as we have seen, apply only to the form, not to the matter, of propositions. Here, again, we find that logic and mathematics are peculiar. Plato, under the influence of the Pythagoreans, assimilated other knowledge too much to mathematics. He shared this mistake with many of the greatest philosophers, but it was a mistake none the less.

—from *A History of Western Philosophy* (1945)

Questions

1. Consider the arguments put forward in *Ion*. Do we currently think more highly of a performer's singing because he or she is smart? Or think less because he is not very intelligent? Do we assume anything about his knowledge in other areas? Do you think singing or engaging in any other performing art enhances the performer's understanding? If so, his or her understanding of what?

2. In *Shorter Hippias* we are confronted with the paradox that an intelligent liar may actually be admired by intelligent and truthful people. Do you think this happens often today? If your answer is no, do you think that there are circumstances when lying is justified? On the other hand, would it be possible to live with nothing but the truth coming from everybody's lips?

3. *Laches* presents a discussion about courage. Do you think that this kind of discussion would take place today along the same lines? Is there a different role assigned today to patriotism in discussions about military courage? If so, why?

4. *Symposium* touches upon many aspects of love, including sexuality. How would you define the expression "Platonic love" after reading this dialogue? Do you think it makes sense to consider sexual desire, or *eros*, and the desire to understand the world as different manifestations of *eros* in human affairs? How is our technological capacity to change the world related to *eros*? Does it even make sense to pose the question in these terms? Why or why not?

5. The belief in reincarnation was not at all widespread in ancient Greek religion. However, in *Phaedrus*, Socrates describes in some detail the process of the reincarnation of the soul. Do you think this is a belief he held firmly, or is he simply presenting it as a means to argue his position more forcibly? Compare this aspect of *Phaedrus* with the myths told by Socrates at the end of *Republic* and *Gorgias*. How are they different? Do some aspects of the various myths contradict one another? Could this be part of what the Athenians considered intolerable from a religious point of view?

6. Is Socrates' acceptance of his death in *Apology* problematic? Do you see signs of stress or fear? If so, how would you describe these signs? What could Socrates have done differently in order to avoid capital punishment? Why didn't he do it?

7. Do you find the proof of the immortality of the soul offered by Socrates in *Phaedo* convincing? In the final analysis, does the proof rely on rational arguments or on irrational belief? What other proofs of immortality have been offered later in history?

8. Compare the end of *Laches* with the end of *Protagoras*. What is similar? What is different? Does Socrates appear more convinced that a new teacher is needed in *Laches* than in *Protagoras*? What kind of teacher do you think Socrates has in mind, if any?

FOR FURTHER READING

Books Mentioned in the General Introduction

Kahn, C. *Plato and the Socratic Dialogue: The Philosophical Use of a Literary Form.* Cambridge and New York: Cambridge University Press, 1996.

Morkot, R. *The Penguin Historical Atlas of Ancient Greece.* London and New York: Penguin Books, 1996.

Nails, D. *The People of Plato: A Prosopography of Plato and Other Socratics.* Indianapolis, IN: Hackett Publishing Company, 2002.

Nightingale, A. W. *Genres in Dialogue: Plato and the Construct of Philosophy.* Cambridge and New York: Cambridge University Press, 1995.

Parker, R. *Athenian Religion: A History.* Oxford and New York: Oxford University Press, 1996.

Vernant, J.-P. *The Universe, the Gods, and Men: Ancient Greek Myths.* New York: HarperCollins, 2001.

Waterfield, R. *The First Philosophers: The Presocratics and the Sophists.* Oxford and New York: Oxford University Press, 2000.

Translations

The standard edition in English of all of Plato's dialogues and letters, including works whose authenticity is disputed, is now *Plato: Complete Works*, edited and with an introduction by J. M. Cooper (D. S. Hutchinson, associate editor), Indianapolis, IN: Hackett Publishing Company, 1997. The dialogues are also available separately from the same publisher, with introductions and notes by the respective translators. Excellent translations of the dialogues are also available, with introductions, from Penguin Classics, Oxford World's Classics, Yale University Press, and Cornell University Press.

The following are translations that I have consulted:

Benardete, S. *Plato's Statesman: Part III of The Being of the Beautiful.* Chicago: University of Chicago Press, 1986.

Hackforth, R. *Plato: Phaedrus.* Cambridge: Cambridge University Press, 1952.

―――. *Plato: Phaedo.* Cambridge: Cambridge University Press, 1955.

Nehamas, A., and P. Woodruff. *Plato: Symposium.* Indianapolis, IN: Hackett Publishing Company, 1989.

————. *Plato: Phaedrus*. Indianapolis, IN: Hackett Publishing Company, 1995.

Pangle, T. *The Laws of Plato*. With notes and an interpretive essay. Chicago: University of Chicago Press, 1988.

Saunders, T. J., ed. *Early Socratic Dialogues*. Harmondsworth, UK, and New York: Penguin Books, 1987.

Skemp, J. B. *Plato: The Statesman*. Bristol, UK: Bristol Classical Press, 1987.

Taylor, C. C. W. *Plato: Protagoras*. Oxford and New York: Oxford University Press, 1996.

Tredennick, H., and H. Tarrant. *Plato: The Last Days of Socrates*. London and New York: Penguin Books, 2003.

Historical and Cultural Context of Plato's Dialogues

Boedeker, D., and K. Raaflaub, eds. *Democracy, Empire, and the Arts in Fifth-Century Athens*. Cambridge, MA: Harvard University Press, 1998.

Bremmer, J. *The Early Greek Concept of the Soul*. Princeton, NJ: Princeton University Press, 1983.

Dover, K. J. *Greek Homosexuality*. Cambridge, MA: Harvard University Press, 1978.

Jones, A. H. M. *Athenian Democracy*. 1957. Baltimore, MD: Johns Hopkins University Press, 1986.

Kerferd, G. B. *The Sophistic Movement*. Cambridge and New York: Cambridge University Press, 1981.

Morgan, K. A. *Myth and Philosophy from the Presocratics to Plato*. Cambridge and New York: Cambridge University Press, 2000.

Ober, J. *Political Dissent in Democratic Athens: Intellectual Critics of Popular Rule*. Princeton, NJ: Princeton University Press, 1998.

Ostwald, M. *From Popular Sovereignty to the Sovereignty of Law: Law, Society, and Politics in Fifth-Century Athens*. Berkeley: University of California Press, 1986.

Schiappa, E. *Protagoras and Logos: A Study in Greek Philosophy and Rhetoric*. Columbia: University of South Carolina Press, 1991.

Tarán, L. *Parmenides*. Princeton, NJ: Princeton University Press, 1965.

Veyne, P. *Did the Greeks Believe in Their Myths? An Essay on the Constitutive Imagination*. Chicago: University of Chicago Press, 1988.

General Works on Plato and His Philosophical Legacy

Annas, J., and C. Rowe, eds. *New Perspectives on Plato, Modern and Ancient*. Cambridge, MA: Harvard University Press, 2002.

Fine, G., ed. *Plato.* 2 vols. Oxford and New York: Oxford University Press, 1999.

Kraut, R., ed. *The Cambridge Companion to Plato.* Cambridge and New York: Cambridge University Press, 1992.

Melling, D. *Understanding Plato.* Oxford and New York: Oxford University Press, 1987.

Zuckert, C. *Postmodern Platos: Nietzsche, Heidegger, Gadamer, Strauss, Derrida.* Chicago: University of Chicago Press, 1996.

Works on the Dialogues in This Selection

Allen, R. E. *Socrates and Legal Obligation.* Minneapolis: University of Minnesota Press, 1980. (On *Apology* and *Crito*.)

Benardete, S. *The Rhetoric of Morality and Philosophy: Plato's Gorgias and Phaedrus.* Chicago: University of Chicago Press, 1991.

Bobonich, C. *Plato's Utopia Recast: His Later Ethics and Politics.* Oxford and New York: Oxford University Press, 2002.

Bostock, D. *Plato's Phaedo.* Oxford and New York: Oxford University Press, 1986.

Ferrari, G. R. F. *Listening to the Cicadas: A Study of Plato's Phaedrus.* Cambridge and New York: Cambridge University Press, 1987.

Geach, P. T. "Plato's Euthyphro: An Analysis and Commentary." *Monist* 50 (1966), pp. 369–382.

Hobbs, A. *Plato and the Hero: Courage, Manliness, and the Impersonal Good.* Cambridge and New York: Cambridge University Press, 2000. (See pages 76–113 on *Laches*.)

Hunter, R. *Plato's Symposium.* Oxford and New York: Oxford University Press, 2004.

Irwin, T. *Plato: Gorgias.* Oxford and New York: Oxford University Press, 1979. Translation and extensive philosophical commentary.

Morrow, G. *Plato's Cretan City: A Historical Interpretation of the Laws.* Princeton, NJ: Princeton University Press, 1960.

Murray, P., ed. *Plato on Poetry: Ion; Republic 376e–398b9, 595–608b10.* Cambridge: Cambridge University Press, 1996. This book requires knowledge of Greek beyond the introduction, which is well worth reading on its own.

O'Brien, M. J. *The Socratic Paradoxes and the Greek Mind.* Chapel Hill: University of North Carolina Press, 1967. (See pages 96–107 on *Shorter Hippias*.)

Reeve, C. D. C. *Socrates in the Apology.* Indianapolis, IN: Hackett Publishing Company, 1989.

Rowe, C. J., ed. *Reading the Statesman. Proceedings of the III Symposium Platonicum.* Sankt Augustin, Germany: Academia Verlag, 1995.

Stalley, R. F. *An Introduction to Plato's Laws.* Indianapolis, IN: Hackett Publishing Company, 1983.

Taylor, C. C. W. *Plato: Protagoras.* Oxford and New York: Oxford University Press, 1976. Translation and extensive philosophical commentary.

Yunis, H. *Taming Democracy: Models of Political Rhetoric in Classical Athens.* Ithaca, NY: Cornell University Press, 1996. (See pages 136–237 on *Gorgias, Phaedrus,* and *Laws.*)

(continued)

(continued)

ℬ
BARNES & NOBLE CLASSICS

If you are an educator and would like to receive an
Examination or Desk Copy of a Barnes & Noble Classics edition,
please refer to Academic Resources on our website at
WWW.BN.COM/CLASSICS
or contact us at
BNCLASSICS@BN.COM

All prices are subject to change.